JUMP!

www.**rbooks**.co.uk

JUMP!

JILLY COOPER

BANTAM PRESS

LONDON • TORONTO • SYDNEY • AUCKLAND • JOHANNESBURG

TRANSWORLD PUBLISHERS
61–63 Uxbridge Road, London W5 5SA
A Random House Group Company
www.rbooks.co.uk

First published in Great Britain
in 2010 by Bantam Press
an imprint of Transworld Publishers

A CIP catalogue record for this book
is available from the British Library.

ISBNs 9780593061534 (cased)
9780593061541 (tpb)

Addresses for Random House Group Ltd companies outside the UK
can be found at: www.randomhouse.co.uk
The Random House Group Ltd Reg. No. 954009

The Random House Group Limited supports the Forest Stewardship
Council (FSC), the leading international forest-certification organization.
All our titles that are printed on Greenpeace-approved
FSC-certified paper carry the FSC logo.
Our paper procurement policy can be found at
www.rbooks.co.uk/environment

Typeset in 11/12pt New Baskerville by
Falcon Oast Graphic Art Ltd.
Printed and bound in Great Britain by
CPI Mackays, Chatham, ME5 8TD

4 6 8 10 9 7 5 3

To my daughter-in-law Edwina Cooper and my son-in-law Adam Tarrant with love and gratitude for the immense kindness and encouragement they gave me while writing this book.

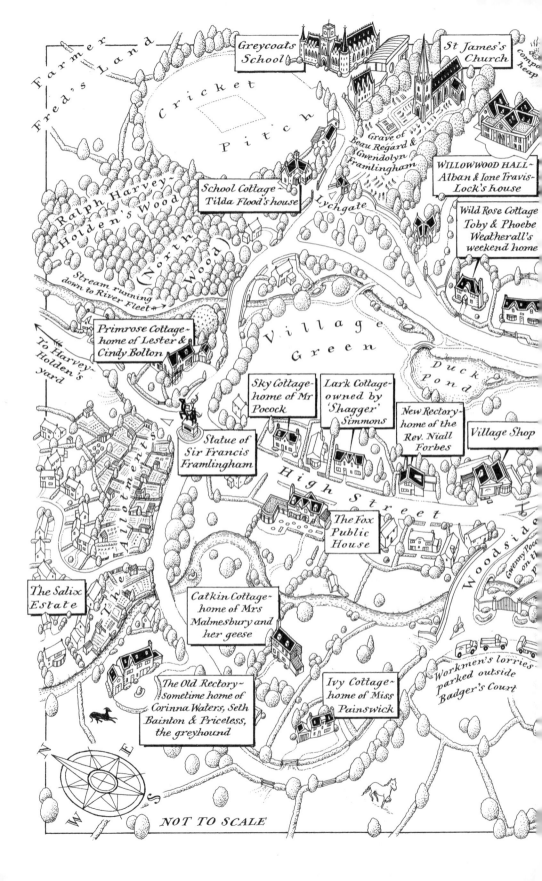

Farmer Fred's Land

Greycoats School

St James's Church

compost heap

Cricket Pitch

Ralph Harvey~ Holden's Wood (North Wood)

Grave of Beau Regard & Gwendolyn Framlingham

WILLOWWOOD HALL~ Alban & Ione Travis-Lock's house

School Cottage~ Tilda Flood's house

Lychgate

Wild Rose Cottage Toby & Phoebe Weatherall's weekend home

Stream running down to River Fleet

Village Green

Primrose Cottage~ home of Lester & Cindy Bolton

Duck Pond

To Harvey-Holden's Yard

Sky Cottage~ home of Mr Pocock

Lark Cottage~ owned by 'Shagger' Simmons

New Rectory~ home of the Rev. Niall Forbes

Village Shop

Statue of Sir Francis Framlingham

High Street

The Fox Public House

Woodside

The Salix Estate

The Allotments

Gwenny Poc... on th...

Catkin Cottage~ home of Mrs Malmesbury and her geese

The Old Rectory~ sometime home of Corinna Waters, Seth Bainton & Priceless, the greyhound

Ivy Cottage~ home of Miss Painswick

Workmen's lorries parked outside Badger's Court

N E S W

NOT TO SCALE

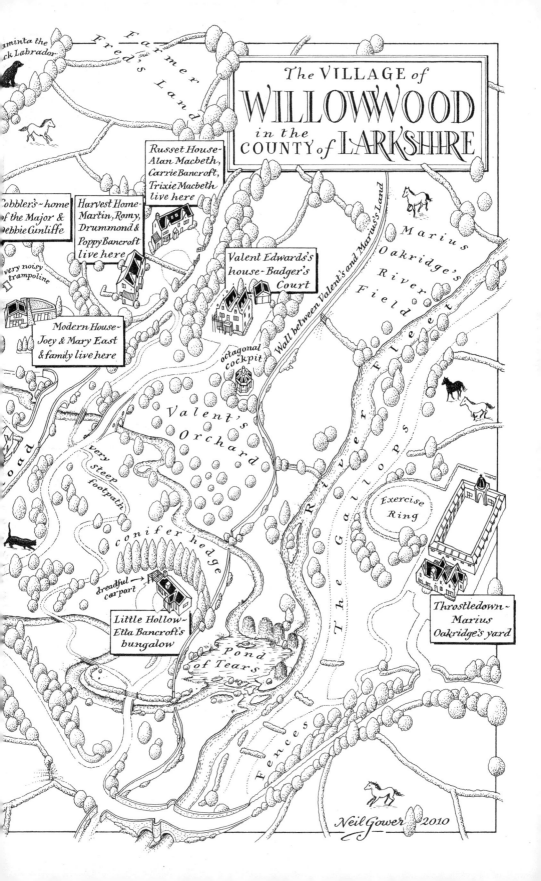

The VILLAGE of **WILLOWWOOD** in the COUNTY of **LARKSHIRE**

Farmer Fred's Land

...minta the ...ck Labrador

...obbler's ~ home ...f the Major & ...ebbie Cunliffe

very noisy trampoline

Harvest Home ~ Martin, Romy, Drummond & Poppy Bancroft live here

Russet House ~ Alan Macbeth, Carrie Bancroft, Trixie Macbeth live here

Modern House ~ Joey & Mary East & family live here

Valent Edwards's house ~ Badger's Court

Marius Oakridge's River Field

Wall between Valent's and Marius's Land

octagonal cockpit

Valent's Orchard

very steep footpath

conifer hedge

dreadful carport

Little Hollow ~ Etta Bancroft's bungalow

Pond of Tears

The Gallops

River Fleet

Exercise Ring

Throstledown ~ Marius Oakridge's yard

Fences

...oad

Neil Gower 2010

CAST OF CHARACTERS

WOODY ADAMS — A delectable Willowwood tree surgeon.

EDWARD ALDERTON — Rupert Campbell-Black's nineteen-year-old American grandson, a gilded brat and former flat jockey who's spending a year at his grandfather's yard in England to try his luck at National Hunt racing.

PARIS ALVASTON — Dora Belvedon's boyfriend and ice-cool Adonis, now in Upper Sixth at Bagley Hall and dickering between Cambridge and RADA.

ANGEL — The youngest stable lass at Marius Oakridge's yard, Throstledown.

ARIELLA — The new young mistress of Bluebell Hill.

CHRISTOPHER AND CHRISTINE ASHBY — Known as Chris and Chrissie. Landlord and lady of the Fox, Willowwood's pub.

SETH BAINTON — Drop-dead gorgeous actor, known as Mr Bulging Crotchester, who with his considerably older and more famous mistress, actress Corinna Waters, lives part of the year in Willowwood in a house inappropriately called the Old Rectory. Seth and Corinna have an open partnership.

SAMPSON BANCROFT	A hugely successful field marshal of industry specializing in property and engineering. A charismatic shit, whose failing health in no way diminishes his ability to bully and control.
ETTA BANCROFT	Sampson's delightful but dreadfully downtrodden wife.
MARTIN BANCROFT	Sampson and Etta's self-regarding son, who gives up the City in favour of fundraising with a celebrity-tapping bias. Has houses in Chiswick and Willowwood.
ROMY BANCROFT	Martin's even smugger wife, who makes a fetish about being a stay-at-home mum. Despite enchanting looks, an egomaniac.
DRUMMOND BANCROFT	Martin and Romy's fiendish five-year-old son.
POPPY BANCROFT	Martin and Romy's four-year-old applause junkie.
CARRIE BANCROFT	Martin's sister. Workaholic – hugely successful in the City, a failure as a wife and mother. Prefers to be known by her maiden name but in reality is Mrs Alan Macbeth. Houses in Knightsbridge and Willowwood.
BERTIE AND RUBY BARACLOUGH	Bedding billionaire and his jolly wife. A devoted couple and very new racehorse owners.
DORA BELVEDON	Fifteen-year-old smart cookie. Besotted with horses, dogs and Paris Alvaston. Has a somewhat dubious ability to flog stories to the national press, redeemed by an extremely kind heart.

LESTER BOLTON	As short in inches as he is on charm. Internet tycoon specializing in porn. Has recently acquired romantic Primrose Cottage in Willowwood.
CINDY BOLTON	Lester's child bride, an extremely successful porn star.
BRUNHILDA	An Animal Rights activist.
JOHNNIE BRUTUS	A narcissistic Irish jockey.
RUPERT CAMPBELL-BLACK	Owner/trainer who bestrides the racing world like a colossus. Despite being in his mid-fifties, still Mecca for most women.
TAGGIE CAMPBELL-BLACK	His enchanting second wife, an angel.
XAVIER CAMPBELL-BLACK	Rupert and Taggie's adopted Colombian son – a point-to-point rider.
BIANCA CAMPBELL-BLACK	Rupert and Taggie's ravishing adopted Colombian daughter, best friend of Dora Belvedon.
ABERDARE 'DARE' CATSWOOD	A complacent, handsome amateur jockey with a very rich father.
JAMIE CATSWOOD	Dare's brother, later pupil assistant to Harvey-Holden.
BLUEY CHARTERIS	Rupert Campbell-Black's retained jockey, about to retire – every jockey in the land wants his job.
COLLIE	Marius Oakridge's long-suffering head lad.
LADY CROWE (NANCY)	Martinet, MFH (Master of Fox Hounds) and Marius Oakridge's most loyal owner.
MAJOR NORMAN CUNLIFFE	Retired bank manager who has wormed his way on to every committee in Willowwood. Closet letch, despite respectable exterior.

DEBBIE CUNLIFFE	The Major's wife. A bossyboots and madly competitive gardener. Known as Direct Debbie because of her appalling lack of tact.
JOEY EAST	A wonderful builder and jack of all trades. Part of the Terrible Trio syndicate with Woody and Jase, Joey has just landed a plum job masterminding the complete gutting and rebuilding of Valent Edwards's house, Badger's Court.
MARY EAST	Known as Mop Idol, Joey's very comely wife who cleans for the Travis-Locks and Seth and Corinna when they're down in Willowwood.
VALENT EDWARDS	Brusque but intensely charismatic widower and a man of the people in his middle sixties. Ex-Premier League goalkeeper remembered for his legendary save in Cup Final. Leaving football, his hawk-like goalkeeper's eyes have found gaps in every market, making him a major player on the world stage. Valent has caused huge excitement in Willowwood, buying the big house, Badger's Court.
TILDA FLOOD	The village schoolmistress – excellent and loving primary teacher, whose pretty face is ruined by very buck teeth. Gagging for marriage and a family, Tilda has developed a passion for Shagger Simmons, Willowwood's beast of a bachelor.
NIALL FORBES	Vicar of St James's, Willowwood. In despair over his dwindling congregation and as yet un-disclosed fondness for his own sex. Niall is drinking rather too much of his parishioners' sherry.

DENNY FORRESTER	Harvey-Holden's embattled head lad.
MARTI GLUCKSTEIN	Rupert Campbell-Black's red-hot lawyer.
CRAIG GREEN	The village leftie – Green by name and Green by nature.
RALPH HARVEY-HOLDEN	A controversial, networking trainer, whose Ravenscroft yard lies to the north of Willowwood.
LYSANDER HAWKLEY	Rupert Campbell-Black's assistant, brilliant at bringing on horses.
HINTON	Etta Bancroft's gardener at Bluebell Hill.
JOSH	Handsome stable lad working for Marius Oakridge.
RAFIQ KHAN	A magnificently moody Pakistani with matchless looks and militant tendencies. After a stint in prison for suspected terrorism, where he learns to love and look after racehorses, Rafiq is trying to make it as a jockey.
BILLY LLOYD-FOXE	Ex-Olympic showjumper and much loved BBC sports correspondent.
JANEY LLOYD-FOXE	Billy's wife, a totally unprincipled journalist.
AMBER LLOYD-FOXE	Billy and Janey's ravishing daughter. A cool beauty determined to make it in National Hunt racing, where she is encountering bias against women jockeys.
ALAN MACBETH	Carrie Bancroft's husband. His talent as a writer is somewhat dissipated by a thirst for alcohol, only equalled by a taste for winners. Alan's unsung skills as a househusband, on the other

	hand, have contributed hugely to Carrie's success.
TRIXIE MACBETH	Carrie Bancroft and Alan Macbeth's long-legged teenage daughter, disastrously lacking in parental attention and totally aware of her overwhelming sex appeal.
OLD MRS MALMESBURY	Willowwood biddy who saves badgers and habitually gets the wrong end of the stick.
MICHAEL MEAGAN	One of Rupert Campbell-Black's stable lads.
MICHELLE	A seductive, scheming stable lass at Marius Oakridge's yard.
SILAS 'SHADE' MURCHIESON	Sexy but shady arms dealer and owner with more than twenty horses in training and definitely something of the night about him.
NUALA	An Animal Rights heroine.
'KILLER' O'KAGAN	King of the Irish jockeys, who rules the weighing room, goes brutally to work on horses with great success and has no scruples whatsoever.
MARIUS OAKRIDGE	An obsessive, brilliant trainer, who bonds with horses but woefully lacks the small talk necessary to charm owners. Marius's yard, Throstledown, is to the south of Willowwood.
OLIVIA OAKRIDGE	Marius's wife and, to many, the only good thing about Marius. Olivia's charm makes up for her husband's lack of diplomacy as she works her backside off cherishing horses, stable jockeys and owners.

INDIA OAKRIDGE	Marius and Olivia's five-year-old daughter.
BLANCHE OSBORNE	Sampson Bancroft's *maîtresse-en-titre*.
BASIL OSBORNE	Blanche's complaisant husband.
JOYCE PAINSWICK	Formerly Hengist Brett-Taylor's dragon of a secretary at Bagley Hall, retired to a cottage in Willowwood and missing school life dreadfully.
JASON (JASE) PERRY	A farrier who mostly shoes racehorses, consequently best gossip and worst tipster in the world. Partner of Woody Adams and Joey East in a racing syndicate entitled the Terrible Trio, which has a good deal more fun than success.
HAROLD POCOCK	Willowwood widower and gardener to Ione Travis-Lock. Runs the allotments, which mean a lot to him, and as Tower Captain rules the St James's bellringers.
CHARLIE RADCLIFFE	Long-suffering vet.
BONNY RICHARDS	Valent Edwards's trophy mistress – a stunning, hugely fancied actress determined to be taken seriously, paranoid about media interest in her sex life and gold-digging ability.
ROGUE ROGERS	Prince Charming of the Irish jockeys, who battles with Killer O'Kagan for weighing-room rule. Awesome rider of horses and women, Rogue is forgiven his bad behaviour because the racing world needs stars.
TOMMY RUDDOCK	Marius Oakridge's sweet-natured stable lass, no beauty – therefore adored more by the horses than the opposite sex.

RUTHIE	Etta Bancroft's cleaner at Bluebell Hill.
'SHAGGER' SIMMONS	A City Slacker – but shrewd financially. A bachelor bruiser, he owns a weekend cottage in Willowwood. Has an on-off relationship with Tilda Flood, who longs for a ring but is more often left looking after Shagger's holiday lets.
CECIL STROUD	A red-hot QC.
BRIAN TENBY	Sampson Bancroft's lawyer.
ALBAN TRAVIS-LOCK	Charming, self-deprecating, newly retired British ambassador who has mostly served in Arab countries. Desperately missing embassy life and spending rather too much time in the Fox with Alan Macbeth.
IONE TRAVIS-LOCK	Alban's formidable wife – with her sister the last living descendants of Sir Francis Framlingham, whose twelfth-century stone effigy lies in St James's church, Willowwood. After forty years as an ambassador's wife, Ione, a serious gardener, has returned to Willowwood Hall to reclaim her rights as lady of the manor.
TRESA	A seductive blonde stable lass working for Marius Oakridge.
VAKIL	A sinister Pakistani stable lad working for Ralph Harvey-Holden.
JIMMY WADE	Former stable lad at Ravenscroft, in prison with Rafiq Khan.
CORINNA WATERS	A very famous and still beautiful actress in her late fifties who lives with Seth Bainton. Corinna and Seth have an open partnership.

TOBY AND PHOEBE WEATHERALL	Newishly weds with a house in Fulham, who weekend in Wild Rose Cottage in Willowwood. Phoebe, very pretty, works in an art gallery. Toby, rather pink, white and chinless, works nervously for Carrie Bancroft in the City, but is a nephew of Ione Travis-Lock, which means they are asked everywhere. Toby is a great friend of Shagger Simmons, who both he and Phoebe think is a hoot.
JUDGE STANFORD WILKES	A wise, not-so-young judge.

THE ANIMALS

ARAMINTA — Alban Travis-Lock's black Labrador, missing embassy life even more than her master.

BAFFORD PLAYBOY — Shade Murchieson's awesome bay gelding, trained by Ralph Harvey-Holden. A bully.

BULLYDOZER — A huge, sweet Irish gelding belonging to Shade Murchieson.

BARTLETT — Etta Bancroft's Golden Retriever.

CADBURY — Dora Belvedon's chocolate Labrador.

CHISOLM — A rescued goat – companion to Mrs Wilkinson.

COUNT ROMEO — A very lazy equine narcissist devoted to Mrs Wilkinson.

GWENNY — Harold Pocock's black cat, who moves house mid-story.

DILYS — A sheep, companion to Furious.

FAMILY DOG (DOGGIE) — A short-legged sweet-faced hurdler, owned by the Terrible Trio syndicate.

FURIOUS — A delinquent rescued racehorse, destined for a career move into polo or eventing, but returning instead to National Hunt racing.

HORACE	A Shetland with attitude.
ILKLEY HALL	Shade Murchieson's equally awesome black gelding, trained by Marius Oakridge.
JUDY'S PET	A horse.
OXFORD	A foxhound.
STOP PRESTON, OH MY GOODNESS AND HISTORY PAINTING	All horses trained by Marius Oakridge.
LOVE RAT	Rupert Campbell-Black's most successful stallion.
LUSTY	Love Rat's son, Rupert Campbell-Black's most successful liver chestnut National Hunt gelding.
MISTLETOE	Marius Oakridge's lurcher.
NOT FOR CROWE	Incurably greedy tailless wonder, owned by the Terrible Trio syndicate.
PRICELESS	Seth Bainton's beautiful black greyhound.
SIR CUTHBERT	A doughty dapple-grey warrior. Trained by Marius Oakridge. Owned by Nancy Crowe.
MRS WILKINSON	The Village Horse.

JUMP!

1

Bullies and dictators are everywhere, not just imposing their stranglehold on vast companies and entire continents but also creating reigns of terror within small businesses and even marriages.

Sampson Bancroft was both a Hitler at work, where he kept 50,000 employees worldwide on the jump, but also at home where he imprisoned, albeit in a beautiful Dorset house called Bluebell Hill, Etta, his sweet wife of forty-five years.

Sampson Bancroft had been so phenomenally successful in both property and engineering that legends were woven around him.

On one occasion, having reached a deadlock while trying to sell a thousand Bancroft engines to the Chinese, he had stunned the meeting by suddenly announcing:

'If you'll excuse me, gentlemen, I have to go and fuck my secretary.'

Although this was interpreted to bemused Chinese officials as a family crisis, by the time Sampson returned forty minutes later the world's markets had shifted dramatically, a foreign power had threatened China and the deal was closed. No one was sure what Sampson had been up to but 'having a Bancroft' became City terminology for a quick shag.

Sampson's courtship of his wife Etta in the early sixties, known as *A la recherche du temps perdu,* had also gone into folklore. Sampson, then in his twenties, was already running his own company, Bancroft Engineering, when on the way out to lunch he had spotted Etta, the latest temp, tearing out her lustrous curls in the typing pool.

Learning on his return that she had just been fired for hopeless incompetence by the personnel lady, Sampson fired the personnel lady.

Arriving home to her parents' house in Thames Ditton, a tearful Etta, terrified of confessing she'd been sacked yet again, found Sampson's dark green XK120 parked outside. Such was the brutal splendour of his blond looks and the force of his personality that he and Etta were engaged in a month, to the delight of her elderly parents, who were relieved that their dreamy, unworldly daughter would be so well provided for.

But even during their courtship, Sampson always put Etta down, and frequently quoted W. H. Davies's 'Sweet Stay-at-Home':

> I love thee for a heart that's kind,
> Not for the knowledge in thy mind.

It was Etta's kind heart, ironically, that had most infuriated Sampson over the years. She would slip his money to charities or friends or visiting workmen, and listen endlessly to girlfriends' problems on the telephone: 'Oh, you poor, poor thing, how awful.'

Sampson also resented Etta's passion for animals. As an only child, she had been particularly close to the family fox terriers and to Snowy, the grey Welsh pony, which her parents had scrimped and saved to buy her and whose photograph still adorned her dressing table. Sampson, who gambled thousands daily on the stock market, hit the roof whenever he caught her putting a tenner on a big race.

He was even angrier when he discovered that Roddy Smithson, the local riding master in Dorset, knowing Etta loved greys and hoping she would visit his stables more frequently, had offered her free access to a lovely dapple-grey mare. Sampson promptly forbade any further contact. He also removed his considerable custom from the local garage, on learning that the manager was servicing Etta's Golf for nothing.

Sampson loathed men who effortlessly attracted women, particularly when, like himself, they were tall, blond, rich and arrogant. Etta's pin-up, the owner-trainer Rupert Campbell-Black, whom she'd hero-worshipped since his showjumping days in the seventies, was therefore anathema.

Sampson resented his wife for being so lovable. For a start Etta was so pretty, her complexion delicate as apple blossom, her soft curls the glowing light brown of woods before the leaves break through in springtime, and her eyes, the dark blue of clouds ushering in an April shower, were never far from tears or laughter. She also had a lovely curvy figure (which Sampson had kept in check by weighing her once a week), slender ankles and the natural grace of a dancer.

But it was not just Etta's prettiness. When Sampson wasn't around, her natural high spirits and cheerfulness broke in.

She had such a loving smile, indicating she was really pleased to see you, such an infectious laugh, such a gentle voice, interrupted by squeaks of excitement, such a sweet, confiding way of tucking her arm through yours and asking after your wife or your sick grandchild or how your exams had gone, as if she really minded.

The words 'that bastard Bancroft' were never far from the lips of those familiar with the set-up. It was common knowledge in Dorset that Sampson not only bullied Etta insensible but kept her very short.

Why hadn't she left him? For the same reason that birds often don't escape when the cage door is left open: she had lost the ability to fly. Then she couldn't leave because disaster struck.

Except for the rare sporting injury, Sampson had never been ill. His superhuman energy had enabled him to work all day and make love all night. Then, during a long winter in the early 2000s, his secretary noticed Sampson nodding off in the afternoon and even during crucial meetings.

In May, the firm's annual cricket match took place, traditionally held on Sampson's birthday to provide yet another showcase for his prowess. Even into his seventies he had taken wickets and knocked up the odd forty runs. This year he was bowled first ball and dropped two easy catches.

At the dinner afterwards, Sampson, who never forgot a face, blanked half the distinguished guests, and his normally rabble-rousing speech to the faithful was slurred and rambling.

Leaving the hotel, he had tripped and hit his head on a pillar and ended up in hospital. Here blood tests revealed Howitt's – a dreaded, degenerative heart disease.

An outraged Sampson turned to the internet. Finding a prognosis not only of blindness and the collapse of organs and muscles but also of searing pain and probable dementia, he rolled up at a board meeting next day and once again collapsed. As his resignation became official, shares in Bancroft Engineering went into temporary free fall.

Back at Bluebell Hill, where he was confined to bed or a wheelchair, Sampson could no longer terrorize Etta by appearing massive-shouldered and six foot three in doorways, his eyes as cold as a lake at twilight.

Instead he bellowed from all over the house but, except for the occasional very pretty carer allowed in to read or sit with him, he refused to let anyone but Etta look after him.

'I can understand that,' cooed an admiring district nurse. 'Mr Bancroft is too proud a man to let a strange woman see him naked.'

That had never been Sampson's problem, thought Etta wryly, remembering the serial mistresses he had kept throughout his marriage. But ever kind-hearted, aware that Sampson could no longer walk, was in dreadful pain, felt mocked by the books in his library that he could no longer read, and was finding even children's crosswords increasingly difficult as his mind and his grasp on reality slid away, Etta felt desperately sorry for him.

Nor did their two children provide much solace. More than forty years ago Etta had nearly died giving birth to two hulking twins, Martin and Carrie, neither of whom she had managed to breastfeed. They seemed to have inherited Sampson's contempt for their mother. Whenever she had tried to cuddle them they had gone rigid and wriggled out of her arms.

Not that they got on any better with each other, perhaps because when they were children Sampson, with stopwatch poised, had set them constantly at odds, not just on tennis court or sports track or in icy swimming pool but in endless history, geography and general knowledge tests.

As a result both twins were indelibly competitive. Dark, handsome, square-jawed Martin and heavy-faced Carrie, who was even more successful in the City than her brother, gazed belligerently out of silver frames on Sampson's desk.

Neither child had been assiduous in visiting their stricken father, who admittedly wasn't keen on his grandchildren and roared with rage when they switched television channels or rampaged across his painful feet.

When five-year-old Drummond managed to bugger both the stairlift and Sampson's reclining chair on the same morning, his father Martin had threatened to smack him. Whereupon Sampson, to the rapture of Martin's wife Romy, had growled that nothing could be achieved by smacking children – then spoilt it all by saying the only answer was to shoot them.

Since then, while claiming 'Dad was such a joker', both Martin and Carrie had found it hard to tear themselves away from their brilliant careers. To assuage their consciences, however, they encouraged others to descend on Bluebell Hill:

'Dad's so desperate for intellectual stimulus and cheering up and Mother's got nothing to do.'

This led to Etta further exhausting herself cooking and putting up for the night Sampson's friends, or his ex-mistresses and their husbands. Street angel, house devil. Sampson managed to be polite, even genial, to them while remaining foul to Etta. Tiredness from continually disturbed nights made her absent-minded, groping for names or why she'd come into a room, which irritated Sampson more than ever.

Early on in their marriage they had been nicknamed Sampson and Delicious because Etta had been so engaging. Even now Sampson's visiting ex-colleagues and friends, many of whom he had cuckolded, squeezed her waist. Like Penelope's suitors, they appreciated what a rich and charming prospect she would be, if anything happened to Sampson.

'We know it's just as tough for the carer,' they whispered as they thrust ribboned boxes of Belgian chocolates into her hands.

'So nice to see you relaxing, Etta,' said their wives tartly. 'London's so tiring.'

Etta's solace throughout her marriage, when Sampson had spent so much time away, had been her girlfriends. Now home all day, Sampson grew increasingly jealous, loathing it when they dropped in or chatted to Etta on the telephone. As she had felt compelled to refuse their invitations, they had drifted away.

Etta's refuge was her exquisite garden, created over thirty-five years, in which her sense of design and colour had had the chance to blossom. She'd been working on a flame-red rose to be called Sampson when he'd fallen ill. In her greenhouse, she grafted plant on to plant, creating ravishing new species.

Her other comfort, apart from her bird table and reading poetry and novels, was Bartlett, her ancient Golden Retriever, who she took on increasingly slow walks round the countryside, wondering who would go first, Bartlett or Sampson. Was there life after Sampson? she was bitterly ashamed of wondering. A patient could live with Howitt's, although it would increase its hideous grip, for twenty years.

2

One March morning, nearly two years after Sampson was struck down, Etta woke in rare excitement. Despite having been roused several times in the night to turn Sampson over and readjust his pillows, she remembered that the guest-free day ahead coincided with the first day of the Cheltenham Festival. If she could settle Sampson in his study with a video of an enthralling Test match or a Grand Prix, she could sneak off to watch the races in the kitchen – particularly as her pin-up and Sampson's bête noire, Rupert Campbell-Black, had a horse running in a big hurdle race.

After that the day went downhill. Sampson, who insisted on opening the post, discovered a letter from one of her few remaining girlfriends enclosing Etta's £100 winnings on a horse called Tigerish Tom: 'Such a brilliant tip, darling, here's your share. Hughie and I put on a hundred and celebrated with a wonderful dinner at the Manoir last night. Hope Sampson isn't giving you a horrid time.'

Sampson's roar of rage, 'You're not allowed to bet, Etta,' rose to a bellow when he opened a receipt for another £100 from SHAC, the animal rights group battling to close down the laboratories in Huntingdon.

'How dare you support them, Etta! D'you want to kill me? How can they ever find a cure unless they test on animals?'

Worse was to come. As a result of a warm dry spell, spartan Sampson had turned off the central heating. Last night the temperature had plummeted and now he was bucketing around in his wheelchair, demanding the whereabouts of the hot electric pad which eased the pain in his back.

Etta had just said she had no idea when, passing a dog basket in the hall, Sampson caught sight of the flex of the electric pad coming out from under the tartan rug on which Bartlett was happily snoring.

Sampson exploded. Etta fled to the kitchen. When she crept back later with Sampson's midday pills and a glass of claret, she found him in a further rage. He'd been ringing some bloody woman all morning but she'd been permanently engaged. Yet when he thrust the number on a piece of blue writing paper towards her, she realized he'd been ringing his own number and her heart went out to him. Then it retreated as the telephone rang.

'Sampy darling,' cooed a voice as Etta answered it, 'just to let you know it's Cheltenham races and roadworks on the M4 so we probably won't be with you before one.'

Blanche Osborne was Sampson's longest-term mistress. Beautiful, self-satisfied, she had been spoilt by Basil, her complaisant husband, who'd been rewarded for the blind eye he'd turned with excellent deals from Sampson over the years.

'Blanche and Basil will be with us around one,' Etta told Sampson, then, with a surge of spirit: 'I wasn't aware.'

'I told you last week,' interrupted Sampson, 'but you never listen. Why don't you stop being obstinate and get that deaf aid.'

By the time Etta had chucked a leg of lamb in the oven and defrosted a raspberry Pavlova, lit the fire, laid the table in Sampson's study and organized drinks, Blanche, who liked to catch her on the hop, had arrived half an hour early, giving Etta no time to change, put on make-up or hardly wash.

Blanche was looking stunning, her sleek silvery-grey bob enhanced by a red suit with a large ruby brooch on the lapel in the shape of a geranium – no doubt given to her by Sampson. Instantly she went into an orgy of plumping Sampson's cushions, re-buttoning his saxe-blue cardigan, which Etta's trembling fingers had done up all wrong earlier, and smoothing his hair with a dampened hairbrush.

'We must make you look as handsome as possible.'

Basil, who had a puce face and a fat tummy, reminding Etta of Keats's poem about the pot of basil, tucked into a large whisky and the *Financial Times*, while Blanche talked to Sampson. Etta raced back and forth to the kitchen, and throughout lunch, crying: 'You'll need mince sauce', 'Redcurrant jelly?', 'Sorry I forgot the water jug' and 'More cream on your raspberries?'

No one noticed when she went missing. With the sound turned down, she lingered in the kitchen to watch the races.

They had moved on to celery and a very ripe Brie, and

Sampson was beginning to look grey from the exertion, when Etta noticed the clock edging towards three fifteen.

'You need another bottle of red and a glass of port,' she said airily.

Back in the kitchen to open the wine she couldn't resist turning up the sound, mindlessly finishing off the Pavlova as the coloured carousel of jockeys and horses circled at the start. Instantly she recognized Rupert's dark blue and emerald green colours, today worn by Rupert's longtime stable jockey Bluey Charteris, whom Rupert, spurning younger jockeys, had coaxed out of retirement to ride a special horse.

This was Lusty, a magnificent plunging liver chestnut showing a lot of white eye. Home-bred and the son of Rupert's greatest stallion, Love Rat, Lusty had been disappointing on the flat. Once gelded, however, he had won over hurdles, but was still at five the most inexperienced horse in the race.

'Oh!' Etta gave a sigh of longing and took a slug of red out of the newly opened bottle, for there was Rupert himself, gimlet blue eyes narrowed, smooth Dubai tan displaying none of those wine-dark rivulets caused by years of icy winds pulverizing the veins. His thick brushed-back gold hair was hidden by a trilby tipped over his Greek nose. A covert coat emphasized the broad shoulders and long lean body. Goodness, he was heaven.

Having rudely refused to discuss his horse's prospects with any of the press, he had taken the unusual step of going down to the start to calm Lusty. Now, with his arm round the horse's neck, he was repeatedly smoothing his satin shoulders.

The cameras then switched to Rupert's lovely wife Taggie, who, in a big midnight-blue hat with a feather, was biting her nails in the stands.

The horses were coming in, bunching up towards the tape, and they were off, lifted by the most exhilarating noise in the world: the Cheltenham roar. Etta turned up the volume even further to hear the Channel 4 commentary over the rattle of hurdles and the thunder of hooves on dry ground.

Three from home, Lusty was still tucked up in the back watching the leaders battling it out. Bluey unleashed him, hurtling up the field, overtaking everything. Coming up the straight, Bluey glanced back between his legs. The rest were nowhere.

'Come on, Lusty!' screamed Etta, as with the relief of a fox who'd shaken off the pack Lusty sauntered past the post and Cheltenham exploded, hats and race cards hurled in the air.

As two beaming red-coated huntsmen led them back past wildly cheering crowds, Bluey rose in his stirrups to punch the air with both fists and nearly got bucked off by a still fresh Lusty.

Now the cameras were on an exultant Rupert who'd loped up from the start, pumping Bluey's hand, hugging Lusty and Lusty's ecstatically sobbing stable lass, and the crowd erupted once more.

Rupert had mostly deserted jump racing for the flat but the punters loved him, and once again he'd delivered. Taking another celebratory slug, Etta jumped higher than Lusty, as an accusing voice cried: 'We thought you were fetching us another bottle. Sampson's getting very stressed, he must be due his second lot of pills and poor Basil's still waiting for his glass of port.'

'So sorry,' gasped Etta.

'And now you've spilled wine all over your jersey. You really ought to smarten yourself up,' chided Blanche, grabbing the bottle and racing back to Sampson.

Scurrying after her, dripping port like drops of blood on the flagstones, Etta heard Blanche say: 'She was drinking from the bottle and drooling over Rupert Campbell-Black, triumphalist as ever, winning some race at Cheltenham.'

'Would you all like some coffee and we can eat your lovely chocolates?' asked Etta nervously.

'Not if it means you disappearing for another hour to salivate over Rupert Campbell-Black,' snapped Sampson.

He wouldn't bawl her out before Blanche and Basil, that would come later.

Bartlett stirred in her sleep. Etta must walk her before it got dark and the greenhouse needed watering, but Blanche and Basil were showing no signs of leaving.

Blanche was rhapsodizing over the children.

'So good-looking – you must be so proud. So brilliant Carrie winning that High Flyer of the Year award and Martin doing so well in the marathon, he looked almost as dishy as his dad on telly.'

Basil slept.

If she had known they were coming, Etta would have arranged for Ruthie, her daily, to pop in to wash up and stay on to keep an eye on Sampson, but Ruthie had gone to her grandson's school play. The sun was sinking, round and red like Basil, as they finally left. Feeling dreadful, knowing Sampson shouldn't be abandoned in such a choleric mood, even with the distraction of a video of the Bahrain Grand Prix, Etta escaped to walk Bartlett.

Scuttling through drifts of white daffodils and blue scillas, past un-cut-back flower beds, through an unpruned rose walk, she reached the fields. Here she got her daily horse fix, from a lovely bay mare and her plump skewbald Shetland companion. Although they flattened their ears and nipped each other as Etta gave them chopped carrot, the two horses were utterly devoted. If parted, their anguished cries could be heard by half of Dorset.

A proper marriage, thought Etta wistfully.

Bartlett progressed slowly, her waving blond tail gathering burrs, stopping to sniff everything, leaving Etta to admire the sulphur explosion of the pussy willows and leaves escaping like green rabbit ears from the lank brown coils of the traveller's joy. Nature had already carpeted the woodland floor with wild garlic. As she returned through the trees, she could see the faded russet towers and gables of Bluebell Hill warmed by the last fires of the sun.

'Come *on*, Bartlett.'

Bartlett smiled and refused to be hurried.

Where the wood joined the garden, Etta found a sycamore blown down by the recent gales and gave a cry as she noticed that three or four bluebells, trapped beneath its trunk, had struggled out from underneath and were trying to flower. Such was their longing to bloom.

Frantically Etta tried to roll back the tree but it was too heavy. She'd get Hinton the gardener to lift it tomorrow and chop up the logs. Tomorrow she'd prune the roses.

Bartlett was snuffling smugly ahead, searching for a stick or a leaf to take home as a present for Sampson.

There was no bellowing as they entered the house, nor when Etta called out. In the drawing room, she found Sampson slumped in his wheelchair. The television was still on, with Bancroft engines roaring round the track. The telephone had fallen from Sampson's hand. His grey, waxy, outraged face would haunt her for ever. And wilt thou leave me thus? He had been extinguished by a massive heart attack.

3

Martin Bancroft was sailing in the Mediterranean when he heard of his father's death. His inconsolable grief was intensified by guilt at not having visited his father more and by the horrific realization that because Sampson, after making over so much money, had not lived the requisite seven years, his dependants would be stymied by estate duty. Both Martin and Carrie were overstretched by mortgages and expensive extension schemes in London and the country.

Martin was a shit like Sampson, but a more devious one. Although he earned enough to support his wife Romy and his children, Drummond and Poppy, he was fed up with the rat race and his sister's success. Poised to leave the City and switch to fundraising, with a caring celebrity bias, he was much in need of capital.

Martin's wife Romy was a beauty, with large brown eyes, lustrous dark hair and a full, deceptively generous mouth. Her athletic big-breasted figure and clear tawny skin needed little upkeep. She and Martin, who insisted on jogging hand in hand, resembled one of those bouncy couples on the label of a multi-vitamin container.

Romy, like her husband, was intensely smug and self-regarding. Unlike her sister-in-law Carrie, she was also into creative child-rearing and when asked if she worked, would reply: 'Yes, extremely hard as the mother of two little people.'

Five-year-old Drummond, the stairlift wrecker, was an over-indulged fiend. Poppy, a four-year-old applause junkie, would interrupt any adult conversation to demand an audience for a handstand or 'Alla Turca' thumped out on the piano. Both children lived on absurdly healthy food. Juice was a rarity, chocolate or a grain of salt had never passed their lips.

Martin had a handsome oblong face, dark hair slicked back from a smooth, untroubled forehead, and a loud, hearty laugh instead of a sense of humour.

Both he and Carrie had houses in London and adjoining barns in the Cotswold village of Willowwood, some eighty miles from Bluebell Hill. Sampson had bought these barns through his property company and, in some tax dodge and possibly as an act of sadism, had gifted them to Martin and Carrie knowing they disliked each other intensely.

Arriving at Bluebell Hill the morning after his father's death, delighted to pre-empt his sister Carrie, who was hammering out some deal in the Far East, Martin found his mother ashen, staring-eyed, jersey on inside out and in total shock. Even the doctor's reassurance that there was nothing she could have done and the heart attack must have been a complete whiteout could not comfort her.

Etta's own heart sank when she saw Martin had brought Romy and the children, who whooped off round the house.

'We thought you'd need your family round you, Mother,' said Martin. 'Tell us what happened.'

'And left Dad by himself!' cried Romy in horror a minute later. 'But he was supposed never to be unattended.'

'I know,' whispered Etta, 'but Blanche and Basil stayed so late, and I had to get Bartlett out before dark.'

'Always putting animals first,' reproved Martin. 'Has anyone rung Blanche?'

Etta started in terror at the imperious bleep of the stairlift.

'Sampson,' she gasped, darting towards the door, 'you mustn't use it on your own. It's simply not safe.'

Outside she found Drummond sailing calmly up the stairs.

'How did Grampy get up to heaven without his stairlift?' he asked.

Martin immediately commandeered the telephone: 'Yes, it's Father, I'm afraid – a massive cardiac arrest.'

Having rung lawyers and financial advisers and ascertained there was nothing they could do, even though Sampson would only have had to live another year, Martin and Romy's resentment hardened towards Etta.

They also spent a lot of time blocking calls of sympathy. 'I'm afraid Mother's too much in shock to talk.'

Ably assisted by Drummond, they then wandered round Bluebell Hill, tempering their grief as they assessed the value of pictures and furniture and, while claiming to be searching for 'mementos of Dad' to put in their funeral orations, decided what pieces they wanted. Their barn in Willowwood cried out for large furniture.

Bartlett, who picked up vibes, was desperately concerned about Etta. When Ruthie, Etta's daily, gave her the lamb bone from yesterday's lunch, Bartlett left it in her basket and came back to comfort Etta, nudging her and laying a soft golden paw on her knee.

Bartlett had also been fond of Sampson. As soon as the men in black suits took his body away in a zipped-up bag, she had heaved herself on to Sampson's bed and growled at Romy when she tried to shoo her off.

Drummond proceeded to tease Bartlett, plunging fingers like four-point plugs into her eyes and nose, trying to tug her off by her arthritic legs until Bartlett bit him, drawing blood. Whereupon Romy, who believed any atrocity on animals was permissible if it benefited mankind, made a fearful scene and demanded Bartlett be put down.

4

Carrie Bancroft, square-jawed and hefty like Sampson, was not as good-looking as her brother Martin. Tough and aggressive, having witnessed her father bullying her mother, she herself bullied people, particularly women. In the office, she was known as 'Carrie On Bitching', although what is called character in men is often described as being a bitch in women. Carrie was brilliant at hedge funds – Etta still couldn't work out what they were – and the managing director of a very large company. Still steeped in the yuppy ethos of her youth, she rose at five when she was in England, spent token quality time with her teenage daughter Trixie, who was invariably asleep, and jogged to the gym before spending an eighteen-hour day at her desk. After breaking off to dine or go to the opera with clients, she would return to work.

At the office, Carrie insisted on being called by her maiden name. Her charming, dissolute husband, Alan Macbeth, was referred to as 'Mr Carrie Bancroft' (his wife, because of her back-stabbing qualities, was 'Lady Macbeth').

Furious to be trapped in Hong Kong while her brother Martin would no doubt be pulling a fast one, Carrie arrived the following day by helicopter, for which she would later claim expenses from the Trust. She found Martin still commandeering the telephone.

'Where's Alan? He's turned off his mobile,' she demanded, chucking down her briefcase.

'Rang and said he was coming down later,' said Martin acidly. 'He was always a tower of jelly in a crisis.'

Carrie's lips tightened. 'He's interviewing some monk up at Fountains Abbey for his book on depression. How's Mother?'

'Off the wall, in the kitchen.'

Etta, who'd woken five times in the night only to find there was no longer any Sampson to turn, had leapt out of bed dripping with sweat, terrified his breakfast wouldn't be ready on time.

Carrie found her mother mindlessly stirring porridge in the kitchen, gazing at bumblebees glutting themselves on the winter honeysuckle. She had odd shoes on her feet.

'I am so sorry, darling.' Etta tried to hug Carrie, who shook her off.

'Don't, you'll get me going.'

'You must be tired. Would you like to lie down or have some breakfast?'

'I'll have Dad's porridge since you're making it,' said Carrie, then, as Martin and Romy joined them: 'Where's Dad's body?'

'In the Chapel of Rest,' replied Martin. 'I spent most of yesterday afternoon with the undertakers. They were delightful but by the time I'd filled in all the forms, organized the service, the cars, the coffin and the music, I could have been dead myself.' He laughed heartily.

'We decided on a wickerwork basket instead of a coffin,' he went on. 'Romy's offered to decorate it with flowers. She's so artistic.'

'Won't that look a bit cheap?' snapped Carrie.

'Certainly not.'

Etta stopped stirring the porridge and, with a rare surge of dissent, cried, 'Sampson should have a proper coffin. Oak or yew. He deserves one.'

'I don't think so,' said Martin crushingly. 'Dad wanted to save the planet and you know how he hated wasting money. Now if he'd lived longer . . .'

'I'm sorry,' muttered Etta.

'You're burning that porridge,' said Carrie.

Having topped up a bowlful with treacle and cream, she dragged Martin into Sampson's office.

'Is there nothing to be done?'

'Nothing.'

It took Martin and Carrie only five minutes to work out that ravishing Bluebell Hill would have to be sold to pay the massive estate duty. Sampson, like many philanderers, had been unable to bear the thought of his friends moving in on Etta. Aware of her hopelessly generous nature, he hated the idea of her squandering his inheritance on lame ducks and had handed everything over to Martin and Carrie with the proviso they looked after their mother.

By the afternoon, Carrie had conjured up an estate agent who valued the house at between three and four million.

'If it's going to reach top whack, we should get all those rails, stairlifts and hoists out of the house,' mused Martin.

He and Carrie had also in their peregrinations noticed herbaceous borders dark brown with un-cut-back plants, sculptures hidden by overgrown shrubs and trees, ground elder on the rampage, and agreed the romantic garden was too much for Etta.

Their mother was clearly over the top, rushing around making beds, cooking for everyone, trying to answer the letters of sympathy that poured in: writing three times to some people, chucking other letters in the wastepaper basket still in their envelopes.

'Get some cards printed, Mother,' ordered Martin, 'then you can top and tail them.'

Drummond, meanwhile, trailed after his mother assessing loot: 'If you have the Rossetti, can I have the stairlift and the reclining chair?'

While Carrie worked on her BlackBerry, Martin was kept very busy planning the funeral. If they held it at three, they could get away with canapés, sandwiches, cake and champagne, just a glass, and lots of interesting teas, which he and Romy had discovered on a visit to China. Then they wouldn't have to provide people with lunch.

Determined to ensure a working funeral to launch his new career as a fundraiser, he had seized Sampson's address book and files and bought a book of remembrance, so every celeb and captain of industry could sign their name and be tapped for donations or personal appearances later.

What a tragedy, observed Martin and Carrie, that Dad had bought a shredder advertised in the *Daily Telegraph* and spent so much time at the end destroying letters from illustrious mistresses and business acquaintances.

'Family flowers only,' said the announcement in both *The Times* and the *Telegraph*. Sampson would have been delighted that there were enough spring flowers to be found in the garden to decorate both the church and the house, so no one would have to fork out for florists.

'Such a pity cow parsley isn't out,' sighed Romy, 'so pretty and so cheap.'

The only thing Martin needed was for his literary brother-in-law Alan to dig out a few poems so they could get the service sheet printed, but he was still ostensibly interviewing monks up north.

'I'm sure I saw him at Cheltenham on the news just now,' said Romy beadily.

Once the children were in bed, Martin and Romy riffled through the albums to find a suitable photograph of Sampson to put on the service sheet.

'What a handsome chap he was,' sighed Romy. 'And who's that?' She peered at a curling print. 'My goodness, it's you, Etta. You were glam in those days. I can't believe it's you. And who's that gorgeous woman with Sampson? Heavens, it's Blanche – wasn't she lovely?'

'Lovely now,' said Martin warmly. 'Blanche is an awfully sweet person, and quite inconsolable. I talked to her again today.'

At supper of chicken Marengo that had Carrie reaching for the salt and tabasco, Romy tried to shake Etta out of her blank-eyed grief.

'You must talk to Mummy, she's handled widowhood so splendidly. Mind you, she's got so many friends who adore her and keep asking her to stay, she never has a moment to herself. Of course, she can't get enough of Poppy and Drummond.' Then, as Etta gave the rest of her chicken to Bartlett, 'Are you taking anything in, Etta?'

'Yes, you're very kind,' muttered Etta.

'It's good to talk,' said Romy smugly.

'Can you possibly wash a couple of white shirts for me, Mother?' asked Carrie.

Romy was gratified to find a disc of ancient dog sick under the spare-room bed. Martin was gratified that in bed that night, at the prospect of never seeing his father again, he cried his eyes out and buried his face in his wife's splendid breasts, which led to them having very noisy sex.

'Yes, yes, yes, yes, yes!'

Etta, in the next bedroom, put her pillow over her head. On the other side, Carrie's rage redoubled that Alan still hadn't arrived. She suspected he was at Cheltenham.

5

Blond, slight and delicate-featured, Alan Macbeth was a very good writer. He was also a drinker and gambler, whose thirst for winners was only equalled by his fondness for alcohol. Carrie, who liked to project an image of a two-career family, wanted Alan to write more successfully and constantly nagged him to work harder.

In fact Alan had spent a large proportion of his married life as a househusband, enabling his wife's career to soar. Currently writing a book on depression, Alan most enjoyed carousing with his friends and chatting up the crumpet outside the school gates so assiduously that he had been nicknamed 'Mother Fucker'.

Those blond, delicate looks, soft voice and languid manner misled women and more often their husbands into thinking that Alan was gay. Women felt safe with him, until it was too late.

'Being married to a workaholic,' Alan was fond of saying, 'gives you a lot of days off.'

Despite leaving him so frequently to his own devices, Carrie had inherited her father's insanely jealous nature and kept her husband very short.

Alan's arrival at Bluebell Hill the following afternoon co-incided with the end of the Cheltenham Festival. Having had a good win on the Gold Cup, he brought for Etta, to whom he was devoted, a tube of Berocca, a bottle of vodka, a huge bunch of freesias and a white cashmere scarf to relieve the black of her funeral outfit.

'Poor old darling,' he said, hugging her.

'I can't get used to the quiet and him not calling for me,' mumbled Etta. 'So awful I wasn't there.'

'Trust the old bugger to depart in Cheltenham week.'

'Is that where you were?' said Romy reproachfully.

To his wife, brother- and sister-in-law's disapproval, Alan got stuck into the whisky. He then produced a lovely piece of Milton, appropriately from *Samson Agonistes*, for Martin to read.

'Dad loved Bunyan – what about something uplifting from *Pilgrim's Progress?*' suggested Carrie.

'Giant Despair had a wife and her name was Diffidence,' quipped Alan. 'Sums up your dad and mum to a T.'

Then, when they looked disapproving, he suggested Carrie might 'read the bit about Mr Valiant-for-Truth and the trumpets sounding for him on the other side. We could hire a trumpeter to play the Last Post.'

'That would cost money,' complained Martin. 'Dame Hermione is singing "Where'er You Walk" for nothing.'

'Drummond wants to get up and describe all the nice things he remembers about Grampy,' said Romy, putting on a soppy face.

'Shouldn't take long,' murmured Alan, looking down his list. 'And for you, Romy . . .'

'I prefer to source my own material. I've found this lovely piece about only being in the next room.'

'I love it,' said Martin, crinkling his eyes engagingly. ' "Call me by my old familiar name." '

'Stingy old bugger, in Sampson's case,' muttered Alan, who'd detested his father-in-law, a dislike that had been reciprocated.

Carrie often vanished to work in Sampson's office, but she and Martin also kept sloping off round the house earmarking loot.

'Don't they remind you of the Walrus and the Carpenter,' Alan remarked to Etta, 'sobbing over the oysters? Boo hoo, I can manage the Sickert if you can accommodate the Nevinson.'

Etta didn't laugh. Getting ice out of the fridge for Alan's whisky, she proceeded to drop four cubes into Bartlett's water bowl. She was haunted by a memory of Sampson sitting on the edge of the bed looking bewildered, not knowing where he was, like a torch battery running out. She shouldn't have left him.

Alan wandered upstairs to talk to Hinton, the gardener, who was dismantling the hoists in Sampson and Etta's bedroom. He and Ruthie, he said, though shaken and worried about their own future, were determined to look after Etta as long as possible.

'Poor soul's pushed herself too far. I wish she'd rest. The boss made her use teabags twice. He was so tight with money.'

'I'm tight without money,' sighed Alan, aware that he'd over-spent at Cheltenham. Wandering downstairs and finding Romy and Martin sipping sherry in the drawing room, he poured himself another large whisky.

'If you're writing that book on depression,' said Romy beadily, 'perhaps you could counsel Etta. I'm drawing a blank. She's selfishly refusing to listen, and I'm such a good listener.'

'All roads lead to Romy,' observed Alan and received a scowl from his brother-in-law.

Alan wished he hadn't embarked on the bloody depression book. The advance had all been spent. Observing his wife, brother-in-law and Romy, however, Alan didn't feel any of them were suffering from depression, more like suppressed euphoria. They were at last free of Sampson's domination and anticipating riches to come. It was as though Saddam Hussein's statue had crashed to the ground like a felled oak.

Alan, however, was desperately worried about Etta, who'd been bullied into a gibbering wreck by Sampson and, if her children got their way, would swiftly exchange one tyranny for another. He must protect her.

On the way to bed, having turned on Teletext to look at tomorrow's runners, Alan noticed that one of the expected guests at the funeral, an arms-dealing billionaire called Shade Murchieson, had a good horse in the 3.00 at Ludlow. Swaying upstairs, he found his wife already in bed, wearing a red wool nightshirt, working on her laptop, and went into the bathroom to clean his teeth.

'So what's the form?' he asked.

'We'll have to sell.'

'Poor darling Etta.'

'You always stick up for her. She can't be left rattling around in a huge house with only her memories.'

'Particularly when you're going to get four million for it.'

'Someone's got to think about money in our house,' snapped Carrie and regretted it. In blue-striped pyjamas her husband looked about fourteen.

'I don't believe you've been interviewing monks,' she snarled. 'Romy saw you at Cheltenham.'

'Yes, yes, yes, yes,' came sobbing confirmation from next door.

'Jesus!' cried Carrie, who also longed to be made love to.

'Death always makes people randy,' grinned Alan, snuggling under the duvet beside her. Next moment he was asleep.

Hell, I shouldn't have nagged him, thought Carrie. Unclenching her fists, she slid one hand between her legs.

Alan, who'd only been pretending to go to sleep, thought how nice it would be to see their daughter, Trixie, tomorrow. He'd missed her terribly since she'd been packed off to boarding school by Carrie, who'd been fed up with him chatting up the day-school mums.

Trixie at thirteen was alarmingly aware of her lethally emerging sex appeal. Like a principal toyboy, she had inherited her mother's ragged dark hair and her father's slenderness and delicate features. She was also clever. Alan often left her reading a book in the drawing room at night to find her still there finishing it in the morning.

Carrie was not domesticated. 'My wife can't even boil a rabbit,' Alan was fond of saying. But despite living on hamburgers, crisps and chocolate, Trixie looked surprisingly healthy.

Occasionally the family would be rounded up for photographs for an upmarket newspaper, where Carrie would appear most unusually making marmalade or playing Scrabble with Alan and Trixie.

'I'm a genius at juggling,' Carrie would tell reporters.

'Which consists of tossing Indian clubs around and bashing anyone who steps out of line,' observed Alan.

Carrie had sent Trixie to Bagley Hall, an independent boarding school only a few miles from the barn at Willowwood. Martin and Romy, on the other hand, were delighted Willowwood was in the catchment area of an extremely good state primary, so they wouldn't have to fork out.

6

The funeral was gratifyingly well attended. The high street was jammed by black-windowed, chauffeur-driven Astons, Mercs and Rolls-Royces. Eight helicopters landed in the field below the house. Private jets had to land at Bristol airport.

'If Mother hadn't been so possessive about her garden we could have had a runway here,' grumbled Martin.

But he was delighted by the presence of Bart Alderton, whose airline had always used Bancroft engines, Kevin Coley, the pet-food billionaire, Freddie Jones, the electronic maestro, Larry Lockton, who was intending to flog a supermarket, Gareth Llewellyn, who had done property deals with Sampson, racehorse owners Lazlo Henriques and Shade Murchieson, whose horse had just won the Champion Hurdle at Cheltenham, plus many more who hoped to network and do business before the afternoon was out.

The church was packed. A marquee with a video link catered for the overflow, mostly local geriatrics and Sampson Bancroft employees.

'Come to see the old bugger's really dead,' said Alan.

At the chancel steps a large, very handsome photograph of Sampson was lit up. His loud, commanding voice reverberated round the church, as one of his legendary speeches to the CBI was relayed on a big screen. The service sheet was adorned with a picture of him looking boyish and windswept in his first car.

Halfway up the church a row of pretty carers, who'd tended, read to and flirted with Sampson, sobbed to a counterpoint of keening from Sampson's mistresses, led by the *maîtresse-en-titre* and public partner Blanche Osborne, who arrived in designer black and a David Shilling fascinator. Martin, who'd always had the hots for Blanche, found her a seat in the family pew.

'Just spent three hours in make-up,' grumbled Sampson's other mistresses.

All eyes were inevitably drawn to the widow, who looked frozen, and arrived in a dowdy black coat and too summery a black straw Breton. Shopping trips to London, even taking in Chelsea Flower Show, had been ruled out once Etta had started looking after Sampson. She wore little make-up because as she dressed she had kept hearing Sampson's voice demanding: 'Why are you putting that muck on your eyes?'

Blanche rose to admit Etta to the family pew, pointedly kissing her rigid cheek, saying loudly: 'Don't reproach yourself, it could have happened to Sampy at any time.'

'She left Daddy alone to die,' hissed Carrie.

'For Christ's sake,' muttered Alan, who'd been ringing his bookmaker, 'Sampson left your mother enough during their marriage.'

Carrie had shocked the congregation by rolling up in a white shirt, black tie and dark grey pinstripe Savile Row suit.

'She should have worn a hat and a skirt for her father's funeral,' Blanche whispered to Martin.

Dame Hermione Harefield, the great diva, a close friend of Sampson, was the next to arrive: a Scottish widow in a long black velvet cloak with the hood up. Seeing Blanche ensconced, Hermione insisted on forcing her large bottom into the family pew, so Etta was rammed even closer to Blanche. Hermione's partner Sexton Kemp, a genial, charming film producer, and Blanche's husband Basil sat in the row behind.

'Why the hell did you allow Dad to shred his correspondence?' Martin chided Etta.

The congregation was getting restless, but the church stilled as Trixie sauntered in. She was wearing a black dress lifted above her groin by a huge leather belt slung round her hips, a black beret on the side of her head, turquoise patterned tights and flat pumps. Ignoring her mother's imperious wave summoning her to sit next to her in the family pew, Trixie sat down next to her father in the row behind and kissed him.

Up came the coffin, like a vast floral shopping basket.

'Biodegradable,' Martin explained to Blanche.

Bio-degrading, thought Etta. Sampson should have had oak.

'Sampy in the basket,' whispered Trixie to her father. They both shook with laughter.

The service kicked off with 'Eternal Father', because Sampson had been briefly in the Navy. Romy's fine singing voice was drowned by Dame Hermione's and taxed by a sadistic organist playing an octave too high.

'"Man walketh in a vain shadow and disquieteth himself in vain: he heapeth up riches, and cannot tell who shall gather them,"' warned the vicar.

Despite Trixie's defection, they were such a tight fit in the family pew that Etta and Blanche had to share a hassock embroidered with a white rabbit when they kneeled down, their knees rammed against each other. Etta wished Bartlett was sitting next to her; she hated leaving her all confused at home.

Dame Hermione sang 'Where'er You Walk'.

The vicar, who'd enjoyed an excellent crate of claret from Sampson every Christmas, had wanted to pay tribute to his old friend but had been pushed aside by Martin, who, in a very white shirt, black tie and dark suit, cut a much handsomer figure than his sister. The mistresses gazed at him hungrily, as he told them how heart-warming and humbling it was that they'd all turned up 'to burst our lovely church at the seams'.

'I'm Martin Bancroft,' he went on pompously. 'Today is a thanksgiving service, a celebration of a brilliant man, a field marshal of industry. Dad suffered from a deadly degenerative heart disease called Howitt's, terrifying in that it destroys organs, muscles and brain, wrapping itself around the sufferer like a boa constrictor, causing excruciating pain. I know Dad would have liked me to express his gratitude to all the nurses, carers and doctors who looked after him so selflessly.' Martin smiled around.

'What about Granny?' said Trixie loudly.

'This illness can linger on for twenty years,' droned on Martin, 'and although I would have given the world for another five minutes with Dad, God was merciful.'

The captains of industry were getting restless – all on their BlackBerries, typing with their thumbs, increasing their millions, checking emails and texts. They had deals to close, mistresses to pleasure, shares to buy, conference calls to take.

Shade Murchieson, whose horse was favourite in the 3.00 at Ludlow, said 'Fuck' very loudly when it only came fourth. Trixie got the giggles. She thought Shade was cool.

'This is going on too long,' complained Drummond, catching the mood.

'If this is Grandpa's funeral,' grumbled Poppy, 'where's Grandpa?'

'In that basket, stupid,' said Drummond.

The audience rocked with laughter.

Time for the readings: Carrie was meant to kick off with Mr

Valiant for Truth arriving in heaven and the trumpets sounding for him on the other side, followed by the Last Post.

But she suddenly lost it, couldn't get any words out and burst into tears.

An anguished Etta was about to run and comfort her but was forcibly restrained by Martin, secretly thrilled that his sister had screwed up, as the organ tactfully launched into 'Dear Lord And Father'. Etta looked up at a stained glass window of knights in armour fighting, and identified with a plump strawberry roan sidling away from the conflict.

'Still small voice of calm,' sang the congregation.

No voice could have been less still, small or calm than Sampson's, thought Etta, and blew her nose on a piece of kitchen roll, so far removed from the lace handkerchief wafting Miss Dior with which Blanche mopped her eyes.

'If Etta had died first,' Blanche whispered to Dame Hermione, 'Sampson would have married me.'

'Or me,' said Dame Hermione loftily.

'Or me, Etta's lost her looks,' reflected the mistresses.

But to their husbands and the captains of industry, Etta was still appealing. She might have lost the enticing youthful plumpness of a Golden Delicious, but with the light falling on her soft curls, her bewildered blue eyes, her sweet profile and lovely skin, she was infinitely touching.

Brian Tenby, the family lawyer, however, thought differently. Not poppy, nor mandragora shall lull you to that sweet sleep which you had yesterday, he thought pityingly, when you hear the will tomorrow and realize Sampson's left you nothing. Penelope's suitors, of whom he had been one of the most ardent, would cool off dramatically when they heard.

Martin Bancroft had often been told he had a lovely voice. He let it break and wiped his eyes as without passion he read:

> 'Nothing is here for tears, nothing to wail
> Or knock the breast . . .
> Nothing but well and fair,
> And what must quiet us in a death so noble.'

The captains of industry next admired Romy's splendid bosom, which heaved as she spoke of Sampson only being in the next room.

'Not bloody far enough,' muttered Alan.

Outside, it was a lovely day. The sun streaming through the stained glass windows cast rakish scarlet and emerald streaks on the congregation's hair and a blue rinse on little Drummond's blond curls. Hardly able to see over the lectern, he charmingly listed the things he loved about Sampson: 'Grampy loved tomatoes and *The Simpsons*. Grampy was always pinching my chips.'

Poppy then sang a song and refused to leave the lectern until the congregation, led by her mother, applauded loudly.

Trixie, who'd been texting throughout the service, got up to read from Robert Louis Stevenson and nearly gave Uncle Martin a coronary with the shortness of her skirt. How could anyone, reflected the captains of industry, have flesh that was so firm yet meltingly soft at the same time?

'Under the wide and starry sky,'

she began meditatively,

'Dig the grave and let me lie:
Glad did I live and gladly die,
And I laid me down with a will.

This be the verse you 'grave for me:
Here he lies where he long'd to be;
Home is the sailor, home from the sea,
And the hunter home from the hill.'

Closing the book, she smiled round at the congregation. 'Grampy also liked short skirts,' she drawled, mocking her little cousin Drummond. Next moment her mobile rang and she got the giggles again. 'That'll be Grampy, asking when we're going to get stuck into the Bolly. He loathed hanging around.'

Laughter rocked the church, as an apoplectic Martin leapt to his feet to take up his position on the chancel steps beside Sampson's photograph.

'I want you all to know,' he boomed, 'this week I've travelled the road to Damascus. As a result I'm giving up the City and going to devote my life to fundraising – kicking off by launching the Sampson Bancroft Memorial Fund to aid research into Howitt's.' More sobs and clapping. 'I know many of you wanted to send flowers. I hope instead you'll make donations to find a cure for this hideous recently identified condition. Sampson, you'll agree, was a man who made a difference. I want to make a difference too.'

'And a fucking fortune,' murmured his brother-in-law.

'Now who's going to kick-start me?' asked Martin.

Shade Murchieson, a show-off, carefully laid a wodge of £50 notes on the silver collection plate, putting everyone else on the spot.

Prayers followed, because the vicar was determined to have his innings. The church would also need a new roof after it had been taken off by Dame Hermione.

Then Martin was on his feet again: 'Just to prove Dad was a fun person and never square,' and the organ and the trumpeter, who also wanted his innings, launched into 'Cherry Pink And Apple Blossom White', which Sampson had once sung to Etta. The audience went laughing and bopping into the sunshine, through the daffodils in the churchyard to the huge grave into which Sampson's body was lowered.

Clutching Martin's hand, half fainting, Blanche chucked a bunch of crimson-flecked geraniums into the grave. They were immediately covered in earth.

7

Back at Bluebell Hill, guests spilled out on to the lawn to admire the view and Etta's exquisite sweeps of pink and purple cyclamen, sky-blue scillas and white daffodils, deep blue grape hyacinths mingling with a crowd of pale purple crocuses and crimson polyanthus. Everyone was speculating how many mil the house would go for while agreeing it looked 'a little tired', like poor Etta.

Inside, a distressed, trapped Bartlett had been sick everywhere, giving Etta a feeling of normality as she rushed round wiping it up, realizing with stunned horror that she'd never be bathing or washing Sampson's huge body again.

'Have a drink, Granny.' Trixie handed her a brimming glass of champagne. 'You were so brave not to cry.'

'My problem is I'm too sensitive,' sighed Blanche, emerging from the downstairs loo where she'd been repairing her face. She must buttonhole Martin and see that the £50,000 a year that Sampson had promised her would hold good.

'I'm too caring as well,' agreed Romy, removing her hat and shaking her hair free and steering Blanche into the drawing room. 'Mummy turned me to face the mirror the other day and said: "Who's that?" I said, "It's me." "That's the person you've got to look after," said Mummy. "Put yourself first for once."'

'How is your mother?' said Blanche, who didn't want anyone put first except herself. 'Still living in Weybridge?'

'She's in Ibiza,' said Romy, 'first holiday in years. She's been wonderful helping out with the kids. They call her Granny Playbridge – they hardly know Etta,' added Romy, thinking how nice that little button-back, coral-pink chair in the corner would look in her bedroom.

'I can't believe Sampy is no more,' quavered Blanche. 'So glad I saw him and brought him some comfort the day he died. The lamb was too rare. He liked it well done, and Etta drooling over Rupert Campbell-Black upset him. I can't help thinking that if she had been more caring, Sampy might still be alive.'

Outside, the captains of industry were exchanging cards, finding customers, discussing deals. Larry Lockton had sold his supermarket.

Shade Murchieson, who had made several fortunes selling arms and explosives to the Americans to flatten Iraq, was lobbying for a multi-billion deal to rebuild its infrastructure.

Martin, meanwhile, was racing around pressing the flesh, grumbling about the snide obituaries in the left-wing papers: 'So full of errors. Dad was in such terrible pain, there has to be a feeling of liberation, but golly I'm going to miss the old boy,' he told everyone. 'Please sign the Book of Remembrance, and put your email address so we can keep in touch.'

'That dog's got to go,' insisted Romy as Bartlett, who had friends among the guests, left blonde hairs on black clothes. 'Easy on the bubbly, Alan.'

The mistresses roamed round, eyeing up possible new benefactors.

'How many horses have you got?' Trixie, perched on the balustrade showing even more leg, asked Shade Murchieson.

'Far too many.'

'Who trains them?'

'Some are with Rupert Campbell-Black.'

'Granny's pin-up.'

'And the rest with Marius Oakridge in Willowwood.'

'My parents have got a barn there. Do you think he'd give me a holiday job?'

'He might, I'll introduce you.'

As a man accustomed like Sampson to terrifying people, Shade liked Trixie being totally unafraid.

Occasionally bellows rent the air as Drummond, who'd been at the champagne, bombed around at crotch level.

'Oh God,' muttered Trixie, 'here comes Grampy's squeeze in pursuit of a new backer, you better watch out.'

'Hello, Trixie, how are you?' cried Blanche. 'I'm almost part of the Bancroft family, Shade. May I call you Shade?'

Out in the cruel sunlight, compared with Trixie, Blanche looked like a middle-aged Barbie doll whose veneer was cracking.

*

Etta was too numb to notice or be relieved Basil and Brian Tenby were no longer squeezing her waist, fingers splaying to caress her breast, murmuring endearments. Rumour was trickling around that she wasn't going to be a very rich widow. Penelope's suitors were in retreat.

She was also much too busy haring round seeing the vicar was looked after, chauffeurs were provided with something to eat and introducing people, groping to remember names of those she knew really well. Her tired brain was like a biro that has to be pressed round and round before the ink comes out.

Several old girlfriends, frightened off by Sampson, had turned up and were hugging her: 'There's a frenzy from death to burial, darling. At first you're frantic, everyone asks you to dinner to hear the grisly details, then silence, so do come and stay in the summer.'

'Don't move for a year,' advised others, 'until you know what you really want, you've made it so lovely here. Thank God you've got Bartlett.'

Martin had rabbited on for so long in church, and also ordered the waitresses to go slow with the champagne, that the Great and Not-So-Good were looking at their watches and muttering about leaving. Pilots were revving up. Etta, however, rushed round filling glasses, to Martin's disapproval:

'Go easy on the bubbly, Mother, not everyone has chauffeurs to drive them home.'

'On sports days in America,' Trixie told Shade, 'they have chauffeurs' races. We could have one now.'

In the summer house, Martin found Carrie ringing Hong Kong on the house telephone and raised an eyebrow.

'I better warn you,' Carrie replaced the receiver, 'Blanche has just told me Dad promised her fifty thousand a year after he died.'

'Don't think there's anything in writing. Hopefully Dad shredded it.'

'Well, she's told Dame Hermione, who now wants paying for today.'

'Sampson remembered me in his will and in his willy,' giggled Trixie, putting on Dame Hermione's deep, deep voice. 'Will you buy me a racehorse?' she asked Shade.

'Fond of your grandfather, were you?'

'No, he was a monster and vile to Granny.'

'Would you like a drink?' asked Alan and Etta in unison, as they met on the terrace waving bottles. Etta glanced up at the sky and shivered: 'I do hope Sampson's OK in heaven.'

'Not sure God will be too happy having such an alpha male up there,' said Alan. 'Sampson's probably fired St Peter and the Holy Ghost already. Oh cheer up, darling, you're in shock now but your life will be so much easier and more fun.'

'Granny Playbridge is in Ibiza,' announced Drummond, wolfing chocolate cake when his mother wasn't looking. 'Granny Dorset is in shock.'

'Where's shock?' asked Poppy.

The Astons and the Mercedes were departing.

'Shade Murchieson's got an SM 1 number plate, how naff,' said Trixie in disappointment.

'Stands for sado-masochist numero uno,' said Alan. 'Don't get too close to him, darling, he's not a nice man.'

'The waitresses don't need tipping, Mother,' snapped Martin, just restraining himself from reminding her that it wasn't her money any more.

8

Next morning, with none of the old teasing affection in his voice, Brian Tenby, the family lawyer, read the will and broke the news to Etta that all the money had been left to Martin and Carrie on condition they looked after their mother.

'I'm sorry, Etta, Bluebell Hill will have to be sold to pay estate duty.'

The answer, Martin assured his mother, was for her to move to Willowwood and make a fresh start.

'There are too many memories here to remind you and indeed all of us unbearably of Dad.'

'Martin and I want you to move to Willowwood,' urged Carrie, for a moment not checking her messages, 'into a charming bungalow – we've already applied for planning permission – in the valley below our barns. Joey East, an excellent local builder, can knock it up while you're winding down here. It'll probably take six months to sell.'

Seeing Etta mouthing in bewilderment and dismay, Martin took up the cudgels.

'You've been so busy caring for Dad, you haven't had time to get to know your grandchildren. "Who's Granny Dorset?" Poppy asked the other day and that's really not good enough. Granny Playbridge has been a tower of strength, but she's got a part-time job now and won't be able to drop everything and whizz over from Weybridge. I told her not to worry because you, Mother, would be stepping into the breach.'

'What about Ruthie and Hinton?' stammered Etta.

'They'll find other work,' said Carrie. 'Whoever buys here might take them on. It was what Dad wanted. We couldn't influence the will in any way.'

'But I love it here. I could let out rooms . . .'

'You've got to face up to the fact that you've got no money except your old age pension,' said Romy bullyingly. Her plan was that while she and Martin set up the Sampson Bancroft Fund and took on other charities, her mother-in-law could look after Poppy and Drummond.

'I've looked after my children single-handed,' she went on sanctimoniously. 'I need some me-time.'

Etta looked round the pretty primrose-yellow-walled room and out at the white blossom of the blackthorn exploding all over the valley.

'I don't want to go,' she whispered.

'Blanche was saying how stressed Dad was on Sunday; how he hated being left alone,' said Carrie brutally. 'If he'd lived another year, none of this would have happened. If you move to Willowwood, you can ferry Trixie back from Bagley Hall during exeats and keep an eye on her in the holidays. That will free me up to travel and Alan to get on with his book.'

Etta could have so done with Alan as an ally, but unable to face his mother-in-law's crucifixion he had sloped off to London. She stumbled to the downstairs cloakroom, where, surrounded by the photographs of Sampson's sporting achievements, she threw up her breakfast cup of Earl Grey. As she rinsed her mouth from the tap, she noticed drawing-room ornaments – the sleeping wooden lion, a Staffordshire dog and a Rockingham Dalmatian removed from Poppy and Drummond's ravening fingers – sidelined but resigned on one of Sampson's filing cabinets.

Had she killed Sampson? Weighing herself, she discovered she'd lost ten pounds, glancing down at new greenish veins rising on the backs of her hands she felt so guilty she agreed to everything.

There now seemed to be so much to do, so many hundreds of letters to answer, direct debits to cancel, clubs writing for subscriptions, charities hoping Sampson would give them a donation, hospitals reminding her Sampson was due for a check-up and sending her pamphlets telling her how well they were doing, pension policies to unravel, endless forms to be filled in, bills and funeral expenses to be paid, people ringing up. Carrie and Martin had refused to take Sampson's booming voice off the answering machine, so lots of people assumed he was still alive.

Leaving Etta to pick up the funeral bills, Carrie was still wrangling over expenses for flying back from Hong Kong.

'I've always called Etta "Mother" and kept her in the loop

because I didn't want her to be jealous of Martin's and my close-ness,' Romy told everyone, insisting that Etta come to Willowwood for Easter.

'So you can suss out the area and see what a fun village you'll be living in.'

Then Romy spoilt it by banning Bartlett.

'Harvest Home is not a Bartlett house, I'm afraid. Drummond's asthma has been awful since we've been staying here.'

'Then I can't come,' stammered Etta. 'I need Bartlett.'

'Ruthie can look after her for a weekend.'

Bartlett took matters into her big blonde paws by being desperately sick in the night. An X-ray revealed a large tumour.

'I don't want her to suffer,' whispered Etta.

'Well, she is suffering, I'm afraid,' said Mr Hollis, the vet, who came out to Bluebell Hill the next day.

Bartlett, unlike most dogs, loved the vets, particularly Mr Hollis. Wagging her feathery gold tail, she staggered out to meet him, gathering up a Bonio as a present, before her back legs collapsed.

'Couldn't she last a bit longer?' begged Etta. 'Not sure I can go on without her.'

'She's in a lot of pain, Etta,' said Mr Hollis, tapping the bubbles out of the pink liquid in his syringe.

Most poignantly of all, Bartlett held out her paw to Mr Hollis for the fatal injection. Then, as Etta held her close, Bartlett turned and smiled reassuringly at her mistress as if to say good-bye. Etta choked back a sob and hugged her but a second later, as Bartlett keeled over like a rag doll, was unable to suppress a great howl of anguish.

'Are you sure she's dead?' she sobbed, stroking Bartlett's silken gold ears.

'Quite sure.' Mr Hollis put a hand on Etta's heaving shoulders. 'I know how much she meant to you. I'll carry her outside.'

Hinton, Etta's great friend – they had pondered so many plant-ings and colour schemes together – had dug a grave in the orchard and planted a hastily knocked-up wooden cross beside it. Bartlett was buried in her tartan rug, with her favourite rubber snowman and a tin of Butcher's Tripe. Etta left on her collar and disc.

'So perhaps Sampson might find her in the underworld.'

'Bartlett's more likely to go to heaven,' said Hinton, blowing his nose.

'Might make it less easy to sell the house if the dog's buried there,' observed a beady Romy, who was still hanging around ear-marking loot for their barn and who was watching from the kitchen window.

'Etta's far more upset over the death of a smelly old dog than over Sampson,' she added disapprovingly.

'Good for her to cry, poor soul,' said Ruthie furiously. 'She was wonderful to Mr Bancroft.'

Etta had a hundred things to do but she wandered sobbing round the wood finding bluebells for Bartlett's grave.

Trixie rang her from boarding school that evening.

'So sorry to hear about Bartlett. No dog could have had a nicer home. Did you know that when you arrive in heaven all the dogs you've had come racing across a sunlit lawn to meet you? I know Bartlett will be leading the pack.'

9

Country Life had long been Etta's favourite magazine. She always enjoyed fantasizing about the houses advertised in the opening pages. Now, to her horror, Bluebell Hill was in it, and sold terrifyingly quickly to a young couple who'd made a fortune in Hong Kong, had one child, were planning more, and who promised not to dig up Bartlett.

'We love animals,' said Ariella, the pretty wife. 'We've got an ancient ginger tom who survived the flight back from Hong Kong, so he'll probably soon be joining Bartlett in the orchard.'

Etta was hardly allowed to meet them in case she was too generous in the negotiations over furniture and fittings. Ariella had loved the big Prussian-blue sofa in the drawing room, but Romy had earmarked that for the barn.

Martin, fulminating as he went through the Book of Remembrance over the people who hadn't sent a donation to the Sampson Bancroft Fund, was busy cancelling Etta's direct debits.

'Now you haven't got a dog, you'll be able to drop Battersea, the Blue Cross and Dogs Trust, and cancel that covenant with the Bournemouth Symphony Orchestra.'

It was now early May and the young couple wanted to move in in five months. As a result Etta was frantically busy clearing up and had only a couple of opportunities to visit Willowwood while her bungalow was being built.

At least it had space for a pretty garden nestled in a wood of weeping willows, and had a stream running by. To the south, across the river, was a valley of fields full of sleek racehorses, gallops and flights of hurdles and fences. To the east was the orchard of a ravishing Georgian house surrounded by parkland. To the north up the road was the village of Willowwood. The

Georgian house, Badger's Court, had just been bought by a billionaire, a widower called Valent Edwards, who Martin claimed 'had known and admired Dad'.

'So he'll be a nice neighbour for you, Mother, when he moves in, which probably won't be for a year or two. The house needs so much throwing at it.'

'Probably ripe tomatoes,' quipped Alan. 'So many of his builders' lorries keep blocking the road.'

Etta felt slightly lifted from her despair, particularly when she was driving away and a string of racehorses clattered past, their laughing riders, several on their mobiles, raising their hands to acknowledge her decreased speed.

There were evidently two trainers in the area, Marius Oakridge and Ralph Harvey-Holden. She wondered whose horses these were.

Though ever conscious of Sampson glaring down on her from on high, Etta was still having the occasional bet, comparing runners over coffee and cake every morning with Ruthie and Hinton, who she was delighted the young couple were taking on.

She was still too shocked to bother much about curtains and carpets for the bungalow. Romy had taken some measurements for her, so some of the prettier Bluebell Hill curtains could be turned up. Romy, Carrie and Martin all pooh-poohed any panic Etta might have about downsizing, as she packed up her cherished pictures, china and furniture:

'Don't worry, Mother. Anything you can't find room for, we'll accommodate in our barns.'

Sampson had left various much too good pictures to his mistresses. And, alas, he hadn't shredded the letter promising Blanche £50,000 a year.

But Etta was still overwhelmed by indecision, chilled to the marrow as ridiculous tears swept over her. How could she throw out her cigarette cards of all the Grand National winners and horse breeds? How could she discard her volumes of poetry and her pony books, *Moorland Mousie*, *National Velvet* and all the Pullein-Thompsons, or her father's favourite books, Dornford Yates, Sapper and John Buchan, or her records. There was no room in the bungalow for the cabinets of sheet music or the Steinway, which was going to Romy and Martin. Perhaps later she might be able to squeeze in a little upright. Music and reading had sustained her through so many long nights when Sampson was away.

Romy was also being horribly bossy about the clothes Etta kept putting into different piles.

'If you haven't worn something for a year, give it away.'

So Etta dispatched two carfuls to the local charity shop. Then, out shopping the day before she left, she saw two of her dresses, one black velvet, one pale blue denim, hanging disconsolately in the window and felt so sorry for them she rushed in and bought them back.

The week she left, Hinton and Ruthie gave a little party for her, inviting several of the locals, and presenting her with some beautiful white and pale pink roses for her new garden.

'If you want any plants from here, give us a ring and we'll bring them over,' said Hinton.

'We're going to miss you so much,' said Ruthie.

Suddenly Etta was hit by the realization of the sweet people and the beautiful house and garden she was leaving. Who would feed the birds every morning and the carp in the pond and the badgers and foxes at night? Who would rescue plants that were being smothered by other plants? Who would take carrots to the bay mare and the skewbald Shetland down the valley? Who would find the first coltsfoot and cry with joy over the first violets?

10

Etta arrived in Willowwood on a warm October afternoon. Sunlight was breaking through shaggy grey clouds and lighting up yellowing willows and drifting blue spirals of bonfires. Ruthie and Hinton's pink and white roses obscured any view in her rear mirror, telling her she must look forward, not back. Her heart lifted at a large sign saying 'Go slow, racehorses', and another saying 'You are entering the Little Valley of the Racehorse'.

As she drove past pretty grey-gold cottages, Etta hoped they might house potential buddies. She wished she were better at bridge. Bridge and dogs were supposed to be the best way for widows to make friends.

Her bungalow, Little Hollow, had been built at the bottom end of the village. As she dropped down a dark green tree tunnel, she was greeted by a frightful din of drilling and hammering issuing from Badger's Court. As she turned left over the stream, Martin and Romy awaited her at the gate smiling and waving, with Drummond and Poppy holding a banner saying 'Welcome to Granny Dorset'.

'How kind,' gasped Etta, then her delight turned to horror as she caught sight of her bungalow. It had been clad in fearful marzipan-yellow stone, without a single creeper or shrub to soften it.

Even worse, where on previous visits her little kitchen, drawing room and even littler bedroom had looked out on to Badger's Court, its orchard and lovely park, a vast dark hedge of mature conifers had been newly planted, totally blocking her view and casting her tiny garden into shade.

'Those trees weren't there last time,' said Etta faintly.

'No,' Martin laughed heartily, 'Valent Edwards, who's bought the place, is having a relationship with Bonny Richards, the actress, who's pathological about her privacy, so Valent doesn't want anyone looking in.'

'But what about my view and my light? Nothing will grow there.'

Worse was to come. Crossing her bedroom to a second window, she was confronted by a cement mixer. Even Martin was looking sheepish that the rest of Etta's garden, to the north, which led to a rough track up through the woods to Carrie and Martin's barns, had just been concreted over to provide parking space for his and Carrie's second cars.

'With Larkshire weather, one must have a four-wheel drive,' explained Martin.

'We're a five-car family now,' said Romy roguishly, 'although . . .' She looked doubtfully at Etta's ancient white Polo, green with moss and still coated with Bartlett's blonde hairs.

'I'm not being picked up from school in that tip,' grumbled Drummond, sticking his tongue out at his grandmother and chucking Poppy's Barbie into the cement mixer.

Etta took another horrified look at the mature conifers, asking over the hammering and drilling: 'Might Next Door thin out those trees?'

'Unlikely,' said Martin. 'Valent Edwards is a distinct addition to the village, not to mention Bonny Richards. I'm sure they'll contribute significantly to Dad's fund and Badger's Court would be the ideal venue for fundraising events. Romy and I have lots of plans. Their relationship is very new. He and Bonny need their space. I don't want to antagonize them.'

'You can still see your beloved horses across the valley from the kitchen window,' teased Romy, 'even better when all the leaves come off the trees.'

'But I've only got that patch of shade under the conifers to put my new roses.'

Suddenly the empty bungalow seemed claustrophobically crammed with bullying, square-faced Sampson replicas. She must try to stand up for herself.

'Plant them in our garden.' Romy appeared to be bestowing a huge favour – let's humour the old biddy. 'Just as you can enjoy your pictures on our walls, your furniture in our barn.' She smiled warmly at Etta. 'We want you to treat our home as your home and live as family.'

'And as a fucking unpaid nanny,' drawled Alan, sauntering in carrying a plate piled high with smoked salmon sandwiches, a magnum of Veuve Clicquot under one arm and a bottle of brandy under the other. Plonking them down on the window ledge, he hugged Etta.

'Angel, how are you? So lovely to see you. Christ, it's dark in here.' He switched on the lights. 'Who on earth planted Birnam Wood and put that ghastly parking lot outside?'

'Been in the P-U-B,' mouthed Romy to Martin, who snapped, 'Don't be negative, Alan. You know perfectly well the aggro it causes in Willowwood, cars blocking the road.'

'If you live in a community, you must think of other people,' said Romy sanctimoniously.

'So you've deprived poor darling Etta of any garden so you could dump your Chelsea tractors here.' Alan glanced round the room. 'And where's that bath you promised her?'

'Stop stirring it, Al.' Carrie stalked in, having just arrived from London in yet another Savile Row suit. 'Martin and I came to the conscious decision that baths use up too much water, which would push up Mother's bills. Showers are better for the environment. Hello, Mother.' Carrie turned to Etta. 'Hope you like your new home.'

'It's a fucking abomination,' said Alan furiously.

'Please don't swear in front of the kids,' cried Romy.

Right on cue, Drummond ran through brandishing Barbie, covered in cement, followed by his screaming sister.

'You're a fucking spaghetti Bolognese,' he yelled.

'There, you see,' Romy turned on Alan, who was edging plastic glasses out of his pocket.

Carrie was back on her mobile, working on million-pound deals. With her spare hand, she was peeling the cellophane off Alan's plate of smoked salmon sandwiches.

'Those are for Etta,' snapped Alan, opening the bottle of champagne.

'I haven't had any lunch,' said Carrie, helping herself to the sandwiches.

'Nor have I,' said Martin, grabbing two more, before handing the plate to Etta. 'Come on, Mother, keep up your strength.'

Etta's legs were shaking, but as yet there was nowhere to sit down.

'Get that inside you.' Alan handed her a brimming glass.

'That's too much,' snapped Carrie, grabbing another sandwich. 'You know how Dad hated Mother drinking.'

'And she's got a lot of sorting to do,' said Martin. 'We must unload the Polo for a start.'

'Surprised you don't want her pissed, so you can grab all the loot.' Alan filled up his own glass and put down the bottle.

'That is obnoxious,' spluttered Martin.

A full-dress row was averted by the arrival of a Pickfords removal man to check this was the right house. The pantechnicon had nearly been decapitated by the tree tunnel, he grumbled, and he hadn't liked the look of the rickety bridge across the stream.

'Hello, Mrs B,' he fondly greeted Etta, who had cooked him breakfast back at Bluebell Hill. 'Bit of a change.'

Drummond, who'd been finishing off his grandmother's champagne, was soon directing the removal van to wrong parts of the bungalow. Poppy, trying to help, dropped Etta's favourite Staffordshire dog.

'You should have packed it properly,' reproved Romy.

Martin kept chiding Etta over the number of books she'd brought.

As soon as the sofa was installed, Alan, who loved horses, got stuck into *Moorland Mousie*.

'Mother cannot throw anything away,' Martin apologized to the removal men. 'She's even brought her old dishcloths.' He held up a carrier bag in distaste.

'That's my underwear,' said Etta, and when she started giggling she found she couldn't stop.

An hour later, Hinton's roses stood on the concrete like arrivals at a party waiting to be introduced.

'I'm never going to fit everything in,' wailed Etta.

'Storage awaits at Harvest Home and Russet House,' said Romy.

'You're not taking that painting of Bartlett,' said Etta, fired up by a second glass of champagne. 'Take this one of Daddy.'

Martin raised an eyebrow. 'We'll also take the Munnings.' He grabbed an oil of a lovely dark brown mare with a blond foal. 'It's too big for here.'

'No it is not,' said Alan, grabbing it back, knowing it was Etta's favourite painting.

'Children, children,' sighed Romy. 'I want Mother to open my moving-in present.'

It was a huge alarm clock with a double bell.

'So you'll wake up in time to take the kids to school. But don't worry, you're not on parade until Monday, so you can sort your-self out,' said Romy, who was now tearing smoked salmon out of the last sandwich and handing it to Drummond.

'What in hell are you doing?' demanded Alan furiously.

'Drummond is gluten intolerant,' said Romy fondly.

'I'm glutton intolerant,' snarled Alan. 'Those sandwiches were for Etta.'

Carrie was peering into the removal van at two portraits of Sampson. 'I'll take the Emma Sergeant. You can have the John Ward, Martin.'

'Those two are going to kill off your mother,' said Alan as later, pushing aside willow fronds, he and Carrie climbed the two hundred yards up the wood to their barn, Russet House, which lay beside Harvest Home on the edge of the village.

'Can't you understand,' stormed Carrie, 'Mother will be just as useful to us? She can not only ferry about and keep an eye on Trixie, who's quite out of control, but also do dinner parties and domestic stuff for us. And free you up to finish that book,' she added, letting a willow frond whizz back and hit him in the face. Constantly suspicious of her engaging husband, Carrie also planned to use Etta as a spy.

Only after the removal men had manoeuvred her and Sampson's vast double bed into the tiny bedroom did Etta realize there was no room for the stool to her dressing table, nor to kneel and say her prayers to plead for acceptance and serenity.

Following Romy's measurements Ruthie had taken up the lovely bedroom curtains: light mauve and dark purple violets that had hung in Etta's bedroom at Bluebell Hill. In Etta's new bedroom they now hung six inches too long and muddied by removal men's feet.

Seeing his mother shivering, Martin exhorted her not to worry. 'Dad's huge duvet folded double will keep you warm.'

'I miss Sampy so much,' Romy mopped her eyes, 'seeing all his things here.'

'These came for you this morning.' Martin thrust a handful of letters into Etta's hand as they left.

Now the sledgehammers and drills of Badger's Court were silent, loneliness swept over Etta. She could have coped if she'd had a lovely bath to soak in or, more importantly, if Bartlett were still alive. She'd never feel herself until she had an animal with whom to share her life. Why did her children paralyse her with fear as Sampson had done? Why hadn't she visited the bungalow more often and laid down the law about conifer hedges and hard standings?

Listlessly she opened one of the letters. It was crammed with glow stars to put on the ceiling, and contained a card from Trixie: 'Darling Granny, Good Luck in your new home.'

Etta burst into tears. How could anyone ever call this hellhole a home?

11

Willowwood, clinging to one side of a steep wooded valley, was one of those sleepy Cotswold villages with a village green, a high street flanked by grey-golden houses, a lichened church and a pub called the Fox, because the politically correct former land-lady had lopped off the words 'and Hounds'.

To the north was the Salix Estate, inhabited by the less affluent members of the community: some old villagers, and some wilder elements given to dumping rubbish, playing too loud music and chucking fireworks. There was also Greycoats, an excellent village school, which put at least £45,000 on the house prices.

'So lovely that Drummond and Poppy will grow up with lots of local friends,' gushed Romy.

Along the bottom of the valley meandered the River Fleet and descending into it, like a host of blondes racing down to wash their hair, was a wood consisting entirely of weeping willows. The same willows, their leaves curling with the approach of autumn or falling to reveal golden stems, ringed the village and adorned the village green – hence the name Willowwood. There was a legend in the village that every time a boy was born a willow must be planted.

Rushing or trickling, depending on recent rainfall, through the village and accompanied when it reached the woods by a grassy footpath was the stream which passed Etta's bungalow, flowing into a rushy willow-flanked pond and out again, down to the river.

Willowwood was such a lovely village that its inhabitants were as appalled by Etta's bungalow as Etta herself.

How the hell had Martin Bancroft got planning permission?

People were entirely sympathetic towards Valent Edwards, who must have planted the mature conifer hedge so the lovely grey eyes of Bonny Richards didn't have to gaze on such a monstrosity.

On the Monday after Etta arrived, Romy and Martin set off on a fundraising course on how to entrap celebrities, leaving her in charge of Drummond and Poppy. Etta promptly goofed by putting chocolate, crisps and ham sandwiches made with white bread in Drummond's lunch box, which turned him into more of a fiend than ever.

Returning to the barn after school, Drummond had complained he'd seen a big rat in the potting shed, locked Etta in when she went to investigate, ate a box of chocolates she'd been sent as a moving-in present, and became so hyper he beat up his sister for letting Etta out.

Returning to screaming chaos, Romy ticked Etta off roundly. Poppy then announced that Granny was going to get a puppy.

'You are not getting a puppy, Mother,' exploded Romy. 'It would chew up everything and dirty our lovely barn. Drummond is allergic to dogs. And frankly, Etta, aren't you a little too old? It's rather selfish to take on a puppy that might outlive you. You'll be kept quite busy enough getting to know your grandchildren.'

The following morning, returning to the bungalow having dropped off Drummond and Poppy at their school, Etta began worrying about what she could give them for tea without poisoning them. And how the hell could she find a home for the towers of books on the floor, the clothes on her bed and the pictures propped against the walls before Romy bagged them for the Willowwood Autumn Fayre?

Her despondency was interrupted by a knock on the door.

Outside were a jaunty chocolate Labrador with a bunch of yellow roses in his mouth, and a very pretty teenager with a round pink face, blonde hair drawn back in a ponytail, large suspicious pale turquoise eyes fringed by thick blonde lashes, a tiny nose and a full, sweet but determined mouth. She was wearing a dark blue man's sweater, which hung to the knees of her ripped jeans. Not as tall but older than Trixie, Etta thought, putting her at fifteen.

Her manner was formal, her voice piercing, as she announced: 'Welcome to Willowwood, Mrs Bancroft. My name is Dora Belvedon. This is Cadbury who has brought you some flowers.'

But as the beaming Labrador proffered a fat paw, he reminded Etta so much of Bartlett's last moment that she burst into tears.

'I'm so sorry,' cried Dora, 'you poor thing. After death and divorce they say moving house is the most stressful experience and you've had both.'

Ushering Etta back into the bungalow, Dora handed her a piece of kitchen roll and made her a cup of coffee into which she tipped a large slug of Alan's brandy, as Etta explained about Bartlett.

'I miss her so much, she gave a paw like Cadbury. I wanted to get a puppy. There must be such lovely walks round here, but my grandson Drummond is allergic to dogs.'

Forbearing to say that most of Willowwood was allergic to Drummond, Dora said Etta could walk Cadbury whenever she wanted.

'Why don't you come for a walk with us now to cheer you up? I'll tell you who everyone is.' Then, looking at the clock: 'It's at least an hour and a half before you pick up your grandchildren from school. You don't really need a coat,' Dora helped a submissive Etta into a Barbour and wrapped a blue and white striped scarf round her neck, 'but people feel the cold at times of stress.'

'You are kind. Where d'you live?' asked Etta.

'I'm staying with Joyce Painswick,' said Dora. 'She was school secretary at Bagley Hall, where Trixie your granddaughter and I go, but she's recently retired to Ivy Cottage, just up the road. Perhaps you could go to the cinema together. She seems a dragon but she's got a heart of gold. I can't live at home at the moment. My mother's very high maintenance and is on the hunt for a new backer.'

Rather like Blanche, thought Etta with a shiver.

Crossing the wooden bridge over the rushing stream, on reaching the road Dora turned right towards the village. Parked all along the verge were vehicles whose owners were working on Badger's Court. Two lorries had stopped outside the gates for a gossip, blocking the road to the fury of a stout bald man with a bristling moustache who was driving a very clean Rover.

When hysterical tooting failed, he leapt out and started shouting, only pausing to shake his fist at Cadbury, who was lifting his leg on a sign saying 'Valent Edwards apologizes for any inconvenience caused during construction'.

Dora giggled and ushered Etta past the furore. 'That's Major Cunliffe who lives in the village. A recently retired bank manager who's got himself on every committee. He's known as Nosy Parking because he's always making a fuss about cars parking in front of his gates or sticking out two inches into the high street.

'Now Badger's Court,' Dora tucked her arm through Etta's, 'has been bought by Valent Edwards, Mr Attractive and Affordable. That stands for the cheap but nice-looking houses he sells in their millions to first-time buyers. He keeps inventing things. He's working on a new fuel to replace gas and electricity and something else to abolish waste. He's got a company called Small Print, which explains contracts and things far quicker and cheaper than any lawyer, and another one setting up care homes with people "of one's own class", as my mother would say. His wife died in the Cotchester train crash three years ago, but he's just shacked up with Bonny Richards who's half his age so all the men are drooling.

'You'll notice not a blade of grass on the verge, because of locals climbing up to gawp over the wall. Valent's arrival has caused intense excitement in Willowwood.'

As Dora and Etta peered in through the vast heraldic gates, the big house seemed to gaze out over the rubble with an air of expectancy, awaiting her new owners.

'Cadbury adores the workmen.' Dora let the dog off his lead so he went bounding towards the house. 'We can retrieve him and have a good snoop. Valent's putting in a heated swimming pool here, a tennis court, a gym and solarium, an underground cinema and a little theatre where Bonny can strut her stuff. Valent's office in the old cockpit will be amazing, according to Joey East. Joey's wonderful, I'll introduce you, he can put his hand on anything – plumbers, sweeps, electricians, stone wallers – and do most of it himself. He's just landed this plum job masterminding the complete gutting and rebuilding of Badger's Court, which is a good thing as he has four children and he gambles.'

Although there was no one in earshot, Dora lowered her voice dramatically, adding a wonderful air of mystery and conspiracy, then crying, 'Cadbury, Cadbury,' as she followed the dog over mountains of rubble, round piles of sand and craters full of black water.

'Valent's so mad for Bonny to move in, he'd buy her anything, even her own production company to make films for her to star in.'

'Have you met her?' asked a panting, fascinated Etta.

'No – but Joey tipped me off last time she came down, so I climbed up that,' Dora pointed to an ancient walnut tree, 'and had a watch.

'Bonny's a bit subtle and still waters: crisp white shirts and grey linen trouser suits. It's difficult to have a shag round here, you'd get rubble trouble, but she and Valent disappeared for yonks into an upstairs room, so I don't think it's platonic, and Bonny's shirt didn't look crisp and white when she came out.'

'You do know a lot,' said Etta in awe.

'My mother's stingy about pocket money so I tip off the press from time to time. They're obsessed with Bonny Richards.

'There's so much rubble and bashing down of buildings in Willowwood,' sighed Dora, 'that if the Martians landed they'd probably think they were in the middle of a war. Now this little house on the left,' she added as they moved on, 'is Ivy Cottage, where I'm staying with Miss Painswick. And this house, Catkin Cottage, belongs to Old Mrs Malmesbury, who keeps geese.

'And this lovely but somewhat decrepit house,' went on Dora as the road curved round to the right towards the top of the village, 'is inappropriately called the Old Rectory and belongs to Corinna Waters and Seth Bainton. You can only see the very top windows like eyes looking out over the trees, so people can't tell how badly they're behaving.'

'Not *the* Corinna Waters?' squeaked Etta in excitement. 'She's marvellous. I loved her in *The Cherry Orchard*, and she and Seth were wonderful in *Who's Afraid of Virginia Woolf?* and Seth was so sexy as Valmont.'

'You're quite a groupie, Mrs Bancroft,' said Dora approvingly.

'My son Martin and his wife are on a course, among other things, to get celebrities involved in raising money for charity,' explained Etta. 'Do you think Corinna, Seth and Bonny might . . .'

'I don't think so.' Dora shook her head until her ponytail whacked her ears. 'The only charity Corinna and Seth would subscribe to is themselves.

'They come here to relax from prying eyes, or pretend they do. Corinna gets cross if she isn't recognized. Seth is seriously naughty. Corinna likes the privacy to sunbathe in the nude – body's a bit past its best, think she's about ten or fifteen years older than Seth. Major Cunliffe, the one leaning on his horn just now, pretends to be birdwatching, but he's looking through his binoculars at Corinna. You can see the Cunliffes' garden from here, blazing with colour on the other side of the village green.

'I wouldn't think,' mused Dora, 'that there's a huge amount of love lost between Bonny Richards and Corinna. Both regard themselves as serious actresses, although everyone, including my mother, wants to get off with Valent Edwards. I don't know why, he's quite rude and seriously old, at least sixty-five.

'Seth Bainton is well fit for an older man,' acknowledged Dora. 'He's a great friend of your son-in-law Alan, Mrs Bancroft. I think he and Corinna are a bit into wife-swapping, or partner-swapping as they're not married. Seth is known as Mr Bulging Crotchester,' giggled Dora as they set off up the road, 'and he's mad about your granddaughter Trixie, but then all the men are. She's the hottest girl at Bagley Hall except for my friend Bianca Campbell-Black.'

'Rupert's daughter?' sighed Etta. 'Rupert really is gorgeous.'

'My mother adores Rupert too, even though he's extremely rude to her, sensible man. She doesn't approve of Seth Bainton but she fancies him rotten. Seth has an excellent greyhound called Priceless, who he refuses to castrate so he's always jumping on other people's dogs and crapping in the high street. Debbie Cunliffe, she's the bossyboots with the brilliantly coloured garden, married to the major, would like both Seth and Priceless castrated. She organized a meeting recently to discuss ways Willowwood could be improved. Seth suggested a casino, a betting shop, a massage parlour, and Debbie and the Major going back to Surrey. Debbie was furious.'

'Seth's awfully attractive,' said Etta, accepting a toffee from Dora, hoping it wouldn't pull her bridge out.

Reaching the top of the village, they passed a lovely eighteenth-century house covered in scaffolding, iron bars and platforms on all levels.

'Awful,' spluttered Dora. 'Like some woman with curlers, braces on her teeth and having every inch of her body lifted. This house, believe it or not, was called Primrose Cottage. It's been bought by a dreadful porn billionaire called Lester Bolton, known as Bolton Wandering because he's such a groper. He paid two mil for Primrose Cottage, has renamed it Primrose Mansions, and is chucking another four mil at it, and not moving in for a year or two either. He can't cock it up too much because English Heritage is breathing down his neck.'

Etta couldn't stop laughing and patting Cadbury.

'Bolton,' went on Dora, 'has a child-bride second wife called Cindy, the most frightful giggling chav who calls herself an actress and stars in all his porn films.'

12

After providing and receiving so much information, Dora and Etta had a rest on a bench on the edge of the village green, admiring the houses clustering around it. 'Such a sweet village,' cried Etta, then, catching sight of the church clock rising above the ring of golding willows: 'I mustn't be late.'

'You've got at least forty minutes.'

But Etta had been distracted by the most beautiful Elizabethan house. Set back from the village green, it peered out of narrowed windows, was partly hidden by venerable trees and had a magic garden, all soft colours merging like a rainbow. How could anyone get delphiniums flowering in October and such a pastel profusion of roses?

'Willowwood Hall,' explained Dora. 'Alban and Ione Travis-Lock live there. They've just come back from some Arab country where Alban was ambassador, with masses of servants and bodyguards following his every movement. He's seriously clever and speaks loads of languages. But the moment he retired, there wasn't even a car to meet him at Heathrow. So unkind.

'Everyone kowtows to his wife Ione, because she was a Framlingham before she married. Framlinghams have lived in Willowwood Hall for ever. Ione looks like one of Auden's Dowagers with Roman noses. Oh look, there she blows.' Dora leapt behind a telephone box that said 'no coins allowed' as a terrifying woman, not unlike the witch in *The Wizard of Oz*, hurtled past on a bicycle. 'That's Ione off to set up her stall outside Tesco's and bellow at customers for not recycling their packaging. She's terribly Green. Alban, her husband, will be straight into the pub to have a large whisky and a bet.

'Oh, look again!' Dora grabbed Cadbury as horses came

clattering by, doing road work for the coming season. 'That's Sir Cuthbert, the oldest horse in the yard, and History Painting, the yard star, and Stop Preston, who's seriously naughty, and Oh My Goodness, isn't that a cool name? She's the one showing a lot of white eye, making her look permanently surprised.' Dora beamed and waved at all the riders.

'They're Marius Oakridge's horses,' she went on. 'His yard's that way.' She pointed south. 'Ralph Harvey-Holden's to the north and twenty miles up the road is Rupert Campbell-Black's yard at Penscombe.'

'How thrilling,' said Etta, then, terrified of being late: 'I must go.'

'We've got half an hour,' said Dora airily. 'Since Alban Travis-Lock retired Ione has returned to reclaim her rightful place as lady of the manor, but she's got competition from pretenders like Debbie Cunliffe and Romy Bancroft, who is another cow and so smug. Romy insisted on doing the flowers last Easter and brought branches of may blossom into the church. Ione nearly had a heart attack – may's so unlucky. Romy doesn't know anything about the country,' went on Dora furiously. 'Oh whoops. So sorry, Mrs Bancroft, I quite forgot Romy was your daughter-in-law. She's seriously beautiful and a much better mother than mine will ever be.'

'It doesn't matter.' Etta was ashamed at how enormously comforted she felt.

'Trixie's great, as I've said,' Dora went on hastily. 'And Alan, your son-in-law, is really nice, he bought me a gin and tonic in the pub last week and a packet of pork scratchings for Cadbury. He's always buying rounds. He's really popular and a very good journalist when he writes. I'm going to be a journalist when I leave school.'

'And be a wonderful one,' said Etta warmly. Moving down the village green they reached a sweet little house covered in red vine with a lovely but untended garden.

'That's Wild Rose Cottage,' said Dora. 'Toby and Phoebe Weatherall live there at weekends. Toby's Ione Travis-Lock's nephew. He earns quite a lot in the City working for your daughter Carrie.'

'Really?' squeaked Etta. 'Does he like her?'

'I think he's a bit scared of her. He's rather a wimp.'

As they passed a duck pond on the right, with Cadbury straining on his lead to put up the ducks, Dora hissed: 'Quick, put on a pair of dark glasses,' as they reached a square house with a front garden crammed with frantically clashing dahlias and chrysanthemums. 'This is Debbie Cunliffe's splash of colour. She's always having rows with Ione Travis-Lock, who thinks Debbie's flower arrangements in the church are too gaudy.

'Her husband, the Nosy Parking Major, is always bellyaching about people driving or riding too fast through Willowwood – all jockeys drive too fast and overtake on the inside. Debbie is frightfully tactless, she's known as Direct Debbie. Their house is called Cobblers, says it all really.' Dora grinned.

'Now this pretty hideous modern house next door belongs to Joey East, Valent's site manager, I told you about him. Joey built it himself,' confided Dora, 'and got away with murder because he knows all the planners, so he didn't have to bribe anyone. The Major and Debbie loathe having Joey next door because of the loud music and his four children bouncing around on the trampoline.

'The only other ugly house in the heart of the village is built straight on to the high street opposite the pub.' Dora lowered her voice. 'Niall Forbes, the vicar, lives in it. Seth and Corinna riot around in the Old Rectory and Niall – who's as gay as a daffodil, incidentally – is fobbed off with the New Rectory, a horror with no front garden so everyone can peer in to see what he's up to.

'Next time I'll include a tour of the high street, the church and the school, and tell you the legend of Willowwood. It's so romantic,' promised Dora.

In the distance Etta could hear children shouting in the school playground and disloyally wondered who Drummond was murdering. They had walked almost in a circle to reach fields stretching away on the eastern side of the village. Above woods of willows flowing down to the river stood two imposing but adjacent barns, Harvest Home and Russet House.

'You don't need to be told anything about the people who live there,' said Dora, 'although I've probably said far too much about Romy.'

'It really doesn't matter, I've had such a heavenly time,' cried Etta. As they took the steep footpath on the right of the barns that ran down through the woods to Etta's bungalow, Cadbury leapt into the stream, bouncing around, snatching at great mouthfuls of water.

To the left through thinning trees, they could see the extent of the work going on at Badger's Court.

'Poor Niall, the vicar, is desperately low.' Taking Etta's arm so she didn't slip, Dora had to shout over the din of the builders. 'No one really goes to church except Martin and Romy sometimes, Direct Debbie and the Major, Painswick who I'm staying with and Old Mrs Malmesbury who keeps geese. She's very deaf and yells to poor Niall to speak up.

'And of course the Travis-Locks, who've got their own pew and a door from their garden into the church. Niall's so petrified of Ione he can hardly get a syllable of sermon out, and she's always bullying him to urge the congregation not to flush the loo and to bicycle to work. And he's useless at refereeing rows between flower arrangers and bell-ringers. But he's rather a boozer, so lock up your brandy if he descends on a pastoral visit. Now here we are at your bungalow.'

'Which makes even the New Rectory look like a period gem,' said Etta bitterly.

'Well, the yellow blends in nicely with the autumn colours,' said Dora kindly.

'It's been such a treat. You have both cheered me up so much,' said Etta, hugging Cadbury. 'Oh, look at that glorious horse,' she added in wonder as a huge black gelding with a zigzag of white blaze came pounding past, hooves sending up sparks from the road.

'That's Ilkley Hall,' said Dora. 'He belongs to Shade Murchieson, a rich and incredibly difficult owner. Half of his horses are with Rupert and half with Marius Oakridge. Marius is terrified Shade's going to take his horses away and send them all to Rupert because Rupert's more successful. Shade likes to keep trainers on the hop.'

Etta remembered Shade Murchieson at Sampson's funeral, saying 'Fuck' when he got an email that his horse hadn't won. Shade of the brutal good looks and the hard, indifferent eyes.

'Hang on a sec.' Etta rushed into the bungalow and rushed out again waving a beautiful royal-blue collar studded with brass dog's heads. 'I noticed Cadbury's collar's a bit worn. I'd like you to have this one, given to Bartlett for her last birthday.' Etta's voice trembled. 'She never wore it.'

'Thank you so much,' said Dora. 'I love it to bits and it will really suit Cadbury, thank you so much, see you very soon.'

13

Etta's day got better and better. She managed to pick up, feed and get pyjamas on Poppy and Drummond and supper of baked potatoes and beef stew into the oven at Harvest Home before Martin and Romy returned from a day spent wrestling over the legal aspects of fundraising.

'You've no idea how hard it is even to print raffle tickets these days,' grumbled Romy.

Clinging on to willow branches, Etta walked for a second time down the steep path, wishing Bartlett was waiting with waving tail and big loving brown eyes, only to find her son-in-law waving a bottle on the doorstep.

'Carrie has gone to Tokyo, so I thought I'd drop in and see how you were.'

'Wonderful,' cried Etta. 'Sorry about the mess.' She removed a pile of Dornford Yates so Alan could sit on the sofa.

'As long as we can find the corkscrew.' Alan rootled around in the kitchen drawer. 'You must get a special hook for that utterly crucial instrument.'

'I've had such a good day,' sighed Etta. 'An absolutely darling child called Dora banged on my door with those lovely roses and such a sweet dog, which she says I can walk. She took me on a tour of the village and told me all about Valent and Bonny, and the Travis-Locks – we saw her biking off like a Valkyrie – and the Major and his wife Direct Debbie and lots of gossip about Seth and Corinna, and Ilkley Hall pounded by. Nor did I know that someone called Toby Weatherall, who lives here, works for Carrie.'

'I don't know for how long.' Alan filled two large glasses to the top with red. 'Toby's pretty thick and chinless and addicted to long weekends slaughtering wildlife, which doesn't fit my wife's 24/7 work ethic.'

'But Dora's such a darling, so clever, and so kind to geriatrics like me.'

'Dora has a lot of artistic older brothers and sisters, and a much older father, who died a few years ago, who she misses dreadfully.'

'She doesn't like her mother very much.'

'Anthea's an absolute bitch who doesn't give Dora any money, so combined with a truly kind heart, she has a dubious ability to flog stories to the nationals, so watch it. Dora's now staying with Miss Painswick, an old biddy who used to be the school secretary.'

'Who lives in Ivy Cottage,' said Etta triumphantly. 'Dora suggested we went to the cinema together.'

'You need someone more exciting than that.'

Etta noticed Alan was looking unusually smart in a blue and yellow striped shirt and light blue corduroy jacket. His blond curls, usually rumpled after a day of writing, were brushed smooth. As he bent over to top up her drink, she smelled lemon aftershave and toothpaste.

'I shouldn't,' she said, putting her hand over her glass. 'I'm terrified of turning into an old soak.'

'Marius Oakridge's horse Stop Preston is running at Stratford on Thursday.'

'I saw him today, he's gorgeous.'

'He's a very good horse, but rather given to mulish antics. Why don't you come?'

'I've got to look after Drummond and Poppy,' said Etta wistfully. 'Martin and Romy are still on their charity course.'

'I'll put on twenty quid for you,' said Alan, then idly, 'Did Dora say anything about Bonny Richards and Valent?'

'That she climbed up a walnut tree and saw them disappear into an upstairs room for hours and hours, and Bonny came down with her shirt crumpled.' Etta put one hand on her hip like Dora and thrust out the palm of the other.

'Not platonic then,' grinned Alan, wondering if it was worth ringing his old newspaper, but he'd lost the taste for selling stories. They always expected one to do more work following them up.

'How's the book going?' asked Etta.

'Backwards. I'm bored rigid with depression. Perhaps I should interview you.'

'I'm fine. Today's really bucked me up. There's going to be tons to watch in the village. Everyone adores you and Trixie, according to Dora. The dear child sent me some glow stars to stick to the ceiling.'

'That's nice.' Alan drained his drink, rinsed his glass and put it in the dishwasher. 'I better go home, I've not done enough work yet.'

Kissing his mother-in-law, he went out into the night, but turned left to where he'd parked his car earlier, rather than right and home to Russet House. If Carrie was going to use Etta as a spy, Alan was going to use her as an alibi.

14

Later in the week, having spent an awful morning getting Drummond and Poppy off to school with suitably E-zero and organic lunch boxes, sending off change of address cards: 'Mrs Etta Bancroft has moved to Blot on the Landscape bungalow', and writing to insurance companies and people who hadn't realized Sampson was dead, Etta was delighted to receive another visit from Dora and Cadbury in his new royal-blue collar. They carried her off on another familiarization tour. It was such a mild, sunny autumn morning that Dora pointed out two men, stripped down to their tight jeans, who were sunbathing in deckchairs on Valent Edwards's flat roof.

'That's Woody Adams and Joey East, Valent's site manager, the one who built his own house in the village. Woody's the local tree surgeon, stunningly good-looking. If he appears at the window when old ladies are playing bridge, they promptly revoke.

'In fact, if I hadn't got a gorgeous boyfriend,' Dora flashed a white blob on her mobile at Etta, 'who's at an audition as we speak, I could easily be tempted by Woody.

'Joey, the other man in a deckchair, is a terrific boozer, probably sleeping off a hangover. He and Woody and Jase, the local farrier, who's the worst tipster in the world, have a syndicate. They own a horse called Not for Crowe.

'Such a sweet story: Lady Crowe, who's a big owner round here, read the catalogue for Rutminster Sales and put in a bid for a chestnut gelding, but retreated in horror when she saw him in the flesh. So a label saying "Not for Crowe" was hung from the poor thing's head collar. Woody, who's such a softie, felt so sorry for him he bought the horse for the syndicate and they called him Not for Crowe.

'I think Lady Crowe got it right,' sighed Dora. 'He's a darling but he comes last in every race. They've got a second horse, a dark brown with a white face called Family Dog, who came third at the Penscombe point-to-point, but there were only three horses in the race. They've asked me to join their syndicate.' Dora beamed with pride.

Willowwood was such a beautiful village, thought Etta, scattered as it was over the steep hillside, all higgledy-piggledy, so fields reared up above houses, and cars and cows appeared to be running along the rooftops. It had such a mixture of big houses on the green, terraced houses on the high street concealing charming gardens and winding paths leading up to other houses, jewelled by equally pretty gardens.

Etta felt so sad she hadn't got a garden. But it was the beauty of the stone, like a looking glass, turning grey on cloudy dull days, platinum blond in the noon heatwaves, soft rose red at sunrise and sunset, rich gold on this sleepy, midge-flecked October morning, that made the place so lovely.

Reaching the very top of the village, Etta and Dora turned right, down into the high street, passing a statue of a handsome Cavalier with long stone curls, waving a plumed hat and astride a splendid pacing horse.

'That's Sir Francis Framlingham, Mrs Travis-Lock's great-great-great-great-great or something who was a bigwig in the Civil War. It was all fought round here, you can see bullet holes in the church.'

Turning off the high street, Dora led Etta up a lane and some stone steps through the lychgate into the churchyard, on to mossy, springy grass cushioned by the dead.

'What a beautiful church.' Etta admired the soaring spire and glinting gold weathercock.

'Twelfth century.' Dora was about to push through the big oak door when she glanced at the noticeboard in the porch.

'Oh bugger, run for it. Flower de-rangers at eleven thirty.' Then, at Etta's startled look: 'Mrs Travis-Lock and Debbie Cunliffe are about to do the flowers and have wildly opposing views on colour schemes and who decorates what bit. And I for one don't fancy telling you the Willowwood legend about Mrs Travis-Lock's rellies with her butting in all the time. I'll give you the history tour next time I'm down here.

'Look,' she hissed, dragging Cadbury and Etta behind a large plague stone as stack-heeled shoes and thick flesh-coloured ankles topped by a vast clashing orange, scarlet, crimson, bright yellow, royal blue and purple herbaceous border came scuttling past, revealing from the back a seal-like body in a strawberry-pink coat and skirt and iron-grey curls more sculptured than those of Sir Francis Framlingham.

'That's Direct Debbie,' said Dora, falling about with laughter, 'frantic to get inside before Ione rolls up.' Then, at the crunch of wheels on gravel and the crash as a bicycle came through a side door into the churchyard: 'Too late, too late, here comes Ione with flowers of delicate hue in front and back basket. Birnam Wood's going to be in collision with Birnam Wood Two any minute.

'And here comes Painswick, who I'm staying with,' whispered Dora, as a woman in her late fifties and a blue tent dress, who had the face of a disenchanted Pekinese and her arms full of bronze chrysanthemums, ran up the path.

'Painswick's quite religious but she can't have a comforting crush on the vicar because, as I told you, he's gay,' said Dora, as they retreated down the steps and headed back to the high street.

'Now that house, Sky Cottage, belongs to Pocock, a lonely widower, who keeps himself busy running the allotments and calls himself Tower Captain because he organizes the bell-ringers. He's a very good gardener and works for Mrs Travis-Lock and formerly for your son Martin, who sacked him.'

'Oh dear,' sighed Etta.

'Because they wanted a low-maintenance all-lawn-and-trampoline garden and Pocock likes borders and flowers.

'One of Willowwood's greatest tragedies,' Dora rolled her eyes dramatically as she pointed to a sweet little house with a yellow door, 'is that Lark Cottage over there used to be rented by Rogue Rogers when he was first retained by Marius Oakridge, before he became champion jockey. Rogue was seriously wild, and evidently pulled everything except curtains. After he left, blondes were found under the floorboards. I wish he still lived there.'

'He's a wonderful jockey,' agreed Etta.

At that moment, a tall man shot across the road into the pub.

'That's Mrs Travis-Lock's husband, Alban,' hissed Dora. 'No one's offered him another job since he left the Foreign Office, not even some stupid quango to boast about at drinks parties, so he's very sad with no one to boss or influence. Their black Lab, Araminta, is also having a nervous breakdown; she's so used to policemen on guard duty petting her and cooks in the kitchen feeding her midnight snacks, poor dog. Mrs Travis-Lock's not the sort of person to indulge husbands or Labradors. She's refusing to cook Alban any lunch, so he goes to the pub,' Dora lowered her voice, 'putting away rather too many with your son-in-law and Seth Bainton when he's around.'

As they drew level with the pub, assailed by a heavenly smell of garlic, red wine and roasting meat, Cadbury sniffed excitedly. Etta, who'd been living on cheese on toast, boiled eggs and latterly Drummond and Poppy's leftovers, felt wonderfully hungry and very daring.

'Shall we have lunch in the pub?'

'That would be cool,' said Dora. 'Are you sure? One of the good things about the Fox is they allow in dogs.'

15

Outside the pub, an inn sign of a jaunty fox in a red coat riding a grinning hound attempted to pacify the anti-hunting brigade. Inside, the message was less ambiguous: horns, hunting whips, bridles, foxes' brushes and pads on silver mounts, even a stuffed fox in a glass case fought for space on the whitewashed walls with gleaming horse brasses and photographs of hunt servants drinking outside large houses, hounds spilling through the village and in full cry across khaki fields.

'That's me on my pony Loofah,' Dora pointed to a ferocious child, flaxen pigtails flying, hurtling along with the leaders, 'and that's Marius Oakridge, the trainer. His father was Master for yonks. Marius is completely one-track – "What war in Afghanistan?" – he never stops working, even hunting he's always trying out young horses or schooling them.'

'He's gorgeous.' Etta peered closer. Even surrounded by a laughing group, knocking back glasses of port and accepting pieces of fruit cake, Marius, on a sidling chestnut, looked isolated, his pale face guarded, still and thoughtful.

'That's his stunning wife, Olivia, on the grey,' added Dora, 'and that's Claudia, the wife of Willowwood's other trainer, Ralph Harvey-Holden. She left him last summer, because he's so jealous and threatened to sell some horse she adored. And that hound's called Oxford. He was walked as a puppy by Old Mrs Malmesbury, and often runs home to her at Catkin Cottage if the hunting gets boring.'

Etta felt terribly guilty. Sampson had thoroughly disapproved of her going into pubs. She was, however, so touched by Dora's kindness, particularly when Dora immediately introduced her to Chris the landlord, who was fat and jolly, with a big smile, slicked-back dark hair and tired bloodshot eyes, which winked a lot.

'Chris runs this place brilliantly,' explained Dora, 'particularly because he allows dogs in. This is Cadbury's favourite pub.'

Cadbury thumped his tail expectantly.

'Chris, this is Mrs Bancroft who's just moved into Willowwood.' Hearing the name, Chris's smile dimmed then returned to full beam as Dora added, 'Alan's mother-in-law.'

Putting down the glass he was polishing, Chris pumped Etta's hand. 'Any friend of Alan's, who incidentally has spoken very warmly of you, Mrs Bancroft. 'Ave one on the 'ouse.'

'How incredibly kind, are you sure? I'd love a small glass of white wine. I've got to pick up my grandchildren later.'

'And you don't want to be drunk in charge of a monster,' said Dora. 'I'd like a Coke if that's OK, Chris.'

'We were hoping we might have some lunch?' asked Etta. Somehow having food in a pub made it less decadent.

'All up there.' Chris pointed to a blackboard. 'Fishcakes is nice. Pheasant's tasty, so's Irish stew.'

'How lovely, fishcakes for me.'

Dora, thinking of a doggie bag for Cadbury, said she'd like steak and chips.

'That's an awfully big glass, thank you,' gasped Etta. 'So cosy and such a lovely fire and, even better, *At the Races* on television.'

'Local Derby at one thirty,' said Chris as Etta wandered towards the set. 'Marius Oakridge and Harvey-Holden have both got horses running in the maiden hurdle at Stratford. Harvey-Holden's maiden proved a bit of an 'urdle for him.' Chris winked at Etta. 'He named an 'orse Claudia Dearest after his missus, and she's pushed off.'

'Poor man,' cried Etta, 'how humiliating.'

'He's not very nice,' said Dora. 'He doesn't feed his horses or pay his staff enough, and he works them much too hard, and he threw Claudia's saddle out into the pouring rain.

'I was going to take Mrs Bancroft round the church and tell her about the Willowwood legend,' Dora added to Chris, 'but Mrs T-L and not much C and Direct Debbie were about to have a punch-up.' Then as Chris coughed and gave her a warning look, Dora swung round to find Alban Travis-Lock lurking in an alcove behind the racing pages of *The Times*.

'Hello, Mr Travis-Lock,' Dora changed legs briskly, 'you haven't met Mrs Bancroft.'

Alban leapt to his feet, nearly concussing himself on a low beam, and offered to buy Etta and Dora a drink as an excuse to fill his own glass.

'That's so kind, I've got one,' said Etta.

'Put one in for Dora and Mrs Bancroft, Chris,' called out Alban. 'Same again for me.'

Travis-Lockjaw, thought Etta, as Alban spoke through clenched teeth. He had receding hair, a domed forehead, big mournful turned-down eyes, a snub nose above a long upper lip and a big mouth. Not unlike an elder-statesman orang-utan campaigning for the preservation of the species.

Cadbury, hopeful of pork scratchings, put his head on Alban's brown corduroy thigh.

'Cadbury is deeply in love with Mr Travis-Lock's Lab, Araminta,' said Dora.

Noticing Alban had a most charming smile, showing large but well-tended teeth, Etta said: 'Dora tells me you were a wonderful ambassador.'

Alban blushed. 'One did one's best, thank you, Dora,' and noticed that now Mrs Bancroft had taken off her Barbour, her ancient and shrunk navy-blue jersey showed off her pretty breasts and eyes.

'Have you had a bet?' asked Dora.

'Well, Jase the farrier was in yesterday and said he'd put on Claudia Dearest's racing plates, and she was an absolute cert, so I think most of Willowwood's backed her.'

'Alan was going to back Stop Preston,' volunteered Etta, wondering if he'd remembered to put something on for her.

They had lunch together near the television. Etta found herself perched on a stool shaped like a fox's head. Her crab fishcakes were utterly delicious and she noticed Alban wolfed up his Irish stew with similar relish. Dora gave most of her steak to Cadbury.

Alban glanced wistfully up at a photograph of a lawn meet outside Willowwood Hall.

'That's your gorgeous garden,' exclaimed Etta, 'and that's you in a topper.'

'Nineteen ninety-five,' said Alban, 'back on leave before the posting to Cairo. The one thing I looked forward to in my retirement was buying an ex-chaser and going out three or four days a week. Now it's banned.'

'I've had some excellent runs this season,' Dora assured him. 'The hunt meets at the pub in the second week in November,' she added to Etta. 'Hounds charged the bar last time, Oxford's sister led the stampede. You'll have to come and cheer us on.'

Etta took a deep breath. 'I'm so sorry, I don't approve of hunting – poor fox.'

'Poor fox killed Old Mrs Malmesbury's gander last week in

broad daylight,' said Dora sternly. 'He plucked him then ate him, there were feathers everywhere.'

'I know, I know.' Etta shook her head.

Seeing the distress on her face, Dora changed the subject.

'This pub is where Joey, Jase the farrier and Woody meet to discuss their syndicate every Wednesday. Their dream is to put Not for Crowe and Family Dog in training with Marius, but I don't think he'd take them, sweet as they are.'

'Doggie's a Shetland,' mocked a pretty girl with long red hair wearing a tight white skirt through which could be seen a leopardskin thong. She had come over to take their plates away. 'Everything OK?'

'Delicious,' sighed Etta.

'That's Chris's wife,' whispered Dora. 'Her name's Chrissie, which confuses things. Joey fancies her like mad even though he has a very pretty wife, known as Mop Idol, who cleans for Mrs Travis-Lock.'

'She does,' said Alban happily.

'Because they're always producing children,' giggled Dora, 'Joey's known as "Go Home for Lunge".'

Alban choked on his drink.

'And talk of the devil, here come Joey and Woody to watch the local derby,' crowed Dora.

Joey had an all-weather face, foxy, knowing and sensual, a chunky body and the air of one at ease with his fellow men. A gold pen was tucked into his black woolly hat.

Now that she could see his face, Etta appreciated Woody was indeed a beauty, with wonderful broad shoulders, a lean long-legged body, thick blond curls flecked with sawdust, a smooth forehead, high cheekbones, kind, darkly shadowed, greeny-blue eyes and a beautifully soft mouth.

Dora, in her element, was about to introduce Etta but the two men just nodded and didn't come over.

'See your boss has been down to Badger's Court enjoying empty bedrooms 'ere with his lady friend, Joey,' shouted Chris, waving the *Daily Mail.*

'Didn't tell me,' snapped Joey, who'd signed a confidentiality agreement not to spread any gossip about Valent and Bonny, and much regretted tipping off Dora, in a moment of weakness, about last week's visit. Not wanting her to thank him in public, he kept his distance.

Woody, who had been responsible for planting the mature conifers round Etta's garden, was also looking sheepish.

The runners for the one thirty were circling the parade ring.

'There's Stop Preston,' said Dora, going towards the television.

'We saw him in the flesh,' squeaked Etta.

'Mrs Bancroft's moved into the bungalow next to Valent's,' Dora told an approaching Joey. 'She needs bookshelves and her pictures hanging. She's mad about horses. What are you two on?'

'Claudia Dearest. Jase said she'd walk it. And an each way on Asbo Andy.'

'Claudia looks a bit peaky to me,' said Dora.

'Harvey-Holden paid five grand for that mare,' said Chris disapprovingly. 'But when his missus, Claudia, pushed off, he sold her to that syndicate for fifty grand.'

Harvey-Holden, a little man in a flat check cap, could hardly be seen for the syndicate – thick-necked hoods bulging out of their brown shiny suits – that surrounded him.

'Look at them hanging on his every dishonest word,' said Joey.

'You had a bet?' asked Woody, looking Etta in the eye for the first time.

'I'm not sure. Alan, my son-in-law, fancied Stop Preston.'

'Looks bloody well,' said Joey, as the gleaming bay bounded round, shoving his stable lass into the rails. 'Dubious who's leading who. Here's Marius.'

'Gloomy as ever,' said Chris.

'Gets very strung up,' said Chrissie.

'Shade will string him up if Stop Preston doesn't win,' observed Woody.

Etta felt so sorry for Marius as he was joined by Shade, who was wearing a belted camel-hair coat, and talking and talking, gesticulating, rings flashing, when Marius, clearly jangling with nerves, wanted to distance himself.

'Look at Shade kissing Olivia on the mouth, bloody letch,' said Joey. 'Shade doesn't rate "Awesome" Wells as a jockey,' he went on. 'According to Jase, he wanted Rogue Rogers to ride Stop Preston. Awesome is so thick, if Marius gives him instructions he forgets them by the time he's up. But he rides bloody well.'

'Preston looks fantastic,' sighed Dora. 'Oh dear, he's bucked Awesome off.'

'Must be hard for Marius,' said Alban, circling downward-pointed fingers to indicate to Chris that he wanted to buy another round, 'keeping all these ambitious owners happy. Rupert Campbell-Black can afford to tell them to eff off.'

The horses were down at the start, Shade's orange and magenta colours rivalling the yellows, reds and rusts of the turning trees. Preston was tugging at his bit, bouncing on the spot, eyeballing the competition, thinking up new naughtiness.

Next moment the group round the television were joined by a bustling, self-important figure with a horizontal moustache.

'Are they off yet?'

'Not quite,' said Chris. 'Your usual, Major?'

Major Cunliffe had a gin and tonic and turned to Alban.

'Our lady wives are still in the church.'

'Going to be secateurs at dawn,' said Alban gloomily.

The Major had backed Asbo Andy. 'Can't stand that chap Oakridge, damn rude whenever I ask him for a raffle prize.'

'Ride on his wife's the best prize he could offer,' leered Chris. 'She's a cracker.'

At first Stop Preston planted himself at the start. Then he decided he didn't like being left behind and tore after the others, pulling so hard he overtook everyone except Asbo Andy and Claudia Dearest, who suddenly ran out of petrol, despite her jockey beating the hell out of her. The pub was in uproar.

Overtaking both of them, Stop Preston looked round for companions, wondering whether to feel lonely.

'Come on, Stop Preston,' yelled Dora.

'Come on, Asbo Andy,' bellowed the Major.

'Don't give up, Preston. You can do it,' screamed Etta, as Asbo Andy passed him again.

As if hearing her, Preston rallied and passed Asbo Andy once more to win by a head.

'And we might see Marius Oakridge smile for a change,' said the commentator.

'That horse is exhausted,' complained Joey, as a fallen-away Claudia Dearest limped in last. 'I'll murder Jase.'

Etta's squeals of excitement had crescendoed as Stop Preston passed the post. Glancing down, to her horror she found she'd been clutching both Alban and the Major's hands, which she dropped instantly.

'So sorry,' she blushed furiously, 'I got carried away. Oh well done, Marius, hasn't he got a lovely smile. My son-in-law Alan was backing Preston and said he'd put something on for me, but he's probably forgotten.'

As her mobile rang, she jumped in terror. It was bound to be Carrie or Romy catching her gambling and drinking in the pub. She must talk slowly and carefully.

'Hell-o.'

'Darling, it's Alan.' Etta slumped with relief. 'What a win! Nothing could stop Preston. I put twenty pounds on for you and got him at 10–1. That's two hundred quid.'

'Oh my goodness.' Etta collapsed on the fox-mask stool. 'Oh, thank you. Did you back him? We must share it.'

'I put on much more,' said Alan smugly. 'Where are you?'

'In the Fox,' whispered Etta, looking around nervously.

'Put me on to Chris.'

'I'll lynch Jase,' said Joey, 'I was going to back Preston.'

'Hello, young man,' said Chris, taking Etta's mobile. 'Certainly, no problem. You're right, my son, she's a lovely lady.' Chris handed back the mobile, opened the till and peeled Etta off a stack of tenners.

'I'm to pay you now, in case Alan forgets.'

'You don't have to,' stammered a deeply embarrassed Etta.

'You take it, Etta, while the goin's good,' urged Joey.

'And count it,' said Woody.

'Well, it must be drinks on me.' Etta turned to the Major. 'What would you like, Major Cunliffe?'

The Major was gratified. 'You know my name?'

'Dora told me you do so much for the village.'

'About the perving and the nosy parking,' mumbled Dora.

'I shouldn't let a lady buy me drinks.'

'Please help me celebrate.'

'Well, I won't get much done this afternoon, I'll have another G and T.'

'A gin and tonic,' Etta told Chris, 'and another whisky for Mr Travis-Lock,' then when Alban demurred, 'you haven't got far to go. And you too, Joey and Woody.'

'I've got some trees to cut back, so I'll have a Coke or they'll shout at me for taking too much off.'

'Joey?' asked Etta.

'As I haven't got to climb trees this afternoon, I'll have a pint, thanks, Etta. You're as good at remembering names as an American.'

'Dora briefed me about everyone,' said Etta. 'And she told me about Not for Crowe. And what will you have, Chris and Dora?'

As she handed everyone their glasses and pork scratchings for Cadbury, the sun came out, gilding the high street, the church and its weathercock.

'Such a charming village,' sighed Etta.

'And such a charming addition to the village,' brayed Alban, raising his dark brown glass of whisky to her.

'Hear, hear!' said the Major enthusiastically.

'Cheers, Etta,' echoed Chris, Joey and Woody.

'What are we going to back in the next race?' asked Dora.

*

Alas, the Major was so captivated, he went home and told his wife Debbie (who'd just done fifteen rounds with Ione Travis-Lock and was smarting over her despised splash of colour) about Etta.

'She'd had a flutter on Preston – little devil finally came good. Marius actually smiled at the presentation. Etta – that's Martin and Carrie's mother – won two hundred pounds and was so excited she bought drinks for all of us.

'Charming lady, knew what regiment I was in. Alban T-L was very smitten.' The Major glanced at his emails: Parish Council, British Legion, Rugby Club, Rotary Club. 'Think she'd be a willing hand at coffee mornings.'

Debbie, who was sourly ramming rejected pillarbox-red dahlias entitled Bishop of Llandaff, George Best and Alan Titchmarsh into a toby jug, said she wasn't sure how pleased Romy and Martin would be.

'Martin's mother is supposed to be minding Poppy and Drummond, keeping Harvest Home shipshape and preparing meals, not betting and carousing in public houses.'

Debbie couldn't wait to ring Romy, who couldn't wait to yank Martin out of a sales pitch workshop. Etta's euphoria, induced by her session in the Fox, had rubbed off on Drummond and Poppy. They were playing snakes and ladders, enjoying egg and tomato pub sandwiches and watching *Scooby-Doo* at the bungalow, when Martin rang in a rage.

'Romy and I feel utterly let down, Mother. What will people think, a widow, still in mourning, encouraging lunchtime binge drinking.'

'I didn't,' squeaked Etta.

'Imposing yourself on the menfolk of Willowwood, calling Joey East and Alban Travis-Lock by their given names, encouraging Woody to undertake dangerous tasks with drink inside him. The Major was so appalled he couldn't wait to tell Debbie. You were leading Dora Belvedon astray, and exacerbating Alban Travis-Lock's drink problem with large Scotches – Ione will be incensed – not to mention picking up Drummond and Poppy in that condition. Rather early to blot your copy book so dramatically.'

'We were having fun,' protested Etta. 'Dora and Woody drank Coke, and everyone gave me such a lovely welcome.'

'You're missing the point, Mother. Has the government thrust on binge drinking passed you by? You know how Dad loathed you drinking and gambling. Also, as we are struggling to support you, isn't it rather selfish to squander your winnings so quickly?'

'Your turn, Granny,' said Poppy as Etta put down the receiver. 'Why are you crying?'

16

At the end of October the weather turned windy and very cold. Leaves rained down. Houses were suddenly revealed behind newly bare trees. Willow spears choked Etta's stream like shoals of goldfish. Desperate for a garden, she looked up shade-tolerant plants in a big book, hoping they'd grow in the shadow of her towering conifer hedge, and decided to dig a flower bed.

Returning from dropping off the children one freezing cold morning, she noticed Joey's filthy white van parked in the road. On the back someone had written: 'I wish my wife was as dirty as this.' 'Me too,' someone had written underneath. And underneath that someone else had written: 'Also available in white.'

Etta smiled, and looking over the wall saw Joey and Woody working on Valent's land, blowing on their fingers, and later took them extremely welcome mugs of leek soup and bowls of black-berry crumble which she'd made for the children's tea.

When in turn they put up bookshelves and hung the Munnings of the mare and foal and her flower paintings, she insisted on paying them twenty pounds. Soon they were popping in every day for a cup of tea and a gossip, Joey to talk about his wild children and his volatile marriage and Valent Edwards, Woody to confide how many tree surgeons were being forced out of business by Health and Safety.

'I got so much work offered I could easily employ two or three assistants but I'd be clobbered by insurance. Four hundred pounds last year, four thousand this one. It's a closed shop, the insurance companies employ a gang of inspectors to examine your equipment.'

'Everyone wants to examine your equipment,' mocked Joey.

'Wherever he rolls up to sort trees, you see wives hanging out of the window.'

'But the husbands always put you down,' sighed Woody, 'saying they'd do it themselves if they had the time. The real battle is views versus privacy. "My neighbour's perfectly happy for you to cut down those trees," they say, so you pick up your axe, then the neighbour rolls up with a shotgun.'

'No cream?' joked Joey, the morning Etta provided hot scones and home-made bramble jelly. As she got a carton of cream out of the fridge, Woody patted his flat stomach: 'We'll have to get out of our jeans into elasticated waistbands soon,' he teased.

Sitting at the table in Etta's dark kitchen, he confessed he felt hellishly guilty about planting the mature hedge that blotted out her sunlight.

'Valent insisted to please Bonny Richards, and when he asks, you jump. I would have planted hawthorn or beech, but I assumed you'd be an old cow like Romy. Sorry, Etta.'

'Romy's always shouting at the lads for making a noise drillin' or hammerin',' grumbled Joey. 'Then she went ballistic when they wolf-whistled at her in a tight jumper. Affront to her dignity, she said.' Joey laughed. 'Front was the operative word. She made Martin ring up Valent and complain. Valent took no notice.'

'Bonny Richards doesn't want anyone spying on her,' explained Woody. 'Journalists were renting houses all round her place in London. You don't look like a member of the paparazzi, Etta, although I'm not sure I'd trust that Dora.'

As the dark, merry eyes of Joey, who'd been given half the *Daily Mail*'s fee by Dora, met Etta's, they shifted.

'What's Bonny like?' asked Etta.

'Bit skinny for me, likes to preserve a respectable image but covered plenty of sheet miles in her time,' said Joey. 'She's tryin' to improve Valent. "If you stop droppin' your haitches, I'll drop my knickers" sort of thing. She thinks he's rough and she hates the country, so Valent's trying to tempt her with the house. God, these are good.' Joey reached out for a third scone.

'Finish them,' cried a delighted Etta – it was such heaven to cook for people who liked her food. 'When's Valent moving in?'

'Depends on her, probably end of next year. He paid four mil, done up proper it could go for 12 mil. Reassures the locals if a lovely 'ouse is restored, improves the whole village, puts every-one's prices up.'

'Yours included,' said Woody, who lived with his mother on the Salix Estate.

'I like your house, Joey,' said Etta. 'Nice and roomy for all your children.'

'Willowwood don't think so. Direct Debbie and Phoebe and Toby are petrified Woody's going to chop down trees round it so they'd 'ave to look at something common that ruins their rural idyll.' Joey laughed fatly and unrepentantly.

Woody put down the *Racing Post* and picked up Etta's garden plan.

'Those are the plants – foxgloves, hostas, Solomon's seal, ferns – I'm hoping to put in,' she explained.

'Shade-tolerant.' Woody shook his head. 'I'm sorry, Etta. I'll dig out a flower bed for you and bring you some manure from the stable.'

'Oh, how kind! Dora was telling me about your syndicate. I'm so pleased you saved Not for Crowe.'

'You'll have to come and see him race, or we'll bring him over to see you. He never stops eating, he'd love your cakes. Syndicate's cheap in the summer. He's been outside, now he's got to come in and go racing.'

Later they showed Etta a video of Not for Crowe and Family Dog, who had a broad, cheerful face and very short legs. Both horses looked as though they could easily get overtaken by the donkeys at Grange-over-Sands.

One evening, Niall Forbes the vicar, slim, blond and baby-faced (fractionally aged by wearing spectacles), dropped in to welcome her. 'I do hope you are a worshipper, Mrs Bancroft,' he said, in a high, fluting voice, and then asked Etta if she was straight yet.

You're certainly not, thought Etta, as Niall downed four glasses of sherry. Under Etta's sweet, sympathetic gaze, he tearfully confessed that last week he'd broken the news that he was gay to his parents.

'They were so good about it. But after I'd gone to bed, I couldn't sleep and came down for a cuppa and found my father crying his eyes out in the study. I wanted to hug him, but felt it might make him uncomfortable.'

'You poor boy,' said Etta. 'Why don't you send them a card, just telling them how much you love them and what wonderful parents they've been. Parents always think it's their fault.'

'I'll try.' Niall wiped his reddened eyes. 'I must go,' then, as the light from the opened door fell on the rich brown turned earth: 'I see you've been gardening.'

'Woody's been so kind, digging up this bed for me.'

'Oh Woody!' The vicar's sad face lit up. 'Such a nice chap. I saw him swinging round the trees in his harness and asked him to trim my hedge, enough to let in some light but not to allow Debbie Cunliffe to peer in. Sorry, that was dreadfully unchristian, but I expect you know what I mean.'

'I certainly do.' The horrible sneak.

'Honestly, you couldn't see where Woody had trimmed it, such a nice chap. God bless you, Etta, see you in church,' said Niall, and nearly falling over a crate of empty milk bottles he stumbled off into the night.

Across the valley, Etta could hear a horse neighing. She wondered if it was Stop Preston, and wished she could visit Marius's yard to thank him for the pale blue jersey she'd just been able to afford, despite squandering the rest of her winnings on boozing in the Fox. Going inside, she hastily hid the empty sherry bottle in the bin in case a spying Romy accused her of drinking alone.

Etta's heart lifted every time she saw Harvey-Holden's and Marius's horses clattering through the village, or being taught to jump fences and hurdles. Often she watched Olivia Oakridge bumping over the fields on her quad bike, bringing hay to horses that were still turned out. Invariably a troupe of horses would follow the bike, clearly they loved her.

There was lots of gossip about Marius. The weather had been awful and he couldn't afford to put in an all-weather gallop, Woody and Joey told Etta. Jase the farrier had also overheard Marius and Olivia rowing.

'Olivia's jogging a lot, she ought to be jogging horizontally on top of Marius,' said Joey.

Trixie had longed to get a holiday job with Marius, but even though Shade Murchieson, whom she'd met at her grandfather's funeral, had put in a good word, Marius had told her there were no vacancies.

'He hasn't got any spare cash,' reported Jase. 'He's laying off staff and acting as his own travelling head lad. He had to lead his horses up himself at Bangor the other day. If he drops his prices any more, we'll be able to send Not for Crowe there.'

Whenever she drove through the village, Etta hoped to catch a glimpse of Seth and Corinna or Valent and Bonny or even Lester Bolton the porn millionaire and his chav wife. But none of them showed up. She was absolutely shattered looking after Poppy and Drummond, trying to find things for them to do. Drummond was even bored when she took him to see the sharks in the aquarium in Bristol, complaining they looked much smaller than they did on television.

He had an answer for everything. When Etta urged him to eat up his carrots because they'd help him see in the dark, Drummond replied that he would rather have a torch.

17

One afternoon, desperate for a horse-fix, Etta took Poppy for a walk along the top road towards Ralph Harvey-Holden's yard. As they admired some sheep in a field, Poppy took Etta's hand and asked, 'Is it black nose day?'

A slight breeze was unleashing more leaves.

'Every time you catch one, you get a happy day,' said Etta.

Soon she and Poppy were racing round shrieking with excitement. Belting after a spiralling olive-green ash frond, Etta nearly fell over a quad bike tucked into the side of the road. On it, surprisingly far from home, was Olivia Oakridge talking into a mobile: 'Thank God we got away with it this time.'

In front of her on the bike, clutching the handles, was a child with her mother's dark auburn hair and innocent, kittenish blue eyes. Etta thought how pretty they both were. As Olivia switched off her mobile, saying she had to come up here to get a signal, she appeared overflowing with happiness, which seemed at variance with her husband's lack of form. Perhaps they'd had a winner.

'You must be Mrs Bancroft. Dora's told me about you and your spectacular win on Preston, and you must be Poppy. This is India, she goes to the same school as you. You must get Granny to bring you over to see the horses.'

Profoundly grateful for something to fill an afternoon, Etta did just that the following day and it was a huge success. Marius was at the races, so everything was much more relaxed.

'Pooh, what a stink,' complained a horrified Drummond when confronted by the muck heap, but he was soon caught up watching the horses being brushed down, skipped out and watered and in helping the stable lads take round hay nets and feed buckets.

India bore Poppy off to meet Horace, her skewbald Shetland pony, who refused to move an inch until he'd been given several whacks. Poppy was even more excited when Josh, a merry-eyed, red-headed stable lad often seen riding or driving much too fast through Willowwood, lifted her up for a ride in front of him on Oh My Goodness.

Etta was in heaven, so busy hugging the horses and patting the swarming pack of lurchers and Jack Russells that she hardly noticed how run-down everything was. Paint was bubbling and peeling, railings were chewed, doors gnawed and most of the horses wore hand-me-down rugs.

She was enchanted to meet Stop Preston, whose huge blaze was splashed over his face like whitewash. He was delighted to eat Etta's carrots and a whole packet of Polos. Graciously receiving her words of gratitude, he kept nudging her.

'As if butter wouldn't melt in his mouth,' called out Olivia, arms full of exercise rugs she'd just taken down from the washing line. 'He'll probably refuse to go down to the start next time.'

Ilkley Hall, on the other hand, flattened his black ears and darted his teeth at Etta.

'He's missing Collie, our head lad, who's gone to the races with Marius. Look, you can see your house across the valley.'

Glancing across, Etta was fascinated to see the cricket pitch, the village green, Willowwood Hall, more of Badger's Court than from her own garden, and the high street, a gleaming parting up the centre.

Oh dear, like a star in a haze of willows, the colour of French mustard now their leaves had gone, a light was shining in Etta's bungalow.

'Mrs Travis-Lock will slap your wrists,' said Olivia. 'She's an old duck really, just bossy.'

'What a beautiful valley,' sighed Etta as they looked over yellowing fields falling down to the river.

'In the old days trees were cut down so you could see your enemies coming. Marius had to gouge a gallop out of the hillside. It's very steep but it gets the horses fit, and we've got a lot of turnout area. It's also very exposed, which hardens the horses – and their trainer,' said Olivia cryptically.

'They lead a four-star life, our horses,' she went on slightly defensively. 'We don't have holidays, the horses do. Marius is up at five and out in the yard at ten o'clock, putting on another rug, giving them some more hay. Come and have some tea.'

'Have you got time?'

As Olivia ran off to answer the telephone in another room, Etta examined the lovely kitchen, where horse photographs were joined on the wall by India's drawings. A big sofa was covered with dogs, and rugs where dog paws had torn the upholstery. A large ginger and even larger tabby cat snored in baskets on higher shelves. Any animal smell was driven away by the scent of a huge bunch of white lilies in a dark green vase and apple logs, flickering and crackling merrily in the fireplace.

Returning, Olivia switched on the kettle and said Poppy and Drummond were having tea in the stable lads' cottage.

'You haven't met Marius,' she went on, getting a last loaf out of the bread bin and putting two slices under the grill. 'When I met him, I used to pray he'd be as forthcoming to my friends and my family as he was when we were alone.'

She looked so slim and gorgeous, with her windswept curls, tight jeans and a turquoise jersey which turned her eyes green.

'Do you ride in races?' asked Etta.

'Not much since I had India. I lost my nerve at the prospect of having half a ton of horse falling on me, but I break in the young horses and go to the sales.'

Etta, still looking at the photographs, found a familiar face: 'There's Shade Murchieson.'

'Do you know him?'

'Not to speak to. He came to my husband's funeral, and gave a fantastic donation to help fight the illness that killed him.'

'Shade's very generous.'

Olivia took out the toast, spread it with butter and, after scraping off the mould, home-made strawberry jam.

'Sorry there isn't any cake,' she said, handing the plate to Etta. 'Shade's a terrible bully. He's always rowing with Marius, who can't be too rude because we need the money. Rupert Campbell-Black just tells him to fuck off. Shade tried to persuade Rupert to pull strings to get his son into Harrow, where Rupert went. Rupert said you have to put them down at birth, or lack of birth in your case.' Olivia burst out laughing. 'Isn't that too dreadful?'

Etta was in heaven, two terriers on either side and one on her knee, all with wood shavings in their fur like Woody.

'Do you terribly miss your husband?' asked Olivia, collapsing on the sofa beside her, then answering herself. 'I think it'd be awfully restful without one. No more "Where's my blue shirt, where are my car keys?" '

She had a sweet way of rattling off these remarks that took the sting out of them.

'It's so lovely of you to have us over,' said Etta. 'India must come over to us. So exciting meeting all your horses in person –

or in horse – after we've admired them as they ride out. When's Preston going to run again? How old is he?'

When no answer came, she realized Olivia had fallen asleep, russet-curled head resting on the back of the sofa, like a poem about autumn. Her mug of tea, however, was at a dangerous angle. When Etta got up and removed it, Olivia woke with a start.

'So sorry, so rude of me.'

'I know you get up at five,' said Etta. 'I often see your light across the valley.'

They had all enjoyed themselves and Etta drove home in tearing spirits. But that evening, she received another sharp telephone call from Romy.

'Drummond should never be taken near horses, Mother. He's having great difficulty breathing and he said he was absolutely terrified and Poppy's just told me she wants a pony like India Oakridge. We are not a horse family, Etta. We don't want to go down that road – all that expense and time and snobbishness. And Drummond said they had fish fingers, frozen peas and tomato ketchup.'

Etta felt intensely irritated. Drummond was a bloody little liar and the children had loved every moment of it.

She did, however, feel guilty when she met Niall the vicar next day in the post office. She'd so meant to go to church but on Sundays Romy liked to go to Matins with Martin and expected Etta to cook lunch. When she returned, full of Christian spirit, she would complain that everything had far too much salt in it.

'I know salt is a generation thing, Mother, but it is bad for you.'

At Evensong time, Martin and Romy would be working on the Sampson Bancroft Fund and Etta would be putting the children to bed. Afterwards she'd walk home through the wood, which got very dark and made her long for Bartlett's reassuring presence.

At least she'd won over Mr Pocock, Mrs Travis-Lock's gardener, who'd previously given her a very cold shoulder because Martin had sacked him. This was because Etta had rescued his black cat, Gwenny, who, when chased by a passing Alsatian, had taken refuge up one of Etta's conifers. When Pocock came to collect Gwenny, he found her purring on Etta's knee, having polished off half a tin of sardines.

'She's such a lovely cat.'

Pocock had burning yellow eyes, a big beaky nose, a crest of grey hair sticking up like a bird of prey and a lean sinewy body. He was very dismissive of Etta's concreted-over garden and mature conifers.

Noticing the still empty bed Woody had dug out, which was now fertilized courtesy of Not for Crowe and Family Dog, and learning that Etta was saving up to buy some plants, Pocock said he might find her something that would flourish there.

'Ferns, hostas, goat's beard.'

'Cowslips, hellebores, foxgloves, primulas, there's a heavenly white one called Moonbeam,' piped up Etta in excitement. And they were off.

Three cups of tea and three slices of chocolate cake later, Pocock was telling her about Mrs Travis-Lock.

'She's very Green, Etta, if I may call you Etta? Won't even use slug pellets. She ought to use them on her neighbour Mr Lester Bolton. I ought to retire, but it's lonely being a widower, so I'll keep going as long as I can.'

With Gwenny mewing under his arm, he set off into the dusk.

18

The next day, Romy took the children off to visit Granny Playbridge and Etta was roused from a rare lie-in by a pounding on the door. Mr Pocock had arrived with a boot full of yellow-leaved hostas, magnificent ferns, a tree peony, a big clump of foxgloves and a splendid goat's beard.

'Those six are primulas and those roots are lily of the valley.'

'Oh, you darling, darling man. Where did you get them from?'

'No names, no pack drill, Etta, but quite a lot from Badger's Court. Joey doesn't know a daffodil from a delphinium. He's planning to knock down a major wall by a flower bed, so we're saving them from certain death. I'll bring you some hellebores and white primulas tomorrow.'

'Oh, oh,' Etta was close to tears, 'thank you so much. Would you like some breakfast?' Then, remembering there was only half Gwenny's sardines in the fridge, she was relieved when he said he'd got to be at Mrs T-L's by nine.

'But thanks, and thanks for rescuing Gwenny. You spoiled her, she turned up her nose at cat food this morning.'

Etta felt absurdly happy. What a kind chap. What marvellous plants. The *Aruncus*, or goat's beard, such a lovely name, was the tallest and had better go at the back. She was just digging a hole when Dora rolled up in the highest excitement, with Cadbury leaping and bouncing around her.

'Mrs Bancroft, gossip, gossip, gossip. What are you doing?'

'Putting in shade-tolerant plants.'

'That is so perfect!' Dora went off into fits of laughter. 'Someone who is not Shade-tolerant is Rupert Campbell-Black. His daughter Bianca, my best friend, rang me yesterday morning to tell me.

79

'Shade,' began Dora, one hand on her hip, the other gesticulating wildly, 'had ten horses with Rupert, or rather he did have but he made the fatal error of making a pass at Rupert's wife Taggie. Taggie wasn't going to tell Rupert because he's soooo jealous, but Michael Meagan, one of the Irish lads, who hates Shade, tipped him off. Anyway Shade had the temerity to roll up at Penscombe next morning and Rupert, who has the shortest fuse in Christendom, howled, "Get orf my gallops *now* and get your horses, all your fucking horses, out of my yard now."'

'Good God,' said Etta, putting down the *Aruncus* and leaning on her spade.

'Well, Shade drove off in a fury, and three hours later he got a hysterical call on his mobile to say all ten horses had been delivered to his offices in St James's Square by high-speed lorry and were crapping everywhere. They had to be led to St James's Park to await further instructions.'

'Good God,' repeated Etta, leaping forward to rescue the Solomon's seal from Dora's pacing feet.

'So I rang Colin Mackenzie, and he raced back from Newbury and it's all in the *Mail* today.' Dora brandished the paper in triumph.

'Gosh, a double-page spread,' said Etta, examining the pictures of Shade, Rupert and Taggie. 'Isn't she beautiful?'

Shade is quoted as saying: 'I kissed Taggie Campbell-Black on the cheek. I was euphoric my horse had won a race and she's my trainer's wife. Such behaviour is standard. I feel very sorry for Taggie, who's a lovely woman.'

'Shade's threatening to sue,' went on Dora gleefully, 'claiming Rupert's endangered at least five million pounds' worth of horse-flesh.'

'Poor horses, they must have been terrified in London. Where will they go?'

'Well, Shade's other ten were already with Marius, so they've gone there. Poor Marius has plenty of empty boxes. But Shade won't like that because he likes to play trainers off against each other, and he likes his horses to win, and Marius is having an even worse year than Ralph Harvey-Holden.

'Taggie's terribly embarrassed, but Colin Mackenzie agrees with me: Rupert's used the whole thing as an excuse to get rid of Shade, who demanded more attention than all the other owners put together. He's known in the yard as Needy Gonzales. 'Plants partial to Shade,' giggled Dora as she watched Etta tread in the goat's beard.

'Would you like a cup of tea and some toast and marmalade?' asked Etta.

'Yes please,' said Dora. 'And now, shifting from the profane to the sacred, my heavenly boyfriend Paris is having a driving lesson, so I've got an hour or so to kill. Shall I take you round the church and tell you the legend of Willowwood?'

'I must get these plants in.'

'You can do that this afternoon.'

As they set out for the village, coming out of Badger's Court was a Water Board van with Leakline printed on its sides.

'I ought to drive round in that,' smirked Dora. 'I must say that was a brilliant scoop . . .'

'How is your boyfriend?' asked Etta.

'Got his part in *Othello*. He's playing Cassius, who in the play is described as "having a daily beauty in his life". I hope Paris doesn't, and I'm the only one.'

The weeping willows in the churchyard were all bare. Nearby yews retained a few of their gold leaves in their dark branches like loose change.

'Sit, Cadbury,' said Dora as they went into the church. 'That's where Pocock and his pals ring their bells,' Dora pointed left to the tower, 'and that font blazing with colour is Direct Debbie's handiwork.'

Near the chancel steps lay a stone knight wearing chainmail.

'Nice,' Dora stroked the little whippet lying against his crossed feet, 'that they had dogs in bed with them even in those days. The knight is Sir Francis Framlingham the first, Ione Travis-Lock's umpteenth great-grandfather. He went on a crusade and beat the hell out of Saladin.

'But in that window,' Dora indicated a handsome man with a pointed beard and long dark hair astride a knowing-looking white-faced horse, 'is the eighth or ninth Sir Francis and that's his beautiful grey charger, Beau Regard, who was home-bred. Beau Regard and Sir Francis had never been parted and were almost more devoted than Sir Francis was to his lovely young golden-haired wife, Gwendolyn, who was expecting their first baby.

'Now it really gets romantic. Sir Francis wrote sonnets to Gwendolyn – actually my boyfriend Paris writes me sonnets too – and in her honour planted a wood of weeping willows all round the churchyard, because their cascading yellow leaves and darker yellow stems in winter reminded him of her flowing hair before she pinned it up.

'Well,' Dora sat down in a pew, picking up a hassock on which a weeping willow was embroidered, 'the Civil War was raging

81

round here at the time, and there are lots of priest's holes in Willowwood Hall where the King's men sought asylum.

'Sir Francis, who was a very good friend of General Fairfax and a leading light of the Cavaliers, went off to fight for the King. Like Napoleon's horse Marengo, Beau Regard was pure grey, so Sir Francis's men could recognize their leader in battle. Alas, it made him a Roundhead target. Wounded at the battle of Naseby, Sir Francis crawled into the bushes and managed to fasten a letter he'd been writing to Gwendolyn, telling her how much he loved her, to Beau Regard's bridle, before setting him loose. Beau Regard refused to leave his master, but when he was fired on by the enemy he took off so fast, no one could catch him.

'Gwendolyn was about to give birth when Beau Regard staggered up to the gate, neighing imperiously. He'd found his way home – a hundred miles – with a bullet in his side, his grey coat drenched in blood. When one of the grooms removed his bridle they found the letter for Gwendolyn, who managed to read it before she died giving birth to a son, little Francis.

'Poor Beau Regard was distraught his master wasn't there.' Dora rolled her eyes in horror and dropped her voice. 'Even when the bullet was dug out, he pined away and died a few days later. Meanwhile, poor Sir Francis escaped and stole home after dark (even though the house was being watched by Cromwell's men) and was absolutely gutted to find both his wife and his beloved horse had died. So he buried them side by side in the churchyard.

'Now I'll show you their grave.' Dora ushered Etta out into the churchyard, where a west wind was sending hundreds of gold willow leaves across the yellowing grass. They were greeted by an ecstatic Cadbury.

'Here it is.' Dora pointed to a flat moss-covered slab surrounded by a rusty iron fence entwined with brambles.

'Rather unorthodox,' mused Etta, peering at the almost indecipherable lettering, 'burying them together.'

'Sir Francis owned the church. He could do what he liked,' said Dora. 'I expect they've got separate coffins, although a shaggy horse to hug on cold winter nights might be a comfort. And the willow saplings Sir Francis had planted were watered by his tears,' she went on dramatically. 'The big round pond on the edge of Marius's land below your bungalow is rumoured to be salt water from the same tears. Whenever it overflows, little streams cascade down the hill to the River Fleet.'

'That is so exciting,' cried Etta. 'Thank you, Dora.'

'You can read all about it in a little booklet they sell in the village shop.'

'But you have such an eye for detail.' Etta ran back and put a couple of pounds into the collecting box. 'This church is so beautifully kept.'

'Painswick does the brass,' said Dora, putting Cadbury on a lead as they walked back to the high street. 'Have I told you about Painswick? Poor old duck's dying of heartbreak over Hengist Brett-Taylor, our glorious ex-headmaster at Bagley Hall. She was his PA and when he went inside for some pathetically small crime she couldn't stand working there without him so she retired here on an excellent pension, but she's sad and lonely and misses the rhythms of school life. I'm sure the reason she allowed me to camp out at Ivy Cottage is so she can rabbit on about Hengist and the old days. I must rush back there and tart up before I meet Paris.'

Etta returned to her shade-tolerant plants, ashamed to be cast down by such a sense of loss. Poor Miss Painswick. Poor Sir Francis and Lady Gwendolyn, but at least those two had known reciprocated love, however briefly. As did Dora, running off in a glow to meet Paris.

Etta had loved Sampson so passionately at the beginning, but realized he'd never loved her except in a violently possessive way. All she felt now was guilt that she didn't miss him, but she was conscious all the time of his disapproval, when she left the soap in the basin or ate a second piece of cake, or wrote her name in a steamed-up window.

But as she got home to the bungalow, she was greeted by Gwenny Pocock mewing round her feet, and the telephone ringing.

'Joyce Painswick here,' said a prim voice.

'What a coincidence, I've just been admiring your wonderful brass in the church.'

'*Midsomer Murders* is on tomorrow evening. I wondered if you'd like to come and have supper.'

'How lovely!' Etta perked up immediately. 'I'll bring a bottle. I might even bring two.'

19

Etta was excited and astounded at the end of November to receive an invitation to a drinks party at Willowwood Hall – so flattering when Alban Travis-Lock had only met her briefly in the Fox.

'Sorry I haven't called,' Ione Travis-Lock had scribbled on the back. 'Do hope you can make it.'

Romy and Martin were most put out to discover Etta had been invited as well as themselves. Who would babysit?

'I will,' announced their ravishing niece Trixie, who'd returned to Willowwood for a few days ostensibly to revise for exams.

'I don't see enough of my dear little cousins,' she added, smiling sweetly at a disapproving but hopelessly susceptible Uncle Martin. 'I need Dad to write my coursework and I'm going to take Granny shopping to buy her a fuck-off dress.'

'Don't be obnoxious,' spluttered Romy. 'Your grandmother is still in mourning.'

'Mourning becomes Electra,' mocked Trixie. 'Then I'll find Granny a fuck-off black dress. Dora said Granny had them all drooling in the Fox the other day.'

Fleeing to the kitchen, Etta reflected that Trixie must have inherited her fearless genes from Sampson.

Everyone in Willowwood was unbelievably flattered to be asked to the Travis-Locks' 'do', as Debbie Cunliffe called it, until they discovered that absolutely everyone had been invited, even Craig Green, the village leftie, and Pocock, who loathed Craig. Martin, who had sacked Pocock, would have to face him.

Also invited were Old Mrs Malmesbury, who wasn't on speaking terms with Farmer Fred because he was threatening to cull the badgers. His land lay to the east, between that of Marius and Harvey-Holden, who were also not speaking to each other or to Farmer Fred because he was always starting up noisy machinery when their stable lads rode out on nervous young horses. Mrs Travis-Lock's parties were rather like the tapestry in the Cluny Museum in Paris, where the lion lies down with the lamb and the greyhound with the rabbit, and when warring factions, if not suspending battle altogether, agree to a temporary truce.

As Dora, who was waitressing, pointed out, 'The Major and Direct Debbie, who can't stand Ione, have cancelled a golfing weekend in Spain, your daughter Carrie is coming back from a conference in Tokyo and the Little Boltons, the porn billionaire and his ghastly chav wife, have booked into the five-star Callendar Hotel for the weekend because Primrose Mansions won't be finished for another twenty years. It'll be Playboy Callendar Hotel if Cindy has her way.'

All the women intended to dress up to the nines, thanks to a rumour that Valent Edwards and Bonny Richards had been invited because Mrs Travis-Lock wanted to shoot down Valent's plans for a runway. Joey had already told Etta they were on Valent's yacht in the Caribbean. Seth Bainton and Corinna had been asked but hadn't bothered to reply.

'Damn rude,' said Ione Travis-Lock.

Etta would have been terribly nervous if Woody and Joey hadn't been invited and Dora hadn't said they'd look after her. Wicked as her word, Trixie had found Etta a sassy black taffeta dress, tight-fitting and with frills at the neck, and then lied that she'd bought it for a tenner from a charity shop.

'I forgot to get one,' Trixie replied airily when an unbelieving Romy demanded to see the bill.

Trixie, in league with Dora, also gave Etta a soft grey eyeshadow, a glittering pink lipstick called Purr and a beautiful floral scent called For Her, and persuaded Etta to have her hair cut and highlighted by Janice, the wife of Jase the farrier, who worked part-time in the village shop.

The result was gratifying. As it was pouring with rain, Woody gave Etta and Dora a lift in his white van which said 'Stump Grinding Assessment' on the side.

'You look awesome, Etta,' said Dora in amazement, 'and that is a cool dress. And as you're going to an even cooler house, Mrs T-L doesn't believe in central heating, you'd better bring a shawl.'

'You look great,' agreed Woody. 'Like a film star.'

'You mustn't get your lovely new hair wet,' added Dora, nearly spiking out Etta's eye with a red umbrella.

On the way they stopped at Ivy Cottage to pick up Joyce Painswick, resplendent in a crimson tent, who had become a firm friend after she and Etta shared macaroni cheese, watched *Midsomer Murders* together and admired endless photographs of Hengist Brett-Taylor.

It took quite a lot of tugging to get Painswick into the cab of Woody's van.

'Good thing you and I and particularly Woody have small bottoms,' whispered Dora.

As they splashed and jolted up the narrow lane that was pitted with craters by the endless rebuilding of Badger's Court, Woody said, 'Mrs T-L will bawl us out for not walking.'

'She can't, we're lift-sharing,' said Dora, adding dramatically, 'and I must warn you all not to think you've strayed into *I'm A Celebrity* when you go into the downstairs loo and find billions of worms heaving in a dark vat. This is Mrs T-L's wormery, which devours household waste and turns it into liquid fertilizer.'

Among the parked cars they saw Joey's filthy van, with 'I wish my wife was as dirty as this' written on the side.

'Mop Idol's not dirty,' protested Dora. 'Poor thing cleans for Mrs T-L and according to Joey has to brush and wash up everything because Mrs T-L thinks Dysons and dishwashers and tumble dryers use too much energy.'

Inside, the party was well under way. Joey and Chris from the Fox were in the kitchen tarting up sweet cider with dark ale and spices in vast saucepans. Mop Idol, comely and slim despite four children, was having her bottom pinched as she took round big jugs of the stuff.

Dora was soon handing round lentil bake.

'That's Toby and Phoebe Weatherall from Wild Rose Cottage,' she hissed, pointing out a chinless pink-and-white-faced young man in a dark suit and a very pretty girl looking the picture of innocence in a tartan gym tunic with a white collar and with her long mousy hair held back by an Alice band.

'Toby's pushing round the drink because he's Mrs T-L's nephew and they've been invited to kitchen sups later,' went on Dora. 'They've only been married a year and are still unpacking their wedding presents. Everyone thinks they're an awfully sweet couple because they're younger than anyone in the village except children, so they're asked everywhere. Toby works for your daughter, Carrie. Phoebe's a terrible freeloader. Freebie, I call her.'

Alban Travis-Lock, in a decrepit dark blue smoking jacket and no tie (which wrong-footed most of the men, who'd been made to wear ties by their wives), had surreptitiously kept whisky, which could be mistaken for mulled cider, aside for Toby and Alan, his drinking chums at the Fox.

As Woody was promptly hijacked by Ione to put more logs on the fire and Painswick, in her role of junior church flower arranger, to hand round courgette and butternut squash tart, Etta was abandoned in a yelling throng, all looking round for Bonny and Valent.

Willowwood Hall, long and low-beamed with narrow windows, had many small downstairs rooms in which to play Hunt the Hostess.

The walls were covered with landscapes needing a clean and ill-lit family portraits which looked down on lots of Middle Eastern memorabilia – sculptures of Anubis, Isis and Osiris and a bronze of Gordon of Khartoum – picked up during Alban's Foreign Office days.

Anxious to see the garden, Etta could only make out lichened sculptures and sweeping lawns frilled with white cyclamen. Inside, spectacular orchids, jasmine, stephanotis and gardenia wafted their sweet seductive scents, but the ceilings were so low the men had to bend over and fall down cleavages to hear anything, and the rooms were too dimly lit to allow much lip-reading.

Having just washed her hair and filled her ears with water, Etta was depressed she really was going deaf, but thrilled when she suddenly noticed a portrait of the eighth Sir Francis Framlingham astride a prancing, even more curly-maned and knowing Beau Regard; and there was a lovely oil of golden-haired Gwendolyn.

Turning, she found Alban Travis-Lock looking at her in admiration.

'No wonder Sir Francis Framlingham planted so many willows in Gwendolyn's memory,' said Etta.

Leading her into a library, which contained every book in the world on willows, Alban pointed to a picture of Beau Regard appearing ghostly and bloodstained through the trees.

'Oh,' gasped Etta, 'have you ever seen his ghost?'

'Only on his way home from the Fox,' quipped Alan, popping his head round the door. 'Sorry we're late, Carrie's on her way. Is it true Bonny and Valent are coming? I hear he's bought a yacht bigger than the *QE2*. He's not? Probably terrified Ione's going to lecture him on his carbon footprint. Hello, darling,' he kissed Etta, 'you look gorgeous . . .'

'Doesn't she,' brayed Alban.

Alan was wearing a red silk tie covered with stalking green panthers – the sort of Tie Rack tie that women give their lovers as goodbye presents on Paddington station.

Oh goodness, I hope he's not going to leave Carrie, thought Etta, I'd miss him so much.

'I need a huge drink,' said Alan.

As they went back into the drawing room, Etta was taken aside by Major Cunliffe, who was wearing a maroon bow tie to match his complexion. He apologized for grassing her up after their session at the Fox.

'Most enjoyable occasion, let me replenish your glass. I probably reported back a little too enthusiastically to my better half on a lovely new neighbour. She gets a tad jealous. Hope you didn't get into trouble.'

'Oh no, no,' lied Etta.

The Major went on to say how fulfilled he was by the retirement he had 'taken early' because the personal touch had gone out of banking. He was just waxing lyrical about his rain gauge and how many millimetres of water there had been that month, when his wife Debbie, like a bull mastiff in drag, bore down on them.

'Sorry Ay haven't called you. You must come and have a noggin at Christmas when we've got Norman's mother staying.'

'Cow,' hissed Dora, 'Debbie's about half a minute younger than you.'

'I hear Lester Bolton's bought half of North Wood from Harvey-Holden, Daddy,' Debbie told the Major.

'Harvey-Holden's short of money,' he replied, 'and disappointed all Shade's horses have gone to Marius, not to him.'

20

Lester Bolton, porn billionaire and master of the newly titled Primrose Mansions and now twenty acres of North Wood, was not enjoying himself. No one had greeted him. Small, plump, predatory, he had a dyed red comb-over, and the pushiness and puffed-out cheeks of a squirrel. He was incensed that so much village riff-raff, with most of whom he had rowed, had been invited. His goal for the evening had been to compare trophy partners and accumulated fortunes with Valent Edwards.

Cindy, his child bride, in a pink fascinator and a dress of insufficient pink chiffon, tossed her blonde hair and giggled incessantly. Major Cunliffe's eyes were out on telegraph poles devouring her bouncing boobs and the rest of her tattooed and perma-tanned body.

'Isn't there any bubbly, Alban? I'd like some bubbly.' She was pouting up at her host as her eight-inch heels sabotaged his ancient oak floor.

'Aren't they gross?' a passing Dora hissed. 'Lester needs a mounting block to get into his Chelsea tractor, and he's bunged the planners so much, probably in porn films, Primrose Mansions is going to have more extensions than Cindy's hair. I won't offer you any lentil bake, it's vile.'

Cindy Bolton was now telling Alban and his nephew Toby, who were swaying over her like poplars, about the calendar she was making: 'I get to take my kit off in every picture but it's tasteful.'

'Is that one of those holiday lets?' demanded Old Mrs Malmesbury, who as well as keeping geese and walking hound puppies, always got the wrong end of the stick.

'No, Shagger's staying at Lark Cottage this weekend,' Alan reassured her, then lowering his voice to Etta, 'Desperate to sniff out the whisky,' as a big man with a huge nose and lank straight hair emerged from the kitchen, looking frustrated.

'That's Michael Simmons, known as Shagger,' explained Alan. 'Took over Lark Cottage from Rogue Rogers last year, but mostly lets it and leaves poor Tilda Flood, who's unaccountably crazy about him, to look after the place.'

Etta recognized Tilda Flood, who had sticking-out teeth on which you could land a helicopter and who taught at Greycoats, but whom Etta had never spoken to because she took a higher class than Drummond's.

Etta was amazed therefore when Tilda came over and introduced herself, saying how much she was looking forward to teaching Drummond in a year or two's time.

'I gather he's a very bright little boy,' she added. 'His behaviour has been so much less challenging this term, it must be your influence.'

Etta wanted to hug her.

Tilda had the blonde, cropped, easy-to-wash hair and flat sing-song accustomed-to-being-listened-to voice of a female cabinet minister. If only she had those teeth fixed, thought Etta, one could appreciate her lovely figure and pretty hazel eyes, which constantly flickered in the direction of Shagger Simmons. He was now greeting Toby Weatherall, Ione's chinless nephew, with a flurry of 'Who won the three thirty at Newton Abbot?', 'What odds did you get?', 'What's happened to Dominic?' and 'What's Jasper up to?'

'Things any better at work?' asked Shagger finally.

Toby shook his head. 'Bloody tough. Hardly been shooting this year. Bloody boss expects one to work weekends.'

'Toby, you must meet Etta,' interrupted an embarrassed Tilda.

Toby looked blank. Shagger, to save his friend, thrust out a big red hand and squeezed Etta's, which was harbouring pieces of lentil bake and butternut squash tart, which went squish. An appalled Shagger shot off to wash his hands. Tilda handed Etta a paper napkin.

To prevent further indiscretion, Etta said, 'I think you work for my daughter Carrie.'

The penny and Toby's jaw dropped and his delicate pink and white face was suffused with red. 'Good heavens, yes, quite forgot. She's great to work for, inspirational, press always ringing up for interviews, brilliant woman, brilliant.'

'I still don't understand hedge funds,' confessed Etta.

'Not sure I do,' Toby giggled nervously. 'Shagger and I used to share an office, got so bored we'd telephone each other all afternoon. Bit different now, feel you're at the hub of things.'

'Your wife and your cottage are both so enchantingly pretty,' said Etta.

'Christ, Ione's got a can of worms in the bog,' grumbled a returning Shagger, who had a loud, ugly carrying voice. 'What's this about Bolton buying a chunk of wood from H-H? He'll need cover, better have a word.'

Turning, he went slap into Direct Debbie.

'Hello, Shagger.' She spoke without affection. Shagger's holiday lets, often binge-drinking hen parties, kept her and the Major awake. 'Hello, Tilda,' she added. 'You and Shagger engaged yet? Never know the score with you. Ought to buck up or you'll miss the boat.'

Noticing Tilda's stricken face, Etta squeezed her hand and said, 'Fiancée's such a dreadful word.'

'Better than spinster,' said Tilda bitterly.

'Better go and chat up Bolton.' Shagger sidled off.

'Aren't Mrs Travis-Lock's gardenias amazing?' cried Etta, desperate to change the subject.

'Ione's an old hypocrite.' Debbie hardly lowered her voice. 'Must have her greenhouse blazing all year round to produce blooms like that, and she ticks Normie off for washing the car every day and using a patio heater.'

Lester Bolton was finally managing to have a word with his hostess.

'I am a big art person, Ione,' he was telling her, 'but I prefer a contemporary look. That piece out there is more to my taste.' He was peering out of the window across the lawn.

'That's a cider press,' said Ione briskly, 'responsible for your drink tonight – although we added ale from a local brewery. I hope you're using local suppliers?'

The rooms were so full, it was easy to miss people. Martin Bancroft, who had grown a beard to give himself a more caring aspect, was on the rampage, pressing the flesh. He had no time to waste on his mother, who was showing too much bosom. He was now doing a number on his hostess.

'I am determined to get Valent, Bonny, Corinna and Seth' (none of whom he knew) 'on side, Ione, love your hairdo. Hope I can drop in one evening for a chat about the Sampson Bancroft Memorial Fund.'

'How pretty your mother is,' said Ione, who'd been un-impressed by Sampson's huge carbon footprint, and whose ability

91

to cut across others wouldn't have disgraced the champion jockey Rogue Rogers. 'I must go and talk to her.

'You must come to tea one afternoon,' she told Etta. 'It's a friendly village. Pity so many of the big houses are empty, so much building going on. I've written to Valent Edwards several times about solar panelling and insulation, so much cheaper if you install them at this stage.

'Joining things is the best way to meet people,' she went on. 'The Theatre Club's excellent and the Willowwood Players put on super things at Christmas. I cannot get Corinna and Seth involved, though you'd think being actors . . .'

Etta, at least three glasses of cider up, found herself liking Ione, who resembled the school lacrosse captain you'd had a crush on. She remembered Dora's description of 'Dowagers with Roman noses . . .'

Britannia, eco-warrior, tall and commanding, Ione had a strong face not enhanced by anything except conviction. Her greying, raven-black hair was drawn back into a bun, and her eyebrows bristled above fine dark eyes that must have enchanted Alban some forty years ago.

'Such a lovely party,' sighed Etta.

'Joyce Painswick tells me you're a keen gardener and might help out with the church flowers.'

Ione was fed up with Debbie's splash of colour and last week had been forced to yank out several catsick-yellow chrysanthemums.

'Oh lovely,' her voice softened, 'Olivia's come after all. Have you met Craig Green, Etta?' she added. 'He's so knowledgeable about compost. Do introduce yourself.'

'I wouldn't,' hissed Dora, filling up Etta's drink. 'He's got avocado dip all over his beard. And gets up to the allotments before anyone else and pinches all the water. Pocock hates him.'

As Ione swept off to greet Olivia, she was waylaid by Romy, radiant in red velvet.

'So good of you to take time to talk to Mother, Ione. She's going to help me and Martin with fundraising and in the summer she'll be doing cricket teas.'

The eyes of a hovering Major gleamed. Perhaps he and Etta could address Tory party envelopes together?

'Frankly, Ione,' Romy drew closer, 'Mother is used to a life of dedication looking after Martin's father. She needs to be kept busy.'

'I would have thought she was kept quite busy enough looking after your children,' said Ione sharply.

'Oh, Mother's so enjoying Poppy and Drummond. I hope you're settling back into Willowwood life, Ione. If you need any help with finding plumbers or builders . . .' Then, unaware that Joey was in the kitchen, 'Do you know Joey East, a mine of information?'

'Joey's family have been working for us for generations,' said Ione icily.

'And if Alban's ever at a loose end,' steamrollered Romy, 'Martin says the Cricket Club's always needing umpires.'

'Darling child!' Escaping, Ione kissed Olivia on both cheeks. 'How charming you look.'

Olivia did. She wore a shirt of stiff white satin, open at the neck to show off the smooth tan of outdoor life and stopping short above a floating pair of black silk trousers which emphasized her slenderness. A diamond butterfly nestled in her newly washed russet curls.

Hoping at last to meet Marius, Etta was disappointed when Olivia said, 'Marius is still at the races. I've brought Shade Murchieson, one of our owners. He's just parking his juggernaut. I hope that's OK? Shade needs cheering up. One of his horses was killed at Worcester this afternoon. Marius is so gutted, he couldn't face a party. Awesome Wells, who was riding her, is distraught.'

'Not Ilkley Hall?' asked Ione in horror.

As Olivia shook her head, wafting Eau d'Issey, the butterfly glittered. 'No, a lovely, really progressive five-year-old mare called Snowball's Chance, who came from Rupert Campbell-Black. So Marius was desperate for her to run well. She was in the lead then had a massive haemorrhage in the air.'

'I'm so sorry, you need a drink.'

'Bloody bad luck,' agreed a small man with curiously dead snake-like eyes in a ratty little face, prematurely wrinkled from so much wasting. Etta immediately recognized him as Ralph Harvey-Holden. Having followed Olivia into the room, he reached up to kiss Ione on the cheek. 'Sorry I'm late.'

'Ralph had a maddeningly good afternoon,' said Olivia. 'He's been getting drunk with ecstatic victorious owners ever since.'

As Harvey-Holden laughed, the snake-like eyes shifted round the room to check if anyone was rich enough to buy horses. He'd hoped to do a number on Valent. But if Lester Bolton could afford to buy twenty acres of his wood, he might be up for some horses. Harvey-Holden crossed the room.

As Shade Murchieson, who hadn't bothered to wear a tie, waited in the doorway for admiring recognition, Cindy Bolton looked wildly excited, further messed up her blonde hair and jacked up her breasts.

'Phwoar, he's well fit.'

'Aren't you cold? I've brought you a cardigan,' said Ione, waving a dishcloth-grey relic.

'I'm fine.' Cindy had no wish to hide any lights under bushels. 'This is the kit I wore to the Grand National, which was even colder than your home, Ione. Lester and I love horseracing.'

Shade Murchieson had an even vaster carbon footprint than Valent Edwards. Having made a fortune selling weapons that had bombed the hell out of Iraq, he'd just secured a massive contract to take part in the rebuilding of that country. Here was an opportunity for conversion and donation.

'Welcome to Willowwood, Mr Murchieson,' said Ione warmly. 'We must talk later. Get him a drink please, Dora.'

'What's this?' asked Shade, as he took a slug a minute later. 'Yak's piss?'

Mop Idol, next in the queue, rushed up and offered Shade some parsnip chips.

'He keeps those on his shoulder,' said Alan waspishly. 'The big creep.'

Martin rushed up next.

'Shade, Shade.' He pumped Shade's huge ringed hand with both of his. 'So grateful you came to Dad's funeral. Sampson Bancroft,' he added when Shade looked blank.

'Oh, Sampson.' Shade nodded. 'Clever guy, tried to persuade him to have a horse in training.'

'Bit chancy for Dad.' Martin laughed heartily. 'If you've got a mo, I'd love to discuss his fund, such a heartbreaking illness,' but Shade had murmured excuses and set off in pursuit of Olivia, who was talking to Etta.

'You must come over and see the horses again. India loved Poppy.'

'When's Preston running again?' asked Etta.

'In about ten days' time, come and watch him. Dora,' hissed Olivia, 'can you find Shade something slightly less repulsive to drink?'

'Leave it to me.' Dora glided off.

Olivia introduced Etta to Shade, who said he'd heard she'd moved to Willowwood and in a rich, deep, very put-on voice asked her how she was getting on.

'OK? Good.' Then turning back to Olivia, who was refusing a slice of lentil bake: 'You ought to eat, darling, you haven't had anything since breakfast.'

'Except you,' murmured Olivia.

Goodness, thought Etta, that's why Shade's horses had all gone to Marius. She said how sorry she was about Snowball's Chance.

'Horrible.' Olivia bit her lip. 'I try not to love them, but you can't not with horses. I'd only known her a few days, but enough to adore her. One moment the world was at her feet, the next she's a lump of dead meat.'

'It wasn't your fault, sweetheart.' Shade put an arm round her shoulders.

'Can't you smell the testosterone? Must come from handling two billion.'

Hearing Shagger's voice, Etta thought he must be talking about Shade, until Shagger added, 'Make a cracking bloke.'

'Cracking the whip more likely,' said Toby Weatherall gloomily.

Turning round, Etta saw Carrie in the doorway. She wore a black velvet trouser suit and a white silk shirt, her short rain-soaked black hair brushed back from her forehead. How pale, tense and tired she looked, thought Etta helplessly. If only I understood big business and could discuss her latest deal with her.

Nodding to Alan, seeing her mother was talking to the great Shade Murchieson, Carrie crossed the room and pecked her cheek.

'Where's Trixie?'

'Babysitting for Martin and Romy.'

'She OK?'

'In great form, come home to revise.'

'Pigs would fly.' Carrie raised a disbelieving eyebrow. 'You OK?'

'Fine,' said Etta.

'Odd to see you without Dad.' Then, totally ignoring Olivia, Carrie congratulated Shade on his Iraq contract and started to quiz him about a possible Japanese recession.

'Here's a whisky for Shade,' whispered Dora, who'd been making notes in the kitchen. 'I've put in a couple of cloves to make it look authentic. For God's sake don't let on to Ione.'

Harvey-Holden was outraged when his sales pitch to Lester Bolton was interrupted by the Major and Old Mrs Malmesbury, whom he wanted to offload.

'Are you a jockey, like Ralph?' Mrs Malmesbury asked Lester Bolton. 'You're the right height. Lose a few pounds though.'

Seeing Lester turn purple, Harvey-Holden said quickly, 'And I'm no longer a jockey, Mrs M. I'm a trainer, so I get far more nervous.'

'What's this about you buying North Wood, Lester?' asked

Major Cunliffe, in his role of chairman of the Parish Council. 'Hope you're not planning to develop. Price of timber's rocketing, even sell sycamore now.'

'I intend turning it into a Harboretum as a showcase for my wife, Cindy. I'm looking for an estate manager,' said Lester grandly.

'Has to be at least a thousand acres to be counted as an estate,' snorted Mrs Malmesbury. 'Must have a word with Farmer Fred, think he's shooting badgers.' And she stumped off.

'I'd cull the lot,' snarled Harvey-Holden. 'Horses always putting their feet down the setts.'

'Old bag should be in a bin,' said a nettled Lester. 'Thousand acres indeed.'

21

Miss Painswick's new navy-blue court shoes were killing her, so she persuaded Etta to join her on a faded chintz sofa, from which Etta retrieved two half-eaten pieces of lentil bake.

She noticed Shade still pretending to listen to Carrie's views on the Japanese stock market, while his hand like a giant tarantula wandered over Olivia's boy's bottom.

Alan, who had a kind heart, was rescuing Niall the vicar, who'd been cornered by Direct Debbie demanding support for her church flowers. She was talking about her roses as if she personally knew the people they were named after: 'Gordon Ramsay, Anna Ford, Alan Titchmarsh, Angela Rippon and Cliff Richard in the same bed make a lovely splash. *The Times* was saying only yesterday bright colours attract butterflies. Ione's so high-handed about gardens. Pocock does her donkey work. Normie and I do all our own. My favourite dahlia is the Bishop of Llandaff,' she went on, 'such a brilliant scarlet. Would you believe it, I got a hundred Bishops from a single plant this year.'

'Good God,' said Alan, 'that's nearly a synod.'

Shagger was now trying to sell insurance to Lester Bolton: 'There are some dangerously overhanging trees along the footpath.'

Phoebe Weatherall meanwhile had buttonholed Woody as he slid in to put more logs on the fire: 'Our cherry tree's fallen down, would you have a moment to chop it up? We'll be needing some logs for Christmas.'

'She'll never pay him,' Painswick muttered to Etta.

Cindy Bolton was doing a number on a handsome blond hunk with a badge on his dark green fleece saying 'Thank you for looking after my dog'.

'How sweet,' cooed Cindy. 'What kind of pooch have you got, Jase?'

'I haven't. Found the badge at a service station. Sure pulls the birds.'

Cindy shrieked with laughter. 'What d'you do for a living?'

'I'm an equine podiatrist.'

'How fascinating.' Hiccuping, Cindy accepted more cider.

'Your hubby's bought North Wood.'

'Where he intends to create a Harboretum.'

'Woody's the man to help you,' grinned Jase. 'He'll trim your bush any time.'

Cindy's shrieks were so excessive that Lester, who disliked competition, beckoned her to join him and Shagger.

Abandoned, Jase sat down beside Etta.

'Jase Perry,' he said. 'I'm the third of the Terrible Trio. Heard a lot about you, Etta, and your cakes.'

Etta blushed and introduced Painswick. 'This is Jase, the famous farrier.'

'I'm only an equine podiatrist at parties.' Jase shook his head. 'Sad day, I replated Snowball only yesterday. Knew her at Rupert's too, sweet little mare, held the hammer in her mouth while I did her feet. Would have taken her plates off tomorrow. You never get used to empty boxes.'

'I'm so sorry,' said Etta, thinking how nice he was. 'It must be nerve-racking shoeing racehorses, they're so skittish.'

'Terrifying, but you get the best gossip. People tell you anyfing when your head's under a horse's belly, no eye contact. Like being a minicab driver or an 'airdresser like my wife.'

'She did my hair beautifully,' said Etta.

'Why's Shade taken his horses to Marius?' enquired Painswick, who wished she'd brought her knitting.

'More to do with that,' Jase nodded at Shade's rotating hand, 'than Marius's form at the moment. Marius can be a grumpy bugger. Hope Shade doesn't take his horses and his missus at the same time.'

As Joey appeared from the kitchen with another jug, he winked at them, but was accosted by Phoebe. 'Joey darling, can I have a top-up? One of our drains is blocked. I wonder if you'd have a mo.'

'See what I mean?' muttered Painswick.

Pocock, leaving the party in the kitchen, filled up Etta's glass, which enabled her to tell him how well his plants were settling in, and how lovely all his plants in this house were, and how sweet

Gwenny had popped back last week and curled up on her bed. Envying Gwenny, amazed how different Etta looked tonight, Pocock said he'd got some Christmas roses for her.

Etta noticed poor Tilda the schoolmistress hovering disconsolately as Shagger, having had his insurance pitch to Bolton constantly interrupted by Cindy's giggles, ignored her pronouncement that she'd made his favourite fish pie for supper and sidled off to talk to his friend Toby.

Harvey-Holden was about to renew his attack on Lester when he was pre-empted by Martin: 'I'd love a chinwag with you about my father's fund, Lester.'

'Who's that talking to Shade and Harvey-Holden?' asked Lester.

'That's Olivia Oakridge, a most attractive lady,' said Martin.

'Needs her boobs enhancing and her teeth veneering,' said Cindy dismissively. 'Do you know they've got creepy-crawlies in the toilet here and Ione's planted pansies in her hubby's shoes?'

'Anyone we know?' said Alan, who was drunk.

'I ought to go.' Etta, also feeling drunk, got to her feet.

'Don't,' called out Olivia. 'Come and talk to us.'

'Ilkley Hall's so beautiful,' Etta told Shade, 'and so macho.'

'Like his master,' purred Shade.

Seeing her mother-in-law laughing rather too loudly with Shade and Olivia, Romy tried to catch her eye to tell her to leave, but she was too late. The last descendant of Sir Francis Framlingham had clapped hands that had never seen a manicure. Summoning as many guests as possible into the drawing room, Ione exhorted them to join the Compost Club for the benefit of global cooling, recycling, and the beauty and fecundity of their gardens.

Etta glanced at Alban leaning against the wall, listening so politely and patiently, as he must have had to do all his career, to potentates and difficult heads of state, smoothing paths, but now centre stage no longer. Glancing round, he caught Etta looking at him and gave her a smile of such sweetness.

'We all have holes in our lives,' Ione's voice was rising, 'so why not refill your hole with compost?'

'I'll fill your hole with something much more exciting,' murmured Shade into Olivia's hair.

Olivia laughed and wriggled against him.

Mrs Travis-Lock then drew attention to her wormery, urging guests to get one of their own.

'Pooh,' said Cindy, at which Jase the farrier started snaking his hand along, opening and closing his fingers and thumb like a devouring worm. Everyone fought the giggles – even more so when Ione paused for breath and Mrs Malmesbury could be heard haranguing Farmer Fred from a nearby room: 'Cows with TB defecate near badger setts.'

'Hope they use forest-friendly loo paper,' whispered Dora.

Ione, however, carried on unfazed: 'And with Christmas not too far away, I implore you to buy Christmas trees with roots which can be replanted, to take your Christmas cards to the recycling banks afterwards, and to leave sellotape off your parcels so the wrapping paper can be used again.'

'Then the dung beetle lays eggs in the cowpat and badger comes along searching for grubs and beetles under the cowpat and catches TB, poor fellow,' yelled Mrs Malmesbury.

'Oh shut up, Mrs M,' called out Ione. 'Tonight I hope you're all biking or walking home, but first I want you to join the Compost Club.'

Such was the force of her personality and her audience's desire for her to also shut up that most people signed up, promising a subscription of £20 per annum.

'I'm going to sort out our garden,' vowed Phoebe, who had managed not to join. Then, smiling at Etta: 'We haven't met, Mrs Bancroft, but I hear your garden in Dorset was lovely. Will you come to tea and advise me?'

'Don't you dare,' hissed Dora and Alan simultaneously.

'I haven't really got a garden here,' said Etta.

'You can always put creepers in tubs up your walls,' said Ione briskly. 'I'll earmark some speedy growers. They'll need some compost. Come on, Etta, join the Compost Club.'

'Bungalow-ho-ho,' whispered a grinning Alan, then, as Lester Bolton wrote out a large cheque and handed it to Mrs T-L: 'The little creep ought to spread it on himself. He might grow a few inches.'

Martin meanwhile was hopping. All these people could have contributed to the Sampson Bancroft Fund.

'I hope we may receive you at Primrose Mansions when it's finished,' Cindy was telling Jase. 'It's so cool to be an equine podiatrist.'

Woody, who was shy and had hidden in the kitchen talking to Pocock and cider-brewing Joey, appeared beside Etta and said, 'I tell people I'm an arborist at parties.'

'Cindy probably thinks that's something to do with boats. Sorry, that was bitchy.'

'You been OK?' asked Woody. 'I'll take you home when you want. This drink's disgusting but it seems to be doing the trick,' he added, as Mrs Malmesbury nearly fell off the arm of the sofa. 'She's a good old girl, still does her own shopping at Tesco's, goes wide round the bends but she's OK coming up on the straight.'

Seeing the delectable Woody and Etta laughing together, both the vicar and Shagger bore down, asking Etta how she was getting on in Willowwood.

'Etta's great,' said Woody, 'best cake-maker in the world.'

'How wonderful! Might you make something for our Christmas Fayre?' asked Tilda. She was shadowing Shagger, to his intense irritation.

'How are things?' he asked, pointedly turning to Woody.

'Crazy since the gales.'

'Why don't you take on an assistant?'

'Insurance gone up too much.'

'Call me.' Shagger posted a card into Woody's breast pocket, letting his fingers linger against Woody's chest. 'I'll get you a better deal.'

'Have a Fairtrade nut,' said Tilda, waving a bowl between them.

'Shagger's only interested in rough-trade nuts,' observed Alan, returning from the kitchen with another large whisky.

As the guests were thinning out and Mop Idol was gathering up glasses, Araminta, the black Labrador who missed embassy life, and an adorable springer spaniel puppy were allowed to bound into the room.

'Oh how lovely,' cried Etta, moving forward, but Harvey-Holden, irritated at being lectured by Ione about his inorganic yard, had already picked up the puppy by the scruff of her neck. He roughhoused with her until she shrieked, then dropped her from a great height on to the floor.

Beastly man, thought a horrified Etta, then was distracted by Shagger's great red hand shooting out to grab and down a three-quarters-full glass.

'That's Alan's whisky,' she squeaked loudly.

A squeak overheard by most of the guests, who had difficulty not laughing, except Ione, who looked at the empty glass: 'Whisky, surely not?'

'I must be mistaken,' stammered Etta.

'Go back to Harvest Home at once, Mother,' said Martin icily, 'and check on the kids.'

'Don't go, Etta,' said Woody and Joey.

'Trixie's at home,' Alan pointed out.

'Is that your gorgeous granddaughter, Etta?' asked Shade.

'Mother,' said Martin ominously.

Olivia raised an eyebrow. 'Do bring Poppy over to see the horses again.'

'I don't want Poppy to get involved in ponies,' snapped Romy. 'She's got so many other interests.'

'A pity,' said Olivia lightly. 'Horses teach children to love and to cherish.' She smiled up at Shade, then, turning to Etta: 'Come and have supper without Poppy, we'll find you a nice man.'

'Utterly inappropriate,' exploded Romy. 'Etta has just lost the most wonderful man.'

And Etta fled, hardly having time to grab her coat and stammer thanks for a lovely party before a going-away present of a jute bag, with 'Join the Jute set' on the side, was thrust into her hand.

'Goodbye, Etta,' called out Alban, kissing her as his wife went round dimming the lights even further to encourage everyone to go.

'Give me the sun,' cried Alan theatrically. 'Your wife's going to do us for drink biking, Alban.'

'Go home,' chided Ione. Despite his leading her husband astray, she was fond of Alan and amused by his antics.

Ralph Harvey-Holden, having not sobered up after the races, invited Cindy and Lester to join him as well as Olivia and Shade for dinner.

'That'll set him back a few bob,' observed Jase. 'Surprised he can afford it. Hasn't paid me for months.'

'Don't forget, Mr Bolton,' Ione called after a departing Lester, 'solar panels provide hot water, and you'll halve your electricity bills with a wind turbine. Save money yourself and save the planet.'

'Shut it, you bossy cow,' muttered Cindy. 'Why the 'eck doesn't she have lights down her drive?'

Next moment, Lester had tripped over his lifts and landed in a flower bed, pulling Cindy on top of him.

'Pooh,' shrieked Cindy. 'Think of all those worms wriggling round underneaf you, Lester.'

'You must feel among friends,' said Alan.

Waving Miss Painswick off into the gloaming, a still giggling Etta swayed back to Harvest Home. Alban and the Major had kissed her good night. Pocock had asked her if she'd like him to organize her an allotment. Woody had invited her to join him and Jase in the pub. She'd refused reluctantly, sad to see the dreadful Shagger spurning a disconsolate Tilda's fish pie and belting after them.

Willowwood, with far too many lit-up windows for Ione's liking, looked like an opera set. Stars glittered like diamond earrings in the bare trees, while Orion, arms raised like a victorious returning jockey, bestrode the valley. The moon, emerging sad, white-faced and hollow-eyed from behind a black cloud, reminded her of Beau Regard. Wet willow fronds brushed her face like lank hanging locks on a ghost train.

Arriving thankfully ahead of Romy and Martin, Etta found Poppy and Drummond watching the adult channel and eating forbidden chocolate, and Trixie on the leather sofa in Martin's den ferociously snogging red-headed Josh, the best-looking of Marius's stable lads, who exited quicker than any three-year-old out of the starting stalls.

Buttoning up her shirt, diverting any reproach, Trixie said: 'Dad's just texted me saying: "Great dress, Granny was the belle of the ball." He and Mum have joined Lester, Shade and Ralph Harvey-Holden for dinner.'

22

Etta's thank-you letter crossed Ione's, saying how nice it had been to meet Etta at last and how she looked forward to receiving Etta's cheque. Etta sighed. For the same reason, she was dreading Christmas and all the money she would have to spend on presents, not just for the family but for Drummond and Poppy's teachers and for every time they were invited to a children's party. Romy always conveniently forgot to reimburse her. But at least Etta needn't bother with fairy lights and a tree this year because both her children were going skiing: Romy and Martin to Courchevel, Alan and Carrie off to the Rockies.

Both sides apologized to Etta for abandoning her the first Christmas after Sampson's death.

'Anniversaries are always painful,' pointed out Romy. 'It's as hard for Martin as for you, Mother. He needs to get away to achieve closure.'

Etta reassured everyone she'd be fine. In fact she was passionately relieved at a chance to catch up on sleep and get Little Hollow into some kind of order.

As Christmas approached, she had the added hassle of Trixie home for the holidays. With Carrie flat out at the office and Alan pretending to work on his book, Trixie was left her to her own devices and vices: smoking, drinking, slamming doors, coming in late, and hanging a NO ENTRY sign outside her bedroom.

Poppy and Drummond were revving up for their nativity plays. Poppy made an adorable angel, but screwed up by ignoring her parents and yelling, 'Hello, Granny,' when she caught sight of Etta in the audience.

'When Santa got stuck in the chimney, he began to shout,'

chanted Drummond. 'You girls and boys won't get any toys unless you pull me out.'

They wouldn't get any anyway, reflected Etta. Romy and Martin had announced they weren't giving presents this year, just making a contribution to charity: their own. Sampson Bankable, as Alan called it.

To counteract Ione's compost push, Martin and Romy gave a fundraising Christmas party at Harvest Home to which they asked Valent and Bonny and Seth and Corinna, who again hadn't replied. Etta, who'd done all the cooking, couldn't help feeling resentful that it was her and Sampson's splendid oak table that she was laying with her own glasses and lovely silver candlesticks, a wedding present from her godmother. Sampson's portrait by John Ward, not remotely daunted by the soaring barn wall, glowered down, daring her to make a fuss.

Martin was practising his after-dinner pitch just before the guests arrived, when he dispatched Etta to the Fox to get beer for Valent in case he turned up. He was, said Martin, 'the kind of rough and ready chap who'd drink that sort of thing'.

'Joseph was a carpenter, bang, bang, bang,' shouted Drummond.

Outside it was bitterly cold and starless with a yellowish tinge to the sky. Shagger's cottage, Phoebe and Toby's cottage and the village shop were in darkness, but Etta could see Niall at his computer, probably wrestling with all the Christmas sermons. She wondered if the blue spotted mug beside him contained sherry.

Aware of a shiny face, an old brown jersey and seated trousers, Etta crept into the Fox. She was immediately hailed by Chris the landlord, wearing a too-tight pink shirt and a Father Christmas hat.

'Long time no see, Etta. Have one on the 'ouse.' He held up a jug of lurid reddy-orange liquid. 'Foxy Lady, our Xmas special, first one on the 'ouse for a pretty lady.'

'Oh goodness,' squeaked Etta, 'it does look delicious.' Noticing branches of holly topping the hunting pictures, and paper chains and tinsel round the necks of hounds and foxes, she added, 'Doesn't the place look festive? Oh, I really shouldn't,' as Chris thrust a large glass into her hand. 'What's in it?'

'Secret,' said Chris. 'Orange and cranberry juice and a bit of et cetera.'

'Wow,' gasped Etta, taking a gulp. 'I mustn't stop, I came to get some beer.'

'Bitter or lager?'

'I don't know. How stupid of me. It's for Valent Edwards in case he turns up at my son's party.'

'He won't,' said a voice. 'He and Bonny are in the Maldives. So you can relax.' And a great furry kiss was planted on her cheek.

It was Joey, who with Jase and Woody was discussing their syndicate and handing over the December money to sustain it, which meant an excuse for a piss-up. Not for Crowe had run out in a hunter chase that afternoon. They had to save enough to put him into training.

'Horrible day's racing,' sighed Joey. 'Harvey-Holden ran an unfit horse. Jockey thrashed it over the second last and it fell and broke its neck. Denny Forrester, H-H's head lad, was already plastered. Heard him and H-H shouting at each other in the lorry. Bloody disgrace.'

Joey then produced the latest photographs of Family Dog to show Etta. She was the sort of person people showed things to, reflected Woody, because she was always so interested and enthusiastic. He thrust a second Foxy Lady into her hand.

'Such a sweet horse,' cried Etta.

'He is,' agreed Joey. 'Ilkley Hall cost a hundred and fifty grand. Doggie cost two grand. It's what's inside that counts.'

'I could run faster than Doggie,' mocked Chris.

'I like your pink shirt,' said Etta.

'Men in pink, make the girls wink,' guffawed Chris.

'This is a delicious drink. How soft is it?' asked Etta.

'The Driver's Friend,' said Chris piously.

'You need another to sustain you on the walk home,' said Joey. 'Snow's forecast.'

'You might see that Beau Regard in your woods,' warned Chris. 'Rumoured only to appear in the snow. Loses hisself against the white background, so you can only see the blood and the gashes.'

'Old wives' tale,' snapped Woody, not wanting Etta to be frightened.

'Craig Green saw a great white thing in the woods last year,' said Jase.

'Probably his mother-in-law,' said Woody.

'That Romy's lucky to have you as a mother-in-law, Etta,' said Joey.

'Oh heavens,' said Etta in horror. 'I forgot I must get back. Thanks for the lovely drinks.' She fled towards the door.

'I'll walk you back,' said Woody.

'Good King Wenceslas looked out,' sang the radio.

King Wenceslas and the vicar, who, seeing Etta and Woody

emerging from the Fox, rushed out and invited them in for a cup of coffee.

'I must go,' squeaked Etta, and fled.

Returning beaming and hiccuping to Harvest Home, Etta had forgotten the beer, which didn't matter as Valent Edwards hadn't turned up. But alas, she had forgotten the potatoes roasting in cream and chutney in the top of the Aga, which had charred and blackened like volcanic waste, and was bawled out by Romy.

'Chill, Aunt Romy,' reproved Trixie, who was waitressing and had been at the vodka. 'You can always enter it for the Turner Prize.'

Later Etta dropped and smashed one of her own gold-leaf-patterned plates when she was serving out the chocolate torte. Martin couldn't shatter his caring image by yelling at his mother in front of his amused guests, but once they had gone, only writing cheques for a collective £350, he and Romy weighed in.

'You've let us down again, Mother, after all we've done to make you welcome. You're simply not pulling your weight. Not only are we supporting you but we're also putting so much work into the Sampson Bancroft Memorial Fund because we know how much it means to you.' Martin glanced up at his father's portrait, brushing away a tear. 'You're letting Dad down too.'

'Father Christmas, Father Christmas, he got stuck,' intoned Drummond, who was peering down the stairwell. 'Coming down the chimney, what bad luck, what bad luck.'

Thank God the whole family were off in the morning, thought Etta, but Romy was bound to leave the dinner-party washing-up and a host of instructions about ironing and cooking.

Lighting her torch, fighting back the tears, Etta wearily set out down the icy path, through the wood to her bungalow. Despite her sadness, her heart lifted at the beauty of snowflakes falling on the bowed willows. This would be a night for the ghost of Beau Regard to appear.

As she dropped downhill, Badger's Court to her left was in darkness. She could no longer see any lights in the village and shivered. Even ancient, crippled Bartlett and incapacitated Sampson had been a comfort in the old days. If only she still had Bartlett.

She was so exhausted she fell asleep the moment her head touched the pillow, only to be roused by a cannonade of exploding fireworks – perhaps someone was having a party on the Salix Estate. Then she heard screaming and neighing. Was it the ghost of Beau Regard calling her? She pulled her sodden pillow over her head.

Next morning, heaving a sigh of relief to hear cheerful bang-ing and the whine of machinery from Badger's Court, and happy that she didn't have to run the gauntlet of Drummond and Poppy, Etta woke to thick snow. The hedge of mature conifers was weighed down and no longer blocked all her view.

Turning on the television, she was greeted by the hideous news that Harvey-Holden's yard, Ravenscroft, had burnt to the ground during the night. No humans had died, but all the horses had perished. Etta hadn't liked Harvey-Holden at the party, but felt desperately sorry for him, the owners and all the stable lads. That must have been the screaming and neighing she had heard.

A later bulletin announced that five fire engines had been called to the scene and battled to contain the blaze. Despite so many crews, flames had spread to the tack room and the office, only just sparing the house.

Harvey-Holden's staff were mostly foreign.

'We heard the horses crying,' said a distraught, swollen-eyed Polish stable lass. 'They were cooked meat when we found them. Even worse, all were lying in the same position, their poor heads pointing away from the fire.'

Etta was appalled: poor, poor Harvey-Holden. She immediately wrote him a letter of commiseration, sending him a hundred pounds she'd saved up for a winter coat.

At first, according to the village shop, the fire had been started by a cigarette in the hayloft. Willowwood swarmed with reporters and the snow still fell. Two days later, news leaked out that Harvey-Holden's travelling head lad, Denny Forrester, who'd been rowing with his boss at Ludlow, had shot himself, leaving a crazed email. This said he'd been drunk and smoking in the yard because he was so stressed and had set fire to the place because he was so fed up with Harvey-Holden.

A devastated, grey-faced Harvey-Holden then appeared, talking to Chris Vacher on *Points West*.

'I cannot think why Denny Forrester did it. Smoking was utterly forbidden in the yard. Denny had been drinking all day; he was upset because he'd screwed up with one of our best horses at Ludlow. He hadn't been up to the job recently, fretting about his mortgage, and I admit I reprimanded him. But I was very fond of Denny. I've lost a good friend and a generally fantastic head lad.' Harvey-Holden's voice broke. 'But how could he have committed a crime of such barbarity? I love my horses, they're my friends. I thought Denny did too.'

Harvey-Holden's ratty little face had crumpled, and as he

sobbed Etta had wanted to jump through the television set and comfort him.

By contrast to such horrors she was slightly cheered up to get Christmas cards from the Cunliffes, the Travis-Locks, Mr Pocock and Miss Painswick, and strangely comforted to receive a card from the young couple who'd bought Bluebell Hill. They said how blissful they were, and hoped she'd come and see them, adding that Ruthie and Hinton, who'd sent Etta a bottle of sherry, had worked out really well and often spoke of her and hoped she had got a dog.

Dora, who'd been saving up to spend Christmas in Paris with her boyfriend Paris, sent Etta a bottle of Baileys and said wasn't it 'the most hideous thing' about Harvey-Holden's horses and that 'revolting Shagger' would be hopping if he'd insured them.

Niall the vicar, worried that Etta was having Christmas on her own, dropped in, drank most of Ruthie and Hinton's sherry and reported with round eyes that Ione Travis-Lock had been roaring round the Salix Estate yelling at people to turn off their Christmas lights, and wasn't Woody the most charming chap?

As Romy and Martin had left for the ski slopes, Carrie Bancroft, determined to extract her pound of flesh, hijacked Etta for a dinner party on 23 December. Guests, mostly high-flyers from the City, had been emailed CVs of the other guests. Alan got drunk.

The party had meant extra beds to be made up in case these guests got snowed in and stayed the night. Etta noticed an open Pill packet beside Trixie's bed, wondered if it was for the benefit of Marius's glamorous red-headed stable lad, and would have tackled Trixie if she hadn't suddenly become so ratty and door-slamming.

Carrie and Alan were off to the Rockies the next day.

'Much cheaper than Courchevel,' Alan told the guests. 'And I won't have to mortgage the barn every time Trixie has a hamburger.'

Trixie had agreed to go with them, but was acting up at the prospect of being stuck with two warring wrinklies for ten days.

Alan was sweet and appreciative about the dinner party. Carrie was ungrateful and very critical. 'The onions weren't done, Mum, and the whole thing lacked flavour. You've been cooking too much for Romy and Martin.'

Thank God no one needed to stay the night. But once again there was general irritation that the major players, Shade and Valent, hadn't bothered to answer. So rude. Joey, however, had already told Etta that Valent and Bonny had moved on to the Seychelles.

'Keeping his eye off the ball, like Mark Antony distracted by Cleopatra,' mused Etta.

'Whatever,' agreed Joey. 'Bonny 'ates cold weather even more than the country, so they won't be down for a month or so.'

And it was cold. Etta's hand had shaken so much that morning she hardly needed to turn on her electric toothbrush.

23

Once again, after midnight, leaving Carrie talking to America, Alan passed out and Trixie locked in her room, Etta, singing 'Don't give up now, little donkey,' set out on the perilous journey down the icy white path to Little Hollow. Her spirits, as before, were lifted by the beauty of the snow. Ancient sycamore and oaks had become suddenly youthful with their twigs thickening and their bent backs wrapped in Arctic fox furs of snow. The weeping willows crouched like shaggy white English sheepdogs. Close up, their tiny buds were flattened against their stems to escape the vicious east wind. Even the towers of Etta's mature conifer hedge soared like a diamanté cathedral in the moonlight, their branches rising and falling in benediction over her plants.

After the heat of rushing around in Carrie's kitchen, Etta relished the bitter cold. At least it wasn't thawing, so the beauty would still be there in the morning. Although her torch was fading, she decided, instead of going in, to take a little ramble in the woods. Suddenly she saw white leaves trembling ahead, and gasped and crossed herself in terror as she caught sight of a horse's white face drenched in blood – the ghost of Beau Regard.

Forcing herself to move closer, she was horrified to find the ghost was real, a filly tightly roped to a high branch of a willow, with a huge open gash across one closed-up eye. Although desperately weak, she was clearly terrified, shrinking as far away as possible, nearly strangling herself in the process.

Her legs were suppurating and ripped to pieces, her donkey-grey body a mass of cuts and bruises, and as though a musket ball had been gouged out, blood seeped from her neck.

She was also skeletally thin, and from the scraped-away snow and scattered earth Etta could see that someone had been trying

111

to bury her alive but had left in a hurry. In her one open dark eye was total panic and dreadful pain.

What monster, thought Etta in outrage, could have dragged her deep into the wood and abandoned her to her fate on the coldest night of the year?

'Oh, you poor angel,' she moaned, tearing off her coat and wrapping it round the filly's collapsing, shuddering body.

She then tried to untie the rope but in her struggle the filly had pulled the knot too tight. Her body went rigid, trembling at any contact.

Nor could Etta get a signal on her mobile.

'I'll be back in a minute, darling, please don't die.' Sobbing with rage, Etta stumbled back to Little Hollow, rang Woody and Jase and left a message on Joey's mobile, telling them where the filly was. Then, snatching a couple of blankets and a knife, Etta rushed back and cut her free. Although she was still trembling frantically and desperate to escape, the filly, too weak to move, collapsed in the snow.

Woody and Jase were there in twenty minutes, held up by the difficulty of getting a trailer into the wood, the wheels slipping and whirring up the snow. At the sound of voices, the filly made another desperate attempt to get up, to hide anywhere, but again she slumped, shuddering helplessly.

Woody and Jase were appalled.

'Bastards, bastards,' hissed Jase, who dealt with horses every day but had never seen anything so dreadful.

She was so thin, the whole of her pelvic frame could be seen as well as her spine and ribcage.

'Only answer is to shoot her.'

'Oh please no, try and save her,' pleaded Etta.

Jase pointed towards her neck. 'Some druggie seems to have attacked her with a chisel,' then, pointing to her feet, 'She's not wearing plates.'

'We must find somewhere to put her,' begged Etta.

'Never get her back through the wood,' mused Woody, 'better take her to Valent's. He's away another month. There's a gate up there into Badger's Court. There's a downstairs room with a couple of storage heaters we could use. Place'll be gutted in a few weeks, but Valent likes somewhere to work if he comes down.'

The filly put up no resistance now. Somehow, slipping and swearing, they managed to lift her into the trailer, then bumped her as little as possible over the rough track, as they tripped over tree roots, fallen branches and old bramble cables, before crossing the orchard to Badger's Court. Here they installed her in

Valent's study, which had a chandelier and an Adam fireplace. The storage heaters were immediately switched on.

It was the only room intact in the building. The floors had been ripped out and the dividing walls knocked down, leaving only a shell with windows and cornices.

In the study, however, which must have been a little drawing room, all the works of Walter Scott still filled a bookshelf. The walls were primrose yellow and on the stripped wooden chimneypiece stood an invitation: 'Mrs Hugo Wilkinson at Home'.

'We'll call you Mrs Wilkinson,' said Etta.

The filly's sunken eye, razor-sharp bones and old-fashioned-radiator ribs made her look prematurely aged, but after a glance at her teeth Jase said she was young, probably only three or four.

They decided it was too late to call out a vet. But despite the snow, Woody and Jase proceeded to go east, south and west, bringing water and wood shavings from Woody's carpenter's workshop, oldish good-quality hay, because new hay was too rich, from Not for Crowe's stables and tubing to pour water into her to rehydrate her.

Mrs Wilkinson was soon tucked up in a bed of shavings three feet deep and banked deeper up the wall so she could really snuggle up and not roll over on her back and be unable to get up. Joey flipped when he arrived and caught sight of her.

'I'll get the sack. Valent will be gutted.'

'Room's going to be gutted anyway,' reasoned Woody. 'Poor little girl, keep your voice down, she's terrified.'

In the light from the chandelier they could now see how hideously cut about and infected was her poor body and how she flinched at any touch, as if awaiting further torture.

'Who could have done it,' raged Etta, 'dragging her into the wood, leaving her to die?'

'She's been knocked about the head.' Jase examined the huge cut across her right eye. 'Probably lost the sight in this one.' Then, examining the deep gash on her neck and mopping it gently with disinfectant, he added, 'Reckon someone gouged out her microchip to escape detection. To have one means she must have been born after 1999.'

As he examined her legs, he shook his head in horror.

'Think she's been tangled up in wire, perhaps in a car crash. Gypsies were here last week but they've moved on.'

Joey went off to get a camera he kept in his Portakabin: 'Better photograph the evidence.'

'She's so totally starved and dehydrated the most important

thing is to get some water into her,' said Jase, stroking her shoulder.

It was not a pleasant task, inserting tubing into the filly's nostril and down through her oesophagus. The greatest danger was directing the tube into her windpipe by mistake and drowning her. Jase and Woody held her head and body still as Joey poured the water.

Unable to witness such helpless terror, Etta bolted back to Little Hollow. Then she unearthed Sampson's duvet, king-sized to accommodate his massive shoulders, and a yellow, light blue and orange striped duvet cover in his old school colours. On her return Etta taped it up to Mrs Wilkinson's ears for extra warmth.

Woody had found a kettle meanwhile and produced some very strong, sweet black coffee. 'Even more delicious than Foxy Lady,' said a grateful Etta.

By the time they'd drunk it, it was three in the morning and she insisted they went home.

'So must you,' chided Joey.

'You've all got to work tomorrow.'

Jase opened the thick Prussian-blue velvet curtains. The snow was still falling softly, wrapping up the world, like Sampson's duvet round Mrs Wilkinson.

'I don't,' he said. 'No racing, it's Christmas Eve.'

'I'm going to stay with her,' said Etta firmly. 'Martin and Romy have gone skiing.'

'I better get back to Mary,' said Joey. Mop Idle had been jealous in the past of Joey's roving eye.

'Thank you all so, so much,' stammered Etta.

'We'll be back first thing,' promised Woody, thinking of the sailor he'd picked up in Cheltenham and left in his bed, who'd probably robbed him and shoved off by now.

'I doubt she'll last the night,' Jase murmured to the others as they went out into the moonlit rose garden.

24

Etta stayed with Mrs Wilkinson all night, stroking her, praying, watching, worrying, telling her about the lovely life that awaited her if she pulled through.

'I'll never let anyone be unkind to you again.'

Despite her fears, Etta felt a strange peace and happiness, remembering her Pony Club days with Snowy, thrilled that she had something to love again. Woody, arriving with a loaf of bread to make toast and a jar of honey, found them both asleep in the wood shavings.

Mrs Wilkinson even accepted a piece of toast.

Later in the morning of Christmas Eve, Jase's friend Charlie Radcliffe, the most admired local vet, turned up to examine her. The snow and bitter cold had taken its toll. By daylight they could see that her iron-grey coat was brown and crusty from malnutrition. She was still too weak to stand or walk on her own but she was eating and drinking.

'Well done. You've saved her life,' Charlie told Etta. 'She certainly wouldn't have survived another night outside. But there's a long road ahead. Whatever got entangled with her legs has given her an infection,' he added as he dressed and bandaged her sores. 'Someone's been laying about her with a shovel and Jase was right, they certainly tried to hide her identity. She's had a microchip gouged out.'

Etta's voice broke. 'Someone's done perfectly dreadful things to her.'

'We'd better report it to the RSPCA or the ILPH,' said Charlie. 'They could winch her and get her on a drip in a veterinary hospital.'

'Oh please don't.' Etta was almost hysterical. 'They'll take her away.'

'Well, she'll die because all her internal organs will get crushed if we don't get her up off the ground. If she's too weak to stand, we'll have to winch her.' Charlie looked up at the ceiling. 'We could hang a sling from those beams.'

Charlie, who was wearing a bow tie, check shirt and horn-rimmed spectacles, had crinkly dark hair, pugnacious features and the belligerent, exasperated air of a pathologist in a television whodunnit, but he had the gentlest hands. After they had slung Mrs Wilkinson up he gave her a massive shot of antibiotics.

'Keep tubing her, she ought to take in at least four gallons a day. And keep her off any new hay or concentrates, they might give her colic.'

Etta ran home and collected her wireless and some leg warmers she'd been intending to chuck out. Now she taped them to Mrs Wilkinson's bandaged legs with Elastoplast, wrapping them in baking foil to make her even warmer.

She also dragged one of Valent's leather chairs back into the office and settled into it, to be on a level to stroke a hanging Mrs Wilkinson, who gradually relaxed, twitching her ears in time to the carols from King's College, Cambridge.

At moments the filly's eye would glaze, her whole body shudder and shrink into itself. Thinking she was losing her, Etta would sing, 'Don't give up now, little donkey, Bethlehem's in sight,' in a quavering treble, because the song always made her cry.

She must have dropped off because she was suddenly roused by church bells rollicking out across the frozen air. Pocock, the Tower Captain, was on great form ringing for Midnight Mass.

Poor Niall. Etta had promised to go, but hoped the congregation would be swollen by families home for the holiday. At least she was appropriately spending Christmas night in a stable.

'I'm sorry I'm not in church, God and Niall,' prayed Etta, 'but please save this sweet horse. Happy Christmas, Mrs Wilkinson,' she added, kissing her on her pink nose.

25

After three days, Mrs Wilkinson gave the first whicker of delight, when Etta returned from stocking up at the village shop. After six days, she was able to stand for a second, come off the sling, had normal droppings and had perked up no end. Etta started feeding her boiled barley and linseed bought by Jase from the local feed merchant, two-thirds water to one-third of barley with a little jug of linseed. Etta boiled it overnight in a big pan on the stove in the bungalow. Mrs Wilkinson found this delicious and very comforting on a cold winter's morning and was soon licking her bucket clean.

Etta also mixed in a small amount of sugar beet for slow-release energy: four smallish feeds at 7am, 12pm, 5pm and 10pm every day. Seeing Mrs Wilkinson respond, Etta was utterly captivated and during the evenings read Walter Scott from the bookshelf out loud to her. She seemed to love the swinging rhythms of 'Lochinvar' and 'The Lay of the Last Minstrel'. She also liked music, particularly when Etta sang to her.

Etta was touched too that Mrs Wilkinson preferred to have everything fed to her by hand and, even when she came in to dress the filly's wounds, had stopped shrinking away.

After ten days, she managed to walk to the door, swaying like a toddler on its first outing, then fell over again as she tried to leap away in terror because Joey had dropped in with some carrots. Jase and Woody couldn't keep away either. After the pub closed, Chris and Chrissie arrived with Friday's special, bread and butter pudding, and were gratified when Mrs Wilkinson accepted a second and even a third helping.

Her right eye was still closed and Charlie Radcliffe confirmed she had lost the sight in it, but the other eye, dark blue, big and beautiful, no longer looked on the world with terror. She was still woefully thin, her pelvic bones protruding, but gradually a lovely thoroughbred filly was emerging.

Etta was alarmed that news of the rescue was spreading round the village. People visiting the sick were also motivated by an opportunity to see what sort of cock-up Valent Edwards was making of Badger's Court. Miss Painswick, Pocock and Gwenny the cat, who would curl up in the wood shavings, all made frequent trips. Niall the vicar popped in bringing barley sugar and on the second Sunday after Christmas a sprinkling of parishioners were exhorted to pray for the continued recovery of Mrs Wilkinson.

'Is she the woman who's moved into the Old Rectory?' boomed Old Mrs Malmesbury.

Rumours still swirled about Harvey-Holden's fire and Denny Forrester, the head lad, who had allegedly topped himself.

'Doesn't add up,' said Jase. 'Denny was a dote, loved his horses, he'd never have burnt them to death.'

'Poor darling, at least you were spared that fate,' said Etta as she began reading *Ivanhoe* to Mrs Wilkinson.

Etta had, however, been touched to get a sweet note from Harvey-Holden, saying he was determined to rebuild his yard, that he had been moved to tears by her kind letter and very generous cheque and hoped she'd come and have a drink one day soon.

Perhaps Mrs Wilkinson could be the first new horse he trained, thought Etta.

Being Willowwood, there were vastly different estimates of the insurance money Harvey-Holden would be able to call on.

'Lucky he didn't use Shagger as a broker,' observed Woody.

Returning to Little Hollow one frosty morning, Etta met the postman delivering a postcard from Trixie: 'Sorry I was bloody, most of the ski instructors gay.'

Joey, after a boozy and expensive Christmas with his four children, kept trying to inject a note of reality into the pantomime. Valent couldn't swan around with Bonny Richards for ever, he had empires to run – he must roll up sometime and unless Mrs Wilkinson was ejected fairly soon, someone would be caught at Badger's Court red-handed.

If Joey was edgy about Valent coming down, Etta was even more worried about the return of Martin and Romy from France and Carrie, Alan and Trixie even earlier from the Rockies. She'd be scooped up into their lives again and how would she escape to look after Mrs Wilkinson? Martin, with his obsession for getting

Valent Edwards on side, would be furious, Romy hated animals, and what about Drummond's asthma?

'Perhaps she'll give the little sod a serious attack,' said Jase.

'Don't worry, Etta, if the worst comes to the worst, Wilkie can move in with Not for Crowe and Doggie,' Woody said.

Everyone was having great fun inventing parents for Mrs Wilkinson.

'Her sire could be Rugger Jonny,' suggested Joey, 'and her mother Near Miss.'

When the Macbeths returned from what seemed to have been an embattled holiday, Carrie promptly drove up to London, Alan sloped off on some date of his own, and Trixie, who was going back to school the next day, descended on Etta and commandeered her landline.

'The reason I wouldn't snog you,' Etta could hear her shouting, 'is because you've got a hairy back, a fat ass, narrow shoulders, a huge tummy and you're a pompous geek.'

'That's a boy called Boffin Brooks who goes to Bagley Hall and who turned up in the Rockies,' she told Etta, as she picked at the shepherd's pie Etta had made for her lunch.

Afterwards Trixie pretended she was going back to Russet House to pack and mug up for her exams. She had, however, developed a crush on Woody, the buffest and fittest, and had observed him and her grandmother sloping off to Badger's Court twice that morning.

She therefore followed Etta and rumbled her secret.

'I promise I won't tell anyone,' said Trixie, collapsing in the wood shavings beside a trembling Mrs Wilkinson. 'Just let me stroke her, she's really sweet. I'll look after her while you go and prepare the fatted calf for Uncle Martin.'

Etta had already made two shepherd's pies, one with salt for Trixie and one without for Martin and Romy, but got them muddled. Martin and Romy, replete and bronzed from skiing and living in a five-star hotel, were not impressed.

'You could have made us a nicer meal, Mother,' complained Romy. 'This is so salty, I'll be up drinking water all night.'

'We're tired,' Martin announced the moment supper was over. 'You've had a good break, nice if you could put the kids to bed.'

Etta was gratified when Poppy hugged her.

'I've missed you, Granny, snow's boring. Yours were the only presents we got. Will you read me two stories?'

Drummond wanted a story, but only one.

'You can go now,' he said coolly. 'I want to play with my willy.'

On the way home, Etta popped into Badger's Court to check on Mrs Wilkinson and found Trixie asleep there, her head on Mrs Wilkinson's shoulder, their dark and white manes entwined. Once more swearing Trixie to secrecy, Etta sent her home.

26

As Valent Edwards landed the Lear at Staverton, he wondered how difficult it would be to install a runway in Willowwood. The locals, spearheaded by that monster Ione Travis-Lock, had kicked up enough fuss about a helipad.

Valent was not a man who ever admitted to tiredness, but Bonny Richards had been a very exacting companion. She had upset his routine. She was always two hours late for everything, which drove him demented.

Since he'd met her, he'd spent £30,000 on very beautiful teeth but wasn't any more inclined to smile in photographs. He had lost two stone, worked out in the gym and ceased to look laughable in bathing trunks. Women had always run after him, more, he suspected, for his success than his sex appeal, but it was wonderful for his ego to have such a beauty on his arm and in his emperor-sized bed, although it was an effort to keep his tummy in. He had refused to wear lifts so he'd appear much taller than Bonny even when she went out in six-inch heels. He had refused to dye his hair or his eyebrows, but had cut his thick, iron-grey hair short so it didn't flop around when he was sailing on the vast new yacht that Bonny had persuaded him to buy. He refused to admit it made him seasick.

Bonny was terribly demanding and hot on her rights. On holiday she had thrown not only tantrums but his mobile and his BlackBerry into the swimming pool to get his attention. She had also engaged him in a colossal amount of sex and shipping. Having kept him up half the night, she would drag him off to visit museums and temples whenever they drew into port.

Having attempted to improve his mind and his figure – 'No desserts, Valent' – Bonny had set about him socially. Along with the make-up artist, agent and personal trainer, she'd also invited on board a voice coach, ostensibly to prepare her Southern accent to play Maggie, her latest television part, in *Cat on a Hot Tin Roof*, but in fact to teach Valent to talk proper.

And when Valent had lost it, and shouted he was not going to talk like a 'fooking fairy, how now bluddy brown cow', Bonny had replied that he had only to listen to himself to prove her point.

As a final straw, Redwin, the voice coach, had made a pass at him.

Valent had been born in Bradford sixty-five years ago into a mining family. His dad had loved his mum. He had loved his wife Pauline and had never been into one-night stands, which went against his Chapel background. This was also why he had half committed himself to Bonny but had still not given her a ring.

Bonny didn't drink, which was great for her flawless complexion but not for jollity. Valent, a workaholic, liked to unwind on holiday, read a dozen biographies, watch football on Sky, drink rather too much and put on half a stone.

As a goalkeeper who had once played for a Premier Division club, he had arthritis in both hands but also the hawk eyes that didn't miss a field mouse. As a great racehorse will find a way through a testudine of closely packed, galloping quarters, Valent saw gaps in the market: retirement homes with people of your own background, and 'Attractive and Affordable' houses for young couples that were cheap and charming to look at, and came with a red rambler rose in a blue tub to grow up the wall. Happy Prentice placed bright and trustworthy youngsters, who hadn't necessarily blossomed at school, in friendly flourishing companies. Another company provided sympathetic people to help you downsize, while a gently massaging rubber hand successfully winded babies and helped couples to avoid sleepless nights. His laboratories had produced an energy source and a method of disposing of waste. His latest product, Rinstant, saved a mass of water by enabling hand-washed clothes or even hair to be rid of soap or shampoo after a single rinse. Although he didn't need it himself, he was working on a cure for baldness.

But even Valent couldn't find a cure for a broken heart.

In Duty Free, he discovered he had bought Rive Gauche, Pauline's favourite perfume, and a bottle of Benedictine, which she had loved; just as when at home, he still found himself making two cups of builder's tea in the morning.

She had died in the Cotchester train crash three years ago, just at the moment when he'd decided to stop spending his life in Concorde and superjets and devote some real time to her. Now it was too late . . . His son wouldn't speak to him because of Bonny. This was not helped by Valent forgetting his and his wife's and his grandchildren's birthdays. Now he expected Pauline to be there when he got home, expected her voice on the end of the telephone longing to hear about his trip, delighting in every new achievement.

When he'd started to go through her things, he found every note he'd ever sent her, and gave up. She wasn't dead, it hadn't happened, he must sail his yacht across the Styx to find her.

Valent had houses in London, Geneva, New York, Cape Town, the Caribbean and now Willowwood, which was the one Pauline had longed for. She had so wanted to move to the country, with fields and woods for the grandchildren.

The row had erupted earlier in the day when he and Bonny reached his big white house in St John's Wood and Valent had announced he was flying down to Willowwood to check on the builders instead of going to a 'Luvvies' party with Bonny and her friends.

During the shouting match that followed, Valent had uttered the deadly words, 'Pauline wasn't a bitch like you, so shut oop.'

Now he was feeling like hell.

27

Patches of snow lurked on the lawn and the piles of rubble at Badger's Court. The black craters were frozen over. Electric gates hadn't been installed, so Valent drove straight up to the house, surprised, despite the extensive security measures, to find a dim light on in his temporary office.

Marching in, he bit the inside of his cheek instead of his chewing gum and gave a terrified gasp as he caught sight amid the gloom of a white-faced horse. Beau Regard, Christ! His blood froze, his heart pounded and he was about to run for his life when he took in, beside the horse, an old biddy in a dirty blue twinset, with wood shavings in her messy grey hair. Then he realized that the rest of the white-faced horse was small and greyish and at his bellow of:

'What the hell is going on? Get that fooking animal out of here or I'll call the police,' it struggled to its feet and hurled itself, trembling, against the jutting Adam fireplace.

'Oh, please don't shout,' begged the old biddy. 'She's terrified of raised voices, particularly men's.'

Putting her arms round the trembling filly, she tried to calm her.

Valent was wearing a navy-blue cashmere overcoat with the collar turned up. His square broken-nosed boxer's face betrayed all the outrage of a football manager denied a penalty in injury time.

'What the hell's she doing here?'

'I thought you were still abroad,' stammered Etta. 'I'm so sorry, it's so cold outside. I'll pay for any damage. She was abandoned in the wood. We – I mean I – rescued her.'

She mustn't shop Joey.

Valent realized the old biddy wasn't that old, probably his age in fact, just tired and unmade-up, with hair like a hurricane-trashed bird's nest.

To make matters worse, Martin had heard the shouts and Drummond had sneaked: 'Granny's got a horse next door.'

'Don't be silly, Drummond.'

'Not. I heard Trixie telling Dora on the phone.'

Seeing lights on in Badger's Court, knowing Valent was away and hoping to ingratiate himself by flushing out a burglar, Martin rushed over and caught Etta in flagrante.

'What do you think you're doing, Mother?'

'Saving Mrs Wilkinson's life,' cried Etta, suddenly fired up. 'I found her tied to a tree, starving, close to death. At first I thought she was Beau Regard. I'll move her as soon as she's strong enough. There, darling.'

'That horse must be put down,' roared Martin. 'Look at its ribs. I'm so sorry,' he turned to Valent, 'it'll be out of here first thing tomorrow morning.' Then, turning on Etta: 'And how could you have used Father's duvet, it's sacrilege. I've told you you can't have pets, Mother.'

'She'd been tortured, she's been so brave. You ought to have seen her a fortnight ago.' Etta clutched at straws and Mrs Wilkinson.

'A fortnight?' thundered Martin. 'How dare you despoil Mr Edwards's house for that long! She'll be put down in the morning.'

'No!' pleaded Etta. 'She's such a fighter.'

'Go home, Mother,' ordered Martin. 'We'll discuss this later. You ought to be thoroughly ashamed of yourself. And don't forget you're taking the children to school tomorrow. Romy has to catch an early train.'

Martin swept Valent off for a drink at Harvest Home, giving him an uncharacteristically large brandy and proud to introduce Romy, his beautiful suntanned wife. He quickly briefed her on Etta's transgression, with particular emphasis on the sullying of Dad's duvet.

'My only excuse,' he turned to Valent, 'is that Mother is like an old door, ha ha, unhinged by my father's death. Dad kept Mother's outlandish behaviour under control. She's addicted to lame ducks – or rather horses,' Martin crinkled his eyes, 'in this case. Even worse, she's involved my young niece Trixie in this deceit.'

'The room is going to be gutted anyway.'

'Nevertheless, I can't apologize enough, Valent. We will of

course pick up the bill for any damage. Mother is here to look after our children, not dead horses. I'm so sorry you lost your wife, Valent.'

'I didn't lose her,' snapped Valent. 'She was killed.'

Not missing a beat, Martin launched into a pitch for the Sampson Bancroft Fund, during which a ping brought Valent a text message from Bonny.

'I'm sorry, I was stressy, call me.'

Mistressy, thought Valent, but felt happier.

Romy meanwhile was studying Valent and decided that in a rough and ready way he was very attractive indeed. A determined chin, jawbones honed by chewing gum, nose broken by a punishing last-minute goal in a cup final, hard eyes the dark green of a Barbour, close-cropped hair more dark than grey, an athlete's body that had thickened but not run to flab, and a tan even richer and darker than Martin's. Here they were, major players, with their winter tans. Romy was going to enjoy working with Valent Edwards. She was sure he'd had a father or a grand-father who had died in pain. Badger's Court would be ideal for functions. Willowwood Hall was obviously lost to compost.

'I expect you knew my father, Sampson Bancroft,' said Martin, pointing to the portrait.

'I met him,' replied Valent. An even more ruthless alpha male bully than himself, he remembered. He had disliked Sampson intensely. He disliked Martin even more – the pompous arse.

'Thanks for the drink,' he drained his brandy. Then, more to irritate Martin than anything else, he added, 'You've talked me into it, the horse can stay for a bit.'

Horrified, Martin stopped in his tracks.

'No, no, the horse must go. Mother can't afford to keep it anyway. You're too kind, but we know that room's due to be gutted. And you don't want mountains of horse poo and late-night neighing.'

'How's Bonny?' asked Romy, as she followed Valent to the front door, lingering under the hall light, so he could appreciate her eyes, even tan and lovely breasts. 'I hope we're going to have the pleasure and privilege of meeting her soon. I so admire her oeuvre.'

Valent said nothing. He walked back up the lime avenue to Badger's Court, crossed the grass, avoided falling down a badger sett and treading on the only snowdrops, to find Etta sobbing into Mrs Wilkinson's shoulder.

'We'll save you, darling.'

She jumped as Valent entered the room, frantically wiping

tears from her cheekbones, her face red and blotchy like a bruised windfall. Mrs Wilkinson struggled to her feet and collapsed into the corner awaiting new torture, her panic-stricken eye darting round for escape. But as Valent moved forward and ran a big, name-braceleted hand over her shoulder, caressing it, she quivered for a moment and lay still.

'There, there, good little girl,' he murmured, kneeling down beside her. 'You can keep her here for the time being,' he said roughly, 'until they start on this room, and when the weather picks up there's an orchard behind the house with plenty of good grass.' Then, as Etta mouthed in amazement and started to cry again, 'Oh, for God's sake, what's the matter now?'

'I'm not used to good luck,' muttered Etta, 'nor is she.'

Continuing to stroke the mare, Valent stopped Etta's flood of thanks by asking why she was called Mrs Wilkinson.

'There was an invitation on the mantelpiece, rather a smart one: "Mrs Hugo Wilkinson: At home. Drinks 6.30," so we called her Mrs Wilkinson.'

'Well, she is at home now,' said Valent, giving her a last pat and getting to his feet. Then, with the first flicker of a smile lifting his face: 'I'm so bluddy glad she wasn't the ghost of Beau Regard.'

28

Martin and Romy were outraged Valent had given sanctuary to Mrs Wilkinson, but reluctant to antagonize a rich and powerful neighbour. They felt they could no longer force Etta to give her up.

'How can you possibly afford to keep a horse, Mother? Who is going to pick up all the feed and vet's bills?'

Etta had been wondering the same thing. But quickly the village came to her rescue. Joey and Woody were so grateful to Etta for not shopping them to Valent that they offered free hay, feed and shavings until summer came. Jase pitched in, offering shoeing and to pick up any vet's bills. (Charlie Radcliffe owed him.) Tilda the village schoolmistress, learning from Drummond about his grandmother's poor horse, suggested the children make her a patchwork rug. Miss Painswick, the out-of-work dragon, grew devoted to the 'dear little soul' and popped in with carrots every day.

Ione Travis-Lock, on her eco-warrior kick, aware that manure was a capital activator for compost, offered to pay for any of Mrs Wilkinson's droppings. Alban and Alan, who were mad about racing and had surreptitious bets most days, took to looking in with a packet of Polos after the Fox closed in the afternoon, and after a good win at Stratford bought Mrs Wilkinson a smart new head collar and grooming kit. Chris and Chrissie were so delighted by Mrs Wilkinson's continued devotion to bread and butter pudding that they put a tin on the bar entitled 'Mrs Wilkinson's Fund'.

Even the Cunliffes contributed their old wheelbarrow, after the Major gave Debbie a smart new one for Christmas. And Toby and Phoebe gave her a salt lick as a late birthday present.

'Make her drink more, not something that's needed in your case,' mocked Shagger.

Most excited of all was Dora, when she popped in in late January.

'Mrs Wilkinson's got a long back and she's long over the loins, great for a jumper,' she cried in ecstasy. 'You may have a serious horse here.'

Gradually Mrs Wilkinson recovered, her dull brown coat turned a glossy steel grey and her confidence grew. Big ears waggling, she began greeting her regular visitors with delight, searching for treats in their pockets with her pale pink nose, gently nudging and head-butting, or laying her head on their shoulders and going to sleep.

To Joey's horror, Woody sawed in half the oak door leading to Mrs Wilkinson's stable, so she could look out into Valent's building site of a garden and see her admirers approaching.

'That door was a beauty, Valent'll do his nut.'

Etta pondered and pondered on what she could give Valent to repay him for his kindness. Miss Painswick, who was a great reader of *The Times*'s social pages, reminiscing about the Great and Good she'd met while working for Hengist Brett-Taylor, came rushing in on Valentine's Day, brandishing a list of the day's birthdays. It included a picture of Valent, who was sixty-six, and a little piece listing his achievements.

'So he's really called Valentine,' sighed Etta. 'How romantic.'

'Why don't you send him a Valentine email from Mrs Wilkinson?'

'I expect he gets cards by the sackful,' said Etta, but she drew a picture of Mrs Wilkinson asleep in her wood shavings and underneath wrote:

> The rose is red, the violet's blue,
> I'm snug in bed, all thanks to you.

'I'm going to buy him an almond tree,' Etta told Miss Painswick, 'which will flower and brighten the dark days of winter. I'd like to create a rose and name it after him: dark red shot with black, with a heavenly smell.'

'Steady on,' reproved Miss Painswick.

Speculation was endless about how Mrs Wilkinson had come to be so horrifically treated and what had actually happened to her.

One afternoon, when Dora was gossiping to Etta, Pocock rolled up to collect some manure for Mrs Travis-Lock's garden, brandishing a shovel. Mrs Wilkinson, who'd been peering out nosily, screamed in panic, stood back on her hocks, cleared the half-door and shot across the grass over a six-foot hedge, just missing a pile of rubble on the other side. Only after careering round Badger's Court, narrowly avoiding skips, JCBs and Portakabins, did she allow herself to be caught.

'Blimey,' Pocock whistled through his remaining teeth, 'that is some horse.'

'Isn't she?' beamed Dora. 'And we must remember she doesn't like shovels. We better start a syndicate: you, Mr Pocock, Jase, Joey, Woody, Etta and Painswick. She'll need this year to get her strength back,' she went on in excitement. 'Then next spring she can go point-to-pointing. I'll start taking her hunting in the autumn. I know you think hunting's cruel,' she added to Etta, who was comforting a shuddering Mrs Wilkinson, 'but it's very kind to horses. They love it and it's the best way to get Mrs Wilkinson going. My pony, Loofah, used to blow out after a mile, but a season's hunting got her fit. They don't account for many foxes these days. The stupid bird of prey who's supposed to finish off the fox was gobbled up by hounds the other day.

'I'm going to be Mrs Wilkinson's press officer,' she added.

As spring turned into summer, Charlie Radcliffe recommended Mrs Wilkinson be turned out for a few hours each day. 'As long as she's well rugged up, I'm a great believer in Dr Greengrass.'

It wasn't a success.

'Dear little soul needs some company,' Painswick confided to Dora as they watched Mrs Wilkinson shivering, despite the warmth of the day, magenta rug up to her ears, which twitched constantly, checking for danger, one eye rolling and searching for Etta. Eternally pacing, she walked off any weight gain as she wore down the perimeter of Valent's orchard.

'Etta doesn't want to abuse Valent Edwards's kindness.'

'Hum,' mused Dora, 'we'll see about that.'

'How's young Paris?' asked Painswick fondly.

'Awesome,' sighed Dora. 'He's got a part in *The Seagull* in the summer holidays, and he's bang in the middle of his 'A' levels. So am I, GCSEs actually, not that you'd know it. On top of this Paris is so cool, he passed his driving test first time before a history paper yesterday. As soon as exams are over, I'll bring him to see you, Miss Painswick. D'you know we've been seeing each other for eighteen months?' Dora added proudly.

29

Paris Alvaston thought it a measure of his great and abiding love for Dora Belvedon that he was driving his father's illicitly borrowed Rover and towing his mother's equally illicitly borrowed trailer down to Hampshire on the eve of a crucial Greek 'A' level in order to rescue a goat from a research laboratory.

The moon was setting. The constellation Hercules, symbolizing resource and bravery, was straddling the heavens with his customary swagger. A heady scent of newly mown hay and honeysuckle wafted in through the open window. White flocks of daisies cowered on the verge as the trailer crashed from side to side in the narrow lanes as Paris, used to an automatic, ground the gears and tried to control the added weight behind him.

Matters were not helped by guests driving home from dinner parties or the pub. A Mercedes which seemed to fill the road was on his tail now, shining powerful lights straight into his rear mirror.

'The goats are being tortured in decompression experiments,' Dora was telling him in her shrill and indignant voice. 'They're coaxed with food into a big steel chamber, then imprisoned for twenty-four hours to recreate the conditions on board a submarine.

'Have you ever heard of anything crueller? Goats have the same sized lungs as humans. For really fat people, they test on poor pigs. The air pressure is decreased and quickly brought back to normal to simulate a quick escape from a submarine. This makes bubbles of air form throughout the body, causing brain damage and agonizing pain around the joints. Poor, poor goats, can you imagine anything worse than being trapped in an iron lung for twenty-four hours?'

'Very easily,' muttered Paris as the trailer lurched back and forth like a drunken hippo, just missing an approaching Bentley.

'Shockingly, any findings have already been proved, and these experiments are just repeats. Enlightened countries like France now use computers, but the bloody MoD keep on testing.'

'For Christ's sake, shut up, Dora,' hissed Paris, as Rover and trailer mounted the verge to let through a large lorry.

'Only about ten miles to go.' Dora examined the map with the torch she had borrowed from Etta. 'The laboratory flanks the golf course and the goats are turned out in a little field. The Animal Rights people have been climbing over the fence throughout the week so the goats won't be scared when we smuggle them out tonight.

'Nuala, my contact, is so lovely, really slim and pretty with rhubarb-pink hair. She and her boyfriend have moved house to be nearer the laboratory so they can step up the campaign to stop the tests. The results were no use when the Brits were called in to help after some Russian submarine disaster. All the trapped sailors died anyway. Nuala's got homes for eight of the goats, and I've offered another one.

'How d'you know this friend of yours, Etta, will accept a goat?'

'She's got such a kind heart, she'd rescue an elephant. You're driving beautifully. No wonder you passed first time.'

Dora's blonde curls and round pink face were concealed by a black balaclava. She loved adventures. Paris only just stopped her slapping a 'www.thegoats.com This company sponsors torture' sticker on the windscreen of the Rover.

He ought to be back at school with a wet towel round his head, washing down uppers with black coffee and mugging up Homer. Paris had to get an 'A' in memory of his late classics master, Theo Graham, whom he had loved so much, who'd instilled in him a love of the ancient world and left him all his money. Places at Cambridge, Oxford and RADA were dependent on 'A' level grades.

'You'll walk it,' said Dora.

'Not if I end up in prison for goat-napping.'

'Here's the golf course,' crowed Dora. 'I've got a collar and lead for our goat. I'll have a disc printed as soon as we get her back to Willowwood.'

The volunteers, all slim, all dressed in black, their features hidden by balaclavas, welcomed them in lowered voices. Nuala, Dora's friend, introduced them to the leader, Brunhilda, who had a very firm handshake and thanked them for coming.

The moon had set, the car doors of the last departing golfer had slammed, the last light was off in the clubhouse. A dog barked. A van, filled with straw and food to entice the goats, had been parked under the trees on the fairway.

'We're aiming to rescue kids of about six months, who may not have been tested on yet,' said Nuala, as she drove Paris and Dora over the golf course towards the field. 'But we've all fallen in love with one older goat, a real character, much naughtier than the others. She keeps trying to eat our clothes and refuses to share apples with any of the other goats. I think she'd be the right sort to cheer up and protect your poor, nervous mare.'

'We've got a collar and lead,' whispered Dora. 'She'll have a lovely home. Etta, the mare's owner, is bats about goats.'

Arcturus, brightest star of the constellation of Bootes the Shepherd, shone down on them. Hercules brandished his sword and cudgel, egging them on. Dora, trying to still her chattering teeth, slid her hand into Paris's, as under the trees on the fairway, eyes growing accustomed to the darkness, they watched Brunhilda run forward to get to work with her wire cutters.

As half a dozen black-clad figures crept stealthily through the hole she'd made, a flock of goats like silver ghosts ran bleating excitedly towards them.

'Aren't they adorable?' whispered Dora, wriggling through the hole, forgetting to be frightened.

'This is Chisolm,' whispered Nuala, 'leading the stampede.'

Pure white Chisolm gleamed in the starlight like a unicorn. White-bearded, high as Paris's waist, she accepted a Granny Smith and tried to eat Paris's black sweatshirt as he buckled on her new blue collar and attached a lead.

'Isn't she good,' sighed Dora, giving her a piece of melon as they led her towards the hole in the fence.

'We'll come and get you next time,' she called back to the thirty-odd goats who'd been unlucky.

'Not bloody likely.' Paris jumped as an icy hand clawed his face, but it was only the wet leaves of an overhanging ash tree.

'Couldn't we take another?' pleaded Dora. 'I'm sure your mum . . .'

'Don't be fucking stupid,' snarled Paris, who, having spent the first fifteen years of his life in a children's home, had a profound distrust of the police and flinched every time he saw headlights on the road below. He was already drenched in sweat.

'It's so biblical,' sighed Dora as they followed the other volunteers, one leading three little goats, the rest leading two. 'And Chisolm already walks to heel.'

Once out on the golf course, however, the goats, intoxicated by this brave new world, took off in all directions, tearing leaves off trees and hedges, not sharing any of the urgency of the volunteers who were risking prison to save them. The language was fruitier than over any missed drive or putt as the goats tugged their rescuers into bunkers and across fairways in the darkness.

'Come back, you fucking animal,' hissed Paris, falling down the ninth hole as Chisolm towed him across the green, rearing up on her hind legs and attacking a field maple. 'Come bloody here, or you'll be back in that compression chamber and we'll be in the nick.'

'We are not giving up,' whispered Dora furiously. 'And don't swear at Chisolm or they won't let us have her.'

Paris tugged, Dora pushed, Chisolm resisted and the lead broke. Paris unbuckled his trouser belt.

One by one, the little goats, tempted by treats, allowed themselves to be loaded into the waiting van. Only Chisolm refused to budge until she'd stripped every leaf within reach off the maple tree. 'We can't waste any more time,' ordered Brunhilda. 'We'll have to take her back and swap her for one of the young ones.'

'No, no,' wailed Dora. 'Mrs Wilkinson needs her. We can't leave her.'

True to her capricious nature, and tempted by Nuala's Polos, Chisolm decided to join the other goats in the van. She was even amenable to being loaded into Paris's mother's trailer, until the ramp slammed on her and she realized she'd lost her companions, when she tried to kick and butt the walls down. 'She'll probably settle down soon,' said Brunhilda, shaking hands with Paris and Dora. 'Thanks very much, and give us a ring tomorrow.'

'If there's a problem,' advised Nuala, 'you could always put her in the back of the car.'

'Whatever,' said Paris wearily.

Luckily the roads were emptier going home. Hercules had long sheathed his sword and gone to bed. Bootes had led his flock over the hill, and Capricorn the goat had appropriately risen. There was a pale apricot glow on the horizon.

Chisolm, having wheedled herself into the Rover, scattered currants all over the back seat, polished off the midnight feast of digestive biscuits, grapes and tomato sandwiches prepared by Dora, and now rested her head on Paris's shoulder as the convoy rumbled towards Willowwood.

Dora was asleep, curls flattened by her discarded balaclava. Fiery aeroplane trails criss-crossed the angelic blue. Paris looked at Marius's gallops, bare sweeps of grass dotted with occasional clumps as though some giant had missed them whilst shaving. Willowwood's pale green willows barely moved above the ice-blue river.

In about four hours Paris would be taking his Greek exam. It felt rather pagan to be bringing home a goat, when his academic career was going to be sacrificed. His adoptive father, the bursar at Bagley, would not take kindly to such an exploit. Nor would the school. He needed a shower. Chisolm, nibbling his hair, smelled far sweeter than he did.

In the driving mirror, he could see Chisolm had long yellow eyes with a black hyphen for a pupil, a pink nose, pink ears, and a white coat turned rose by the rising sun.

'You're an escape goat,' he told her.

In retrospect, he was proud he hadn't crashed the car. It was quite an achievement the day after he'd passed his test.

Coming out of Little Hollow to take in the milk, Etta discovered Dora and a most beautiful youth with silver-blond hair, strange pale grey eyes and an even paler face, leading a white goat up the path.

'Hello, Etta,' said a beaming Dora. 'This is Paris, my boyfriend. We've brought you a companion for Mrs Wilkinson. She's a frightful show-off. Her name is Chisolm and she's really tame.'

'Oh my goodness, isn't she lovely,' stammered Etta. 'Where did you find her?'

'We rescued her from a hideous fate.' Dora rolled her blood-shot eyes. 'Paris was so brave, he lifted her up and shoved her into the back of the car when she tried to kick out the trailer. We've got exams in a couple of hours so shall we put her in the orchard?'

'Oh goodness,' exclaimed a worried Etta as Chisolm started to eat the white roses in a blue tub by the front door, 'I'm not sure what Valent Edwards will say. He's been so kind letting Mrs Wilkinson stay, I don't want to abuse his hospitality, and I'm not sure what Mrs Wilkinson will think.'

Despite the growing heat of the day, Mrs Wilkinson shivered in the orchard, gazing into space. She looked up listlessly as Dora led Chisolm towards her. At first they gazed, then sniffed, then nuzzled each other.

'How sweet,' cried Dora, giving them each a Polo. 'They're really bonding.'

But as she undid Chisolm's lead, Mrs Wilkinson gave a scream of rage and chased the goat round and round the orchard, until Chisolm took a flying leap over the fence.

'Goat's the one who ought to go chasing,' observed Paris, as Dora finally managed to catch her.

'Don't be so spiteful, Mrs Wilkinson,' pleaded Dora.

As if she heard, Mrs Wilkinson trotted to the gate, called out to Chisolm, and they sniffed identical pink noses. When Chisolm was returned to the field, they both began to graze peacefully.

'That was fun, just like the Famous Five,' beamed Dora as they climbed back into the bursar's Rover. 'We should have brought Cadbury. What shall we rescue next?'

30

Returning from Washington a week later, Valent Edwards was irritated to find himself driving through a downpour towards Willowwood, ostensibly to find out why the builders were taking for ever but actually to check on Mrs Wilkinson. Sprinting through the rain to his one-time office, where he noticed the imposing oak door had been sawn in half, he heard a bleat and discovered Mrs Wilkinson curled up beside a large white goat. Etta, who was sitting in the straw beside them reading *The Oldie*, leapt up in embarrassment. She had been having tea with Painswick and was wearing a blue denim dress and looked much more attractive than he'd remembered her.

'I'm so sorry, so very sorry,' she stammered. 'Mrs Wilkinson was so lonely and nervous of being turned out by herself into your lovely orchard, Dora and her boyfriend Paris rescued this dear goat. They adore each other and now Mrs W goes outside. She'd be in the orchard today if it wasn't raining and the grass is doing her so much good.'

As if to prove her point, Mrs Wilkinson scrambled to her feet, whickering and nudging Valent with pleasure.

'She recognizes you,' said Etta in delight. 'She's so grateful for all you've done for her and so am I.'

Valent scratched Mrs Wilkinson behind the ears.

'And I haven't thanked her for her valentine,' said Valent, suddenly aware that he'd pronounced the words 'thunked' and 'vulentine'. Bonny's voice coach had made him so self-conscious.

'Oh, you got it,' asked Etta, 'and it was your birthday on the fourteenth too.'

'Lousy day for a birthday.' Valent got a packet of Polos out of his pocket. 'You find loads of coloured cards on the doorstep and

137

imagine they're valentines from glamorous birds, and they turn out to be lousy birthday cards. And when I wanted to go out to celebrate and get wasted in the evening with my mates, I was expected to take Pauline,' he paused, 'and now Bonny out for a romantic Valentine's dinner.' Suddenly he smiled, lifting the heavy forbidding features like sun falling on the Yorkshire crags.

He's gorgeous, thought Etta in surprise.

Hearing Mrs Wilkinson crunching Polos, Chisolm leapt to her feet, shoving Mrs Wilkinson aside, giving little bleats and butting Valent's hand. Once she'd been given a few Polos, however, Mrs Wilkinson shoved her firmly out of the way.

'Wouldn't have done that at Christmas,' said Valent approvingly, 'and she looks very well. Where'd you find the goat?'

'From some dreadful laboratory, but despite all the horrible tests she went through and apart from a slightly dodgy knee and a cough she seems to be fine. I'm sorry I didn't tell you about her. I wanted to send you a photograph, but she's so affectionate, she rushes up to the camera before you've got time to take a picture.'

Chisolm started to eat *The Oldie*.

'I must go and find Joey.' Valent petted goat and horse and turned towards the half-door.

'I'm sorry about that too,' muttered Etta. 'Mrs Wilkinson just loves gazing out and talking to your builders. It's given her so much more confidence.'

'More talking than building, judging by the progress of the last few months,' said Valent dryly, 'but I'm glad they're both thriving.'

'Dora's already tacked up Mrs Wilkinson,' Etta told him, 'and although she bucked and kicked at first, Dora thinks she's already broken, so she was probably a flat horse.'

Nice lady, thought Valent, delighted to see how Etta had perked up, and how pretty she looked with her pale skin tanned, her hair washed and her dark blue eyes no longer swollen and bloodshot.

As he made his way through the puddles, hearing the rain slapping on the hard summer leaves, he noticed a little tree he was sure hadn't been there last time. Next moment Chisolm had leapt over the half-door and, butting and nibbling, escorted him to his car.

When Dora started hacking Mrs Wilkinson out, Chisolm trotted behind them, and when autumn came, she taught Mrs Wilkinson to climb up banks and eat blackberries off the bushes. They were soon denuding Valent's trees of apples and pears.

When Charlie Radcliffe came to check on Mrs Wilkinson, her new goat friend had got so possessive, she stamped her cloven foot and butted Charlie out of the field. When Charlie had recovered his dignity and his medicine case, he thought the whole thing very funny.

'Little bugger nearly got me in the nuts,' he pronounced from behind the safety of the gate. 'You've done a fantastic job, Etta. Mrs Wilkinson looks wonderful, and she's certainly fit enough to go hunting.'

The following week Joey mounted Mrs Wilkinson for a ride round the orchard, which ended with her carrying his fifteen-stone bulk round the valley.

'She's incredibly strong,' he reported in amazement.

Meanwhile Dora, who'd been riding Mrs Wilkinson all over Larkshire, jumping anything in her path, also spent a lot of time teaching her tricks: making faces, sticking out her tongue for a Polo, shaking hooves and bowing. Chisolm, as had been noted, was very quick with her little horns. Both of them spent hours kicking and heading a football.

31

A captivated village had a whip-round to pay for the cap when Dora took Mrs Wilkinson hunting for the first time. Early in November the West Larks Hunt met at Willowwood Hall. Having alerted people with a notice in the Fox, Dora expected a good turnout, but was apprehensive of how Mrs Wilkinson might react. Her fears increased when Etta refused to go along.

'But Mrs Wilkinson has got to hunt six times to qualify to run in a point-to-point,' protested a horrified Dora. 'She's such a progressive horse, you can't deprive her of the chance.'

'I accept that hunting may be good for Wilkie, but I'm not coming to support it,' said Etta. 'Nor is Chisolm. Hounds might eat her. I'm sorry, Dora.'

Denied her two comfort blankets on the day, Mrs Wilkinson neighed with increasing desperation. But it would have been hard to say who looked better: Mrs Wilkinson, with her pewter coat gleaming, neat plaits and newly washed white and silver tail, or Dora in her dark blue riding coat, snow-white stock for which she'd abandoned her Pony Club tie, and new black leather boots. These had been bought with the proceeds from several stories – including the rescue of Chisolm.

If only Paris could see me now, thought Dora, waving her whip at passers-by and admiring her reflection in the village shop window as she trotted up the high street. So sad Wilkie was blind in her right eye and couldn't admire herself as well.

Willowwood Hall, dozing in the low-angled morning sun, swarmed with horses and riders, gossiping and knocking back drink. An already trembling, sweating Mrs Wilkinson was further unnerved to be greeted by loud cheers.

The atmosphere was unusually relaxed because Ione had been

called away to chair a Compostium in London. This enabled Alban to sex up his wife's innocuous cider cup with lashings of brandy and sloe gin. Nor was there anyone to bellow if hounds, horses or foot followers (mostly retired people in flat caps or pull-on felts and dung-coloured coats) absent-mindedly trod on a precious plant.

In compensation, in between handing round flapjacks, fruit cake, Kit Kats and trays of drink, Mop Idol and Phoebe clanked Compost Club collecting tins.

It was a beautiful day with enough cloud for the sun to idle in and out, casting magic shadows on rolling downs and gold cascades of willows, then lighting up ash-blond stubble and rich brown ploughed fields. Huge proud trees rippled gold, orange and olive green against the rough grass as hounds roved around Ione's orchard and garden, and strayed out through the door into the churchyard. Dirty white, freckled, beige and white, brown, black and white, their amber eyes darting, they leapt to snatch a passing sausage, jumped up lovingly on anyone who stroked them, or rolled joyfully in the grass and piles of leaves.

If only Etta could see how adorable hounds were, thought Dora, she couldn't have stayed away.

'Oh, do shut up, Wilkie,' she snapped, as Mrs Wilkinson jumped all over the place, screaming for Chisolm.

'Come over here,' shouted Woody, looking as beautiful in the formality of hunting kit as the ginger Not for Crowe, who was hoovering up Ione's veggie snacks, looked ugly.

Beside them, skiving from Badger's Court, talking into two mobiles and marking the *Racing Post*, was Joey, who was mounted on the other syndicate horse, Family Dog, or Doggie, whose white face looked remarkably cheerful, despite his belly ruffling the fallen leaves as he buckled under Joey's fifteen stone.

Seeing her two horse friends, Mrs Wilkinson calmed down a bit and blew in their nostrils.

'Where's Etta?' asked Woody.

'Not coming,' said Dora sadly. 'Thinks hunting's cruel.'

'I like people who stick to their principles,' said Painswick, who'd brought a dashing green trilby to match the green and blue scarf Hengist Brett-Taylor had given her for Christmas. She immediately presented Mrs Wilkinson with a Polo, which she rejected with a tossing head.

'My, we are off our food,' said Painswick, giving the Polo to Family Dog. Immediately Not for Crowe heard crunching, he had to have one too.

'You do look splendid, Wilkie,' added Painswick, 'and so do you, Dora dear.'

They were joined by a beady Direct Debbie in a ginger trouser suit.

'You exactly match Crowie,' giggled Dora.

Direct Debbie's bright red lips tightened.

'How did you get the day off, young lady? Half-term's long gone.'

'Amber Lloyd-Foxe always has exeats from Bagley to hunt with the Beaufort,' protested Dora.

'Indeed,' agreed Painswick, 'Amber ran the beagle pack at Bagley. Her father, Billy Lloyd-Foxe, was one of our nicest parents.'

'Anyway this is research,' answered Dora. 'Hunting comes in our GCSE set book, *Pride and Prejudice*, with Young Lucas saying, "If I were as rich as Mr Darcy I would keep a pack of hounds and drink a bottle of wine a day." Sensible guy.' Defiantly Dora reached over and grabbed a glass of port from Phoebe's tray.

Phoebe, as pretty as the day but ever on the scrounge, was trying to persuade Woody to lop the beech hedge that grew between Wild Rose Cottage and Cobblers, in return for an un-limited supply of Bramleys.

'You know how your old mum loves stewed apple, Woody.'

'Hello, Debbie.' Turning, Phoebe pecked Debbie on her mastiff jaw, 'Woody's going to trim our beech hedge so you'll get your sun back.'

'Tree loader,' snarled Dora.

Hunting was anathema to the Cunliffes. How could the Major's traffic-calming plans operate with people unloading their horses and leaving filthy Land-Rovers and lorries so arrogantly all over the village? The Major was having a seizure because Marius Oakridge's trailer was blocking his drive.

'Oh, is Marius here?' asked Phoebe in excitement.

To enrage Debbie, dogs had relieved themselves all over the verges, village green and no doubt her lawn, from which she'd hoovered up every leaf that morning. And now the foot followers were photographing Ione's garden and letting out their terriers without a pooper scooper in sight.

Having hidden a pair of secateurs and trowel in the jute bag handed out at Ione's Christmas drinks, Debbie intended to nick or dig out as many cuttings and plants as possible. She was also determined, if she could escape Pocock's bird-of-prey eye, to annex Dame Hermione Harefield, a glorious gold rose, which would feel so at home at Cobblers beside Angela Rippon, Anna Ford and Cliff Richard.

Pocock himself was not happy. That morning he had been forced to rake up thousands of leaves before mowing the lawns and now they were strewn with leaves again. This time of year, he dreamed of leaves and more recently of Etta Bancroft, such a lovely lady.

Even sadder that Etta hadn't shown up was Alban Travis-Lock, who was walking round filling people's glasses from a big jug. He had longed to hunt once he retired, but last autumn had mounted one of Marius's chasers and it had carted him across country almost to the motorway, and he'd completely lost his nerve.

He pretended he'd backed off because the ban had made hunting so tame. Now he longed to surge off into the falling leaves with the rest of the field. If only he could have poured his heart out to Etta and gazed into her kindly blue eyes . . . Instead he poured himself another drink. He'd better go and kick-start Ione's nephew Toby, who would much rather have been shooting.

Toby had run for his school and once had an Olympic trial. Now, outside the kitchen, he was gloomily rubbing bloody meat into his running shoes to lay a trail that would ensure the hunt a fast and furious run. At his destination, five miles away, a hunt lorry waited with a bucket of meat to reward hounds.

'Better get going,' urged Alban. 'They'll be moving off in twenty minutes.'

'Head off across the fields, then left at the bridle path,' suggested a hunt servant shrugging on his red coat. 'We'll go round by the top of the village and pick up the scent in North Wood. Good luck,' he added, walking off to find his horsebox.

'Safe journey, Toby Juggins,' called Phoebe, leaning out of the kitchen window as her husband set off down Ione's rosewalk.

'Wiv any luck hounds will gobble up hubby, then I'll be in wiv a chance,' chortled Chris from the Fox, winking as he put more full glasses on to a tray for Phoebe to carry out.

'You are wicked,' she said, going into peels of laughter.

'Better go and open up,' said Chris. His wife Chrissie would be making moussaka, in the hope of brisk custom, once the hunt set off.

Outside, Phoebe met Major Cunliffe, who was writing down the number of a silver Mercedes parked on the grass. Replacing the Major's glass with a full one and popping a cauliflower floret into his mouth, she murmured, 'I'm having such trouble with the gas board, Normie, could you bear to sort out the bill for me?'

'You could start by paying it,' murmured a hovering Alan.

Checking she was unobserved, Debbie Cunliffe pulled up a clump of *Corydalis ochroleuca*, when in flower a lovely off-white instead of the common yellow, and nicked a root of the Japanese saxifrage Fortune. Ione had even printed the Japanese name on its discreet black label. Silly old show-off. Debbie jumped out of her skin at a frantic jangling as Martin roguishly clinked a Sampson Bancroft Fund collecting box against a Compost Club tin thrust out by Phoebe.

'Cheers,' laughed Martin.

Next moment, a large speckled hound with a rakish brown patch over one eye had detached himself from the pack and rushed over to a newly arrived Old Mrs Malmesbury. Whimpering with joy, tail whacking back and forth, he put both paws on her shoulders, nearly sending her flying.

'Hello, Oxford,' she bellowed, 'how are you? Walked him and his sister three years ago,' she told a grinning Alan and Alban, 'never forgotten me. Damn nuisance when he was a pup, dug holes in the lawn, dug up my bulbs, chewed up every shoe and boot in the house, took my beloved dachs off hunting for days, had to lock him in the stable. Nice dog.' She patted Oxford affectionately before reaching out for a glass of sloe gin. 'But I'm not walking any more puppies.'

'Perhaps Mrs Bancroft could take on a couple,' said Dora. 'She misses her dog Bartlett dreadfully.'

'I think Etta's got her hands full enough with Mrs Wilkinson and that pestilential goat,' boomed Charlie Radcliffe, cigar in one hand, glass of port in the other, as he bucketed up on a big blue roan with thick furry ankles. 'How's my little patient. Looks splendid,' he added, then as Mrs Wilkinson turned whickering towards him, 'She's such a sweet horse.'

'She is,' agreed Dora. 'I still think Etta would enjoy walking puppies.'

'Do better with a little dachs,' boomed Mrs Malmesbury. 'Hounds don't make good pets, they need to work.'

'So do I,' sighed Alan, 'or I'll never finish *Depression*. But who could work on such a lovely day? What d'you fancy in the three thirty, Alban?'

'Ilkley Hall, normally, but Marius is so not in form.'

'Rupert Campbell-Black's Lusty'll win,' said Joey.

32

So many people had come up and patted Mrs Wilkinson, she'd stopped yelling her head off. The crowd were also excited to see Olivia Oakridge on Etta's favourite, Stop Preston.

'He's lost his taste for jumping after a nasty fall, thought a day out might cheer him up,' Olivia was telling Charlie Radcliffe.

Chatter stopped completely as Harvey-Holden arrived on a spectacular bay gelding who glowed like a new conker. Always after a story, Dora edged up and overheard him telling Olivia that his yard was nearly rebuilt after the fire and filling up with horses.

'That one's seriously nice,' said Olivia.

'Very seriously,' said Harvey-Holden. 'Called Bafford Playboy. Bought him in Ireland. He's for sale, at a price.

'Oh Christ,' he added bitchily as Niall the vicar strolled up the drive, 'here comes Goldilocks. God, he was a pest when the yard burnt down, kept rolling up to counsel me and drink all my drink.'

Niall had been ordered by Ione to bless the hunt, but without her here everyone had forgotten, so he got stuck into the sloe gin and sausages instead, and blessed Not for Crowe, his hand itching to stroke Woody's long muscular thigh at the same time.

Not for Crowe nibbled the vicar's prayer book.

Niall had competition when Shagger charged up, scattering foot followers on a huge, dark brown cob which was clearly unnerved by Shagger's loud, harsh voice and which he was having great difficulty controlling. Despite being a dreadful rider, Shagger was wearing a red coat, for the privilege of which he'd paid the hunt a large sum. He also sported a top hat on the back of his head, so his straight black forelock fell over his face.

'Needs a kirby grip,' observed Miss Painswick beadily.

'Can't raise his hat, needs both hands to cling on,' said Dora.

'Where's Marius?' Harvey-Holden asked Olivia.

'Towcester.' Olivia straightened one of Preston's plaits, adding that Marius didn't want to get shouted at by Lady Crowe, the Master, who was one of his owners.

'He hasn't given her a winner for two years. She's been bloody loyal.' Olivia shook her head when plum cake was offered. 'Sentimental attachment to Marius's father, I suppose. Did you know Lady C was his mistress?' She lowered her voice. 'Hard to believe today, but they used to tie up their horses all over Larkshire and disappear into the bushes. Charlie Radcliffe swears they didn't miss a beat when hounds ran right over them one day . . . Ah, here she is.'

Both gold hands of the church clock edged towards eleven as Nancy Crowe, the Master, arrived. A long-term friend of the Travis-Locks, she had a beaky nose, a line of crimson lipstick instead of a mouth, yellowing skin like a wizened apple, and cropped, dyed black hair. Far more heterosexual than her masculine appearance suggested, she had run the hunt for twenty years. Her horse Terence looked older than her, but would last until she retired. Her voice was as loud and rasping as her name.

'High time you were mounted,' she yelled at Alban, as she tossed back a glass of port.

'Is Spencer out?' asked Alban, lighting her cigar.

'Given up. Seventy-eight now, had to get off and widdle eighty times last time we were out.'

'That's *the* Lady Crowe,' whispered Woody to Dora, 'who turned down Crowie.'

Ears sloping like a basset, eyes closed like an old crocodile, still plump from summer grass, his skimpy tail nearly chewed off by the cows with whom he'd summered, Not for Crowe could never be described as a picture, even less so when he hoovered up Ione's courgette and walnut tart and curled his lip back.

'She rejected Crowie?' raged Dora. 'She'll eat her words, the stupid bitch.'

A group of hunt saboteurs who'd crept in via the churchyard were of the same mind. As Lady Crowe approached them, their tattooed and dreadlocked leader shouted out, 'You fucking bitch.'

'You are entitled to call me the latter,' shouted back Lady Crowe, 'but I haven't indulged in the former activity for twenty years.'

The crowd roared with laughter.

146

'Don't you insult our master, you cheeky bugger,' yelled Charlie Radcliffe as he thundered towards the saboteurs on his mighty blue roan.

'Look out, Brunhilda,' yelled the dreadlocked leader to a big girl in black.

Dora turned green. Brunhilda had been the leader on the goat raid. That night Dora's face had been hidden by a balaclava, but today's leader was now videoing the hunt. What would they think? Goat saviour one day, fox murderer the next. Dora and Mrs Wilkinson retreated behind a yew hedge.

Creeping out five minutes later, Dora retreated again as a smart silver car drove up and out jumped her eldest brother, Jupiter, who was not only MP for Larkminster and head of the New Reform Party but also a governor of Bagley Hall, who didn't approve of bunking off. Jupiter proceeded to announce, to loud cheers, that the New Reform Party would repeal the ban on hunting once they came to power, and shot back into his car again.

'It's going to be Crowie's year,' a returning Dora comforted Woody. 'If Marius is doing that badly, he'll really drop his prices and you'll be able to afford to send Doggie and Crowie to him.'

Woody admired the curves of Ione's limes. He'd done a good job there.

As she surreptitiously snipped off another of Ione's roses and slipped it into her bag, Debbie called out disapprovingly, 'My goodness, here's Tilda Flood. Amazing how many people have taken the day off.'

Tilda had got into the habit of taking her class on much enjoyed nature rambles. It had seemed a fun idea to bring them to see the hunt. With shrieks of joy, the children gathered round Mrs Wilkinson, whose picture was on their noticeboard. Soon she was shaking hooves with them.

Tilda meanwhile was looking round, desperate to catch a mid-week glimpse of Shagger in his red-coated glory.

'Where's Mrs Bancroft?' asked the children in disappointment.

'Looking after Chisolm and Cadbury,' said Dora.

Not all factions were so benign. Re-entering the garden, the saboteurs crept up on Tilda, berating her for encouraging blood sports in the young.

'You ought to be struck off, you buck-toothed cow.'

Tilda went crimson. Where was Shagger in her hour of need?

'Don't be rude to my teacher,' shouted little India Oakridge furiously. 'Hounds kill foxes in seconds. If they're shot, trapped or poisoned they spend days dying in agony. Foxes are murderers anyway.'

'You little pervert,' yelled Brunhilda, 'who brainwashed you?'

'At least her brain's washed,' shouted Alan. 'You lot don't look as though you've touched a bar of soap in days.'

As the crowd bellowed with laughter again, Tilda mouthed a 'thank you' to Alan.

Time to move off. Toby had laid his bloody trail through the faded bracken over a splendid array of hedges and walls.

'Good morning and welcome, ladies and gentlemen,' shouted Lady Crowe to a counterpoint of excited yelping and barking. 'I'm delighted to see so many of you here, supporting the hunt, spending precious petrol on such long distances. I'd like to thank Alban and Ione for their splendid hospitality and beautiful garden.'

A photographer from the *Larkminster Echo* was snapping away. Having taken a nice shot of Lady Crowe, he turned his attention to the group of admirers around Mrs Wilkinson and Not for Crowe. Anxious to get in the picture, Debbie shoved her bulk between the two horses, whereupon the eternally greedy Not for Crowe, mistaking her jute sack for a nosebag, delved inside, drawing out a rainbow riot of cuttings, including several Hermione Harefields.

'Stop it, you brute,' squawked Debbie, whacking Not for Crowe on his ginger nose with her scarlet fold-up umbrella and frantically shoving cuttings back into the bag.

'Don't hit Crowie or I'll report you to the RSPCA, you great bully,' shouted Dora.

Oblivious to the uproar, Lady Crowe wished everyone a good day. Then, with a triumphant blast on the horn, she cried out, 'And I would like to reaffirm that the West Larks will continue to hunt within the law.'

'Unlike Mrs Cunliffe,' raged Pocock, furiously eyeballing Debbie.

'Don't make a fuss, Mr Pocock,' whispered Painswick. 'It's Mrs Wilkinson's day. Good luck, Dora,' she cried.

'Good luck, Mrs Wilkinson,' chorused the children. 'You won't hit her with that whip, will you?'

'No, that's to open gates,' explained Dora, who was in her element. 'Thank you all for coming,' she cried graciously and, leaping on to Mrs Wilkinson, clattered off down the drive to much clapping and cheering.

'Don't know that mare, looks well,' called out Lady Crowe.

'Thank you, Master. I'm qualifying her for the point-to-point.'

'Going to ride her?'

'I'd like to,' said Dora proudly.

'She yours?'

'No, she belongs to Etta Bancroft.'

'So this is the famous Mrs Wilkinson?'

Dora nearly burst with pride. Off they went with a manic jangle and rattle of hooves, fifty riders, pursued through the village by a convoy of cars and motorbikes.

Held up by traffic, Dora, realizing she'd tipped her saddle too far forward, dismounted and undid Mrs Wilkinson's girths to adjust it. Just at that moment, Harvey-Holden trotted past on his spectacular new horse and Mrs Malmesbury, who was parked just ahead and gave way to no one, remembered she'd forgotten to pick up the *Telegraph* from the village shop. Without a glance in her rear mirror, she backed straight into Mrs Wilkinson.

'You fucking stupid old bag,' howled Harvey-Holden. Next moment, Mrs Wilkinson had swung round and bolted down the hill, not stopping until she reached Little Hollow, leaving behind Dora holding the saddle and screaming expletives.

Etta had spent an utterly miserable morning. The thick white cobwebs woven into the conifer hedge reminded her of Bartlett's moulting fur. To comfort a lonely and agitated Chisolm, she'd let her out of her box, whereupon Chisolm had taken off down the road and joined a convoy of ramblers.

Etta had just grabbed her car keys and was setting off to retrieve her when she heard a rattle of hooves and met Mrs Wilkinson at the gate, reins flapping, saddle and Dora missing. She was in a dreadful state, eyes rolling, shuddering in terror. Etta was just trying to calm her when Dora rolled up, raging with humiliation.

'Bloody Wilkie, making me look such an idiot, bloody Mrs Malmesbury. I've got to take her back.' She was about to slap on the saddle.

'You will not,' said Etta firmly. 'Something terrified the life out of her. Chisolm's pushed off, I was just going to look for her.'

'Chisolm will come back, she's got a disc,' said Dora sulkily. 'I can't give in to Wilkie.'

'You damn well can. What happened?'

'Well, we know she's spooked by shovels and cars backing into her,' said Etta, when Dora had cooled down and finished telling her the story. 'I wonder if that's how she got those terrible scars on her legs. I'd better go and find Chisolm, I've got to pick up Poppy at one.'

*

149

Miss Painswick ended up in the Fox with Alan, Alban and Pocock, enjoying Chrissie's moussaka and having a good laugh over Debbie's plant raid.

'Very cutting edge,' quipped Alan.

It was such a lovely day, Miss Painswick had left her sitting-room window open. On her return, she thought she was hallucinating when she saw Chisolm stretched out asleep on her newly upholstered pale blue sofa under a half-eaten copy of *The Times*.

'Chisolm is a distinct addition to our little circle,' announced Painswick as she handed her back to Etta. 'At least she left me the social and television pages. How about scrambled eggs and *The Bill* this evening?'

33

Gradually Mrs Wilkinson grew in confidence and, despite having only one eye, gave Dora some wonderful days out. Working without realizing it, the little mare was learning her trade, discovering how to take the shortest route and to jump all kinds of fences at the gallop. She was loving every minute of it, mixing with other horses, dogs and humans and finding it both steadying and exciting.

To qualify for a point-to-point, she had to hunt six times. On the sixth occasion Dora caught flu, so a heroic Alban Travis-Lock took out Mrs Wilkinson instead. With a flask of brandy in every pocket to steel his nerves, he could hardly shrug into his riding coat. Long legs nearly meeting under Mrs Wilkinson's belly enabled him to cling on.

Cheered on by Alan, who joined the foot followers, Alban gave Mrs Wilkinson her head and had a marvellous afternoon.

'He ended up absolutely rat-arsed,' Alan told Etta later, 'sobbing, "Thank you for giving me back my nerve," into Mrs Wilkinson's shoulder. Must be tough living with Ione, she hasn't forgiven him for knocking over her wormery the day hounds met at the Hall. Wilkie must be incredibly strong to carry him all day.'

The West Larks point-to-point – to be held on 21 March, the first day of spring, was drawing near. Who would ride Mrs Wilkinson? Dora longed to. She had enraged Farmer Fred and the secretary of the golf club galloping all over their land. She had spent ages teaching Mrs Wilkinson to jump. She was the perfect weight for a jockey, but only sixteen and totally inexperienced. In addition, Paris, who loved her, considered it far too dangerous.

Visiting her friend Bianca Campbell-Black, Dora sought the advice of Bianca's father Rupert, who was watching racing all over the world on half a dozen monitors and gazing gloomily at a laptop. Despite having daughters who were brilliant event riders and polo players, Rupert thoroughly disapproved of women jockeys.

'Paris is right. And National Hunt's far more dangerous than flat. It's like going off to the Front. Need to be half-mad to do it. Jump jockeys average a fall every thirteen rides – not the place for a girl. They're not strong enough to hold horses up.'

As Dora's face fell, Rupert suggested she try his god-daughter, Amber Lloyd-Foxe, who had ambitions to become a jump jockey. Rupert felt guilty because he'd refused to give her any rides.

Then, seeing Dora was still despondent, Rupert confided that he was having trouble writing his incredibly opinionated and inflammatory column in the *Racing Post*. If he told her what to say, would she be able to ghost it for him occasionally?

'Certainly,' replied Dora, perking up, 'as long as we can split the fee and write nice things about Mrs Wilkinson.'

Dora had had a terrific pash on Amber Lloyd-Foxe, who when she was at Bagley Hall had exeats to hunt with the Beaufort, and received more letters from boys than anyone else. She was also a heroine, having broken into Parliament with Otis Ferry and scuffled with politicians over the hunting ban.

Amber, like her journalist mother, Janey, liked the fleshpots, and had consequently abandoned eventing as not commercially viable. Despite her famous father, Billy Lloyd-Foxe, who was an Olympic medallist, a BBC equine correspondent and a star on *A Question of Sport*, Amber was finding it hard to get rides, due to other trainers' prejudice against women jockeys – although they were quick enough to offer her rides of a different kind.

Egged on by Painswick, who reasoned that if Amber rode in the point-to-point Amber's ex-headmaster Hengist Brett-Taylor might turn up to cheer her on, Dora wrote to Amber offering her £100 to ride Mrs Wilkinson, 'a fantastic novice mare'.

To Dora's amazement, Amber accepted and came down in early March to school Mrs Wilkinson over some fences. These had been hastily assembled in Valent's orchard by Joey's builders, whose eyes were out on stalks because Amber was languid, blonde, very beautiful, and made Mrs Wilkinson look like a different horse.

Etta, who came to watch, was enchanted to see how well she was going and how wonderfully Amber rode her. With her blonde mane and long eyes the tawny gold of winter willow stems

Amber could have been Gwendolyn on a white-faced Beau Regard.

It's an omen, thought Etta in ecstasy, but was rather disappointed when Amber pulled up and, on being introduced to Etta, pronounced Mrs Wilkinson not bad but very green and small.

'She can't be fifteen hands. She also drops her off hind over fences.' Amber turned to Dora: 'You could try schooling her over a diagonal pole.'

You could be a bit more enthusiastic, thought Etta. She did hope Amber wouldn't use her whip on Mrs Wilkinson.

'Who's she by?' asked Amber, after Etta had rushed off to pick up Poppy from school.

'We don't know,' said Dora.

'And her dam?'

'We don't know that either.'

'Christ, why hasn't she been DNA'd?'

'Etta doesn't want to,' confided Dora. 'She's terrified the rightful owner might want her back, not that he'd have any right after the horrific way he treated her. Etta found her tied to a tree in the middle of winter.'

'Well, that's that then.' Amber jumped off without even bothering to pat Mrs Wilkinson. 'Didn't you realize she can't enter a point-to-point without a passport and a sire and dam?'

'Oh God, we've registered her name with Weatherbys and got her some lovely silks, beech-leaf brown with purple stars, which will really suit you. And I've got a certificate from the Master to say she's hunted six times.' Then, as Mrs Wilkinson nosed around for Polos, 'No one said anything about sires and dams. That's shocking actually,' exploded Dora, 'like saying Paris can't go to Cambridge because he doesn't know who his natural parents are.'

Amber took off her hat, pulled off her toggle so her blonde hair swayed in the breeze like the willows around her and reached for a cigarette.

'The only solution would be to enter her in a members' race. This is limited to horses owned by local farmers or members or subscribers to the hunt. Then you could put "breeding unknown" under Mrs Wilkinson's name in the race card. Is Mrs Bancroft a member of the hunt?'

'Not exactly,' sighed Dora.

'Well, she better become one tout de suite, or there isn't a hope in hell of Mrs Wilkinson running.'

Etta was digging her garden three days later when Dora rolled up with Cadbury, looking furtive.

'Mrs B, I mean Etta, there's something I must tell you. As Mrs Wilkinson's owner, you have to become a member or a subscriber to the hunt in order that she can run.' Then, at Etta's look of horror: 'It's the only way we can swing it. The members' race is the only one that allows horses without a passport.'

'No,' snapped Etta, shoving her trowel so furiously into the earth she punctured a lily bulb, 'I'm not supporting the hunt.'

'We don't kill foxes any more. Oh perlease, Etta, you can't deprive Mrs Wilkinson of a brilliant career. Amber thought her exceptional,' lied Dora, 'and drove all the way down here. We can't let Amber down.'

'I don't care.' Etta threw down her trowel. 'I must go and collect Drummond.'

Fate, however, lent a hand. The following morning Dora popped in and found Etta making chocolate brownies.

'Oh Etta, I've just bumped into Mrs Malmesbury in floods. A horrible fox got her goose yesterday in the lunch hour (when she'd just slipped down to Tesco's) and plucked the poor goose alive then killed her. Feathers everywhere. Geese mate for life and her poor blind gander is absolutely heartbroken and keeps calling for her, "Ee-ee-ee-ee," and bumping into things, "Ee-ee-ee." Foxes kill for the hell of it.' Seeing Etta's eyes fill with tears, Dora pressed home her advantage. 'Just imagine the poor old boy going sadly to bed tonight, "Ee-ee-ee," without his wife. Foxes are bastards – "ee-ee-ee." Please, please join the hunt.'

'Oh, all right, but only for this season. How much is it?'

'Only about four hundred pounds.' Then, as Etta gasped: 'But it's already been paid for.'

'What d'you mean?'

'I've had a whip-round. Alban, Alan, even the Major coughed up (but don't tell Debbie), even Debbie (but don't tell the Major) – Chris and Chrissie, the Terrible Trio, of course, Tilda, Painswick and Pocock. They all chipped in. Phoebe promised but I expect she'll conveniently forget.'

'They can't,' protested Etta. 'I shouldn't support the hunt and I can't allow other people to pay for me to do so, they can't afford it.'

'We can,' said Dora stoutly. 'We all love Mrs Wilkinson, we're so proud of the way you've brought her back from the dead. We all feel we've got a stake in her. She's the village horse.'

'I must contribute something,' squeaked Etta, sadly bidding farewell to the lovely sea-blue suit in the Blue Cross shop she'd hoped to wear on the day.

'You can pay the entry fee and Amber's cap if you insist,' said

Dora kindly. 'God, these brownies are yum. That's only a hundred pounds.'

And the dashing blue stetson as well, thought Etta.

After she'd given the children their tea, Etta rang Alan, who'd contributed more than a hundred pounds to her membership fee. 'Oh Alan, Sampson so disapproved of racing, he'd have died at the thought of my being an owner. And I'm so anti-blood sports I feel I'm going to pieces in every way.'

'Paris is worth a mass,' said Alan reassuringly. 'And Willowwood's so excited. Mrs Wilkinson's given us all an interest.'

34

Race day dawned cold and breezy but still without rain.

'We're going to win the turnout prize if nothing else,' vowed Dora to Etta as she plaited up Mrs Wilkinson. 'That mane and tail conditioner made her mane so thick and shiny. No, darling,' she added as Mrs Wilkinson irritably thrust out a foreleg for a snack, 'you've got to hoist yourself over those fences. And I mustn't forget to take water away an hour before the race.'

Mrs Wilkinson gave a whicker of welcome and Chisolm bleated in excitement as Painswick bustled in with the *Racing Post*.

'Look, you're all in the paper. Here we are,' she said as the pages blew around. ' "Number 13, Mrs Wilkinson, grey mare", dear little soul. "Owned by Mrs Etta Bancroft, trained by Miss Dora Belvedon." '

'Well, someone had to,' mumbled Dora, going rather pink and concentrating on the last plait.

Oh goodness, what would Romy and Martin say if they saw the race card? Etta turned pale. Thank God they'd taken Poppy and Drummond away for the weekend.

As Painswick got an apple out of her bag, Mrs Wilkinson brightened, but Chisolm rushed forward and grabbed it.

'Afraid she mustn't eat before the race,' said Dora. 'What are the odds?'

'Fifty to one. Doesn't she look lovely?'

'So do you,' said Etta.

Painswick was looking very flash in a dashing blue hat with a feather, to pick up the blue in Hengist's scarf.

'I just dropped in to say I won't be needing a lift,' she said smugly. 'I thought poor Old Mrs Malmesbury needed taking out of herself after the wicked fox killed her poor goose,' Painswick looked straight at Etta, daring her to try to chicken out, 'so I invited her to join us at the races. She's driving me.'

'God help you,' muttered Dora.

'I've brought some supplies for the picnic.' Painswick waved a carrier bag which Chisolm eyed with interest as she edged forward to be petted.

'Who else is in Wilkie's race?' asked Dora.

'Family Dog and Crowie, of course,' said Painswick fondly.

'And Rupert Campbell-Black's son Xavier, who was at Bagley with Amber, riding an old soldier called Toddler. Harvey-Holden's got Judy's Pet, and Bafford Playboy ridden by Olivia Oakridge.'

'That'll win,' said Dora.

'Don't be defeatist,' reproved Painswick. 'I'm sure Amber will ride Mrs Wilkinson to victory.'

Mrs Wilkinson, however, had other ideas. When Joey and Woody rumbled up in the lorry already containing Not for Crowe and Family Dog, even when her buddy Chisolm bounded up the ramp, Mrs Wilkinson flatly refused to load, going into a quaking, rolling-eyed, rearing and plunging panic. It took all Dora, Woody, Joey and Etta's strength to stop her hurtling off across Valent's orchard.

Coaxing with nuts had no effect, nor did Dora trying to ride her into the lorry, and when everyone including Painswick tried to hoist her up the ramp, she went crazy, kicking, striking out with her foreleg crashing to the ground, and flailing in panic.

'Stop it,' yelled Etta, flinging her arms round Mrs Wilkinson, trying to still her violently trembling body. 'You can't make her go. She was just like this when I found her, only she was too weak to struggle. This could set her back permanently. She's not going to run.'

'Then I'll hack her there,' cried Dora, rushing past a stable door covered in good luck cards to fetch her tack. 'It's only five miles to Ashcombe.'

'She'll be far too tired to run.'

'We've gotta declare in half an hour,' said Joey, who was fast losing his temper. 'I've put everyone's money on. Half Willowwood has had a punt. Let Dora ride her.'

'No,' wailed Etta.

'I do think you are being rather selfish, dear,' said Painswick, wiping Mrs Wilkinson's froth off her coat.

'Am I?' Etta straightened one of Dora's lovingly executed plaits.

'Yes,' said Joey, 'she'll be fine. She's kept going all day out hunting.'

'We can't let Amber down,' said Dora, sliding a bridle over Mrs Wilkinson's head. With Joey's help she was tacked up in a trice.

'Go across country,' advised Woody, giving Dora a leg up. 'Lester Bolton's got the road up winching in a new cinema to show off his wife's horrible films.'

'I don't want Wilkie to go,' cried Etta. 'She's my horse, and what I say . . .'

But Mrs Wilkinson had taken matters into her own newly shod hooves. Frantic to put as much distance between herself and the lorry, she set off down the drive while Dora shouted back, 'Can you ring Amber and tell her we're on our way? And don't forget the silks. She'll be fine, trust me, Etta.'

As Woody put an arm round Etta's heaving shoulders, Chisolm, unmoved by such events, was polishing off Painswick's last tomato sandwich.

35

Amber Lloyd-Foxe had arrived at Ashcombe unusually early. Believing Mrs Wilkinson hadn't a hope in hell, she had last night gone to a party, met a gorgeous man and ended up in bed with him. Now she was fighting a hangover and remorse for being so unprofessional. To clear her head she had twice walked the course, which unwound over two fields bleached khaki from lack of rain and lying at the bottom of a valley. The valley itself was divided by a nearly dried-up stream which the runners would cross by a water jump and a grassed-over bridge.

Huddled in her Golf in the car park, Amber lit another cigarette. Hoping it was the man from last night, she was disappointed when Etta rang to say Dora was hacking over and hoped to make the declaration.

Trust Dora to cock it up, thought Amber crossly. She should never have accepted the ride. She'd tried to stop her father driving down, but he'd switched off his mobile.

There was a far smarter and larger crowd of all ages than she'd expected, mostly in khaki camouflage. The racing fraternity, who Amber always thought of as the Check Republic because they always dressed in check tweeds, the men in check tweed caps, were out in force. Loads of Sloanes and Aggies from the Royal Agricultural College, with lurchers, Labradors and little terriers on leads, clustered round the boots of Land-Rovers for warmth and sustenance.

Studying the race card, Amber found her name, and Mrs Wilkinson, described as 'a first season youngster, unraced over fences or the flat'.

Next moment she heard raised voices, and looking up recognized Shade Murchieson, olive-skinned, black-browed, his handsome sensual face contorted with rage. A pale fawn cashmere coat, thick leather gloves and a dark brown Homburg set him exotically apart from the other racegoers, but he'd look foreign if wrapped in a Union Jack. He was also a big owner. Amber lowered her window.

Shade was shouting at a man with his back to Amber, who, although as tall and broad-shouldered, was far more slightly built. His thick dark brown curls spilled over the high neck of an ancient bottle-green check coat. Amber could just see even thicker dark eyelashes and the edge of a beautiful jawline. His ears were red with cold and his fists clenched.

'Will you fucking well stop ringing my lads and my jockeys, giving them totally conflicting instructions and pestering them for information on my horses?'

'They're my horses, remember that,' shouted back Shade, 'and as I pay you an inordinate amount to train them, I expect you to deliver occasionally.'

'How can I, with you hanging round the yard, butting in, wrecking morale, ordering them not to try? Don't push me, Shade, or I'll call the police. And stay away from my wife.'

For a second Amber thought the man in the bottle-green check coat was going to hit Shade, then he swung round and half strode, half stumbled past her. And Amber caught her breath because, despite being white with anguish and fury, he was lovely looking, like a Croatian male model, with slanting dark eyes, high cheekbones and a beautiful passionate mouth.

Then she realized it was Marius Oakridge, who was having another horrendous run of form. What were he and Shade doing here? Glancing down at her race card, she discovered Olivia Oakridge was riding Bafford Playboy, which she had a feeling Shade had bought at a vast price from Ralph Harvey-Holden and which was now being trained by Marius. Flipping through the rest of the field, she reckoned Playboy would win. Olivia, despite her kittenish exterior, took no prisoners.

Looking up, Amber saw that Shade had got back into his Mercedes, number SM1, and was smiling into his mobile.

Where the hell was Dora?

'My horse, my horse, a kingdom for a horse,' grumbled Amber.

At last a much graffitied white lorry rumbled into the car park, and Joey and Woody jumped out and rushed off to declare. They were followed by an ancient Polo containing Chisolm, who'd travelled all the way with her head on a tear-stained Etta's shoulder.

'I'm here,' Amber leapt out.

160

'I'm so, so sorry,' said Etta, handing her the silks. 'Mrs Wilkinson refused to load. Dora should be here any moment.' Then, trying not to cry: 'You won't use your whip on her, will you?'

Amber felt so sorry for her she said she'd guard Mrs Wilkinson with her life.

Fighting through the crowd, Amber changed in a freezing tent with a cracked mirror. Nor did the clashing reddy brown and purple do anything for her flushed hungover face. At least Mrs Wilkinson as an unraced mare with a woman rider only had to carry 11 stone 2 lb, as opposed to the 11 stone 12 of Bafford Playboy, who'd won two point-to-points in Ireland.

As Amber carried her saddle in the direction of the roped-off circle serving as a paddock, she was flabbergasted to see from the bookies' boards that Mrs Wilkinson was joint favourite with Playboy at 5–1.

'Hello, Amber, just put a lot of money on you,' whinnied Toby Weatherall, raising his brown curly-brimmed hat. 'Terrific write-up in the *Racing Post.*'

'In Rupert Campbell-Black's column, no less,' chirped Phoebe. 'You are lucky to have friends in high places. Do introduce us, Rupert's so gorgeous and his son Xavier's riding in the same race as you.'

'What *are* you talking about?'

'Here.' Toby thrust the *Post* at Amber. Rupert's cold, beautiful, unsmiling face headed the column, which ended with a para-graph urging everyone to hotfoot it down to the West Larks point-to-point, where Amber, an extremely promising amateur jockey, daughter of his old friend and iconic showjumper Billy Lloyd-Foxe, would be riding Mrs Wilkinson, a brilliant novice, in the members' race.

'Oh my God.' Amber flushed even more with pleasure and dropped the *Racing Post,* which promptly blew away. 'Rupert's never, ever encouraged me before. No wonder the odds have shortened. I can't believe it.'

Nor could Rupert, who was incandescent with rage but could hardly admit to the racing world that his column had been ghosted by a schoolgirl.

Next moment Richard Pitman had jumped out of a car. 'Hi, Amber, tell me about this wonder horse.'

'She should be here any minute,' said Amber.

Dora had great difficulty holding up an utterly traumatized Mrs Wilkinson, who'd cantered or galloped most of the way. She was only now slowed down by the racing traffic still flooding into the ground, so Dora rode her along the verges. She certainly wouldn't win the turnout prize, her coat ruffled with sweat, her legs and white face mud-splattered.

Willowwood had turned out in force, enjoying communal hospitality from the Travis-Lock boot, where Chris was serving Bull Shots, red wine and chicken soup. Phoebe was sitting on the Land-Rover bonnet, telling everyone that she'd just learnt that naughty Amber had been at an all-night party the previous night. Debbie Cunliffe had just returned from a stroll round the trade stands. The Major was bellyaching about sloppy parking and how many more cars he'd have fitted in, and how there hadn't been any rain in his rain gauge for ages. The Cunliffes were on non-speaks with the Travis-Locks because of Ione's latest plan to have a wind turbine clanking away between their gardens.

Ione had only just forgiven Alban for overturning her wormery. The moment she pushed off to enquire into the possibility of a Green stall next year, Pocock, in brown suit and tweed cap, the vicar, still in his dog collar from Matins, and Alban got stuck into the red.

Tilda Flood was looking wistful because Shagger had pushed off to socialize with Toby, who seemed to know everyone. She was cheered up, however, by a large gin and tonic handed her by Alan. Painswick, who arrived white and shaking after a bumpy ride with Mrs Malmesbury, also opted for a G and T. Old Mrs M was already on her second Bull Shot.

No one was making inroads into Ione's forced rhubarb crumble or butternut squash quiche, or even Chris and Chrissie's sliced beef Wellington or Etta's egg sandwiches, because they were all too nervous about Mrs Wilkinson, Family Dog and Not for Crowe.

'Lucky Joey got our bets on first thing,' murmured Alan to Alban. 'Mrs Wilkinson's shortened to 4–1.'

'Wilkie's so thirsty, can't she have a little drink of water?' pleaded Etta.

'Not before the race. Just run a wet sponge round her mouth,' insisted Dora as they resaddled up Mrs Wilkinson behind Joey's lorry to avoid the vicious wind whistling through the bare trees.

Next door, in Marius's lorry, a bounding Bafford Playboy was being saddled up by a sexy but very sulky Titian-haired stable lass called Michelle. Watching her were Shade and Olivia Oakridge, wearing a Puffa over Shade's magenta and orange colours.

'Rupert must know something to have tipped Mrs Wilkinson in the *Post*,' said Olivia.

'When has anything Rupert said ever had any credence,' snarled Shade. 'Only thing you've got to do is beat his arrogant little toad of a son, Xavier, and that scraggy old has-been, Toddler.'

'I'm sorry Marius has buggered off to Chepstow,' sighed Olivia.

'I'm not,' said Shade, then to wind Olivia up, he added, 'That's a stunning girl,' admiring Amber's endless legs in white breeches and shiny brown-topped boots, as she loped towards Joey's lorry. Michelle, the sulky red-headed stable lass, gave a smirk of satisfaction.

The firmness of the ground had reduced the runners to eight. Not for Crowe looked even more gloomy as he padded round the parade ring, Family Dog more cheerful. Joey, riding Crowie, had given up Etta's cakes for two months and just made the weights.

'What did you have for breakfast?' shouted Chris, hanging over the rail.

'A carrot,' shouted back Joey.

The vicar's heart twisted at how pale and thin Woody looked as he saddled up Family Dog.

There were cheers for Farmer Fred's son, Harry, on a chestnut called Nixon, and for Nancy Crowe's son, Jonathan, on a black cob called Marvellous. Jonathan had the same wizened face as his mother and looked almost as old.

Punters gazed approvingly at a very pretty dark brown mare called Judy's Pet, trained by Harvey-Holden and one of the first horses in his fightback. She was owned by a Mrs Judy Tobias. Neither she nor Harvey-Holden was present but a dashing local amateur called Aberdare 'Dare' Catswood was riding the mare.

Quietly plodding round the paddock was Rupert Campbell-Black's ancient warrior Toddler with a seen-it-all-before look on his kind white face.

A rumble of approval greeted Bafford Playboy, a lovely old-fashioned chaser, heavy in the quarters and rippling with muscle.

'That's the horse Shade bought from Harvey-Holden and gave to Marius to train,' murmured Alan to Alban. 'But not for much longer, they had an awful row in the car park. Lovely horse.'

Shagger stole off to have a bet.

The Willowwood contingent huddled together on the ropes for warmth. Etta stood among the owners in the centre of the parade ring, a forlorn figure in her old grey coat – if only she could have afforded that one in sea blue.

'Poor little soul's invested so much love in Mrs Wilkinson,' observed Painswick, speaking for everyone. 'It'll break her heart if anything goes wrong.'

A great cheer went up when Mrs Wilkinson, still in a borrowed red rug which fell to her fetlocks, was finally led in by Dora.

'Must have shrunk in the wash,' shouted a wag.

She was easily the smallest runner, shying nervously, eye darting everywhere, searching the crowd until she caught sight of Etta and dragged Dora over to her, whickering with pleasure, nearly sending Judy's Pet flying.

'Isn't that darling,' said Tilda to Alan.

But as the public took in Mrs Wilkinson's lack of inches and her one eye, her odds began to lengthen dramatically.

The bell went for the jockeys to mount.

'I don't have to give you any instructions,' murmured Shade. As he gave Olivia a leg up, Michelle the stable lass couldn't fail to notice his hand moving up her thigh.

The crowd cheered again in real excitement and Shade's face blackened as Rupert Campbell-Black, the trainer who had rejected him, stalked into the paddock, followed by his son Xavier, wearing Rupert's famous dark blue and emerald silks.

'What a treat.' All the women in the crowd and Niall the vicar patted their hair.

It was as though the north wind had blown in from the Arctic as Rupert looked through Shade and, nodding bleakly at Olivia, asked her, 'Who's your fat friend?'

Shade went purple.

Rupert then caught sight of Dora. 'I want a word with you.'

'Later,' said Dora, quailing inside, 'I'm just getting Mrs Wilkinson sorted.'

'So this is Mrs Wilkinson,' said Rupert softly. 'Brilliant novice indeed. Did they cover a donkey with a woodlouse?'

'Don't be horrible,' flared up Etta. 'You wait till the race is over.' For years she'd dreamed of meeting Rupert, and now her idol had an entire body of clay.

'Here's Amber and her father,' cried Dora in relief.

The crowd was in heaven. Rupert, and now Billy Lloyd-Foxe, the darling of the racing world. A couple of punters who'd been in the bar started singing the *Question of Sport* theme tune.

Billy was also a bit drunk. There were no buttons on his overcoat, not many on his shirt, but his smile warmed the day.

'What a darling horse.' He patted Mrs Wilkinson. 'Isn't she sweet?' Then, turning to Etta: 'Thank you so much for giving Amber the ride. I had a small horse once called the Bull. God, he could jump and he tried so hard.' Turning back to Amber: 'Just put her to sleep in the back, darling. Keep out of trouble and move up slowly.'

'You won't use your whip,' begged Etta, noticing Amber was carrying one.

'Only to whack off Xav and Dare Catswood,' said Billy.

'Hi, Amber,' shouted Xavier, riding past on Toddler. 'Let's catch up on the way round.'

'Hi, Amber,' called out the handsome Dare Catswood on Judy's Pet. 'How about dinner tonight?'

Shade gave Amber a smouldering glance as she set off.

'Safe journey,' he murmured. Good thing to keep Olivia on her toes. Sod Rupert! He couldn't wait for Bafford Playboy to win by ten lengths.

36

Nancy Crowe and a huntsman in red, both mounted, arrived to take the jockeys down.

The Willowwood gang retired to a little hill where they could see the whole oblong course round which the horses had to gallop twice and jump sixteen fences. Amid the wintry bleakness of the day, there were signs of spring, blossom foaming on the blackthorn and blurs of crimson, violet and ruby where the buds on the trees were bursting through. Down at the start, marked by two rugger posts without an adjoining bar, Mrs Wilkinson, trembling violently and already hepped up, was further upset when Bafford Playboy bashed into her, half a ton of snorting muscle, sending her flying. Olivia, who didn't like Shade ogling blondes, didn't even apologize.

The other jockeys were discussing tactics.

'Mine likes to make all.'

'Mine idles when she gets in front.'

'I'm going to hold mine up,' drawled Dare Catswood.

'I'm going to try and stay on,' quavered Woody.

Chisolm took advantage of everyone's preoccupation to eat a Bakewell tart, half a bunch of grapes and a blue woollen glove.

Etta felt sick. God would smite her down for supporting the hunt. She had stupidly put her old age pension for this month on Mrs Wilkinson, but was far more distraught that she might lose her darling horse as she had lost Bartlett.

'It's all right,' whispered Alban, squeezing her hand. 'She carried me all day out hunting, this'll be a doddle.'

'May God bless our little village horse,' cried Niall. 'And bring her safely home, and Not for Crowe and Family Dog as well.'

'Have another Bull Shot, Mrs Malmesbury.' Alan waved a thermos.

'Not too many,' said Painswick nervously.

Chisolm ate another Bakewell tart.

The huntsman's horn rang thrillingly round the valley and they were off. Mrs Wilkinson was so hidden by the larger horses that no one could see her, until she dropped her off hind, caught the top of the second fence, somersaulted wildly and crashed down on to the rock-hard ground, throwing Amber ahead of her.

There was a stunned silence, then Etta wailed with horror and stumbled off down the hill towards them. She could see both the checkered flag and the orange flag frantically waving, summoning doctor and vet.

Willowwood was in uproar.

'We might as well go home,' said Alan, tearing up his betting slip. Phoebe and Tilda burst into tears. Below them Etta had nearly reached the course. Amber was lying on the ground nursing her hurt pride when Mrs Wilkinson scrambled to her feet, shook off the dust and nudged Amber in her ribs: 'Buck up, we've got a race to win.'

Amber staggered up, remounted, they set off and magic occurred, as if Mrs Wilkinson had sprouted wings and flown over the trees. No one could believe what they were seeing.

Intoxicated by the rattle of her feet on the firm ground, enjoying a left-handed track where her good eye was able to focus on crowds lining the route, Mrs Wilkinson was soon skipping joyfully over the fences, a look of intense concentration on her white face, her tongue hanging out like a little girl writing an essay.

Gradually, as she cleared fence after fence and the gap narrowed between her and the rest of the field, the crowd started roaring.

'I'm seeing things.' Alan pressed his binoculars against his blond eyelashes.

'Come on, Wilkie,' screamed Miss Painswick. As Mrs Wilkinson flew past Family Dog and Not for Crowe, who'd both been pulled up, Woody and Joey gave a cheer. Clearing the big blackthorn hedge, she overtook Farmer Fred's Marvellous and Jonathan Crowe's Nixon, and drew level with Xav Campbell-Black on Toddler, who, as his long dappled legs devoured the course, was twice her size.

'Still no time for that catch-up,' yelled Amber as she left Xav behind. 'Come on, you gorgeous little girl.'

Mrs Wilkinson flapped her long ears. Ahead Amber could see hulking bay and sleek dark brown quarters.

'Come on, Wilkie.' Amber drummed her heels even faster into Mrs Wilkinson's ribs. Next minute, they had shot between Bafford Playboy and Judy's Pet.

'Three more to jump, we can do it, Wilkie.'

Then Playboy and Judy's Pet both rallied, Olivia thundering up the inside and blocking off Mrs Wilkinson's view of the crowd, Judy's Pet closing in from the right. For a moment, Mrs Wilkinson panicked and faltered.

'Good girl, Wilkie,' yelled Amber, 'you're doing brilliant. Get out of my way,' she screamed as Olivia bumped her, crossing the bridge. Sandwiched between the two horses as they jumped the last fence, Mrs Wilkinson stayed resolute, and although desperately tired, battled on until Judy's Pet fell away and it was just her and Playboy, who'd bumped her once too often. Eyeballing him furiously, Mrs Wilkinson put on a phenomenal last spurt, shoving her head forward and winning by a whisker.

Ione Travis-Lock screamed her head off and was amazed to find herself hugging Direct Debbie. What did wind turbines matter?

'Photograph, photograph,' howled the punters, including Shagger, who'd backed Playboy, but there was no one to photograph finishes at point-to-points.

Fortunately the West Larks Hunt stewards were biased in Etta's favour. Dora had kept them amused throughout the season, Amber had fought hunting's corner by protesting against the ban and nobody liked Shade Murchieson, so they declared Mrs Wilkinson the rightful winner.

As Dora raced up to welcome Wilkie, covering her with kisses, Marius's sulky red-headed lass clipped a lead-rope on Bafford Playboy and told Olivia Oakridge, 'You ought to be on *Police Five*. You was robbed.'

Dare Catswood, who'd come third on Judy's Pet, shook Amber's hand.

'Well done, offer for dinner's still open any time.'

Etta meanwhile had struggled back up the hill to the overjoyed party from Willowwood.

'I cannot believe this, I cannot believe this.'

'Yes, you can,' said Painswick. 'I'll look after Chisolm, run down and lead her in.'

'Just a sec,' said Ione, getting out a handkerchief and mopping up Etta's tears.

'Use my compact,' said Debbie, turning Etta's cheeks bright orange. 'How about a bit of lippy?' She applied a dash of scarlet.

'There,' she brushed some mud off Etta's coat, 'you look lovely.'

'Like a less gaudy lipstick,' whispered Phoebe.

'Enjoy your moment,' ordered Debbie, propelling a stunned Etta towards the finish to join an ecstatic Dora and Amber and fling her arms round a heaving, panting Mrs Wilkinson, who, however tired she was, still gave a faint whicker.

'Well done indeed,' said Lady Crowe as she led them in.

Next moment they were joined by an escaped Chisolm trailing her lead.

'Punch the air with your fist, Etta,' exhorted Dora.

Amber was too cool to betray her elation. Think of winning like this every day.

'Good horse,' she drawled to Etta. 'I'd like to ride her again.'

Carefully Tilda pieced together Alan's betting slip and handed it back to him. Shagger was livid.

'Why didn't you tell me she had a chance?'

Rupert's irritation with Dora, on the other hand, evaporated as ecstatic punters mobbed him, thanking him for tipping the winner.

'We must get another horse,' said Joey as he and Woody led back Crowie and Doggie.

Etta received £100 as the winning owner, which she split with her jockey and her trainer, then spent her share on champagne, which was drunk in the Fox that evening out of Mrs Wilkinson's splendid silver cup. She was also presented with a video of the race, which when shown on the pub's big screen flabbergasted everyone. Most horses slow up to jump but Mrs Wilkinson, once she got going, made up a length with every fence, skimming them like a swallow to land running and carry on.

They also noticed how beautifully Amber rode, not bobbing about like many women but crouched down over Mrs Wilkinson like a man, like her father Billy, knowing exactly how to take her weight off a horse in the air.

Everyone in Willowwood except an outraged Shagger seemed to have backed her. Etta had made £1,800, Woody £600. Joey, who'd perilously risked half Valent's workmen's wages, had pulled in enough to buy another horse, although he wasn't telling Mop Idol.

Alan and Alban had also bet heavily and were thrilled to pay off their credit card bills. Direct Debbie and the Major had both made £300 but weren't telling each other. The vicar's street cred had rocketed because his prayers for Mrs Wilkinson had been answered. Old Mrs Malmesbury had put on a fiver, which would enable her to buy a new goose for her poor blind gander.

'What's this about an Indian in a turban living at the bottom of your garden?' she asked Ione and Debbie.

'Not an Indian turban, a wind turbine,' explained Ione.

'Turban, turbine, all the same thing. Too many foreigners.'

Ione's eyes met Debbie's and they managed not to laugh, happy to be friends.

Toby and Phoebe, who'd borrowed a fiver off Tilda which she'd never repay, were peeved because they'd only got their money on at 4–1.

As a result of Dora's publicity skills, Rupert's tipping an outsider, Amber's glamour and famous name, and Mrs Wilkinson's romantic rescue in the snow, the story made most of the papers.

Martin Bancroft was not pleased:

'At least donate your winnings to the Sampson Bancroft Fund, Mother, we've got lots of bills to pay. So insensitive to call yourself Mrs Etta rather than Mrs Sampson Bancroft in the race card. Dad would have been so hurt and we need all the publicity we can get.'

'And the pushiest of them all is charity,' observed Alan.

The rest of Willowwood, on the other hand, were enraptured. A move was definitely afoot to form a syndicate.

Etta, however, was feeling so depressed she was grateful to be invited by Painswick, flush from her £150 win, to share a celebratory drink the following evening.

Painswick was particularly excited because Hengist Brett-Taylor had rung, asking her to pass on his congratulations. Etta once more admired handsome Hengist and his greyhound, Elaine, in the framed school photograph on the wall. Dora, Paris, Amber, Xavier Campbell-Black and right at the back a youth with rumpled dark curls who was blatantly smoking a cigarette were also pointed out to her.

'That's Cosmo Rannaldini, the late Sir Roberto and Dame Hermione Harefield's son, so naughty but such a charmer. He owns several racehorses.'

After a second glass of champagne, Etta unbuttoned not just about Martin's bullying but how worried sick she was. If Wilkie went into training, she'd have to have a DNA test to find who her sire and dam were.

'She must have some excellent blood,' said Painswick, who was now knitting Mrs Wilkinson a warm red hood for next autumn.

'Her owners might claim her back,' said Etta despairingly, 'and what trainer shall we use? Harvey-Holden wrote me such a nice letter and he's rebuilding his yard. Wilkie might do better with just a few horses and Marius just looks so cross. Oh Joyce,' she took a gulp of champagne, 'Wilkie looked so sweet lying down in her stable last night. She was so tired after hacking home yet so happy at all the patting and praising. I know I've got to give her the chance to go into training, but it'll be like sending Martin off to prep school.'

'No bad thing if he went back,' said Painswick with a sniff. 'Might knock off a few rough corners.'

37

In the following week, Etta received offers for Mrs Wilkinson from the finest trainers in the land. She refused them all but yielding to pressure from Martin, Carrie and her Willowwood friends, who felt she shouldn't deny Mrs Wilkinson a brilliant career, she allowed her mare to have a DNA test.

Sensational findings came back that Mrs Wilkinson was a five-year-old named Usurper. Her sire was Rupert's Derby-winning stallion Peppy Koala, her dam a National Hunt mare called Little Star, who'd won several races. More disastrously it transpired that Usurper had once belonged to Shade Murchieson and Harvey-Holden. She'd been born on 6 March.

'She's a Pisces and she's got the same birthday as Ouija Board,' said Dora ecstatically. 'No wonder she pissed all over that point-to-point. She's going to need lots of counselling, like my sister Emerald, before she meets her real parents.'

Joey, to protect a distraught Etta, tipped off the police, who immediately rolled up at Ravenscroft to interview Harvey-Holden, waving photographs of a bloodstained, lacerated Mrs Wilkinson from when Etta first rescued her. Harvey-Holden immediately protested he had no idea how his filly had got into that condition. He would never have dreamt of hurting her.

Shade, he said, had bought her for his daughter Chantelle's eighteenth birthday, but Shade's ex-wife, from whom he had parted with colossal acrimony, had refused to let Chantelle accept the filly. Usurper had been returned to Harvey-Holden to await further developments. Harvey-Holden had been very fond of the filly and wanted her back.

Etta's fears intensified because Harvey-Holden's fortunes had changed dramatically. He had not witnessed Mrs Wilkinson's point-to-point victory because that weekend he'd married a very rich, very large widow called Judy Tobias.

Tipped off in the Fox by Joey, Alan arrived to commiserate and brief Etta.

'Judy Tobias, now Judy Harvey-Holden, talk about Tobias and the Devil,' said Alan, helping himself to a large glass of red, 'is a big, blowsy philanthropist, horribly politically correct and heavily, she couldn't be anything else at that size, into animal welfare. So H-H better start treating his horses better. Jude evidently fell in love when she saw H-H crying on television after the fire.

'Taking her to bed must be like a ferret mounting a hippo. With any luck H-H will get squashed flat before the next National Hunt season. If she walked past that window she'd darken the room more than Valent's mature hedge. Oh cheer up, Etta darling. They'll never be allowed to take her back to that dump.'

In the days that followed, the on dit was that Judy's money would enable H-H to rebuild his yard to the lushest specifications, adding new gallops, a solarium, an indoor school the size of a football pitch and an equine swimming pool for Jude to romp in.

'Which means lorries rumbling through Willowwood wrecking the roads, holding up the traffic,' observed Alan. 'Joey will no doubt get the contract to build it.'

Deadliest of all, Jude was determined to help H-H fight the case for the repossession of Mrs Wilkinson with a crack QC called Cecil Stroud.

Martin Bancroft was appalled by the news. On returning a week later from fundraising in America, he set out for Little Hollow, determined to persuade his mother to give back Mrs Wilkinson at once. Judy Tobias, particularly if she were going to be living round the corner, was someone to get in with. Martin was outraged to find his egregious brother-in-law and that slyboots Dora Belvedon in situ drinking a bottle of Moët.

'Cecil Stroud has never lost a case, Mother,' were his opening words. 'You'll end up in prison for horse-rustling.'

'No, she won't,' crowed Dora. 'Marti Gluckstein's going to act for her.'

'Don't be fatuous,' thundered Martin. 'How can Mother possibly afford him?'

'Rupert Campbell-Black's helping with the bill,' drawled Alan, then, at Martin's look of disbelief: 'Never look a gift horseowner in the mouth.'

Rupert had been secretly gratified that all the press had picked up on the fact that he had recognized Mrs Wilkinson's star quality and tipped her in the point-to-point. He loathed Shade, 'Mr Chip and Grievance', and Harvey-Holden, the little twerp. Mrs Wilkinson had turned out to be the daughter of one of his favourite stallions, which was good for business, and if he helped Etta out she was more likely later to sell him Mrs Wilkinson. He had therefore instructed his friend Marti Gluckstein QC, who'd got him out of numerous scrapes over the years, to look after Etta.

Willowwood, devastated at the prospect of losing Mrs Wilkinson, also vowed to chip in if Etta needed help. A shell-shocked Etta was overwhelmed with gratitude but she knew that honour demanded she pay back her benefactors.

38

The court case opened at Larkminster Magistrates' Court, during a heatwave on a Tuesday in late June. Etta, Alan, Alban, the Major, Debbie and Painswick, whispering as though they were in church, sat in a waiting room flipping through old magazines. Painswick was excited to find a picture of Valent and Bonny Richards in *Hello!*

'He'll be moving in soon. Surely they ought to be working on Badger's Court,' observed Debbie, nodding disapprovingly through the window at a smoking Joey and Woody. Alan should have been working too, but as no one could be more depressed than Etta, he could justify this as research.

Miss Painswick had now discovered a glamorous picture of Seth and Corinna, who were also rumoured to be returning to Willowwood in a week or two. Pocock, who did their garden as well as Ione's, hadn't therefore felt justified in taking the day off. The vicar had.

'Surely he ought to be visiting the sick,' chuntered Debbie.

Tilda was heartbroken not to be present but couldn't desert her children. She had, however, instructed her class to draw a poster of a grey horse appearing through willows, with a large caption, 'Mrs Wilkinson belongs to Willowwood'. Joey and Woody, alerted by Dora, were brandishing it for the press outside the court. Shagger, Toby and Phoebe, who'd sent a good luck card, were all in London.

Etta, who was valiantly trying to be cheerful, had thanked everyone a hundred times. She sat mindlessly gazing at a sign which said 'Usher', beneath which were three yellow arrows pointing downwards as if he'd passed out on the carpet. The receptionist, who'd kicked off her shoes, Alan noticed, had nice ankles.

Small claims courts are usually presided over by a magistrate, but in more complicated cases a judge is called in. On this occasion, Judge Stanford Wilkes, a sometime barrister who would understand the complications, sat in the courtroom at one end of a long table, surrounded by books and files, making notes with a green malachite fountain pen. The judge had small but amused eyes, thick grey hair with a five-eighths parting, and a grey and black beard and moustache which emphasized a kind, firm mouth.

'Rather attractive,' murmured Etta, feeling slightly comforted as they filed into court.

'Wearing a wedding ring,' murmured back Painswick, wondering if she would be too much like a tricoteuse if she got out her knitting.

'Think we can take our jackets off?' asked a sweating Major. 'The court is very small for so many people.'

'That's why it's a small claims court,' said Alan.

Bright blue curtains blended into the cloudless blue outside. On the white wall was a very dull etching of Regent Street, Swindon, and a surprisingly undull print of lots of naked nymphs and warriors in helmets enjoying an orgy.

'Looks like one of Seth and Corinna's parties,' whispered Alan.

On the judge's right was Marti Gluckstein, who looked like a leather eagle, watching everything, poised to swoop on any lapse. Next to him sat Etta, gazing at the photograph of Mrs Wilkinson lying entwined with Chisolm, which Dora had put on her mobile. After today, would she be gone? She must not cry.

Yesterday, when it had been chilly, Dora and Trixie had frog-marched her into Larkminster to buy a periwinkle-blue cotton jersey suit.

'I can't afford it,' Etta had protested.

'If you're going to be broke,' said Dora, 'you might as well be really broke.'

'And if you look pretty, the judge will rule in your favour,' said Trixie.

Alas, today the cotton jersey was too hot. Etta rammed her arms together to cover the damp patches. Unable to sleep last night, she had got up and found Mrs Wilkinson lying down in the orchard and, sitting on her plump grey quarters, had chatted to her and Chisolm as the sun rose, praying that they'd still be together in the evening.

She was unable to look Harvey-Holden in the eye in case he had really done those terrible things to Mrs Wilkinson. In a sharp new cream suit, he was reading about his proposed new super-yard in *Horse and Hound*, but his hands clenched and unclenched on the magazine.

Fortunately Martin and Romy were fundraising in Bristol and, worried that Drummond and Poppy might be corrupted by a potential jailbird, had bussed in Granny Playbridge to hold the fort. On the judge's left sat Cecil Stroud QC, a smoothie with a deep throbbing voice, a dark brown toupee, and black eyebrows big as steeplechasing fences, which he raised to great effect.

On the train down, he and Marti Gluckstein had agreed to wrap the matter up in a day.

Facing the judge at the far end of the table were rows of chairs, the left-hand side occupied by Etta's supporters, the right hand by Judy Tobias. Each thigh in her pink trouser suit was as large as a young sow. Her ankles flopped over her flat red shoes and her breasts, jacked up together, created a vast cleavage.

'My God, they are big,' muttered Alban.

'Jude the Obese,' grinned Alan. 'We could go pot-holing down her later. She must have bought that colossal diamond herself.'

'Quite a pretty face,' conceded Alban, noticing how fondly, as she made copious notes in a mauve diary, Jude's black starfish-mascaraed eyes rested on the ratty little profile of Harvey-Holden, who totally ignored her.

'He ought to get her on the horse walker,' said Alan.

Niall glanced round the packed room. If only his church was a quarter as full. Since he had come out, his mother had gone into deep depression at the prospect of no grandchildren.

'Respect is so much more important than love, Niall. Surely you could find some nice girl?'

Harvey-Holden obviously had, thought Niall with a shudder. And how could he meet a nice man? Vicars couldn't go clubbing. He admired Woody's strong suntanned neck in the row in front of him and longed to stroke it, his heart twisting with loneliness.

The usher came over and told them the proceedings were about to begin and they should address Judge Wilkes as 'sir'. Then, pausing beside Alban, he murmured: 'My brother was in the army in the Middle East, sir. Said you were the best person from the Foreign Office they ever had. Said you really understood the Arabs.'

'Good God.' Alban, already flushed from the heat, turned maroon with pleasure and leapt to his feet. 'How awfully kind of you to say so. Made my day. Thank you so much, and to your brother. What regiment was he in?'

But the usher had put his finger to his lips, as Judge Wilkes cleared his throat and welcomed everyone.

177

'I'd just like to point out that once a decision is made on this case, it is unappealable.' Then, with a half-smile: 'My word is law.'

Woody turned and smiled at Niall. 'You better get praying, Rev.'

'Awfully kind of that chap,' said Alban.

Cecil Stroud opened the batting, claiming Mrs Wilkinson was an extremely valuable mare of impeccable pedigree, who must have been stolen from Ralph Harvey-Holden's yard, but had been believed to have perished in the fire.

Marti Gluckstein consulted his notes.

'After the fire, your client claimed insurance on the mare.'

'And will shortly be paying it back,' said Cecil Stroud firmly.

'Can he explain why Mrs Wilkinson was found in such an appalling condition?' asked Marti.

'She was always a strong and wayward filly, sir. My client's theory is that whoever stole her couldn't get a tune out of her and beat her up, perhaps additionally trying to starve her into submission and denying her water to weaken her, a common practice among reprehensible trainers.'

'Your client should know,' observed Marti dryly.

'Objection,' snapped Cecil Stroud. 'Whoever treated Usurper so badly, leaving her to die in the snow, gouged out her microchip to avoid detection.'

'Why didn't Mr Harvey-Holden report the mare missing?'

'Because he assumed she'd perished in the fire. His horses had been so badly burnt, it was impossible to identify them afterwards,' said Cecil as though he was explaining to a half-witted child.

'But if he believed her to have perished in the fire on the twelfth of December,' persisted Marti, 'and she was actually found by Mrs Bancroft on the twenty-third of December, this would not have been enough time for her to be reduced to such a skeleton. Had Mr Harvey-Holden starved her himself? If not, surely she would have had to go missing several weeks if not months earlier.'

Cecil Stroud had been about to object but changed legs like an Olympic dressage horse:

'My client was going through a very upsetting marriage break-up at the time. He was further traumatized by the fire at the yard and when his head lad, Denny Forrester, confessed to starting the fire. My client thinks it likely that Mr Forrester, who admitted in his suicide note to being in financial straits, secretly sold some of the young horses to passing travellers for cash. One of these, he believes, could have been Usurper.'

' "A traveller came by," ' murmured Alan, ' "Silently, invisibly/He took her with a sigh." '

Marti Gluckstein looked at the pointers Rupert had given him.

'I put it to you, sir, that travellers wouldn't abandon a horse if it were untrainable, they'd flog it for meat money. Someone wanted to destroy this mare without trace.'

Despite his cool linen suit, Harvey-Holden was dripping with sweat. Impossible to have a face so still, thought Etta with a shiver, like a ferret not moving a whisker that might alert his prey.

Cecil was clearly not going to expose H-H's lack of charm and his squeaky little ex-jockey's voice by allowing him to give evidence.

Marti Gluckstein continued to peg away to find the truth.

When one of Harvey-Holden's stable lads, a middle-aged Pakistani called Vakil who looked even shiftier than H-H, was called to give evidence, he said he remembered his boss fussing over Usurper but couldn't recall when she left Ravenscroft.

'Surely any decent yard,' asked Marti, 'keeps daily records of what a horse eats, what medication she's on and whether she's been ridden out or schooled. On what date did these details about Usurper cease?'

'I cannot say,' replied Vakil. 'All records were destroyed in the fire.'

'How very convenient,' observed Marti.

Judy Tobias also gave evidence.

'H-H adored Usurper and all his horses. After the fire, he was a broken man.'

'Probably because you sat on him,' muttered Dora and as Etta's supporters rocked with laughter she was told to shut up by the judge.

Cecil Stroud gave her a filthy look and dropped his voice like a cello. 'My client was extremely fond of Usurper. He was devastated to learn what suffering she had endured. After the heartbreak of the fire that destroyed his yard, he longs to salvage something from the ashes.'

'Hear, hear!' murmured Judy Tobias.

'In addition, Mrs Wilkinson won her first point-to-point so convincingly, she obviously has a glittering future. As a pensioner, Mrs Bancroft could hardly put her into training.'

The bright blue curtains were then drawn and a video was shown of the race, including the fall and Mrs Wilkinson nudging Amber to remount. It had the entire court cheering and laughing, particularly when Mrs Wilkinson shook hooves with the stewards afterwards.

'A horse of great charm and character,' observed Cecil Stroud.

After this they adjourned for lunch. Etta couldn't eat a thing because it was her turn to give evidence next. Her pretty new blue suit was miles too hot. If only she could have taken off her jacket like the men, who were lifting their spirits with stiff drinks.

'What is your interest in horses, Mrs Bancroft?' was the judge's first question once they were back in court.

'I had a pony when I was a child and I've always loved them.'

Then she described how mutilated and terrified Mrs Wilkinson had been, and how it seemed, from the scraped snow, as if someone had been trying to bury her alive. She told how Joey and Woody had risked their jobs moving her into Valent Edwards's house, which was warm and dry, because they were so upset by her plight.

'Why didn't you call the police or the RSPCA?' asked Cecil Stroud sternly.

'Because she was learning to trust me, and was so poorly we daren't move her. I felt she'd suffered enough,' said Etta in a voice so low, everyone strained to hear her. 'And truthfully because I'd fallen in love with her and didn't want anyone to take her away.'

'Oh Etta,' sighed Alan, shaking his head.

Cecil Stroud's mocking eyebrows nearly dislodged his toupee.

'So you stole her,' he snapped.

'I rescued her,' said Etta firmly.

'Thank you, Mrs Bancroft,' said Judge Wilkes, 'you explained yourself very clearly.'

Charlie Radcliffe then gave evidence, saying Etta would have been stealing a skeleton. The filly had no body fat or muscle. Her anus was severely sunken. The whole of her pelvis could be seen, as well as her spine and ribs.

'How long would it have taken a horse to reach this state?'

'Months.'

'No more questions.'

Woody, looking impossibly beautiful, told the court that he'd never seen a horse so terrified, but she was too weak to struggle. Jase, saying he'd worked with horses all his life and had never seen such a bad case of cruelty, then produced the photographs Joey'd taken when they first rescued Mrs Wilkinson. These were so hideously heartrending, even the judge mopped his eyes.

Niall, in his dog collar, who'd been terribly moved by Woody's testimony and by the fact he'd never known Woody's real name was Wilfred, then took the stand:

'Mrs Bancroft's caring nursing saved Mrs Wilkinson, but the whole of Willowwood in fact has rallied to her cause. Mrs Wilkinson has become a little local celebrity, and would miss the attention dreadfully if she were forced to go back to her original owner and the anonymity of a racing yard.'

Dora then leapt to her feet:

'Dora Belvedon, sofa surfer. I can't bear the thought of Mrs Wilkinson in a strange yard shaking hands and never getting rewarded with a Polo again.'

She gave a sob, and the judge told her, quite gently, to sit down and not interrupt.

'It seems Mrs Wilkinson is a very popular horse.'

However, there was no getting away from the fact that Etta should have reported finding Mrs Wilkinson to the authorities, who might have been notified of her loss by Harvey-Holden's staff, who could equally have restored her to health. Had Etta and her friends possibly realized what a good horse Mrs Wilkinson was, queried Cecil, and therefore not reported finding her?

As the day dragged on, growing hotter, Etta found herself increasingly detesting Harvey-Holden. The more terrible the cruelty revealed, the less his dead, rat-like features and his serpentine eyes seemed to react. His breath was so sour – even divided by the table, it nearly asphyxiated her. The case, however, seemed to be going his way when it was adjourned until the following morning.

39

H-H was so certain he was going to win that he pushed off to Royal Ascot next day to work the boxes and chat up potential owners. Judy Tobias, however, did turn up, wobbling in this time in white, like a vast blancmange, still writing copiously in her mauve notebook.

Etta, who'd changed into the old denim dress she'd retrieved from the charity shop because the periwinkle blue didn't seem to be bringing them any luck, discovered the temperature had dropped and she couldn't stop shivering. She felt very cast down that Dora hadn't bothered to show up, nor had the Major and Debbie. Joey and Woody still brandished Tilda's poster outside the court, but wondered if the willows would soon be weeping for Mrs Wilkinson.

In court, even Alan was looking worried. Marti Gluckstein resembled an eagle who's mislaid a fat rabbit, as Cecil Stroud launched triumphantly into his final summing-up.

I'm going to lose her, thought Etta in anguish.

But suddenly there was a kerfuffle and cries of 'Court's sitting, sir,' and a tall dark man stalked in like an army with banners. How attractive he is, thought Etta, then realized it was Valent Edwards. He was wearing a brown suede jacket, chinos and a blue check shirt. Putting a reassuring hand on Etta's shoulder, he apologized to the judge for barging in.

He then, by sheer force of personality, turned the case as he described the terror and desperate state of Mrs Wilkinson the first time he'd seen her, about a fortnight after Etta had rescued her. Bonny Richards had been ironing out his Yorkshire accent but it slipped back as his passion grew.

'I have never seen an animal so scared of humans. She was the most pathetic sight, blinded in one eye, collapsing on the ground, crashing round my office ... The one person she troosted was Mrs Bancroft and it was her luv that saved that horse. If Mr Harvey-Holden luved her so much, why didn't he recognize her when he saw her out hunting? Or Mr Murchieson, who had owned her, recognize her when she won the point-to-point?'

'If you come outside, you'll see how she's blossomed.'

Everyone surged out into the sunshine, where they discovered Joey's trailer and a grinning Dora. Next moment out clattered Mrs Wilkinson and Chisolm. Giving a great throaty whicker, Mrs Wilkinson bustled across the courtyard to get to Etta, nudging her delightedly, followed by a skipping, bleating Chisolm. Mrs Wilkinson then turned to her Willowwood friends, greeting them with equal pleasure.

Everyone cheered, except Jude the Obese, who complained the whole thing was a stitch-up. Judge Wilkes, however, beamed and asked to be introduced to Mrs Wilkinson, who shook hands with him until he was butted by a jealous Chisolm.

Back in court, the judge enquired as to the whereabouts of Harvey-Holden, only to be told by his wife that he'd been called away to tend a very sick animal.

'Probably Shade Murchieson,' quipped Alan.

The judge then asked Etta whether, as a pensioner, she could afford to keep a racehorse. Whereupon Valent stepped in again and said there was so much goodwill and affection for Mrs Wilkinson in Willowwood that if Mrs Bancroft needed help, he felt sure everyone would oblige. 'Mrs Wilkinson has become the Village Horse.'

This was greeted by a roar of agreement. Judge Wilkes then summed up: 'This dispute is about a horse. We do not know who perpetrated these dreadful crimes on Mrs Wilkinson.'

'He didn't call her Usurper,' hissed Dora, 'that's promising.'

'So I am unable to make a deprivation order, in addition to putting a ban on him or her ever keeping a horse again. But it is within my power to decide to whom I give this horse. The fact that she is a very valuable mare is of no consequence when one considers the evidence that she would no longer be with us today if it hadn't been for the quick thinking and loving care of Mrs Etta Bancroft. I therefore give the mare, Mrs Wilkinson, formerly known as Usurper, to Mrs Bancroft.'

Cheers rocked the court.

'Oh, thank you, thank you,' sobbed a joyful Etta, who hugged everyone else but found herself too shy to hug Valent.

After she'd wiped her tears away, she and Valent and Mrs

Wilkinson posed for the photographers, marshalled by Dora.

'I don't understand how on earth you got Mrs Wilkinson to load,' stammered Etta. 'No one else has.'

'I told her to get in and not be silly,' said Valent with a smirk. He was in an excellent mood. He'd recently put ten million into a hedge fund providing bulldozers to China, which had risen by 600 per cent in the last fortnight, making him 60 million.

Hearing a furious squawk behind him, he turned to find Chisolm gobbling up the last of Jude the Obese's mauve notebook.

'That was invaluable evidence!'

'I thought your side believed in destroying records,' said Valent icily.

'Valent's only done it to dispel his Tin-Man-without-a-Heart image,' snarled Shade when he heard the result. 'From now on we're going to bury the bastard, and Mrs Bancroft and fucking Rupert Campbell-Black.'

40

In a daze of happiness, Etta read reports of the case the following morning. VALENT TO THE RESCUE, shouted the *Mail* under a lovely picture of Valent, Chisolm and Mrs Wilkinson. Etta was also surrounded by gardening books, plotting ways in which she could surreptitiously enhance Valent's garden as a thank-you present. Outside, the fields were alight with pink campion, dog daisies and foxgloves.

'Should I make him a wild flower garden?' she asked Chisolm, who, having finished up Etta's bowl of cornflakes, was sitting on the sofa, eating her own picture in the *Sun*.

Demanding attention, as she peered over the fence and round Etta's conifer hedge, was Mrs Wilkinson.

'You're mine, mine, mine,' cried Etta, as she rushed out waving a carrot.

But she had reckoned without Martin, who was determined to repossess his mother. She was needed as a nanny, Granny Playbridge having retreated in tatters after a stint of Poppy and Drummond. The weeds were soaring in Harvest Home's garden. The cricket season was under way, he had hit a fine six through Tilda Flood's window, and he needed Etta to do the teas.

He therefore rolled up at the bungalow and weighed in: 'You must sell Mrs Wilkinson at once, Mother.'

'I can't,' gasped Etta, 'the judge awarded her to me to look after.'

Chisolm bleated in agreement.

'Get that goat out of here! If you sold her, you'd be self-sufficient, could afford a decent car and the improvements you wanted on this place – and frankly you wouldn't be a drain on Carrie and me any more. It's been a struggle.'

'Cooee, cooee.' He was joined by Romy, lovely as June in a deep rose-red dress – the effect of warmth somewhat diminished by the cold look she gave Mrs Wilkinson's silver point-to-point cup and Etta's winning owner's glass bowl.

Didn't Etta realize that since Martin had nobly left the City to raise money for the Sampson Bancroft Memorial Fund, she and he had suffered a considerable loss of income?

Martin had also discovered Sampson hadn't been quite so loved that people felt compelled to give generously. Some had been extremely rude. They therefore wanted Etta to pay back the £50,000 they'd forked out for the bungalow, which she could if she cashed in on all the publicity and sold Mrs Wilkinson well and at once.

Etta's heart sank. She also felt honour bound to pay back Woody, Joey, Jase and Charlie Radcliffe for their endless free help, and what about Rupert?

Reading her thoughts, Martin returned to the attack:

'Rupert can only have bankrolled your court case because he's expecting you to sell Mrs Wilkinson to him.'

'What about Chisolm?' quavered Etta.

'Oh, she'd lead a far more worthwhile life sustaining a family in Africa,' said Romy. 'Shoo, shoo, out of here.'

In answer, Chisolm raised a cloven hoof and scattered currants over the kitchen floor.

After they'd gone, a despairing Etta rang Alan, who suggested she leased Mrs Wilkinson to a syndicate. 'They'd pay her training fees and insurance and share out any winnings.'

But if Martin and Carrie stopped her tiny allowance, she'd have only her state pension to live on and couldn't pay anyone back.

It was a stiflingly hot evening. She could hear the roar of Farmer Fred's tedder as he tossed and turned the newly cut hay, baling it into shining silver cotton reels. The shaven fields gleamed like a platinum blonde in a nightclub, the air was heavy with the voluptuous scent of honeysuckle, elder and wild rose. Such a night to be in love, thought Etta, but not with a horse that was going to be taken away.

She sought comfort in the orchard, where Chisolm and Mrs Wilkinson ransacked her pockets for Polos. She must find a way to keep them. As her eyes strayed to the dark house nearby, still spiky with scaffolding, her thoughts turned to Valent. She put her hand on the shoulder he had touched in court, pressing her cheek against the hand, feeling weak with longing for him to take care of her, Wilkie and Chisolm.

But he had Bonny Richards and had done enough. To comfort

her mistress, Mrs Wilkinson hooked her head over Etta's shoulder and drew her against her warm grey breastbone.

'Something will turn up.'

After a sleepless night, when she had tossed like Farmer Fred's hay, Etta was interrupted at seven thirty in the morning by a call from Alan.

'Let's have a meeting in the Fox to see if the village is prepared to form a syndicate.'

'Might they?'

'We can only try. I'll get on the telephone.'

41

To Etta's amazement, twelve hours later she was in the garden of the Fox, breathing in a heady scent of pink rambler roses and damp earth from a recent shower. With a large jug of pre-ordered Pimm's, she filled up the glasses of the Major, Debbie, Pocock, Painswick, Alban, Jase, Joey, Woody, very brown from working stripped to the waist at Badger's Court, Shagger, Tilda, Dora, Trixie, who'd bunked off from school and was keeping shtum because she didn't want her father to see her new tongue stud, Niall the vicar, and Chris and Chrissie, who'd left Jenny the barmaid manning the shop because most of the drinkers were in the garden. Araminta and Cadbury panted under the walnut tree.

Etta had bought the first round. She wanted to, and Alan had suggested it was a good idea to look rich.

He was just kicking off, asking everyone to drink a toast to Etta winning the court case, when Phoebe and Toby, who were gripped with pre-Wimbledon fervour, scuttled in in tennis gear.

'Sorry sorry sorry, just been finishing a needle match,' cried Phoebe. 'Ooh, Pimm's, how refreshing, yes please, just what we need.'

Alan, whose irritation was only betrayed by a hiss through the teeth and drumming fingers on the table, waited until they were sorted and seated to announce: 'Etta and I have invited you here this evening to discuss the possibility of forming a syndicate to put Mrs Wilkinson into training.'

He looked round the garden at his daughter texting, at Tilda marking SATS papers, at Phoebe whispering to Shagger, at Dora beaming in approval.

'What we need,' he continued, 'is ten people each to take a

three thousand pound share. That's assuming Mrs Wilkinson is worth thirty thousand – in fact she's worth a great deal more, bearing in mind her pedigree and her astonishing performance at the point-to-point, so you'd be getting a fantastic bargain. But we want to make this not beyond people's pockets, so we can keep Mrs Wilkinson in Willowwood.'

At the prospect of forking out so much, everyone was doing sums. Alban, who'd been in the pub since six, was confidently looking forward to confirmation of a £250,000-a-year role heading a quango. Debbie was wondering whether having the most colourful garden in Willowwood was quite enough. She and the Major had enjoyed the court case and the point-to-point so much, it had given them something to talk about at mealtimes. Tilda yawned. She'd been up at six that morning, making up beds for Shagger's holiday lets. She couldn't afford to join the syndicate, but she was depressed by the SATS Level 4 essays she was marking. They were so colourless, dull and unimaginative, from children stuck behind computers all day, when there was so much beauty in the world. People needed adventure.

Chris and Chrissie had just discovered their latest stab at IVF hadn't worked. Chris felt his wife needed cheering out of her despair . . . Joey, Jase and Woody had been in at the start and loved Mrs Wilkinson. Niall loved Woody and would seize any opportunity to be near him.

'As well as the initial three thousand,' explained Alan blithely, 'we'd each have to put in a hundred and eighty-five pounds a month. That's to pay twenty-two thousand a year to a trainer for the gallops, feed, vets, entries, jockeys and transport.'

'Same as Bagley school fees,' volunteered Trixie.

'If I take care of the insurance,' asked Shagger, refilling his and Toby's glasses from Etta's Pimm's jug, 'can I have my share free?'

'I have to be straight with you,' said Alan, ignoring him. 'Eighty per cent of owners never have a win.' Then, looking around: 'But if we do win, the jockey gets 10 per cent of the winnings, the trainer 10 per cent, and the owners a socking great 80 per cent. We won't make a fortune, but as we take off to race meetings round the country, we'll have one hell of a ball.' The scent from the garden was getting stronger as a gold full moon with a halo rose out of the trees to watch the fun.

'Also you don't all have to have an equal share,' Alan rallied the doubters. 'If you feel three thousand is too much, you can split it between two or three.'

Gathering up a second jug waiting on a side table, smiling shyly, Etta began to fill up everyone's glasses.

If I joined this syndicate, thought Alban, the Major and Pocock, I could get closer to this sweet woman.

There was a long pause and even longer faces as everyone redid the sums and decided it was one hell of a commitment. They could hear the roar of Farmer Fred's combines and the pat of tennis balls. Then Miss Painswick put down her knitting and announced that 'Bagley Hall gave me a good pension. I've got a few savings. I'm very attached to Mrs Wilkinson and I'd like to be part of her future.'

'Oh Joyce.' Etta grabbed her hand.

'Oh well done, Miss Painswick,' said Dora, 'Hengist would be proud of you. I'd like to have a share but I'm not sure I can afford a hundred and eighty-five pounds. I've got "A" Levels next year, so I won't have time to flog so many stories.'

'I'll take a half-share with you, Dora,' said Trixie, stopping texting in her excitement.

'With what?' demanded Alan.

'You'll help me, Dad. You won't have to pay school fees any more if I go to Larkminster High.'

Pocock, who would soon be working extra time for Corinna and Seth, then said he'd take a half-share with Miss Painswick.

'Good for you, we'll chip in too,' said Chris. A horse would take Chrissie's mind off the baby. 'We can't sell Mrs Wilkinson to some 'orrible owner who might not cherish her. She belongs to Willowwood.'

Jase, Woody and Joey, though they were committed to Not for Crowe and Family Dog, agreed to take a fourth share.

'Just over sixty pounds a monf,' said Joey, who was yet to tell Mop Idol about a third horse he'd bought with his point-to-point winnings.

Debbie glanced at the Major, who polished his spectacles and nodded.

'Father and I have always wanted a Mercedes when we retired,' said Debbie, 'but we'd rather have a racehorse!'

'Oh, come on, Toby. We're both working, and if the Cunliffes are joining . . .' pleaded Phoebe. Then, turning to Alban: 'And you come in too, Uncle Alban. And you and Tilda could take a share, Shagger.'

'I suppose we could manage it,' said Tilda, hiding her blushing face in another turgid essay. Anything to provide an ongoing link with Shagger. She'd just have to take on more coaching.

'Even with Etta, that's only nine shares,' said Shagger crushingly. 'We haven't got enough people.'

'Yes, you have,' said a deep, husky voice and in walked a tall, dark, very suntanned man in a black shirt and jeans, who was followed by an equally beautiful sleek black greyhound. As everyone surged forward to kiss him or shake his hand, except Phoebe, who scuttled off to the Ladies to take the shine off her flushed post-tennis face, Etta realized it was Seth Bainton.

'What are you doing here?' asked an utterly delighted Alan.

'I'm back in England for a good nine months,' said Seth. 'We're doing a BBC film of *The Seagull* and after that Corinna is off to the States in a tour of *Macbeth*. And next year there's talk of *Antony and Cleopatra* at Stratford.' Then, breaking away from his well-wishers, Seth added, 'And you must be Etta Bancroft. Alan told me how pretty you were and about the syndicate. I'm desperate to have a share in Mrs Wilkinson, such a sweet horse. I love her big white face, looks as though they ran out of grey paint.'

And Etta melted because he was absolutely gorgeous.

'She must run a lot at Stratford so I can nip out of rehearsals and cheer her on,' he added, taking Etta's hands. 'And lots of Sundays as that's my day off.'

'That's one day the vicar can't do,' giggled Trixie.

Within five minutes, such was Seth's exuberance and charm, they'd agreed to form a syndicate.

These are my friends, thought Etta joyfully. If they have shares in Mrs Wilkinson, nothing can go far wrong.

'What a heavenly dog,' she said, patting the black greyhound's sleek body, which was even more toned and muscular than his master's. The dog proceeded to look down his long nose at Araminta and Cadbury, rotate his tail and stand on his toes, before crossing the garden and leaping on to the bench seat with the most cushions.

'What's his name?' she asked.

'Priceless, in all senses of the word,' said Seth. 'This calls for another drink.'

'Several drinks,' said Alan. 'We must decide on a trainer.'

'Let's go for Marius,' suggested Seth. 'He's so near and Olivia's so sweet. Harvey-Holden's a no-go after that horrendous court case. Isa Lovell's broken away from Rupert and only just started up on his own, and he's a tricky bugger.'

'We ought to ask Rupert,' protested Etta. 'He did lend me his lawyer for the court case.'

'He's too big and too opinionated,' said Seth, who didn't like competition. 'Meanwhile Dermie O'Driscoll's too far away. Robbie Crowborough's bent. Corinna's nephew paid thirty-five thousand for a horse that Robbie claimed had never been beaten. In fact it had never actually raced, just stayed in a field so it developed laminitis then broke down.'

'We won't go to Robbie,' interrupted Alan, seeing alarm on people's faces. 'Let's check out Marius.'

'Who will approach him?' asked Major Cunliffe, who'd had several up-and-downers with him over speeding racehorses.

'I will if you like,' said Alban, feeling a surge of authority. 'Known him since he was a boy. Now what would everyone like to drink?'

'This calls for champagne,' said Seth.

'I do hope Marius will allow us to see lots of Mrs Wilkinson,' said a suddenly worried Etta.

'You can always wave across the valley at her,' suggested Woody.

How sweet he is, thought Niall, then out loud, 'I'm afraid I can't run to a share in Mrs Wilkinson – yes, I'd love a glass of fizz please, Seth – but I hope when she goes racing I can pray for her success and safe return.'

'Bless this horse,' grinned Seth.

He had such merry dark eyes and a wonderful laugh, decided Etta, which immediately made people feel better. She was horrified to find herself thinking what fun he'd be in bed.

'Will Marius let us drop in?' she asked.

'Well, he is rather anti-visitor,' admitted Alan, 'but Olivia will be very accommodating, she's so easy-going.'

'Pity Wilkie can't be a weekly boarder,' said Trixie.

'Cheer up, darling,' whispered Alan. 'You've just made twenty-seven thousand. Nine shares at three thousand pounds each in Mrs Wilkinson. Thirty thousand minus your three thousand share.'

Etta clapped her hands for quiet.

'I can't thank you all enough for helping me,' her voice trembled, 'but if Mrs Wilkinson retires from racing, would it be OK for me to try and buy her back?'

Later, Alban insisted very unsteadily on walking Etta home through the gloaming to her bungalow, commenting on the frightful mess Valent's builders were making at Badger's Court.

'Can't leave well alone.'

'He's been angelic to Mrs Wilkinson,' protested Etta.

'Surprised he didn't slap scaffolding on her as well.'

Outside her bungalow, as Etta groped for her key, she had a feeling that if she asked Alban in for a drink he'd accept. Only because he wants another drink, she thought humbly. But as she turned to say good night, he suddenly blurted out:

'Awfully glad you've come to live in Willowwood, Etta, think we'll have a lot of fun with Mrs Wilkinson,' and he planted a kiss only half a centimetre off her mouth, which was half open in surprise.

'I'm pleased too,' she stammered and scuttled into the house.

'How can we possibly afford another horse,' cried a despairing Mop Idol, when a drunk Joey finally got home, 'with four children to feed and little Wayne's christening to pay for? I can't clean any more houses in Willowwood.'

Little Wayne's christening took place the following Saturday afternoon at the parish church, with the ceremonious planting of a willow in the churchyard afterwards to mark the birth of a son. Lots of Ione's compost was used to bed the tree in. Niall was thrilled for once to have a full church. Sir Francis Framlingham's effigy in the church was garlanded with roses, a white ribbon was tied round the neck of the little whippet at his feet, and lilies and willow fronds placed on Beau Regard and Gwendolyn's joint grave.

Tilda's children, who had sung charmingly in church, now accompanied by their parents and other villagers, gathered round to watch the tree ceremony, performed by Ione Travis-Lock, before singing a final hymn and repairing for tea in the village hall.

Alas, Alban had had a hellish morning. In the post he had received a letter turning him down for yet another New Labour quango. He would therefore not be paid £250,000 a year to decide over the next two years whether a lack of playing fields leads to obesity in children.

As a result, he had been getting tanked up in the Fox, ending up putting a full glass to his cheek, so red wine spilled all over his check shirt. When he fell off the bar stool, comely Chrissie, in a miniskirt, low-cut T-shirt and pink boots, offered to help him back across the green, through the churchyard and in via the side door of Willowwood Hall. Unfortunately she had forgotten about the planting of the willow.

In the middle of 'Gentle Jesus meek and mild,' Alban tottered into view. 'Q-U-N-G-O, Q-U-N-G-O, Q-U-N-G-O,' he sang, 'and his name was QUANGO, but it's not quango for Alban,' and he collapsed on top of Chrissie, rucking up her miniskirt to reveal a leopard-print thong between plump white buttocks. As they writhed around between the gravestones, grief and rage twisted Ione Travis-Lock's face. She had seen this all before. Throwing down the spade, she hurdled over the gravestones, roaring, 'Put my husband down,' to Chrissie, and frogmarched Alban home.

Next day, he was shunted off to rehab and wouldn't be joining any syndicate.

42

In late July, Etta and Alan – because he was a friend of Olivia's –
drove across the valley to meet Marius. It was a suffocatingly hot
afternoon with fields yellowing and the ground cracking from
lack of rain. Etta felt sick with apprehension. She was wearing a
new off-white linen trouser suit, which Trixie had persuaded her
to buy.

'You'd better spend some of the money you're going to get
from Mrs Wilkinson, before Romy and Martin swipe the lot.'

As Alan drove past a sign saying 'Horses' and turned into
Marius's long drive, Etta hastily pulled down the mirror to check
her face. 'I don't know how one should look as a prospective
owner.'

'Solvent and undemanding,' replied Alan. 'You look perfect.'

Since she'd met Seth, Etta had found herself taking more
trouble with her appearance. She had lost five pounds, and Trixie
had persuaded her to have her hair highlighted again and cut so
it fell in soft tendrils over her forehead.

Etta tried not to talk about Seth all the time, but now found
herself saying, 'Such fun Seth's joined the syndicate, Corinna
must be quite a bit older than him.'

'Lots, Seth's a bit of a gerontophile,' then glancing slyly at Etta,
'so there's hope for you, darling.'

'Don't be silly.' Etta went crimson and hastily changed the
subject. 'Oh, do look, there's Willowwood from a completely
different angle. There's Badger's Court and Wilkie and Chisolm
under the trees, and Willowwood Hall, and the top of your barn.
Thank goodness you can't see Little Hollow for willows or Marius
would reject us out of hand.'

Throstledown was a long, low eighteenth-century Cotswold

house, tucked into the hillside with gallops soaring below it and fields, including an exercise ring, spreading over the valley down to the river. Looking across from Willowwood, you couldn't see how run-down it was: tiles missing from the roof, drainpipes and gutters rusting, paint peeling on doors and window frames.

'In need of modernization,' observed Alan.

'Rather like me,' sighed Etta. 'Wouldn't Lester Bolton or Valent just love to gut it.'

The garden was also desperately neglected. Etta longed to pull up the weeds and water the wilting plants. No one answered the front-door bell, so they went round the back, past a huge horse chestnut, through an arch topped by a weathercock of a golden bird. Here loose boxes and a tack room and office formed three sides of a square joined up by the back of the house.

Etta wondered if they'd see Josh, the handsome red-headed stable lad who still kept up an on-off relationship with Trixie, encouraged by Alan because Josh had given him some excellent tips.

The place, however, was deserted, except for a few horses brought in to escape the flies, who were half asleep in their boxes. Only one horse, lurking at the back of its box, kept up a shrill, desperate whinnying.

Etta could smell burning and found the remnants of a bonfire beside the nearly dried-up fountain in the middle of the yard.

'That's odd,' murmured Alan, extracting a sapphire and crimson fragment from the ashes and putting it in his pocket. 'Someone's been burning a flag which once was flown almost continually at Throstledown to indicate a winner.' He looked at his watch. 'The stable lads must be still on their break. Anyone around?' he shouted.

Instantly a man appeared at an upstairs window of the house.

'I don't care what paper you come from,' he yelled, 'get the fuck out of here!'

Next moment a bullet whistled over their heads, through the arch, and lodged in the vast horse chestnut.

'We're not press,' shouted back Alan, leaping behind Etta. 'It's Alan Macbeth, Marius. We've got an appointment with you, but not yet with the Grim Reaper. It's about putting a horse in training.'

Marius stared down at them in bewilderment, then shook his head. 'I'll come down.'

He emerged not unlike the Grim Reaper, his eyes bloodshot, his face deathly white above the stubble, except for a faint tracery of crimson veins, caused by drink. His dark hair was tousled and

196

drenched with sweat, yet despite the heat he wore a thick navy-blue Guernsey inside out. A belt on the last notch barely held up his jeans. Thin as a pencil, he could have ridden his horses himself. He reeked of whisky, yet such was his bone structure, he still looked beautiful.

A grey and black lurcher ran out expectantly, looked hopefully around, gave a whimper and slunk back into the house.

'We wanted to talk to you about training our horse, Mrs Wilkinson,' repeated Alan.

Marius led them back into the kitchen, where the lurcher shuddered in its basket. On the table was a pile of unopened post. The telephone was off the hook. *At the Races* was on the television with the sound turned down, a three-quarters empty bottle of whisky on the draining board. On the kitchen table, an untouched bowl of dog food was gathering flies, as was a tin of Butcher's Tripe with a spoon in it.

Propped against a vase of wilting flowers, drawing the eye, was a cream envelope with 'Marius' scrawled on it and a letter sticking vertically out of it. Alan sidled over, dying to read it. Etta longed to fill up the vase and cuddle the trembling lurcher.

'Is it a bad time?' she stammered, as Marius glowered at them. 'We made the appointment with Olivia earlier in the week.'

'Didn't put it in the diary,' said Marius flatly. 'Mind obviously on other things. Nor did she put in the diary that she was leaving me. She's gone,' he added, gritting a jaw already trembling worse than the lurcher.

'I'm so sorry,' whispered Etta.

'She's gone off with Shade Murchieson, taking my child and most of my dogs, and Shade's taken his twenty horses away as well.'

'Christ,' said Alan, appalled. 'Where's he taken them?'

'Not far.' Marius gave a horrible, unamused laugh. 'To Ralph Harvey-Holden. The press have got on to it already. Shade must have tipped them off, he gets off on publicity.'

Alan shook his head. 'This is awful. When did she go?'

'Friday afternoon. Shade moved his horses on the same day, while I was rather appropriately at Bangor, or bang-her.'

Marius reached for the whisky bottle, taking a swig. Then, catching sight of horses circling at the start, he turned up the sound. 'One of my remaining horses is running in the four fifteen at Market Rasen.' Going to the door, he bellowed, 'Tommy! Can you show these people round what's left of the yard?'

As Alan and Etta retreated outside, a hot breeze was nudging the golden weathercock. The shrill, desperate whinnying was continuous now. A stable lass, with fuzzy dark hair, very reddened eyes and a large bottom, emerged from the flat over the tack room, tugging on a rugger shirt and buckling up her jeans.

Introducing herself in a breathy voice as Tommy Ruddock, she said Collie, the head lad, was at Market Rasen, with the yard's best horses, History Painting and Don't Interrupt. She showed them Oh My Goodness, Wondrous Childhood, who was lazy at home but caught fire at the races, and Asbo Andy, who was very naughty and always running away on the gallops.

Etta noticed how pleased the horses were to see Tommy.

'Asbo Andy sounds like darling Stop Preston. He's naughty too, isn't he?' asked Etta, who was then horrified to see Tommy's face collapse as she mumbled, 'Preston's gone to Harvey-Holden. I've looked after him since he was a yearling, it's very hard when they go.' She wiped her eyes with the sleeve of her rugger shirt.

'I'm so sorry, it must be dreadful.'

'Horace was Preston's friend,' sniffed Tommy, leading them towards the next box, where the half-door hid a skewbald Shetland. 'That's why he's yelling his head off. He and Preston have been together all that time too.'

'Poor little thing,' but as Etta stretched out her hand, Tommy pulled it back just in time to stop Horace biting her fingers off.

'He's not himself,' apologized Tommy. 'And this is Sir Cuthbert, the old man of the yard, who belongs to Lady Crowe.'

The dapple-grey horse was turned away from them, his body slumped, his head drooping in the corner.

'He loved a sweet little mare called Gifted Child. They were turned out together this summer. He was Gifted's sugar daddy, very protective, always pushing other horses away. Now she's gone to Harvey-Holden he's heartbroken, won't eat and walks his box.'

'Perhaps he could befriend our horse, Mrs Wilkinson, if she comes here,' suggested Etta. 'Perhaps you could too, she needs so much love.' She noticed a bramble covered in green blackberries poking through the roof.

Moving on to the last box, they discovered a handsome but sulky-looking Pakistani brushing down a beautiful chestnut, which flattened his ears and darted his teeth at them.

'That's our newest horse, and that's our newest lad,' said Tommy brightly as the Pakistani merely grunted in acknowledgement of Etta's 'Hello'. 'He's called Furious.'

'The horse or the lad?' asked Alan.

'Where did he come from?' asked Etta.

Tommy waited until they were out of earshot, then said,

'Larkminster Prison, both Rafiq and Furious. As therapy and to learn a trade while he was inside, Rafiq looked after Furious, one of the prison's rescued racehorses. Furious has settled in but he doesn't like other horses and he hated being turned out. But Marius has found him a sheep friend, and they've finally bonded. Furious stayed out all last night, and Rafiq and I crept out with a torch. Furious had wrapped Dilys, his sheep, round him like a duvet, it was so sweet. He's aloof, Rafiq, but he's a real softie round horses.'

'Mrs Wilkinson has a goat friend called Chisolm,' said Etta eagerly. 'Do you think Marius might let her come here as well?'

'Don't see why not,' said Tommy, 'plenty of empty boxes.'

Tommy showed them the tack room, which smelt of hoof oil, saddle soap, liniment and leather. On the walls were framed photographs of past winners, flanked by overjoyed owners and by Marius and Olivia, radiant and separate in their glamour. Riding many of the horses was a laughing jockey. Etta suddenly realized this was the wild and wicked Rogue Rogers, who'd once lived in Willowwood.

'You poor darling,' said Etta, putting an arm through Tommy's, 'you must miss Olivia terribly.'

'We all do, we just hope she'll come back.'

Alan, looking at Olivia's picture, was strangely uncommunicative.

Tommy then took them back to Marius's office, where he could presumably distance himself from any goings-on in the house. Much tidier than the kitchen, it contained another television also tuned in to *At the Races* with the sound turned down, a laptop, a microwave and a fridge. On the shelves were directories called *Horses in Training* and *Races and Racecourses*, files entitled Blood Tests and Tracheal Washes and individual box files containing the progress and medical history of each horse. Those marked Bafford Playboy, Stop Preston, Ilkley Hall, Gifted Child, etc., had been hurled on the floor and were no doubt destined for the bonfire.

On a desk by the window was a large, dilapidated diary that listed which horses were running where, its pages torn and covered with muddy footprints where Mistletoe the lurcher had leapt up to see who was approaching the office. Now she shivered and swallowed in her basket, her light grey eyes filled with foreboding.

'Poor old girl.' Taking the chair next to her, Etta stroked her narrow striped head. Alan was gazing at a beautiful picture of Olivia, in a new pink hat at Cheltenham. Marius had poured himself another large whisky, and appeared singularly un-impressed when Etta showed him the video of Mrs Wilkinson winning her point-to-point, adding that Rupert's great stallion Peppy Koala had been her sire.

'She's had a terrible time. We don't know what unimaginable hell she went through but it never soured her,' said Etta, think-ing, react, you beast. 'And she's blind in one eye. Amber's a wonderful jockey,' she stumbled on. 'I do hope you'll consider using her, that's if you felt like taking on Mrs Wilkinson. They've established a fantastic rapport.'

Outside, the hot high wind was scattering rose petals like confetti over the parched lawn.

'She's not great at loading,' admitted Etta. 'We had to hack her to the point-to-point, but she's so kind she'd tow the lorry if you asked her.'

It was getting hotter, and Marius hadn't even offered them a cup of tea. At first she thought he was so shattered he wasn't taking anything in, but the next moment he'd got up, removed Mrs Wilkinson's video, handed it back to Etta and switched back to *At the Races* to watch Don't Interrupt running in the last race.

Damn cheek, thought Etta, then said, 'Mrs Wilkinson is the sweetest horse you'll ever meet.'

'Presumably you want me to train the horse, not fall in love with it?' said Marius rudely.

'If it's a problem,' Etta was getting shirty, 'we'll leave it.'

What was the matter with Alan? He was being no help at all.

As Don't Interrupt was beaten by an outsider, they could see the punters racing for the train home.

'Mrs Wilkinson is a lovable and much loved horse,' repeated Etta defiantly.

Next minute an anxious-looking Tommy pushed open the door with a tray containing cups of tea and shortbread.

'I saw Mrs Wilkinson in the paper,' she blurted out. 'Such a sweet face, I love her long white eyelashes. Beauticians would probably suggest her appearance might be improved if she dyed them but I think she looks great.'

Marius put three spoonfuls of sugar in his tea and stirred it thoughtfully. 'It won't be easy,' he mused. 'As a left-eyed horse, she'll need left-handed tracks so she can focus on the rails, and she can't exactly walk to places like Cheltenham or Newbury.'

There was suddenly such a look of desolation on his face that Etta leapt to her feet, took his hand and put an arm round his shoulders.

'I'm so sorry about Olivia. She can't really love Shade. He's such a beast. During the court case, someone told me he blacked his ex-wife's eye.'

'She wears so much make-up, I'm amazed anyone could tell,' said Marius, and he reached for a cigarette. 'Anyway, you still want to bring Mrs Wilkinson here?'

'Yes we do,' said Etta stoutly. 'The syndicate want to come down and meet you, if that's all right?'

'Might be put off by the empty boxes,' then, with a bitter half-smile: 'I'll have to borrow some horses from Rupert Campbell-Black.'

As they left, stable lads were skipping out horses, brushing them, feeding them nuts and hay and changing their water. Etta noticed handsome Josh deep in conversation with Tommy as he pretended to sweep the yard and made a thumbs-up sign to them, 'See you very soon.'

As Alan drove down the drive, he nearly ran over a man with a camera and another talking into a tape recorder, who peered into the window and asked: 'Marius Oakridge?'

'He's not here,' said Alan quickly, 'he's at the races.'

'Any idea where?'

'York, I think he said.'

'Bugger,' said the photographer.

As they entered Willowwood, they turned away two more press, who gave Alan their cards.

'Let us know if you hear anything.'

They were from the *Scorpion*.

'Good thing Dora isn't with us,' murmured Alan, tearing up the cards the moment they rounded the corner.

'Poor, poor Marius,' sighed Etta. 'I loved Olivia when I met her but she has behaved horribly. I do hope Shade will be kind to those sweet terriers and the horses won't miss that darling Tommy too much. Do you think the rest of the syndicate will mind if it's a bit run-down and Shade's taken away all his horses?' she added anxiously.

'Course not,' lied Alan, drawing up outside Little Hollow. 'Give him more time to concentrate on Mrs Wilkinson. Oh look, here's my daughter.'

Trixie was sitting on the doorstep, smoking, reading the *Racing Post* and brandishing five beautiful bright pink roses.

'Angela Rippon,' said Etta in amazement. 'Where did they come from?'

'Josh and I are on again,' said Trixie happily, 'so he leaned over Direct Debbie's wall when he was riding out this morning and picked them, then he came over in his break this afternoon to give me them and tell me the latest gossip. It's all in the *Post* about Shade taking his horses away but they haven't got the whole story.'

'I should hope not, poor Marius,' said Etta indignantly.

She put her key in the door to find Gwenny sitting on the red armchair, Chisolm, having jumped through the window, on the sofa and Mrs Wilkinson peering round the mature hedge, knuckering imperiously.

'You can all wait,' she pleaded, 'just let me get everyone a drink.'

'I'll get it,' said Trixie, taking a bottle of white out of the fridge. 'I know your priorities, Granny: Wilkie, Chisolm, Gwenny and no doubt Seth's greyhound Priceless before long,' she added, winking at her father, but he was too busy reading about Marius in the *Post* to notice.

'How did you get on with Marius?' she asked, as Etta began to cut up an apple.

'Well, he's agreed to take on Mrs Wilkinson, which is wonderful. Such a sweet man, he looked shell-shocked.'

'Not that sweet,' said Trixie, filling up three glasses. 'Shade and Olivia have been having a relationship for ages. She evidently adored Shade's jet, which is not just a fast plane with no people, it's got chairs, leather sofas, a gambling table and beds in butterscotch leather. Well, Olivia said she didn't like the colour and Shade changed it to cream, so he must be keen.'

'Golly,' said Etta, handing a piece of apple to Chisolm and leaning out to hand another piece to Mrs Wilkinson, who was listening to every word.

'Anyway,' went on Trixie, 'it emerges that Marius felt rejected by Olivia and boosted his ego by shagging a stable lass called Michelle, the little tart.'

'Which one's she?' Alan looked up from the *Racing Post*.

'The red-headed bitch nympho – Meesh-hell, they call her. When Marius tried to break it off, she promptly blabbed to Olivia. Michelle was fed up with shovelling shit, so she pretended she was pregnant. "I'm soooo sorry, Mrs Oakridge."'

'Olivia was madly jealous, apparently. I bet she never passed on Shade's message to Marius, that I'd have liked a holiday job in the yard. Anyway, Marius when confronted said it hadn't meant a thing.

'"Maybe not to you," snapped back Olivia, "but it meant a great deal to me and Michelle." It was just the trigger Olivia needed.'

'Golly,' repeated Etta, opening a tin of sardines for Gwenny.

'According to Josh,' went on Trixie, 'Olivia hasn't had a holiday in yonks, and she's fed up with making ends meet and exhausting herself. Shade's probably great in bed in a revolting sort of way and he won't have any difficulty paying school fees.'

'The Fat Controller,' said Alan bleakly. 'He won't like Olivia's terriers scrabbling all over the leather in the jet.'

Back in the kitchen at Throstledown, Marius poured himself another glass of whisky and confronted his bleak future. Not only had he lost a wife to whom he had been unable to express his great love, but with her had gone his child, his beloved terriers and twenty horses, whom he'd taught to jump and had been nursing to perfection to ignite the forthcoming season. These included little Gifted Child, Stop Preston and Ilkley Hall, whom he'd particularly adored and who certainly would not get the same love and attention at Harvey-Holden's.

Marius had also flogged his BMW last month and taken out a large mortgage on Throstledown in order to pay his dwindling staff and feed his horses, who'd soon be coming in from the fields and eating their heads off. He hadn't been in the money since March, which meant no tips or bonuses for the lads, so morale was rock bottom. Cruellest of all, Shade had dropped him a line, saying he was no longer prepared to guarantee Marius's crippling overdraft as he'd only kept his horses with Marius so long because of Olivia.

Wandering into the hall, Marius was confronted by a lovely family portrait in a field in summer which had included Ilkley Hall and Preston. He remembered how long Alizarin Belvedon had taken to paint the picture, how absolutely fed up he, his daughter, dogs and horses had got standing about and how only Olivia had kept the peace.

'Oh dear God,' he moaned, 'please bring her back.'

Driven mad by Horace's incessant whinnying, he was tempted to turn his shotgun on himself. Instead he picked up the photographs Etta had left him of Mrs Wilkinson, whom Harvey-Holden had gone to court with the finest lawyers to repossess.

She looked as though she'd been rescued from a donkey sanctuary, but she had beaten Bafford Playboy and Marius knew how good a horse he was. The only revenge would be to turn her into a world-beater.

It was the same old story. When training was going well, it was great, when badly, it was crucifying. Even though you got up at five and were seldom in bed until after the ten o'clock news, you still had sleepless nights. And you had to smile for the troops.

He reached down and stroked a shuddering Mistletoe.

Tomorrow he must screw up the courage to ask Rupert to take Shade's place in guaranteeing his overdraft for a few months.

As he switched on his mobile, it rang immediately. Hope flared but instead of Olivia's voice it was the velvety soft, Irish mist brogue of Rogue Rogers.

'You poor darling boy. She'll come back. I'll come down and school the horses next week.'

43

Early in September, the syndicate visited Throstledown, lured by an invitation to watch the horses on the gallops followed by breakfast. Everyone turned out except Seth, who was doing a voiceover in London, Shagger, who had a board meeting, and Toby, who was slaughtering wildlife in Scotland.

Tommy, who welcomed them, explained away so many empty boxes by pretending most of the horses were turned out in a distant field, which in fact only contained Furious, because he bit people, and his sheep friend Dilys. Tommy smiled and smiled. Rafiq scowled and looked beautiful.

A week of incessant rain had painted the valley green again and closed up the cracks in the ground. Mist curled upwards from the river like steam off a Derby winner. Cobwebs, silver with raindrops, stretched from blades of bleached grass like fairies' dartboards. The fountain in the centre of the yard was flowing again. Everything sparkled in the sunshine, giving a feeling of optimism.

Once again the visitors were fascinated to gaze at their houses across the valley, their chimneys rising out of the turning trees like children's hands put up in class.

Direct Debbie, wearing a scarlet straw hat to keep the sun off her fat neck, admired the blaze of dahlias and chrysanths in Cobblers' garden, but bristled to see how close to their adjoining fence Joey had pushed the trampoline on which his children had bounced noisily all summer. Debbie had also had several words with Joey and Mop Idol about washing on the climbing frame, loud music and raucous drinking sessions, and was not looking forward to being in a syndicate with such riff-raff.

'Are you ever going to get Badger's Court finished?' she asked Joey sourly.

'Look,' Phoebe put her arm through Debbie's, 'there's Wild Rose Cottage. You will come and help me with my indoor bulbs, won't you?' Then, smiling accusingly at Tilda: 'After your long, long holiday you must be looking forward to a new term.'

'Not so much as Granny, who's been looking after Drummond and Poppy all summer,' drawled Trixie. She was tossing newly washed hair and rolling the shortest shorts even shorter at the prospect of seeing Josh again.

Tilda in fact was just as exhausted as Etta. Having spent her holidays cleaning Lark Cottage, washing and changing sheets and providing loo paper for Shagger's holiday lets, she was now hiding her bitter disappointment that he hadn't turned up this morning. Miss Painswick was also in a melancholy mood. The smell of mouldering leaves and wet earth reminded her of the start of the school year and no Hengist Brett-Taylor to get things shipshape for.

The solar panelling glittered on the roof of Willowwood Hall. Pocock furtively tugged down his cap in case Ione picked up her binoculars and saw he wasn't at the dentist. Joey, taking photographs of Badger's Court to show Valent, and Chris, who didn't need to be back at the Fox until opening time, were eyeing up the more lissom stable lasses, Tresa, a soft-eyed blonde and all smiles, and Michelle, the pouting, sulky redhead, as they tacked up their gleaming charges, and little Angel, the baby of the yard.

'Do you use Pledge on them?' joked Debbie.

The Major, who'd invested in a panama with a British Legion hatband, felt dashing and frisky. There were some jolly pretty fillies around. He smoothed his moustache. Woody was more interested in the yellow leaves already flecking the willows, and the coral keys on the sycamore. There were a lot of trees down in Marius's copses which could be cut up and sold off to help his bank balance. The price of timber had gone sky-high.

Alan had justified skiving by giving a lift to Etta, Trixie and Dora, just back from three weeks in Greece with her boyfriend Paris.

'We saw rather too many ruins,' confessed Dora. 'And remembering how Penelope's suitors neglected poor Argus, I shouldn't have been surprised how foul the Greeks are to dogs. I nearly brought back the sweetest little stray for you, Etta, as a present for looking after Cadbury.'

Now home and broke, Dora was anxious to sell more stories.

'Don't tell her too much,' Etta pleaded to Trixie and Alan, 'or Shagger will have ammunition and Debbie will be so shocked she might persuade the others to try another trainer.'

'Where the hell's Marius?' grumbled Alan as they toured the boxes for a second time.

'I never know what to say when people show me horses,' whispered Tilda.

' "Who's he by?" is a good one,' whispered back Alan, 'or "Great ribcage" or "Wasn't her grandmother Desert Orchid's dam?" '

'What's a throstle?' asked Phoebe.

'A poetic name for a thrush,' explained Tilda. 'You can see a gold one on the weathercock.'

'Don't you want to throstle Phoebe?' whispered Alan.

'Always,' whispered back a surprised but delighted Tilda.

'That Tilda Flood's as boring as the Electricity Board in Monopoly,' Trixie muttered to Dora. 'I think she fancies my dad.'

'Après lui, le déluge,' giggled Dora.

They were now welcomed by Collie, the head lad, who had a kind face, mousy hair and spectacles like a chemistry master at a prep school. He said Marius was still doing his declarations (two actually) but would be out soon.

Josh, Rafiq, Tresa, Michelle, Tommy and Angel, all in jeans, T-shirts and bobble hats, were legged up on to their horses and set out, splashing through the puddles.

Etta, Alan, Trixie, Dora and Painswick then piled into Collie's absolutely filthy Land-Rover and bounded, bumped, skidded and swayed over the fields after them. The others, to the Major's horror, were expected to take their own cars, which were soon splattered with mud. Halfway up the hill, they parked on the edge of the gallops and watched the horses snorting round the exercise ring. Then, led by the dark brown History Painting, who fought Michelle for his head all the way, they thundered thrillingly up the gallops, Sir Cuthbert, the veteran, brought up the rear.

'Aren't they beautiful,' sighed Etta.

'Imagine Mrs Wilkinson leading them,' said Dora happily.

'She'd soon see off History Painting and that custard-haired slag,' said Trixie irritably, as blonde Tresa finally managed to tug the big chaser to a halt and turned, laughing, to Josh as he drew level. Trixie wouldn't admit how pleased she felt when Josh surreptitiously blew her a kiss as he rode back down the hill.

The party from Willowwood was distracted by another string of prettier horses, and even prettier stable lasses, who all smiled and said, 'Good morning,' as they crossed the gallops.

'That looks suspiciously like Rupert Campbell-Black's Coppelia,' murmured Alan.

'It *is* Coppelia,' hissed back Trixie. 'Josh told me Rupert went ballistic when he heard Granny was forming a syndicate rather than selling him Mrs Wilkinson, but he hates Shade and Harvey-Holden even more.

'Josh heard Rupert and Marius having a terrible row last night. Rupert saying the place was a tip and Marius should drag himself out of the Dark Ages. Marius saying if you can't get a horse fit with good hay and oats, you might as well shoot it. But Rupert still sent his horses and lads over this morning to swell the ranks, and Taggie, his wife, is making breakfast for us all when we get back.'

'Who's that redhead?' asked Painswick.

'That's Michelle – Meesh-hell, the little tart who's been – ouch,' as Etta kicked her ankle, Trixie changed tack, 'such a bitch to Tommy, always calling her Fatty and pointing out her builder's bum.'

'Michelle's the one who was shagging Marius,' piped up Dora. 'Everyone hoped he'd sack her when she dumped to Olivia, but she's too good in bed.'

'Oh dear,' sighed Etta. 'You won't tell the press, will you, Dora? If you do, Debbie will pull the Major out.'

'Course not, I never dish dirt,' lied Dora.

'Hum,' said Trixie, 'that Rafiq rides like an angel.'

Back at the yard, Phoebe and Debbie were moaning about the state of the place.

'Aunt Ione says the house hasn't been touched in thirty years.'

'Nor has the garden,' sniffed Debbie. 'Are we sure Marius is the right trainer? He should have been here to receive us.'

Instead they were welcomed by Niall the vicar, who'd walked over, hoping such vigorous activity justified skiving. His nostrils were flaring at the smell of frying bacon from the kitchen.

'I dropped in on Old Mrs Malmesbury on the way. Thought if I met Marius casually, he might be receptive to some counselling. He appears very troubled.'

'And very good-looking, you silly woofter,' muttered Dora.

'Wow,' sighed Trixie, as a bright blue Ferrari roared up the drive, making the returning horses toss their heads and leap about. 'That really is hot.'

It was Rogue Rogers, rolling up to school the horses, his laughing eyes bluer than his Ferrari, who tipped the balance and reassured any waverers that this was the right yard.

'Josh says Olivia was being shagged by Rogue Rogers as well as my dad,' murmured Trixie to Dora. 'That's why they're both absolutely livid about Shade going off with her.'

Today, however, Rogue Rogers was out to charm all the

syndicate, many of whom knew him already from when he had lived in Shagger's cottage in Willowwood.

Back in the house, a very tall, slim and pretty woman with cloudy dark hair and silvery grey eyes was serving up the most delicious breakfast of kedgeree, bacon, sausages, fried eggs and mushrooms fresh from the fields. Rogue made everyone laugh by leaping on to a chair to kiss her, like a perky Jack Russell making advances towards a gentle Great Dane.

'This is Taggie,' he announced, 'the loveliest woman in racing, easily the best cook and married to my incredibly lucky friend Rupert Campbell-Black.'

'Oh Rogue,' blushed Taggie. 'Please help yourselves, everyone.'

'Wouldn't mind if she was on the menu,' muttered Chris to Joey, thinking he might introduce kedgeree in the Fox.

'Oh hello, Taggie,' called out Phoebe. 'I was at school with your step-daughter Tabitha. Does she still see . . . ?' and went into an orgy of names, while Taggie was trying to sort out who wanted coffee or tea or Bull Shots.

'I'm not sure who Tab sees,' she said apologetically. 'Mustard's over there.'

Phoebe, Trixie, Debbie, Tilda, Etta and Dora, even Painswick, proceeded to drool over Rogue as he toyed with a black mushroom, sipped even blacker coffee and, in an Irish brogue softer than the thistledown drifting past the window, assured them they'd chosen the best trainer in the country, 'except Rupert', he added, winking at Taggie.

They were even more excited when he lied that he'd watched the video of Mrs Wilkinson's point-to-point and she looked a very decent hoss.

'Do you know Amber Lloyd-Foxe, who rode her?' asked Etta. 'A very good jockey.'

'Miss Amateur Lloyd-Foxe,' said Rogue dismissively.

'That's naughty.' Phoebe giggled in delight.

'Who spends her life in Boujis,' added Rogue. 'She was lucky to have a good horse under her.'

'She'll be a different horse with you on her back,' simpered Phoebe.

'As long as you don't use your whip on her,' said Etta.

'Not now!' Alan shut her up sharply.

'How do you keep so slim, Rogue?' gushed Phoebe.

'One meal a day.'

'How long have you done that for?'

'Since I was at school. I always put my dinner money on a hoss.'

After breakfast, everyone wanted to have their photograph taken with Rogue. Alan, the Major, Woody and Joey, who knew something about racing, were equally impressed when Rogue took Asbo Andy, Oh My Goodness and History Painting over a row of fences.

'He's so bloody brilliant,' sighed Alan. 'Look how he moves with the horse, cuddles it up on the bit, balances it, gets the maximum ounce out of every muscle, like honey on its back.'

'See the expression of relief on History's face, with Rogue on him rather than Michelle,' observed Dora.

'Josh says Rogue's got the biggest tackle in the weighing room,' said Trixie blithely.

As Etta moved away trying not to laugh, she noticed Rafiq had left the yard, where he had been sweeping up, to watch Rogue, an expression of passionate longing, admiration and envy on his face.

'You ride beautifully too,' stammered Etta. 'We all noticed how well the horses went for you.'

Rafiq started in terror, gazing at her uncomprehendingly until Michelle made them both jump. She shrilly ordered him to stop skiving and get back to work.

'We must go,' said Etta. 'We've taken up enough of their time.'

In the yard, horses were looking inquisitively out of their boxes. Those who'd not been ridden were put on the horse walker, while others were turned out for a few hours.

Tresa, the minxy blonde, was brushing History Painting in his box.

'Where are you racing today?' Phoebe asked Rogue.

'Hereford, then I'm flying to Down Royal in Dermie O'Driscoll's chopper for an evening meeting.'

'Dermie wanted to buy Mrs Wilkinson,' said Etta eagerly.

'Showed good taste.' Rogue smiled round at the syndicate. 'I'm really looking forward to seeing you guys again. Must go and pick up my saddle from the tack room.'

'Funny,' muttered Dora as Rogue slid into History Painting's box.

They were distracted by Marius finally emerging from his office, followed by his shy, striped lurcher who, to Etta's delight, bounded up to her, wagging her shepherd's crook tail.

Marius, even thinner and still deathly pale, was if not charming, at least polite.

'We're probably talking about a January start.' Then, seeing the disappointment in people's faces: 'It takes ten weeks to get a horse to the races but for those new to the game like Mrs

Wilkinson, it'll take four months. She'll walk or trot for a couple of months, then learn to canter and gallop in a straight line, to jump hurdles or small fences, to behave calmly in all circumstances, not to kick or bite, and to jump and turn corners while galloping. If this process is rushed, they fall to pieces.'

'We'll be in touch,' said Etta, thanking him profusely.

As they walked towards their cars, Dora said, 'Damn, I think I left my camera in the tack room, I'll catch up with you.' Scuttling back, she ran slap into a grinning Rogue zipping up his flies as he came out of History Painting's box.

One of the very top jump jockeys, redoubtable, tricky, glamorous, Rogue had nearly given up racing eight years earlier after a hideous fall in which he broke his back and a leg and Monte Cristo, the beautiful and valuable bay he was riding, had to be shot. Marius had carried Rogue, visited him in hospital, kept up his retainer, restored his confidence, got him riding again and helped his struggle back to the top. There was no way Rogue was going to desert Marius now.

The little king of the weighing room, Rogue was tall for a jockey at five foot nine and at nine stone the perfect size. Any lighter, he would have to carry weights. Rogue drove owners, trainers and punters demented, holding up his horses as long as possible before unleashing his thunderbolt to mug the opposition on the line. No one drove horses harder than Rogue, but sensing a horse was beaten, unlike his cruel rival Killer O'Kagan, he put down his whip.

Rogue had adored Monte Cristo and still talked about him in his sleep. Determined never to fall in love again, he had since treated horses as a good secretary would a letter, something to be achieved perfectly but without any emotional involvement.

He was so good a rider, in all senses of the word, that trainers and women were willing to share him.

Being a jockey is like being an actor: you have to be visible to get more rides. Rogue was hugely in demand with other trainers, but always on call if Marius needed him. The bane of the stewards, Rogue deserved a BAFTA for talking himself out of trouble. After a bad ride, as a microphone approached, the words 'Fuck off' could be seen forming on his perfect lips. Racing put up with his bad behaviour because the sport desperately needed stars.

44

A riotous meeting that evening decided to appoint Marius as Mrs Wilkinson's trainer.

The only dissenting voice was Shagger's. Returning from London, still in his City pinstripe into which he had clearly sweated, he protested in his carrion crow rasp that Marius couldn't even win races; that he'd gone 166 days and 48 runners without being in the money.

'Asbo Andy's unbeaten,' protested Etta.

'That's because he's never run,' said Shagger rudely.

Then Seth, also back from London, swept in, and in the husky, deeply persuasive voice that had been selling luxury cruises to listeners, set about reassuring the syndicate.

'What you get from racing isn't money,' he said. 'Put in a hundred pounds, you're lucky if you get twenty back. What you're getting is fun, friendship and excitement, meeting, mixing and networking with great jockeys and owners and wonderful horses.'

And the lost heart quickens and rejoices, thought Alan, observing the rapture on Woody's, Tilda's, Etta's, Pocock's, even Painswick's faces.

So Marius it was.

The syndicate then gathered round a table, with Priceless the greyhound flashing his teeth like a Colgate ad as he rushed in from the kitchen, making the numbers up to fourteen by stretching out on a nearby sofa. First drinks were on the house as the rules were hammered out. Only people who lived in Willowwood could join. The majority vote would prevail on all occasions. Payment of vet's bills, insurance, proportion of winnings dependent on size of stake and allocation of owners' badges at race meetings were all thrashed out. Anyone who backed out, or defaulted for three months on payment, would lose their stake unless they could get someone approved by a majority syndicate vote to take it over.

Major Cunliffe had been mugging up on syndicates and, as an ex-bank manager, he was appointed treasurer. When he suggested that 'Cash sums can be handed over in this pub on the twenty-fifth of every month, but I'd prefer people to pay by Direct Debit,' no one dared look at one another.

'And anyone who defaults will be spanked by the Major,' yelled Alan, getting up to buy the next round of drinks.

Direct Debbie looked very disapproving.

'Debbie will be in charge of good behaviour,' said Seth, feeding crisps to Priceless.

'We must think of a name for the syndicate,' said Etta hastily.

Toby, who'd flown down straight off the grouse moors and looking a prat in knickerbockers, interrupted her, announcing that Shagger, 'a whizz-kid in the City', should be the syndicate's banker.

Alan, however, had observed Shagger's trick of asking for a fiver from everyone to buy some white and red, then, having acquired three or four bottles for much less, pocketing the rest. Equally, Shagger would sidle into a group, bury his fat lips in the cheek of one of the women, buy her a half, slide back into the group and be the beneficiary of succeeding rounds.

Only a couple of days ago, Shagger had edged up to him in the pub to reiterate that if he, Shagger, secured a favourable insurance deal for Mrs Wilkinson, perhaps the syndicate might waive his fee. Remembering how Shagger, with the aid of a vicious Health and Safety inspector, had once ripped off Woody, Alan had snapped that it was most unlikely.

Shagger's methods were entirely opposite to the generous open-ended way Alan operated, aided admittedly by a rich wife, so Alan now suggested it would be better if Major Cunliffe was also their banker. He was more experienced, more local and therefore more available. Everyone except Shagger and Toby agreed. Major Cunliffe went puce with pleasure.

'Ask a busy person,' said Debbie smugly. 'Daddy always finds the time.'

'We still haven't got a name,' said Etta, making notes.

'What about Affordable Horsing?' suggested Seth.

Everyone giggled.

'Why not the Willowwood Legend,' said Trixie.

Everyone liked that, it sounded so romantic.

'Except Beau Regard died,' said Painswick.

'Let's just call ourselves Willowwood,' said Woody, seeing Etta's face falter and moving his thigh away from Shagger's.

'How are we going to get to the races?' asked Joey. 'When Mrs Wilkinson starts winning we'll want to celebrate on the way home.'

Chris the landlord then announced he'd got wind of a second-hand Ford Transit bus that took ten.

'Don't 'spect everyone'll go every time she races,' said Joey.

'Some of us work,' quipped Chris.

'And people can sit on people's knees,' said Phoebe, looking up at Seth from under her pale brown eyelashes.

'We'll provide the picnic,' said Chris, thinking of a fat profit.

'We can all make things,' said Etta.

'And drink ourselves insensible,' said Seth, draining his glass.

'We'll have to find someone sober to drive us,' said Alan. 'How about Alban? Poor sod's just returned from rehab utterly demoralized, off the drink, for ever, if Ione has her way. Desperately needs something to do.'

'He's a seriously slow driver,' protested Toby.

'Better to be safe than sorry,' said Miss Painswick, getting another skein of wool out of her bag.

'Will you approach Alban?' the Major asked Alan pompously. 'I was thinking of asking him to address Rotary on his take on the Arab world.'

'We must paint the bus our colours,' said Tilda in excitement.

'What are our colours going to be?' asked Shagger, filling up his pint mug from one of the bottles of red on the bar.

'Why not a dark green willow on the palest green background?' suggested Phoebe, who worked in an art gallery. 'We must have something that shows up on grey, foggy days.'

'Or a pale green willow on an emerald green background.' Etta was surprised by her own assertiveness. 'It would suit Amber. I do hope Marius puts her up.' Hark at herself, swinging into the jargon.

'Rogue Rogers has lovely kingfisher-blue eyes,' sighed Phoebe.

'Rogue likes wearing silks with horizontal stripes to make his shoulders look bigger,' said Trixie, 'which wouldn't work with our willow tree.'

'Perhaps those clever children at your school could come up with a design,' suggested Etta.

'And you've forgotten your girlfriend's glass, Shagger,' said Alan pointedly, as he tipped the remains of his glass into Tilda's. 'We're going to need more bottles, Chris,' then, as Tilda threw him a smile of passionate gratitude, thought: she'd be pretty if she had those teeth fixed.

'Our vicar,' said Seth, who was admiring Trixie's legs, 'must come along whenever Mrs Wilkinson runs to administer the last rites.' Then, seeing the horror on Etta's face: 'And bless her and pray for her safe return.'

'I do hope she isn't homesick,' sighed Etta. 'It's like sending her off to boarding school with name tapes, a trunk and a fruit cake.'

'And costs about the same,' said Seth, then he put a hand on Etta's arm. 'Don't worry, she'll be fine.'

Etta looked round the group who were all smiling sympathetically at her, and thought, nothing can go wrong for Mrs Wilkinson with all these sweet people rooting for her.

After the meeting dispersed, Alan and Seth, who were friends, both married to powerful women and led each other astray, stayed behind in the pub to get tanked up and discuss a trip to York.

Alan confessed the biography of Walter Scott he longed to write was hardly started. 'I can't get stuck into it. Walter wrote frantically to the end of his life to pay off debts incurred by his partner in a publishing firm. I identify with that aspect of his character. But I'm still wrestling with this bloody book on depression and really I need go no further than Willowwood.

'I'm depressed about being Mr Carrie Bancroft. You're pissed off playing second fiddle to Corinna. Alban's about to slit his wrists missing whisky and the kudos of the embassy. Etta's terrorized by ghastly Martin and my wife, missing her old house and her dog and, from next week, Mrs Wilkinson. Tilda's gagging for a husband. Shagger's a bastard to her, hardly surprising bearing in mind his hopeless passion for Toby. Painswick's eating her heart out for Hengist. Niall's terrified of being outed, and demoralized by his empty church. Chris and Chrissie can't have children, unlikely when they're working and drinking themselves insensible. There's something wistful about the divine Woody. Joey seems pretty happy. Mop Idol's frantically worried about money. Pocock is a poor widower, gagging for a shag. Poor Marius, with Olivia buggering off, is the saddest of them all, poor boy, and that stormy Rafiq's obviously got a few problems. Hey presto, I can interview them all for my book on trips to the races.'

'Trixie seems fine,' said Seth idly.

'She'd be better if her mother took a bit of notice of her,' said Alan bitterly.

'She's utterly faint-makingly gorgeous, she's just got to wait for things to happen to her,' said Seth.

Outside, the constellation Pegasus galloped over Throstledown. Poor gorgeous Seth, on his own until Corinna gets back, thought the female members of the syndicate as they rustled home through the first fallen leaves, all alone in that big house.

45

Two weeks later Mrs Wilkinson moved to Throstledown, along with her football and ten pages of notes listing her likes – being sung to, Beethoven, Sir Walter Scott and bread and butter pudding – and her phobias, which included men with loud voices, pitchforks and shovels, cars backing towards her and people approaching unannounced on her blind side. Marius promptly tore up the notes and Tommy pieced them together again when he wasn't looking.

'Christ, it's a Shetland,' sneered Michelle, which didn't endear her to Etta.

Marius then put Mrs Wilkinson into an isolation box thirty yards from the other boxes, so any infections or viruses could be identified. This return to a racing yard, evoking all the horrors of a former life, totally traumatized Mrs Wilkinson. Trembling violently, hurling herself against the walls, she refused to eat, pacing her box at one moment, standing in the corner, her head drooping, the next, as she cried and cried for Etta and Chisolm.

Even when Marius relented and allowed Chisolm, who'd been driving Etta and Valent's builders equally crackers with her pathetic bleating, to move in, Mrs Wilkinson kept up her desperate whinnying. The first time, three days later, she was taken out for a little gentle exercise, she bucked Rafiq off and clattered down the drive, reins and stirrups flying, back to Little Hollow, neighing her head off at the gate like Beau Regard.

A demented Etta rang up Tommy to alert her as to Mrs Wilkinson's whereabouts.

'Oh thank God,' cried Tommy, 'Rafiq was so worried. It'll be a wonderful birthday present for him that she's safe.'

Leading Mrs Wilkinson back to Throstledown and feeling like a traitor, Etta kept up a stream of apologies.

'I've got to tough it out, Wilkie darling, because you're not mine any more to do what I want with. I can't give the syndicate back all their money.' Most of hers had been handed over to Martin and Carrie to pay for Little Hollow.

Rafiq came down Marius's drive to meet her.

'She'll settle soon,' he said.

Thrusting Mrs Wilkinson's reins into his hands, Etta fled down the drive, hands over her ears to blot out any more frantic whinnying.

'Poor darling, I can't do this to her. If only I wasn't too old to sell my body.'

Back at Little Hollow, she spent the afternoon cooking, but before picking the children up from school she drove back to Throstledown, parking halfway down the drive. Crawling into the yard on her hands and knees so Mrs Wilkinson wouldn't see her, she bumped slap into Rafiq's ragged-jeaned legs.

Rafiq was not in carnival mood, having just suffered the racing yard's birthday rituals of being chucked on the muck heap and drenched with a bucket of water. Nor did his temper improve when Etta thrust a white cardboard box at him, and whispered:

'Happy birthday.' Then, when he looked suspicious, she blurted out, 'It's not a bomb,' at which Rafiq's face darkened and his eyes blazed.

'Sorry,' jabbered Etta, 'such a stupid thing to say. It's a present actually.'

For a second she thought Rafiq was going to bolt, then he took the box, cautiously opened it and smiled broadly.

'What a beautiful cake, thank you, thank you.'

'I only put on one candle, it's a bit twee, because I didn't know how old you were.'

'And you spelt Rafiq right. Thank you.'

'Thank you for looking after Mrs Wilkinson.' Etta winced as another despairing whinny rent the air.

'I look after her. Once she settle, you can visit her more times.'

The pathetic cries followed her down the drive.

'How is she?' asked the builders, going home after at last starting work on Valent's study.

Etta still couldn't relax. She had given supper to Drummond and Poppy, who was gratifyingly upset at Mrs Wilkinson's departure, and had them in their pyjamas at Harvest Home by the time their mother came home.

'How's Mrs Wilkinson getting on? Has she won the Derby yet?' mocked Romy.

Etta wanted to punch her.

Poor Mrs Wilkinson, but at least she had Chisolm for company. Etta's other concern was Seth Bainton, all on his own. I do hope he's eating enough, thought Etta for the hundredth time.

There was nothing on telly on a Tuesday. The only way to assuage acute unhappiness was to do a good deed for another person, reasoned Etta.

After a quick bath, she splashed on the last drops of For Her and applied some make-up. Then, putting half the flapjacks she'd made for Valent's builders in a tin, she set out for the Old Rectory.

The sun had left an orange glow along the horizon. The old house was smothered in yellow roses and honeysuckle growing up to the roof, entwining the gutter, clawing at the windows. Shaking uncontrollably, Etta rang the bell. Relieved there was no answer, she was about to dump the tin and run when Seth's head appeared through the shaggy creepers out of an upstairs window.

'Oh, it's you,' he said in gratifying relief, 'I'll come down.'

Answering the door clutching a large whisky, he immediately poured one for Etta. She was too embarrassed to say she never drank the stuff.

'I thought you were another casserole,' he said. 'Talk about ignorant armies clashing by night.'

He led her into an incredibly messy drawing room, lifted a pile of scripts off one end of the sofa and chucked them on the floor for Etta to sit down.

Priceless the greyhound, inhabiting the remaining part of the sofa, gave her a toothy smile and flicked the white end of his tail in recognition. Etta yelped as her coccyx splintered something, but it was only a Bonio.

The room was more a shrine to Corinna than to Seth. Three portraits of her, one, Etta recognized, by John Bratby, graced the walls, photographs of her and Seth in plays were everywhere, and Polaroids, from photographic sessions, adorned the mantelpiece. As in Marius's house, every surface was covered by trophies, BAFTAs, Oliviers, even an Oscar.

'Hello, darling,' Etta stroked Priceless, then to Seth, she added humbly, 'I thought you might like something to snack on, and brought you some flapjacks.'

'How brilliant.' Seth opened the tin and took one out. He broke off half for Priceless. 'God, these are wonderful. I'm rather over-casseroled. I am a casserole model,' he grinned. 'In fact a boeuf bourguignon was in collision with a coq au vin by the war memorial last night. Come and look.'

He led her off to an even messier kitchen and opened the fridge. Inside were four full casserole dishes topped by cling-film.

'Irish stew from Direct Debbie, Lancashire hot pot from Miss Painswick, shepherd's pie from Mop Idol, coq au vin from your daughter-in-law, Romy, "by my own fair hand," she said. Alan told me you did all her cooking for her.'

Etta felt a surge of irritation. 'I didn't make that. She must have got it from William's Kitchen.'

Seth roared with laughter. 'I'll be too fat to play Trigorin soon. She's very up herself, that Romy. Conversation always comes back to her: "That reminds me of a time when I ..."'

Etta tried not to laugh. He had caught Romy's deep, patronizing tones to perfection.

'Martin's up himself too. I know he's your son, but the first time I met him, not knowing they were married, I told him I wouldn't mind giving Romy one. And he chortled himself insensible, then said, "Actually, old boy, I do that every night. I'm her husband." Yuck, as the divine Trixie would say.'

'Romy is very pretty,' protested Etta.

'Pretty ghastly. Priceless loves Direct Debbie's Irish stew, but then he's Irish.'

As they wandered back, stepping over clothes and books, Etta noticed a copy of *Antony and Cleopatra* spine side up.

'Bloody long part,' sighed Seth.

'Would you like me to hear your lines?' Etta was shocked to hear herself asking.

Seth grinned. 'Romy, Direct Debbie, Ione and Phoebe (no casserole from her, you notice, the little sponger) have each offered an ear, but they'd all start questioning my interpretation and my pronunciation. I'd much rather you heard me. I'll drop in if I may when I'm further down the line, or lines. After *The Seagull* Corinna's touring in *Macbeth* – in America, thank God, as she always becomes the part she's playing. I wish she was doing the Duchess of Malfi and I Bosola, so I could smother her,' Seth half laughed.

'You'll adore Corinna,' he went on in mitigation. 'She's very exacting, but she's fun and wonderful at pulling down the mighty from their country seats. She'll annihilate Romy and Direct Debbie and she'll be a riot on the syndicate bus.'

'She was Sampson's favourite actress,' sighed Etta. 'He'd have so loved to have met her.'

Seth topped up his glass and helped himself to another flap-jack. 'These are bloody good. Do you miss him?'

'Yes . . . no,' said Etta. 'I miss what he expected. I feel guilty about reading in the bath, eating between meals and putting on weight.' She squeezed a spare tyre. 'He'd have hated that, he used to weigh me every week. When I'm alone I talk to him. He doesn't answer,' she gave a shrug, 'but he didn't much when he was alive.'

Then she gave a cry of anguish. 'I didn't mean to be disloyal. I'm sorry. I just feel so utterly miserable about Mrs Wilkinson going into training.'

'The heart is a muscle like any other, and must be exercised,' said Seth gently. 'Let's discuss the syndicate, who are all so excited about her future.' He topped up her glass. 'I adore your son-in-law, Alan, and Trixie's enchanting. Tilda's a kind old rabbit and Woody, Jase and Joey are great and I like old Painswick. Beneath that heaving mono-bosom is a heart of lust and passion craving for Hengist Brett-Taylor.'

'Really?' giggled Etta. 'Is he nice?'

'Gorgeous. Shagger's hell, "a bitter heart that bides its time and bites", and Toby's a drip. Phoebe's a professional poppet, a raging snob, flings herself on to people's knees, "Any room for a little one?" '

'You don't fancy her then? She's so pretty.'

'Absolutely not. Chris and Chrissie are on the make, affection beaming out of one eye, calculation out of the other. They aim to do very well with the Fox as the established syndicate meeting place.'

'She's terribly sad about babies,' protested Etta.

'The vicar will be our fag ship, and bless your sweet horse. Alban's a dote, vulnerable as a giraffe. I quite like the Major, but his wife's a bossyboots.'

'She made you a lovely Irish stew,' said Etta reprovingly.

In agreement Priceless began chewing the wooden arm of the sofa.

'So funny.' Seth gave a shout of laughter. 'You know how obsessed she is with dogs not crapping? Well, she's now stuck up a large sign outside her garden saying "Please do not let your dog defect here".'

'Oh how lovely,' giggled Etta. 'Imagine all those illegal immigrant dogs being turned away.'

'Ione is a bossyboots too,' went on Seth. 'She was livid last year because Corinna told her trick-or-treating grand-children to fuck orf. She's always bullying us to tidy up our

221

garden. She must be going through the climate change of life.'

Etta found she was laughing all the time now.

Seth was wearing the same black jeans and black shirt over a pale grey T-shirt, which complemented his sensual, smiling, sun-tanned face and his dark, tousled hair, which was just silvering at the temples. She could listen to his deep voice for ever and watch that firm but full-lipped mouth moving. And he was so confiding and indiscreet and mimicked everyone brilliantly, and was so interested in Wilkie.

'She always squeals when I use the dandy brush on her,' confided Etta. 'If only you could tell animals you haven't deserted them for ever. That Tommy's so sweet.'

'Worth a whole tonful of bricks,' said Seth. 'Shall we heat up some of your daughter-in-law's coq au vin?'

When they had, they agreed that Romy's coq had definitely been cooked by William's Kitchen.

Finally, when Etta reluctantly tore herself away, Seth and Priceless walked her home.

'I'll never get elected to the Parish Council if anyone spots us,' said Seth, tucking his arm through hers.

Priceless, once outside, was galvanized from utter torpor, tossing his head back, beckoning them onwards, seizing Seth's hand gently in his mouth to lead him on, then bouncing off, rustling maniacally through dry fallen leaves.

'What a heavenly dog,' sighed Etta.

'Isn't he?' said Seth. 'If occasionally I can't get back from the theatre, do you think Trixie might walk him for me?'

'I'm sure she would,' said Etta. 'She loves dogs, and if she can't, I will.'

When they reached Etta's door, Seth kissed her on both cheeks. 'I feel I've made a really lovely new friend. Here's to you and Mrs Wilkinson.'

46

Across the valley that evening, Tommy, who had risen at five thirty to start work at six, retired to the grooms' quarters over the tack room, which she shared with Rafiq. They were very primitive, with no carpets, erratic hot water and windows which banged in the wind. Here they had a tiny bathroom, kitchen and sitting room, and separate bedrooms. Sometimes Rafiq sleepwalked and he would be found next morning asleep in the tack room or by the fountain. Alternatively Tommy was roused by his screaming as he was racked by nightmares. She longed to go in and comfort him, but he had a barbed-wire hauteur which deterred her.

Falling into bed around nine, Tommy was so tired that not even Mrs Wilkinson's anguished hollering could keep her from sleep. But waking at midnight and rising to go to the loo, she found Rafiq's door, which was always firmly shut, wide open. Oh God, was he sleepwalking again? Racing downstairs, out into the yard, she was amazed not to hear Mrs Wilkinson neighing.

She could see a light on in Collie's house. She knew he was unable to support a wife and children on the pittance Marius paid him. He kept disappearing up the hill to get a signal on his mobile, probably fixing interviews. All the owners loved Collie. He was approachable and knew, and was prepared to discuss, their horses, and he kept peace and order in the yard.

If Collie went, would Marius give his head lad's job to Michelle, who was such a bitch?

'Move your fat arse,' she'd shouted at Tommy that very evening.

But as Tommy lurked in the tack-room doorway, a figure, wafting scent and with red hair turned green by the moonlight, stole across the yard and let herself in through Marius's kitchen door.

223

Oh God, thought Tommy, Michelle wouldn't be up to the job, she didn't really like or understand horses. And if Marius went broke, all the remaining horses would go, and poor Mrs Wilkinson and Furious would become victims of a broken home.

The trees and boxes cast ebony shadows, while the little weather throstle gleamed silver. Beneath it was Josh's flat. Through roughly drawn curtains, Tommy could see Tresa's bottom rising and falling much more energetically than it ever did on the gallops. Poor little Trixie, so mad about Josh, thought Tommy, but she was so stunning she'd soon find someone better.

Where was Rafiq? She was amazed by the silence. Tiptoeing across the cobbles, trying not to wake the horses, she passed a snoring Furious wrapped round Dilys, his sheep, then from the isolation box she heard music. Creeping up, trying not to rustle the leaves, she found Rafiq singing some beautiful Pakistani lullaby in Mrs Wilkinson's furry grey ear. Arms round her neck, he was stroking her continually. Her head was hooked over his shoulder, her eye drooping. She was nearly asleep.

Tommy melted. Lucky, lucky Mrs Wilkinson. As she crept across the yard, she heard a dull knucker. A bored History Painting was in need of conversation and a Polo. Glancing across the valley, through the thinning willows Tommy could see a light in Etta's bungalow.

On the tack-room landline, she punched out Etta's number.

'Yes? Who's that?' Etta's voice was breathy with panic.

'Sorry to bother you. It's Tommy, I thought you'd like to know, Mrs Wilkinson's fine. Rafiq's taking a particular interest in her and he's in her box, singing her to sleep.'

47

Rafiq Khan was a twenty-five-year-old Muslim of great beauty, with thick black curls, palest tawny skin the colour of milk chocolate and lightish grey eyes, which set him apart from his countrymen. A few of his family had settled near Birmingham. The majority lived in Pakistan, on the Afghan border.

Rafiq had always been a firebrand, and hero-worshipped his charismatic and militant cousin Ibrahim. Endowed with an exquisite voice, Rafiq had dreamed of becoming a pop star, but his family had steered him firmly into reading science at a higher education college in the Midlands. Here he was recruited to the militant cause and got caught up in terrorist activities. His fervour had been fanned to fanaticism by an American bomb attack on a wedding in Afghanistan which killed several cousins and a girl he loved.

He had, however, chickened out of a plan to blow up a football match – a plan that was actually foiled – because he didn't want to die or kill people and, just before, had heard his potential victims chattering away in familiar accents.

When subversive literature, videos of other American bomb attacks on Muslim people and a poster saying 'Allah loves those who fight for him' were found in his college room, Rafiq was arrested. He refused to reveal any sources and was given three years, several months of which he spent in gaol before being transferred to an open prison near Larkminster.

Here he met Hengist Brett-Taylor, Miss Painswick's adored ex-boss. The former headmaster of Bagley Hall, Hengist had been gaoled for three months for cheating on behalf of Dora's boyfriend Paris Alvaston, by rewriting his GCSE history paper.

Rafiq, with his arrogance, beauty, colour and terrorist

sympathies, was targeted by many of the rougher Islamophobic prisoners, who mocked him for expecting to be rewarded with scores of virgins in paradise, and who either wanted to beat him up or bugger him insensible.

At first Rafiq detested Hengist Brett-Taylor, who was just the sort of authoritarian, empire-building bastard who had raped and split up India. Rafiq could imagine Hengist, having occupied some Raj palace, sitting with his booted feet up on a jewelled marble table and yelling instructions in a booming voice.

Hengist, however, an ex-England rugger international, had protected Rafiq from predatory inmates and they had become friends. Hengist, who taught history, entirely agreed with Rafiq about the atrocities inflicted on the Muslims throughout the ages.

For hours they discussed the Crusades.

Richard Coeur de Lion in the first Crusade, pointed out Hengist, was exactly like Tony Blair in his deplorable squandering of resources that were desperately needed at home. Hengist also quoted Steven Runciman that the Crusades were 'nothing more than a long act of intolerance in the name of God'.

He then insisted that Saladin, far from being the fiend portrayed in history lessons, was an absolute sweetheart, who treated prisoners with infinite mercy and forgave his enemies, until Rafiq wanted to hug him.

Hengist, like most great headmasters, had the ability of the morning sun to find a chink in the tree canopy and beam down on a wild garlic leaf or a first bluebell. Rafiq blossomed in his attention.

Larkminster Prison at the time was pioneering a scheme started in America, in which prisoners looked after retired or rescued racehorses, restoring them to health, so these horses could hopefully move on to other careers such as polo, eventing, dressage or as hunters or hacks.

Rafiq had ridden all his life in a terrain where horses were often the quickest way to travel. Not uncalculating, he also adhered to the Muslim proverb, 'Believe in God, but tether your camel.'

Although Sergeant Macnab, the prison officer who ran the stables, was a notorious bully, Rafiq initially saw working there as an opportunity to escape. Egged on by Hengist, he offered his services.

On the first day down at the yard, however, Rafiq saw the happiness on the face of a sullen old murderer who'd bonded with a tricky bay mare. Each had at last found something to love and be loved by. All the twenty prisoners enjoyed looking after their charges and the horses were thriving. Rafiq was allotted a trouble-maker called Furious.

Furious had been found in a roofless stable, suffering from rain scald, a skin disease in which scabs form and pustulate because of the acidity of the rain. Hair then comes off, exposing bare skin and lesions, and birds sit on the lesions and attack them. Furious had become so hungry he'd eaten half the wood partition between his and the next-door stable, in which another horse had already died.

By this time Furious had radiator ribs rising to a razor-sharp backbone and long untrimmed hooves. He was a walking skeleton, covered in skin smeared with dung and sweat marks, and completely lacking in flesh and muscle.

The policeman who found him was all for putting him out of his misery.

'Why shoot him?' said the ILPH inspector. 'If we do, we'll lose the evidence. We're going to rebuild him.'

The trainer, who'd gone bankrupt, was tracked down and sent to prison. After six months of loving care Furious came together, but as he grew well he became increasingly tricky and literally fighting fit.

Rafiq, who loved horses, soon won Furious's trust and a few weeks later proudly paraded the glossy, gleaming chestnut before Hengist and the prison governor. He showed how biddable Furious had become by adjusting the horse's noseband so it most flattered his face and kissing him on the white star on his forehead.

'Don't turn him into a woofter like yourself, Khan,' mocked Sergeant Macnab, who was hovering in the background.

It was a prison rule that because of the insurance, none of the inmates were allowed to ride their charges, only look after them. Rafiq, however, was so incensed by Macnab's insult, he vaulted on to Furious and took off over the six-foot prison wall, hurtling across the fields, jumping every fence and disappearing into the hills.

'Bloody hell,' said the prison governor to Hengist, 'that's the last we'll see of him.'

Just as they were sending out a search party to trail Rafiq in the hope he might lead them to a terrorist cell or even his wicked cousin Ibrahim, Rafiq came galloping back, jumping the last two fences, soaring over the prison wall, pulling up a docile, delighted Furious.

'This is a great horse. He must go back into training,' Rafiq announced haughtily. But as the prison governor moved forward to make much of Furious, the horse flattened his ears and tried to bite him. 'But only with me to look after him. Muslims, contrary to propaganda, love animals,' went on Rafiq. 'Saladin better man than your St Francis. When they meet, St Francis offer to walk on hot coals, just to prove his love for God. Saladin just smile gently and say, "My God doesn't need me to prove my love." '

After Hengist left prison, Rafiq continued to look after the prison horses for another eighteen months. He learnt almost as much from a friendship he forged with an inmate called Jimmy Wade, who had worked for Harvey-Holden. Jimmy had been imprisoned for passing on information for reward and deliberately pulling several favourites. During their long conversations, Jimmy admitted he had broken the law because stable lads' wages, particularly those paid by H-H, were so lousy, he couldn't keep up his mortgage.

Both he and Rafiq had followed Mrs Wilkinson's court case. During their conversation, Jimmy had confided that he knew the dreadful fate of Usurper before she became Mrs Wilkinson and the unimaginably cruel way she had been treated.

'They torture Muslims like that in detention camps,' shuddered Rafiq, 'They slash you with razors and rub in salt. They cut off your penis so you can't breed any more terrorists.'

The British police, seeking information about Ibrahim, hadn't been any too gentle either.

Jimmy and Rafiq had made plans to keep in touch and find work in the same yard. Rafiq was therefore devastated to learn, shortly after his friend's release and only a month before his own, that Jimmy had been knocked down and killed by a car. Rafiq therefore had twin secrets he was desperate to keep, the whereabouts of his cousin Ibrahim and the true story of what had befallen Mrs Wilkinson.

During his stint in gaol, Rafiq had gained a certificate in stable management, which enabled him to work in a racing yard. Hengist, who had written regularly to Rafiq, was determined to find him a job when he came out. There was also the problem of Furious, who, despite being castrated, was increasingly colty except when he was with Rafiq, and for safety's sake ought either to be destroyed or to leave the prison at the same time.

Rupert Campbell-Black was not prepared to take on either Rafiq or Furious.

'I don't want him blowing me up. And he might not like Xav having a Muslim girlfriend. Give him to Harvey-Holden, nice if someone blew up that little weasel. He's so far up Judy Tobias's massive arse, I'm amazed he can see. Or try Marius, he's broke and having a rough time. At least your Paki'll be cheap and Marius is so short of horses he might take on Furious. He must be only four or five.'

So a month before Olivia walked out and Alan and Etta approached Marius with a view to his training Mrs Wilkinson, Rafiq had moved to Throstledown as a stable lad and Marius had bought Furious from the prison for almost nothing.

Marius found Rafiq a truculent, tricky little bugger, but watching him on the gallops, he noticed how the boy could coax the last ounce of speed out of a horse with his hands and heels. Furious too could both jump and gallop and had the makings of a really good horse, if his vicious temper could be sorted out. Having got him a sheep friend, Dilys, Marius realized he must set about finding Furious a rich owner. In the yard, a sign saying 'Please don't stroke me, I bite' was hung outside his box.

The same could be hung outside Rafiq's bedroom, reflected Tommy. Her father, a detective sergeant, had tipped her off that MI5 and the police were keeping Rafiq under surveillance and not to get too close to him.

Tommy couldn't help it. She dreamed of Rafiq pulling her into his arms just as Furious wrapped himself round Dilys the sheep.

48

Later in September, Marius had a stroke of luck. A bedding billionaire called Bertie Barraclough, ennobled for his services to sleep and sexual enterprise, telephoned asking Marius to find him a horse he could give to his wife, appropriately named Ruby, for a ruby wedding present.

Bertie and Ruby, a devoted, very jolly couple, who looked as though they'd spent the forty years of their marriage romping on Bertie's vast bouncy beds, had met Marius and Olivia at some horse awards ceremony in London. Although enchanted by Olivia, they had been shocked when she ran off with Shade Murchieson, who had crossed Bertie once too often in business. Feeling very sorry for Marius and not knowing anything about horses, Bertie turned to him for advice. Marius could have waited for the sales in October. Needing the money, however, he decided to offer them Furious, and asked them down for breakfast and to watch the last lot of the day, which was virtually the only lot because there were so few lads and horses left.

Another problem was the horse himself, who'd probably bite Ruby's plump jewel-laden fingers if she tried to stroke him. Only with Rafiq was he remotely biddable. But smouldering Rafiq, who dreaded Furious being sold in case his new owner took him to another trainer, could not be relied on to show Furious off to best advantage.

Tommy, petrified Marius would sack Rafiq for scuppering any deal, offered to ride Furious herself. Marius agreed and put an outraged Rafiq up on Oh My Goodness. As the horses left the yard, fortunately just before the Barracloughs arrived, Furious carted Tommy then threw himself down on the track, hurling Tommy over his head into a hawthorn bush, to the noisy amusement of Michelle, Tresa and the rest of the lads. None of them, however, was keen to take Tommy's place, so Marius ordered up Trixie's feckless boyfriend, Josh, a good if flashy rider who modelled himself on Rogue Rogers.

It was a glorious morning with the valley silvered by a first frost and the leaves turning gold to match Furious's radiant chestnut beauty. All went well on the gallops, as an enraptured Bertie and Ruby stood hand in hand watching Furious thunder past.

'Why's he called Furious?' asked Bertie.

'Because he's fast and furious,' replied a doting Ruby. 'I can't wait to lead him in. You can wear the topper you wore to the palace, Bertie.'

Next, Josh, crouched over the horse's ears in his best Rogue Rogers fashion, tried to take Furious over a row of fences. Furious, with other ideas, jammed on his brakes, nearly propelling Josh over his head, and tried to eat the first fence.

'How sweet, he's having his breakfast,' cried Ruby.

Furious then took a massive bunny jump over the fence, went into a frenzy of bucking, kicking and farting, and unshipped Josh, who, crash-landing and smashing the mobile in his pocket, launched into a frenzy of expletives, right in front of Ruby and Bertie, who strongly disapproved of swearing in front of a lady. Furious cleared the gate and set off down the drive to Willowwood.

Etta, that same morning, had returned from dropping Drummond and Poppy off at school. Despite Tommy's assurance that Rafiq's singing was soothing Mrs Wilkinson and that she had acquired two admirers, the veteran Sir Cuthbert and a black gelding called Count Romeo who belonged to Marius's brother Philip, Etta missed her and Chisolm more and more unbearably. She had gritted her teeth and stayed away for three weeks, but like a stalker had constantly trained her binoculars across the valley.

Today she could see Mrs Wilkinson with her black and dapple-grey admirers, plus Chisolm and Horace the Shetland, turned out in a different field above Marius's drive. It was hidden from the yard and gallops, which were currently full of activity. Etta's resolve broke.

If she stole over now, she could snatch a few undetected minutes with Mrs Wilkinson. Stuffing the pockets of her moth-eaten grey cardigan with Polos, carrots and chopped apple, she set out down through the wood, slipping and clutching at willow fronds, crossing the river by a little bridge. Panting up fields, far more frozen because they faced north, she clambered over the rusty iron railings into Marius's drive. There she heard a clatter of hooves and saw the most beautiful chestnut galloping towards her, reins flying, stirrups clashing.

'Oh, you darling creature,' cried Etta. Then, as if she were urging Drummond to do up his laces: 'Stop, stop, you'll trip if you're not careful.'

Reaching into her pockets for an apple, she held out a flat palm to the horse, who ground to a halt, snorting wildly, rolling big hazel eyes.

'Come on, sweet thing, I'm sure you're hungry.'

Furious decided he was. He accepted an apple quarter and when he had polished off the rest of it, accepted two more before starting on the carrots. By this time Etta had put his reins back over his head, pushed his irons up the leathers, and was stroking his satiny neck.

'You are lovely,' sighed Etta. 'I better take you back to Marius,' then, as Furious nudged her pockets, she realized regretfully that she had only Polos left for Mrs Wilkinson. Perhaps she had better come back another day. But as she led him towards Marius's main gates, she caught sight of Rafiq scorching across the fields below on Oh My Goodness, and a Land-Rover containing Ruby and Bertie and a white-faced Marius at the wheel thundering towards her. Marius was out in a trice.

'Gimme that horse.'

But as he edged towards them, Furious flattened his ears, stamped his foot and lunged at Marius.

'Stop that.' Etta shook his bridle reprovingly. 'You mustn't bite people, have another Polo.'

Marius's drive was flanked on either side by sporadic hawthorn hedges. Having reached a gap, Etta glanced up and caught sight of Mrs Wilkinson and her entourage. A second later, Mrs Wilkinson gave a great rumble of joy and careered towards them, nearly crashing into the fence.

'Oh Wilkie!' Chucking Furious's reins to Marius, Etta ran to the railings and Mrs Wilkinson, who, whinnying, nickering, nudging, placed her head over Etta's shoulder to draw her close.

'Oh my angel,' sobbed Etta, holding her tight, rejoicing in the rumbling warmth of her body, breathing in her new-mown hay smell, soaking her charcoal-grey shoulder with tears. 'I've missed you so much.'

Their passionate embrace was only disturbed by Chisolm, who raced bleating down the hill and put her hooves up on the railings to greet Etta, butting away Count Romeo, Sir Cuthbert and Horace the Shetland to get a share of the Polos.

'That's the kind of relationship I want to have with my horsie,' cried Ruby.

So they won't buy Furious, thought Marius bleakly.

Ruby, however, was leaning over the fence gazing at Count Romeo. He was a big black athlete, with a white blaze and four white socks, and he strutted like a superstar basketball player.

'That is the most beautiful horse I've ever seen,' she gasped. 'Couldn't we buy that one instead, Bertie?'

Marius had in fact acquired Count Romeo six months ago when he was drunk, spending £20,000 altruistically given him to buy a horse by his younger brother Philip. Seduced by Count Romeo's looks as he had been by Olivia's, Marius got him home only to realize he'd acquired a complete turkey. Count Romeo was incurably lazy, stupid and so vain he admired his reflection in every puddle. Marius had even put a mirror in his box so he could worship himself all day.

The Count had now fallen in love with Mrs Wilkinson, but kept getting bitten, kicked and seen off by his wily rival, Sir Cuthbert.

Marius was sure if he trebled the price and split the difference, his brother Philip would be only too happy to be shot of the Count, so he told an overjoyed Ruby he'd see what he could do, but it might cost them.

Nothing, said Bertie proudly, would be too much for his little lady.

'I wouldn't want to hurt Furious's feelings,' whispered Ruby.

'He's so beautiful, he'll find a home soon,' said Etta, wiping her eyes and her nose on her sleeve and handing Ruby her last Polo to give to the Count, and the love affair was consummated.

After Rafiq arrived and Furious greeted him with equal ecstasy, everyone retired to the yard for coffee and bacon butties, cooked by Michelle, which the rest of the yard thought was very sinister.

The sun had dried off the frost enough for them to sit in the garden and Mrs Wilkinson and Chisolm were allowed to join them.

Looking at the weeds choking the parched and dying herbaceous plants and the shaggy lawn, Etta decided a grazing goat and horse could only improve things. When Ruby and Bertie sloped off to have another love-in with Count Romeo, Etta took a deep breath and asked if she could tidy up Marius's garden.

'I'm sorry, I don't mean to interfere,' she quailed as his haggard face hardened. 'I expect Olivia did the garden.'

'Yes,' said Marius coldly. 'Anyway I can't afford it.'

'I wouldn't want paying,' stammered Etta, 'not at all, and it would only be a few hours a week. It would give me a chance to see Mrs Wilkinson. I miss her so desperately. I had a big garden in Dorset and I miss that so much too. It would be such a pleasure.'

For a moment Marius glared at her.

'OK,' he said brusquely. 'Probably be good for Mrs Wilkinson, she's missed you too, and thanks for catching Furious before he killed someone.'

At that moment, Ruby and Bertie returned.

'Count Romeo is such a charmer,' sighed Ruby. 'Can your brother possibly be persuaded?'

'I'll see what I can do. He's getting married quite soon, perhaps you could throw in a Bertie Bouncer Kingsize,' said Marius. For the first time he smiled and they all laughed, because his stony despair had before been so palpable, it was like seeing a corpse come back to life.

'Tommy's been telling me about your syndicate with Mrs Wilkinson, Etta, if I may call you Etta,' confided Ruby. 'I hope we'll have the pleasure of receiving you in our box at the races, bearing in mind Mrs Wilkinson and Romeo are such friends, and Tommy was saying they both might be ready to run in a few weeks.'

From that day, Mrs Wilkinson cheered up. Rafiq, who was passionately grateful to Etta for saving and loving Furious, sang to her, Tommy cosseted her and Etta dropped in for an hour or two a day to garden, during which time Mrs Wilkinson and Chisolm trailed round after her.

There were also her two equine admirers.

Sir Cuthbert belonged to Nancy Crowe, the local MFH, who, because of a sentimental attachment to Marius's father, left the horse with Marius, even though he'd been off for two seasons with a tendon problem. Sir Cuthbert had been a good servant to the yard, coming second and third on numerous occasions. Heartbroken when little Gifted Child had been taken by Shade to Harvey-Holden, he had transferred his affections to Mrs Wilkinson. Now they called and called to each other when separated. Mrs Wilkinson knew Sir Cuthbert's approaching footsteps from twenty other horses and set up a din. Once united they would spend hours kissing and grooming each other. Count Romeo, looking on longingly, was occasionally let into the circle. Horace the Shetland, given to Romeo as a friend, had got a crush on Chisolm, who butted him away with her horns less and less.

'Love is in the air,' sang Rafiq.

As the weather grew colder, Mrs Wilkinson was stabled with Cuthbert and Romeo on either side.

'It's so sweet the way she pushes her hay through the hole in the wall to Sir Cuthbert when he's hungry,' Tommy told Etta. 'And when she's hungry she scrapes her food bowl up and down the wall or drops it and rattles her empty water bowls.'

Adoring making people laugh, Mrs Wilkinson started doing the tricks Dora had taught her for the lads: pulling faces, shaking hooves, unpeeling a banana before eating it, curtseying and playing football with Chisolm.

'Next time we play football against Rupert Campbell-Black or Harvey-Holden, she and Chisolm better be in the side,' said Josh.

'We'll need them anyway,' said blonde Tresa gloomily. 'If Marius lays off any more people we won't be able to field a team.'

Etta, now visiting most days, was making friends, particularly with Rafiq, Tommy and little Angel, at sixteen the youngest member of the yard.

'I love working here,' Angel told Etta. 'I rode out two lots this morning and had a shag in the tack room.'

'Really,' said Etta.

There was a lot of yard bitching about Michelle, who was getting more and more up herself.

'When I go inside to pray, Michelle say, "Why don't you ask Allah to teach you to ride?"' stormed Rafiq.

'How rude,' squeaked Etta. 'You ride beautifully.'

Michelle, who clearly resented the fact that Rafiq didn't respond to her charms, never stopped bitching at him. Every time there was a reference to terrorism in the papers, she'd say, 'Oh, that's your lot again.'

'And she put poor little Angel, because she's young and pretty, on the most difficult horses,' raged Rafiq, 'and she cheeky Collie the whole time, and he's her boss. Collie complain to Marius who always defends Michelle.'

The morning after this conversation, the entire yard heard raised voices coming from Marius's office. Next moment Mistletoe the lurcher shot out and took quivering refuge in the tack room between Tommy's legs.

'There isn't any more fucking money to give you,' Marius was shouting.

Collie had started as a boy, looking after the hunt horses when Marius's father was Master, and had worked his way up to the glory years when the Throstledown flag was always flying. Marius had then made Collie head lad and given him and his wife a four-bedroom house as a wedding present with only £40,000 of mortgage left to pay.

Having for years invested his heart and expertise in nurturing Ilkley Hall, Gifted Child, Preston and most recently Bafford Playboy, Collie, although not showing it, had been devastated when Shade took these and his other horses away. He hated seeing them at the races, hepped up, unsettled, calling out to him, but now winning glory for Harvey-Holden, who was going from strength to strength and continually sneering about Throstledown's decline.

Collie was accustomed to running a winning ship, and bringing peace and harmony to the yard. Olivia had been his great pal and he missed her too. In turn Collie worried about Rafiq, who every night rolled up his mattress and rode it, practising changing his whip from one hand to the other, obsessively watching videos of Rogue Rogers, Killer O'Kagan and Bluey Charteris. Rafiq had a very short fuse and had nearly lost it the other day, when Michelle threatened Furious with a pitchfork. Something must explode soon.

Marius, meanwhile, was impressed with Mrs Wilkinson but wasn't having much success in teaching her to load or accept a male rider on her back. She did, however, tolerate Rafiq with his soft voice, silken hands and fluid body. But Marius was no more ready to allow Rafiq to ride her in races than Amber Lloyd-Foxe, even though Amber was so determined to become a professional that she'd taken a foundation course at the British Racing School. Now qualified as a conditional jockey, she was allowed to carry 7 pounds less in races until she'd notched up twenty wins. Knowing Mrs Wilkinson's first race must be soon, she rang in every day asking for rides. She even offered to work for nothing if Marius allowed her to school the horses.

Michelle had great delight in fielding these calls until Amber shouted, 'The only way to get put up is to sleep with the trainer, and you know all about that,' and hung up.

49

By late autumn Mrs Wilkinson was flying over hurdles with Tommy on her back and Marius was so pleased with her progress, he entered her for a midweek maiden hurdle at Worcester. The Willowwood syndicate became frightfully excited, revving up for their first race. They had exerted huge self-control and stayed away, but had constantly pestered Etta for news of their horse.

Many had missed dropping in to see her at Badger's Court. Alban and Pocock had called in as an excuse to see Etta, Dora and Trixie on their exeats and Joey and Woody on their breaks. Alan had come for black coffee when swaying home from the pub, Miss Painswick for a gossip and Chris and Chrissie bearing bread and butter pudding, which in the pub had been renamed 'Mrs Wilkinson's Favourite'.

Neither Shagger, the Weatheralls nor the Cunliffes had visited in the past, but now boasted about 'our horse in training, sired by Rupert Campbell-Black's Derby winner'.

The Cunliffes had returned early from Lanzarote and the Major had most unusually ducked out of a meeting of the Willowwood Improvement Society, which he was supposed to be chairing. Instead he emailed the rest of the committee to watch the 2.15 at Worcester on Wednesday, where they might see 'a most familiar face' in the winners enclosure.

As the race was midweek Shagger, Phoebe and Toby took a day's holiday and the train down from London, having emailed most of the City, Fulham and Chelsea to say that Rogue Rogers would be riding 'my horse in the 2.15'.

To everyone's disappointment, Seth was filming. Dora and Trixie were stuck in school. Dora, however, alerted the press to look up the court case and the point-to-point at which Mrs

237

Wilkinson had beaten Bafford Playboy, who had since won three races. Niall the vicar was equally fed up to have a two o'clock funeral but had exhorted his tiny congregation to pray for 'the safe return of our Village Horse on Wednesday'.

Joey just skived, leaving his indignant team – all fans of Mrs Wilkinson – applying wallpaper at £8,700 a roll to the dining room at Badger's Court, with a portable television. They all had huge bets.

Direct Debbie bore Miss Painswick off to Cavendish House to do some shopping. In the next-door booth, Painswick heard a mobile playing 'Edelweiss' and Debbie's voice saying: 'Indeed – the two fifteen at Worcester. Our National Hunt horse, Mrs Wilkinson, will be making her hurdling debut under rules.'

To mark the solemnity of the occasion, Miss Painswick splurged on an olive green coat in Whiskas brown to go with the blue hat to match Hengist's scarf and emailed her old boss that he might see his protégé Rafiq at the races. Debbie, meanwhile, bought a royal-blue trouser suit and a vermilion sombrero to brighten the greyest day.

A heartbroken Pocock didn't dare abandon Ione midweek. Tilda too was unable to leave her class, who'd all drawn good luck cards for Mrs Wilkinson and would be allowed to watch the race in the staff room at the end of the dinner hour. Tilda, as Romy and Martin were being thoroughly unhelpful, had heroically offered to take Drummond and Poppy home after school to give Etta a chance to celebrate after the race.

'If she wins, you'll be guest of honour at the pub that evening,' promised Alan, who was not getting on with his book on depression.

Etta, who couldn't afford to buy anything new, took her charcoal-grey coat to the cleaners, to rid it of Cadbury and Priceless's hairs and muddy paw prints. She tried pulling her old pale blue beret on to the left side of her head, but her ear stuck out hideously through her hair on the right. At least that looked better than the check cap and matching scarf with snaffles on in tan, easily Etta's worst colour, which Direct Debbie and Painswick had brought her back as a treat from their shopping trip.

Expectation, however, was wildly high.

Two days before, Jase the farrier put four light racing plates on Mrs Wilkinson's little feet, 'so she'll no longer feel she's running in gumboots'. Jase returned, as usual, full of gossip. The yard was going from bad to worse. Marius, drunk, had accused Collie of sleeping with Olivia. Collie was so enraged, everyone was terrified he was going to walk.

Collie, not Marius, would accompany Mrs Wilkinson to Worcester on Wednesday because Marius was running a new horse, Count Romeo, belonging to a rich new owner, Bertie Barraclough, at Rutminster. Marius had had great difficulty finding a race bad enough for Count Romeo to win.

Bertie had hired a box and invited his entire board to watch. Ruby Barraclough would also have gone ballistic if, in an attempt to persuade Count Romeo to concentrate, Marius had hidden his beauty behind blinkers.

Expectation was terrifyingly high here as well.

Race day dawned. Down at five thirty, as the constellation of the swan began her flight and Leo the lion sank into the west, Tommy loved to be first out to feed and water the horses. They were all so pleased to see her. Mrs Wilkinson, already banging her bowl, was very put out to be limited to reduced racehorse nuts, little water and no hay, so she wouldn't be bloated before her race.

'It's your big day, darling,' Tommy consoled her. 'The honour of Throstledown is at stake.'

Yielding to her phobia of lorries, Marius allowed Tommy and Rafiq to take Mrs Wilkinson, whinnying continually for Chisolm, and History Painting, who was entered in the fourth race, to Worcester in the trailer.

Tommy drove past the great cathedral, through the town to the beautiful oval racecourse surrounded by trees and with the river running along the north side. She then felt a bit silly parking the little trailer beside huge lorries belonging to Isa Lovell, Harvey-Holden, Dermie O'Driscoll and Rupert Campbell-Black, all elaborately decorated with designs of horses jumping or loping past winning posts. Harry, the lorry park attendant, however, welcomed everyone with equal warmth.

Tommy liked to relax young horses by getting them to the course three hours before their race. Now she set about plaiting up Mrs Wilkinson.

As Mrs Wilkinson's first race was taking place in November rather than January, the spanking new Ford Transit Chris was getting sprayed with the Willowwood colours wasn't ready, so Alan, Etta, the Major and Debbie, Painswick, Joey, Woody and Chris piled into a hired minibus. A very subdued, dried-out Alban Travis-Lock, bossily directed by the Major, took the wheel. Etta, trying to cheer up Alban, took the seat behind them.

'Isn't this the most exciting day of our lives?'

If only she had something more glamorous to wear, but at least Seth wasn't there to witness her dowdiness.

In deference to Alban, Chris was surreptitiously pouring Bloody Marys out of a thermos into paper cups and circulating them to everyone else in the bus. How proudly they read about Mrs Wilkinson in the *Racing Post*, which tipped her to win.

'Probably because Marius has put up Rogue,' said Woody.

'He's never ridden her before,' protested Etta.

'Marius believes horses need someone experienced on their backs in their first race,' said Alan. 'Rogue had a pony under his arse before he could walk.'

'Got a pony under him today,' guffawed Joey.

'Ponies stop at fourteen two,' said Etta indignantly. 'Mrs Wilkinson's fourteen three.'

It was a bitterly cold day, with the trees wrapping their remaining leaves round their bare limbs and a vicious east wind sweeping those they had shed across the course. But nothing could dim the syndicate's expectations.

How proudly they collected their red owners' badges at the gates to tie on to lapel or bag, how proudly they repaired to the Owners and Trainers bar, where Etta insisted on buying the first round. How proudly they took their places in the owners' stand and watched Rogue Rogers win the 1.15 by ten lengths. He was also riding the favourite in the 1.45, so a win on Wilkie would mean a treble.

'There's a lot resting on your shoulders, kiddo,' chided Tommy as she polished the pewter coat of Mrs Wilkinson, who was increasingly put out by the lack of food. An inch of water in a bucket was no substitute.

The syndicate were returning to the bar when Shagger, Toby and Phoebe arrived from London. Phoebe, looking enchanting in a little green wool suit and a fur hat, immediately cried:

'Who's going to buy us a drink?'

'Have a coffee to warm you up,' said the Major, who was getting wily.

Shagger, still sulking at not being banker and getting his hands on a pot of money, had no intention of buying a round, so Alan ordered everyone except poor Alban a glass of red.

'You look gorgeous, Debbie, that is a serious hat. You must lead Mrs Wilkinson in,' raved Phoebe as the scarlet sombrero blew off for a third time and Woody scuttled away to retrieve it.

'What a pity Trixie and Dora aren't here to add a bit of glamour for the telly,' continued Phoebe, who actually loved being the baby of the party, 'but at least they won't shout at me for wearing fur. You look stunning too, Miss Painswick. I couldn't sleep a wink all night, I was so nervous.'

240

Etta, who hadn't slept either, felt sick. The hurdles suddenly looked huge and she felt so responsible for all these friends who'd kept having even bigger bets.

Having cheered on Rogue to win his second race, they hurried down to the pre-parade ring, gathering round an open stall to watch Tommy and Rafiq tacking up Mrs Wilkinson, who gave a thunderous whicker of welcome when she saw Etta and her friends.

Before a race, to check the girths aren't pinching, a horse's forelegs have to be stretched out one at a time.

'Aaaaaaah,' went the syndicate, as Mrs Wilkinson, without any prompting, proffered each leg in turn to Rafiq.

Tommy meanwhile was sponging her face and mouth with water. 'Because she's not allowed to drink anything,' she explained.

Like me, thought Alban wearily. He could murder a quadruple Bell's.

Rafiq had his arm round Mrs Wilkinson's neck, constantly stroking and calming her. Tommy, in a dark blue jacket and black trousers, her face red from exertion, her unruly dark hair restrained by a blue scarf, waited until she was about to lead Mrs Wilkinson up to the paddock before whipping off her tail bandage, undoing six little plaits and applying a squirt of mane-and-tail spray, so Mrs Wilkinson's tail exploded in a crinkly white fountain. Even Shagger cheered.

'She looks wonderful! Thank you, Tommy,' cried Etta.

She looked wonderful in the paddock but very small, which elicited more jokes about Shetlands and 'shrunk in the wash'. As she led Mrs Wilkinson round anti-clockwise, the public ringing the rails could see that Tommy had hung a black patch over her blind eye.

The favourite was a lovely bay mare called Heroine, who was trained by Harvey-Holden. H-H's ferret-like face contorted with fury as he caught sight of Mrs Wilkinson, then turned into a sneer, his upper lip curling more than the brim of his brown felt hat.

'What's that pony's handicap?' asked Heroine's owner.

'Having Marius Oakridge as a trainer,' snarled Harvey-Holden. 'Her odds, for some unaccountable reason, are even shorter than her legs.'

On the bookies' boards and on the big screen, Mrs Wilkinson was now second favourite at 5–1. Etta felt even sicker.

Tommy won the turnout.

'Pity she can't do something about her own appearance,' said

Michelle, who was about to tack up History Painting for the next race.

The jockeys were flowing into the paddock.

'Don't our silks look lush on Rogue?' sighed Phoebe, as in emerald green with a pale green weeping willow back and front he was waylaid by photographers and television presenters.

Etta noticed the contrast between the slim, emaciated jockeys with their ashen, often spotty faces and frequently cut lips, polite and formal as little corporals, and the fat, shiny-suited owners flushed from hospitality.

Rogue looked different. For a start he had a tan, his hands were as big as a prop forward's, his shoulders huge and muscular. On his collar was printed the words 'Venturer Television', on his breeches it said 'Bar Sinister'.

'I'd like to sponsor Rogue's thighs,' giggled Phoebe, as he strutted towards them, speculative eyes turned turquoise by the Willowwood colours, slapping his whip against muddy boots, going for the treble.

'Connections', as owners, trainer and stable lad belonging to an individual horse are grandiosely known, hung on his every word, straining to hear, as if he were George Clooney or Prince William.

'I've studied the video, she's a decent hoss,' lied Rogue. 'I'll settle her mid-division and hont her round.'

'Please don't hit her with that whip,' Etta couldn't help saying.

'Shhhhhh,' hissed the horrified syndicate as though Etta had farted in church.

'Rogue needs his whip to guide her,' snapped Alan.

'We mustn't wish you good luck, it's unlucky, so break a leg,' called out Debbie heartily.

On their way to watch the race, Etta bumped into Amber Lloyd-Foxe, who was riding in a later ladies' race and looked very upset.

'I should be riding her,' she pleaded to Etta, 'please put in a good word.'

Up in the Owners and Trainers, aware that owners invariably hug each other if their horses win, Shagger placed himself next to Woody. Etta was shivering so uncontrollably, Alban put his greatcoat round her shoulders so it fell to her ankles, like Mrs Wilkinson's rug. God, she's sweet, he thought wistfully.

Everyone had their mobiles poised to report victory.

Back in Willowwood, the whole of Greycoats was now watching on the school television. Dora and Trixie were watching at Bagley Hall. Joey rushed downstairs to put on another hundred for himself and Woody. If she won at 5–1, that would pay the mortgage and the gas bill.

Through his binoculars, far down the course on the left, the Major could see the jockeys circling. For once the piss-taking Rogue was the butt of their humour, as they patted him on the head from the superior height of their horses.

'Oh Daddy,' said Debbie, taking the Major's hands, 'this is a dream come true.'

'Good thing to have a grey,' Alban told Etta, 'always identify them.'

Through her shaking binoculars, Etta could see only that Mrs Wilkinson wasn't happy, her coat white with lather as she gazed longingly in the direction of the stables and the lorry park.

'I can't look.' Phoebe put her hands over her eyes. 'Tell me what's going on.'

'Are you ready, jockeys?' called the starter. 'OK, then off you go,' and encouraged by a steward cracking a whip behind them, off they went.

Except for Mrs Wilkinson. Feeling her hanging back, Rogue gave her a couple of hefty whacks. Next moment, she'd veered left, ducking under the rails, scraping him off as, with lightning reflexes, he kicked his feet out of his irons, and depositing him on the grass before scorching off to the lorry park.

'Hurrah,' yelled an overjoyed Harvey-Holden from behind the stunned syndicate, 'that's one less horse to beat.'

'I can't look,' cried Phoebe. 'What's going on?'

'Bugger all,' said Chris as the rest of the runners thundered by on the first circuit.

Harry, the lorry park attendant, grabbed Mrs Wilkinson as she hurtled towards him. By the time Tommy caught up with her, the race had been won by Heroine and a gloating Harvey-Holden.

Collapse of stout syndicate.

Everyone was flattened with disappointment.

Etta was in tears. 'I'm so dreadfully sorry.' Alan and Miss Painswick gave her their handkerchiefs.

Alan tried to comfort her. 'Lots of owners never get a winner.'

'We should have brought Niall with us,' said Woody. 'He'd have prayed us into the frame.'

Everyone, to Etta's white, horrified face, was very sympathetic.

'I must go to her.' She wiped her eyes. 'Rogue shouldn't have hit her. Why didn't Marius tell him?'

'Jockeys are paid to use their crops,' spluttered the Major the moment Etta ran off down the steps. 'Rogue's had two wins already. Proof of the pudding. This has cost us three thousand plus a hundred and eighty-five pounds a month.'

'I wasted a day's holiday,' pouted Phoebe.

'We came back from Lanzarote,' grumbled Debbie.

'I'm sure she'll win next time,' protested Painswick. 'I expect something frightened the poor little soul.'

'All trainers go through lousy seasons,' said Shagger contemptuously, 'but Marius is having a lousy decade. We should have gone to Harvey-Holden,' he added. Looking down, they watched a returning Heroine being clapped back to the winners enclosure.

At least I won't have to fork out for the champagne and I'll have lots of people to interview about depression, thought Alan.

'What happened to Mrs Wilkinson?' cried the children at Greycoats.

Major Cunliffe's committee, who'd stopped proceedings to watch the race, had a good laugh to see 'a most familiar face' looking absolutely livid.

50

Rogue returned from the race with only his pride hurt. Temporarily denied his treble, he needed to collect his saddle and pull himself together for the big race on History Painting. On his way he bumped into a jubilant Amber.

'Aren't you going to debrief connections?' she mocked. 'I was taught to work out what happened in a race and why it happened, so you can talk positively to the owner and trainer.'

'Fuck off,' snarled Rogue, disappearing into the weighing room to change silks and receive more mobbing up.

Etta found Mrs Wilkinson in the stables, head down, trembling violently from head to foot, with Tommy hugging, stroking and desperately trying to comfort her.

'Rogue said he'd watched the video.'

'He says that to everyone.'

Etta's mobile rang. It was a spitting Dora.

'It was all Rogue's fault for giving her those reminders.'

Back in the bar, a grey-faced Joey downed a treble whisky. Having already lost £500 on Mrs Wilkinson, he was just wondering whether to try to recoup his losses by backing History Painting in the next race when his mobile rang, and he went even greyer.

Valent had rolled up at Badger's Court unexpectedly, just as the ceiling collapsed in the dining room taking all the £8,700-a-roll wallpaper with it. Joey would have to get a taxi straight back to Willowwood.

Joey had in fact met Collie for a drink in the Fox the previous night. Both men had children at Greycoats. Collie told Joey if he didn't get any winners today, he was handing in his notice. Marius was drinking far too much. Trainers should either be charming to owners or get inside the heads of their horses. Marius, at the moment, was doing neither.

'Where might you go?' Joey had asked. 'Christ,' he said when Collie told him.

History Painting and Rogue fell three out in the next race, which was won by Harvey-Holden with Shade's horse, Gifted Child.

'Still waiting for Mrs Wilkinson to come in?' he called out bitchily to Alan and Alban, as he loped off yet again to the winners enclosure.

Marius had an equally dreadful time at Rutminster, where Bertie and Ruby Barraclough felt even more humiliated than Major Cunliffe. Count Romeo had been absolutely useless, trotting up at the back of the field, fooling around, gazing at seagulls and sheep.

Since the court case, Valent Edwards had been sorting out businesses in India and China. Back in England he had been goaded by Bonny Richards, who, determined to have a minimalist house in London, had been pressurizing him to throw out Pauline's stuff. Not realizing Mrs Wilkinson and Chisolm had gone to Marius, she'd also been nagging him to get them out of Badger's Court or they'd soon be claiming squatters' rights.

'I'm not going to live in the house if they're there.'

Valent had therefore returned unexpectedly to Willowwood to find Mrs Wilkinson's stable being knocked down and rebuilt and his entire workforce, with no manager in sight, watching Mrs Wilkinson screw up on a portable television.

Legend has it that it was Valent's ensuing roar of rage that brought down the ceiling of the dining room and all of the £8,700-a-roll wallpaper. This resulted in an extremely unpleasant hour for a returning Joey.

When Etta got back to Little Hollow, her telephone was ringing. It was Valent.

'How dare you send Mrs Wilkinson to a two-bit yard and a crap trainer without telling me,' he roared.

'Marius was local,' stammered Etta. 'We wanted to be able to go on seeing her.'

'I didn't allow her to camp out in my study for nearly two years for that.'

'I know. I'm so sorry.'

'Or come back from China to win her back in the court case.'

'I know, I know. You saved her from Harvey-Holden.'

'She'd be better off with him. At least he gets winners.'

For once Etta was glad the mature conifers were protecting her from Valent's wrath.

'Marius hasn't had a winner for two hundred and twenty days. It's absolutely goot-wrenching, he hasn't even got anyone manning his phone. I've been trying to get through all day. Why didn't you send her to Rupert Campbell-Black? He helped you enough giving you his lawyer.'

'I know,' sobbed Etta, 'I'm so sorry, but Rupert's too big, too impersonal. I was frightened he'd be tough on her, she's so sensitive.' God, she sounded like Phoebe.

'Well, you picked the wrong trainer. Collie's leaving.'

'No,' gasped Etta. 'Collie's wonderful.'

'He can't survive on the pittance Marius pays him, so he's off. Who owns Mrs Wilkinson now?'

Etta quailed. 'We all do, all the Willowwood syndicate.'

'Joodge Wilkes gave her to you,' snarled Valent.

I couldn't afford to keep her, Etta wanted to plead. If she'd told Valent, he might have bought Wilkie for her. He'd done so much, she was terrified of imposing any more.

As if reading her thoughts, Valent shouted, 'You might have given me first refusal.'

'I'm so sorry.'

'No good being bluddy sorry, it's a bluddy disgrace. You've let me down and you've let Joodge Wilkes down.'

'Where's Collie gone?' whispered Etta.

'To Harvey-Holden,' said Valent, and hung up.

Harvey-Holden had always relied on cheap foreign labour, Poles, Ukrainians, Czechs and Pakistanis, who tended to form little ghettoes and speak only in their own languages. He needed the emollient Collie to hire and fire, rebuild morale and then unite people.

Collie had been seduced by the wonderful yard being built and paid for by Jude the Obese, and the house with four bedrooms and a lovely garden that Harvey-Holden was prepared to give him. Olivia, whom he'd adored but never slept with because he loved his own wife, would be around acting as a buffer between him and Shade the impossible.

He longed to be part of a winning team again. Best of all, when he walked into the yard, was the rumble of joy from Playboy, Ilkley Hall, little Gifted Child, wayward Preston and all Shade's other horses, which he'd loved and understood. Now they would be his again.

51

Marius was almost as devastated by Collie's departure as by Olivia's, but again he was too proud and too obstinate to beg him to come back. The story, leaked by Harvey-Holden, was soon all over the racing pages. This upset Marius as well as his owners.

Bertie Barraclough, for example, was very unhappy with Count Romeo. After the fiasco at Rutminster, Marius entered the horse in a maiden hurdle at Stratford. Giving the ride to Rogue, he told him to get his bat out. As a result, the handsome Count was up with the leaders. Then he suddenly caught sight of himself on the big screen, swerved right, cantered across the track to admire himself, to the hysterics of the crowd, and came in last.

'Racing is all a question of whether,' quipped Harvey-Holden, 'whether Count Romeo is going to get off his fat black arse or not.' This was quoted in the *Racing Post* and read by Bertie, who disapproved of bad language.

Rogue was so angry he shouted at Marius in the unsaddling enclosure, 'Go back to school. I'm not riding for you any more until you learn to train horses.'

There was speculation in the yard as to who would take over Collie's job. Josh, Tresa, Michelle and Tommy were all in the frame. But Marius was notoriously bad at decisions and appointed no one. Foul-tempered by day, by night he drowned his sorrows, staggering out with a torch long after evening stables to give his horses a last handful of feed and check their doors were shut. Invariably, next morning Tommy would find the wheelbarrow turned over, feed scattered all over the yard, and would hastily sweep up before the other lads appeared.

One particularly freezing morning, when Tommy was admiring the winter stars and breaking ice on the horses' water bowls, a flash sports car drove up. Bulked out by two pairs of long johns, breeches, three polo necks, a body protector, a fleece under the jacket, a scarf, a bandanna under the hat, ear muffs and gloves, the figure jumping out was unrecognizable. All anyone could see was the eyes.

'Like those burkas your women wear,' said Tresa dismissively to Rafiq, who was shivering worse than Mrs Wilkinson because he couldn't afford many clothes.

'Who the hell is it?' Josh asked Tommy, as Marius legged the stranger up on to a new horse who hadn't been on the horse walker or done any road work. Now, wired to the moon, the horse put in a mighty buck, then galloped down the drive, raced towards the gate into the road and screamed to a halt without unseating her.

'She can certainly ride,' said Tommy.

During two more lots, the stranger had both her horses flying like angels. Later, when everyone was having breakfast, she took off her hat and bandanna.

'God, one gets sweaty under these things.'

It was Amber Lloyd-Foxe.

Michelle, who never bothered to ride out when she had a period, was furious when she found out.

'What's she doing here? I hope Marius isn't considering her for head lad. That class always stick together. She probably went to school with Marius's sister.'

'Bollocks, she's only nineteen,' said Josh. 'She just wants to ride races.'

Amber, hearing Collie had gone and Marius was short-staffed, had not only offered to ride for nothing, merely to get experience, but also to help out in the yard, even to drive the lorry.

Reluctantly, Marius agreed and, also reluctantly, noticed how beautifully Mrs Wilkinson went for her over both fences and hurdles.

'You ride very well for a girl,' Rafiq told her.

'I ride very well full stop,' snapped Amber.

Rafiq, Tommy, Angel, even Josh and Tresa were delighted to have her around, because it bugged the hell out of Michelle that Amber wasn't remotely afraid of her.

It was also noticed that Rogue had made it up with Marius and was coming down more often to school horses. To begin with he indulged in horseplay on the gallops, pulling the bridle over Mrs Wilkinson's head, goosing Amber, leaving a welt on her bottom when he whacked her with his whip, but after she slashed him across the face with her own whip he backed off.

52

As Mrs Wilkinson had hardly exerted herself at Worcester, Marius shortly afterwards entered her for another maiden hurdle at Newbury, where a different mix of the syndicate turned up to cheer her on. Shagger, utterly sceptical of the mare's ability, persuaded Toby to stay in London for some City lunch. Ione and Debbie were too busy battling over next Sunday's church flowers. They were united, however, in their displeasure that Niall the vicar had been persuaded he needed a day off and gone to the races. Why couldn't he bless Mrs Wilkinson before she left Willowwood?

Nor was Ione pleased that Alban had been hijacked again to drive the Ford Transit, which Chris the landlord had finally collected. Handsomely resprayed in emerald green and decorated on both sides with pale green willows and the words 'Willowwood Syndicate', it was now being revved up outside the Fox.

'Isn't it lovely,' cried Etta. Weighed down by carrier bags, she came running up the high street. 'Oh, thank you, Chris.'

'Mrs Wilkinson better win today so we can pay for it,' said Chris, winking at everyone as he loaded a groaning picnic hamper and a large box of drink.

He was staying behind to man the Fox as it was the turn of pretty, wistful Chrissie, who still hadn't managed to get pregnant, to go to the races. Scuttling past driver Alban, who she'd last seen when they grappled on the churchyard grass during little Wayne East's christening, she found a seat at the back.

'Now you be'ave yourselves,' teased Chris, further winking to mitigate the cheekiness, or Mrs T-L will have something to say when you get 'ome, Alban.' He banged on the bus roof as it set off to Newbury.

'You could always hang Chris out of the window and use him as an indicator,' observed Alan.

The instant they rounded the bend, Joey put back the gold pen he'd taken out of his woolly hat to mark the *Racing Post* and, announcing he was going to snog in the back, moved seats to join Chrissie and pour her a large brandy and ginger.

The bus was impeded by a huge lorry delivering an indoor swimming pool to Primrose Mansions, whereupon Alan leapt out and redirected it to Harvey-Holden's yard.

'Jude the Obese can use it as a bidet,' he told the giggling passengers. 'Poor Alban – must be hell driving a lot of piss artists,' he muttered, filling his glass with Pouilly Fumé and handing the bottle on to Seth.

'Hell,' agreed Seth. He'd just finished filming in several episodes of *Holby City*, and was feeling exhausted but exuberantly end-of-termish. 'But I wish he'd get his finger out or we'll miss the last race.'

Alban was indeed sad. To save water, at his wife's insistence he was wearing a wool check shirt for a third day. He was chilled to the marrow because Ione believed in extra jerseys rather than central heating. Finally, he'd heard that a £200,000 job to chair an independent review of an independent economic review accused of government bias had fallen through because he was considered too right wing.

If only he could have poured his heart out to Etta. How pathetic to be jealous of Pocock, who'd taken the seat beside her.

Major Cunliffe would also have liked to sit next to Etta. Freed of his wife's beady chaperonage, he was feeling flirtatious and was delighted, as inky clouds massed on the horizon, that his grim forecast looked correct. Up the front, he was again acting as Alban's satnav, which didn't speed up the proceedings particularly as Alban kept slowing down to identify the inhabitants of the great houses along the route.

'That's Robinsgrove, Ricky France-Lynch's place. His wife Daisy did a lovely oil of Araminta.

'That's Valhalla,' he announced ten minutes later, 'where the late Roberto Rannaldini lived. Absolute shit but brilliant musician.'

As he turned up the wireless to drown the Major's directions, the bus was flooded with Beethoven's Ninth Symphony.

'Rannaldini's son Wolfgang married Tabitha Campbell-Black. I was at school with both of them,' piped up Phoebe, who'd come without Toby because she'd got a crush on Seth. He looked even more gorgeous in that black pea jacket with those bags under his naughty eyes.

Phoebe was not over-pleased when Trixie, playing truant from yet another school, flagged down the bus thirty miles outside Willowwood, disappeared into the upended-coffin-shaped loo and emerged in black boots and tights, a groin-level shocking-pink coat and a black trilby decorated with a pink rose.

'You'll run out of schools to get expelled from soon,' reproved Alan.

'Fat chance,' sighed Trixie, taking a swig from her father's bottle. 'With Mummy standing by to offer to build them a new science block, I'll get in anywhere.' She smiled at Seth.

Alan knew he should send her back to school, but he was so proud Seth thought she was pretty. Trixie, however, fancied Woody and took a large drink and the seat next to him.

Down the bus, Dora, also playing truant, had three mobiles to her ears and was reading the *Racing Post.*

'What does it say about Mrs Wilkinson?' asked Woody, who had rather nervously taken another day off from the big job of clearing Lester Bolton's wood.

'It says,' giggled Dora, 'connections have decided to persevere with Mrs Wilkinson because of her very promising homework. More than can be said for Trixie and me.'

'What do they say about Count Romeo?' Marius had entered him in the same race.

' "At least Mrs Wilkinson won't come last," ' read Dora. ' "That place is reserved for that dreadful lazy pig Count Romeo." '

'Goodness,' gasped Etta, 'I hope Bertie and Ruby Barraclough don't read that. They're threatening to ask for their fifty thousand back.'

'That's Rupert Campbell-Black's place,' shouted Alban, pointing to a beautiful golden house against a background of beech trees. The bus nearly keeled over as everyone rushed to the right to have a look. 'Declan O'Hara lives in the Priory across the valley,' added Alban.

'Declan's daughter Taggie, who married Rupert, cooked breakfast for us the day we met Marius,' called out Phoebe.

Guiltiest of all syndicate members was Tilda Flood. Yesterday, with lowered eyes, she had asked for the day off for 'personal reasons' and not elaborated. Whereupon the head, Mrs Hammond, aware how often and how uncomplainingly Tilda covered for staff members when their children were ill, had urged her to go. Tilda rolled up in a new dark crimson suit and medium-heeled brown boots bought especially to impress Shagger, only to learn when they were halfway to Newbury that he'd ratted without telling her.

Aware that she'd risked her job with a lie, Tilda burst into tears.

'Don't worry,' Seth hugged her, 'you'll have much more fun without him and it'll give us blokes a chance. Come and sit here beside

Alan.' This gave him the opportunity to move nearer to Trixie.

Alan poured Tilda a large drink and soon decided she was much less skittish and silly when Shagger wasn't around.

'Mrs Wilkinson's the first horse I'm not frightened of,' she confided. 'I like petting them and feeding them carrots, but with a fence between us.'

'D'you feel that way with men?' teased Alan. 'That's a very pretty suit.'

'Bit too bright for the races,' stage-whispered Phoebe to Miss Painswick. 'You should wear brown and greens, camouflagey things that blend into the countryside. Trixie's pink coat is completely OTT.'

Phoebe then launched into hostess mode.

'You should be sitting next to Niall, Tilda, singletons together. Nice seeing Etta next to Pocock, both lonely people.'

'Alban, Pocock and the Major all have crushes on Granny,' snapped Trixie, who was painting her nails purple.

'That's ridiculous,' hissed Phoebe. 'Etta's quite the wrong class for Uncle Alban.' Then, raising her voice: 'Sure you're going to be warm enough in that thin suit, Mrs Bancroft? You should invest in a thick coat. I saw such a lovely snuff-brown one in Larkminster with a big bow, it'd really suit you.'

'I'm not great in brown. It'd look lovely on you.'

'Oh no, it'd be much too mature for me.'

'I'd invest in a pair of earplugs first,' muttered Dora. 'Yes, Seth Bainton, he's just done a stint in *Holby City*,' she added into her mobile.

Joey's arm along the back seat had drifted down to stroke Chrissie's white neck.

Etta was aware of Pocock's bony body pressing against hers each time he leant across to make disparaging remarks about everyone's gardens as they passed. She tried to chat cheerfully to hide how devastated she'd been by Valent's harsh words after the Worcester disaster. She'd never dreamt he'd be so bothered over Mrs Wilkinson. Horrified he thought her ungrateful, she had written a crawling letter of apology, wondering which of his six houses to send it to, and planted a lot more bulbs and shrubs in his garden, where Joey's men had finished. She couldn't stop fretting and felt so guilty about the sweet judge who'd given her the horse.

Oh, please let Wilkie redeem herself today.

Looking up, she saw they were overtaking two lorries with WILKINSON on their sides, promoting Wilkinson's shops. Everyone was delighted by such a good-luck sign and giggled that Mrs Wilkinson must be branching out.

After they accelerated on to the motorway, Niall called for a two-minute silence to pray for the safety of Mrs Wilkinson. It was a bit difficult as Beethoven's Ninth had just reached the third movement, with the incessant drumroll sounding like the thunder of horses' hooves.

'Turn it down,' barked the Major.

Noticing what fun Woody seemed to be having with Trixie, Dora and Seth, Niall prayed to be delivered of his hopeless passion. He hadn't been able to concentrate on writing his sermon yesterday, with Woody swinging his lean body round in his harness as he pollarded the church limes.

Flashing orange balls on either side of the road warned of fog. Hoar frost silvered the tops of trees and the ploughed fields. Would the going be too firm for Mrs Wilkinson?

As they entered the outskirts of Newbury, singing along to the 'Ode to Joy', the traffic slowed to a crawl. They passed a ghostly church hidden in the trees, with a canal beside which people were walking their dogs or sitting together on benches. How lovely, Etta mused, to sit with Seth and hear his deep voice quoting poetry: ' "So well I love thee as without thee/I Love nothing." '

On a roundabout a racy metal sculpture reared up of a woman with high, pointed breasts playfighting with a man with a dangling willy.

Probably the effect I'd have on Seth, thought Etta.

'Why hasn't he got a hard-on?' asked Seth.

'Probably gay,' said Trixie.

Crossing the river with its willows, swans and fleet of coloured barges lifting the grey day like jockeys' silks, they reached a sign saying 'Welcome to historic Newbury'.

'Will be 'istoric if we get there on time,' grumbled Joey.

They were driving across a common, down a road flanked with leafless poplars as though a flock of witches had parked their broomsticks in a hurry and rushed off to cheer on Mrs Wilkinson.

'Come on,' groaned Trixie.

Ahead at last was the great red-brick stand with its flags, glass doors, little triangular turrets and gold-numbered clock over the weighing room. The roofs of the hospitality-stand rose like egg white whipped into points.

'Tommy'll be walking her around the parade ring by now,' fumed Dora. 'We won't even see Mrs Wilkinson saddled up and I've alerted all the press to look out for Seth's first appearance as part of the syndicate.'

Thank God Tommy's there, nothing can go far wrong, thought Etta.

53

Much earlier in the day, Tommy had been woken by Mrs Wilkinson irritably banging her food bowl against the stable wall. Running downstairs, she found kind Sir Cuthbert shoving hay to her through the hole in the wall.

'She mustn't eat on race days.'

Count Romeo was still asleep, looking so sweet, his handsome head tucked between his curled-up forelegs.

'You mustn't let me down, Wilkie,' begged Tommy. 'Or you, Romeo, or you'll get sold despite your good looks.'

Alas, Michelle had been getting at Marius for not making her head lad, so in a weak and last moment he told her she could go to Newbury instead of Tommy, and lead up Mrs Wilkinson and later History Painting. The easy-going Tommy, protective as a lioness over her horses, had flipped.

'Mrs Wilkinson's only just got used to loading. She trusts me, so does Romeo. She'll be traumatized by Rogue riding her again and she needs me to calm her down. Michelle doesn't know anything about Mrs Wilkinson, she doesn't care about horses,' she shouted at Marius, who shouted back at her not to be so fucking insolent and spoilt.

'You think you're bloody God around horses. You went last time, it's Michelle's turn today.'

So Tommy handed in her notice.

It was arguable who was more distraught, Tommy as she led a trusting Mrs Wilkinson up the ramp and then abandoned her, or Sir Cuthbert, left behind with a bleating Chisolm, as his lady love set out with his rival Count Romeo.

'Rafiq and I'll keep an eye on Wilkie, don't worry,' Amber told Tommy as they rumbled off down the drive.

Amber was driving because Rafiq, with his police record, was having difficulty getting a licence. Michelle, who had taken the seat by the window, was pleased to be leading up Mrs Wilkinson. She had a crush on Rogue. Marius, who was foul-tempered and talked in his sleep about Olivia, wasn't proving a satisfactory lover. Although he refused to put Amber or Rafiq up on Count Romeo or Mrs Wilkinson, Michelle was jealous of Amber. The way Rogue constantly mobbed her up and Marius was so hard on her were disturbingly indicative that neither man felt neutral towards her.

Rafiq certainly didn't either. The haughty crosspatch was always doing things for Amber, skipping out, haying and watering her horses. She noticed his thigh was four inches from her own but comfortably rested against Amber's.

Both of them were furious that Tommy had been left behind. Rafiq had wanted to take her part against Marius, but was terrified of losing his job.

'Tommy really loves her horses and invests everything in them,' said Amber, for once shaken out of her normal languor.

'And I don't?' snapped Michelle.

'I didn't say that. It's just Marius being bloody-minded.' Amber groped for a cigarette, which Rafiq lit for her. 'By forcing Tommy into handing in her notice, he doesn't have to pay her redundancy money. And why the hell's he put Rogue on Mrs Wilkinson? She won't go for him.'

'Rogue can ride anything.' Michelle took out a make-up bag and started doing her face so the punters could admire her when she led up Mrs Wilkinson.

Amber was almost more fed up with Marius giving the ride on Count Romeo to the famously thick jockey Andrew Wells, known as 'Awesome'.

Awesome's claim to fame was some years ago when while working his way up as a conditional jockey he had forgotten to load one of Marius's horses, entered in the second race at Wincanton. He had therefore saddled up the young Ilkley Hall, which had been destined for the third race but won the second easily. Terrified of Marius's wrath, putting Ilkley Hall in blinkers to hide his distinctive white zigzag blaze, Awesome saddled him up again for the third race, which he also won without breaking sweat.

When Marius discovered the truth, that he'd acquired a brilliant staying chaser for next to nothing, he forgot to be angry and because Awesome was such a natural and sympathetic rider, used him when he needed a second jockey.

'Bloody stupid, putting him on Count Romeo,' fumed Amber. 'Village idiot squared.'

Michelle's freckles were now covered with base and blusher, her mean green eyes enlarged by shadow, her thin mouth by coral gloss. She was darkening her pale lashes and swore as she nearly rammed the mascara wand into her eye when Amber jammed on the brakes.

'Sorry,' murmured Amber, 'thought that deer was going to jump out.'

Rafiq smirked, and as Mrs Wilkinson's stamping grew more panic-stricken, he launched into the Pakistani lullaby that had soothed her before. Immediately the stamping stopped.

The moment he finished, as they turned off the motorway, Amber took over. ' "Early one morning/Just as the sun was rising/I heard a maid singing/In the valley below." ' She looked at Rafiq under her lashes.

Michelle was angrily reading the *Daily Express*.

'Another suicide bomb, expect you lot were responsible.'

'Shut up, Michelle,' said Amber furiously.

'I can say what I like, it's a free country.'

'Not any more it ain't. Here's a song from the Crusades,' Amber told Rafiq.

'Gaily the troubadour touched his guitar,' she sang, in her pure, clear treble:

> 'When he was hast'ning home from the war
> Singing from Palestine hither I come,
> Lady love, lady love, welcome me home.'

'War in the Middle East's still going on,' said Michelle sourly.

'Not between Rafiq and me, it isn't.'

Amber took her hand off the wheel and held Rafiq's.

'Singing from Palestine hither I come,' sang Rafiq. 'Lady love, lady love, welcome me home.'

'For God's sake concentrate on the road,' spat Michelle, furious with Amber for encouraging that sullen beast. She couldn't wait to get to the races and have a good bitch with Rogue or tell Marius how insolent they were being.

Rancid with animosity, they rolled into the racecourse.

An hour later, Michelle had just tacked up a restless, sweating Mrs Wilkinson when Marius raced up, already reeking of whisky. Rogue, who always left everything to the last moment, was stuck in traffic and wouldn't make the race in time.

'Let me ride her.' Amber stubbed out her cigarette, leaping to her feet. 'I know her. Don't risk another cack-handed man getting bucked off. I've got my saddle.'

Marius glared at Amber. Behind her he could see Michelle frantically shaking her head.

'OK,' he growled. 'Get a move on, you've got to go through the scales fifteen minutes before the race.'

But he spoke to the air, as Amber grabbed the silks and her saddle and fled to the weighing room under the big gold clock, which told her she'd only got ten minutes. Fortunately the valet there was a friend of her father's, loved him on *A Question of Sport*, and with lightning speed fitted her up with boots, breeches, body protector, knee guards, undershirt and whip.

Michelle was absolutely furious.

'I'm not leading up that bitch. Rafiq can lead Mrs Wilkinson, I'll lead Romeo.'

Rafiq was equally furious. He'd really worked on Count Romeo, who was wearing a sheepskin noseband, in the hope that he might concentrate on that rather than the world around him. The Count looked sensational and would probably win the turnout and the £50 that would have enabled Rafiq to ask Amber out for a drink that night. Instead he was left with Mrs Wilkinson, who was sweating up, probably ashamed of the sloppiest plaits in the world.

Because the meeting was midweek, and cold and dank, the crowd consisted of serious racegoers rather than the kind who roll up for the champagne and to be looked at. All the same, Seth was being mobbed by autograph hunters and was now being interviewed by *At the Races*. In shot behind him, Trixie could be seen taking swigs from a bottle and alerting friends on her mobile.

Etta, distressed to receive a distraught telephone call from Tommy, was relieved to see Mrs Wilkinson being led up not by Michelle but by Rafiq. She was further relieved when the big noticeboard announced a jockey change to Amber Lloyd-Foxe.

A lot of women in the crowd wished they were on the handsome Rafiq as he prowled round the paddock stroking and singing under his breath to Mrs Wilkinson, who was psyching herself up for battle with Rogue.

There were some good horses in the race. Oliver's Travels, a big bay, was the favourite. Stop Preston, whom Etta liked, had been deliberately given a 'very easy ride' in his last race, resulting in him finishing last. This meant longer odds and a lowered handicap. Today, his jockey, Johnnie Brutus, Irish, feline, outwardly delicate but hugely strong, would get his whip out and annihilate the opposition. Harvey-Holden and Shade had consequently had massive bets in utter confidence of victory.

Neither Shade nor Olivia was present. Keen to avoid Marius and punch-ups, they had gone with Collie to Uttoxeter.

'Talk about a donkey derby,' bitched Harvey-Holden as Mrs Wilkinson jogged past followed by Count Romeo, desperate to bury his head between her quarters.

Preston, who'd always been so jaunty and boisterous when he was trained by Marius, was sweating up and didn't seem happy.

Nor was Phoebe happy. 'Shame it's not that gorgeous Rogue on Wilkie any more, I've already put on a fiver.'

'Amber's ten times more gorgeous,' snapped Alan. Amber, as green with nerves as the Willowwood silks, which clung enticingly to her long high-breasted body, came over to talk through chattering teeth to the syndicate.

'If Mrs Wilkinson wants to make it, I'd let her,' said Marius, who was commuting between Willowwood and a disillusioned Bertie and Ruby Barraclough, who hadn't bothered to hire a box this time.

'Handsome is as handsome doesn't,' grumbled Bertie, who wanted his £50,000 back. 'If you pay that money, you expect your horse to at least finish.'

Today Romeo wasn't even being ridden by the champion jockey. Awesome Wells, however, had huge brown eyes, long blond lashes and a sweet little boy's face. He never took in the trainer's instructions but loved chatting to owners.

'What a good idea!' he was saying to a slightly mollified Ruby and Bertie. 'I must try that.'

'Get on, Awesome,' snapped Marius.

Michelle, to Rafiq's rage, won the turnout, and posed for a photograph with Bertie, Ruby and Count Romeo.

A bell ordered the jockeys to mount. Suddenly Ruby descended to her knees in the churned-up parade ring, exclaiming, 'Dear Lord God, please help Count Romeo,' and nearly getting trampled underfoot by Oliver's Travels on his way out.

'Get up, Mother,' ordered Bertie.

'Unlike Count Romeo,' sneered Harvey-Holden as Ruby scrambled to her feet. 'That horse is so lazy, if he falls over on the gallops he can't be bothered to get up.'

'Good luck,' chorused Willowwood, as Marius legged up Amber.

'That's unlucky,' piped up Phoebe. 'Say "Break a leg" as they do on stage, don't they, Seth?'

'Good luck to you both,' a beaming Awesome Wells called out to Bertie and Ruby.

Willowwood, nerves fortunately cushioned by alcohol, retreated to the Owners and Trainers.

Looking down the flat, oblong course flanked by woodland as jagged as a growing-out mane, Etta noticed more poplars. More witches had rolled up to watch Mrs Wilkinson. Trixie took Etta's hand. 'She'll be OK.'

'I just don't want her to be bumped about too much and lose heart.'

Across the course, they could see horses circling with intent, the jockeys' colours shifting like shaken Smarties.

Michelle and Rafiq, having let their charges go, waited unspeaking by the Hampshire stand, on the right of the grandstand, for their return. Michelle had insisted on keeping the turnout money so bang went Rafiq's drink with Amber. Please God, bring her and Mrs Wilkinson safe home.

Marius, preparing for ritual humiliation, retreated to the bar.

54

The starter on his rostrum called them into a barging, bumping start and they were off. Mrs Wilkinson was at the end of her season. Once they were racing, Count Romeo, who was fooling around at the back, suddenly realized he'd lost her. Catching sight of her lustrous, newly washed white tail disappearing round the first bend, he hurtled down the course after her. He was so incensed that she totally ignored his shrill call, he forgot to be idle and overtook her to get her attention. Mrs Wilkinson in turn was so outraged to be headed, she fought back and overtook him, grinding her teeth and lashing her tail, so he overtook her, and on it went.

Count Romeo gave every hurdle a lot of air while Mrs Wilkinson skimmed them, but Romeo displayed such a turn of foot he caught up between fences and didn't even pause to check his mane on the big screen.

'And Shade Murchieson's orange and maroon silks are moving up,' said the commentator, as Johnnie Brutus got to work on Preston, giving him not at all an easy ride as he thundered down, passing everyone to take the lead.

'Come on, Wilkie,' howled Willowwood.

'Romeo, Romeo,' screamed Ruby Barraclough.

Thwack went Johnnie's whip again and again, clunk went his booted heels into Preston's ribs, but he couldn't catch the lovers. Encouraged by the mighty roar of the crowd, Mrs Wilkinson made a heroic last effort and, throwing herself forward, overtook the Count by a pale pink nose.

Miraculously Marius's horses had come first and second, to bring him racing out of the bar, spilling whisky everywhere.

The Willowwood syndicate were yelling their heads off. Alban, braying like an old mule, was hugging Etta. Seth was hugging Trixie, what a body. Tilda hugged Alan, who turned his head slightly so as not to get bayoneted by her teeth. The Major hugged Phoebe, scratching her with his moustache, and sidled off to hug Etta, as Phoebe sidled off to hug Seth. Chrissie and Joey launched into a wild ecstatic jive, then, as she stumbled against him, he kissed her on the mouth, harder and harder.

Woody found himself hugging Niall and drew away, meeting his eyes. Then, with a bewildered smile, he hugged him again, realizing what a lean, elegant body Niall had.

Dora was on her mobile talking to the press:

'Mrs Wilkinson's seen off Preston and Oliver's Travels.'

Harvey-Holden, on his mobile, was changing colour from sallow to olive green as Shade blamed him totally for Preston's failure and Marius's victory.

Except for her gleaming white teeth and the two pale circles round her eyes where her goggles had been, Amber was caked all over with mud, and so was her brave grey mare. For once Rafiq was all smiles as he ran towards her, patting Mrs Wilkinson over and over again, pulling her ears and hugging her.

'Well done, Amber, well done, Wilkie.'

He looked so handsome with the tears spilling out of his pale grey eyes and his black curls ruffled that Amber was tempted to kiss him. She was only distracted by an *At the Races* microphone thrust under her nose.

'Well done, Amber, great ride,' said a delighted Robert Cooper.

'What a credit to her connections,' babbled Amber. 'She's a one-eyed wonder. Only one eye but the biggest heart in the world. Preston was our only worry and he couldn't get near her, thanks to Count Romeo. Mrs Wilkinson has to be up there, and she sticks her neck out and really tries.'

Mrs Wilkinson loved praise and nudged Robert Cooper's microphone.

'And she's beautifully looked after at home by Tommy Ruddock and Rafiq here.' Amber tapped a bemused Rafiq on the head with her whip.

'Is that really our ice-cool Amber?' said Josh in amazement, as back at Throstledown the stable lads who'd been watching the race were dancing round the yard. Tommy decided not to resign after all, as she joyfully clocked Amber touching her hat with one finger to acknowledge the cheers as she rode into the winners enclosure. Mrs Wilkinson was delighted to disappear under a hailstorm of patting hands.

'Darling, darling, darling little girl.' Etta hugged her, then, looking round at a phalanx of snapping cameramen: 'We must have Rafiq, Amber and all the syndicate in the picture with her. Where is Mr Pocock?'

'He fainted with excitement,' giggled Trixie. 'Painswick revived him with a handkerchief drenched in lavender cologne. She and Dora have taken him to Casualty. Could this be the start of something big?'

'We must go to him,' gasped Etta. 'Poor man.'

'No, we must not,' said Seth, hugging her. 'Enjoy your moment, Mrs B.'

Everyone had had bets on Mrs Wilkinson and Count Romeo and 80 per cent of Mrs Wilkinson's £4,000 winnings would be divided out among them. Ten per cent would then go to Marius and ten to Amber, who was happily telling the press what a wonderful horse Mrs Wilkinson was before going off to weigh in.

On the way she bumped into a just-arrived Rogue. Surrounded by groupies and signing autographs, he looked up.

'Well done,' he said evenly.

'Thank you. What price Amateur Lloyd-Foxe now?' demanded Amber.

They were knocked sideways by an ashen Johnnie Brutus, who'd been threatened with the sack as Harvey-Holden's stable jockey for not winning on such a heavily backed Preston.

Meanwhile, in the winners enclosure, Awesome was talking to Ruby and Bertie, who were ecstatic that their glossy black boy had come such a close second.

'He ran green,' admitted Awesome, 'but halfway round he got the hang of it, desperate to keep up with his lady friend, overtaking horse after horse to get to her. Only got beat by a whisker. Nice horse, a true Romeo, like to ride him again.'

'You shall, you shall,' cried a tearful Ruby. Then, falling to her knees again: 'Oh, thank you, thank you, Lord.'

The Willowwood syndicate were being mobbed.

'We're getting ten times as much attention as last time,' said Phoebe, happily rearranging her fur hat. 'That's because Seth's here.'

'It's because we won,' snapped Alan, 'and because Dora worked so hard.'

Niall was in a daze. Could it really have happened? Even now Woody was smiling shyly across at him.

Mrs Wilkinson was as tickled pink as her nose. She had drunk water from a yellow bucket, she wasn't remotely tired, could easily have gone round again, was greeting all her friends, ecstatically nudging microphones and tape recorders, and listening with pricked ears to all the questions.

Then suddenly she glanced up, gave a deep-throated whicker of welcome and dragged Rafiq across the winners enclosure to leave white slobber all over the navy-blue cashmere coat of Valent Edwards.

'Well done, Mrs Wilkinson,' he said, taking her face in his huge goalkeeper's hands and kissing her on the forehead. 'Well done, you little beauty.'

And the photographers, realizing who he was and that they had a picture, went berserk. All the trainers too were licking their lips and, knowing they'd have to get on with the next race, wondering how they could wangle an introduction.

'What's your connection with Mrs Wilkinson?' asked the *Sun*.

'She stayed at my place for eighteen months. I've got a very soft spot for my equine lodger,' said Valentine and kissed her again.

'Lucky thing,' murmured Tilda to Etta. 'Isn't he gorgeous? Oh Etta, Greycoats are so thrilled, do you think Mrs Wilkinson could make a guest appearance?'

'Horses away, horses away,' shouted the Clerk of the Scales, who needed room for the next race.

'You better get her out of here, Rafiq,' ordered Marius, 'or she'll be going up to collect her own cup.'

Mrs Wilkinson didn't want to go at all. She was enjoying her friends and her moment of glory far too much, and Count Romeo, whose face was covered in Ruby's red lipstick kisses, refused to go without her.

Next moment, Valent had turned to Rafiq and shoved a great fistful of greenbacks into his pocket.

'Well done, lad, she looks tremendous.'

'Thank you, sir,' said an ecstatic Rafiq, as, able to take Amber out for an entire crate of champagne now, he set out with Mrs Wilkinson for the stables.

Michelle, leading back Count Romeo, was livid. Bertie wasn't into tipping. She must get Marius to wise him up.

'I must go with them,' cried Etta, who had been quite unable to meet Valent's eyes.

'You can't.' Seth took her arm firmly. 'We're all going up to the Royal Box for a glass of champagne and to watch the race.'

'Doesn't happen very often,' grinned a returning Joey, clutching even more fistfuls of winnings. Then he went pale as he caught sight of Valent, who asked, 'Are those this month's wages?' and decided to forgive him.

'Can Rafiq come up to the Royal Box?' begged Etta.

'No he can't, he's the groom,' said Phoebe scornfully. 'You wouldn't expect Mop Idol to sit on Uncle Alban's right at a dinner party. Oh, whoops,' she added, realizing Joey was just behind her, fortunately too preoccupied with Chrissie.

55

After the syndicate had been photographed collecting Mrs Wilkinson's cup and Marius had been awarded a framed cartoon, Rafiq a photo frame and Amber, as winning rider, a glass tankard, they floated through a solid oak door into the building containing the Royal Box. Etta thought she had gone to heaven. The walls were papered in her favourite sea blue and crowded with wonderful photographs of the Queen in a flowered print dress and the Queen Mother in crimson.

'Hardly wearing camouflage to blend into the countryside,' hissed Dora.

Up the stairs they found more photographs of George V and Queen Mary and the Duke of Edinburgh at the races, of Best Mate and Galway Bay winning the Hennessy, and some adorable Shetland ponies with their tails trailing on the ground.

'Do you think Horace should grow his hair?' giggled Trixie.

'Oh God, this is bliss,' sighed Etta, as they reached a room with more leaping horses, and a gilt looking glass and a tariff from the olden days, when whisky was ten old pennies a tot.

'We wouldn't pay the rent on that,' laughed Chrissie, clutching Joey's arm.

As they were handed the most delicious glass of champagne in the world and watched the video of the race, all they could think was that Mrs Wilkinson, their beloved village horse, had come good.

'Look at the way she stands orf, looks at the fence and really picks up her feet,' said Alban, accepting a glass, feeling he couldn't not on such an occasion.

Everyone cheered as Pocock, looking pale, and Painswick, looking pink after receiving a congratulatory text message from

Hengist which she would never wipe, returned from Casualty. They were also persuaded to have a restorative glass. Everyone cheered even more when Amber arrived.

'Not just a pretty arse,' said Seth, hugging her.

'I've had text messages from Rupert and Taggie, Dad and Mum and my old headmaster, Hengist Brett-Taylor. He sent love to you, Miss Painswick, and to Rafiq,' crowed Amber.

Etta, in a daze of happiness and confusion – she still hadn't spoken to Valent – wandered across the room and up on to a little platform where Royalty must have stood so often to watch a race through a huge window.

The jockeys for the next race were going down to post, idly chatting to each other. It seemed like midnight. The huge course which Mrs Wilkinson had conquered stretched below. The witches who parked their broomsticks had put a good spell on her.

Aware of a footstep on the carpet, she turned, then started. It was Valent, who had been in Darwin mining ore to sell to the Chinese at massive profit but was far more excited by Mrs Wilkinson's victory.

'I'm sorry, Etta, I was so rude to you, I'm bluddy ashamed of myself. I was bluddy out of order,' he added, blushing all over his square suntanned face. 'I just lost it. I'd grown very fond of Mrs Wilkinson. I wanted to be part of her future.'

'I only sold her to the syndicate because I couldn't afford to keep her on my own,' stammered Etta.

'Should have come to me.'

'I didn't want to bother you. I didn't want to abuse your colossal generosity.'

Valent led Etta back into the room where the Royal Box, impressed by such an illustrious guest, had been persuaded to show the video again.

'Look at her little legs in a blur,' said Valent ecstatically. 'Look at the way her ears are pricked the moment she passes the post.'

Marius was also watching the video.

'Why did you do that?' he accused Amber. 'Why didn't you look round? You nearly let Johnnie up the inner.'

'Oh shut up, Marius,' called out Alan. 'Don't be so bloody ungracious. She rode a dream race. Have a drink, darling.'

'She's got to drive the lorry home,' snapped Marius and bore Amber off.

'Bloody paranoid,' said Seth. 'He's so snarled up and suspicious about his staff getting close to owners, terrified they'll take them away to other yards, when they only leave because he's so tricky.'

'I like Marius,' reproved Phoebe. 'Must remember his wife's just left him, poor chap.'

'Oh shut up,' muttered Trixie.

'And two fingers to Shagger and Toby for not bothering to come,' said Dora.

56

'Let's party,' said Valent, bearing everyone off to the Owners and Trainers bar for more champagne. Here owners, trainers and jockeys sat round tables on wicker chairs conducting past-the-post mortems, watching the races on two screens and gazing hungrily at Valent, who had to be good for at least a hundred horses.

Even the big punters, Joey, Alan, Seth and Alban, had only to cross the room to a kind of mahogany witness box, manned by a moustached stalwart, who was taking bets for the tote.

Euphoria nearly took the roof off when History Painting beat Ilkley Hall in the next race.

Valent switched off his BlackBerry, and Etta remembered how glued to theirs the alpha males had been at Sampson's funeral. She watched him working the syndicate, asking questions like a football manager determined to discover the special excellence of each of his players.

Learning Miss Painswick was an out-of-work dragon who'd organized a great public school almost single-handed, he suggested the one thing Marius needed was a decent local secretary.

Pocock supplied the information that Etta was sorting out Marius's garden.

'Perhaps she'll do mine when it emerges from the Blitz.'

'And then Joey could build a few more boxes and repair those already there, which are in a shocking state,' said Painswick.

'Sir Cuthbert can feed hay to Mrs Wilkinson through the hole in their common wall,' giggled Trixie, 'and she and Chisolm eat blackberries growing through the roof.'

'Chisolm ought to come to the races with Mrs Wilkinson,'

suggested Dora. 'It'd be good for Wilkie's image, make the public remember her.'

'The stable lads need better quarters,' said Trixie. 'Josh and particularly Rafiq and Tommy live in a tip.'

'Need planning permission,' said Valent, filling up everyone's glasses. 'Throstledown's in an area of outstanding natural beauty.'

'That's where the Major comes in, he's good with planners,' said Painswick.

'So's Joey, brilliant,' said Alan.

'Must be,' giggled Phoebe, holding out her glass. 'Or how else did he get permission for that hideous house in Willowwood?'

Valent frowned and glanced round. He was relieved to see that Joey and the Major were over by the tote collecting their winnings and, in a rare moment of concord, agreeing not to tell Mop Idol or Debbie how much they'd won.

Valent then sought out Alban, questioning him about an on-going problem he was having with a Saudi oil company. He arranged to have lunch with Alban in London.

'Yes, she was Valent Edwards's house guest, lived in his office for weeks,' Dora was telling the *Daily Mail*. 'He came back specially to see her race.'

Switching off her mobile, she beamed at Valent and was soon telling him about Paris.

'He's such a brilliant actor.' She flashed a picture of Paris and Cadbury. 'He's dogsitting as we speak. He's just back from Cambridge, he's terribly clever.'

'He must meet Bonny, there might be something in her next film,' said Valent. 'Beautiful-looking boy.'

'Isn't he, but he isn't spoilt. He needs masses of love because he was brought up in a children's home, but please don't tell anyone.'

'I won't,' said Valent gravely.

Alan was talking to Tilda, thinking again how pretty she'd be if only her teeth were fixed.

'My father's a wonderful writer,' Trixie's tongue, loosened by champagne, was telling Valent, 'but he doesn't have much incentive because Mummy makes so much money. But she's so busy she doesn't have a lot of time for us. She's in Russia chatting up some Russian oligarch.'

'What do you want to be in life?'

'I would love infinitely and be loved,' sighed Trixie.

'Lucky you've got your nan.'

'Oh, Mum and Uncle Martin are foul to Granny.' Trixie

lowered her voice. 'She's so sweet, look at her talking for hours to the vicar in case he feels left out. His church is so empty, Granny says we've all got to go at Christmas.'

Phoebe was chatting up Seth, who had positioned himself so he could gaze at Trixie. Christ, he wanted her, that untamed mane of hair, that wonderful coltish body.

That's dangerous, thought Valent, clocking the expression on Seth's face. That man was so handsome he could get anyone. He had noticed how Etta's face softened when she looked at Seth.

Moving on, he filled up Phoebe and Seth's glasses.

Bonny hated the idea of the country, he reflected, but if Corinna and Seth were down here she might find it more exciting.

Phoebe was in heaven, two alpha males fighting over her.

'When are you and Bonny going to move in, Valent? We're all agog. I was just saying to Seth it must be difficult being Mr Corinna Waters, and I suppose if you marry Bonny, Valent, you'll be Mr Bonny Richards.'

'Hardly,' said Seth, raising his glass. 'Here's to Mrs Wilkinson, God bless her.'

'I'll drink to that,' said Valent.

'I was so nervous, I couldn't eat a thing earlier,' simpered Phoebe. 'I'd absolutely adore a smoked salmon sandwich. Would that be OK, Valent? All this fizz is getting me quite tiddly.'

When Valent ordered her one, she added to Painswick, 'Wouldn't you like a round too, Joyce?'

'How dare she,' exploded Dora to Trixie. 'There's masses left in the picnic basket for the journey home, bloody pig.'

Noticing Joey and Chrissie outside smoking a very long cigarette, Valent asked Chrissie on her return whether the smoking ban had affected takings at the Fox.

'It hasn't been great,' she began, but was halted by Dora and Trixie approaching Valent with a large brandy.

'Lots of men hate champagne,' said Dora, 'so Trixie and I wanted to buy you a proper drink for being so kind to us all.'

'Why thank you, Dora,' said Valent, unable to hide how touched he was.

'Why don't you join us on the bus home, Mr Edwards?' suggested Trixie. 'It'll be a riot. I can sit on Woody's knee, he's so fit. Tilda can sit on Daddy's knee, from behind you can't see her teeth. Alban's off the drink, or at least he was until Mrs Wilkinson won.' Looking across, they watched a beaming Alban downing yet another glass. 'Perhaps your chauffeur could drive us home? Oh, wasn't Amber cool?'

The Major was very happy. Valent had asked him lots of questions about the finances of the syndicate. Glancing up at a sepia photograph on the wall of racegoers in top hats, he decided he must get out his topper.

Hours later they set out for home. Valent's driver, delighted to see his boss enjoying himself so much, had taken the wheel of the Ford Transit. On its side Trixie had written 'Well done, Mrs Wilkinson' in lipstick, watched by a giggling Etta, who was joyfully clutching Mrs Wilkinson's cup, revelling in the fact that Seth had told her she'd made him the happiest man in the world.

Miss Painswick, sitting next to a much recovered Pocock, was knitting a red hood with one eyehole for Mrs Wilkinson, singing 'Roll out the Barrel' and conducting with a sausage roll.

Maybe she could go back to work part time.

Euphoric to be forgiven by Valent, with a possibility of working next on Throstledown, Joey was snogging in the back with Chrissie.

'My foxy lady,' he murmured, 'I want to see a lot of you.'

Alan, with Tilda on his knee, discovered she had a very slim and exciting body. Carrie was due back from Russia any moment. He'd better persuade Valent's chauffeur to stop at the next service station so he could buy some placatory flowers.

'Romeo, Romeo, wherefore art thou, Romeo, only second to Mrs Wilkinson,' intoned Seth and everyone fell about.

Nice, he thought, that he'd been mobbed today. Very few people had asked after Corinna.

Trixie was happily perched on Woody's knee. Seth, with Phoebe on his knee, had positioned himself so he could look up Trixie's rucked-up shocking-pink coat and shoot her the occasional white-hot glance to unsettle her. Trixie was sad Josh hadn't texted her.

Niall, pretending to write a sermon on paper already covered in drink rings, sat on Woody's inside, aware of Trixie on his knee. The only suitable text would be from the Song of Solomon. He could feel Woody's beautiful arse against his thigh.

They were passing the Membury radio transmitter, red lights gleaming in the grey fog. Ahead stretched rows and rows of brake lights, saying stop, stop, slow down. Towards them came yellow headlights, saying caution, caution. Niall threw back his head. He mustn't let his heart carry him away.

The Major, a nouveau texter, was sending messages to all his committee members, drawing their attention to Mrs Wilkinson's victory.

Alban sat beside Etta.

'Fritefly exciting day, splendid. Mick Fitzgerald said winning was better than sex, got something there. Not all sex of course,' Alban whinnied with laughter. 'Charming chap, Valent, asked me to lunch. Back on the wagon tomorrow.' He tottered off to have a pee in the coffin-shaped loo.

Outside, Etta could see a beautiful full moon gliding out of cotton-wool clouds, the stars kept appearing and disappearing like jockeys. Next minute 'Ode to Joy' had flooded the bus.

Taking Alban's place, Valent filled up Etta's glass.

'The drought is ended,' said Etta tearfully. 'One shouldn't be ungrateful for huge mercies, but I wish she was still living at Badger's Court.'

'She can come back for her summer holidays,' said Valent.

'Oh, thank you.' Etta gave him a kiss.

'Excellent,' murmured Dora approvingly, 'much better for Etta than Alban, Pocock or the Major.'

'Thank God I've paid off my gambling debts and my credit card bills,' muttered Seth, shifting his legs under Phoebe.

'Don't think I'm going to get much material for my book on depression,' muttered back Alan, resisting a temptation to slide a hand over Tilda's breasts. He'd have a hard-on if she wasn't sitting on it.

Reality was about to kick in. The syndicate reached Willowwood around nine, spilling out joyfully on to the village green. Debbie and Ione awaited them – extremely beady, particularly with the vicar. What would the Parochial Church Council say about seeing him on the telly, arm around Mrs Wilkinson, laughing like a jackass? Carrie had also come home from Moscow. She was livid to see Trixie sitting on Woody's knee and Alan wrapped round that stupid Bugs Bunny teacher.

'We won, Mum, we won,' screamed Trixie, falling out of the bus. 'Count Romeo came second. Mrs Wilkinson won, she's no longer a maiden. I think Count Romeo is responsible.'

'Here's to you, Mrs Wilkinson,' sang Niall. 'She's going to be a serioush horshe.'

'And wear spectacles and read Proust,' giggled Dora.

Next moment a furious, beautiful, instantly recognizable older woman came storming across the village green.

'Seth, you little bastard,' she roared. 'Why the hell didn't you meet us at Bristol? I left a message on the machine. Stefan got drunk on the plane, we had to break in, poor bloody Priceless has crapped all over the house and there's no champagne in the fridge. Where the fuck have you been?'

Enter Corinna Waters and Stefan, the Polish houseboy.

'I've been trying to persuade Valent to join the syndicate, Mum, he's so nice,' Trixie told an outraged Carrie.

Joey had left Mop Idol with baby Wayne, who was teething. Mop Idol was seething, particularly because Joey, utterly euphoric at having a winner at Newbury, had passed out in the back of the bus and had to be carried out and deposited on the grass. Pocock had lost his teeth, and later found them in Painswick's knitting bag.

Bonny Richards was so livid not to be able to contact Valent, she had filled up his message box with abuse.

Nor did Alan's service station flowers have the right effect.

'You know I can't stand chrysanthemums,' screamed Carrie, chucking them back at him.

Grabbing them, Alan rushed back to the Fox. Much later, on the way home, seeing a light on at School Cottage, he posted the chrysanthemums through Tilda's letter box, adding on a page torn out of his diary: 'Thanks for a lovely day.'

57

Mrs Wilkinson, observed Seth, was probably the only thing to come out of Newbury Races without a black eye or a hangover. She was not pleased on her return to Throstledown. Not only did a furiously jealous Sir Cuthbert give her a hard time, but Tommy had borne a disconsolate Chisolm off to a packed-out Fox.

Here Chisolm had a ball, eating crisps and licking up quantities of spilled alcohol. As the landlady had returned home plastered, and the landlord had been celebrating Mrs Wilkinson's victory since lunchtime, customers had begun helping themselves.

Fighting her way in late to retrieve Alan and Trixie, Carrie was bawling out her mother for leading them both astray, when an inebriated Chisolm jumped to Etta's defence and butted Carrie out into the street, to roars of applause.

'Little darling, I'll give you a job any night at closing time,' said Chris, as Chisolm nudged him for another alcopop.

Romy and Martin had been as incensed as Carrie to see an over-joyed, tearful, hatless Etta on television hugging everyone. Learning from a sneaking Phoebe of their mother's winnings, Martin next day tried to persuade her to hand them over to the Sampson Bancroft Fund. And why hadn't she persuaded Valent and all the rich people she'd met to chip in as well?

Drummond and Poppy, on the other hand, thought it dead cool. All their friends at Greycoats had been blown away to see their grandmother and Mrs Wilkinson on television and by the fact that Amber had been the only jockey not to whack her poor horse.

Fortunately Etta had already handed her winnings over to the Major to pay for her next six months' subscription.

Meanwhile, over at the yard, Michelle was still nagging Rafiq to give her half of Valent's massive tip, But in a surge of revolt and egged on by Tommy, Rafiq had blued the lot on a second-hand mechanical horse known as an Equicizer.

'Much cheaper to have ridden me,' said Amber mockingly.

But everyone was delighted that Mrs Wilkinson came really well out of her race, eating up all her food. Next morning she trotted up sound and, still fresh, ran round squealing and bucking when she was turned out. By contrast, Count Romeo was very stiff and needed physio.

'Typical male,' said Amber.

Chisolm had a hangover and despite a packet of frozen peas dripping on her forehead kept emitting pathetic bleats. Marius was feeling even sorrier for himself. Despite yesterday's victories, no one had texted or rung to congratulate him. Rafiq had just brought him a cup of tea, which he was trying to keep down, and the *Racing Post*, which irritated him because of the photograph of Amber, Seth Bainton and Mrs Wilkinson – and not him – on the front. Knowing her master was in an eruptive mood, Mistletoe, one eye open, quivered in her basket, yesterday's dinner untouched.

Marius had to get tomorrow's declarations or declaration in before ten o'clock. Hearing the second lot clattering into the yard, he glanced up and froze, for hanging from the peeling flag-post, writhing against a soft wind, was the sapphire and crimson Throstledown flag. He'd burnt it in fury and despair, the first time Alan and Etta visited the yard. Running to the window, sending a pile of unpaid bills flying, he gazed in disbelief. The old flag had been ripped and patched and chewed by puppies. This one was new and beautifully sewn, its jewel colours glowing.

Fighting back both expletives and tears, Marius stumbled out into the yard.

'Where the hell did that flag come from?' he roared. 'You had no right.'

Immediately human and horse heads appeared over the half-doors.

'That was a good day yesterday,' stammered Tommy. 'The Throstledown flag flies for winners.'

'Only if I say so. Where did it come from?'

'Please don't shout,' begged Amber, 'we're all a bit fragile.' Then, as another anguished bleat rent the air: 'Particularly Chisolm.'

'Don't be fucking lippy, who's bloody responsible?' Marius glared round.

'I think it was Alan's idea,' volunteered Josh.

'Etta bought the stuff,' said Tresa.

'Painswick made it, she's brilliant at sewing,' added Tommy.

Perhaps Marius wasn't going to fire them all after all, as he fingered the flag for a moment, unable to speak.

'I still should have been consulted.'

His staff, who'd been used and abused by him for so many months, realized once again what strain he'd been under.

'Where's Michelle?' he snapped.

'In bed and even more fragile than us,' said Amber sarcastically.

Mrs Wilkinson was banging her food bowl against the wall. Chisolm winced and decided to eat the melted peas.

'It was a good day yesterday,' repeated Amber. 'I've had more than fifty text messages, most of them,' she looked at Marius under her eyelashes, 'wanting to know when I'm next going to ride Mrs Wilkinson.'

'Don't push it,' snapped Marius.

Amber, about to snap back, was saved by Pavarotti singing 'None shall sleep' on Tommy's mobile.

'It's Etta,' said Tommy. 'Valent Edwards has been trying to get in touch with you, Marius, can you ring him a.s.a.p.'

Only when Marius tried did he realize his telephone had been cut off for non-payment and his mobile was not topped up. No wonder no one had rung to congratulate him.

Looking round at the chaos of unpaid bills, old *Racing Posts*, a racing calendar covered with drink rings, entry books, directories piled up and not put back on the shelves, empty bottles, cups, glasses, overflowing ashtrays and, most disgraceful, little Mistletoe's dinner uneaten, Marius winced.

He looked up at the flag. To go to all that trouble, they must have thought he'd have winners again. He better start looking for a secretary.

Valent, who rolled up later in the day, was of the same opinion.

'Need someone to organize things, answer the telephones, keep owners up to date and at bay, pay the staff who are working longer and longer hours as there are less of them.'

'Got someone in mind?' snarled Marius.

'Yes,' said Valent.

'Don't be ridiculous,' exploded Marius, 'she doesn't know any-thing about horses and she's a nosey old frump. I need someone with charm and their wits about them.'

Marius was thinking of Olivia, who all the owners had loved. One of the reasons, apart from cost, he hadn't employed a secretary was the faint hope Olivia might come back.

He slumped on the sofa. Mistletoe edged up tentatively and licked his hand.

'Painswick'll free you up for what you're good at – training horses,' said Valent gently. 'You've got a cracker with Mrs Wilkinson.'

'Little horse, got to keep her handicap down, can't have her carrying too much weight.' Ten minutes later, Marius stopped talking about Mrs Wilkinson.

'Nice touch that flag,' he admitted, 'kind of Etta too.'

'Etta's smashing,' said Valent. 'Want to talk to you about Amber, Rafiq and Furious.'

Tilda Flood put her mauve chrysanthemums in a square glass vase in her bedroom. She'd never liked the smell before, but thought what a lovely day she had had and how nice Alan was.

Dora achieved such widespread national and local coverage over the next few days, what with Marius's comeback, Valent's 'horse guest' and *Holby City*'s latest heart-throb bopping with ecstatic vicars, that the rest of the syndicate decided to come to the races in future either to keep an eye on errant other halves or, in Corinna's case, to cash in on the publicity and have a crack at Valent.

The Major was euphoric at getting his name and photograph in the *Telegraph* beside Valent Edwards. He had played the video of the race, freezing on himself in the winners enclosure so many times the tape had scrambled. He was also thoroughly over-excited that Corinna was back and he could spy on her opulent curves through the trees with his powerful new racing binoculars. What a shame that Valent's conifers shielded Etta.

Debbie, flipping through her husband's photographs of the Royal Box, burst into tears.

'I should have been there, I should have been there.'

58

Mrs Wilkinson's next race – the 3.15 Novice Hurdle at Ludlow on a soggy, gloomy fourth Monday in January – was supported by a very different mix of the syndicate.

So many Greycoats teachers were away with flu, Tilda didn't feel she could justify another day off, even though her beloved Shagger had decided to go. To Shagger's disappointment, the fair Woody had cried off to attend a preservation meeting to save a beautiful horse chestnut which grew in Lester Bolton's garden but overlooked the village green. Lester wanted to cut it down because it impeded the CCTV view of Primrose Mansions.

As Woody wasn't going, Niall, who'd thought of no one else since Newbury, was only too happy to respond to Parochial Church Council pressure and stay away too. He had, after all, prayed for a safe outcome for Mrs Wilkinson in church on Sunday.

'I thought the church had Mondays off like Sunday newspapers,' grumbled Dora. 'It's good for Mrs Wilkinson's image to have her own vicar in attendance.'

Having failed all her exams, Dora was outraged to have been gated at Bagley Hall.

'How can I achieve maximum coverage for Corinna Waters's first trip to the races if I'm not on the spot?'

Facing a two-hour journey to Ludlow along winding roads, the minibus, parked outside the Fox, was due to leave at eleven. Alban (who'd only been allowed to go if he didn't drink) was revving up. Ione had rolled up to wave them off, bringing a large thermos of lentil soup to keep out the cold. She was now scowling at the minibus.

'Stop revving up, Alban, it's so wasteful. Those monsters bingedrink petrol.'

279

'Oh, put a sock in it, Ione,' shouted a shivering Alan, who was having a Bloody Mary and a fag outside the pub. 'This bus is carrying eleven people who could all be driving their own cars. I suppose you'd like us to bike to Ludlow.'

Chris, whose turn it was to go instead of his wife, was loading up the boot.

'Poor 'en-pecked sod,' he murmured, laughing fatly.

From the warmth of the pub, Chrissie watched her husband, poised the moment the bus left to ring Joey, who'd virtuously announced that he couldn't justify another day's skiving, Valent had been so decent about it last time.

Inside the Fox, a video of Mrs Wilkinson's last race played continually on the television. A framed photograph of the syndicate flanking her hung on the wall. Phoebe, on a bar stool sipping hot Ribena, was delighted to be the baby of the party again, but with fewer people on the jaunt she might not have the excuse to sit on Seth's knee. But at least Toby had risked the wrath of Carrie Bancroft and, braving the cold, was chatting to Uncle Alban.

A minute to the off, the Major, who'd recorded another half-inch in his rain gauge, was forecasting rain and arctic conditions. Thrilled about seeing Corinna, he rolled up with Debbie, who, not realizing Ludlow didn't have a Royal Box, had invested in a beetroot-coloured trilby with a lilac feather. She was also hopping. Corinna Waters, the great Shakespearean actress, might have the perfect diction that could be heard in the gods, but it could also be heard all over Willowwood.

'She and Seth were rowing and hurling plates all night,' Debbie was now telling the entire pub, 'playing loud music to drown each other and with so many kiddies in the village their language was simply disgusting.'

'Fink Joey's kids could teach Corinna and Sef a few new words,' said a returning Chris with an all-embracing wink.

'That's a lovely one of me,' said Phoebe, admiring the cuttings pinned to the noticeboard. 'I must get Dora to get me a print.'

'The correct procedure,' said a returning Alan, 'is to ring up the picture editor and ask to pay for it. Dora's done more than enough.' He held his glass out to Chrissie for a refill. 'We ought to go,' he told the Major.

'Who are we missing? Seth, Corinna, Etta,' the Major consulted his clipboard, 'that's not like her.'

On cue, Etta crashed through the door.

'I'm so sorry,' she gasped. 'I forgot Poppy and Drummond's lunch boxes and had to go back, and the Polo's got a puncture so I had to walk. I hope I haven't held everyone up.'

'No panic.' Alan handed her his Bloody Mary. 'Seth and Corinna haven't arrived yet.'

'Oh, thank God,' said Etta. She had time to whisk into the loo and do her face.

Once inside, she realized she'd forgotten her make-up bag and she had no foundation to tone down her flushed face or to hide the red veins and dark circles, or eyeliner to enlarge her tired, bloodshot eyes. As she hadn't been able to afford to have her hair streaked and cut since the summer, she'd curled it up, but it had now dropped in the mist and rain and hung to her shoulders – a grey-haired crone, an awful old bat stared back at her from the mirror. What would Seth and Valent think? Not that they'd look at her anyway. She took a slug of Bloody Mary and returned to the bar, where Debbie and Phoebe were of the same opinion. They must smarten Etta up and decided to club together to give her a decent haircut and a smart hat.

Everyone then waited and waited and waited. Toby returned to the warmth of the pub and, lips moving, read *Shooting Life* before moving on to *Country Life*. Etta would have had masses of time to retrieve her make-up bag from Little Hollow. Alan called Seth: 'Where the fuck are you?'

'Madam's been doing an interview for Radio 4, we'll be along in a minute.'

Shagger returned to the attack and accosted the Major.

'You sure we're insured? What happens if Mrs Wilkinson injures herself or anyone else? What about Amber Lloyd-Foxe? I've looked into it, I could provide total cover for Willowwood and you could waive my subscription.'

'Which I haven't yet received,' said the Major.

'Nor should you. Mrs Wilkinson won two and a half thou at Newbury, that divided into ten shares should cover it.'

'Doesn't quite work that way,' admitted the Major. 'Minibus has to be paid for, and the catering,' he lowered his voice, 'was very expensive last time.'

'Thought Valent picked that up.'

'Only bubbly after we won the race. Champagne charged at pub prices and food came to sixty pounds a head.'

'Jesus!'

'Debbie's going to look at special wine offers in Tesco's and I think we'll have to start bringing our own grub. Or having a hot dog at the races.'

'Hardly Corinna's style, where the hell are they?'

'If they don't come in five minutes, we'll go without them.'

'Here they come,' said Chris, as Seth and Corinna came down

the high street, ten yards apart, obviously in the middle of a blazing row.

'They've brought that dreadful dog,' fumed Debbie, as Seth swept through the door, holding it open for Priceless but letting it swing in Corinna's face. Priceless proceeded to greet Etta with delight, sweeping the cuttings off the table with his tail before lifting his leg on the curtains.

'Can't bring that dog to the races,' Chris told Seth.

'I know,' apologized Seth, 'I hoped darling Chrissie might look after him for the day, he's no trouble. For a fee,' he added.

He was followed by Corinna, who smiled around:

'Hello, darlings, we better get going or we'll miss the first race.'

She was wearing a blond fox-fur hat, whose shaggy fringe flattered her long dark crafty eyes, a short scarlet coat, shiny black boots, and she looked a billion dollars.

'Outrageous,' spluttered Debbie.

'Steady on, Mother,' murmured the Major.

'Hiya, Seth,' twinkled Phoebe, 'hiya, Miss Waters.' Then, as they climbed into the bus: 'We've left you the comfy seat along the back so you can spread yourselves.'

'I get sick in the back,' said Corinna rudely, 'particularly when I've got lines to learn.' She picked up Debbie's bag on the third row, threw it across the gangway and settled into the seat next to the window. Seth ostentatiously took a seat two back from her next to Alan. Phoebe sat next to the window in the seat in front of them in order to show off her charming profile.

Toby took a seat up the front next to Alban so they could discuss shooting and people they knew.

Having waved them off, Chrissie rang Joey:

'All clear, but they've landed me with bloody Priceless.'

'Don't worry, I'll find somewhere. We'll have to go dogging.'

Accustomed to playing queens, empresses or other powerful women on stage, Corinna treated other humans as subjects. Only happy if the centre of attention, demanding, imperious, charismatic, she took violently against anyone who criticized or disagreed with her. On the other hand, she took her art incredibly seriously, watching people the whole time, rowing, insulting, enchanting so she could study the hurt and anger or delight in others' faces.

Junoesque with a white opaque complexion, which seemed impervious to booze or late nights, she had a strong face, shaggy shoulder-length dark hair, drooping red lips, and dark eyes that swivelled, not missing a trick. She seldom looked people straight in the face because she didn't want them to suspect the truths she was absorbing about them.

Corinna tended to wear black or brilliant colours, chucking her clothes on like a throw with which one hides a beautiful but dilapidated sofa. Above her black boots, her tights were laddered. There was a food stain on her black cashmere polo neck. Becoming every character she played, she didn't mind looking ugly if the part required it, confident she could be beautiful and irresistible when needed.

As the bus set off north-west through the icy rain, seeing Alan and a boot-faced Seth getting stuck into the red and the racing pages, she ordered Chris to pour her a half-pint of champagne.

Noticing Debbie more beetroot than her trilby and about to explode, Etta, attempting to defuse things, took the window seat in front of Corinna. 'What a beautiful coat.'

'One should always have a red coat in one's wardrobe. It looks good in photographs, even if one doesn't.'

'There's a picture of you in the *Telegraph* today, Miss Waters, you are *so* photogenic,' gushed Phoebe.

'Must have been taken years ago, very airbrushed,' sniffed Debbie.

Seeing Corinna stiffen, Etta said firmly, 'You're much prettier now.'

'Bit tired, darling.' Corinna smiled at Etta. 'Just done *Macbeth* in America, standing ovations in every city, but it does drain you.'

'It must do,' said Etta sympathetically. 'I'm so excited to meet you. My late husband and I were huge fans, he worked in London and never missed one of your first nights.' Then, struck by a chilling thought that Sampson might have been one of Corinna's lovers, she hastily added, 'How did you and Seth meet?'

'We were in *Private Lives*, playing Amanda and Elyot. Critics said we set the stage on fire. The press got wildly excited because Seth was a bit younger than me.'

'Still am,' drawled Seth, not looking up from the *Independent*.

'Naughty Seth.' Phoebe shrieked with laughter, then, turning the page of the *Mail*: 'Oh look, Bonny Richards, she really is pretty.'

Corinna seized the paper. 'Pretty chocolate-boxy,' she said dismissively, then reading on in a simpering little girl voice: ' "Valent Edwards is my significant other," dear, dear, God help us,' then glaring at the picture at the bottom of the page: 'She's got Valent into "a crisp white tunic with silver trim". God, he looks a prat. She goes on: "I want Valent to get in touch with his feminine side." Sounds like a women's football team. Poor sod, he is attractive though.'

'For an older chap he is,' agreed Phoebe. 'Is he joining us at Ludlow?'

'He's not coming,' replied the Major. 'He phoned, very graciously sent his regards but said he'd got too much on.'

'That appalling kaftan for a start,' said Corinna. 'That's a pity, we were promised the great tycoon.'

She got a red book out of her bag.

Feeling disappointed yet relieved because she was looking so awful, Etta asked Corinna what she was learning lines for.

'*Phèdre*. Doing it in Paris, the English are far too philistine to go to a play in French.'

'What's it about?' asked Etta.

'A stepmother falling passionately in love with her stepson. It caused a sensation when it was first produced in 1677. And Patrick O'Hara's writing a play for me called *Virago*. He should know, his mother Maud and his partner Cameron are both impossibly difficult. I like playing impossibly difficult women.'

'Don't need to act,' observed Seth.

More shrieks from Phoebe.

Seth was much quieter and bitchier when Corinna was around, reflected Etta. It must be difficult playing second fiddle to such a star.

The men had marked the racing pages and telephoned their bets, putting more than they could afford on Mrs Wilkinson. The bus was following the first signposts to Ludlow now.

'Housman country,' sighed Corinna.

' "Oh, when I was in love with you," ' began Seth in his infinitely deep, husky voice with the slight break in it that sent shivers down Etta's spine, ' "Then I was clean and brave,/And all around the wonder grew/How well did I behave." '

' "And now the fancy passes by," ' mockingly, Corinna took up the refrain, ' "And nothing will remain,/And miles around they'll say that you" ' she nodded round at Seth, ' "Are quite yourself again." '

There was a silence. Alan filled up everyone's glasses.

'Where's Joyce Painswick?' asked Debbie.

'I thought she and Hengist's scarf were part of the fittings,' said Phoebe bitchily, 'getting her money's worth.'

'Joyce has got a job,' said Etta.

'Whatever as?' asked Phoebe, then choked on her hot Ribena as Etta, with quiet satisfaction, said:

'As Marius's secretary.'

'How ridiculous!' exploded Debbie.

'But she's such a frump,' raged Phoebe, 'and she must be nearly seventy.'

'Ah-hem,' said Alan.

'Well, some people are young at seventy,' said Phoebe hastily, 'but Painswick's so spinny. She'll never cope with Marius's language.'

'Whose idea was it?' demanded Debbie.

'Valent's,' said Alan in amusement. 'He reckons Marius is in pieces. And if Painswick was able to control Hengist Brett-Taylor and six hundred hooligans at Bagley Hall, Throstledown will be a breeze. Didn't you notice an improvement in today's emails?'

'Didn't get certain people leaving on time,' said Debbie sourly.

'Damn, damn, damn,' said Phoebe, filling up her Ribena glass with champagne. 'We want to start a family and it would have been the perfect part-time job for me.'

'Joyce won't last long. Far too bossy for Marius, can't see her appealing to the owners,' sniffed Debbie.

'Joyce is a darling,' flared up Etta to everyone's amazement, 'such a kind heart and a lovely sense of humour. She'll look after Marius and the horses and the lads.'

'Hoity-toity,' muttered Debbie to Phoebe, as Etta stomped off up the bus to talk to Alban and Toby, who were praising Araminta, whom Toby often took shooting.

'I've been told to take at least a thousand cartridges to the Borders next weekend,' Toby was saying excitedly. 'Must go and have a pee.'

'I had a wonderful tip for the two thirty,' Alban turned round and smiled at Etta, 'but alas, I've reached the age when if some-one gives me a wonderful tip I've forgotten it in five minutes.'

59

' "The lads in their hundreds to Ludlow come in for the fair," '
sang Amber as she swung Marius's lorry into the Ludlow road.
'Such a lovely song, one of my father's favourites.'

She was eaten up with nerves. Unlike Newbury, where she'd
been thrown up at the last moment, she'd had several days to fret.

'The last line of the song's so sad,' she continued, rattling away
to Tommy and Rafiq. ' "The lads that will die in their glory and
never be old." '

'Housman's a brilliant poet for jump racing,' she went on. 'He
understood about camaraderie and bands of brothers, soldiers at
the front heroically risking their lives day after day. Jockeys are
the same, riding into the cannon's mouth, never knowing if they
or their horse will come home. Most jockeys are in constant pain
from endless falls or stomach cramps from wasting.

'Rogue says even the jockeys he most wants to beat, like Bluey
Charteris, even an evil bastard like Killer O'Kagan, he misses
when he's not riding every day against them. He hates it when
they have terrible falls.

' "The lads that will die in their glory and never be old." ' As
Amber sang the line again, her voice broke. 'I'm sorry to bang
on, I guess I'm just wound up. I hoped my dad was going to make
it and walk the course with me, but he's not very well.'

'You'll do brilliant,' said Tommy soothingly. 'Must be awful
living in a time of war when you're constantly dreading all your
friends and family being wiped out.'

'I still am,' said Rafiq chillingly. 'In Afghanistan, in Iraq, in
Pakistan. The Yanks bombed a funeral the other day and killed
my uncle and aunt.'

'I'm so sorry.' Tommy put an arm round his shoulders, feeling him tense up then tremble. 'I wish you'd talk more about it.'

And you'd tell your policeman father, thought Rafiq darkly. He'd been up at five, praying for Amber and Mrs Wilkinson and that Marius would get out of blinkers and at least recognize how well the horses went for him and help him get a licence as a conditional jockey.

Back in the Ford Transit, a lurking Shagger descended heavily into the seat beside Corinna.

'You have such exquisite diction, Miss Waters, have you ever thought of insuring your voice?'

'Will you also insure my exquisite dick? I know you'd like to,' said Seth maliciously.

Shagger blushed. He felt ambiguous about Seth, responding to his magnetism but aware of his ability to make mischief as well as love.

'How's little Trixie?' murmured Seth to Alan.

'Gated like Dora.'

Next moment Etta's mobile rang: it was a gated, gutted Dora.

'You'll never guess what utterly bloody Rogue has done. You know, with Killer banned this season, Rogue's determined to nail the championship. He's already got ninety-seven winners. Well, racing at Down Royal's been cancelled because of flooding, so Rogue's flown back to Ludlow and told his agent to pinch rides off as many other jockeys as possible. I've just heard one includes Johnnie Brutus on Bafford Playboy in the two fifteen so Rogue'll be riding against Mrs Wilkinson.

'There's no way Wilkie's going to beat Rogue and Playboy on that right-handed track,' stormed Dora. 'And Marius will go ballistic Rogue's riding for Shade. And it's so unfair to Joey, Alan and everyone who's had massive ante-post bets on Wilkie – but all Rogue cares about is getting his hundredth win.

'The flip side is that the press will be out in force to see if Rogue gets his ton, and Corinna will think they're all for her.' Dora giggled. 'I've just rung Painswick, neighing down the phone pretending to be Mrs Wilkinson and asking her to take poor deserted Chisolm a piece of carrot cake for her tea.

'And Etta, if you get a moment, you won't forget to show Corinna those pictures of Paris. There's a fantastic part for him in *Phèdre* if they bring the production to England.'

60

The sun kept making brief appearances in a sky dominated by inky-blue clouds, either tasselled by falling rain or with rainbows leaping up into them like chasers. Gradually, as the road twisted and turned, stone walls gave way to neat fences, sheep-coloured fields scattered with sheep, blue mountains topped with fir trees and square Georgian houses in white or faded red.

Once again Alban kept slowing down to discuss who lived in the larger ones.

'They put Phoebe and me in separate rooms, last time we stayed there,' brayed Toby, 'so I got into Phoebe's bed. Next moment our host marched in and jumped on us. Bit put out to find me there, then tried to join in.'

'Look, there's a signpost to Much Wenlock,' said Seth. ' "On Wenlock Edge the wood's in trouble." '

'So will we be if we don't get a move on, Alban,' called out Alan.

'Housman was born on the borders of Shropshire and Worcester actually,' said the Major, determined to keep his literary end up.

'Housman was a very difficult, introverted man, rather like Marius,' mused Seth.

'Housman was gay,' protested Alan.

'Marius isn't exactly jolly,' grinned Seth.

'I guess it's worth putting money on Rogue and Bafford Playboy,' said Chris.

Corinna, on her third half-pint of champagne, was pretending to learn *Phèdre*. Etta sat down beside her.

'I hope you don't mind, darling Dora Belvedon's boyfriend Paris is determined to be an actor. Just wondered if you knew of anything for him? He's awfully good-looking, they're still talking about his Romeo at Bagley.'

'No, no, no, no!' exploded Corinna, so everyone in the bus stopped talking. 'Every day the post is a Niagara of demands, every telephone call, every email wants something, a favourite recipe, a doodle, a tile painted, a thirty-minute trip to a studio to talk up some lousy dead actress, a fête to open, a request for a piece of jewellery, a signed T-shirt. Me,' raged Corinna, 'in a T-shirt, free seats for a play, a sponsored walk. Even worse are the endless execrable scripts that thunder through the letter box, the letters from parents demanding help for their children. Find me a director, a producer, most of all an agent. Watch this DVD of my play about recycled gerbils, watch this video of me in *Hamlet*, give me a part in your next play.'

Her rage was terrifyingly eruptive, the spit flying from her lips, mad eyes glittering, emotions going to work on her face like a jockey on the run-in, all the time brandishing *Phèdre* as though she was going to bash Etta on the head.

'I'm so sorry,' whispered Etta. 'It was tactless of me, when you must be so tired.'

'I have no time for myself. I am an artist, but my public devours me,' stormed Corinna. 'I am sucked dry like a lemon.'

Debbie smirked at Phoebe. Serve Etta right for sucking up.

Gazing down at her trembling hands, Etta suddenly saw the photographs she was clutching being taken from her and replaced by a large glass of champagne.

'Shut up, Corinna, just shut up,' ordered Seth. 'You're not Phèdre now, just look at these pix.'

'Take them away,' screeched Corinna, the back of her hand pressed to her forehead.

'Bloody look,' hissed Seth.

There was a long pause.

'Christ, he is beautiful,' admitted Corinna. 'Heart-stopping.' She examined the pictures more closely. 'How old is he?'

'Eighteen,' stammered Etta, 'he's just gone up to Cambridge.'

Corinna glanced up at Seth.

'Hippolyte?' she said. 'If we do an English run.'

'Or Konstantin,' said Seth.

'Tell him to ring me up,' said Corinna. Then, bursting into deep, rather too consciously infectious laughter, she patted Etta's cheek: 'I'm sorry, you were quite right.'

As the bus rumbled into Ludlow racecourse, Etta couldn't stop shaking. Seth helped her down.

'Darling Etta, you're a saint. Corinna's rehearsing the bit of

Phèdre when Hippolyte rejects her. I'm so sorry. You're the best thing about this syndicate. Thank you so much.' He kissed her cheek and the grey day was flooded with light.

Alan shook his head and thought of Housman again:

> His folly has not fellow
> Beneath the blue of day
> That gives to man or woman
> His heart and soul away.

Like Yelena and Serebryakov in *Uncle Vanya*, he reflected, Seth and Corinna descended on the country and affected everyone with their selfishness, passing fancies and disregard for other people's lives.

Despite a dank, wet, cold Monday afternoon, a very creditable crowd had turned out to watch Rogue. Mist drifted round the bare trees like an anxious hostess. The lovely flat course was ringed with small mountains.

'Those must be Housman's blue remembered hills,' said Seth. 'I wonder if he liked horses.'

'He wrote a good poem about carthorses,' said Alan.

> 'Is my team ploughing,
> That I was used to drive
> And hear the harness jingle
> When I was man alive?

'Then he died and his ghost didn't like someone else driving his horses.'

' 'Spect those poor jockeys that Rogue's ousted feel the same,' said Chris disapprovingly. 'That's probably Rogue in that 'elicopter.'

'That'll be a bookie,' said Alan.

'Everyone got their badges?' said the Major bossily.

'Seth doesn't need a badge,' cooed Phoebe, 'everyone knows him.'

Corinna, giving Phoebe a filthy look, grew increasingly disagreeable.

'Christ, it's arctic, no wonder bloody Valent backed out. I'm getting a taxi home.'

Happily, at that moment, a pack of press and photographers, gathered in anticipation of Rogue's ninety-ninth and hundredth, turned their attentions to Corinna, who became all smiles and waves.

'Darlings, isn't it thrilling? Yes, it's my first time jump racing,' she was soon telling Richard Pitman. 'I've come to cheer on my horse, Mrs Williams.'

'*My* horse?' Debbie and Phoebe exchanged expressions of outrage.

'Leave her,' muttered Seth. 'Anything's better than her stupid tanties.'

'I don't know how you put up with her, Seth,' said Phoebe.

Awesome Wells was livid. He'd been riding Oh My Goodness, which had been favourite in the first race, a mares only, and been so certain of victory he'd asked little Angel from Throstledown out to dinner.

Then Rogue had rolled up and taken Dare Catswood's ride on Gifted Child off him. The commentary had the crowd in stitches.

'Rogue Rogers and Gifted Child are taking them along, and Oh My Goodness in the dark blue and purple colours is moving up. And, Oh My Goodness . . .'

Alas, poor Awesome kicked too early. When she hit the front, Oh My Goodness, not liking being on her own, started looking around for friends. She allowed Rogue to hurtle past on Gifted and take the race, his ninety-eighth, to ecstatic cheers.

'Can I borrow fifty quid off you, Tommy?' asked Awesome.

Only two races to go. Rogue won his ninety-ninth and rode grinning into the winners enclosure to cheers and the thud of gloved hands clapping.

'I'd like him for supper,' said Corinna, now thoroughly over-excited by the strange cries of the bookies and the horses clopping clockwise round the parade ring.

Seth was delighted to be even more mobbed than Corinna.

'When's the next *Holby City*?' asked eager ladies.

'Perhaps Corinna should do a stint in *Corrie* to raise her profile,' sniffed Debbie.

Down in the parade ring, Bafford Playboy was flexing his muscles, excited as a dog about to go for a walk. Mrs Wilkinson by contrast was cold and edgy, with no Sir Cuthbert, no Chisolm, no Count Romeo to comfort her. Only Bafford Playboy, a bully who she remembered bashing into her at the point-to-point.

As Corinna reached the parade ring, two women, wearing fur hats like Saturn's rings which showed off their exquisite cheek-bones, suddenly noticed her and squealed in excitement. 'How fritefly exciting to see you, such fans, what brings you to Ludlow?'

'My horse, Mrs Wilson, is in this race . . . Which one is she?' she hissed to Etta.

'Number ten, over there.'

'But she's tiny, no bigger than a donkey,' exploded Corinna.

'Nice horse, very well related,' said a proud hovering Alban, raising his hat to the Saturn ring ladies. 'Her sire was Rupert Campbell-Black's Peppy Koala.'

61

Marius was raw with nerves. He refused to admit how fond he'd become of Mrs Wilkinson. Was he crazy forcing her on to a right-handed track, was the trip too short, would she ever get her little feet out of the mud? There wasn't a blade of grass left in the winners enclosure. Now his wife, who he hadn't seen since she left him, had turned up with Shade and he'd forgotten how beautiful she was, particularly smothered in Shade's furs, which she'd been so violently opposed to wearing in the old days. Collie and Harvey-Holden were with them. Marius looked straight through the lot.

Etta was distressed. Having put a tenner she could ill afford on Mrs Wilkinson, she had mislaid her betting slip. Searching frantically, not wanting to bother anyone, she didn't notice Shagger surreptitiously picking it up and putting it in his notecase.

One more race needed. The crowd cheered, the press gathered, as Rogue, always last to leave the weighing room because he liked to make an entrance, sauntered out in Shade's orange and magenta colours, smiling round, whacking his boots, kissing Olivia on both cheeks and shaking the hands of Shade and Harvey-Holden.

Mrs Wilkinson had beaten Playboy once, so Harvey-Holden instructed both Rogue and Dare Catswood, who was riding Stop Preston, to block Wilkie's good eye and hem her in.

'Amber Lloyd-Foxe will panic and lose it.'

Rogue raised an eyebrow but said nothing.

Amber was already in a state of shock, having barged into the weighing room and discovered Rogue naked on the scales and flashing the biggest tackle therein.

'Don't win by too much,' Marius warned her.

Mrs Wilkinson was allowed three races over hurdles as a novice before she was allotted a handicap, which Marius wanted as low as possible because it meant less weight to carry.

The twelve riders were down at the start, surrounded by even more photographers. Nervous as a cat, poised for his hundredth, Rogue on a vast Bafford Playboy was eight inches taller than Amber, and winding her up.

'Winning isn't everything,' he said reassuringly, and then after a pause, 'it's the only thing.'

He's much less beautiful in a gum shield, thought Amber. Wish he'd keep it in all the time.

'Make sure you're in the frame, darling,' he added as they rode their horses up to look at the first fence, 'then you'll get into the winners and be able to cash in on all my publicity.'

As she glared up at him, he ostentatiously checked his reflection in her goggles.

Mrs Wilkinson was trembling violently, psyching herself up.

'Who's going to make it?' asked the starter.

'I am,' said Dare Catswood.

'I'm keeping mine handy,' said Awesome.

'I'm going to win,' said Rogue.

They were out, bumping and jostling for position on a course which curled off towards the trees round to the right.

The flag fell, the tape flew, they were off. Dare Catswood set a furious pace on Preston to exhaust Mrs Wilkinson, who hated not leading the pack.

Rogue and Amber rowed all the way round.

'Don't crowd me,' she screamed as he sat on her tail.

'You know I'm only looking at your arse.'

Amber was having a nightmare ride. The pace was faster than anything she'd ever imagined as they took off and landed on ground slipperier than turkey fat.

With no right eye, Mrs Wilkinson couldn't see the rail. Frantic to find something on which to focus, she kept hanging left.

'Get off my line, you stupid cunt,' yelled the jockeys as she drifted across them. The track had been ripped to pieces by earlier races. As horses overtook a faltering Mrs Wilkinson, they kicked clods of earth in her good eye.

At the next flight she slipped again, jumped wildly left and would have unshipped Amber, if Rogue hadn't grabbed her silks and tugged her back into place.

'Use your fucking stick down the left side to correct her,' he yelled. 'You're not with the Pony Club now.'

'It'll bloody freak her out,' yelled back Amber.

'Well, yank her back to the right, then.'

Watching the television by the tote, Marius was in agony. How could he have put Wilkie through it? Etta was in double agony, with Corinna driving her nuts. Too vain to wear her spectacles, she bombarded Etta with questions.

'What's that funeral cortège following the riders?'

'Oh, ambulance, doctors, vets and things.'

'Who's in the lead?'

'Dare Catswood and Awesome Wells.'

'Which one's Mrs Willoughby?'

'Wilkinson. She's the grey and Amber's wearing emerald green colours . . . Lying fifth, no, sixth now.'

Etta was terrified seeing Mrs Wilkinson lurch ever wider as they swung into the home straight.

'Taking the scenic route,' yelled Rogue as he and the other jockeys got to work, somehow staying put as their frantically thrusting bodies kicked and pushed and, like weavers with their looms, switched whip and reins to different hands as they thrashed their horses on.

'Which one is Amber?'

'The one in emerald green.'

'Why isn't she whipping Mrs Willoughby like the others? She seems to be going backwards. Where's that good-looking Rogue Rogers?'

'In the lead in magenta and orange.'

'Why can't he ride Mrs Willoughby?'

'Please, Corinna,' cried Etta, 'watch the big screen.'

Mrs Wilkinson had steadied. Ahead galloped Preston and Awesome Wells's chestnut mare Katya Katkin, and ahead of them Rogue and Playboy. But Rogue was having to use a lot of whip, Playboy was not jumping fluently, wearily dragging his feet out of the mud. Harvey-Holden, registered Amber, even with Collie's added expertise, has not got that horse fit enough.

Already the crowd were roaring him home.

'Come on, Rogue!'

'Kick on, son.'

'Come on, Playboy!'

Two out Dare Catswood and Preston fell, horse and jockey lying in a crumpled heap. Very carefully, Mrs Wilkinson landed to the left and jumped over them, allowing Rogue to surge even further ahead.

'He's going to piss all over it,' said Chris in disgust.

'She'll be third. Come on, Wilkie!' cried Etta.

Deafened by the increasing roar of the crowd on the run-in, Rogue glanced back through his legs, realizing he was safely in front, then up at the big screen. Yippee, a hundred up.

Playboy, a young horse, however, decided, rather than run the gauntlet of those cheering, shouting punters and the flashing photographers, to swing right through the gap in the rails on to the steeplechasing course. Before Rogue could yank him back left on to the run-in, he had cleared the next fence.

Like a wireless switched off, the cheers stopped.

Stupid prat's taken the wrong course, thought Amber in ecstasy.

'Now's our chance, Wilkie,' she cried, as Mrs Wilkinson, eyeballing Katya Katkin and grinding her teeth, trundled past the aghast, astounded faces. She was in front by a mud-splattered nose, and despite being briefly headed by Katya, fought back with tremendous courage and stayed ahead all the way to the line.

As Amber pulled up, still shaking, burying her face in Mrs Wilkinson's muddy shoulder, she heard a stream of expletives coming from a returning Rogue and ostentatiously clapped her hands over her ears.

'Dear, dear, why didn't you use your whip to stop him hanging right?'

'We won, we won,' screamed Etta. 'Oh Corinna.'

But Corinna had gone. Having lavishly reapplied blood-red lipstick, she had hurtled down the steps, across the grass, ducking under the rails and running down the course with her arms out.

'With any luck she'll be trampled to death like a suffragette,' said Seth.

Tommy came panting up, hugging Mrs Wilkinson, pulling her ears and crying as she clipped on the lead rope.

'Well done, you took out Rogue.'

'Hubris took him out,' said Amber.

'Hugh who?' said Awesome, cantering up and putting an arm round Amber's shoulders. 'Well done, you took out that fucker.'

Next minute Corinna pounded up, arms out, then, deciding Mrs Wilkinson's face was too muddy to be kissed, snatched the lead rope from Tommy and the microphone from Richard Pitman, so he could interview her rather than Amber.

'We don't need two of us to lead her,' Corinna then said dismissively to Tommy, and strode off to the winners enclosure. The photographers went crazy.

Amber's deadpan face was as mud-speckled as a thrush's egg,

but as she rode into the winners enclosure she touched her green hat, punched the air and grinned in ecstasy, and the crowd roared their applause. Rogue would get his hundredth later on, this was the young conditional's moment.

As she dismounted, Marius was beside her, ex-wife, Shade and Harvey-Holden forgotten.

'That was brilliant. Must have been really hairy. I'm sorry, the trip was wrong, the going was wrong, she's never running right-handed again, but she still won. God, she's got guts.'

'This is the most exciting day of my life,' Corinna was telling the press, as she took up her position next to Mrs Wilkinson.

It was while Amber was weighing in that she heard the horrible news that although Dare Catswood had only wrenched his shoulder, Stop Preston had had to be put down. She then escaped to the women's changing room, which was part of the ambulance room, in which she would probably have ended up if Rogue hadn't dragged her back on to Mrs Wilkinson, and burst into a flood of tears.

'You don't want to do that,' said a soft voice. 'You've got to talk to the press.'

It was Rogue. Having shed Shade's silks, he was dressed in a black undershirt. His face was still spattered with mud, making his smile wider and whiter. As she wasn't wearing heels, his blue eyes were on a level with hers.

'Well done,' he said. 'Aren't you glad I let you win?'

'You did not.'

'I did too, I wanted Marius to put you op for Wetherby next month.'

'He won't, he hasn't. You did not,' sobbed Amber, 'I won on my own.'

Frantically wiping her eyes, she was about to slap his face when Rogue caught her hand and brushed it with his lips, sending a thousand volts through her. 'I'm going to Wetherby too,' he said, 'and I'm going to take you out to dinner, and later in the evening we're going to make peace, not war.' Then, at her look of bewilderment: 'Well done, darling, of course you won and that's one hell of a brave little horse. I better go and win the last race.'

62

Sadness was cast over the day by the death of Stop Preston, who had showed such promise.

'The horses that die in their glory, and never grow old,' sighed Alan.

'Congratulations to Mrs Wilkinson and all her connections,' crackled the loudspeaker.

'Sounds just like Jane Austen,' mocked Corinna as she went up to collect Mrs Wilkinson's cup, watched with differing emotions by the rest of the syndicate.

> 'Oh I have been to Ludlow Fair
> And left my necktie God knows where,'

quoted Seth.

> 'And carried half way home, or near,
> Pints and quarts of Ludlow beer:'

continued Alan,

> 'Then the world seemed none so bad,
> And I myself a sterling lad.'

'Tommy's a sterling stable lad,' observed Seth.

'And she's got such a crush on Rafiq, and poor Rafiq's got such a crush on Amber,' said Alan.

He and Seth, having both made a grand on Mrs Wilkinson, were getting drunk on the way home. Corinna, who'd passed out, was sleeping peacefully in the back. Chris, also drunk, was pouring his heart out to the Major, who was well aware that he and Chrissie had lapsed on their subscription but, unlike Shagger, not through avarice.

'We're frankly havin' to live on the Fox's takings, the rental's so bloody huge. Previous landlady lied about the takings,' Chris was saying. 'Shouldn't have joined the syndicate, haven't got three thousand to put in, let alone the subscription. Smoking ban and drink driving's hit us hard. IVF's cost us a fortune. Chrissie won't be happy until she has a baby.'

Meanwhile back at Badger's Court, in a room intended one day to be Bonny and Valent's master bedroom, Joey and Chrissie made love on an old divan, to which Joey often retreated for forty winks after lunch.

'Oh Joey,' sighed Chrissie.

'Oh Chrissie,' sighed Joey, 'I 'ave longed for this.'

'Oh Joey, that is so naughty,' squeaked Chrissie, feeling something deliciously cold up her bottom.

'No, it ain't, it's Priceless,' said Joey. 'Get that long nose out of there, Priceless.'

'I've got an idea, Chris,' said the Major. 'Let me make a call.' As he retreated to the back of the bus, where Corinna snored lightly, he longed to put a hand on her splendidly heaving breasts.

The full moon peering in through the window must be checking her reflection in my shiny face, thought Etta wearily. She had no right to feel so despondent, except that she was heartbroken about Preston, her lucky horse, and sad about losing her betting slip. Fifty pounds would have paid for her share of the picnic and enabled her to buy something for Tilda for looking after Drummond and Poppy.

She had terribly missed Dora and Trixie on the trip, and Woody and Joey, and the vicar, and dear Pocock and darling Joyce. Etta wondered how she'd got on holding the fort at the yard.

She ought to be overjoyed that Mrs Wilkinson had won. Ludlow was such a lovely course, but somehow winning at Newbury had been more exciting because so unexpected. Also she wasn't sure about Corinna. Somehow it hadn't been as much fun as last time.

Phoebe felt the same.

'The Royal Box was so exciting,' she was complaining to Debbie, 'and everyone didn't rabbit on about Housman, though I suppose it's better than house prices. Frankly, I'm fed up with

Corinna hogging the limelight. Pity Valent wasn't here to buy all that lovely fizz, he'd have kept her in order.'

'I'm quite exhausted, having been kept awake by them rowing all night,' said Debbie, not adding that just as she was dropping off at five o'clock, she'd felt the Major's penis nudging her back: 'Wakey, wakey, here comes snakey,' so she really hadn't got any sleep at all.

The west was dominated by a dark cloud with a chink of fiery scarlet light along the bottom, the remains of the sunset.

'I don't know how Seth puts up with her,' grumbled Phoebe.

'By drinking too much,' said Debbie tartly. 'Mrs Wilkinson's *our* Village Horse, not Corinna's. She's the village whore. I'm going to bail out if she continues to ruin things.'

Up the front, Alban and Toby were still talking about shooting.

'Phoebe won't beat or pick up,' Toby was complaining. 'Last time we went shooting with Georgie Larkminster, we only got a cup of coffee when we arrived, and nothing but Cornish pasties and not a drop of drink at lunchtime.'

The Major's mobile rang. He took it to the back of the bus again and five minutes later strode back down the gangway, taking up his position beside Alban, bristling with self-importance.

'Well, there's good news and very good news. That was Valent ringing to congratulate us all and particularly Mrs Wilkinson and Etta,' the Major smiled in her direction, 'and he wants to join the syndicate if we'll have him.'

'Of course we will,' cried Etta, feeling a glow of happiness as everyone cheered.

'He's going to take Chris and Chrissie's slot,' went on the Major, 'although they'll still be involved, I hope.'

'Not too much at that price,' muttered Debbie.

'How lovely, drinks will be on the house,' piped up Phoebe.

'Now the even better news.' The Major's eyes gleamed. 'He's going to donate his share to Bonny Richards as a birthday gift.'

There was a pause.

'We'll have to put chastity belts on our husbands,' giggled Phoebe, 'but what fun to have some young blood in the syndicate.'

Even Toby looked rather excited.

'Valent wants Bonny to involve herself properly in the community,' explained the Major. 'He's so anxious for her to enjoy living in Willowwood.'

'Here's one member of the community who wouldn't mind getting improperly involved with Bonny,' said Seth.

Etta felt even more depressed.

Everyone, particularly the Major, who'd had his hand up her black polo neck all the time he was talking to Valent, jumped as Corinna's rich contralto rang out:

> 'My Bonny lies over the ocean.
> My Bonny lies over the sea.
> My father lay over my mother
> And that's how they got little me.'

When Etta got home, she was delighted to find Gwenny mewing outside and inside a message to ring Joyce Painswick, however late.

'Wasn't Wilkie wonderful, clever little girl, beating Playboy in those ghastly conditions?' cried Etta, as she tried to hold the telephone and scrape the meat off the chicken leg intended for her supper into a saucer for Gwenny. 'And didn't Amber do brilliantly?'

'Brilliantly,' agreed Painswick. 'I texted Hengist that she would be riding.'

'We missed you and Dora and Trixie so much. How did you get on?'

'I now know how Hercules felt after mucking out the Augean stables,' said Painswick sourly. 'I have never encountered such a mess. The only thing Marius puts away in filing cabinets is bottles. I had to take little Mistletoe and Chisolm for a walk to get some fresh air.

'Marius was absurdly late leaving for Ludlow. Worked himself into a lather over nothing, changed in thirty seconds without even washing, rushed off, then rang up constantly from the car. Had I seen that, not to do that, had X been entered for that. I've never met anyone so disorganized.'

'Oh, poor Joyce.' Etta put the chicken on the floor.

'Not sure I'm up to it.'

'Oh please, you will be. Look how you cherished Hengist. Wilkie needs you, Marius certainly needs you.'

'Huh, not sure he'll ever pay me, he's got bills going back to the middle of last year. How was Corinna? Saw her hogging the limelight. You'd think she won the race herself.'

'Demanding. Actually I thought she was horrid. I can't see why she and dear Seth ... But she's going to have competition. Valent's bought a share in Wilkie for Bonny Richards.'

'Oh dear. Megastar wars. I thought Bonny loathed the country and that everyone was boring and right-wing, particularly the horses,' sniffed Painswick. 'Joey'll have to buck up and finish Badger's Court. I saw across the valley he was giving Chrissie and Priceless a very thorough conducted tour of the place this afternoon. Their conduct left a lot to be desired.'

'Oh dear. Never mind, darling, Wilkie won,' Etta stroked a purring Gwenny, 'and Marius was nice to Amber for a change.'

Tommy came home the saddest. She had acquired fifth-degree burns from the sparks flying between Rogue and Amber. Rafiq hadn't spoken on the journey home, and having settled Oh My Goodness and History Painting, had sloped off to bed, refusing to join the lads celebrating Mrs Wilkinson's victory in the Fox, not even bothering to say good night to Furious.

A confused, exhausted Mrs Wilkinson, missing Etta and being chided noisily on her return by Sir Cuthbert, Romeo and Chisolm, had misjudged the doorway into her box. She had banged her head and taken a long time to settle, so Tommy didn't go to the Fox either.

'You're headed for stardom, Wilkie. You'll soon be a Saturday horse and hear the crowds cheering your name.'

Tommy gave Mrs Wilkinson a last hug. Wondering why she was always comforting things that longed to be with other things, she crossed the yard to Furious, who, ears flattened, was hanging out of the isolation box with Dilys the sheep snoring in the straw behind him.

'It'll be spring soon, and you won't have to use her as a duvet any more.' Tommy took out a packet of Polos, then, as Furious lunged at her: 'Stop it, you've bitten me enough times, or you won't get any of these, and you'll get sold and break Rafiq's heart, even more than Miss Amber Lloyd-Foxe has. You've got to start winning races, and Rafiq must ride you.'

In agreement, Furious grabbed and munched the entire packet of Polos before laying his head on Tommy's shoulder, breathing lovingly into her ear.

'Oh Furious,' sighed Tommy, 'at least you love me. Ouch, you pig,' as he nipped her sharply on the arm.

The following morning Etta rang Joyce in high excitement.

'Is it a bad moment?'

'It's all bad moments. Marius came back drunk and reduced the place to an absolute tip again. Perhaps that's why it's called tipsy.'

'Oh, poor Joyce,' giggled Etta. 'Look, I feel really really mean. Corinna's Pole, Stefan, has just dropped off a beautifully wrapped present with a card saying, "Dearest Etta, sorry I was horrible, come and have a drink soon, all love, Corinna." Isn't that sweet?'

'Fairly. What's she given you?'

'I'm just unwrapping it. Oh, it's a ravishing pink and lilac scarf, with another little card attached.'

There was a long pause, then Painswick could hear Etta laughing hysterically.

'What does it say? Come on.'

'It says,' gasped Etta, ' "Dearest Corinna, Happy fifty-fifth birthday, love Judi D." '

63

Any doubts Bonny Richards might have had about accepting Valent's birthday present were dispelled by the magnificent coverage afforded to Corinna the following day. Most of the papers referred to her wildly successful tour of America, her bold move to play Phèdre in French in Paris, and her forthcoming stint at Stratford.

'Leading lady', was the headline in both *The Times* and the *Independent*, with a ravishing photograph of Corinna leading in Mrs Wilkinson.

'I must get that picture blown up,' cried an overjoyed Corinna.

'Not the only thing,' muttered Seth, who hadn't made any of the pictures.

Nor had Amber. She'd have to get her famous father along next time to pull in the crowds. She was in a complete daze. Had Rogue really said what he'd said? Would Marius let her ride at Wetherby? He was so indecisive. The next meeting was in February. Her evenings not on the Equicizer were spent watching videos of Rogue, noticing how low he crouched over his horses, how well he presented them at fences, how he could think and adjust at full gallop. Then her mind would mist over and she would long and long for him to crouch over her, driving her over the line with those deep pelvic thrusts.

Rafiq also watched Rogue's videos obsessively, learning and churning with hatred. Death to the infidel.

Painswick was driven crackers by Amber's constant texting. Had Marius made any decisions on Wetherby, had he entered Wilkie? Had he entered any horses for Rogue? Rafiq nearly murdered Josh when he hit Furious with a spade for striking out at him with a foreleg.

Tension was running high.

*

Attitudes to Bonny's joining the syndicate were mixed. Would she really grace the minibus rather than Valent's twenty-million Gulfstream jet on the long journey from Willowwood to Wetherby, which would allow loads of time for her and Corinna to insult each other?

Ione was excited by Bonny's Green credentials. Alban, who had met her in London when he lunched with Valent, thought she was 'awfully pretty but hard to understand'.

Having bankrupted herself paying Shagger's syndicate bill, Tilda was scared Shagger would fall for Bonny. Perhaps she'd come and talk to the children at Greycoats.

Joey, who loved Valent, hated Bonny and had had to endure her caprice and criticism whenever she visited the house. He was depressed that Chris and Chrissie had backed out of the syndicate, which would afford him less opportunity to see Chrissie on her own, particularly as Bonny and Valent might soon be moving into Badger's Court.

He had been dispiritedly clearing rubble from the garden in February when Valent and Bonny had paid a flying visit. They had been enchanted to see sweeps of purple crocuses merging with pools of sky-blue scillas, clumps of primroses like day-old chicks merging with the gold aconites and crimson polyanthus and, loveliest of all, the palest pink *Prunus autumnalis* blossom dancing against a dark yew hedge.

'I never believed such a lovely garden lurked beneath the debris,' cried Bonny, but looked less amused when Joey, not without malice, said, 'Etta done that. Etta planted all those fings as a fank-you present to Valent for taking in Mrs Wilkinson.'

The lads at Throstledown were wildly excited about Bonny and fought to go to Wetherby instead of Tommy, who was having a week off to help her sister who'd just had a baby. At the last moment, egged on by Painswick who was aware of Rafiq's depression, Marius decided to run Furious. As the lorry was going all that way taking Oh My Goodness, Mrs Wilkinson and History Painting, it might as well take Furious too. Rogue could ride him in a novice chase. Furious was far too contemptuous of hurdles. At the very last moment, he agreed Amber could ride Mrs Wilkinson.

Amber, who'd never lost sleep over a man, was rattled. She was supposed to be having dinner with Rogue after Wetherby, but he hadn't called her. With his track record, could he resist making a pass at Bonny? Not that Amber cared, but she still spent any fee she might get in advance on having her roots done and her legs and pubes waxed.

Romy and Martin were furious with Etta for losing her Ludlow betting slip – the money would have boosted a dwindling Sampson Bancroft Fund – but they were frightfully excited about Bonny joining the syndicate and wanted an invitation pronto. They'd just landed a battle-against-obesity charity, and felt slender Bonny would be the ideal target role model.

Etta sighed. If only she was still living at Bluebell Hill, she could have given a little party to welcome Bonny.

Instead she bit the bullet and sent her a very pretty card of snowdrops, saying how thrilled everyone was that she was joining the syndicate and how they all looked forward to meeting her when Mrs Wilkinson ran again. She also sent Valent a birthday card from Wilkie and Chisolm.

Willowwood made acquaintance with Bonny sooner than expected when she appeared on television winning a BAFTA.

Etta was touched and surprised when, on the same evening, Corinna asked her round for a drink. She brightened up her pale blue jersey with the pink and lilac scarf Corinna had given her.

When she arrived, Corinna was already three parts cut and watching the awards with Seth, Alan and Priceless who was stretched out on the sofa chewing a nearby table but jumped down flashing his white teeth and snaking his long black nose all round Etta's hips.

Seth handed Etta a glass of champagne.

'Bonny's been nominated for Best Actress in a film called *The Blossoming*,' he explained, 'about a woman who overcomes the trauma of rape and child abuse.'

'Valent sent us a tape,' said Corinna, 'but Bonny mumbles so badly you can't hear a bloody word she says.'

Bonny's acceptance speech was long and tearful, thanking her 'significant other, Valent Edwards', who was blushing and squirming with pride and embarrassment in the stalls.

'Beetrooted to the spot,' said Seth scornfully. 'Talk about Bonny and Clod.'

'Valent looks sweet,' protested Etta.

Bonny was wearing a short strapless pale grey silk sheath dress which seemed to merge into her luminously pearly shoulders, touchingly slender neck and long fawn's legs. She had the huge-eyed, hauntingly sad face of the Little Mermaid. Life would be spent treading on knives.

At that moment, Corinna's mobile rang. It was Phoebe.

'Quick, quick, Miss Waters, so exciting, Bonny's on television, she's won a BAFTA.'

'We know,' said Corinna and hung up.

'Just look at her gorgeous diamonds,' murmured Alan. 'Twinkle, twinkle, little star.'

'Valent must have emptied Asprey,' grumbled Corinna.

Bonny was now paying tribute to everyone who'd helped her on her life's journey.

'Why doesn't she mention Mr Whiskers the gerbil and Gordon the goldfish?' snorted Corinna. As she threw a cushion at the television, lots of feathers fell out. 'I've always thought BAFTA stands for Bloody Awful Film and Television Actress.'

Seth laughed and topped up her and Etta's glasses.

'I wonder if she'll make the races tomorrow,' asked Etta. 'After such celebrations, she'll have a hangover.'

'She doesn't drink,' said Alan.

'That's a hammer blow,' said Seth. 'Christ, you can see why Valent's besotted.'

The Major was also turned on. Debbie, who had wanted to look as nice as possible tomorrow, was irked when her beauty sleep was disturbed again by the Major's cock nudging her coccyx.

'Wakey, wakey,' murmured the Major, 'here comes Snakey.'

Debbie sighed and rolled over.

Before she and Phoebe even met Bonny, they had decided to hero-worship her, knowing how much this would enrage Corinna.

The telephone was ringing as Etta got home from watching the BAFTAs. It was Valent to say he had a meeting in North Yorkshire tomorrow so he and Bonny would be joining the syndicate at Wetherby.

'I'm sending you a DVD of her new film, *The Blossoming*.'

'I'll watch it then we'll have something to talk about,' said Etta, not sure how au fait she was with abuse and rape.

'Bonny comes across as super-confident but underneath she's shy, talks a lot of highfalutin stoof.'

'She's very young,' said Etta, then, regretting it: 'She adores you, lovely the way she singled you out this evening.'

Then she told Valent about Furious making his debut at Wetherby with Rogue. 'I wish Rafiq was riding him, he's the only one who can get a tune out of Furious. If only Marius'd send him on a jockey's course, then he could get a licence. He feels he's not going anywhere and he's so worried about Pakistan. He's such a sweet boy.'

'Wilkie'll be getting jealous,' said Valent. 'Don't forget the orchard's booked for her and Chisolm in the summer. And thunks so much for the bulbs, Etta, the garden looks smashing and thunk you for writing to Bonny and for the birthday card, so nice of you to remember. See you at Wetherby.'

Etta always felt so much happier when she'd been talking to Valent.

64

There are great problems for trainers in having horses owned by a syndicate. You never know when and if a horse is going to run. People take a day's holiday from work, fly down from somewhere, charter a plane or a box, then horses get colic or pull muscles on the gallops. It's desperately difficult to get it right.

Racing is also ruled by the weather. A scorching day of sun or thirty-six hours of deluge or a sharp frost can put a horse out of a race. But it's a brave trainer who pulls a horse if the entire syndicate is descending from all over the country to watch it and is booked into hotels, having cancelled board meetings, sports days, major speeches, and arranged later liaisons with mistresses, only to discover their horse has been withdrawn. Owners, in addition, are often rich men and women used to calling the shots.

Unlike Harvey-Holden, who overran his horses to appease his owners, Marius frequently drove horses miles to races then refused to run them unless the going suited them perfectly, particularly if a horse had been off as long as Sir Cuthbert or was a beginner like Mrs Wilkinson or Furious. Painswick's new job involved a lot of time emailing apologies or fielding expletives.

Due to leave at nine, the Willowwood syndicate set off very late for Wetherby. Stefan the Pole, making Corinna up and attempting to repair last night's ravages, had great difficulty applying lipstick because she kept yelling at Seth. A new short citrus-yellow coat, worn with a big black Stetson, needed different make-up. Tempers were not improved by four hours in a hot bus.

The traffic was frightful. Marius's horses had a nightmare six-hour journey through gales and torrential rain. Mrs Wilkinson arrived in a terrible state, sweating up despite the cold and badly gashed in the shoulder where Furious had bitten her. She was missing Chisolm and Tommy, and Rafiq, the other lad she particularly loved, was preoccupied with Furious.

Deluge followed by brilliant sunshine had dried out the course, a fast-galloping clay track which could get waterlogged in places. Mrs Wilkinson hated soft ground. Marius was tearing his dark brown hair out. It was Bonny Richards's first visit to the races and, as Painswick assured him, most of the syndicate had bought new outfits.

Amber, who took her all-too-few rides seriously, had arrived early and spent a long time walking the course, measuring strides, looking for boggy ground and angles that might cause trouble.

She had also dragged along her father Billy, ex-Olympic showjumper, television superstar. Although he was adored by the public, Billy's job was under threat. Having drunk too much over the years, he was given to fluffing lines and speaking his mind on air. He had expressed horror at possible relocation to Manchester and was also considered 'too posh', which didn't go down well in the penny-pinching, puritan, egalitarian mood at Television Centre. All equine sports were being pruned and plenty of young turks were after Billy's job. His tousled light brown curls were touched with grey, but the enchanting smile and the air of life being a little too much (which it was now) hadn't changed.

Having escaped from the BBC for the day, he was extremely helpful at pointing out hazards.

'Go steady or you won't get round. Ground's bottomless and very wet, tell Mrs Wilkinson to bring her bikini. Don't go for gaps in hurdles, she's got a short stride, might catch her little feet. Very proud, darling, if you win today it's three out of three.'

'Thanks, Dad. Marius is such a shit, he never encourages me or gives me advice. It's just "Why'd you do that?", "Why didn't you do this?" '

'Rupert was like that when we were showjumping,' said Billy. 'Christ, I need a drink.'

A bitter east wind tugged at the last lank curls of old man's beard hanging from the bare trees. It was only eleven in the morning and Billy had smoked all the way round. Amber was horrified how grey he looked in the open air.

'You OK, Dad? Mum playing you up?'

'No, no,' lied Billy.

'Rogue's asked me out this evening,' she couldn't resist telling him.

'Don't get hurt, darling. He's charming, but an even worse womanizer than Rupert used to be.'

'I can look after myself. Don't tell Mum, she's bound to tell the press if Dora doesn't get there first.'

Amber had been so busy, rising early, driving up and walking the course, she hadn't looked at the papers. On her return to the stables, Michelle with a smug smile handed her the *Evening Standard*, which had been brought up by a southern owner.

'Rogue's been a naughty boy again.'

On an inside page was a picture of a plastered Rogue with his arm round an equally plastered, very pretty actress called Tara Wilson, as they emerged from a nightclub at one o'clock in the morning.

'He's always had the hots for Tara,' smirked Michelle.

Determined not to show how outraged and desperately hurt she was, Amber stumbled off to see Wilkie and ran slap into Marius, who, sheltering his mobile from the downpour, was shouting out his code number and declaring Mrs Wilkinson a non-runner in the 3.15.

Then, as Amber gave a wail of horror, he turned on her.

'She's boiled over, sweated up and used all her energy. I'm not risking her on this ground, she's not right.'

And Amber lost it. She wouldn't get paid now and she'd spent a fortune on petrol, getting herself waxed and on a clinging catkin-yellow jersey dress to ensnare Rogue . . . Fucking Rogue, fucking Marius.

'It's pathetic not to run her when she's come all this way. I've just spent hours walking the course, I know where the danger spots are.'

'This going'll put six inches on the fences. Unlike Harvey-Holden, I don't run unfit horses to appease owners,' growled Marius.

'At least he gets results,' screamed Amber. 'It's only a drop of rain.'

At that moment, God turned the tap on, drenching them both. Hearing shouting, Etta ran out of Wilkie's box in alarm.

'Marius isn't going to run Wilkie,' stormed Amber.

Etta's first emotion was profound relief, followed by alarm for Amber, who, as grinning staff from other yards braved the downpour to eavesdrop, would certainly never get another ride from Marius if she didn't shut up.

The syndicate had arrived half an hour ago and immediately repaired to the famous White Rose restaurant in the stands for large drinks and an early lunch. Etta, however, had sloped off to the stables to find a distraught Mrs Wilkinson, reminiscent of her terror in the early days. To compound the image, here was Valent, splashing through the puddles, looming more menacingly than the huge black clouds overhead. He'd go berserk, having brought Bonny up here, if Wilkie didn't run.

Knowing Marius needed a bottle of whisky before telling an owner his horse had broken down, Etta waded in.

'I'm desperately sorry, Mrs Wilkinson's not going to run. She's a little horse and this kind of going puts six inches on the fences,' she stammered, wiping rain which Valent thought was tears off her face. 'And the light's awful and Wilkie's only got one eye, and the mud can kick up into her face, and she didn't travel well. I'm so sorry you've come all this way.'

Valent had just left Bonny in the warmth of the White Rose. Already that morning, he had made a detour in the North Riding with the intention of introducing Bonny over breakfast to his son Ryan, the football manager. Bonny, who was very much aware of and resented Valent's children's disapproval, had needed a lot of coaxing. She had spent a great deal more than Amber on a demure little dove-grey dress, so as not to appear a wicked step-mother. She had also seen photographs of the handsome Ryan and, assuming instant conquest, was furious on arrival at the club to find he had flown off to Spain to look at a new striker.

Ryan loved his father and would have liked to discuss the possible new signing with him but, watching the BAFTAs, he had been dazzled less by Bonny than by the £50,000 worth of diamonds round her slender neck, which she later told the press was a present from Valent. Disliking Valent squandering his in-heritance, Ryan had pushed off to the airport.

Bonny had never been so insulted. Valent, shy and ill at ease among luvvies, had drunk heavily at the BAFTAs. Bonny had not. In the argument that followed about the appalling way he and Pauline had reared their children, Bonny's screams had pierced his hangover like needles dipped in acid . . .

He had felt humiliated and was livid with Bonny for slagging off Pauline. The last straw was Bonny yelling: 'And it's a hangover, not an 'angover, Valent.'

He was about to take it out on Etta, when Mrs Wilkinson's head appeared over the half-door and with infinite tact, she whickered despairingly.

Gratified, Valent moved forward, his angry red face suddenly softening. He pulled her ears, scratched her neck, raked her mane with his huge hands.

'Poor little luv, had a bad journey, did you? Makes two of us.'

Then he turned to an equally apprehensive Amber, Marius and Etta.

'These things happen, right decision. It's so dark today, wouldn't be easy for her to see with two eyes, would it, little girl?'

Mrs Wilkinson nudged him in the ribs in agreement.

'I feel so awful it's Bonny's first race,' stammered Etta. 'Such a long way.'

'Doesn't matter, we want her to run again.' He smiled at Amber. 'Sorry, luv, disappointing for you, but something will come up soon. Let's go and have a drink, we'll leave Bonny to settle.'

Oh, you dear, dear man, thought Etta, as he led them into the nearest bar.

65

It was like a game of consequences. Bonny Richards met Corinna Waters, who'd already downed a pint of champagne at the White Rose restaurant overlooking the entrance to the racecourse.

Bonny, having positioned herself so the light fell on her flaw-less, unlined face, said to Corinna, 'You are an icon, Miss Waters. You have been my favourite actress ever since my father took me to see you playing Hester in *The Deep Blue Sea* when I was a very little girl and I was hooked. I vowed that one day I would portray the suffering of older women. Whenever I seek inspiration I revisit your oeuvre.'

'Charmed, I'm sure.' Corinna took a slug of champagne. 'But I was actually the youngest Hester ever seen in the West End.'

Bonny, however, was not to be deflected.

'My other icon is Sarah Bernhardt.' Then, to show she'd done her homework: 'Like you, Miss Waters, Sarah triumphed as Phèdre.'

'Both legless,' drawled Seth.

'Bastard,' hissed Corinna.

'Hi, Bonny, I'm Seth Bainton.'

Good-looking, unprincipled, terrifyingly charming, Seth smiled down at Bonny, and she made a smooth transition from heroine to hero-worship.

'Indeed I know,' Bonny gazed up admiringly. 'Corinna' (she pronounced it Coroner) 'must be so proud of your versatility, as at home in *Hamlet* as in *Holby City*. With each part, you take us on a journey, truly connecting us with your character.'

Seth was actually blushing.

'Christ, she's awful,' Alan muttered to Joey, then blushed him-self when Bonny told him how much she admired *his* oeuvre and how much she was looking forward to his seminal work on depression.

'A subject on which I should like to exchange views. I feel I could have input.'

'I'm sure you could. What a darling,' Alan murmured to Seth.

'And you must be Etta.' Bonny seized Debbie's hands and was shaking them up and down. 'Valent has described you so often, I feel we are old friends.'

'That's not Etta, Etta's beautiful,' muttered Seth, whose diction was a bit too good and who received a scowl from Debbie.

'This is Debbie Cunliffe, who's lovely in a different way,' said Alan hastily. 'Etta's gone to the stables to check on her precious Wilkie.' Then, seeing Bonny's eyes narrow: 'She'll be along in a tick.'

'And you must be Debbie's spouse, who makes everything run like clockwork.' Bonny gave a bemused and ecstatic Major a little kiss.

'And you must be Shagger, I can see why you've earned your naughty nickname. And I know Alban. How are you, Alban? Valent has so enjoyed engaging with you.'

'Fritefly kind, very good of him.'

Corinna, after a late night and four hours on a bus, was edging towards a table in the dark of the restaurant. Bonny, trailing admirers, headed for one near the big floor-to-ceiling window overlooking flower beds and the entrance to the course, and where the harsh north light fell lovingly on her wild-rose complexion.

Everyone in the restaurant was nudging and craning. Older men, mostly members of the Check Republic, straightened their silk ties, whipping on their spectacles to look then whipping them off to seem more attractive, seeking identification from their wives. 'Who's she, who *is* she?'

Many recognized Corinna and some of them Seth. He slid in next to Bonny, who pointed to the seat opposite which was equally exposed to the harsh light, crying, 'I want my icon to sit there.'

Fractionally mollified, Corinna sat down.

'What are you reading?' asked Bonny.

Corinna waved *Macbeth*, which after the earlier tour in America was being given a short West End run. 'I immerse myself in every part, even relearning lines is tough in so short a time.'

'I don't have a problem with lines,' Bonny opened her big eyes even wider, 'but I guess I'm that much younger.'

'Your generation don't bother to absorb the meaning,' said

Corinna rudely. 'Valent sent us a tape of *The Blossoming*, couldn't make head nor tail what it was about. None of you enunciate these days.'

'You're probably used to an older theatre audience,' said Bonny sweetly, 'some of them not wearing hearing aids, so you've got to shout.'

'My generation combined clarity with subtlety,' snapped Corinna.

'I found *The Blossoming* very moving,' said Debbie, who had maddeningly plonked herself next to Corinna to be near Bonny, on whose left a grinning Alan had seated himself.

'Do you see Valent as the older man in *The Blossoming*?' he asked.

'There are elements in the movie which are reflective of the politics of our relationship,' Bonny nodded sagely. 'Valent is a guy, intelligent, kind, compassionate' – where the hell was he? – 'and strong enough to stand up to me.'

'Could have fooled me,' muttered Joey, who was still marking the *Racing Post*. 'We better order some grub or we'll miss the first race.'

Joey was not really enjoying himself. He knew from Bonny's frosty looks she didn't approve of him skiving and being part of the syndicate. He missed Chrissie and his mate Woody. This lot were a bit posh. He was also very worried about Woody, who was getting himself snarled up trying to save the Willowwood Chestnut, the beautiful tree in Lester Bolton's garden that had provided conkers for generations of Willowwood children.

Bolton, hell-bent on felling it, had been heavily but surreptitiously backed by the Major, whose view of Cindy Bolton undressing was blocked by the tree.

Woody had taken yet more time off that he could ill afford to attend the last day of the enquiry. But the Major, randy old goat, reflected Joey, must be so sure of victory, he'd come to Wetherby instead.

'Are you married, Alan?' Bonny was asking.

'Not in this postcode,' quipped Alan. She really was pretty.

'My first boss,' Shagger boomed up the table, 'told me: if you're not at the races three days a week, my boy, you're fired. That's where your clients are. I hope you'll become one of my clients, Bonny.'

'Isn't Shagger amusing?' Bonny murmured to Alan, then calling down the table: 'And you must be Toby and Phoebe, who live in Wild Rose Cottage, my favourite house in Willowwood.'

'I cannot tell you what big fans Toby and I are, Bonny, congrats on your BAFTA,' cooed Phoebe.

Toby, in a new yellow, red and brown check suit which looked good on his tall lean body, was quivering with excitement.

'I work in a gallery,' added Phoebe. 'I hope someone's painting you, Bonny, you are so lovely.'

'Lovely,' sighed Seth to Alan. 'Delicate as a wood anemone.'

More like bindweed, thought Joey darkly, white, innocent face concealing the murderous tendrils that curl round and round the towering plant before toppling it.

'*The Blossoming* sounds so moving,' cried Phoebe, who was gazing at Bonny in such wonder that Debbie was getting quite jealous.

'Shall we order some grub?' said Corinna.

'The point is,' Phoebe hissed to Shagger, 'is Valent paying? Because if he isn't, I'll skip the first course.'

'And I'll have cheese and biscuits,' said Shagger.

'I am so hungry,' said Alban and ordered Yorkshire pudding and onion sauce for a first course and Yorkshire pudding and roast beef for a main course.

'You can have Yorkshire pudding and treacle for dessert,' said Debbie, consulting the menu.

'Good idea,' said Alban.

No one was anxious to fork out for an entire round.

'Get another bottle of champagne,' Corinna ordered Seth.

'I'll get it,' said Alan.

Bonny, who was vying with Corinna to dazzle the waiters, announced that she'd like a glass of water. 'And a castle of sweet seasonal melon with elderflower-scented compote.'

'As a starter?' asked Phoebe hopefully.

'No, as a main course.'

Shagger, whose huge hairy nostrils were twitching as roast loin of pork went by, looked as though he was going to cry.

'You ought to get something hot inside you, Bonny,' said the Major heartily.

'Preferably yourself,' said Seth.

'Don't be disgusting,' snapped Debbie.

'If Valent's paying,' whispered Phoebe, 'I'll have smoked salmon, if not, I'll skip a starter.'

'I'm going to have steak and French fries,' said Joey. 'I've got a monkey on Wilkie to do the business, good little girl.' Then he glanced up at the television: 'Fuckin' hell.'

'Joey,' thundered the Major.

'She's not running.'

Sure enough, on the blue ribbon along the bottom of the screen beside 'NR' in the 3.15 were the words 'Mrs Wilkinson'.

'Fucking hell,' said Alan and Seth simultaneously.

'What's going on?' demanded the Major.

'Mrs Wilkinson's been withdrawn.'

'But we've come all this way,' squawked Debbie, 'and booked a room.'

'Marius ought to be sacked, why in hell hasn't he notified us?' said Shagger, who hadn't had a bet. 'Toby and I have taken a day off work.'

'I'm so sorry.' Running up the table, Phoebe put an arm round Bonny's shoulders.

'I'll phone Oakridge,' spluttered the Major.

Marius of course wasn't answering his mobile.

'Can't organize a piss-up in a brewery,' seethed Shagger.

Painswick's number was engaged too.

'Perhaps that's why Etta and Valent have been so long down there,' said Alan. 'Poor little Wilkie. Shall we go down to the stables?'

The runners were already going down to the start for the first race.

'We're owners, we should have been consulted,' puffed the Major.

'We've come all this way in the bloody minibus,' said Corinna furiously. 'Seth turned down a commercial. And we won't get to go into the parade ring.'

'This is most disappointing,' said Bonny, who was clearly furious.

Next moment Valent stalked into the restaurant, blue collar turned up, hair dark with rain, and the room went quiet, such was his impact.

'He was in *Midsomer Murders*,' said a Check Republic wife.

'No, I'm sure he was Mr Rochester a few years ago. Very dishy,' said her friend.

'No, he was in *The Bill*.'

Valent as usual looked as though he brought the stormy weather in with him, black brows lowered, mouth set, followed by a cringing, apologizing Etta. He strode straight up to the table. Lunchers hastily pulled their chairs in to let him through.

'What's going on?' blustered the Major. 'Oakridge is refusing to answer his mobile. Damned disgrace. We've come all this way, no one's consulted us.'

'Is Wilkie OK?' asked Alan.

'She wasn't, worked herself up into a terrible state,' said Valent. 'Furious took a piece out of her. I'm sorry you've come so far but Marius is quite right not to run her. Very gutsy of him. It's too dark, going too heavy, like quicksand, mud flying around. She's a great little mare, let her live to fight another day. She'll not let us down.' Then he glanced ruefully up the table at Bonny flanked by Seth and Alan. 'Sorry, luv, I'm afraid that's racing for you.'

'Oh Valent.' Bonny's eyes filled with tears and, running down the table, she disappeared into his arms.

'We'll all get our money back and put it on Furious instead,' said a relieved Valent. 'He belongs to Marius, who said anyone who wants to can go into the paddock to see him off.'

'I'm so sorry,' stammered Etta, opening her purse, 'I'd like to buy a round.'

'Don't be silly, luv.' Valent looked round at the hungry, apprehensive faces, the hovering waiters, the empty glasses. 'Better have some more bubbly. I'd like a pint,' he told the hovering waiters. 'Now what are you all going to eat?'

'I'd like smoked salmon for a starter,' said Phoebe.

'I'd like smoked salmon and roast loin of pork,' said Shagger.

'This is Etta, Bonny,' said Valent.

Relief was the primary emotion on Bonny's face as she looked Etta up and down. 'Delighted to meet you,' she said truthfully.

'Come and sit opposite me, Valent,' called out Corinna, who'd been busy powdering and lipsticking.

'Go and get dry, Etta,' ordered Valent.

Such a sweet man, he made everything all right, thought Etta, dizzy with gratitude as she dried her hair on the roller towel in the Ladies. God, she looked tired, the shadows under her eyes were darker purple than Debbie's hat.

Taking the seat next to Alan on her return, she whispered, 'Bonny is so beautiful.'

'Only if you shut your ears and think of England,' he whispered back. 'The pillow talk would be excruciating, although it'd be a good sleeping pill. There was a terribly funny moment when she went up to Direct Debbie and said, "Oh, you must be Etta, Valent's told me so much about you" and evil Seth said not nearly sotto voce enough, "That's not Etta, Etta's beautiful."'

'Seth didn't,' gasped Etta. 'He didn't?'

Alan laughed. 'He did, angel. Seth's got a very soft spot for you, got a very hard spot for Bonny.'

'Seth said I was beautiful?'

Ringing to check if Painswick was OK, Etta found her very indignant.

'Marius didn't bother to tell me he'd scratched Wilkie.

Telephone's never stopped ringing, people wanting to know if she's OK, complete strangers. She's got a lot of fans.

'Chisolm's driving us all crackers, she never stops bleating. She escaped to the village and got into Ione's vegetable garden. She's eaten Michelle's scarf, don't tell her. Wish Furious good luck. Rather horrid for Rafiq having Rogue on his precious baby.'

66

Furious didn't have an owner except Marius. That afternoon he nearly didn't have a jockey.

Rogue and Dare Catswood got caught up in traffic after a smash on the A1. Dare Catswood left his car in the road and ran all the way to Wetherby, making it just in time. Rogue, held up by all the policemen gathered round Dare's car, didn't.

'I expect he's got caught up with another girl,' mocked Michelle.

'I expect he's scared of Furious, the great wuss,' snarled Amber.

At that moment Rogue rang Marius.

'I can't get through, terribly sorry. I might make the ride on History Painting.'

Driven crackers by the Major and Painswick's grumbling, Marius, who'd reached screaming pitch, was forced to give the ride to Amber, who was very reluctant to take it.

'Furious is a bugger,' she snapped. 'He's carted me and decked me enough times and once he's got me on the ground he'll go for me.'

Rain was lashing down, hats being blown away, umbrellas turning inside out like wounded crows, as the runners in the 3.15 splashed round the parade ring. Besides Furious, they included a grey with a lot of ability called Umbridge, which Harvey-Holden had recently run on the wrong trip to keep his handicap down, and Fur Calf, whose name had somehow got through the Weatherbys watchdogs, a lovely dark brown gelding trained by Isa Lovell and owned by Amber's old schoolfriend, the extremely wicked and dangerous Cosmo Rannaldini.

The Willowwood syndicate opted to watch the race from the warmth of the Owners and Trainers bar. The television cameras, whose lenses were pearled with raindrops, picked up the arrival of Cosmo's mother, the great diva Dame Hermione Harefield, smothered in fur, who was making a great fuss about the rain and icy wind endangering her voice as she swept into the bar.

'Why in hell did they make that stupid cow a dame?' grumbled Corinna.

Bonny, however, sidled up to her.

'Dame Hermione, you are an icon, I so admire your oeuvre.'

'What a pleasant young woman,' cried Dame Hermione. 'My son Cosmo's horse Fur Calf is running in this race and there, about to mount, is Amber Lloyd-Foxe, a very old friend of Cosmo's and god-daughter of my very good friend Rupert Campbell-Black. She's riding a horse called Furious.'

Furious at first refused to go into the parade ring, then refused to leave it, spooking at everything, lunging indiscriminately with hooves and teeth at humans and horses. Marius was reduced to legging Amber up on the path down to the course.

'There are good horses in this race,' he shouted as he hung on to Furious's reins. 'Hold him up as long as possible, don't let him tire himself, keep out of trouble and make a late run. He's very forward going,' he added as he jumped free.

'I.e., an absolute sod with no brakes,' snarled Amber.

Rafiq, ignoring her and gazing stonily into space, had noticed Amber's reddened eyes. Maybe it wasn't going so well with Rogue. As he led her down to the start, he addressed her for the first time in days: 'Eeegnore Marius. I know Furious. He hate other horses, let him make it and he will run like a wind to get away from them. He like daylight. You will not see another horse. Good luck,' he added, giving Furious's ear a last pull.

The start was by the B1224. Amber wished she was hurtling away in one of the cars as Furious, tail lashing, ears glued to his head, took a lunge first at Umbridge, then at Fur Calf, then at Ilkley Hall to a chorus of fuck offs.

And they were off, hurtling through the downpour, except Furious, who reared up and nearly right over, before taking off and carting her. After four furlongs, she gave up hauling on his mouth and let him go. Trees and houses flashed by as, bucketing over each fence, he landed running.

'Got a plane to catch?' yelled Dare Catswood as she overtook him and Umbridge.

Having walked the course, she was able to steer Furious away from boggy ground. The rain lashed her face, harder than the jockeys' whips. As other young horses in the race exhausted themselves trying to keep up with her, others were forced by the headlong pace into making errors.

Dame Hermione was giving tongue in the Owners and Trainers: 'Go on, Fur Calf, go on, Fur Calf.'

'Did Dame Hermione really shout fuck off?' whispered Debbie to the Major in horror.

Poor Fur Calf fell at four out, Umbridge at the next.

Looking round to left and right, Amber saw the rain-shiny hats of the rest of the jockeys bobbing like seals in the distance. The race was at Furious's mercy as the winning post flashed by.

'You glorious horse,' gasped Amber, brandishing her whip in the air. Furious punished her by taking about three weeks to pull up.

Rogue, who had no opinion of Furious, had from the motorway seen the horses circling at the start and noticed Amber on board. She'll be riding me later, he thought complacently. For the moment, she wouldn't have a hope of holding up Furious. Contemptuously parking his blue Ferrari at an angle, he loped towards the paddock.

But no one ran faster than Rafiq, as he raced up to welcome Furious, hugging him, patting him over and over again, kissing his sly chestnut face, crying, 'Oh, thank you, thank you,' then praising Allah and patting him again.

'Don't pat him so loudly,' mocked Amber, 'or I won't be able to hear myself boast.' Then she smiled. 'Oh Rafiq, this is an absolutely fantastic horse, he could win a Derby, he could go round again. He's hardly blowing, couldn't blow out his own birthday cake. You were right, I didn't see another horse.'

Looking down at Rafiq's dark, arrogant, sulky face totally transformed by happiness, split by a huge white grin, Amber ignored Alice Plunkett's microphone.

'Welcome me home,' she murmured and bending down, kissed Rafiq long and lingeringly on the mouth, only drawing away as Marius came striding up.

'Amber,' he roared, 'why in hell didn't you hold him up? He's beaten so many good horses by so many lengths, he'll be top weight in his next race.'

'You bloody well try riding him. Don't be so ungrateful,' howled Rafiq, turning on an amazed Marius, at which point Furious, in support, bit Marius sharply on the arm, to distract him from firing Rafiq.

As quickly as it had started, the deluge stopped and the sun came out to admire this wonderful horse. The Willowwood syndicate, who'd backed him for a joke, were ecstatic.

'I'd like to lead Furious in,' cried Bonny and Corinna, reaching for their powder compacts.

'I'm afraid he's not our horse yet,' laughed the Major, 'but by Jove, he ran well.'

'I think we should try and buy him,' said Seth, putting his arm round a cheering, sobbing Etta. 'Your baby's come good, darling.'

'Hasn't he?' gasped Etta. 'But he's Rafiq's baby, he made him, he always had faith.'

Dame Hermione, who'd intended to lead in Fur Calf, was most put out.

Fur Calf's owner, her son Cosmo, was even angrier, eyes blazing, face white with fury above his late father's black astrakhan coat. He had flown back from New York especially and bet very heavily. So had Harvey-Holden, who'd put £10,000 on Umbridge at 30–1 and had expected to clean up.

As Willowwood swarmed down to congratulate Amber and Rafiq, they were overtaken by Rogue, racing towards the winners enclosure.

'That guy's appealing,' observed Bonny.

'All the time,' said Joey.

Having placated and congratulated Marius – 'Desperately sorry, bad crash outside Wakefield. Ill wind though, I probably wouldn't have won on him' – Rogue turned to Amber, who'd probably have slapped his laughing, unrepentant face if she hadn't been clutching her saddle on her way to weigh in.

'Well done, darling, brilliant. You'll probably win Ride of the Week, might win it later.' Dropping his voice, he drew her aside.

'Not with you on my back,' hissed Amber.

'Hush, hush, darling, we'll discuss it over dinner.'

'We will not, you never confirmed it. I've got a better offer.'

'But I've booked 20 The Calls, a lovely hotel in Leeds,' said Rogue softly, 'and the unbridled suite for later.'

'You'd better take Tara Wilson then,' spat Amber. 'She looks as though she needs a good night's sleep,' and she stalked off to weigh in.

The water in the shower was cold, bringing her back to reality. All the joy of winning was extinguished because she'd stood up Rogue. As she talked briefly to the press, she could see him doing a number on Bonny.

As she drove home in the dusk, she passed a crash outside Wakefield, still holding up oncoming traffic for miles. Maybe he had been delayed. Maybe he had just been escorting a drunken Tara Wilson out of that nightclub. Tears poured down her face.

People kept ringing and texting to congratulate her, but each time, because it wasn't Rogue, she had difficulty being polite. She was asphyxiated by the smell of burning bridges.

Bloody jockeys.

Her thoughts drifted towards Rafiq. That had been a great kiss and he'd stuck up for her to Marius and risked getting the sack. Marius hadn't praised her and he hadn't even noticed Rafiq kissing her.

Bloody trainers.

67

All the way home, Michelle and Josh went on and on about the wonder of Bonny Richards. A silent Rafiq, ripped apart by emotions, gazed out at the stars and a sickle moon, with which he'd have liked to cut down both of them. His beloved Furious, after such an impressive victory, would be a target for every owner. His beloved Amber had kissed him and asked him to welcome her home, and she'd clearly had a blazing row with Rogue.

As the lorry left, she had told him she just might drop into the yard later to break the journey home to Penscombe. And Rafiq had found himself saying that, as Tommy was away, why didn't Amber crash out on her bed?

Why had he said that? Now he wouldn't sleep all night praying she turned up.

That was the worst part of being a lad. Trainers and owners swanned off and drank champagne all night while you faced an endless journey home, after which you had to unload, feed, water and settle the horses, fall into bed and be up again at six to ride out. The horses didn't get champagne either, thought Rafiq, only a net of hay.

Without Tommy around he had to put Furious and History Painting to bed as well as a thoroughly depressed Mrs Wilkinson, to whom the races had come to mean lots of clapping and cheering in the winners enclosure. She was in no mood to hear Chisolm's grumbling about boxed ears and indigestion after raiding Ione's veggie patch and eating Michelle's scarf.

Having patted Dilys and given Furious a final good-night hug, Rafiq emerged from their box, wondering if he'd ever been so tired in his life, to find Amber outside, her hair as gold as the sickle moon which, across the valley, was setting into the dark arms of the Willowwood Chestnut.

'I looked in at the Fox, everyone's drinking to you and Furious. I wanted to buy you a drink to thank you,' she said. 'I bought a bottle instead. I've had a few, don't think I ought to drive home. Thought I'd take up your offer of Tommy's bed.'

Josh, already plastered, had urged her to go back and shag Rafiq. 'Might improve the moody sod's temper.'

Rafiq's face betrayed no emotion.

He might kiss me, thought Amber sulkily, but having showed her the bathroom and Tommy's room, he bade her good night.

Amber was touched by Tommy's room. Just as Tommy would never leave a horse's box unskipped out, she had put a clean sheet and a duvet cover, patterned with jaunty Jack Russells, on her bed ready for her return. You could hardly see the walls for photographs of horses Tommy'd looked after, alongside pictures of Rafiq, Etta, Marius, Amber herself and of Tommy's parents and her sister's wedding.

On the mantelpiece were trophies she'd won, and on the shelves books on racing, autobiographies of great jockeys, novels by Dick Francis and Johnnie Francome and slimming videos. They hadn't worked, nor had the exercise bicycle in the corner.

Beside the bed was a rocking horse alarm clock, which neighed, made a sound of galloping hooves and never let Tommy down, and a biography she was reading of Amber's father, Billy. Seeing his sweet youthful face on the cover, Amber shivered at the memory of how pale and ill he'd looked earlier. It was bloody cold in this room.

Having warmed herself up with a shower and washed her hair with Tommy's shampoo, she smothered herself in Tommy's lily of the valley body lotion. It was much sweeter, appropriately, than the sophisticated, sexy Madame that Amber normally wore. She examined herself in the mirror, waxed, highlighted, toned, scented, toe nails painted, raring for Rogue. She looked bloody gorgeous. If she hadn't blown him out, she'd be in Leeds drinking Dom Perignon in a four-poster.

Finding a bottle of white in the little fridge, she took a slug and pulled a face. Too sweet again. Pity to waste herself and him, she thought, catching sight of a rare smiling photo of Rafiq. Everyone knew of his police record, his dangerous past, how only terror of losing his job contained his terrible temper, which he'd lost when he'd stuck up for her today.

In the drawer, she found neatly folded clothes. Tommy's scarlet

327

pyjama bottoms fell to the ground when she tried them on, so she put on a white cotton nightdress.

Taking Tommy's kettle – she could always pretend she was going to fill it for a hot-water bottle – she opened the door, slap into Rafiq. Both jumped out of their gooseflesh.

His newly washed hair was shiny as a raven's wing, his midnight-blue pyjamas, buttoned up to a high collar, looked wet or was it sweat?

'I wash them and put them in dryer, but they didn't dry enough. I wanted to . . .' confessed Rafiq.

'Look gorgeous for me?' murmured Amber. 'And you do, but you better get out of them. You'll find me much more fun than an Equicizer.'

Taking his hand, she led him back into Tommy's room.

They gazed at each other.

'What about Rogue?'

'Only interested in fucking. All Irish jockeys are the same, they go to Mass on Sunday, confess who they've been shagging, say their Hail Marys and carry on regardless. Hail Mary, Hail Amber, Hail fucking Tara.'

'Shut up,' interrupted Rafiq. 'Why you talk so ugly? It doesn't suit you. If you were my girl, I'd lock you away, so no one feast on your beauty.'

'Beauty?' taunted Amber. 'I didn't know you noticed.'

Rafiq ran his hand over her face. 'Lovely eyelash and eyes, proud nose, beautiful mouth, which shouldn't say ugly things.'

Very slowly he ran a finger along her lower lip, then slid his hand round to the back of her head, running fingers through her hair, gazing deep into her eyes, so close that she could smell his clean, sweet breath, his big mouth widening into a nervous smile as he gazed longingly at her lips then back to her eyes for reassurance.

'I know you kiss me to annoy Rogue.'

'Not entirely,' drawled Amber, edging a little nearer. 'Shouldn't you go and pray?'

'For what?'

'For deliverance from the she-devil, who takes love where she finds it. The infidel incapable of fidelity.'

'Once you find love with me,' said Rafiq haughtily, 'you will seek no further.' He stroked her bare arms, his touch so sure yet gentle. 'I am in no hurry, unlike your jockey lovers, to reach winning post.'

Amber unbuttoned his pyjama top, sliding her hands inside and catching her breath. His body was wonderful, silken, sleek, and as hard with muscle as Furious. Pulling him down on the jaunty Jack Russells, she undid more buttons, kissing his chest, running her tongue through the dark down of hair, feeling him shudder. Tentatively his tongue slid into her mouth, feather-light.

He was clearly not going to make the running so she undid the buttons of her nightdress, pressing her breasts against him, hearing him gasp in wonder and she gasped too a second later, as he began to stroke them. The magic touch of his fingers was soothing away the hurt of the day. Dropping his head, he licked one hardening nipple then the other. His tongue was unhurried, roving.

'Oh God, Rafiq, was the Kama Sutra your set book?'

'Wrong country,' murmured Rafiq. 'To us, sex comes naturally. Feel this.' Pushing her back on the Jack Russells, his hand crept up her thigh, millimetre by millimetre, smiling as she gasped and moaned. 'My little infidel.'

'That is so lovely.'

As he pushed two fingers in and out, deeper and deeper, she was reduced to begging until the fingers strayed upwards, as delicate as the fluttering of a butterfly's wings, caressing on and on. It was only when she was shaken by earthquake tremors that she realized she'd come.

'Wow, that was something else.' Then, seeing how moved and delighted Rafiq was: 'Now it's your turn.

'Wow, quadrupled,' she gasped as she pulled down his pyjamas and his cock sprang out. 'That is truly awesome, Childe Roland to the dark tower came, or came because of the dark tower.'

'What are you talking about?'

'Nonsense, wanting you so badly makes me silly. You were so brave to stick up for me earlier, and now you're sticking up for me again.'

'Stop taking piss,' Rafiq cuffed her gently, 'and welcome me home.'

But when Amber crouched down, seizing his cock, tongue happy to pleasure him with an art in which she knew she was expert, he wriggled away. Instead he laid her on the bed, gliding into her with the joy of a speedboat plunging into a warm ocean. Controlled at first, in and out, in and out, changing positions they thrust and arched together. Rafiq could smell Tommy's familiar lily of the valley on Amber's golden breasts and Tommy's shampoo on her hair, which cascaded over the pillow. He could smell Tommy's Polos on her breath.

The jaunty Jack Russells got squashed, as Amber and Rafiq rode finish after finish. They were both so fit, sleep escaped them for at least fifty minutes until Rafiq suddenly shouted a few words in Punjabi and erupted inside her.

He rested his head for an age on her shoulder and she realized he was sobbing. Rolling off her, he turned her face to his, saying with sudden terrifying intensity, 'I love you, Amber, thank you, thank you, you welcome me home.'

He was so vulnerable, she mustn't hurt him. She'd never been good at commitment. Tommy said he was often racked by nightmares and sure enough, he woke sobbing again half an hour later.

As she snuggled against him he confessed he had nothing to offer her. Because of his prison record, Marius had employed him for a pathetic wage and had never bothered to raise it.

'I can give you nothing.'

'You've just given me the most marvellous fuck.'

Rafiq put his hand over her mouth.

'You must stop this horrible language.'

'I don't know anything about you. Why are you so angry?'

'I worry about what will happen to Furious and I am worried about my country. It is more unstable and dangerous than ever as the Americans pour troops into Afghanistan, murder thousands of innocent people and make me hate the West even more.'

'How did you get involved in terrorism?' Amber asked carefully.

'Why you ask these questions?' Suddenly Rafiq was suspicious.

'I want you to be happier. Trust me,' said Amber.

But as he drifted off to sleep again, panic swept her. What if her mother, Janey the journalist, who'd sell any of her family down the river, found out? Imagine the headlines. Oh God, she must protect him. But as she tugged the only pillow under her head, a photograph fluttered out. It was a lovely smiling picture of Tommy and Rafiq together in the garden. Oh God, she mustn't hurt Tommy either.

68

On the day the syndicate went to Wetherby, Woody lost his beloved horse chestnut. The powers of Health and Safety, heavily bunged by Lester Bolton, declared that the tree should be felled. Traces of horse chestnut disease were alleged to have been found which could result in branches falling on unwary passers-by.

Henceforth the great tree's candles would no longer light the village in spring, nor the burnished shingle of its conkers beguile the children of Willowwood in autumn, which was an added plus for Health and Safety who considered conkers weapons of mass destruction. The tree would no longer obscure the CCTV view of the much extended rear of Primrose Mansions. The Major, who, as head of the Parish Council, had backed the felling, could feast his eyes on Cindy Bolton undressing.

A smell of· burning logs was softening the night air, as Woody bumped into the Major outside the Fox the following evening.

'At least you'll make a few bob cutting the thing down, Woody,' joshed the Major, 'and I've no doubt Lester Bolton will give you a cut for disposing of the timb-ah. Ouch,' he squawked, 'ow-ow-ouch,' as Woody's long fingers closed round his short, thick neck, squeezing tighter and tighter.

'Don't ever mess with me again, you fat greedy bastard, or I'll really kill you,' spat Woody. Leaving the Major groping in the gutter for his spectacles and his new check racing cap, Woody stumbled off into the dusk.

This exchange was witnessed by Niall as he returned home from choir practice. He was too shy to run after Woody, but incredibly fit images of him surging up trees in his harness, leaping from branch to branch like Tarzan, had haunted Niall's dreams since Newbury, so he pondered what he had heard in his heart.

Next Sunday's Sung Eucharist was combined with a christening, which meant the church was quite full. Etta was admiring the stained glass window of Sir Francis Framlingham and Beau Regard – so like Mrs Wilkinson – and idly wondering if Niall would run out of drink if he had to give communion wine to so many people, when he launched into his sermon. Taking a deep breath, he exhorted the congregation to come to the rescue of one of the village's most beloved citizens: the Willowwood Horse Chestnut.

Instantly everyone woke up, particularly Ione Travis-Lock who, armed with a spade, which she'd left propped against Beau Regard's tombstone, to plant another willow for another local son, had absolutely no desire to see Cindy undressing.

Striding round to the village shop after the planting, she launched a petition to Save Our Chestnut, which soon attracted hundreds of signatures.

What tipped the balance, however, was Ione's dropping in on Lester Bolton, his first visitor at the officially renamed Primrose Mansions, and telling him he had upset the people of Willowwood more than enough over the past two years. Their gas and electricity had been frequently cut off while his was installed, the traffic had been constantly held up due to deliveries, the roads wrecked by his lorries, and his workmen, making a din worse than the Nibelung, had prevented mothers ever getting their babies to sleep in the afternoon. If Lester ever wanted to be welcomed as a member of the community, he'd better start by leaving the Willowwood Chestnut alone. It could easily be trimmed back to give access to CCTV.

Lester took it well, placating Ione by pointing out the solar panelling, the rain-harvesting plant, and his plans to install a wind turbine and to lower the wattage on his lights up the drive. Finally he promised not to cut down the chestnut.

An eternally grateful Woody dropped a lorryload of apple logs and a crate of red off at Niall's as a thank-you, but was too shy to stay for an answer. The rest of Willowwood, however, who were gagging to find out what Primrose Mansions looked like inside after two million had been spent on it, were disappointed with Ione when Mop Idol imparted the information that her boss hadn't noticed anything in particular – except that Bolton had made out a generous cheque to the Compost Club.

Phoebe and Debbie, who were having a rapprochement because Bonny hadn't, as promised, invited Phoebe to the premiere of her latest film, were delighted when Bolton summoned the Major for a drink the following evening.

'Can't we come too?' pleaded Phoebe.

'No,' replied the Major pompously, 'Lester Bolton wants to talk business with me wearing my Parish Council hat.'

'I bet it's very OK.'

'Very un-OK with Madam Cindy's taste,' sniffed Debbie.

'No, OK as in *OK!* and *Hello!* WAG taste,' giggled Phoebe.

'Take your camera, Normie, and as many pictures as you can.'

Lester Bolton had taken Ione's sermon to heart. He had also seen the papers and the pictures of Valent, Bonny, Corinna and Seth at the races. He was envious of men like Sir Alan Sugar and Sir Philip Green. Like them, he wanted to be recognized in the street.

He was shrewd enough to realize that even the most cut-throat tycoon took on a new persona at the races. Filmed wiping away a tear and hugging a beautiful, panting horse in the winners enclosure, the most ruthless bully could suddenly be regarded as a big softie, and emerge from the financial pages, which women tend not to read, on to the front pages. Look at Valent, the taciturn Tin Man without a Heart, his arm round Corinna one week, Bonny the next. Bertie Barraclough, despite his happy marriage and his religion, was a thug in the workplace.

Lester also wanted Cindy to be recognized as an actress. Fame was the spur. Lester decided to take up racing and invest in some horses.

His first choice as a trainer would have been Harvey-Holden, with whom he'd dined after Ione Travis-Lock's party two years ago, and part of whose wood he had bought and was transforming into an arboretum, but they had fallen out. H-H wasn't good at observing boundaries. Ilkley Hall had nearly run over him and Cindy having a woodland shag the other day and when, at the time, Lester had resisted buying horses, H-H had dropped him. Shade, H-H's biggest owner, had cut him dead in the City the other day. Marius Oakridge's yard and the Willowwood syndicate looked more star-studded and exciting, so in March he summoned the Major to Primrose Mansions.

Picking up a video of Furious winning at Wetherby from the pub, the Major arrived to find the last Portakabin had rolled away and not a chip of gravel out of place. He had great difficulty getting in through the electric gates and, in the dim, Ione-induced lights up the drive, tripped over a garden gnome in a bikini.

The Major was in a lather about seeing Cindy again. The two years out-of-date girlie calendar she'd presented to him remained locked in his den desk with the British Legion cashbox. Frequently he took surreptitious glances at August, showing Cindy's thrusting breasts, or November, which revealed her parted buttocks.

He was almost relieved when fat little Lester, wearing an open-necked very white silk shirt and showing off a 'Dearest Dad' pendant nestling in a copse of ginger chest hair, said Cindy was out pampering herself at a salon in Larkminster.

The Major was then given a brief look at the library, lit by a huge chandelier. It contained a vast screen and shelves crammed with porn videos, of which he glimpsed a few titles: *Young Muff*, *Juicy Snatch* and *The Naughtiest Girl on the Monitor*. The Major felt he'd like to revisit Lester's oeuvre again and again.

' 'Elp yourself at any time, Mijor,' urged Lester. He led his guest downstairs to a bar, which had leopardskin walls, a huge screen and nude photographs of Cindy cuddling a lion cub, and vast leather sofas like beached oxen, covered in leopardskin cushions.

As the progress of his lifts was impeded by the off-white shagpile, Lester clutched on to a lap-dancing pole descending from the ceiling.

'Cindy will give you a personal demonstration one day,' he told a sweating Major.

Also built into the ceiling was the large glass-bottomed swimming pool whose delivery had held up the minibus on the way to Newbury.

On the bar was the *Daily Mail*, with a picture of Bonny and Valent at Wetherby.

'A lovely lady, but not a patch on Cindy.'

Lester opened a bottle of sparkling wine.

'I need your 'elp again, Norm.' He rested their two glasses on the back of a fibreglass nude bending down to touch her scarlet toes and, sitting down, practically disappeared into the folds of a leather sofa.

'I 'old my 'and up, Norm. I've upset the folk of Willowwood, I've stopped the flow of village life. Work at Ravenscroft and Badger's Court 'as been equally extensive, but the properties are outside the village. I want to win over 'earts and minds, engage with the community and send our kiddies to Greycoats. Mijor, I'd like to join the Willowwood syndicate.'

Before the Major had time to express any opinion, Bolton added that he would like to invite all the syndicate to an 'arse-warming party.

334

'Blinis and bubbly. They could bring their cossies, or not,' Bolton winked lasciviously, 'and have a swim in the pool after dinner, or there's a jacuzzi, takes eight.'

Bolton also wanted to treat guests during the evening to a preview of Cindy's latest movie, *Little Red Riding Whip*, which had a horsey theme. He put a DVD in the machine and immediately Cindy could be seen tripping through North Wood in a high wind, wearing nothing but a red cloak.

'See, it's very tasteful.'

'Might be a bit racy, ho ho, for some of our members,' volunteered the Major, taking a large gulp of wine to cool himself down. 'Miss Painswick, Etta Bancroft, indeed my own wife' (who was broad of beam but not of mind), 'and of course the vicar.'

'Show it later in the evening then when the oldies have gone 'ome.'

The Major retaliated by showing Bolton the video of Furious winning at Wetherby.

'Everyone is after this horse since that win. Campbell-Black, Dermie O'Driscoll, Isa Lovell. I could see my way to having a word with Marius Oakridge if you move fast.'

'Would the syndicate buy shares in Furious?'

'I doubt if they could afford it. Many of our members are strapped paying for Mrs Wilkinson.'

'Valent bought in.'

'Only because Chris and Chrissie at the Fox pulled out, and Valent wanted to give his share to Bonny as a birthday gift.'

'I'd be prepared to pay well to buy into the syndicate,' said Bolton, getting pushy. 'I'm sure Etta Bancroft could use the money.'

'Etta would never forfeit her share, she's devoted to Mrs Wilkinson,' said the Major with rare asperity. 'If you bought into the syndicate and in addition bought Furious, you would have more clout. Trainers tend to listen to those with the most horses.'

There was a pause.

'So you're not cutting down the Willowwood Chestnut?' asked the Major.

'Ione decided me,' said Bolton smugly. 'She was very civil. Stayed over an hour.' Then, lowering his voice: 'Did you know she widdles on her compost every night? Got a shot of it in the shrubbery last night.'

The Major choked on his wine.

'Always wanted to make a film about mat-uer women, Ione, Etta, Corinna, call it *The Rude Antiques Show*.' Lester laughed fatly. 'Showy-looking 'orse, that Furious,' he went on. 'Might be the answer. Cindy's going to play Lady Godiva, or Lady Muff Diver, this summer. Furious might suit.'

He refilled the Major's glass and put *Little Red Riding Whip* on again. By the time the wolf had abandoned his grandmother drag role and jumped on Cindy, 'All the better to eat you out with, my dear,' the Major's glasses had steamed up and his too-long Christmas sweater was proving to have its uses.

'Tasty, isn't she, my old lady,' observed Lester smugly.

'Don't you mind the world seeing, well, so much of your wife?' asked the Major.

'I'm always present during shooting,' said Bolton, filling up the Major's glass. 'Perhaps you'd like to come along one day.'

'Indeed,' croaked the Major.

'Now, about the syndicate. You've been good to me, Norm. That holiday villa in Portugal is yours for nothing whenever you and your good lady need a break. Might even see my way to making it over to you.'

At that moment, lights flashed on above, illuminating the swimming pool. It was as though the Major's Cindy calendar had sprung into life, and February and March were following January and racing on through the year as a naked Cindy, back from the spa, her pink breasts, bottom and shaven haven flashing above him, breast- and backstroked through the water. Good God, there was August and November again . . .

'I'm sure we can sort out the syndicate,' he spluttered.

'I'll leave it in your capable hands,' said Lester as he ushered the Major out. 'We'll come and view Furious pronto, but I'm not interested unless Cindy and I can become part of the syndicate.'

69

The Major called a meeting of the syndicate at the Fox the following night, played the DVD of Furious winning at Wetherby and reported the thrilling news that Bolton was anxious to become involved.

Etta was violently opposed from the start. The syndicate was becoming too big and unmanageable, and much less fun since Bonny and Corinna had taken over. She had observed Lester at the Travis-Locks, greedy, predatory, a great fat spider waiting for the flies to come down. If he acquired 20 per cent, as the Major suggested, he could get the Major and Debbie, Shagger, Phoebe and Toby on his side and vote everyone else out.

Etta had hoped for support from Painswick, but after several weeks working for Marius she was aware how desperately strapped for cash he was. Selling Furious for £100,000 might be one way out of the mess, particularly if Bolton bought other horses.

'Let me explain,' urged the Major. 'Mrs Wilkinson has proved herself a winner and is now worth at least fifty thousand. Therefore if Bolton buys in at 20 per cent, he would have to hand over ten thousand, which would mean a grand for each shareholder.' Everyone brightened. 'The moment he buys in, I'll be able to issue you with a cheque and we'd be saving Marius.'

'Can't think why,' sniffed Debbie, 'he's so rude.'

Etta was now the only dissenting voice.

'My dear,' urged the Major, 'Bolton truly won't buy Furious unless we let him into our syndicate. He wants the social standing. We owe it to Marius.'

'And Rafiq too,' said Painswick. 'The poor boy's been crying his heart out, according to Tommy, ever since Michelle gleefully reported how many trainers were after Furious.'

'I don't like Bolton, and I think we should check with Valent who's only just joined,' said Etta. 'He might not like Bolton slobbering all over Bonny.'

'He's too small to slobber over anyone,' said Alan.

'I talked to Bonny,' said Seth idly. 'I called Valent at home but he's still in China buying some electronic toy factory. Bonny didn't seem too concerned about Lester Bolton. She thinks the syndicate's a broad church. Anyway, Etta darling, Alan and I and Valent can handle tossers like Bolton. And it is the answer.'

'I don't trust him.' Etta was fighting back the tears when Seth put an arm round her shoulder, leading her to the fire at the other end of the bar. He sat her down on the fender and, clicking his fingers to Chris, bought her another glass of white.

'Darling,' he gently stroked her hair and then the back of her neck, 'it's the only answer. The Major's pushed Bolton up to a hundred thousand for Furious and ten thousand to buy into the syndicate, which'll be a few bob for you and me.

'More importantly, angel – look at me, Etta,' he forced her chin up with his other hand, giving her the benefit of his *Holby City* sincerity smoulder, 'Marius is about to go under. Poor Joyce Painswick paid the wages out of her own pocket last week.' Then, at Etta's look of horror: 'Rafiq will lose his job and is unlikely to get another, and so will Tommy, and Mrs Wilkinson, the Beau Regard of Willowwood, will be without a trainer. She'll have to go somewhere else and you won't be able to see her all the time, and that will break your heart, darling. And haven't we had fun in the syndicate so far, and we'll have more fun as Wilkie beats everything in sight, and Bolton and Cindy, who I've yet to meet, will provide us with so many laughs. If Bolton wants to throw an arse-warming party for all the syndicate and you and I can romp in the giant jacuzzi while sperm whale Debbie frolicks naked in the sunken pool . . .'

Then, as Etta started to laugh: 'Please, darling, Bonny's given the OK. We've got a majority vote, people are only not endorsing it out of respect for you. They love you, and they want you on our side.' For a moment he was serious, then he laughed. 'Goodness, that soliloquy, silly-quoy, was longer than "Friends, Romans, countrymen". Please, darling.'

A log crashed out of the fire, making them jump, and as Seth brushed the sparks off her old tweed skirt Etta melted in both senses of the word.

'Of course it's OK,' she stammered. 'Thank you so much for

putting things into perspective. Poor Joyce must be reimbursed.'

At that moment Priceless wandered up, snaking his head along Etta's thigh until she rubbed his ears. 'Such a darling dog.'

'I wanted to ask you a great favour. A week's filming has come up, a motoring commercial, marvellous money – only problem is it's abroad. Since Priceless adores you so much, could you possibly look after him for me?'

'Yes, of course.' 'Etta could deny him nothing, but quailed at the rumpus it would cause. She leapt to her feet. 'I must go. I've got to make supper for Martin and Romy, they're due back from skiing.'

'Not until you've finished that drink.'

He clapped his hands.

'Darling Etta has agreed that Lester and Cindy can join the syndicate.'

Everyone looked pleased.

'But we've all got to promise not to let them change its character.'

At that moment the door opened, letting in a blast of icy air, and in swept Romy and Martin, radiant and conker-brown from the Alps.

'We thought we'd find you here, Mother,' said Martin, but not too accusingly because others were present.

'We're celebrating,' said Seth. 'Let me buy you both a drink. You look ludicrously beautiful, Mrs Bancroft. I'm sure Chris can knock up some Glühwein.'

'We can't really, kids in the car,' said Romy, delighted Seth should be seeing her at her best. 'They've had a long journey. We've just popped in to round up Mother.'

'She's busy,' snapped Alan.

'She's had a long break,' joked Martin, but his eyes were cold. Etta, who was still reeling from Seth's stroking soliloquy, jumped up, knocking over her glass of wine.

'Oh God, I'm sorry.'

'That settles it,' said Martin briskly as Etta dropped to her knees, mopping with a paper handkerchief.

'Come on, Mother. No,' he added to Chris, who was approaching with a bottle of white, 'she's had quite enough.'

'She's had one small glass,' protested Alan. 'You're staying, darling.'

'Don't interfere,' snapped Martin.

Priceless wandered back again, weaving his head round Etta's bottom.

'Your mother's very kindly agreed to look after Priceless next week,' said Seth, shooting Romy a hot glance.

'Impossible,' snapped Martin. 'She's far too busy and dogs give Drummond asthma.'

'No he don't,' cried an even browner Drummond, rushing into the bar and hugging Priceless. 'I like him, he's got short fur. Can I have a drink, Dad?'

'You're very tired, little man,' said Romy.

'No I'm not, I'm thirsty,' said Drummond.

'Have a large Scotch,' suggested Alan.

'Hello, Granny.' Poppy came racing in to hug Etta and then Priceless, who flashed his teeth at her, hitting his ribs on either side as he wagged his long skinny tail.

'Come away,' shrieked Romy, snatching up Poppy. 'He's going to bite you.'

'No, that's smiling,' protested Poppy. 'He's pleased to see me.'

'He's coming to stay with Granny,' said Drummond.

'I can take him for walks, he never pulls,' crowed Poppy. 'Skiing's boring. I missed you, Granny.'

'Poppy and Drummond seem to know that greyhound rather too well,' said Romy ominously as she and Martin stretched out in the clean sheets Etta had ironed and put on their bed that afternoon. 'I think Mother may have been minding it already. But we don't want to antagonize Seth and Corinna by forbidding it. They'll be invaluable for attracting punters when we have events.'

'Norman was just telling me Lester Bolton's joined the syndicate,' volunteered Martin. 'We must ask him round. He's very wealthy and desperate to be accepted.'

'Kitchen sups with Seth and Corinna, Bonny and Valent perhaps?'

'Excellent.' Martin put a sunburnt hand on his wife's full white breast. 'Seth's right, you do look ludicrously beautiful.' His hand slid down between her thighs, encountering warmth and wetness. 'Exciting that you still fancy me.'

Romy smiled, closing her eyes, growing wetter and warmer as she thought of Seth. Gratifying to have the two handsomest men in Willowwood in love with her.

The next Becher's Brook was stopping Furious eating Cindy and Bolton alive when they viewed him at the yard. Dora, however, had dreamed up a cunning plan. The moment Marius and Michelle set off to Hereford, Furious was locked away in the isolation box and a very kind, docile chestnut called Cheesecake was imported from the nearest riding school for the day and polished all morning by Tommy and Dora. Cheesecake's blaze was as white as the clouds above, an expression of delight on his sweet face, as he nuzzled the pockets of Cindy's tight white breeches for Polos provided by Dora.

'You must have a ride,' urged Dora.

Cindy's shrieks and giggles, according to her neighbour Alban Travis-Lock, were more earsplitting than the drills screaming on metal of her husband's workmen. As Rafiq and Dora led her round the home paddock, she was in full throttle. All the lads, on a lunchtime break, stifled their laughter and clapped and cheered. Furious, in his isolation box, snorted, neighed, gnawed and scraped his hooves against his locked door.

'Hubby,' announced Cindy, 'is very keen that my next movie should be Lady Godiva.'

'How brilliant,' cried Dora.

'We'll be auditioning mounts soon,' said Cindy loftily. 'Perhaps we should keep it in 'ouse and use Furious. He's so gentle yet so good-lookin', and if I'm going to be getting my kit off I don't want anything too frisky, what's going to buck me off on the cobblestones.'

'Furious would fit the bill perfectly,' said Dora, kissing Cheesecake. 'You two are made for each other. Want to trot on?'

'Might get a black eye from one of my boobs. Perhaps that handsome Rafiq could give me some lessons.'

'He might,' whispered Dora. 'He's been looking after Furious for yonks. He's desperate for him to go to a good owner, so he can go on caring for him.'

'He can care for me any time,' giggled Cindy. 'Phwoar, he's well fit, he looks very pashnit.'

'For Christ's sake smile, Rafiq,' hissed Dora.

'Why's horsey called Furious?' asked Cindy.

'Because he's furious he hasn't had someone as pretty as you on his back before,' said Dora.

Cindy's shrieks of mirth made even Cheesecake bound forward. At that moment, Lester Bolton rolled up in a vast Range Rover, and in a nothing-is-too-good-for-my-Cindy mood.

'If you want this 'orse, princess, he's yours. He's certainly a nice-looking animal. Blood will out of course.'

'And bloody-mindedness in Furious's case,' murmured Dora.

'I love him.' Cindy hugged Cheesecake. 'He and Rafiq are to come and stay at Primrose Mansions on their 'olidays.'

'So glad you made it today, Mr Bolton,' whispered Dora. 'So many big hitters are after Furious, they'll tear their hair out.'

As Marius was at the races, Miss Painswick and the Major accepted the cheque.

'Better frame it,' said Dora.

'It's Bolton that's been framed,' said Painswick. 'Better get Cheesecake back to the riding school before Marius returns.'

'Can't we keep him?' sighed Dora.

Marius was not amused when Painswick showed him the cheque.

'So I've got to deal with that monster on the telephone twenty-four hours a day now.'

'You ought to be very grateful to Dora,' snapped Painswick. 'She masterminded the whole thing.'

At that moment, Dora sidled in.

'Can we have a word about Mrs Wilkinson, Mr Oakridge?' she asked politely.

'No, we may not,' said Marius, pouring himself a large whisky.

'She's not at all happy, and she jumps when you approach her suddenly from the wrong side. She's slumped in her box with her head down. She needs a good win to cheer her up.'

Marius glared at Dora's sweet round face, the picture of innocence, as she continued.

'Companion animals are allowed on most racecourses. Cheltenham's had ducks, hens, sheep, cats and goats. Rupert Campbell-Black's Love Rat wouldn't leave his box without his pony friend. The pony went into the parade ring and down to the start of the Derby and Rupert had to put Love Rat in blinkers so he wouldn't see the pony hadn't started and wasn't racing with him.'

'I know all this,' snapped Marius, looking at his post with slightly less alarm because of Bolton's cheque.

'Poor little Chisolm meanwhile,' Dora stopped to remove a burr from Mistletoe's tail, 'is going into a decline. She's losing weight, her coat's dull. Being abandoned for hours in her box must remind her of being trapped in that terrible compression chamber. And when Wilkie goes out without her she always gets up to mischief, butting Bolton's skip lorry back into Willowwood last week, and if she's shut away, she drives the other horses and the lads crackers with her pathetic bleating. Wilkie, on the other hand, needs Chisolm's reassuring presence. Look what a state she got herself into at Wetherby. And if Chisolm fades away, Wilkie will also go into a decline, and you don't want to jeopardize the career of a world-beater.'

'Shut up, Dora,' howled Marius, curling his hand round the bronze horse Mrs Wilkinson had won at Ludlow. 'Just shut up and get out, I don't need idiot schoolgirls to tell me how to run my yard.'

Head hanging, shoulders heaving, giving pitiful little sobs, Dora had reached the door when an infuriated Marius called out, 'Oh, for Christ's sake, let the bloody goat go along then.'

Dora's tears dried as instantly as a summer shower, and she beamed at Marius.

'Oh, thank you so much, Chisolm will be absolutely delighted. She'll be such a talking point at the races, I'm going to get her a new green collar and lead. Wilkie will have even more fans. Did you know that since Bonny, Seth and Corinna joined the syndicate, she's been getting five hundred hits a day on her website?'

'*Website?*' thundered Marius.

'Of course,' said Dora sweetly, 'and you'll never guess, I've taught Wilkie to lie down – I know Count Romeo does it automatically – but think what a joke it would be if we could get Jude the Obese on her back at the fête and make Wilkie pretend to collapse. She might anyway. And if Bolton parks his Chelsea tractor on the pavement, poor Jude will never get up the high street. She'll be traffic-jammed. What a problem for the Major!'

Seeing Marius was trying not to laugh, Dora said sternly, 'You ought to thank Miss Painswick. She organized the whole thing *and* got Lester to pay up.'

70

Bolton joined the syndicate and was quite awful. At his first meeting at the Fox, which to his disappointment neither Corinna, Seth nor Bonny was able to attend, he suggested chucking out the Ford Transit and going to the races in something smarter.

'I appreciate we need a minibus to retain the corporate feel,' he told the group, 'but if we each put in a grand or two we could afford a Mercedes Sprinter with infinitely superior facilities.'

Seeing Woody, Joey, Tilda, Pocock and Painswick turning green, Etta interrupted that the point of the syndicate was to make Mrs Wilkinson affordable to all of them.

'We keep back any extra money for vet's bills and things.'

'The wages of syndicate is debt,' murmured Alan, ordering red and white.

Bolton then suggested finding a sponsor for the bus and kitting out all Marius's stable lads in smarter gear.

'Tommy looks a mess and Rafiq needs an 'aircut and a smile occasionally. Marius needs six monfs in a charm school. Pretty Michelle is the only one who gets it right.'

Painswick, who was embroidering a church vestment, raised an eyebrow.

It became plain that Bolton was not going to pick up bar and food bills like Valent. At this first encounter, he didn't buy a round and suggested in a loud voice that if they were worried about costs, why didn't they take turns to have meetings in people's homes rather than at the Fox, buy any refreshments from the supermarket so they wouldn't have to fork out pub prices and each bring food on the day. The Major, who'd been shocked by the prices of Chris's hampers, agreed heartily.

'Fun to go to different houses,' cried Phoebe. 'You're welcome at Wild Rose Cottage any time, although you'd have to sit on the stairs. As it's your lovely idea, Lester, why don't we start with Primrose Mansions? We heard from the Major how exciting it is.'

Lester bowed. 'Cindy and I would be happy to receive you.'

'We'll give a pah-ee in the summer,' promised Cindy.

From then on Bolton continually bullied for improvements and was constantly on the telephone to Marius, whose calls were fielded by Miss Painswick. He was unable to understand why horses couldn't run every day. Nor could he appreciate that a lack of rain made the ground too quick for Furious, or that Mrs Wilkinson was still pulled down by her trip to Wetherby.

Bolton's ambition was to showcase his princess, who would prefer a stretch limo to a minibus and was anxious to put a pink bridle on Mrs Wilkinson: 'She is a girlie after all.'

Mrs Wilkinson's first race since Ludlow was a novice hurdle at Cheltenham in the middle of April. Cheltenham had been chosen because it was only twenty miles from Willowwood and wouldn't upset her, particularly as she was being accompanied by Count Romeo, History Painting and, best of all, Chisolm, who stopped bleating instantly she discovered she was coming too.

The day was full of incident. Bolton's electric gates fused shut and Pocock and the Major leapt from the minibus and much enjoyed helping Cindy over them with much shrieking.

Toby's lack of chin dropped.

'Good God,' exclaimed Alban from the driving seat, as Cindy tottered towards the bus, tossing her long blonde hair, flashing boobs, bare shoulders and a massive expanse of mantanned, tattooed bare leg. Hanging from her arm was a pale yellow bag in the shape of a unicorn. Flung round her shoulders, despite the mild spring day, was a floor-length mink.

'How many animals died to give you that coat?' hissed Dora.

'Only my mother-in-law,' giggled Cindy, which cracked up the bus.

Lester followed in a shiny, light brown suit, jewellery flashing in the sunshine. Despite Bolton's call for austerity, Alan was circulating the champagne and everyone was lapping it up.

Corinna was on tour, Valent in China. Bonny, in a neat little grey tweed suit and a white silk shirt, was sitting with Seth, who introduced her to the Boltons.

'A little birdie told me you was thirty-five, Bonny,' shrieked Cindy. 'I cannot believe it, I hope I'm as lovely as you when I get to your age.'

'Where's Valent?' asked Lester.

'Shopping,' said Bonny. 'He bought a mining company in South Africa last week.'

Not to be outdone, Bolton took his BlackBerry to the back of the minibus.

Trying not to mind Seth sitting next to Bonny, Etta feasted her eyes on primroses and celandines starring the verges, above which blackthorn blossom foamed in a tidal wave. White toadflax festooned the lichened walls and weeping willow branches hung like feather boas, with little lime-green leaves and yellow catkins curling outwards.

Cindy plonked herself across the row from Seth and Bonny and in front of Phoebe and Debbie.

'That's so sweet, Lester's "Dearest Dad" pendant and ring,' cooed Phoebe.

'He bought them hisself,' whispered Cindy. 'Hasn't seen his kids in years. I'm his precious little girl. His kids regard me as a fret.'

'That's rather sad,' said Bonny.

'How d'you get on with Valent's kids then?' demanded Cindy.

'I haven't met the boys yet,' replied Bonny coolly. 'We're taking things very slowly. After all, their mother passed away in a train crash. They need to achieve closure. I don't want to threaten them.'

'They couldn't not find you attractive, Bonny,' said Phoebe, 'which might make things hard for Valent.'

'I've seen piccies of Ryan. He's drop-dead gorgeous,' said Cindy.

'Phèdre again,' sighed Seth. 'A woman fatally drawn to her stepson.'

They'd reached the outskirts of Cheltenham, in whose greenhouse atmosphere everything was much further on. The crocuses were over but the white cherry blossom breathtaking against pink-petalled magnolia. Daffodils danced across the parks.

'Books are my life. So many authors have passed through Cheltenham,' Bonny was now saying to Seth.

'I don't read, me,' piped up Cindy.

'I can read you,' said Alan, bending over to admire the tattoo on her shoulder. ' "I love Lester", that's nice. What happens if you split up?'

'I get a kitten called Lester,' giggled Cindy. 'I don't read books, but I'm writing one.'

'You what?' asked Bonny incredulously. 'What on earth about?'

'About me, a hautobiography, a voyage of erotic discovery and how I found fulfilment wiv my gentle little Lester. I've made over forty movies.'

'You must have some terrific stories, do tell us more,' begged Alan, topping up her glass.

Clearly disapproving, Debbie got up and retreated down the bus. The Major moved closer.

'What's next?' he asked, rheumy eyes gleaming.

'Well, Lester is planning to shoot me as Lady Godiva in the Harboretum, riding Furious.'

'Furious might need a stand-in,' suggested Alan.

'And then he wants me to play Gwendolyn.'

'Oscar Wilde's Gwendolyn?' cried a horrified Bonny.

'Dunno how wild she was,' giggled Cindy, 'but she was pashnit about Sir Francis Framlingham, such a romantic story, and we want Mrs Wilkinson, who's grey, to play Beau Regard. If you shot carefully, you wouldn't know she hadn't gotta winkle. Perhaps you could play Sir Francis, Seth – I can just see you in a Cavalier 'at with a fevver or perhaps Marius, he's well fit, phwoar!' Cindy at last lowered her voice. 'Lester's a bit jelly of Marius.'

The stunned silence, no one daring to meet anyone's eyes, was broken by an outraged Phoebe.

'My husband Toby would have inherited the title if Aunt Ione's sister had been a boy. If anyone should play Sir Francis, it should be him. But I know Aunt Ione would fight tooth and nail to stop the Willowwood Legend being made into a porn film.'

'Erotic fantasy, perlease,' cried Cindy. 'Lester's always tasteful.'

Lester, glued to his BlackBerry, didn't rise.

'I'm sure it's out of copyright,' grinned Alan. '*The Willywood Legover*. Let me play Sir Francis, Cindy.'

'The porn is green,' said Seth. 'The best person to play Sir Francis,' he grinned, 'is Alban, our driver. You wouldn't mind getting your kit off, would you, Alban?'

Alban brayed with laughter and nearly ran into a lamp post.

Cindy shrieked as well.

'You'd 'ave to be an 'orseback rider, Allbare. I like that title, Alan, *The Willywood Legover*.'

'It's a travesty,' hissed Phoebe.

'I agree,' said Bonny.

'Not if it were done tasteful,' insisted Cindy. 'Have you ever taken your kit off in a film, Bonny? You'd enjoy it, it's very liberating. You'd need a boob enhancement first, but Valent would pick up the tab, and I'm sure he wouldn't mind in such a good cause.'

For once Bonny was silenced.

Etta gazed at the racing page of the *Mail*, willing herself not to laugh.

'I suppose it turns you on to – er – make this kind of film,' said Phoebe scornfully.

'Naah, you do it over and over and over, tike after tike. Lester's always present, he spanks my botty afterwards if I've under-performed. Makes me go all warm underneaf.'

More stunned silence was interrupted by a cough from Debbie. She was progressing down the bus with a large hatbox, wearing the serene smile of a head waiter bringing in a surprise birthday cake. She nearly knocked off Pocock's flat cap on the way.

'This is a gift from Normie and me, Etta. Enjoy.'

Inside, rising like a vast raspberry summer pudding, was a huge bright magenta stovepipe, the most awful hat Etta had ever seen.

'Gosh,' she squeaked.

'For you.'

'How terribly kind, but I couldn't possibly accept it. It's far too grand for me.'

'Try it on now.' Phoebe leapt to her feet.

'And far too expensive.'

'Furious paid for it,' chortled Debbie. 'I placed a bet on him at Wetherby.'

'It's lovely,' stammered Etta, 'but it would really show up my old coat. It'd look so much better on you, Debbie.'

'This hat will lift any outfit,' insisted Debbie.

'Chapeau, chapeau, and off to work we go,' sang a giggling Alan as he filled up his and Seth's glasses.

'Go on, Etta.' Phoebe lifted out the hat and, as if she were snuffing out a candle, dropped it over Etta's head, covering her eyes and most of her little snub nose.

'Where's Etta?' cried Seth. 'Where's she gone? I can't see her anywhere.'

'Not like that,' chided Debbie, tipping the huge contraption backwards. 'Give me your comb, dear.'

'I'll find it.' Seizing Etta's bag, Cindy scrabbled among a lot of tickets, pencils, Polos and a dog biscuit and unearthed an embarrassingly dirty comb, some grey fluff down its prongs, and handed it to Debbie, who coaxed feathery tendrils on to Etta's forehead.

'There, doesn't she look a poppet?'

'A pleasure dome of high degree,' murmured Seth.

'At least you're not swollen-headed, Etta,' quipped the Major, as Etta hung her head and the hat fell over her nose once more.

'It's lovely,' mumbled Etta from the magenta depths, desperate not to hurt Debbie's feelings. 'It's just a bit smart for me.'

'Not the new you,' said Debbie, tipping the hat again. 'Next week we'll find you a nice skirt suit in town.'

Gazing imploringly down the bus, Etta could see Alan, Woody, Joey and even Pocock creased up with laughter.

Alas, there were no gales blowing at the Cheltenham drop-off point to sweep the hat away into the ravishing green valley, no river to swallow it up.

The hat was so vast, Etta kept bumping into racegoers and knocking them and the hat sideways. Nor with it over her face could she feast her eyes on the most beautiful course in England with its ring of hills, lovely houses and little square church peeping out of angelically green trees, the blue Malvern hills to the left and the three radio masts looking down from Cleeve Hill opposite. Fences, hurdles, rails, cars, copses and helicopters spilled across the course like some divine toy a child couldn't bear to put away at night. Etta could at least breathe in a heady smell of hot horses, frying onions, burgers and scampi.

All around, too, were sculptures of great horses of the past. Cindy promptly handed her cigarette holder and glass of champagne to Alban and clambered on to Best Mate's statue, flashing a leopardskin thong while Lester took photographs.

'Try side-saddle, princess.'

'Isn't she dreadful,' whispered Phoebe to Debbie.

'Dreadful,' replied Debbie. 'Don't take your hat off, Etta, it looks so elegant.'

Bonny was delighted to see Etta so discomforted.

At least Mrs Wilkinson marched into the paddock looking cheerful. She adored crowds and they came running down to the rail to admire her and Chisolm, who trotted round in her new collar and lead, snatching at fading daffodils or any chip, burger bun or ice cream in unwary hands.

'There are thirty-three cameras in the stable block,' an amazed Dora, who was leading Chisolm, informed Tommy. 'Corinna and Bonny should hire a box for themselves.'

'Security is very tight,' observed Tommy.

'So is Cindy Bolton,' giggled Dora.

The crowd were also gazing at Cindy, who, having abandoned her mink to Lester and reached the centre of the parade ring in her six-inch heels, was squawking, 'Oh my God' and 'Phwoar' at the trainers and owners around her. Bonny, aware of not being gazed at as much as usual, had taken off her trilby so the world could appreciate her flawless but bleak face.

'Aren't you frozen, Cindy?' she said disapprovingly.

'No gain without pain,' giggled Cindy. 'Phwoar, here comes Marius, I really fancy 'im. I love mean, difficult fellows, can't fink why his wife left 'im.'

Mrs Wilkinson was looking for Etta. Only when Etta surreptitiously raised her hat as though she were peering through a letter box did Mrs Wilkinson recognize her, break away and tow a giggling Dora and Tommy to her side, bowling over a group of owners like skittles.

Above the parade ring, by a statue of the great Arkle, a lovely willow swung in a breeze which was also tossing around Lester's ginger comb-over, so it fell on his forehead like a giant kiss curl.

Why was Mrs Wilkinson wearing a rug with Marius's initials on and not his? wondered Lester angrily. He'd ordered a rug, with LB on, for Furious.

'She's not going to win the turnout,' said Joey. 'She hasn't come in her coat.'

'Funny fing to come in,' Cindy shrieked with laughter, 'I always take mine off.'

'Hush,' said Debbie in horror.

Marius had just had a word with Bertie and Ruby Barraclough and Awesome Wells, before legging him up on to Count Romeo, who at least had won the turnout. Coming back to the Willowwood syndicate, wincing at the sight of Cindy, Marius saw Amber had joined them, her long blonde plait falling down her green silk back.

Next moment Lester had strutted up and, putting a caressing hand on her arm, was telling her how to ride Mrs Wilkinson.

'Don't let her make it and exhaust herself. This is a longer trip. You've got the Cheltenham 'ill, so don't start your run too early.'

For a second, Marius was speechless, then, fired up by memories of bullying Shade Murchieson, he strode up.

'Am I training this horse or are you?' he said icily. 'Please stop muddling my jockey and take your hands off her.'

'Marius,' hissed Alan in horror, but before Bolton could explode, a voice said, 'Hear, hear,' and Rogue sauntered up, giving Amber's plait a tug. 'How are you, beauty?' then nodding at the rest of the syndicate, 'Seth. Bonny, you're looking good. Etta, where's Etta, under canvas?' He tipped back her hat and peered under it and everyone laughed in relief, as the bell went for the jockeys to mount.

'Good luck, darling.' He tugged Amber's plait again and sauntered off to ride Birthday Boy, the favourite.

'Phwoar, isn't he drop-dead,' sighed Cindy, which pleased Lester even less.

Amber didn't take in a word of Marius's instructions and even forgot to be charming to the syndicate.

I am not over him, she thought in horror.

Despite having to be secretive in order not to hurt Tommy, and Rafiq being in a terrible state about Bolton buying Furious, Amber and Rafiq had had wonderful sex since that rapturous first night after Wetherby. But all that was as nothing compared with her sudden explosion of longing for Rogue.

Thank God Rafiq had stayed behind at the yard. As Marius legged her up, Amber went straight over, landing on her bottom on the other side. As she remounted in embarrassment, she could see Rogue, his long legs hanging down out of his stirrups, laughing his head off as he undid Birthday Boy's four nearest plaits, giving himself something to cling on to.

If only he'd cling on to her, she thought, but as he set off for the start and she saw him flashing smiles at all the pretty women in the crowd, she pulled herself together. She'd got to beat the bastard.

Equally put out was Chisolm, when Mrs Wilkinson was set free to follow Rogue. Dora had to rush off and buy her an ice cream.

High up in the Owners and Trainers, Etta could at least see the race under the brim of her dreadful hat and that Mrs Wilkinson, enjoying the wide undulating track, had gone straight to the front and stayed there.

Amber's ignoring my instructions, thought Bolton, his heart darkening against Marius, who, below them on the grass, stood apart from the crowd, hands clenched on his binoculars.

'Come on, Mrs Wilkinson,' bellowed and screamed Willowwood, as she started her run up the hill.

'Come on, Mrs Wilkinson,' shrieked Cindy. 'Get your fucking arse into gear.'

'Here we go,' shouted Rogue, as he and Birthday Boy stormed past.

No you don't, thought Mrs Wilkinson, grinding her teeth.

Birthday Boy was a young horse. Leading up the hill, he wanted company and started looking around. Rogue picked up his whip and was so busy laying into the horse, who was also carrying 12 lb more than Mrs Wilkinson, that she managed to hurtle up the inner and once again win by a head.

Cindy went into complete hysterics of joy. Chisolm was almost as excited and towed a laughing Tommy down the walkway to meet her dear friend, and a captivated crowd went crazy.

Amber didn't dare look at Rogue and could hardly stammer out a coherent word when the overjoyed syndicate surged forward to congratulate her.

Bonny and Cindy, each determined to hog the limelight, were not pleased to be upstaged by a goat. Chisolm, having eaten the horn of Cindy's yellow unicorn bag, butted away anyone who tried to stand between her and Mrs Wilkinson.

The rest of the syndicate, aware that Marius had been dreadfully rude, insisted that Lester and Cindy, as the newest members, went up to collect Mrs Wilkinson's cup. Even on the podium Lester and Cindy were permanently on their mobiles, reporting on 'our 'orse'.

'Probably ringing each other up,' Seth murmured into the very clean ear of Bonny, who'd been feeling unusually upstaged and gave him a smile of radiant gratitude.

'Surprising he hasn't tattooed LB on Cindy,' she said.

'We all know that stands for Little Bugger,' said Seth and they both creased up with laughter.

Cackling at weak jokes was a sign of burgeoning love, reflected Alan, putting an arm round Etta: a rictus grin beneath her huge magenta hat.

'All right, darling?'

'Of course she is,' cried Debbie. 'We must make sure she wears her lucky hat every time Wilkie runs.'

Etta was in despair. Lester adored going into the winning owners' room on the left of the weighing room to drink more champagne and watch the race again, but he was still hopping mad with Marius. So was Bertie Barraclough. Count Romeo had come last. Bertie was even crosser when Lester, complacent in victory, sidled up and suggested Bertie's bouncing bed sales would rocket if he included a special offer of Cindy's latest erotic fantasy. Marius, felt Bertie, should not lower the tone of the yard by taking on scum like Bolton.

'Beware of winning,' Alan murmured to Marius. 'Bolton will expect it from now on.'

71

Bolton kept up the pressure, urging the syndicate to invest in a flat horse to race through the summer. He was particularly keen on a glossy black mare with four white socks, 'and "useless" written across her forehead', muttered Jase the farrier.

Bolton wanted to call the mare Cindy Kate. He was furious when Marius was disparaging about her prospects.

'God, give me ugly winners.'

Bolton continually infuriated Marius by rolling up un-announced at the yard with clients. He also rang constantly for inside information on Marius's runners – not many because Marius was still struggling to get back on track – and other trainers' horses. He continued to march into the paddock and give Marius's jockeys spurious advice. Rogue always ignored this, particularly after Bolton, while instructing Amber, left his hand a little too long on her succulent thigh.

In her next outing, to Wincanton in late April, Mrs Wilkinson was entered for her first novice chase over two miles. Bolton pro-ceeded to take a box for some of his important clients, demanding an excessive number of owners' badges.

Marius had told Amber to settle Mrs Wilkinson in third or fourth place and pull her up if she got tired. Mrs Wilkinson, how-ever, took to chasing with alacrity, gaining with each fence she carefully jumped, preferring it to the rush and bash-through of hurdles. Out of a large field she came fourth, beating some very good horses. Marius was delighted. Cindy, a symphony in lilac after spending a fortune at Karen Millen, and looking forward to leading in Mrs Wilkinson, was not happy. Nor was Bolton, who made a frightful scene, to the amusement of his important clients, who were fed up with him boasting about his horse and his tasty blonde jockey.

The syndicate was upset by the row, however, and were surprised the Major, as their chairman, seemed so reluctant to call Bolton into line.

'Harvey-Holden's horses are raced every few days, that's why they're so fit,' spluttered Bolton.

Marius snarled back that Mrs Wilkinson tried so hard, she really took it out of herself during a race and needed to rest afterwards. 'I am not going to push her.'

Not could the yard go on substituting Cheesecake for Furious when Cindy dropped in. On one occasion, tipped off by Michelle, she had turned up unexpectedly and flung her jangly braceleted arms round Furious, only for him to take a bite out of her. An enraged Bolton threatened to sue and, asking around, discovered he'd paid far too much for Furious and muttered about wanting his money back.

In his first race for Bolton, Furious had kicked the starter's car and two other horses and refused to start. In the next, he wouldn't even go into the parade ring.

The National Hunt season traditionally ends in April but jump racing continues throughout the summer for less good or less experienced horses or those suited to firmer ground. To appease Bolton, Marius entered Furious for a handicap chase at Worcester on Ladies' Day, which was held in aid of a wonderful local hospice called St Richard's. Bolton, in rare magnanimous mood, invited a party to join his table for lunch in the marquee.

Etta was touched to be asked. Petrified, however, that Debbie would frogmarch her into Larkminster and a pillarbox-red suit to complement the magenta stovepipe, she was relieved when Martin and Romy decided they'd like to accept Bolton's invitation and pick up tips and big fish for their own charities, and left her at home to look after Poppy, Drummond and Priceless.

The syndicate were happy to be back at the lovely wooded course with the river running behind the Owners and Trainers bar.

Marius didn't expect Furious to do anything, particularly as he himself had at last responded to pressure and sent Rafiq away on a course at the Northern Racing School in Doncaster to enable him to get a licence. But at least Tommy, whom Furious tolerated, was leading him up – and as it was summer they hadn't had to go through the battle of trying to clip him.

The lunch tables in the marquee were crammed with glamorous people, but easily the noisiest, most glamorous and stared-at table was Lester Bolton's, which included Shade Murchieson and Olivia Oakridge, Seth and Corinna, Martin and Romy, Alan, Bonny and of course Lester and Cindy with Harvey-Holden, Shade's trainer, popping in for a bite and a glass of champagne between races.

None of his guests liked Bolton but the invitation gave them the opportunity to talk to each other and enjoy an excellent free lunch. Aware he was among peers, the people with whom his princess should be mingling, Bolton had pushed the boat out, offering ever-flowing vintage champagne, wonderful white and red, and a fabulous pudding wine to go with the glazed strawberry tart.

Bolton himself looked absurd. Having observed Alban and Toby at the races, Cindy had persuaded her husband into an avocado-green check tweed suit, into which he was now sweating buckets. She had also talked him into shaving his head, comb-over and all. Lester was now sporting a pancake-shaped spinach-green check cap.

'Don't he look the country squire?' Cindy crowed to Alan, as they sat down to a first course of Parma ham and mango.

'Lester Squire,' grinned Alan, who, noticing the vicious cross-currents at the table, was determined to get drunk.

Bonny looked exquisite in a strapless grey silk dress topped by a shocking-pink and grey striped kimono jacket, with her hair up and tucked into a little pink pillbox.

She had been asked to judge the turnout in the first race and had given the prize to a mare 'with her mane falling on the wrong side', an increasingly impertinent and knowledgeable Cindy had told her scathingly.

'I guess Cindy knows all about comb-overs,' a furious Bonny hissed to Seth.

Corinna, stunning in a violet satin suit and a big black cart-wheel hat, had, to irritate Bonny, taken a public shine to Cindy, asking about her work, expressing huge enthusiasm for Lady Godiva in the wood. 'You're so ravishing, darling, the whole of Willowwood will be auditioning to play Peeping Tom.'

As admirers kept stopping at the table for autographs, 'We're so looking forward to your season at Stratford, Miss Waters,' Corinna would insist Cindy sign their race cards as well. 'This young woman is a serious actress, her autograph will be worth its weight one day.'

Bonny was hopping. She'd skipped her first course and was only drinking water, which didn't add to her merriment. Corinna, suspecting a tendresse developing between Seth and Bonny, was further irritated that Valent hadn't joined the party for her to flirt with.

'Where's your beau, Bonny?' she called accusingly across the table.

'Back in China.'

'You ought to go away together, you must need a break,' said Romy sympathetically.

'We tried,' sighed Bonny. 'Valent doesn't really do holidays. Like Sir Philip Green, he answers telephones in different parts of the world. And he hates sightseeing, not mad about the arts generally.'

'Thinks Hedda Gabler is a footballer,' drawled Seth.

Romy and Bonny shrieked with laughter.

'Bonny and Clod,' murmured Seth.

'Oh shut up,' murmured back Bonny.

'I've always thought me-time was rather selfish,' said Romy, crinkling her eyes engagingly. 'Martin and I believe in we-time, that *we* should take time off together to celebrate our marriage.'

'I believe in wee-wee time,' said Corinna rudely. 'Where's the lavatory?'

Shade, in a beautifully cut white suit and black shirt which set off his dark tan, was being eyed up as much for his good looks as his bank balance.

He was now showing off to Bonny, who was on his left. 'We're campaigning Ilkley Hall next season, starting with the Paddy Power followed by the Hennessy, the King George and the Gold Cup.'

'Why not enter him for Wimbledon, Henley, Cowes and the Grand Prix?' mocked Seth. Shade was just thinking up a withering reply, but as the waitresses removed the first-course plates, a jolly bald man in a pale blue Peter Rabbit coat seized the microphone and was going through the race card, telling people which horses to back in the remaining races.

To Bolton's irritation, he recommended three of Shade's horses but Furious didn't get a mention. Matters were not helped when Harvey-Holden returned for more champagne and a chat with Shade and Olivia.

'Why can't I have a trainer I can engage with?' grumbled Bolton. 'I asked Marius to join us,' he added petulantly, 'but with his usual lack of courtesy he hasn't showed up.'

'For Christ's sake,' snapped Alan, 'it might have something to do with the fact that one of your guests took both Marius's wife and twenty horses away from his yard.'

'What's that?' Olivia swung round.

'Poor Marius,' sighed Cindy, 'I don't know how you could leave him, Olivia. I mean Shade's well fit, but Marius is drop-dead gorgeous. Phwoar! I'd love to cheer him up.'

'Really,' said Olivia icily.

'Reeely.' Cindy leant across and admired the diamond big as a snowball on Olivia's hand. 'That's a nice ring, where'd you get that?'

'Shade gave it to me.'

'Say no more,' giggled Cindy. 'I don't fink Marius could have afforded that.'

A very, very bleak Olivia turned to Alan. 'Isn't she dreadful?'

'I think she's sweet,' said Alan coldly.

As the waitresses swept in bearing roast pork with Calvados and cream sauce, and wild mushroom roulade for Bonny, Cindy turned back to Alan.

'Doesn't Lester mind you lusting after other men?' he asked.

'Naaah,' Cindy hardly lowered her voice, 'not as long as he can join in. Lester enjoys freesomes, but sadly, I don't fink Marius is up for it.'

'How exquisite freesomes sound!' Alan filled up both their glasses.

'Lester likes that stuck-up Michelle – he's fumin' she's not leading up Furious today – and Michelle is seeing Marius so we could have 'ad a nice little foursome. Why don't you join us one evening, Alan? Our jacuzzi takes eight, so does our bed.'

'Gosh!' said Alan excitedly. 'Who else shall we have?'

'Dame Corinna is a bit old to get her kit off,' murmured Cindy, 'but I found it very humbling and heart-warming, being singled out by her as an actress just now.'

'We could ask Seth,' suggested Alan and received a steely look from Martin and Romy.

Shade meanwhile was enjoying himself. It was music to his ears to hear Bolton bitching about Marius, and having patronized the little creep in the past he was prepared today to discuss fluctuations in the porn industry as seriously as if they were billion-pound arms deals.

Alan was then thrown to find himself almost liking Shade, when, as they settled down to their main course, Shade crossed the marquee and seized the microphone in order to praise St Richard's Hospice, saying how miraculous they had been when his mother was dying of cancer.

'They control the pain, families are allowed to stay, their kindness is unbelievable. I cannot thank them enough.' He smiled round. 'Death comes to all of us, but to some,' his deep voice faltered for only a second, 'in better ways than others.'

He then urged everyone to give generously to St Richard's and to spend as much as possible at the auction after the last race.

Everyone cheered and clapped and as he returned to the table, Olivia hugged him: 'Well done, darling, that was great,' and Harvey-Holden patted him on the back.

Romy's eyes gleamed. People were already chucking £20 notes into buckets that were being circulated. If only Shade could become a patron of WOO, their War on Obesity charity.

As the head of fundraising drew Shade aside to thank him, Olivia, so beautiful in her simple little lime-green suit, turned to Alan.

'Please don't hate me,' she whispered.

'I've missed you,' he murmured.

'Me too.'

'Why didn't you warn me you were leaving Marius?'

'I thought you might stop me.'

'Are you happy?'

Olivia gave a half-smile.

'Shade's trying so hard to look after me better than Marius did.'

'I'd like some glazed tart,' Cindy told a waitress.

'Takes one to know one,' sneered Bonny.

'That was so moving,' Romy told Shade as he came back to the table. 'Martin and I have a colossal database but we find the best way of fundraising is face to face. We employ students to confront people in the street and persuade them to give ten pounds a month for African orphans.'

'I'd pay students ten pounds to leave me alone,' drawled Seth.

'Oh get away, I know you don't mean that,' said Romy roguishly.

Glancing round, Bonny caught sight of the *Scorpion*, a copy of which two women at the next-door table were avidly reading. In it some outwardly respectable ageing actress had told all and more to Amber's mother, Janey Lloyd-Foxe.

'I cannot understand why celebs suddenly reveal sordid details about their past,' said Bonny disapprovingly.

'For money,' said Seth, forking up Bonny's rejected mushrooms, 'or to sell books. My sister and I,' he added idly, 'are going to sue our parents.'

'Whatever for, Seth?'

'Because neither of them sexually abused us and consequently gave us nothing with which to spice up interviews or our autobiographies.'

'Oh Seth.' Bonny, who wore no mascara to run, burst into tears.

'Earth's the matter?' asked Seth, reaching across and tugging Alan's yellow silk handkerchief out of his breast pocket and handing it to Bonny.

'I was abused by both my father and my stepfather,' she sobbed.

'Can't really blame them.'

'Seth,' thundered Martin, adding, 'That's what makes you so able to express suffering in your acting, Bonny.'

'Certainly the abuse I suffered informed my life experience, Martin,' sniffed Bonny. 'Through therapy, I recognized I must put myself first for a change. I recognized my own fragility. *The Blossoming* is indeed resonant of my special trauma.'

'Can you pass the potatoes?' demanded Corinna.

'I'm sensitive, me,' piped up Cindy, 'but one has to move on.'

'My goal this year is to internationalize the Bonny Richards phenomenon,' said Bonny.

'That won't be hard,' gushed Romy. 'Charity work would raise your profile. Your voice alone would do it, you have such a fascinating accent.'

'I spent a lot of time in the States.'

'About three minutes,' snarled Corinna.

'Land of the freesome,' giggled Alan, who was already drunk.

72

It was nearly time for the Best Dressed Lady contest. Competitors were powdering their noses.

'Neither of you need do a thing to improve your faces,' Seth told Romy and Bonny, but they still went off to the Ladies.

'I cannot understand your mother-in-law, allowing Debbie to force her into that dreadful hat,' murmured Bonny as she tilted her little pink pillbox.

'Etta's always been a wet blanket,' murmured back Romy, adjusting her gentian-blue picture hat. 'Not up to Martin's wonderful father's speed at all.'

'I can't figure out why she bugs me,' mused Bonny. 'I guess it's the way she hangs on Valent's and Seth's every word like a hysterical spaniel, laughing at their jokes. Do you know what Seth calls her?'

'Tell me.'

'"Sorry with the fringe on top," because she never stops apologizing!'

'Sorry with the fringe on top! How priceless.' Romy burst out laughing. 'Do let's lunch.'

The loudspeaker crackled.

'Will all the runners in the Best Dressed Lady competition please make their way to the winners enclosure to meet their celebrity judge,' ordered the loudspeaker.

'Who's that darling old boy? He looks very familiar,' murmured Bonny as the ladies lined up.

'He's an actor,' said Romy.

'He's off of the telly anyway,' said Cindy.

'I know who he is, he's in *Buffers*,' cried Romy, 'that army quiz game where old generals and war heroes argue over campaigns.'

'So he is. It's Rupert Campbell-Black's father, Eddie,' said Corinna.

'Ooh, I wonder if Rupert's here?' All the ladies looked round in excitement.

As they paraded before him in their finery, letcherous Eddie was like a pig in clover.

Shuffling down the line, he particularly admired Romy's cleavage, Bonny's legs, Olivia's kitten face and the scarlet drooping lips of Corinna, whose make-up had just been touched up in the car park by Stefan the Pole.

Eddie then caught sight of Cindy in pink Versace with her boobs hanging out. Her pink feather fascinator tickled his nose, making him sneeze, as he leaned forward to have a better look. Awarding her first prize as Best Dressed Lady, he was rewarded with an explosion of excited squawks and omigods and kisses.

'Fancy me being better dressed than famous older celebs like Corinna and Bonny Richards,' screamed Cindy.

'Bonny Richards?' asked Eddie. 'Is that Gordon's girl?'

'I gave Cindy that reconstruction,' Lester Bolton told Shade complacently. 'Each boob cost nine thousand.'

This event had been taking place in the winners enclosure while Furious, in an LB-initialled rug, and Tommy, in an LB-initialled sweatshirt, both sweating up worse than Lester in his tweed suit, were walking quietly round the parade ring next door.

Unfortunately, Cindy's prolonged and hysterical victory screams coincided with a woman hanging over the rails and putting up her rose-patterned parasol in Furious's face. Furious spooked, Tommy, caught off guard, let go of the lead rope. Furious took off, clearing the rail and, people swear to this day, the cowering spectators. By the time he was caught, glaring into a bungalow and terrorizing two pensioners, the race was over.

Marius also lost it. When greeted by an even more shrilly shrieking Cindy: 'Oh Marius, our horsey's run away,' he had yelled back, 'It's your fucking fault for making such a bloody awful din.'

'How dare you insult my wife,' yelled Lester, secretly delighted to have even more of an excuse to hate Marius.

This hatred was intensified when Count Romeo, wearing blinkers for the first time to make him concentrate, ran a blinder for Rogue Rogers and took the next race.

And even further intensified when Tommy, in the winners enclosure chucking buckets of water over Count Romeo to cool him down, caught sight of Cindy, waiting as Best Dressed Lady to present the cup. Tommy was so cross with her for spooking Furious, she deliberately drenched her at the same time.

Furious had banged a hock while running around Worcester. Examining it, Charlie Radcliffe got kicked again.

'The sooner you get that brute out of your yard the better,' he roared. 'It's a pit bull. You'll be done for murder soon.'

Marius didn't care. He had looked across the paddock and seen his wife, infinitely lovelier, in beautiful clothes, no longer exhausted, and hadn't returned her shy, tentative smile.

Coming in next morning, Miss Painswick found Marius passed out in the dog basket clutching an empty bottle of whisky, with a shivering Mistletoe on the floor beside him.

'That's not the way to get your wife back,' she said tartly.

73

Goaded by Bolton, nagged by the Major, Marius reluctantly entered Mrs Wilkinson for a novice chase back at Worcester later in June. He grew increasingly worried that the going was too soft. It had rained heavily in the night and as they arrived at the course, behind the Owners and Trainers, the River Severn, the colour of strong tea, was rising steadily.

'Any moment you expect a crocodile to jump out and gobble you up,' observed Alan, whose birthday it was. He was dispensing champagne to a skeleton syndicate in the car park.

Dora, Trixie and Tilda were all tied up with exams. The vicar was taking a funeral. Woody was beautifying North Wood for the filming of Lady Godiva. Joey was flat out at Badger's Court, being appropriately badgered by Bonny to alter things while Valent was still away in China. The paint in the bedroom had been changed five times. For Valent's office, once the home of Mrs Wilkinson, Bonny had ordered a special wallpaper of leaping salmon as a surprise, not least because it cost £9,000 a roll.

Bonny had several times nearly caught Joey in flagrante. On one occasion, Chrissie had to hide in a wheelie bin. What horrors if a nocturnal spying Ione had surprised her with a wind-up torch.

Leaning against a nearby Bentley at Worcester, Bonny was telling Seth about the vast heart-shaped bed she was installing in her and Valent's bedroom.

'Tin man with a heart-shaped bed,' quipped Seth. 'Want me to give it a trial run?'

'If you want to spice up yours and Valent's love life,' interrupted Cindy, 'you orta screw a levver swing into the ceiling. We've got one hanging down the stairwell, it's great for sex. We have to unscrew it when Lester's mum comes to stay.'

As part of the economy drive, the syndicate were enjoying a cold picnic in the car park. Chisolm had proved most useful, eating up Ione's contribution of chopped veggies and home-made dip. She had even drunk two bowls of nettle soup but drew the line at the little pork pies, past their sell-by date, provided by Phoebe.

Having eaten a bag of chips and read the *Racing Post*, Alban was off to put a tenner each way on Mrs Wilkinson.

'D'you think she's got a chance?' he asked the assembled company.

'According to Marius, she was given a good blow on Monday,' said the Major.

'Sounds so rude,' giggled Cindy. 'That's what I'd like to give her trainer.'

'Cindy!' exploded Debbie.

'That is so gross,' said Bonny furiously. 'Must you always vulgarize everything?'

'That's because I'm vulgar, me, Miss Toffee Nose.'

'I wouldn't argue with that.' Bonny turned back to Seth.

'As I was saying, every time Bonny Richards is on the cover, magazines fly off the shelves.'

Alan had brought a tape recorder and was idly making notes for a life of Mrs Wilkinson, for which Valent had given him a five-grand advance. Alan didn't think it would see the light of day, but he had better look keen.

The syndicate had realigned, he reflected. His friend Seth and Bonny were drifting together. Phoebe, aware of a faint neglect from both of them and with feet that were killing her after two days at Royal Ascot, had gone back to being babied by Debbie and Norman. She was now asking Uncle Alban to put a fiver on Mrs Wilkinson, which she would probably never pay back.

Alan thought it would be nice when school broke up and darling Trixie and Tilda could come racing again. He had noticed Painswick blossoming. Marius, grateful to her for work-ing so many weekends, had invited her to the races that afternoon and left Tresa in charge of the office. Painswick had bought a floral-print tent with a matching hat. It was her first time out not wearing Hengist's scarf. Work in the engine room had given her knowledge about the horses, the lads and Marius which fascinated the syndicate, and which would be particularly useful for the book on Mrs Wilkinson – if he ever wrote it.

Pocock had also taken the afternoon off and was advising Etta on her continuing dream of creating a rose called Valent Edwards: dark red shot with black and deeply scented.

'You can use my greenhouse,' he told her.

Etta has no idea how much he adores her, thought Alan.

Bolton, in green gumboots high as waders on his fat little legs, and a Barbour that came down to his ankles, had buttonholed the Major.

'I gave Marius a computerized spreadsheet with potential races on it for all the 'orses in the yard. He hasn't fucking looked at it. I insisted lovely Michelle lead up Wilkie and Furious, he ignored me. When's he going to 'ave an open day, so we can socialize with uvver owners?'

'I'll have a word.' The Major felt his Portuguese villa sliding into the Atlantic. At least he'd forecast the rain and an east wind which was excitingly blowing Cindy's citrus-yellow dress over her fascinator, but was not able to dislodge Etta's magenta monstrosity, which she'd taken off during the picnic.

'Don't forget your lucky hat, Etta,' ordered Debbie as they drifted towards the paddock.

'Don't listen to that old bat,' whispered Cindy, tucking an arm through Etta's. 'Come and 'ave a bevvy at the weekend, I've got loads of 'ats you can try on or we'll find you something nice on the internet. You're a pretty lady, Etta, and Lester agrees.'

'Oh, thank you,' cried Etta, ridiculously touched. 'And you're a darling, Cindy.'

Led up by Tommy, Mrs Wilkinson looked a picture, gleaming pewter and silver as the curly white and dark grey clouds raced overhead. The crowd admired a weeping willow Tommy had imposed by transfer on her sleek quarters and laughed at Chisolm, who'd snatched a large mouthful of pansies from a tub on the way in.

'Hello, Wilkie, hello, Chisolm,' they cried.

Only that morning an old lady had written to Marius asking for a set of Mrs Wilkinson's shoes and a signed photograph.

Bolton was still complaining loudly that Michelle wasn't leading Wilkie up. Having legged up Amber, Marius retired to the bar, fingers caressing a treble whisky.

'Marius Soakridge,' quipped Harvey-Holden nastily.

The syndicate gathered outside the bar to watch the race. Ten horses went down to post. One mare dumped her jockey, jumped the rail and took off into the country.

'Must be Furious's sister,' said Alan.

Etta looked at the cathedral spire rising out of the trees. 'Dear God, bring Wilkie home safely.'

'I do a lot for the planet,' Bonny was saying. 'I couldn't go out with a man who didn't recycle.'

'That's why you've bought Valent an exercise bike,' mocked Seth.

'I'm fed up with all this Green stuff,' grumbled Cindy. 'Ione's got Lester geed up now, said we should have dimmer lights everywhere. She's given 'im a wind-up torch – he's going to need it to find the clit – and she's even got 'im on to solar-powered sex toys now. He put my vibrator out on the balcony to recharge yesterday and it got rained on.'

'For God's sake, shut up,' muttered Bonny.

'They're off,' said Seth, picking up his binoculars.

The sun came out.

Mrs Wilkinson was travelling beautifully. By the end of the first circuit, the field was so close, their black shadows were like nine clubs on a playing card. Mrs Wilkinson was edging up to the leaders. The syndicate yelled in delight at each long glorious jump. Marius was so delighted he came running out to join them.

'Come on, little girl, come on.'

'She's going into the lead,' yelled Seth.

The runners were still on the far side of the course when, four from home, on the big screen Amber could be seen drifting away from the field.

'Stupid, stupid bitch,' howled Bolton. 'She's taken the wrong course.'

'Shit,' hissed an ashen Marius, 'oh shit, she's broken down.'

'Shit,' said Seth, 'I've lost a bomb.'

'What's happened?' gasped an anguished Etta.

For a couple of seconds they could see Mrs Wilkinson hobbling helplessly, Amber pulling up and jumping off, and the horse ambulance hurtling towards her. Then the camera moved back to the rest of the runners, who were galloping round the bend and entering the home straight.

'Wait for us,' begged Etta, but Marius had vaulted over the rail, bolted across the track and vaulted over the far rail before the rest of the runners cleared the final fence and came thundering towards him. Next moment he'd hijacked a Land-Rover and set out to find his stricken charge.

'I must go to her,' sobbed Etta.

'Come on,' cried Cindy, kicking off her six-inch heels. 'Lester can't run in his wellies. See you later, babe.'

'I'm coming too,' cried Phoebe. 'Poor Wilkie.'

'I'm not going,' said Bonny. 'I'm too sensitive to witness an animal's suffering.'

'You'd better have a large drink then,' said Seth.

The rest of the syndicate raced across the wet grass to the stables on the far side of the course. Phoebe and Cindy were in the lead, clutching their shoes, their macs and bags over their arms.

They were followed by a desperately panting Etta, whose hat had fallen off and been run over by the horse coming in last. She was joined by Tommy and Chisolm, who had rushed over from the finish.

'Don't worry, Mrs Bancroft.' Tommy hugged a distraught Etta. 'I'm sure she'll be OK. The ambulance will have taken her to the stables.'

The rain-dark trees hung overhead like undertakers. By the time they reached the stables, Mrs Wilkinson had been seen by the vet and her two front legs had been hastily wrapped in bright blue bandages with cotton wool spilling over the top. Her coat was dark with sweat, her big brown eye with the blue centre heavy with pain. She gave a half-knucker when she saw Etta and Chisolm and fell silent.

Her leg had evidently exploded and had swollen up hugely. The vet, who wore a bright blue shirt to match the bandages, said he had given her two shots of morphine. Etta put her arms round Mrs Wilkinson's neck.

'Oh my angel, my poor angel. Is she going to be OK?'

'I've advised Marius to take her home and let your vet X-ray her in the morning.'

Tommy and even Michelle were crying openly, and so was Phoebe. 'Oh, poor poor horsey,' wailed Cindy.

Amber was sitting on an upturned bucket, her head in her hands.

'I'm so sorry, Etta. She was jumping perfectly, going like a dream. Then she seemed to collapse under me.'

'What's happened, what did the vet say?' gasped Alan, running up. He was followed by Debbie, Painswick and Pocock, who at least hadn't collapsed from shock this time.

'Will Mrs Wilkinson have to be put down?' panted Debbie. 'Will she get better?'

'Poor horse, poor horse,' sobbed Cindy, trying and failing to give her a Polo. 'Has she hurt both her poor leggies?'

'No, you always bandage both,' said Amber.

Everyone was being gentlemanly. No one was saying, 'I've paid three thousand for a share in this horse,' when Bolton barged in.

'I've just joined this fucking syndicate,' he howled, 'and the fucking horse has broken down.'

'And you pressurized Marius into running her, you bully,' howled back Cindy. 'Poor little Wilkie, the grass was too wet and slippery.'

'A good 'orse can run on any ground, look at Arkle,' shouted Bolton.

'We're not talking about Arkle, dickhead.'

Alan, Josephus the historian, was standing outside the box, talking into his tape recorder.

Everyone except him and Bolton was stroking Mrs Wilkinson and telling her what a good girl she was.

How ironic, thought Etta with strange clarity, that in a disaster Wilkie was being wept over, fussed over and patted in exactly the same way as when she won at Ludlow, Newbury and Cheltenham – the agony and the ecstasy of racing.

Alban, who had a bad hip, and the Major, who was scared of coronaries, had just reached the stables.

'We should be told what's going on. Where's Marius?' demanded the Major.

'Gone,' intoned Amber. 'History Painting needed saddling up for the next race. The trainer and the television cameras move on.'

'What did the vet say exactly?' asked Alban.

'I think we better get everyone out of the stable,' said Tommy.

Horses were clattering past the door, going out or returning from races.

How dare you be sound? Etta wanted to shout at them.

'Good thing I was wearing flatties for running,' said Phoebe. 'I felt like Princess Diana in that mothers' race. It's been such fun. We must get another horse.'

'That's my last horse,' quavered Painswick. 'I couldn't have another horse after Wilkie.'

Pocock put an arm round her heaving shoulders.

'Think we ought to clear out and give her some peace,' urged Alban.

Unable to contain her anguish any longer, determined not to frighten Mrs Wilkinson by breaking down in front of her, the same as not crying when Bartlett was put down, Etta stumbled out. Finding an empty stable, she sobbed her heart out.

'Oh please God, let her be all right.'

Suddenly she was aware of darkness as the light from the doorway was blotted out by a large figure. It was Valent.

With a wail, Etta collapsed sobbing against him.

'I'm so sorry, it's Wilkie. I'm so terrified she's going to be put down. I don't want to frighten her by crying. Oh Valent, she's so brave, I love her so much.'

'I know you do.' Valent enfolded her in a great warm bearlike hug. He was wearing a black shirt and a black and white herring-bone jacket. Both were soaked by Etta's tears as he patted her shoulder and stroked her hair.

'It's OK, it's going to be all right. What did the vet say?'

'Lots of meaningless things, meaningless because you can't take them in. I don't want them to write her off and s-s-s-shoot her.'

'No one's going to shoot her, I promise, we'll get her the best vets in the world. You pulled her through last time.' For a moment Etta thought he might break down too, as he went on in a rough, choked voice, 'She's going to need you.' He squeezed her tightly. 'I'm so sorry, luv.'

'Thank you.' Drawing away, Etta tugged the pink and lilac scarf from her neck and blew her nose. 'She was going so beautifully,' she gulped.

'She'll be all right, she's tough,' said Valent, drawing her close again. 'Come on, luvie, get a grip for Wilkie's sake. We'll go and see her.'

They heard a clatter outside and the smell of stables was joined by a waft of Allure.

'Hello, hello-o.' It was Bonny, with a distinct edge to her voice. 'Welcome home, Valent. I thought it was Mrs Wilkinson who needed comforting.'

'I'm so sorry.' Etta leapt away from him, battling a further onslaught of tears. 'Valent was just being unbelievably kind.'

Bonny glanced at Etta's crimson, wrecked, blubbered face incredulously.

'I didn't assume for a second he was being anything else.'

'Don't be a bitch, Bonny,' snapped Valent. 'Wilkie's special to Etta.'

'And to me. I've got a share in her too. I'd have come sooner, but I can't bear to see animals suffering. God, this place stinks.'

'I'm so sorry,' gulped Etta.

As she stumbled towards the door, Seth appeared.

'Oh, there you all are. Hi, Valent, good flight? Great to see you back. Bonny managed to enchant some besotted official into driving us over. She's been really missing you,' he reassured Valent, then, turning to Etta: 'Don't worry, angel, Wilkie'll be fine, she's such a gutsy horse.'

Seth hugged Etta, his body so lean and honed, a panther compared with bearlike Valent.

'I'll look after Etta,' Seth added, 'and leave you two lovebirds to a touching reunion. You're a lucky man, Valent.'

Seeing Valent's face like granite, Bonny decided not to make a scene.

'It's so good to see you,' she told him as soon as Seth and Etta were out of earshot. 'You should have warned me you were coming. Nice jacket, black and grey suit you.' Then, seeing Valent still looking wintry: 'Don't worry about Mrs Bancroft. I've spoken with Romy, her daughter-in-law, such a charming woman, and she says Etta's a drama queen, far too dotty about animals, cries at the drop of a sparrow, and she's had a little too much bubbly today. Martin and Romy are really concerned about her drinking.'

'Etta's a sweet lady,' said Valent sharply, 'and Wilkie means the world to her.'

'And who's been eating too much chop suey?' Bonny poked Valent in the tummy. 'We'll have to get you back in shape, or on second thoughts,' even in the dim light, Valent was dazzled by her beauty, 'let's go back to Willowwood. I can't wait for you to see the improvements I've made and to try out our new bed.'

She couldn't understand why Valent didn't seem to take in what she was saying and insisted on seeing Mrs Wilkinson first.

Finding Bolton still bellyaching: 'I paid three grand to join this syndicate, what compensation do I get if she's a write-off?' Valent promptly told him to bugger off and stop upsetting Mrs Wilkinson. When Bolton refused, Chisolm, like a bossy staff nurse, butted him out of the stable.

'Oh fuck,' said Alan, as the tape ran out.

Word had got around that a big hitter had arrived. Suddenly every trainer on the racecourse made an excuse to stop by and commiserate with Valent and Bonny, who might well be looking for another horse soon.

74

Next day Charlie Radcliffe X-rayed Mrs Wilkinson and diagnosed a possible hairline fracture of the cannon bone. He would X-ray her again in a fortnight and in a fortnight after that, by which time the injury would show up more clearly. After twelve weeks, if nothing more serious had developed, she could very slowly start exercising again, but was unlikely to be race-fit before late spring, which could mean nearly a year off.

Etta, who hadn't dared ask Marius if she could sleep in the stable with Mrs Wilkinson, spent a miserable night, but was thrilled when Valent rang her mid-morning.

'Don't you worry, luv, it could have been a lot worse and later she and Chisolm can come back to Badger's Court to convalesce.'

'How lovely to have her home again,' gasped Etta. 'Are you sure people won't mind?'

'I'm people – and I don't,' said Valent and rang off.

Arrangements for the immediate future were more complicated, however. To give Mrs Wilkinson a chance, she had to be confined to twenty-four-hour box rest in big bandages for at least three months. There was even talk of cross-tying her so she couldn't move around.

Most of Marius's other horses were turned out. Having been canvassed by Bonny, Romy and Martin were deliberately keeping Etta busy. As a result she had far less time to visit Mrs Wilkinson, who sunk into depression, slumped in her box, refusing to eat, head hanging, not even diverted by Chisolm's antics. The mass of get-well flowers from fans, propped outside her box and not eaten by Chisolm, had withered away. There were also murmurs of discontent from the syndicate. Why should they go on forking out for a horse that might not be able to race for a year – with no prize money and escalating vet's bills?

A week later, in early July, Painswick was leaving work when Mistletoe leapt on to her desk, leaving muddy paws all over the medical book and scattering papers.

'Get down, Mistletoe dear,' said Painswick fondly, reflecting that six months ago she'd have hit the roof.

Looking out, she saw Valent getting out of his Mercedes, carrying a big bunch of young carrots like a bouquet and heading towards the tack room, then going with Marius into Wilkie's box. Seeing them return, Painswick turned down *At the Races*, and poured a beer for Valent and a modest whisky for Marius.

'And don't go to bed too late,' she chided him as she set off for home. 'You've got an early start to Fontwell. There's a chicken pie for you and Mistletoe in the fridge.'

'Getting on all right?' asked Valent as Marius turned up *ATR* again.

Marius nodded. 'She drives me round the twist, but she's an old duck and bloody efficient. She sees off Bolton and Bertie Barraclough, even Nancy Crowe.'

Proudly, shyly, he showed Valent the sapphire and crimson cushion embroidered with the words 'God, give me winners', which Painswick had made for him.

'That's neat,' said Valent, and proceeded to give Marius a dressing-down.

'I know it's the pot calling the kettle black, Marius, but you've got to be more diplomatic, socialize more and stop being so bluddy rude and grumpy. You've got to offer owners a more exciting time. They're not just buying horses, they're buying oopmarket fun.

'And Amber mustn't be so snotty, or Rafiq so sulky. Tommy's the only decent ambassadress in your yard and she screwed up when she tipped a bucket of water all over Cindy at Worcester. I heard about that.' Valent started to laugh. 'Must've been bluddy funny though.

'For a start, I think you should give Rafiq a contract as stable jockey.' Then, when Marius looked appalled: 'I rung them up at the Northern Racing College and they said he was bluddy marvellous.'

'And bloody tricky.'

'The trickiness would disappear with a bit of recognition. You'd get a 10 lb allowance for him. You need to win more. You won't get your wife back by losing races.'

'That's fuck-all to do with you,' snarled Marius, picking up the schooling lists.

'And when are you going to replace Collie? The yard lacks direction.'

'Soon. Probably with Michelle. She's already acting head lad.'

'Acting up head lad,' growled Valent. 'She's lippy, bitchy, she can't ride. She hardly ever gets up to ride out, the others have to do five lots sometimes. She cheeks Miss Painswick. All the staff except Josh and Tresa are scared of her and she grasses to Lester Bolton too much.'

'You've been in China,' exploded Marius, 'how d'you know all this?'

'Phone works in China too. I ask questions and I learn a lot. You orta sack Michelle.' Valent thought Marius was going to hit him.

A diversion was then caused by Chisolm running into the office pursued by Horace the Shetland. Having done a lap, scattering magazines and papers, they ran straight out again.

Marius looked at Valent, and they burst out laughing.

I've never let anyone bawl me out like this, thought Marius as he got up to refill his drink. But I trust this man, he's straight.

Valent in turn was wistfully thinking how handsome Marius was and how elegantly he was built. If he looked like that, Bonny wouldn't be giving him the runaround and always bullying him to lose weight. Last night, Valent had nearly fallen off the heart-shaped bed, which ought to have seat belts, and the mirror on the ceiling only showed how out of shape he was.

'What's your take on Mrs Wilkinson?' he asked.

Marius shrugged. 'Not great. Charlie X-rayed her again today. The fracture isn't as bad as we thought but she's terribly low. She's a mare who suffers from depression, tough as hell but easily cast down.'

'We don't want to lose a bluddy good horse,' said Valent. 'I've got a plan. Send her back to my place to convalesce. Trixie, Dora, Poppy and Drummond will all be home for the holidays, and Wilkie loves children.'

Marius was dubious and said he'd have to ask Charlie Radcliffe.

Getting up, Valent thought how pretty Marius's garden looked, with foxgloves, pinks, alstroemerias, delphiniums and roses jostling for position in the beds and spilling over emerald-green lawns. A white rose had been grown up the office wall and peered in, pale and lovely as Bonny.

'Looks good. Place looking much better, but you've got to get rid of Furious.'

'Not mine to sell. I can't afford to buy him back.'

'He's not going anywhere and Bolton will sue you if he does any more damage.'

'He's been better since Rafiq came back.'

What Rafiq hadn't told Marius was that when he came back from the course to get a licence up in Doncaster, which he'd really enjoyed, Furious had greeted him with every affection until he'd entered the box, whereupon Furious had picked him up by the ribs, thrown him into the corner so he couldn't escape and kicked him in the back of the head.

Reluctant to show the terrible bruising, Rafiq had made excuses not to sleep with Amber when she needed him, the night after Wilkie broke down. It had not improved their relationship.

Despite 120 get-well cards from the children of Greycoats, Mrs Wilkinson was not responding, and after a week Charlie and Marius agreed to Valent's plan.

Gleefully Valent rang Etta.

'Mrs Wilkinson's coming home to Badger's Court.'

'But she's not allowed out.'

'She can start in her old stable. Tommy and Rafiq aren't busy. With so many horses turned out, they'll lend a hand.'

'But that's your lovely office,' said Etta, aghast.

'I've decided to turn the cockpit into my office,' said Valent. 'Octagonal shapes are considered very auspicious and it's more peaceful away from the house.'

He didn't add that Bonny, on her latest feng shui kick, had junked the £9,000 wallpaper and redecorated his office in flesh-coloured paint to balance the flow of positive and relaxing energy. Then she'd littered it with seashells and joss sticks, and hung his white kaftan on the back of the door. On the windowsill she had placed a yellow teapot, which according to feng shui encouraged stability in relationships, and given him an orange chair to provide the fire element to boost his career.

Worst of all, she'd thrown out his microwave because electro-magnetic waves weren't friendly, so, if he was hungry, he could no longer chuck in a pizza at one o'clock in the morning. She'd also covered the television in the bedroom and his Lowry with throws because they acted as mirrors, which was bad feng shui.

According to a gleeful Joey, who reported all this to Etta, the mother and father and baby bear of all battles had followed.

Bonny was incandescent with rage. She'd earmarked the cockpit for herself, as a quiet room for learning lines and meditation, and what about the private cinema Valent was going to build for her? Even worse, Mrs Wilkinson would be back in the office, which meant Etta Bancroft and that pestilential goat bleating round the place 24/7.

Immediately she rang Romy, who was appalled and rang Etta.

'You must stop taking advantage of Valent's kindness. Don't you realize Bonny is an artist who needs her personal space? She has incredibly kindly put her name to a beautiful letter launching WOO – the War on Obesity. Do you really want to rock the boat?

'Valent has a sentimental attachment to Mrs Wilkinson, but he'll soon transfer his affections to another horse.'

Etta was mortified, but it was too late. Joey, utterly fed up with repainting and being bossed about, was joyfully transforming the office back into a stable and the cockpit into an office. It meant several months' more work. He wanted to put his elder daughter on the tennis circuit, and he was worried Chrissie might be pregnant. Times was hard.

The change in Mrs Wilkinson was dramatic. Installed in Badger's Court, peering over a newly painted dark blue half-door, she could see the orchard and the valley. Etta was close by and Chisolm, chewing the bark off apple trees and stealing the workmen's lunches, was never far away. Gwenny curled up on her back again, and the syndicate popped in to see her as they'd never felt able to at Throstledown.

She'd perked up in a fortnight and was walking by the end of July. Etta, having been so upset by Romy and Bonny, had also cheered up. Listening to her singing as she skipped out Mrs Wilkinson and rebandaged her legs, Willowwood smiled.

'So lovely for her, having her Village Horse home again.'

75

Etta's apparent ecstasy was not just due to Mrs Wilkinson's return to Badger's Court. One lovely morning soon after she had moved back in, Etta was watering her garden, delighting in the way white and pink clematis and honeysuckle swarmed up the mature conifer hedge as if to catch a glimpse of Valent.

But she mustn't think of Valent, who was on a yacht some-where, supposedly 'mending his relationship' with Bonny.

Etta did, however, still harbour a long-distance crush on Seth and was saving up to see him at Stratford when he opened as Benedict in *Much Ado*.

The stream had dried to such a trickle, she was just sliding her watering can along the pebbly bottom to refill it when Stefan the Pole rolled up and admired Etta's garden saying he wished Corinna and Seth were more interested in theirs, so many plants had died in the drought. Corinna Waters, reflected Etta, was something of a misnomer – but she had been away on tour.

Stefan confided that, pre-Stratford, Seth was running around like a 'blue-iced fly'. He then handed Etta an envelope marked 'Private'.

The letter was on Royal Shakespeare paper.

'Darling Mrs B,' she read incredulously, 'I know I shouldn't write this but I think you're absolutely gorgeous and bedworthy. We must keep it a secret but I wonder if you'd have lunch with me on Wednesday, one-ish at Calcot Manor. I'm not expecting miracles, but if by any chance you're free just turn up and I'll be waiting. Yours adoringly, Seth (Bainton).'

And she'd covered it with earthy finger marks. Rushing inside, Etta had to sit down and read the letter twenty times, leaping up to check in the mirror that she was 'gorgeous and bedworthy' and real.

'Oh my goodness,' she cried, gathering up Gwenny and dancing round the room. 'Could he mean me? "Yours adoringly"?' And Wednesday was tomorrow.

Etta was waltzing on air, worries about syndicates and fractured cannon bones forgotten. Rushing off to Larkminster, she blued most of next month's pension on a dress in lilac linen which brought out the dark violet of her eyes. Such a pretty dress needed new dark blue high heels and a lovely new scent called 24 Faubourg.

And if I'm going to be an Oldie, decided Etta, I'm going to be a golden one, and had blonde highlights put back in her hair.

Wednesday was ideal because Drummond and Poppy were going to some end-of-term party and didn't have to be picked up until four o'clock. As she got out of the shower on Wednesday morning, however, euphoria gave way to despair. If only she could afford some Botox, or her body looked less old and unused, as the morning sun fell on the evening pleating on her breastbone and inside arms. Perhaps the letter was a wind-up.

Driving all dolled up past Badger's Court, she was surprised to see Valent coming out of the gates and waved at him gaily but he just stared and didn't seem to react. Stopping every few minutes to check her face for caked powder or lipstick escaping down wrinkles, she arrived at Calcot Manor, a beautiful sixteenth-century house whose emerald-green lawn defied any hosepipe ban.

Omigod! Omigod! She felt just like Cindy, for there was Seth in the dark of the champagne bar with a bottle of Moët on ice, being drooled at by pretty women at adjacent tables. He looked bronzed and utterly stunning in a dark green shirt and chinos. The beard he was growing to play Benedict had reached the stubbly stage and really suited him in a piratical way.

'Etta!' He looked startled. Perhaps she really was looking good. 'What a coincidence, both of us here on the same day. Have you got time for a drink?'

As Seth was always joking, Etta said she had all the time in the world, at least until she had to pick up the children.

'Such a thrill,' the words came tumbling out, 'I haven't been asked out to lunch for centuries. Sampson would never let me, and after he was ill it was impossible to get away. Thank you for your dear, dear letter, it's the naughtiest, loveliest letter I've ever had. Even if you were a bit plastered, it's been such a boost to my ego.'

And Seth poured Etta a large glass of champagne and on no breakfast, she proceeded, as they downed one bottle and started on a second, to get legless. Under his warm, sympathetic, admiring gaze, as she inhaled great wafts of Terre, his sexy after-shave, she was soon telling him about her life with Sampson – 'I was so in awe of him' – and how worried she was about Carrie and Alan.

'Carrie's a workaholic like Sampson and I'm so sad she and Trixie don't get on and see so little of each other. I love Alan, he's so sweet to me, but he's so wrapped up in his writing.'

'Could I possibly have your autograph, Seth?' asked one of the prettier ladies. 'I'm such a fan of you in *Holby City*, I wish you'd cure my migraines, and we're all coming to see you at Stratford.'

As Seth smirked and scribbled, Etta studied the menu, feeling humble. How could such a gorgeous man ask her out to lunch? She was far too nervous to eat much, which ruled out roast pork, so she settled on grilled lamb's liver and when persuaded to have a starter, opted for melon and smoked duck with grilled figs.

'Could I possibly have your autograph, Seth?' asked another beauty.

'Let's push off to the dining room,' muttered Seth.

This was in a conservatory. Outside, the dark green woods merged with parched fields that had turned yellow in the heat. Etta wished the sun wasn't beating quite so hard on the glass roof, exposing every wrinkle and liver spot and turning her so pink, she should have been keeping cool in the ice bucket.

But Seth was so interested, so kind. In the end she found her-self gushing like the Willowwood stream in winter, talking about Trixie, who was adorable but so wild and hadn't been taking her exams seriously enough. And how difficult she found Romy and Martin.

Seth ended up eating most of Etta's smoked duck, as well as his risotto.

'Stefan,' he told her delightedly, 'calls adultery "adult-tree".'

'Rather like Valent's mature conifers,' giggled Etta.

'Has Romy been unfaithful to Martin?'

'No, no, I'm sure not.'

'Has Trixie got a boyfriend?'

'Well, she had Josh at the yard, but he seems to have moved in permanently with Tresa. Lots of boys ring her up.'

'Did you commit adult-tree when you were married to Sampson?'

Etta went scarlet. 'No, no. You'll be divine as Benedict,' she gibbered, trying to change the subject. 'I loved Kenneth Branagh in the part.'

' "Speak low, if you speak love",' murmured Seth, making Etta's toes curl. 'Was Sampson unfaithful to you?'

'Yes,' said Etta.

'"Men were deceivers ever," ' quoted Seth, letting his deep husky voice drop, ' "One foot in sea and one on shore/To one thing constant never." Did it hurt terribly?'

'Yes. No, I got used to it. Hugs, shared jokes, compliments when you're dressed to go out. These are the things one's supposed to miss as a widow. I never had them as a wife. Sampson hugged other women.'

'Poor darling.' Seth took her hand. 'Your hair looks so pretty.'

'I did it for you.' So used to stroking Gwenny, Priceless and Mrs Wilkinson, Etta found herself running her hand over Seth's chin. 'I thought Benedict shaved off his beard because Beatrice didn't like them.'

'He did, but I have to start the play with stubble, after that I can wear a false beard.'

'It does suit you.'

'I'm getting old like Corinna, I find it more and more difficult to learn lines.'

'You're only a baby,' chided Etta, then humbly, 'As I've said, I'd love to hear your lines if it's any help. Do drop in at any time.'

'Is little Trixie staying in Willowwood in the holidays?'

'It depends on Alan and Carrie's plans. I do hope I can keep her amused, she seems to spend her time on chat shows.'

'Chat rooms,' Seth said, laughing. 'What's the latest on Mrs Wilkinson?'

'Blissful for her to be home. Dear Valent's given her back his old office. Bonny had specially feng shui-ed it to calm him down.' Etta started to laugh. 'Alas, it distressed rather than de-stressed him, so he handed it over to Wilkie. It's done wonders for her. She's so relaxed she keeps falling asleep on my shoulder. Sorry, I'm being bitchy.'

'Bonny is deeply silly.' Seth filled up Etta's glass.

'You think so?' Etta tried not to beam with relief. 'I thought you had rather a soft spot for her.'

'I'm not wild about either of them, Bonny and Clod. He's terribly heavy going.'

'Valent's a darling,' protested Etta, 'and he's been so sweet to Wilkie.'

'He's a yob, a mid-life Croesus,' said Seth dismissively, 'and she's a joke. "Stand aside, Corinna Waters, Bonny Richards appeals to a younger demographic." She's not fit to lick Corinna's boots.'

Etta felt giddy with relief.

With their main course, they moved on to the syndicate.

'We must have some events to increase the camaraderie,' sighed Etta. 'People are getting awfully restless.'

'Let's have a mass orgy,' suggested Seth. 'Lester Squire can film it. He's busy auditioning Peeping Toms. He need go no further than the Major. How's Rafiq getting on?'

'Riding work angelically, but Marius still won't put him up. I don't know how it's going with him and Amber.'

By the end of lunch, Etta, who'd only managed a few lettuce leaves, had spilled French dressing all over her lovely lilac dress. Linking his arm through hers and singing the Hokey Cokey, Seth guided her, shrieking with laughter, towards the Polo.

She was appalled, as she collapsed against the car, to hear herself saying, 'I've thought you were utterly gorgeous ever since you walked into the Fox and joined the syndicate, making everyone else join it too. Once Mrs Wilkinson runs again, we'll be able to see each other more often. I don't want to hurt Corinna, I like her too much.'

'No, we mustn't hurt Corinna,' agreed Seth gravely.

As he opened the door of the Polo, Etta's head fell back and she opened her lips in ecstasy, but Seth only planted a kiss on the corner of her mouth, adding, 'We must watch out for the Neighbourhood Witch. Is it all right if I leave Priceless with you tomorrow?'

'Of course it is,' cried Etta.

Only when she glanced in the driving mirror to see if Seth were waving her off did she notice two fig seeds stuck between her front teeth.

As Seth wandered back to pay the bill, the prettiest luncher sidled up to him.

'So kind of you to give Mummy a treat.'

Seth smiled. 'Have a drink.'

Etta floated home. Such a beautiful day, if only she and Seth could have taken to the woods. She took the side off the Polo going into the school gates. Such a relief Sampson wasn't alive.

Such a relief, thought Drummond, we can chuck Granny's dreadful old car. Later he appalled his parents.

'Pooh, Granny absolutely stank of drink and had to stop and have a wee behind a tree.'

'And she hurt her car very badly,' said Poppy. 'She laughed all the way home and let us have crisps and two slices of chocolate cake for tea.'

Romy and Martin were outraged.

'You've put our kids in jeopardy again, Mother.'

'Just imagine if the police had stopped you.'

'GRANDMOTHER DRUNK ON THE SCHOOL RUN.'

If they hadn't needed help looking after the children during the interminable school holidays and with their dinner parties, they would have sacked Etta on the spot.

Etta refused to tell them with whom she'd been having lunch.

76

Next day Seth, looking even more gorgeous in a plum-coloured corduroy suit and dark purple shirt, dropped off Priceless. Explaining he was criminally late for rehearsals, he asked if he could possibly borrow the good bottle of claret Etta had splurged on especially to share with him, as a peace offering for the director. What fun lunch had been.

It was only after he'd swirled off in a cloud of dust that Etta realized he hadn't left any dog food. So Etta walked Priceless up to the village shop and bought two tins of Butcher's Tripe and a packet of dog biscuits. Priceless was a most beautiful dog, black with a white shirt front and loving, long brown eyes. He was wonderful on the lead, matching his step to hers. But when she let him loose on the edge of the wood, he took off after a rabbit sunning itself in Marius's field and didn't return for an hour, by which time Etta had nearly rung the police. He then lifted his leg on all her tubs, drank noisily out of the lavatory and ate the contents of the two tins and all the biscuits, before going to the door and whining and whining for Seth.

'I know how you feel, darling, I miss him too,' sighed Etta, particularly as she now hadn't any drink to cheer herself up with.

Priceless, however, was a pragmatist. Having thrown all the cushions, including one saying 'Love me, love my Golden Retriever', on to the floor, he stretched out the entire length of Etta's sofa. When Gwenny came in at bedtime, and hissed worse than water spilled inside Romy's Aga, Priceless retreated to Etta's double bed, deciding it was much more restful than the rumpy-pumpy of Seth and Corinna's or whoever. When Etta sat beside him and stroked his sleek black body, his breathing immediately became faster and shorter until he fell asleep.

Etta was so tired that she got into her nightie but found there was only about three inches of space on either side of Priceless, and one side was soon occupied by Gwenny. Etta therefore curled up in a foetal position along the pillows. No doubt Chisolm would join them any minute, followed by the ghost of Beau Regard. If only Seth were there too. Etta took a deep breath and hunched her shoulders in longing. She was just wondering what she was going to live on for the next month when she fell asleep.

Priceless stayed for a fortnight, eating Etta out of bungalow and home, running away less and less, and endearing himself to Gwenny, Poppy and Drummond, who loved it when he suddenly went berserk and did half a dozen laps round the orchard at thirty-five miles an hour. None of this paid Etta's bills, but up at the yard she got a tip from Rogue Rogers: Rupert Campbell-Black's colt, Penscombe Poodle, who was running at Goodwood at 20–1. Seeing Woody in the street, she gave him her last £50 to put on for her.

To her delighted relief, Poodle annihilated the opposition, winning by several lengths. Thank you, thank you, God. Etta was as overjoyed as Rupert in the paddock. To celebrate she rushed out and bought a bottle of Sancerre for herself and a chicken for Priceless, who was the dearest dog. She loved the way he took her hand gently in his mouth to lead her on walks. She was sad Seth hadn't rung but he was probably very busy.

On the way back from the shop, she met Woody in his stump-grinding van.

'Isn't it wonderful?' she cried. 'I hope you backed Poodle too.'

Woody felt the same sickening crunch as when you tread on a snail in the dark. Next moment he had clapped a big grimy hand to his smooth, normally untroubled forehead in horror:

'Oh my God, Etta, I forgot, I am so sorry. I got sidetracked. Oh Christ, here's your fifty quid back.' He unearthed it from his jeans pocket. 'What were the odds?'

'Twenty to one. Don't worry, it's not your fault, Woody, please don't worry.'

But how on earth was she going to feed herself, Gwenny and Priceless and the children for the next month? She'd hoped to use the rest of the money as down payment on a car.

Woody was appalled. Poor Etta, he ought to give her the equivalent but he was desperately broke, paying for a home carer for his mother when he went out to work because she'd started taking all her clothes off at the day centre. Insurance premiums were still rising, and there was a limited amount of work he could take on by himself. He had, on the other hand, done a lot of clearing up in North Wood in preparation for *Lady Godiva*, but Bolton, apart from occasional dollops of cash, was turning out to be a very reluctant payer.

Even a starring role as Lord Godiva only offered £500, which wouldn't repay his debt to Etta. Woody shuddered. He couldn't shag Cindy. More shaming, he had forgotten about Etta's bet because he had caught sight of Niall the vicar coming out of church. He was looking so low, Woody had pulled up for a chat.

Niall was in despair because, with Mrs Wilkinson out of action and the syndicate suspended, no one came to church to hear him pray for her and report on her progress. The congregation had dwindled humiliatingly and the interminable Sundays after Trinity were grinding on.

Woody had longed to hug Niall, but seeing him near to tears, only muttered that he was sure things would pick up. The Lord had struck him down for being so feeble, by making him forget dear Etta.

Matters went from worse to even worse for Niall.

The following Sunday, the Travis-Locks and the Weatheralls, his stalwarts, were in Scotland in preparation for 12 August. Miss Painswick was away, Mrs Malmesbury staying with her sister. Niall, having spent half the week trying to find something inspiring to say about the 6th Sunday after Trinity, rolled up at St James's for the family service, to find Craig Green the organist dispiritedly idling through 'Jesu, Joy of Man's Desiring', Pocock, as single bell-ringer doubling up as sidesman, looking gloomy and Major Cunliffe, the church warden, boot-faced. His wife Debbie, who had gastric flu, had, with the flower show coming up, wasted a lot of precious flowers to make a splash of colour, but there was absolutely no congregation.

'I'm so sorry,' stammered Niall, retreating into the vestry and feeling tempted to drink all the communion wine.

The Major looked broodily at the bronze and red alstroemerias by the hymn list, Bishop of Llandaff on the windowsill and coral begonias on the table as you came in, not to mention the time Miss Painswick had spent on her housemaid's knee, polishing brass.

'No one's coming, we better go home,' he said brusquely. Then, marching Niall into the side chapel to be blinded by red and orange dahlias, the Major suggested that he really ought to think about packing it in.

'There's a feeling in Willowwood you lack vocation and conviction. You've tried but the people in Willowwood need spiritual guidance. Perhaps the church fête at the end of the month would be a good time to announce your retirement. We can discuss it more fully – come and have a jar later in the week – but you should think carefully, Niall. I'm sorry, old chap. Would you like me to put out the candles and lock up?'

'No, I'll do it.' Niall's heart was thumping so hard he expected it to crash out of his ribs. 'I think I'll stay and pray a bit.'

'Do that. Sorry to be blunt, have to be cruel to be kind.'

As the door clanged behind him, Niall looked down at his white surplice, slightly pink from a red handkerchief in the washing machine. What would his parents say? They hadn't really got over the fact that he was gay, how would they cope with a failed priest?

He tore off his dog collar and slumped to his knees in the third pew, catching sight of the little whippet, ever watchful, supporting the bruised, chipped feet of the first Sir Francis Framlingham. Such a beautiful church, such a lovely village, and Niall was beginning to feel such a part of it. He had hoped to do so much good.

He tried to pray, but loss and sadness overcame him, great sobs racking his body. The stained glass saints looking down could offer him no comfort. 'Oh help me, God.'

Suddenly he felt a warm hand on the back of his neck, steadying him when he started violently, then a voice with a soft, infinitely tender Larkshire accent saying:

'Don't be sad, there's no need to be sad, I'm here.'

Staggering to his feet, clutching the back of the pew in front, Niall discovered Woody, looking gentler in a grey T-shirt and jeans than in his regulation tree-surgeon green shirt and trousers and ropes. Concern was written all over his beautiful open face, intense kindness in his big turned-down grey eyes.

'There there, my lamb. Come back home to breakfast and we can talk. Things will seem better.' He put out a thumb, smoothing away Niall's tears. Then, looking down and smiling: 'You're kneeling on the hassock my mum embroidered of a lamb, that's nice. She'd have been pleased.'

He put an arm round Niall's still shaking shoulders.

'Sorry to be such a wuss,' Niall gulped. 'It was just having no one turn up except Major Cunliffe. He said I ought to pack it in, I'd lost the hearts of the people here.'

'Bollocks,' said Woody, then, looking up to the roof: 'Sorry, God. Don't listen to the insensitive bastard. You saved my horse chestnut, now I'm going to save you.'

Standing on the check-tiled aisle, they gazed at each other.

Their mouths, one trembling, one smiling and reassuring, were so close, their eyes meeting, the next moment they were in each other's arms, for a kiss that went on and on and on, until they were both giddy.

'You may kiss the bride,' murmured Woody. 'Don't be frightened, nothing so miraculous as that could be blasphemous. I've wanted to do that for such a long time.'

'Have you?' said Niall in amazement. 'Oh Woody.'

'Come home for a fry-up,' Woody took his hand, 'my mum's been taken out for the day.'

Inside the church, the candles burnt on.

Outside in the churchyard, Niall praised the limes Woody had pollarded so beautifully, like women in tight dresses spilling out at the knee because the leaves shoot like mad round the base. Piling into the stump-grinding van, they rolled back to the Salix Estate.

'I'll tell everyone you've come to talk to me about Mum,' said Woody, locking the front door and leading Niall straight upstairs, where light filtered through already drawn curtains on to an unmade bed. The shelves were filled with books on trees, the walls adorned with photographs of more trees including one of the Willowwood Chestnut in spring, its candles driven crooked by the rough winds of May.

There was no more time to look. Niall was shivering like a poplar, but didn't resist as Woody pulled off his surplice and black shirt, and slowly kissed him on each shoulder.

'You've got a great body.'

'I must sound more of a wuss than ever,' muttered Niall through desperately chattering teeth, 'but I'm a virgin.'

'Very right and proper,' said Woody, 'I don't like slags. I can break you in as I like.'

Niall's trousers fell to the floor as Woody pulled off Niall's shoes and socks. His spectacles were the last thing to go.

'You're so beautiful, Woody.'

'You're certainly not a beast, Niall, you just need building up physically and spiritually, and that is a great penis.'

Dropping to his knees, Woody put his beautiful lips over Niall's cock, sucking and licking, then gently parting his buttocks and probing and jabbing with his right hand, until Niall gasped and gave a sob and shot into Woody's mouth.

This was the only breakfast Woody had until four o'clock in the afternoon, when he cooked bacon, eggs, sausages, tomatoes and black pudding for himself and Niall.

Niall, his eyes drowsy with love, wearing Woody's red and black dressing gown, a present from Etta, said, 'Do you think what we've done is terribly wrong?'

'Terribly right,' said Woody, pouring himself another cup of dark brown tea, 'because we love each other.'

Niall had to dress very fast and pretend he was just making a social call on Woody's mum, when her carer brought her back.

Woody insisted on walking Niall home.

'You oughtn't to go out without your dog collar,' were his parting words. 'I'm going to microchip you, so I never lose you. I love you, Mr Forbes.'

77

Term came to an end at Greycoats, bringing home not only Drummond and Poppy but also a beautiful patchwork rug made for Mrs Wilkinson by the children of Willowwood. It was snugly lined with felt and had a weeping willow embroidered by Tilda on each side.

The presentation was made to Mrs Wilkinson as she hung over the dark blue half-door of Valent's former office. Chisolm was presented with a straw hat which she promptly ate, reducing the children to helpless laughter. Both Mrs Wilkinson and Chisolm consumed so many treats, it was surprising their good and bad legs still held them up.

'When's she going to run again?' the children pleaded.

Poor Tilda looked very tired, thought Etta, who hoped she would get a break now, then remembered that she had to organize Shagger's holiday lets during their busiest time, which meant five or six lots of sheets a week, and seeing the house was clean and tidy. Judging by the wilting balloons on the gate of Shagger's cottage and empties which included a case of Jacob's Creek, twelve bottles of champagne and three bottles of vodka, a hen party had taken place over the weekend.

'They were all asking where Seth Bainton lived,' winked Chris, as Etta walked Priceless past the pub.

Poor Tilda, it seemed so ironic that, when she had a long break and could go to the races, Mrs Wilkinson was out of action. And with the monthly payments eating up her salary, she could no longer afford to take a nice hot holiday.

Meanwhile Etta's crush on Seth, although not over-encouraged, raged on. Priceless was living with her almost full time and greeted his master, when he dropped in, with toothy smiles and head snakings along Seth's increasingly lean hips, but showed no sign of following him when he left.

After a holiday in Ibiza, Trixie was also staying in Willowwood, mostly at her grandmother's, where she retreated to Etta's bedroom to text. She was glued to her laptop or Etta's portable television, sharing the bed with Priceless, her legs longer and browner than ever, her hair longer and messier. She was moodier and more abstracted and irritated by Poppy and Drummond, at whom she kept shouting, so Etta was doubly delighted one evening when Seth dropped in armed with *The Merchant of Venice* and a DVD of himself in *Much Ado*.

While Etta heard him as Bassanio, eyes on the text, quivering at the beauty of the language and his voice, Seth gazed lazily at Trixie, who appeared far more interested in *Hello!* and *Cosmopolitan*.

'*Merchant*'s a difficult play to stage,' said Seth, as he paused to refill everyone's drinks. 'If you make Shylock too much of a villain, you're being anti-Semitic. If you make Antonio too much of a shit, you're being homophobic.'

'Bassanio's a wuss,' said Trixie scornfully. 'He's a gold-digger, and I loathe Portia. I hate teasing, playful women like Aunt Romy.'

'"In Belmont,"' said Seth huskily, '""is a lady richly left;/And she is fair, and, fairer than that word,/Of wondrous virtues: sometimes from her eyes/I did receive fair speechless messages."'

He smiled wickedly at Trixie.

'I still hate her as a character. "Richly left" sounds like Harriet Harman.'

'Seth's doing Antony in the spring,' said Etta, sensing tension, 'and Corinna's playing Cleopatra. Isn't that exciting?'

'Not particularly,' said Trixie, '*Antony and Cleopatra* is sooo boring. Antony's going through the male menopause like my dad and Uncle Martin, and Cleopatra's a silly old tart like Dora Belvedon's mother. Dora won the Most Embarrassing Mother competition at Bagley on Speech Day, she laced her mother's breakfast orange juice with neat vodka. All the Lower Sixths went to sleep during a production of *Antony and Cleopatra* at the National.'

'That would never happen if Seth was on stage,' said Etta warmly.

'The boys only woke up when Cleopatra bared her breasts to plug in the asp,' added Trixie.

'Plenty of asps living in Mrs Travis-Lockjaw's compost heap, according to Pocock,' said Seth.

'Yuck,' said Trixie, 'Mrs T-L pees on it every night.'

'Compissed heap,' murmured Seth.

Trixie's mouth lifted a quarter of a centimetre at one corner. 'Josh took a photograph of her which they refused to print in the parish mag. She'll probably get stung on the bum.'

'Bolton's got a crush on her,' said Seth. 'He roves around Willowwood with a camera at the dead of night. Better draw your curtains, Etta, he likes pretty ladies.'

Etta blushed.

Gwenny came in mewing. Trixie got up – her dark hair so long it reached the top of her legs – and gave Gwenny some cat sweets.

Seth picked up the packet.

'They always tell you to provide drinking water. Ought to insist you provide drinking water and whisky.' He drained his glass.

Unable to bear him going, Etta suggested she pop up to the pub and get another bottle.

'I've got to go,' said Trixie.

'I'll see you home,' said Seth. 'Come on, Priceless.'

Priceless raised his tail a centimetre off the sofa, but showed no inclination, unlike Etta, to follow his master.

It was very hot outside, the sky crowded with stars, the air heavy with the scent of honeysuckle. The stream gleamed silver in the moonlight.

'"The moon shines bright: in such a night as this,"' said Seth. 'Let's take a detour through Valent's garden, they're both away.'

'How do we get out of the locked gates on the other side?'

'I'll lift you over the wall.'

Her face was expressionless.

'How's Josh?' he asked.

'"He doth nothing but talk of his horse,"' said Trixie lightly.

'Good girl, you've read the play,' said Seth approvingly.

Valent's house reared sombre in front of them. With satisfaction, they admired their two black shadows, hers so willowy, his broad of shoulder, svelte of hip. Seth, who seemed to know all the paths, took her arm. She froze for a second but didn't shake him off.

'"In such a night/Stood Dido with a willow in her hand,"' murmured Seth. 'Ker-ist!' He leapt behind Trixie as a great white face loomed over the half-door. 'It's the ghost of Beau Regard.'

'It's darling Wilkie.' Showing tenderness and animation for the first time, Trixie rushed up and patted her.

'Oh lucky horse to bear the weight of Trixie,' sighed Seth.

To her surprise, given he had such a terrible reputation, Seth didn't try to kiss her.

Once home, she texted Dora. 'Granny's got a thumping great crush on Mr Bulging Crotchester.'

Feeling rather flat, Etta made herself a cup of tomato soup and a piece of toast and decided to watch *Much Ado*, but she couldn't find the DVD anywhere. Perhaps Priceless had stolen it.

Aware of Seth's lethal charm, Alan didn't want his mother-in-law to get hurt. The following evening, glad to have an excuse to stop writing, he gathered up a couple of bottles and wandered down to the bungalow. Here he found a shattered Etta trying to referee a squawking match between Drummond and Poppy on whether they should watch *Shrek* or *Harry Potter*.

'You stupid bumhole,' yelled Drummond, hurling a green glass paperweight at his sister.

'Out!' roared Alan, 'O-U-T.' Then, getting four pound coins out of his pocket: 'You can each have two of these if you bugger off until I tell you to come in.'

'Go and see Mrs Wilkinson,' said Etta, giving them her last two carrots.

Outside the back door, she had been sorting out her indoor bulbs, seven white ones in one blue bowl, pink in another, dark blue, pale blue and more white in others. Like making sloe gin, it was one of the rituals of late summer to ward off the cold and darkness of the coming winter. Pocock had very kindly given her the bulbs for looking after Gwenny, but she was not sure she'd be able to afford the gin to go with the sloes.

After pouring two large glasses of red, Alan handed Etta some cuttings. 'Your boyfriend's all over the newspapers today.'

Etta went crimson, had she been rumbled? Then, glancing at them, her face softened. 'Oh Valent, how lovely.'

Valent had been very busy launching a robot made in his Chinese factory called the Iron Man, which ironed everything from shirts to sheets and would forever transform the lives of women.

'And men too,' said Alan, perching on the tenth of the sofa not occupied by Priceless. 'My wife, your daughter, has never liked ironing.'

'How is she?'

'Eruptive. When both the women in my family are at the wrong time of the month, I make myself scarce.'

'How's *Depression* going?'

'Nearly finished,' lied Alan. 'I wish Mrs Wilkinson would get off her arse so I could get on with her life story.'

'I'm so sorry,' said Etta guiltily. Across the valley, she could see

Marius's horses relishing the sun on their backs, lying flat out on the grass with just the occasional flick of their tails. When the sun went down they would all gallop round – to show how much horses enjoy racing each other.

'I'm sure Wilkie will be fit soon. Gosh, these cuttings are lovely. The interviewers really like him.'

Previously the press had emphasized Valent's ruthlessness and killer instinct, dubbing him the 'Tin Man without a Heart'.

'Of course he's got a heart,' protested Etta. 'No matter how busy he is he sends postcards from all over the world asking after Wilkie. More than Bonny does. Do you know Seth can't stand Bonny?' she couldn't resist saying. 'I thought he adored her.'

So did Alan, but he didn't say so.

'He doesn't like Valent either.'

'Seth doesn't like competition. Valent's a heavyweight.'

Alan was full of gossip:

'Lester, another would-be heavyweight, is due to start filming any moment. He's determined to use Furious, so Amber is booked as a stand-in for Cindy in the riding scenes. Cindy told me, "Amber's boobs aren't as good as mine, but on an 'orse, her 'air will cover them." Lester's still interviewing Peeping Toms, the queue went round the village this morning. He even asked Trixie to play Godiva's handmaiden.'

Etta shuddered. 'Loathsome little man, I hope she refused.'

'She did, but only because the money was lousy. As Mrs Wilkinson is off games, Bolton wants his horse, Furious, led up by Michelle, natch, to give pony rides at the fête.'

'He's mad,' cried Etta in horror. 'Furious would savage all the children.'

'Then Drummond must have the first ride.'

'Hush,' smiled Etta, 'Drummond can be a sweetheart.'

As they heard a crash from outside, Etta ran to the window.

'You little beast,' she screamed.

Drummond had tipped all her bulbs on to the tarmac, mixing and scattering pink, white, dark blue, light blue and dark red underneath his father's Range Rover.

'*Such* a sweetheart,' said Alan.

78

Desperate for events to hold the syndicate together, Etta was relieved so many members were going to meet at the village fête and flower show held in Farmer Fred's big field next to the cricket pitch at the end of August.

Although Pocock, Craig Green, Ione and Debbie were expected to win most of the cups, the morning of the fête saw many Willowwood residents sloping off to the local farm shop to buy vegetables, fruit and flowers to pass off as their own in the various classes. The Major, as president of the fête, was very much in command, and finding no water in his rain gauge, had rightly forecast a fine sunny day.

Lester Bolton had donated half a dozen of Cindy's steamiest DVDs to the tombola. The Major had hastily confiscated them and was looking forward to a good watch in his den later. His most exciting duty of the day, however, was to look after Corinna, who had returned briefly from a triumphant tour in *The Deep Blue C-word* (as Seth called it) to open the fête and remind everyone how beautiful she was.

Wearing a huge, shocking-pink picture hat and a scarlet suit, which showed off her splendid bosom and the still slender legs that had captivated audiences in the stalls for so many years, she allowed the Major gallantly to lead her on to the platform and urge the big crowds and stallholders to 'gather round'.

Corinna's speech, written by Seth and Alan, was meant to be a witty take-off of an Oscars acceptance speech, in order to make the inevitable list of thank-yous less tedious.

Corinna's voice could carry to Larkminster but had to compete with a screeching, ear-splittingly loud loudspeaker and the local brass band tuning up. She also made the mistake of ending by quoting lengthily from 'The Land' by Vita Sackville-West, from 'The country habit has me by the heart', to its lovely last line: 'only here/Lies peace after uneasy truancy.' She then ruined the peace by screaming at the band to 'bloody well SHUT UP!'

'She didn't thank anyone,' stormed Debbie, 'or exhort everyone to spend, spend, spend and dig deep in their pockets.'

'She completely forgot to say that it costs ninety-five pounds a day for the upkeep of St James's, that's thirty-five thousand a year,' snorted Ione.

'We first asked darling Bonny Richards to open the fête,' Romy was telling everyone, 'but tragically she's filming.'

Fortunately the *Larkminster Echo*, which had got stuck behind one of Farmer Fred's combines, arrived after Corinna had finished and were terribly grateful when she gave them the original typescript.

'Keep it, my dear, I always write a new speech.'

'How are you enjoying being a member of the Willowwood syndicate?' asked the reporter.

'Alas, I'm hardly ever able to see Mrs Wilkinson run because I'm always working. I so envy Bonny Richards, who's been free to lead her in several times.'

The Major was hovering. 'Are you ready to do a tour of the stalls? Your public awaits you.'

What a beautiful setting, thought Etta, the trees dark, dark green against the parched, cracked yellow of the grass, the pale green leaves of the willows already turning gold, blending in with their gold stems, curling black and yellow leaves already littering the ground. Children shrieked with joy on the bouncy castle, steam engines chooed, and Chris and Chrissie from the Fox were doing a roaring trade in Pimm's laced with cucumber and strawberries.

Mrs Wilkinson was still confined to barracks, but Chisolm, like a carer freed for the afternoon, left an even longer trail of shrieking children as she slyly nicked one ice cream or candy floss after another. She was now eyeing up the fancy cake stall.

'I've seen Seth Bainton, I've seen Corinna, I haven't seen Bonny,' cried the crowd.

Etta, so broke she had no money to spend, was helping Alban on the plant stall, which gave him the excuse to touch her hand and exchange meaningful glances over the delphiniums.

Etta sidled off, however, to watch the dog show judged by Corinna and Charlie Radcliffe. Drummond had shown no interest in walking Priceless, who had been bathed, polished and buffed to gleaming ebony by Tommy and Etta, and who so sweetly matched his steps to Poppy's that the judges had absolutely no doubt about awarding them Best in Show. There was a box of Smarties for Poppy and a huge red rosette and Bonios for Priceless – whereupon Drummond erupted into the ring to punch his sister and kick Priceless's long, delicate legs.

'Stop it, you little bugger,' screamed Etta, dragging him off and shaking him. 'Don't you dare hurt Poppy and Priceless,' and was awarded the biggest round of applause of the day.

Thank God Drummond's parents had been temporarily hijacked by Ione, manning the Green stall, who urged them to share a bath every night, wash their clothes in the water and syphon it off afterwards to use on their plants.

'Did you know,' she told Martin sternly, 'dripping taps waste four litres a day and sprinklers use a thousand litres an hour? Why not invest in this lavatory hippo which saves three litres a day?'

Martin didn't seem keen, so Ione tried to persuade Romy to buy some of the scent she'd made from olive, jasmine and lavender oils.

'Do buy a bottle, Rosie.'

'A beautiful woman never has to buy her own perfume,' said Martin roguishly. 'Come on, dear, I'm pulling in the tug-of-war soon.'

Scuttling back to the plant stall, Etta passed books, cards and bric-a-brac, where she was amused to see a large yellow teapot hadn't yet sold.

'How,' fulminated Debbie, 'did the vicar get a first in sweet peas when he hasn't got a garden?'

Convinced by Woody that he had a great body, Niall was winning back his spurs in Willowwood by sitting in the stocks flashing his six-pack and having wet sponges hurled at him by the village children.

'I'll share a bath with you any time,' murmured Woody, as he dried Niall with a big blue towel.

'Thought he was wet enough already,' sneered Shagger, who'd been away murdering wildlife in Scotland with Toby and Phoebe. He was not the only person to notice a tendresse between Niall and Woody. Shagger was consequently in a belligerent mood, stirring up trouble.

Mrs Wilkinson had been confined to box rest for two and a half months now. Even if she recovered it would take three or four months to get her match-fit. All round the fête field, little pools of discontent were bubbling. Why should they go on forking out £185 a month for Mrs Wilkinson to eat grass?

'Surely Mrs Bancroft isn't the answer for getting a horse right?' grumbled Bolton to Charlie Radcliffe, who shrugged his shoulders.

'These things take time, you can't hurry horses.'

Matters weren't helped that even with a drought and rock-hard ground, which would have suited Mrs Wilkinson, Marius had taken on Doggie and Not for Crowe and found a race bad enough for the latter to come in third. Joey, Woody and Jase were still celebrating, rather too triumphantly for the rest of the syndicate.

To the rage of Direct Debbie and Ione Travis-Lock, Valent's roses, which had been nurtured by Etta, won the Millennium Trophy for Best in Show.

A merry party was gathering round the Fox's Pimm's stall. Miss Painswick, who'd been taking money at the gate, was brought over by Alan. On the way he gathered up Tilda and bought them both a drink.

'You look tired, darling,' Alan murmured to Tilda. 'We've missed you at the races. Do say you're depressed and we can have lunch and I'll interview you for my book.'

'I bought your book on Swinburne at the book stall,' said Tilda blushing. 'Would you sign it for me?'

Trixie, in a very short white smock, turned all the men's heads as she walked round with Chisolm, who was now trying to eat Priceless's red rosette.

'Buy me a drink, Dad,' she asked Alan.

Within seconds, Seth had drifted up and given her a kiss. 'Hi, "my dear Lady Disdain, are you yet living?"' Then he handed her a Pimm's. 'How's your love life?'

'"There is not one among but I dote on his very absence,"' replied Trixie, tossing her shaggy mane.

'Good girl,' murmured Seth, 'you've watched my DVD.'

'It's cool,' admitted Trixie. 'Oh bugger, here comes Malvolio.'

'Hello, Seth. Hello, Trixie,' Martin tugged his niece's hair, 'got your results yet?'

'Next week.'

'Your aunt Romy needs some help on the Nearly New stall,' Martin said pointedly. Trixie ignored him, so he turned back to Seth. 'I need your help.'

'Hide your wallet,' hissed Trixie.

'I've got to make a DVD for our War on Obesity charity, wonder if you and Corinna could give me a bit of coaching. May I drop in?'

'Only if you bring your lovely wife,' said Seth.

Lester Bolton meanwhile was seething. Not only were his lifts killing him, but Marius had been so unbelievably rude when Cindy had announced that she wanted to ride into the fête as Lady Godiva, on her 'frisky mount' Furious. She planned to offer whatever little kiddie was crowned Flower Queen not only a ride but also a part as one of Lady Godiva's children.

'Furious shouldn't be allowed anywhere near children, particularly at a fête,' snarled Marius.

So instead Family Dog and Not for Crowe, with a large placard saying 'I came third at Bangor' round his scrawny neck, were now proudly obliging round the fête field. Led up by Angel and Dora, they were enjoying more treats than Chisolm.

Apart from Angel, the rest of the Throstledown lads had been invited over to Penscombe for the annual rounders match against Rupert Campbell-Black's lads, which was always a great party.

'I'd like to come back to life as a Penscombe stallion,' sighed Josh, 'and have one hundred and fifty mares a year.'

Rafiq, however, couldn't relax at the rounders match when he noticed Michelle hadn't joined them. Of all people, she would have wanted to admire the wonders of Penscombe and have a gawp at Rupert. Why had she offered to stay behind and man the yard? He didn't trust her, and rightly. Hitching a lift back to Throstledown, he found Furious's box empty, Dilys, his sheep, bleating pitifully, and belted down the fields up through the woods to the fête ground.

Corinna had just crowned the Flower Queen when cries of amusement and excitement rose from the field. Cindy, in an eight-denier body stocking, that left zero to the imagination, hair extensions swinging round her ankles, was screaming and squealing as Michelle, tipped £500 by Bolton, led her up to the platform on a plunging Furious.

Furious loathed and feared Michelle, who in the early days had hit him once too often with a spade. Now she was leading him up in a really vicious American gag, which caused him great pain if he took the smallest pull. Despite the pain, Furious, his rolling, darting eyes looking everywhere for escape, leapt this way and that, scattering spectators.

The Major, who'd also been bunged by Lester, seized the microphone: 'Pray silence for Mr Lester Bolton.'

Lester then announced he was offering the Flower Queen a wonderful opportunity to star as Lady Godiva's daughter. In addition, he hoped as many people as possible from Willowwood would turn up at North Wood to be paid as extras and take part in crowd scenes. Details would be posted on the *Lady Godiva* website.

Next moment the steam engine hooted and hissed, the band struck up 'The Galloping Major', the microphone screeched and Furious went berserk. Plunging his teeth into the shoulder of Michelle, who dropped the lead rope, he dumped a shrieking Cindy on the rock-hard ground, lashed out at the platform and the Major and took off through the stalls, kicking down the coconut shy, sending second-hand books, home-made cards, bric-a-brac including a yellow teapot, ten lavatory hippos, plants and cakes flying, charging straight through the microphone wire and upturning the tombola table with a great crash.

Treading on his lead rope, causing himself untold agony, he was now bearing down on the bar. Seth snatched Trixie out of the way and Alan grabbed Tilda as Furious sent the table, glasses of Pimm's and bottles flying. Seeing a way out, Furious, blood gushing from his mouth, hurtled towards the crèche where a dozen village children were painting each other's faces.

'Stop him,' screamed Romy.

He was twenty yards away, ten yards, when a figure leapt out, catching his lead rope, tugging him to one side.

'Steady, boy, steady, boy, it's OK, it's me,' cried Rafiq, who, after being dragged along the ground, managed to jump on to Furious's back and steer him away from the children, until they came to a shuddering halt against a hawthorn hedge.

Leaping off the terrified, maddened animal, Rafiq hugged and stroked him, crooning and murmuring, 'It's all right, boy.'

Next moment, Charlie Radcliffe had panted up with his bag.

'Well done, bloody well done.' Then, as Furious lashed out with his off fore: 'I'll give him a shot.' Seeing blood was pouring from Furious's mouth he asked, 'Christ, what's he done to himself?'

'This fucking gag,' hissed Rafiq, who was drenched in blood too. 'Look what she put on him. No wonder he go crazy, poor horse.' He was ruffling Furious's mane and rubbing his forehead to distract him as the needle went in.

'Now get him out of here. Go through the woods,' ordered Charlie.

But as Michelle rushed up, followed by a limping Lester, Rafiq went berserk.

'You stupid, stupid bitch!' he yelled. 'Why you bring him here and put that gag on him? He's terrified of you anyway, ever since you hit him with a spade.'

'I never,' yelled back Michelle, 'that horse is vicious.'

'So is that gag, you torture him, don't you ever touch him again.'

'Don't speak to a lady like that,' howled Bolton. 'He's my 'orse to do what I like wiv. No good you sticking up for that brute, he's going to the sales next week.' Then: 'Ouch,' he screamed as Chisolm, drunk from hoovering up the cucumber and strawberries scattered round the Pimm's stall, butted him in the groin.

As people picked themselves up and tried to assess the damage, the fête committee decided they were going to need a large cheque from Mr Bolton. The Major, however, found compensation in helping a sobbing Cindy to her feet.

Trixie was horrified how much she'd enjoyed being pulled out of danger and held against Seth's hot, hard body. Tilda ditto, against Alan.

Furious calmed down and was practically nodding off by the time Rafiq had walked him home. Dilys was delirious with joy to see him. She was such a sweet sheep, so loving and so much less self-regarding and greedy than Chisolm. Rafiq fed them both and kept them in for the night.

At around four o'clock in the morning, however, Rafiq and Tommy were woken by hysterical and bewildered neighing.

First to reach Furious's box in her nightie, Tommy opened the door to find Dilys lying in the straw, her coat soaked in blood, her head kicked in. Furious, wool in his teeth, was desperately nudging her, pitifully calling for her to wake up.

Tommy couldn't stop crying.

Rafiq comforted her: 'It must have been the fête and that gag that made him mad.'

When Marius returned from Cartmel the next day, he insisted Dilys be buried in the field behind the house alongside his great horses. After Josh and Rafiq had dug a grave, Furious refused to let them take Dilys away and stood over her, lashing out at anyone who came near. Rafiq had to lead him down the drive while they removed her body. When he was returned to an empty stable, he called for her endlessly.

Later Joey made a headstone: 'Dear Dilys, Furious's faithful companion.'

79

That was the end for Marius, who had been very fond of Dilys. He thanked Rafiq for his quick thinking at the fête. He fired Michelle. He agreed to buy back Furious and promptly entered him for a selling race at Stratford early in September.

Rafiq and Tommy were distraught. Rogue, Awesome and Amber all refused to ride him, not wanting to get carted, bucked off or savaged, so Marius allowed Rafiq a first and last ride.

Rafiq, however, had studied Furious and remembered his first and only win with Amber. He had reared up at the start because she tried to hold him up, and then carted her past all the other horses. Rafiq realized that Furious hated other horses so much that if he were allowed to escape from them and gallop flat out from the start, nothing could catch up with him . . . the answer was to make all.

It was a hot, muggy day. Furious worked himself into a state before the race, getting angrier and angrier, and when he couldn't get at Rafiq he swung his head round, trying to bite the toes off the new boots Rafiq had struggled to pay for.

Rafiq, however, rode him with immense sympathy and kindness, giving him his head, so he hurtled straight into the lead, getting the stride right at every fence. Even when other horses challenged him in the straight, Rafiq didn't pick up his whip but let Furious accelerate naturally. Winning by fifteen lengths, he contemptuously slowed to a trot as he passed the post.

The athlete in victory starts to die. In his moment of glory, Furious was put up for auction. He had never looked handsomer, chestnut coat gleaming, quarters and shoulders rippling with muscle, pink and black oiled hooves flashing in the sun, snow-white star giving his face a look of deceptive amiability and contentment. Tommy invariably won the turnout prize but never had she done one of her charges prouder.

A toff in a trilby with a microphone was revving up the crowd, which ringed the winners enclosure ten deep. Tommy walked Furious round and round as the water thrown over to cool him down dried in the hot September sun.

All day Furious had sensed that Tommy and Rafiq were unhappy. That was why he hadn't bitten anything except Rafiq's boots and had carried Rafiq, such a sensitive rider, so willingly. He nudged Tommy and placed his shoulder against hers as they circled.

It had been a tough race but he'd enjoyed it. He loved the cheers just for him and the ecstatic patting from Rafiq and later Tommy, as she'd run towards him, tears in her eyes, and tugged his ears. But now he sensed her sadness and wanted her to take him back to his box and bask in reflected glory. He wanted to have something to eat rather than biting anyone, so he laid his head on Tommy's shoulder, breathing into her ear.

'We now offer you Furious, a beautiful six-year-old chestnut gelding who won at Worcester as a five-year-old and won very convincingly this afternoon.'

The bidding started at 3,000 guineas and quickly went up to 3,750 then 4,000 guineas.

The horse had won magnificently, but all eyes were also on the stocky little stable lass. White as a sheet, she had forgotten to brush her hair, her full round breasts were rising and falling beneath the beige T-shirt, plump thighs filling the charcoal-grey jeans, sturdy ankles above trainers, eyes cast down like King Cophetua's beggarmaid. A tear trickled like a diamond from her lashes, an indicator of the flood to come. The crowd was drawn to her as much as to the powerful, ungovernable horse, momentarily docile beside her as, bottom lip trembling, he tried to nudge her into cheerfulness.

The bidding was creeping up: 7,750 guineas, 8,000.

'Oh, please let him go to someone who loves and understands him,' prayed Tommy.

Rafiq leant against a tree, puffing frantically on a roll-up. He could see that a well-known trainer, a woman with a tough face, her hair tied back in a red scarf, was bidding against an owner whose trainer hadn't arrived, caught up in the inevitable traffic. The auctioneer pointed his clipboard at a man with a thin ferret's face. Imagining the sadistic pleasure Harvey-Holden would have knocking Furious into shape, Rafiq clenched his fists. Isa Lovell was also bidding. Big bidders usually kept out of the way, in case people got fired up into thinking a horse was worth more. In fact the auctioneer was the only person who knew all the people bidding, looking out for a nod of the head or a raised finger.

The woman in the red scarf was off again. She's so tough, thought Tommy in anguish.

'I'll buy that stable lass,' said a wag, 'she knows how to make a horse look right.'

As the bidding stuck at 12,000 guineas, a telephone bidder slid in at 12,500. Everyone glanced round for mobiles.

'Look how sweet he is,' said a beautiful girl, as Furious laid his head on Tommy's shoulder again.

'I'd buy him for you, darling,' said her boyfriend, 'but I don't think I'd get him in the Aston.'

Harvey-Holden had bid 13,000, the telephone bidder 13,500, 14,000, 14,500 right up to 20,000 – very high for a selling race.

The whole crowd could smell the despair of the sweet-faced stable lass. If the horse were vicious, it might be worth employing her as well to calm him down. There was a long pause.

Harvey-Holden shook his head. Furious was too much of a risk.

'Twenty thousand guineas I'm bid. For the second time of asking. Going, going, gone.' The auctioneer brought down his hammer.

Tommy clung to Furious, looking round defensively, fearfully, as if she would leap on his back and make a run for it. Then, shoulders heaving, she buried her face in Furious's glossy neck.

'Twenty thousand guineas,' repeated the auctioneer. 'Bought in.'

The heaving stopped. Clinging to Furious to hold herself up, looking round incredulously, Tommy noticed Marius chucking away his cigarette.

The bell for the next race was telling the jockeys to mount.

Hugging and kissing Furious, wiping her eyes and nose with his mane, Tommy led him back to his box. She was just rubbing him down when a voice said, 'I thought we'd give him another chance, rather an expensive one, admittedly. That's ten thousand pounds of the bid to pay back to the racecourse.'

As Marius entered the box, Furious flattened his ears and took a bite out of his sleeve.

'Ungrateful sod,' said Marius.

'We're not,' said Tommy in a choked voice. 'Oh Marius, thank you. I know he'll reward you,' and she flung her arms round Marius's neck and kissed his cheek.

For a second Marius was tempted to kiss her back. Since

Michelle had gone, his bed was very empty. Tommy's body would make a comforting replacement.

'He'll win it all back for you,' she mumbled.

Furious looked up and whickered as Rafiq's head appeared over the half-door.

'Didn't Rafiq ride well?' said Tommy.

'He did,' said Marius. 'Well done.'

'He stuck his head out and galloped all the way for me, he is holy terrier.' Rafiq pulled Furious's ears. Then, after a long pause: 'Thanks for buying him back.'

Thus Marius won the undying loyalty and gratitude of Rafiq.

80

Charlie Radcliffe gave Mrs Wilkinson the all-clear at the beginning of September. Let out of Valent's stable where she had been imprisoned for months, she went berserk, tugging the lead rope out of Tommy's hand, charging round the orchard bucking and squealing. Etta, Tommy, Marius and Chisolm held their breaths but she walked back absolutely sound.

'With luck she'll be up and running soon after Christmas,' said Charlie.

'Well done, Etta and Tommy,' added Marius with rare warmth.

Tommy needed every encouragement. With the departure of Michelle, Marius had made Josh rather than her head lad because he felt Josh would be better at keeping order than the gentle Tommy, though he was desperate to hold on to her because she was so good with the horses. Josh had consequently moved into the head lad's cottage that Collie and his family had left. This had been redecorated, recarpeted and fitted with a new shower and kitchen, which delighted blonde Tresa, who had officially moved in with Josh.

The fact that Marius could afford to do up the cottage and buy back Furious convinced observers that he was receiving financial help from Valent.

Back at Throstledown, also in September, Marius held a parade of the horses to attract new owners and to enable existing ones to meet each other over an excellent lunch. Furious the un-predictable was shut away in a far-off field. To distract people from the hairiness of some of the horses' ankles, the prettiest stable lasses, Tresa and Angel, were deputed to lead them past. The yard, however, looked wonderful, newly painted by Joey's men, the buildings in good order, Etta's flowers blooming in tubs and beds. There was definitely a feeling of renewal and optimism.

Unfortunately, Harvey-Holden had a parade on the same day with a band and a marquee, which took away a chunk of the clientele, and so did Rupert Campbell-Black. Rupert's invitation said his yard needed advance warning of any helicopters landing. Lester Bolton would have given anything for such an invitation and would have used it as an excuse to buy a helicopter. He was irked that at Marius's open day, no one bothered to introduce him to Lady Crowe or to Brigadier Parsons, who owned History Painting. He felt he and his princess had been slighted again.

He was also outraged that the moment he sold Furious back to Marius, the horse should win so spectacularly in that selling race at Stratford. He was not, however, as outraged as Carrie Bancroft, when she returned from Russia and discovered Trixie had ploughed all her exams.

'You've been sacked from seven schools. You promised to work at this one. How could this have happened?' yelled Carrie.

'I didn't work hard enough,' admitted Trixie. 'My hopes were slightly too high, I guess. For some beyond-me reason I failed.'

Carrie was even angrier when someone, probably Dora, leaked the story of the straight 'U' grades achieved by the daughter of the Businesswoman of the Year – did high achievers fail their children?

The atmosphere was truly dreadful, particularly when Uncle Martin, who had the hots for Trixie anyway, dropped in at Russet House and suggested that if his sister had been more caring and less of an absentee mother, and Alan not so obsessed with his writing, things would have been different. 'Children need nourishing and encouraging. Frankly you neglect Trixie, Carrie.'

'She does,' agreed Trixie.

Martin indicated he'd be only too happy to be a father figure to his niece.

Meeting Tilda for lunch to discuss depression, Alan turned out to be the depressed one. He cheered up when Tilda said she'd be only too happy to give Trixie some coaching.

Etta, meanwhile, had expressed her worries about Trixie to Seth. 'She's so moody and unhappy, I'm sure it's Josh officially moving in with Tresa.'

' "Partners are all we need of hell," ' smirked Seth and said he'd be only too happy to coach Trixie and act as a father figure in return for all Etta's kindness in looking after Priceless.

'He's no trouble,' lied Etta. When Seth smiled at her she could deny him nothing.

If Etta hadn't had a brilliant win, when she did actually manage to get her money on Penscombe Poodle at Haydock, she would never have been brave enough to give a party to celebrate the end of Mrs Wilkinson's box rest. She chose the second Sunday in September because Romy and Martin were taking their children to Wales for the weekend, which meant they wouldn't be around to demoralize her, nor would their vast Range Rover be monopolizing the carport.

As well as all the syndicate, she asked Chris and Chrissie, Niall, Rogue, Amber and Marius and all the lads and lasses from the yard. She was amazed when so many accepted and particularly touched to receive a telephone call from Valent in China saying he hoped to be able to make it, and how great that Wilkie was better. Marius rang to say he'd be at Uttoxeter, alas, but his staff were really looking forward to it.

Etta decided to make a huge chilli con carne, accompanied by salads, and she picked enough blackberries and cookers, rejected by Mrs Wilkinson, who only liked sweet apples, to make two vast crumbles. Neither Seth, Corinna, Bonny, Lester nor Cindy had replied, which made catering difficult.

'We'll all bring things,' said Painswick soothingly.

Shopping beforehand, Etta discovered that Ione Travis-Lock, who'd just been appointed a Master Composter, had set up her stall outside Waitrose and was bellowing at shoppers to make compost, avoid packaged food and buy fruit and veg from local suppliers. Etta scuttled inside. She had just bought mince for the chilli when she heard more yelling. Edging down the pet food aisle, she discovered Corinna about to detonate:

'I'm afraid we only allow baskets with five items at this till,' an unfortunate check-out assistant was telling her.

'Do you know who I am?' shouted Corinna. 'I'm not going to wait in that queue. I have an interview with the *Guardian* in half an hour.'

'I can't help it, madam.'

Etta cringed beside the ramparts of Whiskas as Corinna started chucking items out of her basket. Curious customers retreated or ducked as tins of pâté, ripe Bries, jumbo prawns and a pineapple came flying past, until only four bottles of champagne and a packet of cigarettes were left.

'Now will you let me through? I am one of the greatest classical actresses of my age, and you treat me like a chorus girl.'

'Chekhov rather than Checkout,' grinned Alan, when Etta told him later.

'I do hope she's in a better mood tomorrow,' sighed Etta, who was making French dressing.

Chris had lent her two trestle tables from the pub, which he put up in the centre of the carport. These she would cover with the only two white damask tablecloths left from Bluebell Hill and use for glasses, silver, plates and food. Chris had only been able to spare a couple of dozen chairs, but the rest of the guests could perch on the little wall Joey had built round the garden she had made under the mature conifers. This was now filled with white flowers – Michaelmas daisies, dahlias, delphiniums, Iceberg roses and lilies – and looked, even Etta admitted, rather ravishing.

It would be a terrible squeeze, but people could always spill out into the road. Painswick, Tommy and Dora had all promised to help, and had already bathed Mrs Wilkinson and Chisolm.

For once Etta felt well organized and was determined to get an early night and try to look pretty, just in case Seth or Valent turned up. Alas, a sobbing Trixie rolled up at midnight. She'd had a dreadful row with her mother, could she sleep on Etta's sofa? It was already occupied by Priceless, who took himself off to Etta's bed.

At two, a terrible thunderstorm broke out. Priceless was terrified. Tranquillized, he passed out on even more of Etta's bed, denying her any sleep as she tossed and turned, wondering if she had enough drink or whether Seth would get away from rehearsals.

81

At least a glorious day rose out of the first mists of autumn, meaning jump racing would soon be taking centre stage. Wandering out, the dew caressing her bare feet, breathing in a smell of mouldering leaves, Etta heard a rumble and a bleat and found Mrs Wilkinson and Chisolm demanding breakfast. Mrs Wilkinson had celebrated her new freedom by rolling extensively, covering herself with green muck.

'Oh Wilkie, you'll need another bath,' wailed Etta.

After that, the morning ran away with itself. A huge saucepan of chilli was bubbling on the hob, salads were in the fridge, dressings mixed, glasses and silver sparkling. Etta had put on a frilly pale pink shirt and pink-striped trousers from the Blue Cross shop and just made up one eye, when she heard imperious tooting. Looking out she was horrified to see Martin, Romy, the children and the bloody Range Rover at the gate. So she rushed out to open it and Martin drove right in within an inch of the trestle tables.

'You're going to have to move those against the wall, Mother.'

'But there won't be enough room for people to sit. Can't you park outside?'

'And block all your guests? We knew you wouldn't cope on your own, Mother, so we've specially cut short our weekend to support you,' said Martin.

'New outfit,' said Romy accusingly, 'we are splashing out.'

'Granny looks cool,' drawled Trixie, wandering out in the briefest of T-shirts. 'What can I do?'

'Get dressed, young lady,' said Martin, 'and clear up your mess in Mother's living room and put back those cushions.'

'Helloo!' It was Painswick bearing a couple of quiches and two bottles of Chablis, and a huge bunch of carrots like an orange porcupine for Mrs Wilkinson, who practically broke the gate down.

Next moment, Priceless emerged from Etta's bed with the munchies, gobbled up Gwenny's breakfast, eyed Painswick's quiches, then trotted purposefully out into the garden with one cushion that Trixie had just put back on the sofa after another.

Next to arrive were Joey and Woody, clutching six-packs. Sizing up the crises, they started opening bottles.

'Now we've got some chaps,' said Martin and was soon bossing them around to move the tables against the garden wall.

Etta's right eye never did get made up. Glancing out of the kitchen window, she was so enchanted to see Valent's red and grey helicopter landing on the helipad, and Mrs Wilkinson and Chisolm leaving their admirers beside the fence and rushing whickering and bleating up the hill to welcome him, that she absent-mindedly added a huge pinch of chilli powder.

'Nothing much wrong with that horse,' said the Major, who'd just arrived with Debbie.

Romy, not believing her mother-in-law was an adventurous enough cook, surreptitiously added another hefty pinch of chilli as Etta ran out of the house to greet Valent. As he walked down to the little orchard gate next to the mature conifer hedge, Wilkie and Chisolm trotted after him.

He was very suntanned and, although he looked more tired and thinner, he seemed much happier. He was wearing a pale blue shirt tucked into jeans and he bent and kissed her on the cheek.

'Wilkie's sound.' He scratched Mrs Wilkinson's neck as she frisked his pockets. 'You wrought another miracle.'

Then he looked round at the crowds piling into what was left of Etta's tiny garden after the aggressive parking of Martin's car and, unlocking the gate, invited everyone to spread out into the orchard, where the apples were reddening or turning gold.

'Yuck, there's poo in the field,' said Drummond loudly.

'Takes one to know one, you little shit,' murmured Joey.

'Mrs Wilkinson is the guest of honour,' said Valent. 'She needs to mingle with her friends.'

Chisolm was already showing off, clambering up trees from which she'd stripped the bark in search of pears to drop down on guests.

Hoping Dora and Trixie would soon turn up to push bottles round, Etta charged about seeing people at least had a first drink.

Valent, grabbing a can of beer, had headed straight for the Throstledown stable lads, singling out Rafiq.

'Well done, lad, you certainly sorted out Furious. When's he running again?'

'Marius hasn't said, he prefers soft going.'

'Well, he must put you up again, bluddy good.'

Valent then said he'd been spending a lot of time in Pakistan, and asked where Rafiq's family lived.

Valent's really, really taking trouble, thought Tommy gratefully, exactly what Rafiq needs.

Carrie and Alan, who'd spent much of the night rowing over Trixie, were the next to arrive.

'Mother, you've been at the bottle,' accused Carrie, examining Etta's gold hair.

'And you look gorgeous,' said Alan.

'Not sure at your age,' persisted Carrie.

'And your hair looks as though you've been pulled through a hedge fund backwards,' Trixie told her mother, as she finally emerged from Etta's bedroom, ravishing in the shortest of strapless blue and white flower-printed dresses, reeking of her 24 Faubourg.

A wolf whistle greeted her. Turning, she saw Seth in the doorway, ostentatiously staggering in under a crate of red.

'That's far too much,' gasped Etta. 'You are kind, you got away from rehearsals in time!' She was so amazed and thrilled to see him, she added another pinch of chilli.

'I've just been hearing about my Millennium Cup,' said Valent, also appearing in the doorway. 'Didn't know you'd been tending my roses as well,' he chuckled. 'Gives me a buzz to beat Ione and Debbie, and your garden looks smashing. Here, let me carry that,' he said, taking the vast saucepan of chilli and putting it on the table outside. 'I'm famished, didn't have time for breakfast.'

'Oh, please help yourself,' Etta handed him a plate. 'Let me get you another beer. I'm so thrilled you came.'

The result, alas, was a chilli hotter than hell. Caring Romy rushed back to the barn and returned with a big chicken pie she'd bought last week from Waitrose and defrosted in the microwave. She took the opportunity to change into a ravishing strapless white dress, which showed a lot of leg and cleavage.

'I was too hot before.'

'Like the chilli,' said Seth.

Most of the syndicate had fortunately brought quiches and pies.

But Valent valiantly, among others, ploughed his way through the chilli, his eyes watering, his face growing redder and redder.

'It's quite inedible, Mother,' said Carrie, picking at a slice of Painswick's quiche. 'If you had fewer guests, I'd whisk them off to a restaurant.'

A mortified Etta rushed round, apologizing frantically and offering people glasses of water. She was then amazed to discover that Joey had dumped a crate of champagne brought by Valent in the kitchen. People were soon knocking this back to cool themselves down.

Much of the rejected chilli ended up in the long grass along the north side of Valent's conifer hedge, where it was finished up by Chisolm, Cadbury and Priceless until real tears poured out of their eyes. Mrs Wilkinson was in heaven, however, bustling about chatting to all her friends, resting her head on their shoulders, shaking hooves, peeling bananas to order, sipping champagne. Chisolm, already pissed, was butting people in the backside.

'Where's Tilda?' asked Painswick.

'Coming,' said Pocock. 'She's got a lot of lessons to prepare.'

Inadvertently, Tilda had recently upset both Romy and Carrie, telling the former that Drummond was developing into a bit of a bully, and his language should be watched.

'Doesn't get that from our house,' Romy had snapped. 'Must be listening to my mother-in-law's builder friends.'

Tilda had been coaching Trixie, and told Alan that the child was desperate for her mother's approval. 'She's really clever, she just needs a reason to succeed, some interest in her future, not just rants when she fails.'

Alan, in a row last night, had been unwise enough to pass this on to Carrie.

'Doesn't Wilkie look well,' said Valent, as she nudgingly followed him round.

'I think the feng shui in the office really worked on her,' Etta couldn't resist saying.

Valent grinned. 'Bonny says I have an excess of Yang.'

'They try to tell us we're too yang,' said Etta. 'Do you remember? Sung by Jimmy Young, or Yang?' she giggled. 'How is Bonny? I'm so sorry about the chilli.'

'It was fine, it's a lovely party.'

Looking round his field he could see Niall, back from Matins, sitting on the grass with Woody and talking to Joey and Chrissie. Chris was opening bottles and buttling.

Valent next questioned Painswick about the yard. 'Marius has gone to Uttoxeter,' she said. 'He works so hard, but he's so thrilled about Furious.'

411

So was Valent, who'd secretly bought him.

Direct Debbie even congratulated Etta on her garden.

'To grow those plants with so little sun is impressive. I'll give you my scarlet kniphofia Percy's Pride to brighten things up a bit.'

Rafiq, still dazed from having such a long and encouraging conversation with Valent, lay on his back looking up at lemon-yellow flowers of traveller's joy. Josh, handsome, tanned and just back from a week in Portugal, didn't know how to handle Trixie, who he had to admit was looking well fit. Lester was bending the Major's ear.

'I want Mrs Wilkinson in my Godiva film. If she can canter around the orchard, she can carry Cindy for a week or so.'

Seth was talking to Trixie.

'Valent is too old for jeans,' he was saying dismissively, 'particularly with those great muscular footballer's thighs.'

'He looks pretty cool for a coffin-dodger,' said Trixie, who was looking at Josh and deciding she was still mad about him.

82

Etta poured drink after drink, continuing to apologize for the chilli. At least everyone loved her crumbles and the salads had gone down well.

She felt suddenly deflated when Valent came up and said he had to go.

'I've got to be in Shanghai for a meeting first thing.'

'You came all the way for Wilkie's party?'

'More or less. Bonny's in London doing a television programme. I'll be back later in the autumn and we'll get Wilkie up and running. How's Alan getting on with her biography?'

'Not much to write about.'

'He can write about today, it's been a great party.'

He kissed her on the cheek and she resisted the urge to cling to him. 'Thank you for the lovely champagne and being so sweet to everyone.'

'Hetta!' Lester Bolton accosted her five minutes later. 'Will you introduce me to Valent?'

'I'm so sorry, he's gone.'

Bolton looked furious. 'We need to have a serious talk about the syndicate,' he said ominously.

Etta was relieved to be distracted by the arrival of Dora, who had passed all her GCSEs and had spent a lot of the holidays teaching Mrs Wilkinson new tricks.

Mrs Wilkinson frequently stuck out her tongue when she was trying hard in a race, or, knowing it would get a laugh, for a Polo. She had now learnt to make faces. When asked to do her John Prescott face, she would screw her mouth and nose up, but, much more dangerously, when asked to do her Tilda Flood face, she curled her lip and stuck out her top teeth, which had people in stitches.

Alas, Trixie in a brief attempt at conciliation had told her mother, Carrie, about this trick. Increasingly irked by the closeness she saw developing between Alan and buck-toothed Tilda, and punchy on too much champagne, Carrie asked Dora to make Mrs Wilkinson do her Tilda Flood face.

Not realizing that Tilda, who'd been dealing with a hot water failure upsetting the holiday-letters in Shagger's cottage, had just wandered in late to the party, Dora and Mrs Wilkinson obliged at length, to screams of laughter.

Witnessing everything, utterly mortified, Tilda clapped her hands over her teeth. Instantly the laughter petered out. Looking round, Dora felt as though she'd missed a step in the dark.

'I'm so sorry, Tilda,' she wailed. 'It's only a silly joke.'

'Come on, Tilda,' called out Carrie. 'Can't you laugh at yourself?'

But a sobbing Tilda had fled up the road, back to School Cottage. She must somehow scrape together the money to get her teeth fixed. She'd been home for the weekend to a mother with eyes full of questions, who so longed for a grandchild to boast about at bridge parties. Learning Tilda was coaching the ravishing Trixie, one of the Greycoats teachers had asked her if she was coming out at last.

Back at the party, this was definitely a Miss Bates moment as an outraged Alan bawled Carrie out for being an absolute bitch.

Carrie was not the only bitch. As Trixie was clearly having a row with Josh in the orchard, Seth returned to the cool of Etta's bungalow with Romy.

'Move, dog,' she ordered Priceless, who ignored her, so she had to sit very close to Seth. Opening the last bottle of Valent's champagne, he filled up their glasses.

'Awful she hasn't got a single photograph of Sampson here,' chuntered Romy. 'There's one of Trixie and that ghastly goat and Mrs Wilkinson and Valent, but none of Drummond and Poppy.'

'She sees enough of them,' said Seth reasonably. 'Sampson sounds a brute.'

'He was Yang personified.' Then Romy added roguishly, 'Have you noticed my mother-in-law has such a crush on you she gave you the biggest mountain of chilli and she trembles every time you speak to her?'

Seth was transfixed by Romy's smiling, full, red lips and the warm brown softness of her cleavage. Were her breasts brown all over? Very tanked up, he murmured that he had a confession to make.

'I intended to ask you to lunch back in July, but Stefan by mistake took my letter to the wrong Mrs Bancroft.'

Romy couldn't stop laughing, peal after peal worthy of Tower Captain Pocock.

'Etta thought you were madly in love with her? Oh Seth, how *priceless.*' She gave the dog a light tap. 'She does give herself airs. Did you explain you meant me?'

'I couldn't disillusion her.'

'That isn't fair, leading her on, letting her look after your dog all the time.'

' "I do love nothing in the world so well as you," ' murmured Seth, taking her hand. ' "Is not that strange?" ' Then, when Romy raised an eyebrow: '*Much Ado* – Act 4. I'm devoted to Etta, she's terrific for her age and must have been stunning in her youth. It was a genuine mistake.'

'When are you going to come and watch Martin's DVD?' asked Romy.

'When he's out,' murmured Seth, running an idle finger down her cleavage.

Next moment Trixie had stumbled past them, tears pouring down her face, and locked herself in Etta's bedroom.

Hearing cries, lots of laughter and whooping outside, Seth went to the window and groaned.

'Oh God, the fair Weatheralls have arrived.'

'Oh, it's little Phoebe,' cried Romy, leaving her champagne and running outside.

'Promise not to say anything to Etta,' Seth called after her, then turning back, hearing sobbing, he banged on the bedroom door.

'You all right, lovely?'

'Bugger off.'

'What you need is a large glass of champagne.'

Catching sight of his reflection in Etta's mirror, Seth was faced with a dilemma. He wanted to look younger, and if he cut his hair short and spiked it upwards with product, he'd look trendy. This, on the other hand, would reveal the lines on his forehead and round his eyes, which would be covered if he combed his hair forward like Mark Antony.

'Come on, babe.' He banged on the door again.

'How are you, how are you, long time no see.' An ecstatic Seth-fuelled Romy pushed Debbie aside and was hugging Phoebe.

'Shagger and Toby are dropping off our stuff, but I wanted to come straight over,' cried Phoebe, who was wearing a grey and white striped smock.

'Have a glass of bubbly,' said Romy.

'No, no, just a glass of orange squash.'

'Have you had a good summer?'

'Heavenly. We had such a great time staying with the Lennoxes. Such a beautiful house. Do gather round, everyone, I've got such lovely news for you all. I'm expecting a baby in February. If it's a boy that'll mean another willow in the churchyard. I want all the syndicate to be honorary godparents.' Then, as Romy, Debbie and even a newly arrived Cindy hugged her: 'I know you'll all be there for me.'

'Roughly translated as free babysitting and presents Christmas and Easter,' murmured Alan to Etta.

'Must go to the lav,' said Phoebe, adding, as Mrs Wilkinson wandered up to her, 'Hello, Wilkie. So glad you're out and about again.' She patted her pink nose. 'How soon can we come and see you racing?'

Toby, hugely congratulated by everyone, was whinnying with nervous laughter.

'Shagger's going to be chief godfather,' he said.

Despite discovering Tilda crying her eyes out at School Cottage, Shagger hadn't stayed to comfort her. Etta's free drink was too important to miss.

Tilda wept on, not answering door or telephone. 'In loveless bowers, we sigh alone.'

Much later, there was another knock. Creeping downstairs, Tilda found a vast bunch of white flowers on the doorstep. Someone must have stripped Etta's garden.

'Darling Tilda,' said the scrawled note, 'so very sorry. We all love you. All love, Mrs Wilkinson.'

83

The syndicate grew increasingly restless. So many had seen Mrs Wilkinson cavorting around at Etta's party, why couldn't she run sooner? Bolton was the chief stirrer: if the mare wasn't race-fit, she could at least play Lady Godiva's horse. This would merely entail a week or so's filming, carrying a naked Cindy through some deserted town with only Peeping Tom as a witness.

But to Bolton's rage, Marius flatly refused. Mrs Wilkinson must concentrate on getting fit, not star in some grubby porn film.

An apoplectic Bolton proposed a motion of no confidence in Marius and demanded a meeting in the skittle alley of the Fox the following Saturday evening, the first in October, coinciding with the beginning of the winter game. Bolton's mood was not improved when Joey greeted him with the news that Furious had 'pissed all over the three fifteen at Fontwell' that afternoon.

All the syndicate were present except for Alban, who'd gone to a charity dinner in Oxford, Trixie and Dora, who were at school, and Tilda, who had a PTA meeting and anyway only owned half a share with Shagger. He was already banging out 'Horsey, Horsey, Don't You Stop' on the skittle alley's ancient upright.

The Major and Cindy, quickstepping round the floor to much laughter, did nothing to dispel the underlying tension. Feeling hillocks of silicone pressed against his Rotary Club-blazered breast, the Major shuddered. What if he were to lose Cindy and his Portuguese villa? Somehow he must ensure victory.

The syndicate sat round a table, armed with drinks and mocked by hunting prints on the walls of fit horses hurtling across country. Willowwood rugger team, who'd thrashed Limesbridge that afternoon, were getting drunk downstairs.

Chrissie, who couldn't bear to miss a chance of smouldering at Joey and learning the outcome of the meeting, was serving drinks in a little bar in the corner.

In his pursuit of the patrician, Bolton was looking particularly absurd in a new mauve cashmere jersey which fell to his calves. His face was bronzed by fake bake, which made him look more like a red squirrel than a grey one. He kicked off, saying he was fed up with Marius's appalling rudeness.

'He insulted my wife Cindy by suggesting she would take part in anything other than a tasteful erotic fantasy, and now he's denying Mrs Wilkinson a chance to star. And what is more, our producer was prepared to offer five grand for Mrs Wilkinson to take part, which would mean around four hundred to each shareholder, which I'm sure you would all appreciate.'

The syndicate agreed they would.

Then Phoebe spoke. In a billowing flowered smock, she was playing the pregnancy card for all it was worth, making everyone carry her glasses of orange squash and even her mobile, on which there was already a message: 'This is the voicemail of Toby, Phoebe and Bump.'

'While we were in Scotland,' she began, 'we met the most charming man called Henry Ponsonby, who runs the most wonderful syndicates. He knows all about horses so he's great at handling trainers, which you aren't really, Normie. They're getting loads of winners and seem to have such fun. Last open day at Nicky Henderson's they had the most delicious lunch and met loads of famous horses, jockeys and owners.'

'Which is more than happened at Marius's open day,' grumbled Bolton. 'I wasn't introduced to anyone that mattered.'

'I may be sticking my neck out,' went on Phoebe, 'but I think we should not only look for a new trainer but also sell Mrs Wilkinson.'

Etta gasped, feeling as though a huge ball had taken out all her skittles.

'I'm sorry, Etta, but I'm giving up work and on one income a hundred and eighty-five pounds a month is too much to pay for a dud horse. If we went to Henry, he'd find us a decent replacement and make sure we had a ball. He's so owner-friendly and there's a confidential owners' line you can ring for information any time.'

'We can always ring Joyce,' protested Etta.

'Of course,' Phoebe was all dimples, 'but she's not on call twenty-four hours a day. Also I think it would be fun for Wilkie to star in a blue movie.'

'Who's she going to shag? Count Romeo, Sir Cuthbert or Horace?' Toby brayed with laughter.

'I can't see why she can't,' said Alan, thinking what a wonderful chapter it would make in her biography.

'Nor can I,' said Joey, who needed the money.

'I'm all for dumping Marius,' said Shagger.

'Ay can't say Ay've warmed to him,' said Debbie. 'He's been so uncooperative with the Major, who's trayed so hard.'

'Marius is very shy,' protested Etta.

'And he's been through a horrid marriage break-up,' volunteered Painswick, alarmed she might soon be without a job. As it was, she was having great difficulty paying her monthly subscription.

'We can't sell Mrs Wilkinson,' said Woody in outrage.

'Even if she gets better, we don't know if she'll be any good,' drawled Shagger.

'And Marius implied there's another thousand-pound vet's bill coming up,' huffed the Major.

'Henry Ponsonby specializes in affinity marketing, which means arranging syndicates that really get on and enjoy each other's company,' said Phoebe.

'We did at the beginning,' said Debbie, glaring at Cindy. 'We need a decent horse to unite us.'

They were interrupted by a burst of cheering from the rugger club and, clanking up the steel staircase, in walked Seth, a leading actor making an entrance.

Priceless lifted his tail. Etta leapt to her feet. Feeling her shaking as he kissed her, Seth said, 'Darling, what's up?'

'Thank God you're here,' she whispered. 'They want to ditch Marius and sell Mrs Wilkinson. Please help.'

Seth was about to reply when Bonny, flushed by pleasantries from the rugger club, appeared behind him.

'Bonny, Bonny,' everyone crowded around, 'we thought you and Valent were abroad.'

Joey went green. He'd done none of the things Bonny had asked for at Badger's Court.

'I've been filming in London. Seth told me this was a key meeting and I'd better show up.'

Alan grinned at Etta and nodded knowingly. 'What d'you both want to drink?' he added, going towards the bar.

'I'd like a large Scotch,' called out Shagger.

'What's been going on?' asked Seth.

'Marius won't let Wilkie star in *Lady Godiva*,' giggled Phoebe. 'Being a thesp, Bonny, you'll know how disappointed she must feel.'

'What you don't realize,' said Alan mock-seriously, 'is that this movie is social commentary. The poor peasants were being taxed out of existence – there were no state benefits in those days. Lady Godiva rode out to save them, she was a heroine. It's so topical. It would make such a wonderfully colourful chapter in her biography,' he pleaded. 'Not much else to fill it until January.'

'You won't have a book at all if you sell her,' implored Etta.

'Where are you staying in London?' Phoebe asked Bonny.

'Just off the Little Boltons.'

'Wish those two were off there too,' muttered Woody.

Etta, despite the danger, got the giggles.

Bolton cleared his throat.

'Let's get on with the meeting. As a majority shareholder,' he reminded them ominously, 'I'd like to donate a Mercedes Sprinter so we've got something decent to travel in. I also propose we sell Mrs Wilkinson.'

'You can't,' cried Etta.

'Let me finish, please. I propose to buy two babies. I've got my eye on a pretty filly I'd like to call Cindy Kate.'

'Oh Lester,' shrieked Cindy, looking up from *Hello!* 'Do let's buy some flat 'orses, racing's so much nicer in the summer. Then we can go into the Royal Enclosure at Ascot.'

'Hardly think she'd get in,' murmured Bonny.

Cindy and Bolton had powerful allies: Shagger, Phoebe, Toby, Major Cunliffe and Direct Debbie, who'd give anything to dump Cindy but liked the thought of the Portuguese villa.

Chrissie polished glasses and edged closer to hear what Woody and Joey were arguing about. Joey, who had terrible gambling debts and had spent too much money on Chrissie, was reluctantly in support of the motion.

'Marius doesn't do flat horses,' said Shagger. 'And I'm sure we'd do better with Harvey-Holden – Ilkley Hall won again yesterday – or Rupert Campbell-Black.'

'*We* would.' Cindy, Bonny and Phoebe licked their lips.

'Isa Lovell's set up on his own,' said Joey, 'and Cosmo Rannaldini's got all his horses with him. Dermie O'Driscoll's taken a yard in North Gloucestershire, which should be a riot.'

'Marius is really working to get Mrs Wilkinson fit again,' cried a frantic Etta. 'He feels sure she'll be back in the New Year. He's so grateful you've been so patient.'

'Funny way of showing it,' snapped the Major. 'There's no guarantee she'll win again. We could all go on pouring money into her for ever.'

'I think we should vote,' persisted Bolton.

'What are the rules, Major?' asked Bonny.

'Members must abide by a majority decision,' intoned the Major, 'and we must hold a syndicate vote before any horse is allowed to run in a selling plate.'

'Mrs Wilkinson can't run at all at the moment,' said Woody.

'Then she must go to the sales,' said Shagger.

'She'd fetch nothing,' said Joey.

'She would as a brood mare,' said Seth. 'Father's Peppy Koala, mother's Little Star.'

'She must go through the ring then. I'm sure she'd find a good home,' said Phoebe.

'Rubbish,' said Painswick. In her fury she dropped three stitches. 'You know no such thing. We couldn't possibly sell the dear little soul like that.'

'Let's follow the democratic process and have a vote,' urged Shagger.

'We can't,' gasped Etta. 'Alban isn't here, can't we try him on his mobile? He wouldn't want to sell Wilkie, nor would Dora and Trixie, let me try and ring them.'

'Alban doesn't have a mobile,' said Alan.

Neither Dora nor Trixie answered theirs.

'They've got better things to do. Bagley's got a dance with Marlborough this evening.' Alan didn't meet Etta's eyes.

'If Wilkie goes, you won't have a book to write,' a distraught Etta told him.

Bonny, talking to Seth, looked round.

'If her career's over, he won't have one anyway.'

'Joey and Woody,' pleaded Etta, 'you were in at the start.'

'Sorry, Ett, but it's a lot of money to fork out each monf, particularly along with Crowie and Doggie,' said Joey.

'I don't want to sell her,' insisted Woody, 'or leave Marius. He'll get her right.'

Bolton glared at Woody. 'I thought you liked working for me,' he hissed.

'You two only have one vote between you, Woody. You and Joey cancel each other out anyway,' pointed out the Major.

'What about Tilda, she's got a half-share with Shagger.'

'Tilda'll do what I choose,' boomed Shagger, looking at Etta. 'She's not Wilkie's greatest fan after the way she was humiliated at your party, Etta.'

'No, I understand, I'm sorry.'

Pocock was dickering. He loved Etta and Miss Painswick. He was very fond of Wilkie. But he didn't like Seth or the Major or Bolton, he hadn't been able to go racing very often because of work and the presence of Alban in the syndicate intimidated him.

Joey went over to Chrissie and the bar because he felt a traitor and wanted to fill his glass.

'Marius hasn't got what it takes,' said Shagger. 'He's so bloody stroppy. If you twist my arm I'll have another Scotch,' he shouted at Joey.

'What's the point of a syndicate with no action?' Toby looked up from the *Shooting Times*.

Etta could see Alan, Seth and even Pocock wavering.

If Valent were here, she thought in panic, he'd never let this happen. It was Valent who'd accused her of betraying the judge when the syndicate was formed: 'He gave her to you, Etta.'

'Valent wouldn't want to sell Mrs Wilkinson,' she cried. 'He loves her to bits, he'd never let her go.'

'I beg your pardon, Etta,' said Bonny icily, 'I think I know what Valent "thinks". You've clearly forgotten that Valent gave me the share in Mrs Wilkinson as a birthday present. It's nothing to do with him if we sell her, or you,' she added rudely.

'Mind your manners, young lady,' snapped Painswick.

'Bravo,' murmured Shagger, smiling across at Bonny and winking at Phoebe. 'Let's have a vote.'

Alan, Seth, Shagger, Bonny, Phoebe and Toby who counted as one vote, the Major and Debbie who counted as another, Bolton and Cindy who counted as two. That was eight votes, Etta worked out with trembling fingers. Joey for and Woody against cancelled each other out, as did Pocock and Painswick. Even if Alban and Trixie and Dora, who counted as one vote, came in on Wilkie's side that was only two votes, three with Etta's, to eight.

'It mustn't happen,' Etta's voice was rising, 'we're betraying her.'

Distraught, she clanged down the iron steps into the street, where she was asphyxiated by aftershave and nearly sent flying by Niall coming into the pub.

'They're going to sell Wilkie, please try and save her,' she begged. Rustling through the leaves, conkers crunching like pebbles beneath her feet, she raced left up the high street then right, across the village green.

Up in the sky Pegasus was jumping over the church steeple. Surely a good omen. Reaching Ione's iron gates, she was greeted by the red and crimson glow of acers, dogwood and parrotia.

The house was in darkness. Ione isn't in, she thought in despair. But drawing close, she detected a slight gleam from low-energy bulbs. Ione, sitting in three jerseys at her desk near the window to catch the last of the light, had a deadline to meet for

Compost magazine. She was writing on the back of recycled paper, teabag on its second innings in her mug.

Etta rang the bell furiously, a waft of icy air hitting her as Ione opened the door.

'Please help,' gasped Etta, 'I need Alban's mobile number. Bolton's called a meeting in the Fox, they're voting to sell Mrs Wilkinson because she costs too much, and they don't believe she's going to come right.' She burst into tears.

'Have a drink,' said Ione.

'No, no, there isn't time. I just thought if I rang Alban, he might talk them round. He's always seemed to love Wilkie.'

'We all do,' said Ione, and gathering up a vegetable marrow lying in the hall as a weapon of mass destruction, not bothering to close the door, she stormed out of the house across the village green and into the Fox.

Gaunt, beaky-nosed, dark eyes flashing, dark hair escaping from her bun, splendid eco-warrior, she stood in the doorway for a second, then, pummelling aside rugger players, made for the stairs.

'We'll have you in the second row, darlin',' called the captain, raising his beer mug, as she bounded up the stairs three steps at a time, bursting into the skittle alley just as the Major was gleefully counting a majority vote.

Pocock leapt behind Painswick.

'Stop, stop,' ordered Ione, brandishing her marrow. 'You can't sell Mrs Wilkinson,' she added in a voice that had silenced Mothers' Unions and army wives in far-flung posts of the Empire. 'She's not any old racehorse now. She's the Village Horse, all the children at Greycoats love her, we all love her, and we'll keep her as long as it takes.'

'We've voted to sell her,' squealed Cindy.

'I don't care!' Snatching the voting papers from the Major, Ione ripped them up and threw them on the fire. 'You ought to be ashamed of yourselves.'

The syndicate quailed. Next moment they all jumped at the sound of clapping. It was Painswick.

'Thank you, Mrs Travis-Lock. Let me buy you a drink.'

'I've got to rush, thank you, but I don't want to hear any more nonsense, particularly from you, Toby, you earn enough in the City as it is.' Then, glancing round the room: 'Too many lights on, Chrissie, and you're not using low energy,' and she was gone.

'My only recourse is to resign,' announced Bolton. 'I doubt if you'll find anyone to take my share, but that's your problem, Major. Come, Cindy.'

'I'm going to send that piccie of her widdlin' on her compost heap to the *News of the World*,' stormed Cindy. 'Bossy old cow.'

'I suppose we better try and soldier on till Christmas,' spluttered the Major.

'Oh, thank you all so much,' whispered Etta, 'I promise you won't regret it.'

She couldn't stop shaking and she couldn't promise any such thing. It had been a terrible blow that her friends Seth, Alan, Joey and Pocock had been prepared to sacrifice Wilkie.

Niall took the initiative, smiling across at Woody, so proud his dear friend had stood out against the majority, then clearing his throat.

'Dear God, look after Mrs Wilkinson, restore her to health, and please rain blessings on our little Village Horse.'

Etta was slightly comforted when Debbie, who was suffering from Viagra-phobia, drew her aside.

'Oh Etta, thank you. I'm so sorry Ay didn't stick up for Wilkie, so pleased the Boltons have gone. Normie's so crazy about Cindy and Bolton's invited us to his villa in Portugal, and she'd have been there the whole time.'

84

Despite the saving of Mrs Wilkinson, Etta felt terribly low and guilty that so many of the syndicate were being forced to fork out more than they could afford. Her illusions of a band of brothers had been shattered. She still loved Alan, Joey, Pocock and Seth, but felt she couldn't trust them any more – and guilt on their parts stopped them dropping in on her. She was passionately grateful to Woody, Painswick and Ione for standing by her and gave them all bottles of sloe gin.

She was exhausted looking after Drummond and Poppy as well as Priceless, whom she adored even though his master, despite his 'pashnit' letter on Royal Shakespeare writing paper, clearly wasn't interested. She mustn't think of Valent, he belonged to Bonny, who Etta didn't think was nearly nice enough for him.

Towards Christmas, the weather turned bitterly cold and racing was cancelled. Wilkie couldn't go on the frozen gallops and the lads, as they broke the ice on the water buckets on dark winter mornings, longed for the spring.

Martin and Romy decided to give a dinner party to raise money for Sampson's Fund and for WOO.

'I hope they serve bread and water,' said Alan, who was not invited.

Those on the guest list included Seth and Corinna, and Bonny and Valent. Martin wanted to tap Valent for cash and get him to lend Badger's Court for fundraising extravaganzas. Having no loyalty, Martin had also invited Harvey-Holden and Jude the Obese. With the all-weather gallops and indoor school Jude had paid for, H-H was able to carry on training and was very busy buying horses for his demanding new owner, Lester Bolton.

Corinna, still on tour in *The Deep Blue Sea*, couldn't make it.

Valent, who couldn't stand Martin and Romy, and who, as the fourth anniversary of Pauline's death in the Cotchester rail crash approached, was hardly in party mode, wanted to refuse, which resulted in a frightful row with Bonny, who accused him of selfishness.

'You come all the way back from China for the widow Bancroft's party. You want me to love living in the sticks, and deny me the opportunity to engage with people. I so enjoy Martin and Romy, who are inviting some congenial locals – you might put me first for once.'

So Valent agreed. He could check on his cockpit office and on Marius and it would be nice to see Etta again.

Also staying with Martin and Romy was Blanche Osborne, Sampson's chief mistress, who had caused Etta such unhappiness. She had just come reluctantly out of mourning, designer black had so suited her pale blonde hair and creamy complexion. She had left her husband Basil behind and, as Corinna was still away on tour, would make up the eight.

Martin decided it would be easier if Etta wasn't present, even if she were only waitressing and clearing away. It would be difficult for Blanche to be herself. And after the court case over Mrs Wilkinson, he was sure Harvey-Holden would be happier if Etta wasn't around, so he had employed Trixie, which he knew would please Seth.

Not prepared to risk Etta's cooking after her chilli con carne fiasco, Romy had bought dinner in from William's Kitchen. But they needed Etta's help in bulling the place up, laying the table and getting Poppy and Drummond supper and into their pyjamas.

'Mummy and Daddy's job is to make money for poor people,' explained Poppy. 'Your job, Granny, is to tidy up.'

Etta had great difficulty preventing Drummond eating all the toffee roulade layered with white chocolate mousse.

'They'll need an ox to feed Jude the Obese,' said Trixie, who was studying the seating plan drawn up by Romy, in order to put the place names on Etta's lovely gold-leaf dinner plates.

'Listen to these ghastly CVs. "Seth Bainton: a most talented and fascinating actor. Bonny Richards: who could have expected someone so gifted and beautiful could be so nice? Ditto Blanche Osborne, very close friend of Sampson Bancroft." Yuckarama, sorry, Granny. "Judy Tobias, charismatic director of Tobias Inc., married to our most successful trainer." That is seriously repulsive.'

Trixie poured herself a large vodka and tonic.

'Romy's put Seth on her right, greedy bitch, and poor sweet Valent on her left and Jude on his left – she'll need the whole side of a table – then Martin next to Blanche with toxic Bonny on his left, and even more toxic Harvey-Holden next to her and Blanche next to Harvey-Holden. What a cosy little eightsome.'

Trixie shoved her cigarette in the bin and downed her vodka as Romy swanned in wearing a red dressing gown, hot and scented from the shower, hair in rollers.

'How many times do I have to tell you to put the dishwasher on eco setting?' she snapped. 'Absolutely maddening, Corinna's decided to come after all. So you'll have to re-lay the table, Mother. I'm not a stickler for even numbers but she might have let us know before. We'll have to shift everyone around and put her between Harvey-Holden and Jude. If you roll up that late, you can't expect a chap on either side. Better add "our greatest Shakespearean actress" to her place card, or she'll act up. I don't know how Seth puts up with her.

'After you've readjusted the placement and got the kids into their pyjamas and banked up the fire, Mother, you might as well push off. Must go and get ready, Blanche will be here in a mo.'

Trixie and Etta looked at each other. Trixie poured herself another vodka.

No doubt Blanche, with her £50,000 annuity from Sampson, will have bought something sensational to wow Seth and Valent, thought Etta.

Trixie read her grandmother's mind. 'I'll put arsenic in her pudding.'

'What are you going to wear?' asked Etta.

'A fuck-off dress,' said Trixie. 'That table looks gorgeous, so do the flowers.'

Blanche, having been told by Romy that there were some fascinating men coming and wanting everyone to understand exactly why Sampson had adored her and preferred her to Etta, looked stunning. She wore crimson taffeta with transparent trumpet sleeves and a nipped-in waist to glorify a total lack of spare tyre. Sampson's huge rubies glowed at her neck. Below her collarbone was also pinned a ruby brooch in the shape of a geranium.

Bonny, even slenderer, looked deceptively demure in a little bleak dress in ivy-green silk, high-necked, but slit to her groin to ensnare Valent, Seth, Martin and the devilish Harvey-Holden, who, like her, was accused of shacking up for money.

Romy, in a fuchsia shift worn off one polished brown shoulder to show that she had no need of a bra, was looking as voluptuous as Bonny looked fragile. She was determined to charm a massive donation out of Valent and captivate Seth, who was troubling her dreams.

Sampson's portrait looked arrogantly down from the twenty-foot high white wall as if to say, 'I could have the lot of them.'

It was a bitterly cold night but a huge log fire crackled and flickered, bringing colour to everyone's cheeks. Trixie hadn't arrived so Martin was forced to open bottles. Jude seemed to have grown even larger like a children's story: the hippo who came to tea.

Urged by her parents, Poppy sat down at the piano and played a Beethoven minuet, irritating the hell out of Blanche and Bonny, who had to shut up. A lot of wrong notes resulted because Poppy couldn't take her eyes off Jude.

'Are you having twelve babies like that lady in America?' she asked the moment she'd finished.

'Time for bed, young lady,' said Martin firmly.

'Good night, darling.' Romy kissed Poppy tenderly.

Drummond then rode his new bike round the room over the corns of Harvey-Holden, who for a second looked sufficiently convulsed with hatred to throttle him.

A diversion was created by Valent's arrival. He had been to see Marius and learnt from Painswick how nearly Mrs Wilkinson had come to being sold. Bonny had been economical with the truth and not told him she'd come down to Willowwood or that Seth had been present.

My Bonny lies over the ocean, My Bonny lies . . .

Valent loathed dinner parties, everyone talking about house prices and schools and asking him for free financial advice.

He also felt a prat. Insisting the dress code for tonight was casual, Bonny had persuaded him, before he left for the yard, to put on a poncy pink flower-patterned shirt, which Bonny had bought for his birthday and which he'd always resisted wearing. And there were Seth, Martin and H-H all in smoking jackets.

As he arrived, Romy was saying playfully to Seth, 'You must talk to Bonny now, because you're not sitting next to her at dinner.'

'How's Clod?' murmured Seth.

'You must not call him that,' murmured back Bonny.

'There's an interesting development, tell you later,' said Seth.

Next moment the men's hands fluttered to smooth their hair as Trixie sauntered in, deliberately provocative in a flower-patterned satin blazer, worn with nothing underneath and the briefest pink satin shorts.

'You're late,' fumed Romy. 'You're supposed to be waitressing, and that's not an appropriate outfit.'

'For God's sake, push around the fizz,' exploded Martin, handing her a bottle.

'I'll open it,' said Valent, taking the bottle from Trixie.

'You look cool,' said Trixie, kissing him. 'If we stand side by side, people'll think we're a herbaceous border.'

'Blanche,' called out Romy, 'this is our neighbour Valent Edwards.'

Blanche left her tiny hand in Valent's huge paw longer than necessary.

'We've met before,' said Valent without warmth.

'I'm sure you'd rather have a beer,' interrupted Trixie, handing Valent a can of Carlsberg, so he turned away from Blanche to talk to her. 'Where's your nan, I mean grandmother?'

'Romy didn't want her here,' hissed Trixie. 'That enamelled stick insect was Grandpa's mistress. She's bound to make a pass at you.'

'Nice pictures,' said Valent, glancing round the room.

'They're Granny's, they shoved her into that bungalow so they could cop the lot. Mum's done the same.'

'How's Mrs Wilkinson?'

Trixie's face darkened. 'Did you know that Seth, Dad, Bonny and all those creeps voted to sell her?'

'I had heard,' said Valent grimly.

'Trixie,' thundered Martin, 'you're supposed to be waitressing.' He looked at his watch. 'Where the hell's Corinna?'

'She'll be along in a minute,' said Seth.

He and Corinna had in fact had a frightful row. Both due to go into *Antony and Cleopatra* at Stratford in February, they had been offered a short provincial tour of their great hit as Elyot and Amanda in *Private Lives*.

Corinna had refused; she was shattered from her last tour as Hester in *The Deep Blue Sea*.

'I'd look like Amanda's grandmother. You do it, it'll keep you busy.'

'They want you,' Seth had said evenly. That was the irking thing. 'They'll only do it if you do it, you're the crowd-puller.'

Corinna had mentally left Hester and was morphing into Cleopatra, the great man-eater. She knew Seth and Bonny were up to something. Her aim for tonight was to seduce Valent. Then she wouldn't have to spend her life on tour and supporting Seth.

85

Corinna arrived half cut in very low-cut black velvet and was irritated when Romy insisted they went straight in. She was even crosser when she discovered she had been seated between that little weasel Harvey-Holden and his mountain of a wife, round whom she couldn't see a millimetre of Valent who was seated on Jude's right.

The oppressive heat from the fire had given Seth an excuse to take off his smoking jacket and reveal the lean excellence of his body. Romy and Blanche on his left and right were drooling over him. Martin was between Blanche and Bonny, who had H-H on her left.

As they tucked into crayfish and salmon ravioli, Trixie, as she poured the Sauvignon into everyone's glasses, announced in a stage whisper that Granny had done the cooking. Blanche and Bonny looked as though they were being poisoned.

Martin and Blanche clinked glasses.

'It's good to see you.'

'And you.'

'Etta was so jealous,' said Blanche, hardly lowering her voice. 'Sampy loved my blanquette de veau, but Etta would never cook veal for him. He also loved foie gras.'

'I know, I know.'

'So strange to see his portrait looking down, I feel he has come home.'

Bloody old cow, thought Trixie as she handed round the pheasant casserole, but she was distracted to feel Seth's warm hand caressing her thigh as she served him.

'Why are you ignoring me?'

'Because you wanted to sell Mrs Wilkinson,' hissed Trixie.

'I'm starving,' Jude told Valent, as she opened up another roll. 'We didn't get tea at the races.'

'Can you pass the booter?' Valent asked Harvey-Holden.

'Butter, Valent,' corrected Bonny. 'I'm making Valent persevere with my voice coach,' she told the table.

'So you said last time,' snapped Corinna. 'Is that why he sounds so much more patrician than you?'

'Thunks.' Leaning forward, Valent raised his glass to her.

'He is rather Neanderthal,' murmured Blanche, turning to Seth. 'What does Bonny see in him?'

'Success,' said Seth.

Bonny was spitting, but decided not to react to Corinna's patrician crack. She turned back to Harvey-Holden, who'd had two wins at Chepstow that afternoon and was boasting about his all-weather gallop which had cost over a million.

'What a pity Mrs Wilkinson can't come back to you,' murmured Bonny. 'Why did you let her go in the first place?'

Harvey-Holden's hand was wrapped round a solid cut-glass tumbler. Next moment it had shattered, spilling water all over the table.

Everyone stopped talking. Harvey-Holden, whose face had gone absolutely dead, had cut himself. Jude jumped to her feet. 'Are you all right?'

'Fine,' he snarled, wrapping a napkin round his hand. 'For Christ's sake, sit down.'

Romy flapped around, crying that it didn't matter one bit that the glass was one of a family set, and mopping up the water and broken glass. Jude insisted on waddling off to the kitchen to find some plasters. Corinna turned to Valent.

'At least I can see you now.' She drained her glass.

'How's your tour gone?' asked Valent.

'Standing O's in every city, but I hate living out of suitcases. Only good thing about staying in hotels, you end up with a lot of free bathcaps.'

'If you cut your hair short, you wouldn't need to wear a shower cap,' cried Blanche reprovingly. 'It would suit you, long hair's so ageing. Why don't you try Shumi in Britten Street?'

When Corinna didn't answer, Blanche smiled across at Valent. 'Have you remembered when we met?'

'With Sampson Bancroft at Downing Street.'

'Oh, you knew Sampy. Wasn't he charismatic?'

'I knew Sampy,' said Corinna, Cleopatra-majestic, helping herself to more red. 'He came backstage and asked me out to dinner. I would have gone but I'd only known Seth a few months, we were

431

playing the Marquise de Merteuil and Valmont and were still in the white heat stage, so I'm afraid poor Sampy got the brush-off. He was furious, I don't think it had ever happened to him before. After that he was never off the telephone, pestering. He came to all my first nights.'

Trixie was laughing openly.

'You deserve another roast potato,' she whispered to Corinna, 'well done.'

Blanche was incandescent with rage.

'I don't believe any of that, Sampy had no need to pester.'

'Perhaps he wasn't getting it at home or away,' said Corinna rudely.

Jude had returned to the table. Although blood was seeping through the napkin round his hand, Harvey-Holden curtly refused any plasters. Valent, unable to get H-H's murderous expression out of his mind, pushed Jude's chair in for her and found her surprisingly congenial to talk to. She had followed his career and congratulated him on his Iron Man invention.

'It changed my life, does all my ironing when H-H's owners come to stay and my clothes, as you can imagine, are quite large.' She laughed, so Valent did, adding, 'I got to know your father well when we were on the Aid to Exports Board.'

Her mother, Jude then told him, had ended her days so happily in one of Valent's care homes.

'Your Bonny's so lovely and doing so well. Must be wonderful for her having you as a partner, so she can be choosy about the roles she takes and doesn't have to worry about money.'

'You've done the same for H-H,' said Valent.

'I hope so.' Jude looked very sad for a moment. 'I hope he'll be less likely to wander, if he feels secure and his horses are doing well and he can be choosy like Bonny about owners.'

'That was a very extreme reaction to Bonny asking him about Mrs Wilkinson. Does he ever talk about her?'

For a second, there was real fear in Jude's eyes.

'No, please don't mention it.'

'Like Corinna's hair,' murmured Valent. 'Who runs your family business now?'

86

Corinna, divided from Valent by Jude's vast bulk, ignored by
H-H, who clearly preferred listening to Bonny and Martin,
irritated by Blanche, who, in revenge for Corinna's Sampson-
baiting, was deliberately chatting up Seth, helped herself to more
red as she boiled up for a row.

Martin was telling Bonny about the War on Obesity.

'You are just the right person to head up our campaign, I know
we'd get huge support from the local and national press, and
people would turn out in their thousands to run five miles with
their favourite celebrity: Bonny Richards.'

Bonny looked delighted.

'Why don't you use Jude?' she whispered. 'Think of the
publicity if we could reduce her by six stone.'

'Brilliant, brilliant,' Martin clapped his hands, 'let's do lunch.
If we could get Jude slim, she'd be so much happier. Valent's a bit
podgy too. I need to talk to him. One of the ways we fundraise is
to get employees to give to a charity straight from their gross
salary. I know Valent's got forty-five thousand employees.'

Martin had notes in his pocket for the presentation he would
make later. Bonny was very lovely, her dress fallen open to reveal
her shaven haven. Martin found it increasingly hard to
concentrate.

'Romy rings up celebs,' he struggled on. 'She has such a lovely
speaking voice, they always give generously.'

Trixie was coming round with the wonderful white chocolate
and toffee roulade.

'That's how you keep your lovely figure,' he murmured, as
Bonny took the tiniest helping.

'Valent's very oedipal,' she grumbled. 'Pauline was more of a mother than a wife, he loves old ladies like your mother fussing over him.'

Across the table, as Jude told Corinna how much she'd loved *The Deep Blue Sea*, Valent got out his BlackBerry to check the football scores and helped himself to a huge dollop of pudding.

'Valent, put some back,' called out Bonny. 'I despair, and put that thing away – it's so disrespectful.'

There was a pause. Romy, getting jealous of the glazed look in Martin's eyes, turned to Seth.

'How's Etta's crush on you getting on?' she asked playfully.

Her 'lovely speaking voice' then carried round the table as with peals of laughter, to Seth's utter horror, she relayed that 'Mother-in-Law thought Seth was after her. He hadn't the heart to tell her when she rolled up, all tarted up, to meet him at Calcot Manor that Stefan the Pole had taken his adoring letter asking me out to lunch to the bungalow by mistake. He'd got the wrong Mrs Bancroft. Isn't it hilarious?'

'Mother was ever a fantasist,' sighed Martin, 'always reading poetry and romantic novels.'

'Seth meant to ask *you* out?' said Corinna softly, who with Bonny and Trixie was glaring at Seth.

'We know where that puts us,' snapped Bonny.

'How priceless Etta thought you were after her,' said Blanche, waving a pink-nailed finger at Seth. 'I do hope you didn't encourage her.'

'Granny's absolutely gorgeous,' shouted Trixie, making everyone jump as she banged down the white chocolate pudding on the sideboard and stormed out.

Seth felt an absolute shit, particularly when Valent also exploded in fury: 'Etta's a luvly lady and still bluddy attractive.'

'Course she is.' Martin, who didn't want to antagonize Valent before the presentation, laughed heartily. 'She's my mother after all.'

'All men were deceivers ever,' said Corinna. Angry, savage and drunk, she held out her glass for a refill. 'You're all the same, having to prove you can still pull and satisfy a young chick.' Then, overwhelmed with venom because Valent hadn't chatted her up, she turned on him. 'If Pauline hadn't died, you'd have dumped her for a younger model by now.'

There was a ghastly silence.

'How dare you, how rude is that!' Trixie came howling back into the dining room, gathering up the pudding as though she was going to ram it in Corinna's face. 'Valent loved Pauline, and haven't you enough sensitivity to realize it's the anniversary of the Cotchester rail crash next week?'

'Don't be so impertinent,' thundered Martin. 'How dare you speak to Miss Waters like that.'

'Because she's a fucking bitch.' Trixie gave a sob and ran out of the room.

'Let's have the cheese board,' said Romy, taking it off the sideboard and plonking it on the table.

Having starved themselves and feeling Etta couldn't have cooked the cheese, Blanche and Bonny cut themselves large slices.

'Dolcelatte was Sampy's favourite cheese.' Blanche turned to Martin. 'I feel your father is watching over me,' she sighed, 'but I think he would want me to be happy and move on.'

'I know he would.' Martin grasped her hand.

Romy smiled at a spitting Seth, who she'd dropped right in it.

'I haven't had a moment to chat to Valent,' she cooed. Turning, she put a hand on Valent's clenched fist. 'I'm sorry Corinna was so hurtful. I know how sad you are, Valent, I'm hoping I can involve you in one of our charities. My goal is to find wealthy folk who are sad or unfulfilled and involve them in a project, perhaps a little African orphan, where they can see the results of their donations. I know we can make your life more meaningful.'

And line your own fucking pockets, thought Valent, looking bleakly across at Blanche, who was saying:

'You're so like your father, Martin.'

Valent wanted to throw up. Martin then pinged a glass and announced that with Ralph Harvey-Holden's help he was approaching the delightful Clerk of the Course at Cheltenham, Simon Claisse, to stage a Sampson Bancroft Memorial race. 'It would mean so much to Mother,' he added to Valent. 'Despite her unseemly crush on a certain person,' he raised his glass roguishly to Seth, 'there will never be anyone else for Mother but Father.'

'Sampson was such a gentleman. Wellington, Cambridge,' sighed Blanche, then, turning to Valent: 'Tell me about yourself.'

Behind Blanche's head, Trixie pulled a face at Valent and stuck her fingers down her throat.

Valent chucked aside his napkin and got to his feet.

'Smashing nosh. You wouldn't get better at the Ivy. I've got to go.'

'But Martin's about to make a presentation,' wailed Romy.

'I'm not going,' said Bonny furiously, 'I'm having far too good a time.'

Valent shrugged. 'Suit yourself.'

'I'll see her home,' chorused Seth and Martin.

Valent turned to Jude, who told him, 'You're lovely to sit next to. Normally men just talk about themselves at dinner parties.'

'Give my best to your dad.' Valent smiled briefly. 'He's a nice man.'

Seeing Trixie hovering in the doorway, a look of trepidation on her face, he crossed the room and kissed her.

'Night, little one, thanks for sticking up for me. See you next time Wilkie races.' Then, turning to an enraged Martin and Romy: 'Thanks for supper.'

Then he turned to Corinna.

'If you'd ever had the privilege of meeting my wife Pauline,' he said softly, 'you'd never have made such a filthy assumption,' and he was gone.

In the hall he picked up one of the bottles of red Bonny had taken from his cellar for Romy and Martin and set out to see Etta, imagining how low she must feel to have been excluded. It was even colder, the bowed willows glittering with frost in the light of a yellow full moon. Odd that trees, when they needed warmth, shed their cover of leaves.

Leaving Romy and Martin's barn, he appreciated for the first time how steep, slippery and treacherous was the path down to Etta's bungalow, particularly when there was no moon and her torch might run out. Swearing as he put his foot down a rabbit hole, he vowed to do something about it.

It was a minute or two before Etta answered the door.

'Who's that?' she cried in terror.

She was wearing an old green dressing gown. Gwenny, hanging on to the sash, tugged it open. Valent caught a glimpse of slightly sagging beasts, a little tummy and a small copse of pubic hair, before she tugged the dressing gown round her in embarrassment. 'I'm so sorry, I thought you were a burglar.'

Aware how red and swollen her eyes were, Etta longed to slap on some foundation and comb her hair.

'I've only popped in to ask after Mrs Wilkinson,' Valent said as he handed her the bottle.

Priceless, who was stretched out on the sofa, flicked his tail but didn't budge.

'Lousy guard dog,' said Valent.

There was a pause. 'Come in,' said Etta, 'I'll get a corkscrew, how incredibly kind.'

Once inside her sitting room, Valent realized the moon was totally blotted out by his mature hedge, planted to protect

Bonny's privacy, and how dark and poky was the bungalow. He vowed to do something about that too.

'So sorry I didn't bother to light a fire.'

Gratified to see a photograph of himself and Mrs Wilkinson on the side table, Valent opened the bottle and filled two glasses.

Etta felt stunned. All she could think of was how awful he should catch her looking so dreadful.

'I talked to Marius earlier,' said Valent. 'Wilkie's doing smashing but they've been held up by the weather. Pity he's not speaking to Harvey-Holden or he could have borrowed his all-weather gallops.'

'How was Harvey-Holden tonight?' asked Etta with a shudder.

'Evasive, never met my eyes once. Very nice wife.'

'How did Trixie do?'

'Brilliantly, best thing about the evening, smashing kid, brave as a lion, gorgeous lookin'. I'll give her a job when she leaves school. Much better guard dog than that thing.'

Etta's sad face lit up. 'I'm so pleased, Martin and Romy and Carrie put her down so much.'

Valent smiled as Gwenny stalked in and jumped on to his knee, purring thunderously.

'What happened at the meeting about Mrs Wilkinson?' he asked.

Etta didn't want to drop Bonny in it.

'Lester Bolton was horribly persuasive and turned people against Marius,' she stammered. 'Some members are finding it difficult to pay their monthly subscription.'

You included, thought Valent.

'Should have rung me,' he chided her, 'I'd have sorted it. Here's my mobile number,' he handed her a card, 'if you get any trouble.'

As she got up to fill his glass, her dressing gown fell open again to show little purple feet.

'Why aren't you wearing slippers?'

'Priceless ate them,' said Etta.

They chatted about the yard. Everyone was happier without Michelle, Rafiq was doing well and had won several races. Furious had disgraced himself running the wrong way at the start at Towcester, then spinning round, which would have upset most jockeys, had caught up and overtaken the rest of the field.

'Marius was ecstatic. He thinks if he can stabilize Furious a little, he's got a world-beater,' said Etta.

Gwenny settled between Valent's thighs, purring like distant farm machinery.

'How was the food tonight?'

'Smashing, congratulations.'

'I didn't cook it. It came from William's Kitchen.'

As he burst out laughing, Valent's weary face lifted.

'Trixie told everyone you'd cooked it all, so a bitch called Blanche Osborne hardly touched anything.' Oh God, he hoped he hadn't hurt Etta, but she looked delighted.

'I'm so pleased you didn't like her, she always made me feel so hopeless.'

'She told Corinna to cut her hair, imagine how that went down.'

Neither of them mentioned Bonny, although Valent longed to pour his heart out. How Bonny had demoralized him, who'd always been pretty sure of himself. How he now doubted his taste in houses, in clothes – he was so glad his overcoat was covering the poncy flowered shirt. Bonny had made him so aware of his ignorance of the arts. She was always criticizing his pronunciation, his manners. Was he making a complete fool of himself, running after someone half his age? One of the reasons he had agreed to go tonight was because he had assumed Etta would be there and she made him feel safe.

Turning to the bookshelves and the books piled up beside them, he found novels and the volumes of poetry Martin had mentioned so dismissively.

'I've never read mooch poetry,' he confessed.

'Borrow this.' Etta handed him the *Everyman Book of Poetry*. 'It's full of lovely stuff.'

'Thunk you, I must go.' Valent took the book and dropped a reluctant Gwenny gently on the floor. He didn't want to burden Etta with his problems.

On his way back to Badger's Court he slipped twice on the path and only saved himself by clutching on to willow branches.

Earlier, back at Harvest Home, having asked Romy why she was such a fucking bitch, Seth wandered into the kitchen to find Trixie furiously chucking pudding plates into the dishwasher. Sliding his hands inside her flowered blazer, encountering bare flesh, he caressed the undersides of her breasts with his little fingers, squeezing her hardening nipples between his first and second fingers.

'I'll walk you home,' he murmured.

For a second Trixie's resistance faltered and she dropped her head back against his chest, then she said, 'You effing won't. I only live next door, if you'd forgotten. And I don't know which is more seriously retarded: voting to sell Mrs Wilkinson or trying to shag Aunt Romy. How could you!'

Wriggling out of his grasp, she escaped out of the back door into the freezing night. Reaching Russet House, finding neither of her parents home, she wandered down the garden and, oblivious of the cold, lurked in the trees.

Sure enough, ten minutes later, Seth and Bonny emerged and set out not down through the wood but along the road towards Badger's Court. Unable to hear what they were saying, shivering uncontrollably, aching with longing, Trixie retreated to her empty house.

'I love, I hate,' she intoned, 'the cause I know not, but it is excruciating.'

Bonny was no more pleased than Trixie that Seth had asked Romy out to lunch.

'Only to take the smug smile off her husband's face,' protested Seth.

'I find Martin very charming,' said Bonny coldly.

'How would you like to play Amanda in *Private Lives* for a few weeks?' asked Seth.

Bonny was excited by the idea, but all thoughts fled out of her head when she got back to Badger's Court and found no Valent.

Having dropped Bonny off, and left Corinna passed out on Martin and Romy's sofa – hopefully she might throw up and serve them both right – Seth dialled Trixie's mobile.

'Hi, babe. How about running me up a whisky and soda.'

Returning back from Etta's half an hour later, Valent discovered Bonny's little bleak dress, her bra, her high heels, her diamond necklace and her bracelet draped up the stairs and Bonny lying naked on the heart-shaped bed with her legs apart. His huge fingers slid in easily, finding her even more slippery than Etta's path through the woods. Was she acting when she sobbed:

'Where have you been? I was so scared. There was no party once you left. I love you so much, Valent.'

Ripping off his flowered shirt, tugging at his cords and his boxers, she pulled him down on top of her.

Afterwards he couldn't sleep and picked up Etta's anthology. On many of the pages, she'd jotted down other quotes.

'And beauty, though injurious,' he read, 'Hath strange power . . . to regain/Love once possessed.'

The following day, Valent ordered Joey to hammer in wooden posts at four-foot intervals down the footpath, for Etta to cling on to when she was walking back and forth. To his amusement, around dusk Martin came banging at the cockpit door.

'Don't know who's been putting up those posts, Valent, probably one of my mother's dubious friends, Woody or Joey, but they must come down, they're an eyesore, I am so sorry.'

'I saw Esau sitting on an eyesore, how many esses in that,' murmured Valent, not looking up from Etta's anthology, then, in a tone that froze Martin's blood: 'I had them put up because your mother could easily slip in wet or icy weather. And I'd like to point out, she's been looking very tired recently. If your children wear you out, think how exhausting it must be for someone thirty years older. Etta should have some life of her own. Now get out, I don't want to hear any presentations,' and he returned to his book.

Before going to bed, Valent glanced out of the window and caught sight of Etta and Priceless going home in the moonlight. As if in a bending race, they were weaving in and out of the poles.

'He likes me, he likes me not, he likes me, he likes me not, oh he likes me.' As Etta wheeled round the bottom pole, she kissed it.

'Valent Edwards thinks Mother ought to have more of a life of her own,' Romy grumbled to Debbie.

'What about an evening class? You can take courses in everything from welding to wine appreciation.'

'Mother's got a degree in that already,' said Romy heavily, 'and we need her to babysit.'

87

Christmas was approaching, the cold spell not letting up. Marius was desperate to gallop his horses, particularly Mrs Wilkinson, who had made progress but needed to be race-fit for a handicap chase in which she'd been entered on New Year's Day.

Marius was very much aware how the increasingly impatient Willowwood syndicate would act up if she didn't run soon – so he tore his hair as he gazed across his white frozen fields, and thought of his loathed and eternally gloating rival H-H, whose horses thundered along the all-weather gallop, and notched up one win after another.

One couple with no desire to see Mrs Wilkinson back on the racecourse was Romy and Martin. What with Gwenny and Priceless and her trips to see Wilkie and Chisolm, Etta had been failing in her duties as their children's nanny. Romy had actually had to cut short a meeting to pick them up from school the other day. Poppy cried all night because no one came to the carol concert at Greycoats.

Martin and Romy had so many charitable functions at Christmas.

'We must capitalize on the moment when people are feeling festive and generous.'

Jude the Obese had very kindly sent them £1,000 after the presentation at the dinner party. Martin had been tempted to launch WOO just after Christmas when people were feeling fat from bingeing, but they'd probably be too broke to give generously. He planned lunches with both Bonny, the proposed spirit of WOO, and Jude, the roly-poly model.

Martin, however, was capable of gross foxiness. Rolling up at the bungalow in early December crinkling his eyes engagingly, he handed Etta an envelope.

'Romy and I think you've been looking very tired recently. We're very conscious you missed out on holidays when Father was failing. Your turn has come, you're going to join us when we go skiing over Christmas, before the kids go back to school.'

In the envelope was a plane ticket to Switzerland.

Etta's heart sank, she'd miss Mrs Wilkinson's first race back.

'I can't, Wilkie's running at Cheltenham.'

'You don't need to be there, you're only a tenth owner. And Ralph Harvey-Holden told me that unless the weather picks up she hasn't a hope.

'Gosh, I'm starving.' Martin opened the fridge, found a little rounded tin of prawn cat food for Gwenny's supper, and seized a piece of sliced bread to make himself a sandwich.

Etta was too stunned by what he had imparted to wise him up, particularly when he pronounced it 'Excellent, glad you're not stinting yourself, Mother. You don't seem very excited,' or 'grateful', he nearly added.

Etta had been looking forward to a few days without them and had planned to ask Rafiq, Painswick and Pocock for Christmas dinner.

'I want to see Wilkie run,' she repeated bravely, 'and who will look after Priceless?'

'Stefan the Pole can do that,' said Martin, who'd gone off Seth since he called Romy a fucking bitch. 'Seth has no right to dump that beast on you. You know what Romy and I feel about pets.'

Differently, Etta suspected, if they were offered an animal charity.

As he stalked off into the night, Martin nearly fell over a smart green and red bird table.

'What on earth's this?'

'Joey and Woody,' Etta gathered up Martin's discarded crusts, 'gave it to me as an early Christmas present.'

'Get rid of it at once,' snapped Martin, 'you don't want to encourage bird flu.'

Carrie, when she heard Etta was going to Switzerland, was outraged.

'You don't care about Mother needing a rest, you just want a free babysitter,' she shouted at Martin. 'I need Mother in the school holidays. It's my turn, Trixie wants someone to drive her around and see she eats.'

'After the way she behaved at our dinner party,' shouted back Martin, 'I would think it was your duty to keep an eye on your daughter yourself. She is seriously out of control. And why can't Alan do that?'

'Alan is criminally behind on his book on depression,' snapped Carrie. She didn't add that he had been spending too much time in the betting shop and, she suspected, with Tilda Flood. He seemed only too willing to attend carol concerts at Greycoats.

Alan was also lagging behind with his book because few of the syndicate seemed depressed at the moment. Joey was going hammer and tongs with Chrissie, the vicar's carol concert had been very well attended and Woody had provided wonderful branches of holly and spruce for the church. Alban had at last got a quango, £200,000 a year to decide whether the nation's adultery figures had decreased since doctors had stopped visiting patients at night.

As a result, Alan had been reduced to inventing more and more case histories. Only last week, he'd made up a Catholic priest depressed at not having any sex. Alas, sending the sample chapter to keep his publishers happy, he had so inspired the publicity department that they were determined to have 'this wonderfully courageous old man' at the launch party and available for interview. Alan wondered if Seth or Alban or even Pocock would dress up as the priest.

As his publishers believed he'd nearly finished *Depression*, they had suggested he write a book on celibacy. As he had designs on Tilda, Alan had said he knew nothing about the subject and would rather write about Mrs Wilkinson and the Willowwood legend.

Etta hated leaving Willowwood. She was absolutely exhausted, having addressed all the Christmas cards Martin and Romy were sending out to possible benefactors. She had washed and packed all Drummond and Poppy's clothes, and was now wondering what to pack for herself.

She had been terribly worried about Rafiq. Every time a suicide bomb exploded anywhere in the world, he felt the ripples of hatred, and he had been unable to ride any races because of the big freeze. Marius, coming to the rescue, had had the brainwave of posting him, Tommy and the lorry to Burnham on Crouch for ten days over Christmas, so Mrs Wilkinson could get fit galloping over the sands, strengthening her legs in the sea water. Tommy and Rafiq were enjoying staying in a B and B, while Mrs Wilkinson and Chisolm lodged with a local trainer.

Etta hoped Valent liked her presents: a bottle of sloe gin and his own copy of her favourite Everyman anthology. She in turn was enchanted by her presents. Marius had given her a tiny greenhouse, in return for tending his garden, Pocock a dozen

Regalia lilies. Joey and Woody's bird table had brought her so much joy, but her best present had been a pair of brown Ugg boots, so blissfully warm and comfortable. Inside was a card: 'No excuse for chilblains now. Love, Valent.'

What a dear, dear man.

While Etta was in Switzerland Painswick was coming in to feed Gwenny and the birds.

'Why not save money and feed Gwenny on the birds?' she had suggested when she had dropped in on Etta earlier and found Gwenny on the windowsill, angrily chattering at two blackbirds.

'I like the robins best,' sighed Etta.

One, which she'd nicknamed Pavarobin because he sang so beautifully, was always waiting in the winter honeysuckle, eyes bright, orange chest thrust out, often hitting her hand as she put out the first crumbs.

'Most of his time,' she told Painswick, 'is spent perched on the table, wings on his hips, ready to attack any bird that approaches.'

'Typically male,' said Painswick. 'Old Mrs Malmesbury calls robins: "souls of the dead".'

Etta hoped Pavarobin wasn't Sampson keeping an eye on her.

She hated leaving the birds and Gwenny, but she was most worried about Priceless. She didn't trust Seth or Corinna or Stefan to look after him.

Wandering into her bedroom to finish her packing, she found him stretched out on her rumpled bed, flashing his teeth, his head resting on one of her Ugg boots, at which he'd been gently nibbling.

'Wish you'd come and pull my sledge,' sighed Etta.

88

Before Christmas, arctic conditions returned to Larkshire, which made flying off to the Swiss Alps and leaving behind Mrs Wilkinson, whom Etta had found in the snow, even more poignant.

Ever since Ione had sided with Etta over keeping Mrs Wilkinson and refused to give Sampson's fund any money, Martin and Romy had given up any attempt to reduce their carbon footprint or take a Green skiing holiday. It was Zermatt or nothing.

Judging by the splendour of their hotel bedroom, which had a blue-velvet-curtained four-poster, a jacuzzi, a vast television and a spectacular view of the Matterhorn, WOO and their other charities must be paying them well.

By contrast Etta had a single bed, no minibar and no television in a tiny room next to Poppy and Drummond, so she was constantly refereeing squabbles.

Returning from a shattering third day hawking the children round skating rinks and toboggan runs and applauding every achievement, while Romy and Martin acquired mahogany tans whizzing down the mountains, Etta found Sky and a huge wide-screen television installed in her room.

Aided by Drummond, she quickly located *At the Races*, where Marius was being interviewed in a snow-covered yard. The children screamed with delight to see Mrs Wilkinson in her patchwork rug and Chisolm in a Father Christmas hat kicking a huge snowball, followed by Mrs Wilkinson peeling a banana and shaking hooves with Matt Chapman, the presenter.

A most uncharacteristically smiling Marius then admitted Mrs Wilkinson was in great form and looking forward to her return. Cheltenham wasn't cancelled because of the weather. The camera then switched to her 422 Christmas cards strung across the office and Miss Painswick reading out some of her fan letters.

Matt Chapman was just telling viewers that tomorrow's race was of great interest because Mrs Wilkinson would be pitted against her old enemy Ilkley Hall, who'd won his last four races, when Martin roared in and, to wails of protest that Wilkie and Chisolm were on the television, switched off the set. Well aware that Drummond had the skills to track down adult movies featuring goats in more questionable activities, Martin promptly rang the manager to complain.

'Take it away, I'm not subjecting my kids to pornography.'

Martin was wearing a banana-yellow ski suit. Etta had a vision of Mrs Wilkinson peeling it off him. Romy followed him, red as her ski suit with rage: 'How dare you order Sky, Etta,' and was followed by the manager, Mr Marcel, who'd already earmarked Martin as a pest.

Marching in, with a grin lifting his black moustache, Mr Marcel announced that Sky and the big screen had been specifically ordered and paid for. Then, brandishing a magnum of Moët and a vast bunch of alstroemerias and pink scented lilies, he added: 'These also are for Mrs Bancroft.'

'They'll be for me,' said Romy, snatching the flowers. 'Don't want them to go to the wrong Mrs Bancroft this time.' Laughing heartily, she ripped open the envelope and read out, ' "Darling Etta, All your friends at Willowwood are missing you, lots of love Mrs Wilkinson and Chisolm." '

Romy's red, turning-to-puce face was a picture: a Francis Bacon cardinal.

'How pathetic, a horse and goat sending flowers.'

'Surprised Chisolm didn't eat them,' said Etta ecstatically.

Who would have known alstroemerias were her favourite flowers? Seth, Valent, Alan, Painswick, Pocock, Marius? She'd planted enough in his garden. She waited until her room had emptied to ring the Major, as head of the syndicate, to thank him. She got Debbie, who said Wilkie was fine, and Cheltenham would be inspecting the course at 8am, to see if racing could go ahead.

'It's very cold here, how's Switzerland?'

'OK. Thank you all for the lovely flowers and champagne and Sky so I can watch the race. I can't believe it.'

'We all chipped in but it was Seth's idea,' said Debbie tartly. 'He was so fed up with Romy boasting to everyone that he'd muddled the two Mrs Bancrofts and meant to ask her rather than you out to lunch.'

'Oh no,' whispered Etta. 'He what? How dreadful, how embarrassing.'

For once Direct Debbie was contrite. 'Oh Etta, I thought you knew, I'm so sorry. And you've been forced to look after Seth's awful dog.'

Etta put down the telephone and died. Poor, poor Seth having to give her lunch and her getting so drunk and trying to kiss him. What a laugh everyone must have had. Oh God.

Then she tried to be sensible. After his first passionate letter, she'd grown increasingly deflated as Seth's behaviour hadn't been remotely amorous. How she had beaten herself up, wondering if she'd repelled him coming on too strong at lunch, when he'd never meant anything in the first place. How he must only have dropped in so often to gaze at Trixie. Wryly she looked at her single bed:

> Take back the hope you gave – I claim
> Only a memory of the same.

Would it be sacrilege to put a teaspoon in the neck of a magnum of champagne and have a glass now?

The flying cork nearly took Martin's eye out, as he popped in wearing a dinner jacket, bound for a New Year's Eve jaunt.

'Mother!'

'I'm not taking your children out tomorrow. I'm going to watch Mrs Wilkinson.'

'Mother!'

'And I'm going to have several glasses of champagne now, so I'm sure you won't consider me a responsible enough person to babysit this evening. Happy New Year, Etta,' she added, and slammed the door in Martin's face.

Then she looked in the mirror. The cowardly lion was roaring.

447

89

If the sea saved Mrs Wilkinson's legs, Cheltenham, putting down enough frost cover for twenty-five football pitches, saved racing on New Year's Day. The covers had now been rolled up like black brandy snaps and sent off to Sandown to save racing later in the week. There was something schizophrenic about thick snow on the surrounding fields and ring of hills, their woods silvered with hoarfrost, and the bright green course below.

Etta stuck to her last and insisted on staying in to watch the race. Poppy and Drummond opted to stay with her, partly because Mr Marcel had presented her with a huge basket of fruit. Etta didn't tell them she'd rung Joey earlier and asked him to put £2 for each child and £30 for herself on Mrs Wilkinson, whose odds had shortened to 10–1. She tried, however, to explain to them about betting.

'If I put on a pound, I get eleven back.'

'Why?' said Drummond, eating grapes.

'If it's 7–4 like Ilkley Hall, and I put on a four pounds, I get eleven back.'

'Why?'

It was frustrating only to get a glimpse of the syndicate gathering in the parade ring. Nice that Ione, in a Saturn-ring fur hat, had accompanied Alban. Perhaps Cheltenham was warmer than Willowwood Hall.

She could see Corinna (who'd told the *Daily Mail* her New Year's resolution was 'to give up smoking and Seth Bainton'), Seth (how could she ever face him again?) and Alan, all in dark glasses, obviously with fearful hangovers. There was Phoebe, voluminous green cloak covering her still non-existent bump.

At least Etta wouldn't have to relay every moment of the race to her. Five minutes to the off – pre-recorded film was now showing the twelve runners circling the parade ring.

All eyes were on Ilkley Hall, the black and beautiful favourite with his white zigzag blaze, and on Michelle, slinky in tight black leather jeans and a waisted scarlet jacket with a red fur-lined hood, as she led him up.

Ilkley Hall was followed by another of Mrs Wilkinson's old rivals, Cosmo Rannaldini's Internetso and by two younger horses, Last Quango, which Harvey-Holden had sold for vast profit to Lester Bolton, and a flashy chestnut gelding called Merchant of Venus, trained by Rupert Campbell-Black.

If only I were there to gaze at Rupert, thought Etta.

She was so nervous, she could feel rivulets of sweat trickling down her sides. She took a huge gulp of champagne.

'Here's Wilkie,' shrieked Poppy. 'Doesn't she look lovely.'

Etta had to fight back the tears as Mrs Wilkinson came dancing out in her patchwork rug. Chisolm, in a red Christmas bow, followed, irked that the public were warming their hands on cups of coffee or soup rather than eating ice creams. Etta was so pleased to see the crowds clapping and smiling as they passed: 'Welcome back, Wilkie, Happy New Year, Chisolm.'

She knew she was being sentimental but as Wilkie jigjogged past, ears pricked, she kept turning her head as though she were searching for Etta, wanting to give that rumbling thunderous whicker of pleasure.

'You'll see her again soon, Granny.' Poppy took Etta's hand.

Oh, there was Lester Bolton, shaved head covered by a brown trilby, and Cindy smothered in white furs like the Snow Queen.

'This is boring,' grumbled Drummond, grabbing the remote control.

'Don't you dare,' snapped Etta.

'Oh look, there's Rupert talking to Rogue, who's riding Merchant of Venus.'

Then she gave a gasp of horror as the list of runners and riders came up, and she realized Killer O'Kagan, back in circulation after his year-long ban, had flown in from Ireland at the last moment to ride Ilkley Hall. The young Irish jockey Johnnie Brutus had been demoted to Last Quango and Dare Catswood jocked off altogether.

Because she in turn had been off since June, Mrs Wilkinson had never come up against the dreaded Killer before.

Oh God, what evil schemes might Shade and H-H be cooking up? For a minute into shot came Olivia in blond furs and Shade in a black fur hat, both richly brown from skiing. By contrast

Killer, skeletal thin but huge across the shoulder, his thumb constantly caressing his whip, was white as the snowflakes tumbling down. Malevolence gave a green tinge to Harvey-Holden's ratty little face. What a terrifying quartet, plotting, caballing.

Etta caught a glimpse of Marius ignoring his ex-wife as much as Amber was ignoring Rogue. Etta had no idea how hopelessly Amber had been thrown earlier in the day to see Rogue lounging, muscular thighs apart, on Channel 4's programme *The Morning Line*.

Although Merchant of Venus had a spectacular turn of foot, Rogue had told the panel, Ilkley Hall would probably win the race. Mrs Wilkinson, he went on, didn't have his cruising speed, but it was nice to have her back and her jockey Amber Lloyd-Foxe would certainly win the beauty stakes. He'd then gone on to talk about the likelihood of his retaining his champion jockey title.

Rafiq, watching at Throstledown, had nearly kicked the television in.

Both Killer and Rogue had already notched up a hundred winners.

'You beat me last year, but I'll have my title back by April,' taunted Killer as they set off down to post at Cheltenham.

Snow was falling faster, mist coming down. Marquees, stands, rails, wings to the fences, wheeling seagulls on the lookout for chips dropped by hungover racegoers, the jockeys' breeches and Mrs Wilkinson's dear white face and Ilkley Hall's zigzag blaze were among the only things discernible through the gloom.

As the jockeys, wearing thicker clothes and gloves, gathered at the start, Amber gazed stonily into space as Rogue circled beside her cracking jokes. Mrs Wilkinson looked so much smaller than any of the others.

Little donkey, little donkey, don't give up, pleaded Etta.

Even Drummond looked up from his computer game, and they were off.

Last Quango went straight to the front, setting a punishing pace for the first few furlongs, then Mrs Wilkinson overtook him, trundling along like a little train, jumping so carefully and, as she cleared each fence, looking ahead for the best place to jump the next one, doing the thing she loved most, racing and listening to the sweetest sound in the world to furry ears on a dank, freezing New Year's Day: the Cheltenham crowds calling her name, 'Come on, Mrs Wilkinson.'

'Mrs Wilkinson is taking them along,' said the commentator.

Etta squeezed herself in joy. 'Taking them along', what a lovely phrase.

'Wilkie's travelling really well,' she told the children.

Too well for Killer, who moved up the inner, galloping beside Mrs Wilkinson so she couldn't see the rails out of her good eye.

Confused, losing her bearings, she took off a stride too early and stumbled on landing. Amber managed to stay in the saddle but by the time she'd righted herself Internetso, Ilkley Hall, Merchant of Venus and Last Quango had all overtaken her.

Mrs Wilkinson also took a while to recover but fortunately, like Valent, she could always see a gap. This time it was in the huddled-together quarters ahead and, trusting Amber, displaying incredible courage, she pushed through despite Killer riding right across her.

'Get off her line, you bastard,' screamed Etta, as Killer, his face even whiter and crueller, his reins deceptively loose in his left hand, thrashed the hell out of Ilkley Hall with his right and, as a fiendish trick, at the same time let the whip repeatedly catch Mrs Wilkinson's good eye as he thundered once more up the inner, pushing her wide on the bend, as they swung into the home straight.

Although wincing and blinking, Mrs Wilkinson's blood was up.

Even though snow was now clogging her good eye, she challenged again, darting back up the inner, stripping the paint off the rail. Killer, enraged, swung Ilkley Hall deliberately left, bumping her, denying her running room. For a second she reeled from the bump but held steady and pushed through.

'Bastard,' screamed Etta, 'lay off Mrs Wilkinson, you fucker.'

'Granny!' said Poppy in horror.

'Get your arse into gear,' screamed Drummond.

'Drummond!' said Poppy, appalled, then, 'Go on, Wilkie, fucking do it,' she screamed as Mrs Wilkinson stuck her white head out, drawing level with Killer as they crossed the line.

Ilkley Hall had won four races since the season began. Mrs Wilkinson had been to the seaside.

'Well done, Amber. If that's not Ride of the Week, I'll eat my hat,' said Derek Thompson, thrusting a microphone under her nose.

'Photograph, photograph, she was robbed,' yelled Etta and everyone else, clocking the way Michelle had thrown a rug straight over Ilkley Hall to cover excessive whip marks.

'Photo, photo,' echoed the commentator.

Ding dong, ding dong, went the airport sound, followed by the loudspeaker announcing a stewards' inquiry.

There was no shaking of hands between the contestants.

'You bastard,' hissed Amber, about to slash Killer's evil, mocking face with her whip.

Mrs Wilkinson had no such reserve. Lashing her tail, flattening her ears, stretching out her neck once more, she bit Ilkley Hall sharply on the shoulder.

'Stop that.' Michelle raised a black leather fist to punch her.

'Don't you dare,' shouted Tommy.

The crowd in the lit-up stands cheered Mrs Wilkinson all the way back to the winners enclosure, where without hesitation she took up her place by the number one post, refusing to let Ilkley Hall anywhere near it.

Etta choked back the tears as she saw the syndicate swarming round and Mrs Wilkinson disappearing under the same hailstorm of joyfully patting hands. Then Etta's heart stopped, for there was Valent, his jaw rigid with muscle, determined not to break down, pulling Mrs Wilkinson's ears, hugging her, gathering up Chisolm to stop her being trampled to death and putting her on Mrs Wilkinson's back so the press got their picture.

For a second the cameras rested on Harvey-Holden's face, so evil that Etta crossed herself in terror.

Then followed an agonizing wait while Killer protested his innocence to the stewards with a conviction that would have earned him a scholarship to RADA.

'If you have to count every time you smack a horse, you'll be done for non-trying because you're not concentrating,' he grumbled.

'He cut across me, pushed me into the rail, took me wide, and repeatedly hit Wilkie with his whip on her good eye,' stormed Amber.

Rogue, having observed things from behind, backed up Amber.

'Killer interfered with her again and again.'

Merchant of Venus had come third. On television, Etta could see a delighted Rupert giving Amber a congratulatory kiss. I would have met him, she thought wistfully, then winced as she thought of Seth. She must stop lusting after younger men.

Finally, after an interminable wait, ding dong, ding dong, and the crackle of the loudspeaker: as a result of the stewards' inquiry, Killer O'Kagan would be suspended for ten days for interference and excessive use of the whip, and the winner was number eight: Mrs Wilkinson.

'Why are you crying, Granny?' asked Drummond.

'Because she's happy,' said Poppy.

Both she and Drummond were even happier when Etta fumbled for her purse.

'I backed Mrs Wilkinson for both of you. Here are your winnings,' and she handed them £20 each.

Mr Marcel, popping in to see if everything was all right, was thrilled to hear of Mrs Wilkinson's victory. Filling up Etta's glass and pouring a quarter each for Poppy and Drummond, he said Mrs Wilkinson was '*très petite et tout coeur*'.

On the television they could still see the Willowwood syndicate ecstatic in the winners enclosure, waiting to collect the silverware.

'Look, look,' cried Poppy, 'there's Uncle Alan kissing Miss Flood. We'll have to ask her about it when we're back at school.'

And there was the vicar hugging Woody and Mrs Travis-Lock doing a war dance with the Major.

'Can we go racing next time, Granny?'

Even Marius looked ecstatic and told the press he'd never expected Mrs Wilkinson to return so spectacularly after six months off. Corinna had once again covered Mrs Wilkinson with red lipstick kisses. Dora made her shake hooves with handsome Lord Vestey, the Chairman of the Course, and Chisolm took a bite out of his yellow check suit.

Finally, after they'd collected Mrs Wilkinson's cup, the syndicate gathered round and said they'd like to send a message to Etta Bancroft, who'd rescued Wilkie in the first place.

'You were right all along, Etta, you kept faith,' said the Major, mopping his eyes. 'We all miss you, it's not the same.'

'Come home soon,' cried Debbie.

'That's you they're talking about,' said Drummond, fingering his twenty pounds and looking at his grandmother with new respect.

Next moment her mobile rang. It was Amber, in heaven.

'Oh Etta, Rupert congratulated me for the first time, and at the bottom of the hill Rogue told me to go for it and I could win. Wasn't she wonderful, and Marius put five hundred quid on her at 10–1. He must trust me now. Only sad thing, Dad couldn't make it.'

As Etta listened, wondering what had become of Valent, she suddenly caught a glimpse of Bonny in a exquisitely cut grey-flannel coat, with snowflakes in her tousled ash-blonde hair, lovely as ever. She was flanked by Seth and Valent, who were both looking so proud.

'It's my first win,' Bonny was telling Derek Thompson, and how it had enriched her life experience, and how spiritual and epic a journey it had been, getting Mrs Wilkinson back on the race track.

'You were nothing to do with it,' Etta shouted indignantly. 'You wanted to dump her.'

'She was a birthday gift from my partner Valent Edwards,' went on Bonny, giving Valent a kiss, 'and I'm a very proud owner.'

'*C'est Bonny Richards*,' said Mr Marcel in awe.

As the syndicate swarmed off to the Royal Box to celebrate, Etta sat down on an apple with one bite out of it, feeling the euphoria drain out of her. Then she felt bitterly ashamed.

It should be enough that Wilkie had made such a dazzling comeback. Why shouldn't Bonny, Seth and Valent enjoy themselves?

'Mummy, Daddy,' cried Poppy as her parents swept in, 'Mrs Wilkinson won, and Miss Flood and Uncle Alan have been on telly and Granny cried and cried.'

It would have been nice if Romy and Martin had been even fractionally enthusiastic. One plus was that Drummond had been totally converted to racing.

'Granny had a bet for me,' he said, waving his twenty-two pounds. 'Can I have a bet tomorrow?'

Fortunately an enraged Martin and Romy were distracted by a journalist, alerted by Mr Marcel, rolling up to interview Etta about her great victory.

'Don't forget to mention the Sampson Bancroft Memorial Fund,' hissed Martin.

Next day the papers were full of Rogue Rogers hitting Killer O'Kagan across the weighing room and also being suspended for ten days. So the battle for champion jockey was still wide open.

Etta returned home feeling very flat, and was vastly cheered by a message on her machine from Valent, saying how wonderful Wilkie had been, and how they'd all missed her at the races.

She was almost more touched that Priceless was absolutely ecstatic to see her. He had lost a lot of weight and he smiled and smiled when he saw her, snaking his head round and round her hips in the most loving way. They were both so tired from not sleeping, they fell into bed, Priceless immediately taking up three-quarters and Etta not minding, even when Gwenny joined them in the middle of the night.

90

To cheer up the gloom of winter, a mega jaunt was planned in early February. The syndicate would watch Mrs Wilkinson run at Warwick, then move on to Stratford to stay in a hotel and see Seth and Corinna open in *Antony and Cleopatra*, followed by a party afterwards.

In the preceding weeks, a great din could be heard issuing from the Old Rectory as the two stars hurled insults and objects and re-enacted the play together. As a demanding, charismatic applause junkie, with the ability to charm, seduce and manipulate, the part of Cleopatra might have been made for Corinna. Having been with Seth for fifteen years in which she had been more successful, she was aware he played around while she was away. Yet on stage as Cleopatra the enchantress, she felt sure she could win him back and was excited by the challenge.

As the din increased, there was great local speculation over Seth's ebony locks, which were suddenly much greyer. Had this been caused by Corinna's tantrums or was grey considered more suitable for the battle-scarred Antony, or was it his natural colour which he'd stopped dyeing black?

One evening, as Oscars and BAFTAs started whistling past his head, Seth escaped. Armed with a big bunch of alstroemerias and a bottle of Moët, reeking of Terre, he banged on Etta's door.

'Darling, darling, I'm so sorry about the two Mrs Bancrofts, I only made a pass at Romy to irritate her tosser of a husband. I only called you "Sorry with the fringe on top" because you're so sweet and always apologizing for everything. Please forgive me.'

And of course Etta did. Priceless was less forgiving. At the pop of the champagne cork he retreated, with a deep sigh, to Etta's bed.

'How are things going?' she asked.

'I feel as though both the Tiber and the Nile are flowing through our drawing room.' Seth filled two glasses. 'If we were doing *Othello* I could smother her with a pillow. She's given up drink to lose weight and reduce any red veins and it makes her really mean. Antony's such a demanding part, I've got 24 per cent of the lines. Corinna's only got 19 per cent and hers are far more beautiful and more dramatic. You must help me to learn mine.'

Etta tried not to melt as he gazed into her eyes and, in his deepest, huskiest voice with a slight break in it, declaimed of love finding a new heaven and a new earth.

'It sounds wonderful,' said Etta as they paused for a break.

'Fascinating plot, the great warrior destroyed by sexual desire,' observed Seth.

'Sampson was destroyed by Delilah,' mused Etta. 'I remember being shocked when I overheard my father saying Eisenhower had a mistress. I thought he meant a schoolmistress and that Ike was a bit old for that.'

'Your son-in-law's got a schoolmistress,' said Seth idly. 'Very keen on her, doesn't notice her teeth any more. Poor Carrie.'

'You didn't think about poor Martin,' said Etta tartly.

'I try not to. A great warrior destroyed by sexual desire,' repeated Seth wickedly. ' "The triple pillar of the world transform'd into a strumpet's fool". Do you think Valent's been destroyed by Bonny?'

Etta struggled out of a sunken cherry-red armchair, which needed re-upholstering, and banged a log to shake out any woodlice before putting it on the fire.

'Course not, Bonny's not a strumpet, and no one pushes Valent around. He recovered the cockpit as an office. According to Trixie his voice was "rattling thunder" when he chewed out Corinna for being foul about Pauline, and he hasn't allowed Bonny to chop suey his house. He allowed Wilkie to stay against her wishes.'

'Macho man,' mocked Seth, kicking back another log which was scattering sparks. 'D'you fancy him?'

'I like him enormously,' said Etta firmly.

In fact she liked Valent so much, she was always thinking of ways to repay him. On a flying visit to Willowwood, Valent had found his cockpit so sweetly scented with her indoor bulbs, he'd taken a couple of bowls back to his house in London. And he'd so liked a big bowl of African violets she'd nurtured for him, he was thinking of using the glowing purple of the flowers and the dusty green of the leaves as his colours when Furious raced.

Glancing out of the window when he arrived one evening, he was surprised to see the lawn of Badger's Court covered in snow. Only when he stepped outside did he discover they were great sweeps of snowdrops, their little heads hanging and nodding like Etta's.

Fed up with Seth spouting poetry all the time, particularly to Bonny, Valent had devoured Etta's anthology, hoping to find lines to quote himself. But his voice coach had made him self-conscious about his Yorkshire accent. He must remember to rhyme 'one' with 'fun', not 'gone'.

> 'Shall I compare thee to a Soomer's day.
> Thou art more luvely and more temperate.'

> 'How do I luv thee? Let me count the ways.'

He hated Bonny mocking him.

Ringing Etta, he was livid when Seth, sounding drunk, picked up the telephone.

'Etta's been absolutely marvellous helping me learn my lines. She's so good at being Cleopatra. Do you want a word?'

As it was only to say he'd liked Etta's poetry book, her hyacinths and her snowdrops, Valent snapped he wouldn't interrupt her, he'd ring another time.

'Give her my love.'

Etta, who'd heaved herself out of the cherry-red armchair, hand out to take the cordless, fell back in disappointment.

'Said he'd ring again,' said Seth.

Later, to wind Bonny up, Seth told her about Valent calling Etta. Bonny was further irritated that Seth wouldn't let her hear his lines. He hated her correcting him all the time, suggesting poncy interpretations.

Romy was even more irritated.

'Why don't you let me hear your lines?' she demanded, trapping Seth with her bicycle as he came out of the village shop.

'You're much too distracting,' murmured Seth, 'I'd want to do other things.'

'Oh Seth.' Then Romy's voice hardened. 'I hope you're not taking that bottle round to Mother–in-law, she drinks quite enough as it is.'

The mega jaunt to Stratford grew. Valent insisted the minibus leave an hour early so that, to please Etta, they could drop in on a snowdrop garden on the way.

457

'How can I wear the same thing to traipse through the woods, go to the races, to the theatre and on to a party?' grumbled Painswick.

'When I was young there was a thing called a dress'n'jacket,' reflected Etta, 'which looked like a coat and skirt until you took off the jacket and discovered a sleeveless dress, but I don't think my wrinkled little arms are up to it.'

She longed to stay in her Ugg boots all day, but didn't want the suede to get ruined if it were muddy at Warwick.

Seth and Corinna were travelling direct to Stratford separately, and Bonny also decided to miss the races and join everyone later at the theatre.

'So she can swan in looking a million dollars,' stormed Trixie, appalled at how much she was longing to see Seth again.

Everyone else was surprised how much they enjoyed the snow-drops, which drifted for miles round a ruined abbey and along a mysterious darkly flowing stream.

'I can joost imagine the Lady of Shalott floating past,' said Valent, showing off his new literary knowledge.

'Yes, and so many different kinds of snowdrop,' cried Etta.

'The common garden snowdrop *Galanthus nivalis* of course predominates,' said Debbie importantly.

'As a symbol of hope in a long winter,' said Painswick.

Pocock, not to be outdone in the poetry stakes, cleared his throat:

> 'The snowdrop, in purest white array,
> First rears her head on Candlemas day.'

When the others looked at him in amazement, Painswick said, 'Who wrote that, Harry?'

'It's an old Larkshire rhyme.'

'Harry now,' whispered Alan, making a thumbs-up to Etta, 'watch that space.'

'When's Candlemas?' asked Etta quickly, to stop herself laughing.

'Feb the third,' said Niall, 'the day Mary presented Jesus at the temple, so it's a day of purity.'

'Like we're going to have today,' said Alan.

'Was it a sort of christening? I suppose Bump will be christened at Toby Jug's family church.'

'You're like a brilliant guidebook, that's lovely to know,' Etta put her arm through Niall's. 'Isn't it beautiful here?'

458

'Not enough splashes of colour for Debbie,' said Alan.

Debbie's lips tightened, then she laughed: 'And you don't know much about purity, young man.'

'Touché.' Alan winked at Tilda.

'You oughta see the snowdrops Etta's planted at Badger's Court,' said Valent. Dropping to his knees, he tucked in a trouser leg which had escaped from Etta's boot, and she found herself trembling as she felt his hands on her leg. She was so happy they were all getting on, like in the early days.

'I don't want to leave here.'

'We can always come back next year,' said Valent.

'Chop chop,' shouted the Major from the minibus, who couldn't wait to get to Stratford and see Corinna in all her glory. 'We'll miss the first race.'

He and Alban had been discussing Lester Bolton's defiant plans for a moat to encircle Primrose Mansions.

'He's intending to divert the Willowwood stream,' said the Major, 'so we'll lose out on water, and also to divert Harvey-Holden's stream into it, so if we have a lot of rain it'll flood the village.'

'We need moat control,' said Alban, braying with laughter.

In the bus, Debbie sidled up to Valent, who was reading *Antony and Cleopatra*, and said that Normie had given her the Iron Man for Xmas.

'Changed my life. Irons shirts better than I do. Normie often wears three shirts a day if he has a lunch and an evening function. Sheets and duvet covers are done in a trice, when the family come to visit.'

'I'm glad,' said Valent, looking as though he really was.

Alban sighed. He was lucky if he was allowed a clean shirt every two days and a bath twice a week.

Woody was opening bottles.

'We must pace ourselves,' said Painswick, accepting a paper cup of white and handing it on to Pocock. 'I'll have half of that.'

'I hope the going's not too heavy for Wilkie,' said Joey, checking his mobile. 'Says it's soft in places but yielding.'

'Just like you,' whispered Alan to Tilda.

'Get on with you.' Tilda nudged him in the ribs, spilling wine all over the notebook in which he was trying to write about Mrs Wilkinson. She didn't seem at all upset that Shagger and Toby were shooting and would only make the theatre.

Valent took a can of beer and another anthology and wandered up the bus.

'Good poem for you here, Alban,' he said.

'Lord Lilac thought it rather rotten
That Shakespeare should be quite forgotten,
And therefore got on a committee
With several chaps out of the city.'

'Good God,' exclaimed Alban. 'Who wrote that?'

'Chesterton in nineteen thirty-three. Nothing changes.'

'Brilliant. Let's have a government inquiry into whether Shakespeare is remembered enough.' Alban adored Valent.

Only Trixie seemed in low spirits as she gazed constantly at her mobile, waiting for messages, snapping at Etta and even Valent when they asked if she was OK.

The general high spirits increased at Warwick where Mrs Wilkinson proceeded to demonstrate that Cheltenham hadn't been a flash in the pan, trundling through torrential rain and a sea of mud to win her novice chase by six lengths. After monkeyish antics at the start in the next race, Furious then carted Rafiq, once again picking off all the other runners and winning by a length.

Count Romeo, despite loathing rain, kept his handsome face dry and mud-free in his red blinkers and came a close second. History Painting won the big race of the afternoon, completing a dazzling day for Throstledown. Marius's euphoria was intensified when Olivia, passing him on the way to the winners enclosure, smiled and said, 'Congratulations.'

This triggered off a blazing row between Olivia and Shade, who later, bumping into Amber, asked her when she was going to have dinner with him.

'When you put me up on one of your horses.'

'It's a deal,' purred Shade. 'A ride for a ride. Call me.'

The only sad note was that one of Harvey-Holden's mares, House Price, had a dreadful fall. They had to leave without hearing what had happened to her.

So off the syndicate set to Stratford, half cut and in manic mood. Having finished reading *Antony and Cleopatra*, Valent sat at the back with his BlackBerry, reflecting that emails were easier to deal with than females. Had Bonny thrown a hissy fit over the visit to the snowdrop garden to give herself an excuse to duck out of the races and slope off to somewhere else in the Stratford area? Corinna always insisted on sleeping for a couple of hours before a performance, which would free up Seth.

Valent used enough private detectives to spy on other companies, but refused to let them loose on Bonny because he felt it was dishonourable and he didn't want to get hurt.

Down the bus, Niall, amid the laughter and the chink of glasses, was wrestling with tomorrow's sermon, based on the contemporary relevance of miracles. The gospel for the day included the miracle of Jesus calming the winds and waves when a storm threatened to overturn the boat which was carrying him and his terrified disciples.

'Why are ye fearful?' Jesus had then demanded. 'Oh ye of little faith.'

Since the gloriously golden Woody had graced his life, Niall believed in miracles, but there was no way to calm the storm if their love affair became public. Tonight he must lay off the drink, as it always took the brake off his inhibitions.

91

The rain was rattling the bus windows like Wilkie's hooves and ebony clouds blotted out any sunset glow as they arrived at the appropriately named Tempest Inn, which was mock-Tudor with low beams and rooms named after characters in the play. The first night party would be held later in the Prospero Suite. Etta found herself in 'Miranda', an embarrassingly lovely room with pale lilac walls, a huge four-poster and a charming watercolour above the fireplace showing Ferdinand and Miranda declaring their love:

> 'Here's my hand.'
> 'And mine with my heart in't.'

Etta was so thrilled about Wilkie and Furious's wins and buoyed up by champagne, she refused to worry about how she was going to pay for it.

Miss Painswick was in 'Trinculo' next door and the Major and Debbie in 'Gonzalo, an honest old counsellor', beyond that. Seth and Corinna, who'd already gone to the theatre, were in 'Ferdinand' beyond that.

'We're in "Stephano",' said Toby, coming out into the corridor. 'Who was he?'

'A drunken butler,' said Alan, 'which figures. Go and get us a drink.'

'Our bed isn't nearly as big as Etta's,' grumbled Phoebe, 'and there are two of us. Shall we see if she'll swap?'

'The vicar's in "Ariel",' said Miss Painswick.

'Who was an irritating little fairy, which figures too,' said Shagger bitchily.

462

'Watch it,' hissed Woody.

'Where the bee sucks/There suck I,' sang Alan.

Bonny was in 'Caliban'.

'Two monsters together,' said Trixie bitterly.

Etta for once was delighted by her appearance in a slinky black skirt and a beautiful white frilled shirt given her by Trixie and Dora for Christmas. She had drenched herself in 24 Faubourg, another Christmas present, which darling Tommy and Rafiq must have bankrupted themselves to give her.

She wished they could have come to the party instead of having to drive the horses home. At least the journey seemed shorter when you had winners on board, and she was so pleased that the two of them appeared to be growing closer.

Everyone had in fact dressed up like mad and, while admiring the vast photos of Seth and Corinna in the foyer of the Royal Shakespeare, excitedly told each other how good they looked, particularly Trixie, dark hair rioting over a fuchsia-pink jacket, tight black satin trousers above pink stilettos.

Then Bonny swanned in with Valent, slim as a wand in another little bleak dress which set off Valent's diamonds, and upstaged everyone. Immediately the theatre audience recognized her and, nudging and squealing like Mrs Wilkinson, thrust their pro-grammes forward to be signed.

'Oh Lord, there's the Bishop of Larkminster, I should have worn a dog collar,' muttered Niall.

Inside, the auditorium was absolutely packed. Although the Major nearly had cracked ribs from being nudged awake by Debbie, for nodding off whenever Corinna wasn't on stage, and Pocock and Joey, who'd been up since five, kept falling asleep, and Phoebe, the Little No Brow, kept tugging Etta's arm – 'What's going on? Who's he?' – the rest of the syndicate enjoyed an awesome performance.

Corinna, in gleaming gold robes, was magnificently command-ing, capricious and beguiling as Cleopatra.

'Is that really our neighbour? Isn't she wonderful?' Tilda whispered to Alan.

Seth, on the other hand, made an unbelievably sexy Antony, prowling around, slit eyes smouldering, as they both set the stage on fire with their passion. Etta felt her crush reignite. There couldn't be a woman who didn't want to clamber on to the stage and rip off his toga.

All the syndicate cheered in the scene when Cleopatra cried:

'Oh happy horse, to bear the weight of Antony!' and Seth, his armour gleaming, could be seen on a back projection riding along on Mrs Wilkinson.

Alan was incredibly proud of his mate.

'Isn't he marvellous?' he whispered to Tilda as he rubbed one hidden hand up and down her slender legs and pretended to make notes with the other. Glancing down the row, he could see Bonny, Trixie, Phoebe, Painswick, Debbie, even Woody and Niall, gazing up enraptured at an oiled, bare-chested, bearded Seth. Etta, having heard his lines, was mouthing every wonderful word along with him.

Valent, a competitive man, noticed this too, and sat wild with envy and jealousy, thinking wistfully that he could never compete with Seth.

'Don't look, Vicar,' cried Painswick, putting her hands over Niall's eyes, when, on a darkened stage, a naked Seth and Corinna could be glimpsed copulating.

'She hasn't shaved,' hissed Debbie.

'Don't interrupt,' snapped the Major, his racing binoculars registering every pubic hair.

'Oh happy whore to bear the weight of Antony,' quipped Alan.

More champagne in the interval kept everyone going.

'Isn't it fantastic?' sighed Etta.

'Jolly good,' agreed Alban. 'Pretty strong stuff. Egyptian women don't behave like that now, more's the pity. Must say, despite the rows, you can see Seth and Corinna still, well, still . . .'

'Fancy each other rotten. I agree, Albie,' said Joey, who was euphoric after huge wins that afternoon.

'I don't agree with you,' said Bonny sharply. 'Seth just happens to be a *very* good, underrated actor. He's so natural, he engages with the audience. Corinna over-dramatizes everything and she's much too old to take her clothes off.'

'Cindy said the same about you,' snapped Trixie and regretted it as Bonny turned on her:

'And what does that mean?'

'When Lester suggested you play Godiva.'

'Don't be ridiculous, Trix,' said Alan hastily. 'Everyone knows Bonny has the most beautiful body in Larkshire.'

'England, Europe, the World, Outer Space,' intoned Trixie.

'Oh look, there's Quentin Letts,' cried Etta.

'Where, where?' said an excited Bonny, temporarily distracted as the five-minute bell called them back.

Where's Valent? wondered a worried Etta, looking at the empty seat at the end of the row.

'O, withered is the garland of the war,/The soldier's pole is fallen . . .' Corinna's whisper of infinite sadness could be heard round the entire theatre, 'And there is nothing left remarkable/Beneath the visiting moon.'

The play's end was so tragic that it took the syndicate a little time to get back into carnival mood.

92

Back at the Tempest Inn, the Prospero Suite turned out to have a mural of great black storm clouds, flashing lightning zipping out of purple waves and mariners being tossed on to the palest apple-green island, on which Miranda and Ferdinand wandered hand in hand, Caliban sulked in the bushes and Prospero could be seen drowning his book.

'Wish I could afford to drown mine,' grumbled Alan.

Tables were grouped around a little dance floor with a disco alternating between golden oldies and the latest pop music in the corner.

'One would expect viols and lutes,' said the Major pompously.

The behaviour of the syndicate, however, grew more like that of Stephano and Trinculo, the play's drunkards, as they tucked into flagons of booze and piles of Shakespearean food: boar's heads, sucking pigs, and mountains of figs and grapes.

'Why no roast swan?' asked Alan.

Cheers greeted the arrival of Seth and Corinna.

'O eastern star!' cried the Major, kissing her hand.

'The lighting was awesome,' Bonny told her, 'you didn't look a day over fifty-five, Corinna. And weren't the sets marvellous? What a good supporting cast and you must be so proud of Seth.'

Unable to come down to earth at once, Etta escaped to her lovely room to tart up.

'I have immortal longings in me,' she sighed.

The play had been so wonderful, but the best part of the day had been Valent hugging her after Wilkie won and his tucking her trousers into her gumboots and feeling his big strong hands on her legs. She hoped they'd have a dance later. She was sure he'd be a terrific dancer, he'd spent enough time dancing round the goal mouth.

She was worried, however, by the way Bonny was leaping to Seth's defence. She hoped Valent wouldn't be hurt and things wouldn't get out of hand. Going downstairs she found a note in her pigeon hole.

'Dear Etta, Sorry, had to fly off to the States to sort out some crisis. Have a good evening, Valent,' and felt winded by a huge charging bullock of disappointment. Turning, she found Seth talking to a boot-faced Bonny.

'Whatever's the matter?'

'Valent's pushed off to the States. The Yanks are kicking up because he's refusing to have his miracle teething gel tested on baby chimps.'

'Quite right,' said Etta warmly.

'For the sake of a few monkeys,' spat Bonny.

'Let's have one other gaudy night,' mocked Seth, linking arms with them both, 'and fill our bowls once more and mock the midnight bell.'

Having acted her heart out, taken a dozen curtain calls and been sought out in her dressing room by the great French director Tristan de Montigny, who was mad about her Phèdre, Corinna wasn't up to another gaudy night and retired to bed after about an hour.

Seth, aware she was an infinitely greater actor than he, psychologically wanted to flaunt his pulling power and decided to play Trixie and Bonny off against each other.

Punishing Trixie for her initial indifference, gradually over the last months he had reeled her in, all over her one moment, pulling up the drawbridge the next, not ringing her for a fortnight, reducing her to desperate uncertainty. Tonight she'd drop into his hand like a ripe fig.

'Such a sad ending,' Miss Painswick was saying to Pocock. 'At least Antony and Cleopatra are together in heaven.'

'Not sure they'd go to heaven,' chuntered Debbie.

'Did you know, in Shakespeare's day, Cleopatra would have been played by a boy in his late teens,' said Tilda.

'Dora's boyfriend Paris would be perfect for it,' said Trixie.

'What bliss,' Niall murmured to Woody.

'Drink up,' said Seth, filling their glasses.

Joey had put his woolly hat on Shakespeare's bust and tucked in his gold pen. He longed to ring Chrissie, but the Fox was laying off staff and she'd be serving in the bar. Pity they weren't celebrating there where they needed the custom.

Painswick was very happy because the yard had done so well. Mrs Wilkinson's health was drunk as often as Seth and Corinna's.

To Alban, not drinking, everyone seemed very silly. But at least he was warm and the food was delicious. Just before the party, Valent had tipped him off about an impending inquiry into the Iraq war.

'With your encyclopaedic knowledge of the Middle East, Alban, you'd be a real asset. And the money'd be great and it's likely to last a year or two. I'm just leaving,' Valent had added, 'but I'd be very grateful if you'd keep an eye on things. Not sure I troost Seth not to let things get out of hand. Don't want Trixie or Etta to get hurt.'

'Certainly not,' said a delighted Alban.

He was now enjoying a lovely bop with Etta. He wondered which room she was in. In the absence of Ione he was far less inhibited, as was Niall, who was dancing with Woody, as was Pocock, who later danced with both Etta and Painswick. Alan danced with Tilda.

The director of *Antony and Cleopatra* rolled up and was soon nose to perfect nose with Bonny.

'You'd make a wonderful Rosalind,' he was saying.

Plastered and forgiving her for being so offhand and cool, the syndicate surged round Amber when she arrived. She had washed her long gold hair and was wearing her clinging catkin-yellow mini, showing off her lovely legs in high-heeled black boots.

'I'd forgotten how gorgeous she was,' murmured Seth to Alan. 'Those awful helmets don't do women jockeys any favours.'

'Wilkie is so gutsy,' Amber was saying. 'Bloody Rogue snatched my whip, we rowed all the way round. Stupid idiot made his run too early, now he's livid he got beat.'

'Beaten,' sighed Alan. 'Did Bagley Hall teach you even less than my daughter?'

'Is Marius coming?' asked Etta.

'Bastard!' snarled Amber. 'After the race he saw my silks were soaked in blood and went berserk because he thought Wilkie had bled. When I explained she'd tossed her head up, practically broken my nose and given me a nosebleed, he just said, "Thank God for that!"'

'Was little House Price OK?' asked Etta.

'Put down on the course,' said Amber dolefully. 'Even Michelle was in floods, probably more because Harvey-Holden just screamed at her, "Forget the horse, just get the fucking bridle back." He's worse than Marius.' Seeing the shocked faces around her, Amber shrugged. 'House Price was lame going down to post. H-H prefers horses to break down on the course rather than at home, so he'll get insurance, not blame.'

Amber took a slug of champagne then looked round the room: 'Which of you lot am I going to shag tonight? Rafiq's gone home with the horses and there's too much competition for Seth.'

'I'm always in love,' Seth was telling a pretty reporter from the *Stage*. 'If not with myself, then with someone else. Was I really good?'

'Awesome, so, so sexy, you ought to be in Hollywood.'

Rogue, who'd won on History Painting, and Marius arrived to more loud cheers. Both were extremely drunk. Marius, talking between clenched jaws, was soon telling Joey and Alan that he'd won enough today for a down payment on an all-weather.

'Then we'll bury that fucker Harvey-Holden.'

The Major, refreshed from his long sleep during the play, was hot to trot. Disappointed Corinna had pushed off, he asked Etta to dance.

'Just like *Strictly*,' called out Phoebe as they quickstepped round. 'I can feel Bump kicking,' she told Debbie, who was guzzling a third helping of sucking pig. 'Do hope it's a boy, it would mean so much to Toby. Wonderful if Valent can produce this gel to stop teething troubles.'

The music switched to the Black Eyed Peas. Rogue, to wind Amber up, had removed Trixie's stilettos, making her two inches smaller than him, and led her off to dance. After some vigorous gyrating, he pressed his cheek against hers and drew her against him. Feeling herself shot into orbit by the biggest tackle in the weighing-in room, Trixie leapt away.

Not as sophisticated as she makes out, thought Rogue in amusement.

'The poetry's wonderful, but I still prefer *Julius Caesar*,' Tilda, reeling from the bliss of not minding being neglected by Shagger, was saying to Alan.

Having escaped Rogue, Trixie took refuge at a table with Woody and Niall, and was reading next Sunday's gospel in Niall's prayer book.

'Jesus cast out devils from two men,' she said furiously, 'and drove them into a herd of swine, which sent the poor demented pigs jumping off a cliff and drowning. Jesus ought to be shot.

Compassion in World Farming and Joanna Lumley would have something to say about that.'

'You have to put it in context, Trixie,' said Niall, 'Jesus and the disciples were Jewish and regarded swine as unclean.'

'The vicar's awfully good-looking without his specs,' murmured Painswick to Etta.

'Come on, Marius, dance with me,' said Amber, swaying in front of him and putting her arms round his neck. She *must* be drunk. He had such a lovely face, so planed and austere, drink never seemed to blur or redden his features.

'You've got to cheer up and stop being so bad-tempered. You've had a brilliant day so enjoy the end of it.' Snakily undulating in front of him, she gazed at his angry closed lips, then she pulled him close and kissed him, on and on and on, until everyone clapped and whooped.

'Nice?' she asked as she broke away.

'Yup. Stop trying to annoy Rogue.'

'Doesn't look annoyed to me.'

Across the floor, Rogue, dancing with Bonny, had undone three buttons of her little bleak dress and was kissing her breastbone.

'Where Pauline's concerned, I want Valent to achieve closure,' Bonny was saying.

'And I want to achieve clothes off,' giggled Rogue, undoing another button.

'Good thing Valent isn't here,' said Painswick disapprovingly, 'or he'd bring in the heavy brigade.'

Suddenly Etta felt very tired.

'Come and join us,' said Seth, who while he watched developments on the dance floor was sitting with the Major and Alban, idly listening to them banging on about moat control. Pulling out a chair for Etta, he filled her glass.

'Bolton's moat's going to flood the village or cause a drought,' warned the Major.

'Someone ought to do something about goat control,' giggled a swaying Trixie, pausing at the table to drain Etta's full glass. 'Chisolm escaped at Warwick and was found in the Owners and Trainers wolfing down all the sandwiches. When the barman threatened to charge her, she charged him. Ha ha ha.' Trixie laughed too long and loudly at her own joke, then collapsed into the chair beside Etta. 'I wish Valent was here.'

'Were here,' said Seth absent-mindedly.

'He always makes things safe.'

'And he could pick up the bill,' said Shagger, waving an empty bottle at the next table. 'We're running out of champagne.'

'That's horrible,' flared up Etta, 'Valent's the most generous man in the world,' then blushed as they all stared at her.

'Valent has picked up the entire bill,' said Joey, switching off his mobile and coming out of the dark corner. 'That's why we're all here.'

'Good God,' exclaimed Alban.

'"For his bounty, there was no winter in't."' Alan glared reprovingly at Shagger.

'Mrs Wilkinson and Valent,' said Seth, a slight edge to his voice as he raised his glass. He had noticed Bonny and Rogue going outside twenty minutes ago to 'have a smoke'.

Bonny didn't smoke, nor did she normally drink.

'Corinna's old enough to be Seth's mother,' she was complaining to Rogue as they returned to the tables.

'Probably *is* his mother,' grinned Rogue, ostentatiously wiping off lipstick. 'Whatever turns you on.'

Bonny's mobile rang. 'Oh Valent, dearest, where are you? I miss you so much.' She ran out of the room.

What a tart, thought Etta. 'I'm off to bed,' she said.

'Must you, darling?' Seth escorted her to the door but didn't discourage her. 'Thank you so much. I'd never have remembered all those words if it hadn't been for you.'

'They sounded glorious.' Then, in the hope that if he were in loco parentis, he might behave better: 'Will you keep an eye on Trixie? Rogue's fun but he's a bit of a wolf.'

'Of course,' said Seth, kissing her.

As the disco launched into 'American Pie', everyone seemed to surge on to the dance floor.

'I'll come with you, Etta,' cried Phoebe. 'You are lucky to have that lovely room all to yourself.'

Etta was too depressed and exhausted to offer to exchange it. She'd just taken off her make-up, cleaned her teeth and got into her nightgown when the telephone rang.

After she picked it up, there was a long pause.

'Etta, this is Alban.' Even longer pause. 'Wonder if you'd like a nightcap? I could bring a bottle round. You looked so awfully pretty tonight.'

'That is so kind,' cried Etta, trying to sound sleepy, 'but it's a bit late. But thank you so, so much, sweet dreams.'

Gosh! Five minutes later, the telephone rang again. It was the Major.

'You were looking very tasty this evening, young lady. Fancy a noggin?'

'With you and Debbie?'

'Old girl's hit the hay, just yours very truly.'

Etta tried not to laugh.

'So sorry, Normie, it's really sweet of you, but I'm a bit tired. Thank you so much for thinking of me.'

Gosh! Two minutes later it rang again.

'Etta,' stammered a hoarse voice. 'Got a big bar of drink here, wonder if you'd like to share it?'

It was Pocock. After all the lovely plants he'd given her, Etta felt a brute saying no.

Collapsing on her bed with hysterical laughter, she fell asleep.

93

The Major – a great warrior brought down by sexual desire – was stalking the passages. He couldn't waste his Viagra. The soldier's pole must not fall. He leapt behind a sculpture of Ben Jonson as he saw Seth knock on Bonny's door and slide inside. He'd be busy for a few hours.

Padding along the passage, moustache erect, the Major found Corinna's door open. He tiptoed inside.

The bedside light was still on, a bottle of champagne on its side dripping its last dregs on to the carpet. A newspaper lay open at a rave review and a lovely picture. The Major folded it neatly.

Corinna was naked, her long legs apart, lips protruding. An arm thrown back on the pillow raised one big floppy breast higher than the other. Her tummy was concave, she was snoring slightly but still looked 'As she would catch another Antony/In her strong toil of grace.'

The Major had been unbearably moved by her on the stage, holding his programme over his erection throughout her last scenes. Overcome by lust, glancing down at his stumpy but loyally erect penis, parting his Paisley dressing gown: 'Long and thin goes right in,' whispered the Major, 'but short and thick does the trick.' Switching off the bedside light, he climbed on top of her.

'Wakey wakey, here comes Snakey or rather Aspie. The nobleness of life is to do thus.' He gave a thrust.

It was not quite necrophilia because Corinna did wake up, groaning with delight as his bristling moustache rearranged her pubic hair as he kissed her between the legs until she was flowing like the Nile. Then, plunging into her, he felt her iron muscles tightening round his cock. By Jove!

' "Give me my robe . . . I have/Immortal longings in me," ' she mumbled.

Did she mean her dressing gown, white and silken and tossed over an armchair? Evidently not, for Corinna held out her arms. The Major had found new heaven and new earth.

Rogue Rogers, clocking with fury Amber going upstairs with Marius, joined forces with Seth, who had plans for a foursome.

'Just like bridge. Shall we ask Alan to join us as well?' asked Rogue.

'Christ no, he's Trixie's father and a journalist and I don't fancy Tilda's teeth on my dick.'

The moment Bonny had come off the telephone to Valent, she had nodded at Seth and disappeared upstairs. Shortly afterwards he had followed her. Registering this, trying not to cry, Trixie fled upstairs to her room, which was called 'Alonso', then realized she'd left her new pink high heels in the Prospero Suite. Opening the door, she went slap into Seth, wearing nothing but a pair of black jeans, from which his body reared sleek, muscular, perfect.

Trixie gave a sob. 'Go away.'

'Silly child.' He shoved her back into 'Alonso', pulling her against him.

He smelt of drink, sweat, Terre, his musky, sweet aftershave and, too late, as his lips came down on hers, of Allure, Bonny's favourite scent.

'Why are you being so mean?' she sobbed.

'I had to punish you,' murmured Seth. 'You were so arrogant, Lady Disdain, you needed bringing into line.'

Then he kissed her properly, as he had done so often when he was coaching her, holding her upright as her knees gave way, pouring bliss into her. As he pulled away, she stammered: 'I've been so unhappy, you were so cool in the play then so cold at the party.'

'Not any more.' Taking her hand, he frogmarched her down the passage. Only when she was inside 'Caliban', with the door shut and locked, did she realize Bonny was lying naked in the centre of a large four-poster.

'No,' gasped Trixie, 'not with her, I can't.'

'Yes, you can, little bitch, you'll adore it.' Bonny's words were slurred, her eyes crossing with drink. 'It takes a woman's touch.' She reached out to Trixie's breasts. 'Beautiful,' she murmured, unbuttoning the pink satin coat, cupping, squeezing, caressing. 'Come on, baby.' Her touch was unbelievably gentle.

'I can't,' Trixie leapt backwards, 'it's gross.'

'That's not very polite,' said a soft Irish voice, 'when you're going to have such a lovely time.'

Next moment, iron arms that had driven and thrust a thousand winners past the post gathered her up, ripped off her leggings and pants and laid her beside Bonny.

'Rogue, how could you?' sobbed Trixie. 'Get me out of here.'

'You'll love it, angel.'

Suddenly a very large four-poster became very small as four heaving bodies took over.

'Get her wet first,' ordered Seth.

So Bonny knelt between Trixie's legs and got to work, tongue and fingers sliding everywhere.

'Stop that,' screamed Trixie, bucking like Furious.

'Just shut up,' snarled Seth, clamping a hand over her mouth to silence her, yet at the same time smiling into her eyes and gently stroking her face with his fingertips. 'Relax, babe, don't let me down.'

The three of them were so beautiful and so practised, Trixie felt she was the only lousy actress in one of Lester Bolton's grubby porn films. She closed her eyes after that, trying to blot out who was shoving what into her, tears, and God knows what else, trickling down her face.

How ironic that when she finally opened her eyes again it was to read, on the wall above, Caliban's loveliest lines.

'Be not afeared. The isle is full of noises,
Sounds, and sweet airs, that give delight, and hurt not.'

She gave a wail of anguish. 'Let me go, please, please.'

'She's not enjoying it, poor kid,' said Rogue. 'Let her go.'

'Give her time,' said Seth, trying to grab her ankle as she leapt from the bed.

As she managed to unlock the door and stumble into the corridor, his last words were: 'If you breathe a word about this, you'll never see me again.'

Etta was so fast asleep, it took several rings before the telephone roused her.

'Darling, so sorry to wake you, it's Alan.'

'W-what, what's happened, is Trixie OK?'

'Fine, fast asleep in "Alonso". Darling, is it OK if I say the party didn't break up until three and then I had a late nightcap or daycap in your room?'

'Whatever for?'

'Carrie rang, doesn't believe I wasn't up to no good, so I said I was with you.'

'Oh Alan, you are her husband.'

'I'll explain, I promise.'

Etta was just dropping off again when the Major rang.

'Normie here, Etta. I woke Debbie up when I came in, is it all right if I say I had a late nightcap with you?'

Seth woke her around five, sounding unusually rattled.

'Etta darling, Rogue and I were having a drink in Bonny's room, "Caliban". Valent rang in and stupid me, not thinking, picked up the telephone. I hung straight up, but I don't want him to put the dogs on me. Can I say I was with you?'

'Seems Valent need not have booked so many rooms,' said Etta acidly. 'Did you keep an eye on Trixie?'

'I saw her into bed, she was fine.'

After he'd rung off, Etta lay back in bed helpless with laughter. She hadn't bothered to draw her curtains. A silver-white semi-circle of moon peered in.

'Join the party,' said Etta. 'There's nothing left remarkable.'

It was not just the moon that had been visiting last night, most of the syndicate seemed to have had a party in her room.

Good thing Dora hadn't been around seeking stories.

Shagger, with no thought of Tilda, had been up all night feasting his eyes on the pink and white face of Toby, as he poured out his heart about the difficulty of holding down his job working for Carrie, and the responsibility of impending fatherhood.

'Is paralysis a symptom of pregnancy, Shag? Phoebe never moves an inch these days to cook supper or iron a shirt.'

On a chair in the corridor, a returning Shagger found Niall's prayer book open and covered in drink rings and, better still, bumped into Niall emerging from Woody's room, which was named 'Sebastian'.

'Where the bee sucks, there suck I,' murmured Shagger, 'Hope you haven't been led into temptation, Vicar.'

'Etta's just left, quite the party animal,' said Niall blithely. 'So little opportunity for the syndicate to get together. Time flew, we were discussing Mrs Wilkinson's campaign.'

'Camp's the operative word,' sneered Shagger.

'Must rush back to Willowwood for Early Service,' cried Niall.

476

Outside, as he waited for a taxi, he called Etta.

'Could you bear to say you were celebrating Mrs Wilkinson's victory with Woody and me in "Sebastian" until dawn?'

'Who's Sebastian?' asked Etta.

94

Amber woke from an excellent night's sleep. She was delighted with Mrs Wilkinson's win yesterday. She had no hangover. She had been miffed last night that no sex had taken place. Marius had twice called her 'Olivia darling', but before he passed out he had promised her a ride on History Painting. This all meant she could face Rafiq, who got so stormily jealous, with a clear conscience and drive down to Exeter without any fear of being breathalysed.

In the old days, she'd have got legless or stoned and gone on the pull. Now she was twenty, she had become so much more mature and professional and was really getting her career together. She must spend more time in the gym so she was really fit to ride History Painting.

It was getting light outside. Hearing desperate sobbing as she passed 'Alonso', she found the door ajar and Trixie slumped on the bed, naked except for a white hotel dressing gown. There was sick all over the carpet and on the pillow. The room reeked of rotten alcohol.

'Go away,' wept Trixie, 'I can't talk. Leave me alone.'

Grabbing a box of tissues, soaking a towel, Amber cleaned up, threw the pillowcase on the bathroom floor and gave Trixie a glass of water.

'Whatever happened?'

'I can't tell, I promised not to.'

Amber sat on the bed, pushing Trixie's damp hair back from her sweating forehead and feeling even more mature.

'Tell me, babe, I won't tell anyone.'

'It's Seth,' howled Trixie. 'I don't know how it happened. I loved him so much. He pursued me and pursued me, ringing me at school, texting me the whole time, sending flowers. I didn't want to know. I kept asking him if he had any attractive grandsons. Gradually I got hooked.'

'Hardly surprising, he's well fit.'

'He was so loving when he was coaching me, then he backed off, didn't answer my calls or texts, all over that vile Bonny. Last night he totally blanked me, but when I came out of my room he was waiting. He kissed me so lovingly and led me back into what I thought was his room and it was Bonny's.'

Trixie was crying so much, Amber could hardly distinguish what she was saying.

'B-b-bonny was on the bed starkers, Seth made her shag me. It was hideous, she kept smacking and pinching me and laughing at me for being crap in bed, then Seth joined in. Oh God, I feel so dirty.' She blew her nose on the duvet cover.

'Not your fault, babe.' Amber felt more mature by the minute as she stroked Trixie's hair. 'Threesome's nothing. Loads of grown-ups do it. Like jumping on everyone else's horses at the end of Pony Club camp. Bloody Seth shouldn't have forced you, even if he was drunk.'

'It was a foursome,' whispered Trixie, 'Rogue was there too.'

'Rogue,' screamed Amber, 'Rogue! The bastard, how dare he, the bastard.'

'He was laughing his head off and very drunk. Bonny kept ticking him off for not concentrating,' confessed Trixie. 'He was always into group sex when he lived in Willowwood.'

Amber couldn't speak for fury, so Trixie carried on.

'Bonny was drunk too. She doesn't drink normally. She showed off terribly, proving how brilliant she was at blow jobs and things, oh yuck.'

'The bitch,' whispered Amber. 'The bitch, how dare she.'

'Please, please don't tell anyone.' Trixie looked terrified. 'Granny would die if it got out. She thinks the world of Seth. And Uncle Martin and Romy would be so censorious. Mummy'd kill me, she doesn't understand love, and Daddy's so wrapped up in Tilda Flood.' The desolation in Trixie's voice for a moment distracted Amber from her own misery.

'Rogue ought to be shot.'

'Please don't say anything to him, or Seth says he'll never see me again. How can one hate someone so much and still adore them?'

Seth last night had been slightly disconcerted, on reaching 'Ferdinand', to be greeted by a sleepily replete Corinna:

'Darling, thank you for the best fuck I have ever had.'

But he cheered up when he read his reviews on a hotel laptop. For once they compared very favourably with Corinna's, which were so good she wouldn't give a stuff who'd been shagging who last night.

Bonny was not so sanguine. After her first furious text, Seth had ordered a fry-up and shut himself in the bathroom to call her.

'Have you seen the internet, such fantastic notices . . . How are you, Bon-Bon, you looked ravishing last night – fun, wasn't it?'

'How could you let that happen?' shrieked Bonny. 'What in hell did you slip in my drink? It could constitute rape, that little tramp is sure to tell Dora and it'll be all over the papers. When I think of the efforts I've made to safeguard my reputation . . . And I can't see Rogue staying shtum either. How *could* you?'

'I'll square Trixie,' reassured Seth.

'And I've had an email from Martin Bancroft, who wants me to be the War on Obesity icon. If word gets out, they'll pull the plug.'

Seth had had enough. 'Oh shut up,' he said, 'I've got a headache. That's room service just arrived. The good news is my agent's just emailed me that there's big interest in you playing Gwendolyn.'

'Gwendolyn Framlingham – over my dead body,' shrieked Bonny, remembering Cindy's dismissive remarks about her boobs. 'I wouldn't work with those two.'

'Wilde's Gwendolyn, dumb-dumb, for the BBC. They want me to play Jack Worthing and, wait for it, they're going to offer Corinna Lady Bracknell. See you.'

Etta lay on her bed giggling hysterically.

'Our revels now are ended,' she read on the wall above, 'These our actors,/As I foretold you, were all spirits and/Are melted into air, into thin air.'

So no one had got off with anyone.

Room service then arrived with an enormous breakfast of bacon, sausages, tomatoes, fried bread, two fried eggs, mushrooms, orange juice, croissants and apricot jam.

Etta rang Miss Painswick.

'Joyce, I've been sent a huge breakfast by mistake, please come and share it with me and have a post mortem.'

'Mr Pocock rang and asked if I'd like a nightcap,' said Miss Painswick smugly as she accepted another mushroom. 'Must have been tiddly but I said no because I'd got my curlers in. Who d'you think got off with who?'

'I don't know,' said Etta, spreading marmalade on a piece of fried bread, 'but the Vicar, Seth, Alan and the Major (yes) rang me and begged me to confirm that they'd spent half the night drinking in my room, which they certainly had not.'

Flattering in a way, she mused, that they'd turned to her, yet rather unflattering was the assumption that if they *had* been with her, their other halves would assume nothing could possibly have occurred.

'Shall we take the sausages back to Priceless,' she said, 'and the rest of the croissants for Pavarobin and the bird table?'

95

Amber hurtled down to Throstledown in a red mist – road rage, Rogue rage. Why was she so devastated? Was it because underneath she believed, despite Rogue's scores of women, that a special spark flickered between them that, if allowed, would flare into a conflagration? Or was it, more shamingly, jealousy? Bonny was stunning and made no secret of her dislike of Amber. Rogue had always said how silly Bonny was, but silliness, when allied to beauty, never deterred men. And why wasn't she jealous of poor victimized Trixie?

Pink aeroplane trails were playing noughts and crosses with the departing stars and a rosy glow in the east echoed her red mist as she stormed up Marius's drive.

In the yard Mrs Wilkinson was banging her food bowl against the wall – winners deserve breakfast. Chisolm, hooves up on the stable door, bleated hello. From Sir Cuthbert's box she could hear singing.

> 'Gaily the troubadour touched his guitar,
> When he was hast'ning home from the war.'

Rafiq often sang the Crusader's song with which she had first taunted him. As he emerged, she noticed the black smudges beneath his bloodshot eyes and how drawn he looked, having done all the hard work last night while she partied. Them and us. But his face lit up when he saw her.

> 'Singing from Stratford hither I come,
> Rafiq Khan, Rafiq Khan, welcome me home,'

sang Amber.

This is reality, she thought, the way Rafiq trembled as he kissed her, so tentatively and then so passionately.

An equally exhausted Tommy, looking rough and pug-like as she came out of History Painting's box, shot back in again, burying her face in his big, dark brown shoulder while he nudged her sympathetically and repeatedly. He was such a kind horse. They both jumped as Amber's voice said, 'Wake up, you two. Can you walk him up to see if he's sound? You'll never guess what: Marius says I can ride him at Wincanton next week.'

Amber schooled History Painting several times in the following days, impressed by how beautifully and carefully he jumped for a big horse. Concentrating on the race ahead, she tried to forget Rogue. But when she rang up Marius to confirm the ride, he denied all knowledge of giving it to her.

'D'you honestly think I'd put you up on my best horse? Rogue's riding him.'

'But you promised at Stratford, you promised.'

'You must have heard wrong.'

'I did not. You must have been too bloody drunk to remember.'

'If you don't learn some bloody manners, you won't even ride Mrs Wilkinson again, so shut up,' howled Marius and hung up on her.

Such was her rage, though aware she was treating with the enemy, Amber texted Shade Murchieson. She hoped Olivia wasn't peering over his shoulder, remembering that the last time they'd met he'd offered her a ride for a ride.

Within ten minutes he'd texted back.

'As promised, a ride for a ride.'

She was to come to his Larkshire house at midnight that evening and ring when she got to the gates. Not a please or thank you: what had she unleashed? To ward off evil, she'd put on her lucky pants, white lycra but with snazzy lace panels, which she'd worn every time she won on Wilkie.

It was a viciously cold night. The stars glittered as though Olivia had scattered Shade's diamonds over the sky. Shade's house, lowering, dark, four-square, like him, loomed up at the end of a long drive.

Shade himself let her into a vast hall with a glossy oak floor and serious pictures. Amber recognized a Lowry and a mournful Landseer hound rather like Alban, alternating with glassy-eyed stags and bisons' heads. Shade, resplendent in black evening trousers and a frilled cream shirt, wore even more scent than she did. His dinner jacket and black tie hung over the chair. The central heating was stifling, even a bra was too hot.

Shade had just flown down from London. Immediately he boasted of the ministers and bankers with whom he's been dining, indicating, as he poured her a glass of Krug, that a peerage was imminent.

He'd taken her into the drawing room to show off more serious pictures on wallpaper covered in glittering humming-birds.

'Cool paper,' murmured Amber.

'Should be at ten thousand a roll.'

'And that's Degas,' said Amber, admiring an oil of jockeys and horses circling at the start.

'I've got another Degas in the Lear.'

'Shame if it crashed.'

'It's insured. Bring your drink upstairs.'

'Am I worth ten thousand a roll?' asked Amber.

'That's what we're going to find out.'

Shade's bedroom – Amber wondered if it were Olivia's too – was even more stifling, an approaching storm indicated by the matching thunder-blue curtains, window seats and wallpaper. A massive stretch of sheepskin rug covered the floor. A vast bed, with a leather headboard, hung with straps was the only furniture.

Shade stood in the doorway staring at her. He was definitely attractive in a repulsive sort of way – well over six foot with dark olive skin and wide but not heavy shoulders. His eyes, large, black-coffee-coloured to keep you awake at night, with heavy lids and the thickest black lashes, had already stripped off her clothes. His smile was all-knowing, predatory, a panther selecting a plump gazelle. His unbuttoned shirt showed the slight reddening of a recent chest wax.

'You're well fit for a geriatric,' taunted Amber.

'You're too young to need the lights dimmed,' quipped Shade, pressing a button and flooding the room with *Romeo and Juliet*.

'Oh lovely.' Amber sang along for a minute, remembering with a stab of anguish singing with Rafiq to an accompaniment of stamping horses on long journeys. What the hell was she doing here?

'A ride for a ride,' Shade reminded her.

'Then you ought to play the Post Horn Gallop instead of Tchaikovsky.'

'And you ought to be in the parade ring. You've always disturbed me, you spoilt, upmarket bitch. Get your kit off.'

As Amber pulled off her pale grey jersey dress and unhooked her bra, Shade breathed a little faster and ran big, warm, pudgy hands over her very high, springy breasts.

'I must be worth a monkey each way,' mocked Amber to hide her sudden excitement, as Shade tugged her roughly into his arms, then kissed her surprisingly expertly, big tongue tickling her lips, sucking then gently exploring, then stabbing her mouth.

Then as he ripped off her lucky pants, sliding equally expert fingers into the sticky cavern between her legs, she cried out with pleasure, adding, 'Oh, lucky Olivia.'

As Shade drew away, she thought he was going to hit her. 'Shut up about Olivia,' he said sharply. 'I said get your kit off.'

As she sat back on the bed, Shade took off his clothes. He was magnificent stripped. He must live in the gym.

'A picture of muscle and good health that caught every eye in the paddock,' mocked Amber. Leaping up, she took a couple of turns round the room, cantering, tossing her long gold mane and calling out, 'Mount please, jockeys, let's go down to post.'

Goodness, that glass of Krug on an empty stomach had unhinged her.

'And that's some post,' she added, seizing his penis, which soared higher than his navel, then running her tongue round the knob. 'Are you going up the inner?'

'Stop making stupid jokes,' snarled Shade.

Grabbing her, he chucked her on the bed and without pre-amble thrust his penis deep inside her, back and forth until she cried out in amazement and a little pain. But she still kept up the patter.

'Don't go to the front too early.'

'Going too firm for you?' countered Shade, giving a few more thrusts. Then he pulled out and rolled on his back, pulling her on top of him, giving her two very, very hard slaps on her bottom.

'Ouch!'

'Stop playing silly buggers then and prove you're good enough to ride my horse.'

'It was a done deal,' hissed Amber, burying her teeth in his shoulder, 'a ride for a ride, or I'm going home.'

'OK, OK,' conceded Shade, as she began to move, crouching low over him, thrusting and driving, muscles gripping his cock with all her strength, riding the finish of her life.

She was gratified to see his heavy eyelids closed, to hear the groans of pleasure, as she kissed the bite mark on his scented shoulder and tried to read if the tattoo said 'Olivia'.

Suddenly, he wriggled out from under her. Sitting on the edge of the bed, he made her kneel between his legs, ramming his cock into her mouth, shoving with real violence until she gagged. Thank God she hadn't eaten since breakfast. She couldn't scream.

Just before she choked to death, Shade had changed positions, making her lie back on the bed, tipping her legs right over in a U-turn. Her knees rested on her shoulders, her toes against the leather headboard, so he could ride his own finish, forcing deep inside her, then, ramming a long finger up her exposed anus to tighten the fit, he exploded inside her. For a moment he let his full weight collapse on her, then he rolled away.

'I thought you'd rammed the winning post up me as well,' gasped Amber.

Shade laughed or, rather, flashed his teeth.

'Well done, definitely winners enclosure.' Then he added brusquely, 'Now get dressed. I've got a conference call from Beijing,' he glanced at his vast watch, 'in a few minutes. Use the bathroom in there, then hop it.'

Amber didn't move. 'A ride for a ride. I need proof.' There was steel in her voice.

'I gave you my word.'

'Doesn't mean a thing.'

For a second they glared at each other. She was so beautiful, so golden against his dark blue silk pillows, and so fearless. Shade was more jolted than he cared to admit.

'My mother's a very dangerous journalist,' said Amber. 'My father works for the BBC. You don't mess with us, Mr Deadly Night Shade.'

She wasn't moving. Shade was in a hurry. Even though it was the middle of the night, he reached for his mobile and punched out a number. The other end took some time to answer.

'H-H, good morning. Change of plan. That new Irish horse running at Wincanton next week, what's it called? Oh yes, Bullydozer. I want you to put up Amber Lloyd-Foxe.'

Amber could hear the howl of protest rising to a crescendo at the other end.

'It's my fucking horse, I say who rides it.' Shade hung up.

'Bullydozer is a very good name for its owner,' said Amber.

'Did you enjoy that?' Once more Shade's hand slid between her legs.

'Not a lot. There is something called the clitoris, in case you'd forgotten.'

'I know. Tonight was for me. Next time, I'll make you yell your head off. Now bugger off.'

Rafiq was all delicacy, Shade all brutality, she reflected.

As she drove out through the gates, she heard his helicopter revving up, and swore as she realized she'd left her lucky pants behind.

96

Amber was terrified Shade would rat. Declarations have to be in by ten o'clock on the previous day, reaching the *Racing Post* website around lunchtime. Checking with shaking hands and pounding heart, Amber yelled with joy. Ten horses were entered in the 3.15 Edward Thring Cup at Wincanton tomorrow, including Bafford Playboy ridden by Killer, Rogue on History Painting, Awesome Wells on Count Romeo and Amber Lloyd Foxe (who had the 7-lb advantage of being a conditional jockey) on Bullydozer.

If only Dora was in England to tell all the world. Amber rang her father, who was thrilled.

'I'll try really hard to get down there. Saturday afternoon's a bit of a bugger. So much going on.'

Amber was gratified to be emailed by an agent nicknamed 'Special' Donaldson, who she'd been pestering for months.

'Good luck in the Edward Thring. Let's do lunch.'

The big time – at last. If only she hadn't left her lucky pants at Shade's.

Marius, who'd been to Sandown the previous day and stayed overnight to look at a couple of horses, was going straight to Wincanton. Amber, knowing Harvey-Holden wouldn't welcome her at Ravenscroft, took advantage of Marius's absence to ride out at Throstledown on the Saturday morning.

Everyone was transfixed with interest.

'How in hell did you swing that ride?' asked Josh, as he legged her up on to a new, worried-looking bay mare called School Fees.

'Natural talent,' crowed Amber.

'You're mad,' said Tresa, as they rode out through the drizzle. 'H-H will murder you, he's psychotic about anyone involved with

Mrs Wilkinson. Marius will murder you for riding one of Shade's horses, particularly if you beat Rogue and History Painting.'

'I've beaten Rogue often enough,' scoffed Amber.

Rafiq said nothing. He and Amber had already rowed furiously about her taking the ride.

'H-H has a different agenda.'

'Marius should have kept his promise.'

'Why he promise in first place?' hissed Rafiq, who had heard rumours of goings-on at Stratford.

As they pounded up the gallops, past bleached fields and beech trees flashing their silver trunks and crows' nests in the rising sun, Amber really got to work on young School Fees.

'Go easy,' shouted Josh in his new role as head lad, as he caught up with her. 'You're not riding a race yet.'

'I'm not getting a chance to ride Bullydozer beforehand,' shouted back Amber, who had been studying videos of the horse with declining confidence. He looked a brute and a huge one at that.

As they rode home, a deer shot out of a copse, School Fees spooked and Amber, who'd been fretting about seeing Rogue again, flew through the air. There was a sickening crunch as she landed in the long blond grasses, then pain blotted out all thoughts of Rogue. Suppressing a groan and cursing, she struggled to her feet as Rafiq, who'd caught School Fees, cantered back, his face full of concern.

'You OK?'

'Absolutely fine.'

'Let me look.' He jumped off.

'It's OK for fuck's sake,' lied Amber, her wrist aloft. She couldn't miss the ride of a lifetime.

By the time she got to Wincanton, her wrist was agony and very swollen. She didn't let on to Tommy or Rafiq, who would have stopped her riding. Instead she took four Nurofen and swore Awesome Wells to secrecy.

'Are you sure you're up to it? Bullydozer pulls double, no, quadruple,' warned a worried Awesome as he bound up her wrist with vet wrap behind the lorry. 'I must remember not to tell Bertie that new mare Marius sold him, which I've got to ride in the two forty-five, is fucking useless.'

So's my wrist, thought Amber.

Having weighed out, in return for Shade's magenta and orange silks, she handed over her saddle to Harvey-Holden. She was shocked by the venom in his twitching, sallow face, the quivering hands itching to throttle her, the acid sourness of his breath.

489

'It'll be the last time you wear these colours,' he hissed. 'What in hell did you give Shade to get this ride? You may be OK on clapped-out donkeys. Bullydozer's in a different league. You just see how you fuck up,' and he was gone.

Jolted to the core, Amber managed to wriggle into her body protector and the silks, pulling the sleeves down over her vet wrap and wrist brace, before the valet helped her on with her breeches, boots and helmet. In the mirror her face was grey and sweating. Was she insane to carry on?

Then Rogue erupted into the weighing room in just dark blue underpants and leapt on to the scales.

'Traffic's so bad, I had to undress in the car and streak through the car park,' he told his grinning valet, who was waiting with his racing clothes.

In order to put on the transparent ladies' tights jockeys wear under their breeches, Rogue whipped off his dark blue underpants. Amber fled.

Entering the paddock in a haze of pain, she saw Bullydozer, a huge dark bay bucking bronco. Michelle and Vakil stood on either side of him, hanging on to a lead rope attached to a vicious bit.

Michelle, with Harvey-Holden's encouragement, had confined Bullydozer to his box for two days and stuffed him with oats. This had necessitated Vakil twice clouting him across the head with a spade before they could get a bridle on him earlier. Determined to win the turnout, Michelle had also rubbed baby oil into his face, which made it shine but had also made his reins slippery.

Bullydozer was the biggest horse in the paddock and demonstrably the most bloody-minded and out of control.

'How's Wilkie, how's Chisolm?' the punters called out to Amber.

'Left them at home.'

Billowing black clouds promised rain any minute. There was Shade, looking much less attractive in a belted camel-hair coat and a fedora, and Olivia looking bleak, both talking to evil Killer, who was also wearing Shade's colours to ride the mighty Bafford Playboy.

Big bright bay Playboy, despite his frivolous name, had grown into a bully like Shade, his owner. In the yard at home and out in the field, other horses nervously deferred to him. On the racecourse he was equally determined to assert his mastery, as was his jockey, Killer.

Killer wanted his revenge on Amber for getting him suspended for ten days at Cheltenham. Both he and Rogue were on one hundred and twenty-five winners apiece.

As Rogue sauntered into the paddock, the crowd nudged each other and smiled. History Painting's owners, Brigadier Parsons, his wife and two pretty daughters, surged forward adoringly to hear the master's words.

Beside them, Marius, as grim as the day, was deliberately ignoring his ex-wife and Amber.

'What are you planning, Rogue?' asked the Brigadier.

'To make all. A few will do the same, a few could pop out later. History Painting has won from the front and will do so again.' He whacked his boots with his whip.

'Enjoy your ride, hope it goes well, Rogue, come back safely,' exhorted the Brigadier's pretty ladies.

Oh shut up, thought Amber, as she nervously approached Harvey-Holden, who was, however, charm itself when he spoke to her in front of Shade and Olivia:

'Remember to hold Bully up for the first circuit at least. He's fast but he may not stay, so make a late run.'

Shade put a big leather-gloved hand on Amber's shoulder. He'd enjoyed their last ride and planned another.

'Good luck, Amber.'

Bullydozer won the turnout and, kept back to be photo-graphed with Michelle, was the last to leave the parade ring. Feeling Amber on his back, he went up and nearly tipped over, squealing with pain as Vakil swore and jerked on his mouth to bring him down.

'Have fun,' Michelle whispered evilly to Amber. 'Nice change to have someone Olivia hates more than me.'

As she and Vakil unclipped their lead ropes, Bullydozer took off, thundering diagonally across the golf course in the middle of the track, down to the start.

'I got a birdie here once,' Awesome was saying, calling out, 'Are you OK, Amber?' as she hurtled past him, her good hand hauling helplessly on the reins.

Bullydozer was a hand bigger than History Painting. As Rogue reached out, catching the horse's reins to steady him as he passed, Bullydozer nearly pulled him out of the saddle.

'Morning, Miss Lloyd-Foxe,' said Rogue, righting himself. Then, noticing how pale she was: 'What did you and Marius get up to at Stratford?'

'Much less than you,' spat Amber. 'Let go of my horse. Poor little Trix, how could you?'

Rogue was fazed only for a second.

'We were all hammered. You should have joined us.'

'Don't be so fucking stupid. Trixie's only fifteen, you've crucified her.'

'She didn't stay long. Bonny was sensational, she'd get an Oscar in one of Bolton's erotic fantasies.'

Amber had no strength to slap his mocking face.

'You're just a tart.'

They reached the start, the banter flying as the jockeys circled.

'I'm going to get two hundred winners by the end of March,' boasted Rogue, patting History Painting and undoing the bottom plaits of his mane.

'How d'you know?' asked Awesome admiringly.

'I've put ten grand on myself, does concentrate the mind.'

The starter looked at his watch:

'Who's going to make it?'

'I am,' said Killer, glaring round.

'I might not,' muttered Amber as Bullydozer leapt about. Amber daren't ride him down to look at the first fence in case he took off.

She caught Killer staring in her direction, pale squinting wolf eyes hidden by his goggles, thin lips curling in an evil smile. Amber tugged her silk sleeve down over her glove. The Nurofen was wearing off.

Up went the tapes, Bullydozer set off quick enough to win the Derby.

'Too fucking fast, I'm making it,' yelled a furious Killer, particularly when a totally out-of-control Bullydozer cut straight across him, barging into Playboy like a drunken dodgem car.

Killer didn't take prisoners of either sex.

'Get off my line, you fucking cunt.'

Changing tactics, Rogue decided to cruise at the back on History Painting so he could once more feast his eyes on Amber's delectable bottom – they must suspend hostilities. Seeing her tugging on Bullydozer's mouth, he felt a stab of fear. She was pulling one-sided, having no effect. Slowly, slowly Killer was edging her into the rail dividing the steeplechasing track from the hurdle track, which ran along beside it. They were out in the country, hidden by a clump of trees and a small building where the stable lads camped out. Any moment Killer was going to ram an elbow into Amber's ribs and hoist her over the rail: 'You're going hurdling, you bitch,' and Amber would have no strength in her right hand to tug Bullydozer back. To his horror, Rogue realized the wings of the next fence were hurtling towards her. She was going to crash into them.

492

Killer was drifting back to the right so no one could blame him. Amber had lost her balance, and her saddle – hadn't Michelle tightened the girths sufficiently? – was slipping to the left.

Picking up his whip, Rogue thrust History Painting forward, forcing their way between Amber and Killer, reaching up because Bullydozer was so much bigger, grabbing Amber's wrist so she screamed in agony, tugging her upright, grabbing her reins with his other hand, holding her until she managed to right herself, as somehow, taking most of the brushwood with them, they survived the next fence.

'You stupid, stupid bitch, what have you done?' yelled Rogue, then glancing down he saw the wrist brace and vet wrap. 'Jesus.'

'Let me go, go on,' gasped Amber, whiter than the daytime moon, as they hurtled round the bend into the home straight.

Fortunately Bullydozer had realized the race was longer than the Derby and decided to pull himself up. So Rogue, mindful of his two hundred wins, beetled off, made one of his spectacular last-minute runs and mugged an enraged Killer and Playboy on the line.

Killer and an even angrier Harvey-Holden called for a stewards' inquiry. Amber had cut across Playboy and bumped him several times. Without this he'd have been several more lengths ahead and Rogue would never have caught him.

'Neither Marius nor Shade will ever put you up again,' gloated Harvey-Holden. He didn't want to make too much fuss in case Rogue reported Killer for intimidating Amber.

Amber sorted things by fainting in the middle of the inquiry and the strapped-up wrist was discovered.

'I'm so sorry,' she stammered when she came round, 'I had a fall on the gallops this morning. I thought it was OK to ride. I was wrong, I couldn't hold him up, he barged into Playboy.'

An X-ray revealed a broken wrist and broken thumb.

The stewards agreed there wasn't much point suspending her. According to the course doctor, the wrist would have to be pinned and she wouldn't be riding for at least three months anyway, so they put it down to unintentional interference.

'You've been very stupid,' the Stipendiary Steward, who was a friend of her father's, told her sternly. 'If it doesn't heal right, you have only yourself to blame. And I hope you'll be suitably grateful to Rogue, who saved your life or at least your riding career. He not only pulled you straight but managed to pull up your horse – one of the most spectacularly brave pieces of—'

'The horse was tired. He pulled himself up,' said Amber sulkily.

'Don't be so ungrateful,' snapped the Stipe.

493

97

Amber spent a week in Larkminster hospital and in a lot of pain after an operation to set and pin her wrist and thumb. But the pain in her heart was worse. No matter how many flowers and cards poured in from friends and from the public – 'Please get well soon, Mrs Wilkinson needs you' – she kept thinking of how she had put her life on hold, determined to make it as a jockey, and if she were off for at least four months, as the doctors now forecast, everyone would forget her. She was suicidal.

Marius, though delighted History Painting had won the Edward Thring Cup, was not going to forgive her for riding for Harvey-Holden. Nor was Shade:

'How dare you ride with a broken wrist, making me look a prat.'

'Special' Donaldson had cancelled lunch, and who was now going to ride Mrs Wilkinson?

No matter how much Tommy and Rafiq and her sweet father, Billy, tried to reassure her this was just a blip in her career, Amber sank into despair.

Matters weren't helped by Rogue all over the papers and television winning Ride of the Week for his gallant rescue, or when Amber's unprincipled, scoop-crazy mother, Janey, interviewed Rogue for the *Daily Mail*. THE BRAVE SIR GALAHAD WHO SAVED MY AMBER'S LIFE was accompanied by sexy photographs of Rogue, stripped to the waist, flaunting his six-pack, highlighted brown hair tousled, kingfisher-blue eyes flashing.

Having just clocked his one hundred and thirtieth winner, Rogue was quoted as saying: 'One should always be ready to help young and inexperienced riders.'

'Sir Gala-had everyone in sight,' howled Amber when she read the piece, 'how dare he call me young and inexperienced . . .'

She wasn't even mollified when Rogue sent her two dozen red roses.

On the Saturday after the accident, she was visited at midday by an old schoolfriend. Milly Walton was looking so urban chic and ravishingly little girlish, in a pale pink smock and brown leggings. Perching on Amber's bed, reading her cards and eating her grapes, Milly tried to divert her with London gossip about all their mutual friends and the parties Amber had been missing, which she might now have time to go to.

As Amber was still looking wintry and bored, Milly tried to interest her with the information that she had a new boyfriend – a jockey.

'You're mad,' snapped Amber. 'For a start, jockeys are useless in bed. They're only interested in coming as fast as they can.'

'This one is fantastic,' protested Milly.

'Can't be a jockey then.'

'He is. He's called Dare Catswood.'

'Dare's an amateur,' said Amber scornfully. 'Amateurs are different, they have to work harder for a ride.'

Milly giggled. 'Well, I think he's hot.'

'Jockeys get thoroughly spoilt.' Amber was on a roll now. 'Once they've got a licence everyone wants to hop on them, like a bus in the rush hour.'

'You *have* changed,' sighed Milly. 'At school you were crazy about Rogue Rogers, had pictures of him all over your study . . .'

'Rogue lives up to his name, he's really like a bus in the rush hour, just comes more often and in more lanes. Even the roses he gave me got brewer's droop in twenty-four hours. He's the worst of the lot.'

In mid-rant, Amber suddenly clocked that Milly wasn't laughing any more, just looking horrified and deeply embarrassed.

As she swung round, Amber's heart failed, for standing in the doorway was Rogue. Beneath the peak of his blue baseball cap, on which was printed the words 'Italian Stallion', his eyes were shadowed and tired, his laughing face unutterably bleak.

'R-rogue,' stammered Amber, 'what are you doing here?'

'On my way to Chepstow, thought you might like these.'

He threw a huge bunch of freesias on the bed, followed by Richard Dunwoody's autobiography.

'On second thoughts, not,' he took back the book, 'you don't seem to like jockeys.'

'She was only joking,' stammered Milly. 'I know she's a huge

495

fan really, so am I. She always took the piss out of everyone when we were at school.'

'Perhaps she should go back there and learn some manners.'

'Rogue, I'm sorry,' wailed Amber, but Rogue had turned on his heel, slamming the door behind him.

Amber cried for the first time since she broke her wrist, howling even louder when Milly discovered a little card inside the freesias, 'Darling Amber, I'm so sorry, please come back soon. All my love Rogue,' in Rogue's handwriting.

She was utterly inconsolable.

98

Dora, having passed eleven GCSEs, decided to leave Bagley Hall because she was fed up with her mother moaning about the fees. Choosing to take a gap year, she was in New York in late February, staying with her half-sister Sienna and her husband Zac, when she received a long email from Alan:

Darling Dora, we all miss you. Hope you're fine. I thought I'd give you an update on the syndicate. I'm really pissed off because my Life of Wilkie has hit the buffers again because Amber's been sidelined for four months with a broken wrist and there's no one to ride Wilkie – who's due to run at Rutminster early next month.

The tragedy is that the last time she ran and won, the syndicate had such a fantastic time afterwards at the après stage *Antony and Cleopatra* party, they're frantic for another opportunity to behave badly.

From what I can gather, Alban and the Major both pulled Corinna. Amber disappeared upstairs with Marius. I draw a veil over Painswick and Pocock. Seth was off pleasuring Bonny and God knows who else and the Vicar and Woody are looking very smug.

Valent pushed off before the orgy, said he had a crisis at work, but I guess, being an alpha male, he was pissed off with all the women drooling over Seth, who incidentally was magnificent as Antony.

On the luvvie front, Corinna, on the grounds that Dame Judi shines in comedy, agreed to play Lady Bracknell in a BBC production of *The Importance of Being Earnest*, due to start any minute, only to discover that Seth's playing Jack Watling and, far, far worse, Bonny's been cast as Gwendolyn.

Corinna proceeded to throw her toyboys out of the pram, screaming that Bonny was far too lower middle to play her daughter. Seth, being a bitch, told Bonny, who threw a hissy fit, particularly when Seth suggested she use the same voice coach she employed to iron out Valent's Yorkshire accent.

Corinna, meanwhile, to bone up on her patrician vowel sounds, keeps inviting a thoroughly over-excited Alban round for drinks.

Tomorrow to fresh Woodies and parsons new.

God knows what a den of depravity we've unleashed.

One big piece of gossip is that Collie's left Harvey-Holden – they fell out because Collie didn't like the way H-H treated his horses and the fact he hired Michelle the moment Marius fired her. Anyway, Collie's up-sticked and gone to work in Ireland. Harvey-Holden's made sinister Vakil his head lad. I think the RSPCA should be told.

But to go back to our syndicate, the upshot is they're all frantic for another jolly so they can misbehave again. Wilkie is booked to run at Rutminster in ten days' time. Marius is tearing his hair out over who to put up. There's talk of Awesome Wells. Any ideas? Please come home soon. Love to Paris

Dora emailed back instantly:

All that stuff must go in Wilkie's biography – particularly the Major and Corinna – wow! The only person to ride Wilkie should be Rafiq, they'd adore each other and he's a fantastically gentle rider. All love Dora.

Alas, more gossip had reached Rafiq that Amber had got off with Marius at Stratford. Raging with jealousy, Rafiq had been particularly truculent and bolshy towards Marius, which didn't predispose Marius to reward him with any rides, especially as Furious had done a leg and been confined to even more bad-tempered box rest than Amber.

Unwilling to risk a tongue-lashing if he approached Marius direct, Alan asked Etta, who was so fond of Rafiq, to plead his cause.

99

Valent Edwards suspected he spent so much time abroad because he missed Pauline, most agonizingly when she wasn't there when he returned home to England.

As he flew back to Willowwood at the beginning of March, to sadness was added exhaustion. Over the past five years, among his myriad activities had been sorting out a wayward New York bank called Goldstein Phillipson, who'd originally invited him on to their board to add gravitas.

Now they were making a fortune, he was revolted by the obscenely large bonuses the board were intending to pay themselves, including him. So Valent had resigned, refusing to accept the bonus. His fellow directors were outraged, terrified that once word of his defection got out, shares would plummet, so he'd agreed the news should be kept from the press for a few weeks.

Valent felt very bad about abandoning the junior staff of Goldstein Phillipson, who had become friends on his many visits. As a condition of his temporarily keeping quiet, he had asked if his bonus could be divided between these junior staff, but he wasn't very hopeful. The fights had been bloody.

He was also depressed about Bonny. If she was going to spend the next few months filming or touring with Seth, the inevitable must happen, if it hadn't already. Yet she swore she loved him, was angling for marriage, and made scenes if he suggested things weren't right.

'It's a generational thing, Valent. You cannot expect me to engage with football.'

She had great plans for him to help her develop her own make-up, fragrance and clothes labels. 'Bonny Richards should be as universally known as Kate Moss.'

Arriving at Badger's Court late in the afternoon, he was cheered to see that the great sweep of snowdrops had been replaced by gold and purple carpets of crocuses, pale blue scillas and an emerging host of white daffodils. Etta had been at work.

'And then my heart with pleasure fills,/And dances with the daffodils,' Valent quoted happily.

He was still reading a poem from the Everyman anthology every day, no longer just to upstage Seth but because he really enjoyed them. Today, most appropriately where Goldstein Phillipson was concerned, he'd read a poem by George Herbert which started:

'I struck the board, and cried, No more.'

There still seemed to be a lot of rubble and bulldozers around but at least his octagonal office in the cockpit was finished. He gave a sigh of satisfaction. Joey had framed and hung the signed photographs of Gordon Banks outwitting Pelé in the World Cup, and of the Colombian goalie who had prevented an England victory with a legendary scorpion save, kicking up his legs behind him to stop the goal.

Most importantly, on his desk was the photograph of his son Ryan, his wife Diane and the grandchildren. Valent had been working on a new lighter-but-tougher football boot to prevent so many injuries to the vulnerable top of the foot.

He longed to involve Ryan in the marketing. He had dreams of buying Searston Rovers, the fast-rising local football team, and putting Ryan in as manager. Ryan, however, was still violently opposed to Bonny and a more chilling voice inside him said if the all-too-handsome Ryan came back into the fold, Bonny would surely ensnare him.

'Christ,' Valent opened a can of beer. 'I strook the board and cried no more.'

He looked out towards Etta's bungalow. As he'd planted those stupid trees to protect Bonny's privacy (goings-on, more like) he couldn't see if her lights were on. Dribbling a football, signed and given him by Bobby Moore, across the room, he opened a window and heard robins and blackbirds singing in dark trees silhouetted against an orange sunset.

There was a thump as a plump, fluffy black cat landed on his desk, mewing importantly. Her rusty purr was more like a crow's caw as she weaved around him, butting his arm, blinking at him with fearless lemon-yellow eyes.

Valent helped himself to another beer from the fridge and poured the cat a saucer of milk, which she sniffed and rejected.

'Faddy cow,' said Valent, and dialled Etta's number.

500

Digging her garden in the twilight, Etta was soothed by the stream that hurtled over yellow and brown pebbles and brushed against the first primroses and coltsfoot. There was a soft violet blur on the trees, the first little green kiss curls on the willows. Birds, who had fallen on her bird table a week ago and emptied it in half an hour, were now abandoning it to sing to their loves. She was gratified that Pavarobin, who now took crumbs from her hand, had not deserted her. He was keeping a shiny black eye out for worms as she turned over the liver-chestnut Cotswold earth.

It was a few moments before she realized the telephone was ringing and rushed inside.

'Valent here.'

'How lovely. How are you?'

'Fine,' lied Valent. 'Have you lost a furry black cat?'

'It's Gwenny, Harold Pocock's cat actually, but she's sort of moved in.'

'If I had sticking-out ribs or one eye, or no collar, would you rescue me?'

'Of course.'

'Would you like an Indian?'

'I'd rather have a Pakistani.'

'You what?'

'Sorry, that was silly. I didn't mean to be ungracious,' Etta took a deep breath and plunged straight on, 'but, oh Valent, I truly believe Rafiq would be the best person to ride Wilkie at Rutminster next week. He's such a beautiful, sensitive rider and he's having such a rough time. He loves Amber and she's being a bit of a "b" to him. Amber told me she didn't sleep with Marius at Stratford. What a lovely hotel that was, thank you, but Rafiq's convinced she did, so he's being stroppy with Marius, who's punishing him by not giving him any rides and about to sack him. But I know Marius would listen to you, he really respects you.'

As he'd lent Marius the money to pay for his new Gold Cup jumps and his all-weather track, and guaranteed his overdraft and bought Furious, Marius should, thought Valent.

'OK, I'll have a word. Now, would you like an Indian?'

'Yes please. How lovely.'

'Any preferences?'

'I adore meat and spinach and prawns, nothing too hot,' and then she burst out laughing. 'Although you wouldn't think so after that dreadful chilli I gave you last summer.'

'I'll be round in half an hour.'

Etta panicked. She hadn't walked Priceless yet but as it had started raining, he was refusing to leave the comfort of the sofa.

Washing-up from Poppy and Drummond's supper was still in the sink; washing to be ironed hung from the radiator, and Gwenny's and Priceless's half-eaten bowls were still on the floor. As she used to shut the kitchen door to hide the chaos during dinner parties at Bluebell Hill, now she shoved bowls, washing up and washing into the kitchen cupboard. Even so, she only had time to scrub the earth out of her nails, clean her teeth and slap some base on her flushed face. She had to tip her bottle of 24 Faubourg on its side to press out the last drop.

Oh help, was it too forward to put on scent? Better than smelling of cat food. Anyway she was far too old for anyone to fancy her. She ought to light the fire, and as it was the end of the month there was only half a bottle of cheap white in the fridge.

Wearing just one Ugg boot, Etta hopped outside to pick some pink polyanthus for the table and ran slap into Valent. He had put on a red jersey and looked tired and lined, and, to Etta's relief, much less powerfully glamorous. Could she detect a faint trace of aftershave over the curry fumes? But then he probably wore an expensive brand that had lasted since this morning.

He dumped a carrier bag full of foil dishes, two bottles of red and Gwenny on the kitchen table, and accepted a glass of Etta's white. Priceless jumped down, flashed his teeth at Valent, but, deciding he didn't like curry, retreated to the sofa.

Gwenny, unable to find her bowl, mewed indignantly round the kitchen cupboard, which also contained the vases, so Etta had to put the polyanthus in her tooth mug.

'God, this is a treat,' she sighed, as she unpacked prawns, tikka masala, lamb rogan josh, spinach, mixed vegetables, and a paddy field of rice. 'I'm so used to packed dinners for one,' she went on. 'I wonder what they put in them,' she squeezed her waist, 'I've never had such a spare tyre before.'

Dinners for one, thought Valent, ashamed at the tears pricking his eyes.

'Here's something to fatten you up. Put it in the fridge,' he said, handing her a chocolate tart and a half-pint of cream.

'How deliciously decadent,' cried Etta. 'I won't tell Bonny. Gosh, sorry, I didn't mean . . . Bonny's lovely, and I so love my Ugg boots. I'm going to wear them all through the summer.'

'Good, and you've made this place right cosy,' said Valent, looking round.

And big as you are, you don't dwarf it, thought Etta, as Valent tugged the red armchair for her and the sofa, plus Priceless, for himself up to the kitchen table. Taking a corkscrew, he opened one of the bottles of red.

'Thank you so much for putting us up in such a fabulous hotel in Stratford,' gabbled Etta, as she spiked up a large prawn.

To her amazement, as he filled up her glass, Valent asked if she'd enjoyed 'Miranda', her room, and her four-poster. Did he keep tabs on everything?

'It was heavenly, but a bit wasted on me. I mean, I'm sure there were couples more deserving who could have enjoyed it.'

'Evidently,' said Valent dryly. 'I gather everyone ended up having a party in your room.'

'Er, well, yes. Do have some of this chicken tikka, it's such heaven and the wine's gorgeous.' Etta took a gulp, praying he wasn't going to quiz her. Perhaps the only reason he was there was to cross-question her about Bonny.

'You moost have all drunk tap water,' persisted Valent. 'You didn't order any room service for your party, or put anything on your bill.'

'Some people,' stammered Etta, 'did get a bit carried away. You provided so much lovely drink at the party that they asked if they could say they had a nightcap in my room.'

'Who?' insisted Valent.

'Oh well, the Major and Alban and people, but I'm so old, their wives wouldn't be remotely jealous anyway.'

Valent looked at Etta, her big dark blue eyes imploring him not to push her, little white teeth biting her lower lip instead of the prawn and spinach on her fork.

'Roobbish,' he said, and reaching across and running a finger down her blushing, anguished face, proudly quoted:

'No spring nor summer beauty hath such grace
As I have seen in one autumnal face.'

'Oh how kind.' Etta turned even pinker than the polyanthus.

'I've been stoodying your poetry book, except that Bonny would say I should have rhymed "one" with "sun", not said "wan". There's nothing "wan" about your face. Eat oop.'

'Everyone pronounces things differently,' said Etta. 'Alban says "orf" and "corsts".'

She was about to tell him Corinna was trying to ape his and Ione's accent for Lady Bracknell, then decided it was a bit close to Bonny being too common to play Corinna's daughter.

'You've chosen all my favourites,' she cried instead, spooning up lentils.

Valent then said he'd enjoyed the extract from *The Canterbury Tales* so much he'd bought the book, and wasn't Alban exactly

503

like Chaucer's perfect gentle knight, even to his wearing understated camouflage clothes.

'What other poems do you like?' asked Etta.

' "I struck the board, and cried, No more," ' said Valent, and he told her about Goldstein Phillipson and how guilty he felt abandoning middle management and the younger staff.

'Was that the crisis you had to sort out when you couldn't make the party after *Antony and Cleopatra*?' asked Etta. 'We all missed you so much, particularly Trixie.'

Not meeting Etta's eyes, or admitting he couldn't bear everyone drooling over Seth, who was so good-looking and so much younger, Valent lied that it had been about the new lighter-but-tougher football boots. Then, his tongue loosened by wine, he told her how he longed to work with Ryan again.

'I luv him, Etta, and I used to talk to him every day when Pauline was alive. I miss him, but he doesn't approve of me and Bonny.'

He was about to say how lucky she was having children living nearby, but having earlier seen Martin bossily pounding the streets with Jude the Obese in the twilight, he decided she wasn't and moved on to the possibility of buying Searston Rovers.

'They have a wonderful player called Feral Jackson.'

'How do you know that?' asked Valent, impressed.

'He's a friend of Dora's. Wish she'd come back, she's so sweet.' Etta got the chocolate tart out of the fridge and cut a large slice for him and, 'bugger Bonny', tipped cream all over it.

'Do you miss football?' she asked. 'You were brilliant at it.'

'Playing in goal taught me to watch and concentrate,' explained Valent. 'It's dangerous, you get kicked in the face, and in the hands when you fling yourself at people's feet, everywhere really. And it's not spectacular. Everyone remembers the forty-yard goal or the score backwards over the head, but not the great saves.'

'Unless you're Gordon Banks,' said Etta, who'd been shown the photographs in the office by Joey. 'And that amazing Colombian scorpion save. You're a hero too. That save against Holland . . .'

Valent was impressed and smiled: sunlight on the Yorkshire crags again.

'I wish Bonny thought so.'

'How is she?' Etta decided to take the bully by the horns.

'I've been away. She's rehearsing, which she luvs.' Then he confided that Bonny always made him conscious of his age. 'I know I'm too old for her.'

'You're not, you look really gorgeous and you're really young at heart. Look how Trixie and Rafiq and Dora and Tommy adore you.'

'Bonny's Ryan's age.' Valent looked down at his uneaten chocolate tart. 'God, what a waste. I was a war baby.'

'The badgers will adore it.' Etta removed his plate. 'Shall we open that second bottle?' she asked hopefully. It was so nice having him sitting on the sofa, idly stroking a supine Priceless.

Valent picked the bottle up, then found it had a screw top which his big hands couldn't shift.

'Fucking arthritis. That comes from being in goal.'

'Give it to me,' Etta shoved the top between the front-door hinges, letting in a blast of cold air. They could hear a gaggle of Mrs Malmesbury's geese going to bed. After a couple of turns, the bottle opened.

'Thank goodness Sampson isn't alive, he would have been furious with me for spoiling the paintwork.' Etta filled up their glasses.

Curious, but suspecting she didn't like talking about Sampson, Valent asked if she had any other gossip.

'Mrs Malmesbury's having a problem with her geese.' Etta removed the plates and the chocolate tart, popping another bit in her mouth. 'God, I'm a pig. Now here is a point.' Etta paused, waggling a finger at Valent. 'Mrs Malmesbury's youngest goose, Spotty, was shared by two young ganders, but when the older goose, who was the girlfriend of the much older gander, Honky, got eaten by a fox, Spotty the young goose promptly flew over the fence, abandoning her two young gander lovers, and moved in with Honky the old gander, who was desolate without his mate.' Etta absent-mindedly broke off and ate another corner of chocolate tart. 'So you see, like Bonny and loads of other women, she found an older mate much more attractive.'

'Yeah, yeah.' Valent smiled, thinking how he liked watching Etta's face as she talked.

'Anyway, the two young ganders were so furious, they got poor old Honky down, pulled out his feathers and pecked out one eye, like poor Wilkie, but it made no difference to young Spotty. She still adores her old Honky even with one eye, and leads him around everywhere.'

'So you think I ought to wear an eyepatch?' said Valent dryly. 'And talking about eyepatches, how's Mrs Wilkinson?'

When Etta had finished telling him, he promised to ring Marius first thing and say Rafiq must ride her.

'Oh, would you?' said Etta in delight. 'That's so kind. If he doesn't make it as a jockey Rafiq ought to become a pop star, he's got such a beautiful voice. Wilkie really loves him singing to her and waggles her ears in time.'

Valent suppressed a yawn. 'I must go.'

Gwenny thought better and jumped on to his lap, her tail fluffed up like a Christmas tree. Hearing a fox barking outside, Priceless leapt down and rushed sniffing and snorting to the door.

'Has Seth given him up completely?' said Valent in disapproval.

'Well, he can't take him on tour.'

'He must eat you out of house and home. And Gwenny?'

'Pocock's sort of given her to me. I think,' she added, seeing Valent look even more disapproving, 'he rather fancies Joyce Painswick. He keeps nagging her to let him take the ivy off her cottage, says it's pulling out her brickwork.'

'Bonny's pulling out my brickwork.' Valent realized he'd spoken aloud. Christ, he must be pissed. Then, reluctantly, 'I *must* go. Everything all right up at the yard?'

'OK. Marius needs more winners. He's still eaten up missing Olivia.'

'Geese mate for life,' said Valent. As he opened the door Priceless shot off into the night.

The rain had stopped, the mature conifers were wearing stars as tiaras, narcissi scented the air.

'Good night, Etta.' Valent took hold of both her arms. There was a bit of a mish-mash as he kissed her on the forehead and she tried to offer him both cheeks, so they laughed.

'Chinking cheeks is a bit luvvie for me, I like tooching flesh.' Valent put his lips to her fringe.

'Thank you so much,' said Etta. 'It was really lovely.'

'Could we do this again,' asked Valent, 'and have a home fixture next time?'

'Yes please, and you will put in a good word for Rafiq, won't you?'

100

Amber was overwhelmed with jealousy when she learnt Rafiq was going to ride Mrs Wilkinson on Friday at Rutminster. She bombarded him with advice, until he was both confused and panic-stricken.

He had also learnt from stable gossip that Harvey-Holden had regrouped his army. Bullydozer was in the same race and Harvey-Holden and Vakil had taken the poor horse into the indoor school, subjecting him to their private and particularly brutal form of schooling, and deprived him of water to make him more biddable. Killer, his jockey, having been beaten for a second time by Mrs Wilkinson, was in even less of a mood to take prisoners.

Seeing Bullydozer in his box before the race, Tommy had peered over the half-door and was horrified to see the cuts on his legs inflicted by Vakil's pitchfork. Seeing Tommy, he ran trembling to the back of the box.

'Poor old boy.' When she surreptitiously offered him a Polo, he nearly took her hand off. He trusted no one.

As Rafiq walked apprehensively into the parade ring, his olive skin looked the muddy green of a real olive. He was so desperate not to let the yard and Tommy down. Since he'd been given the ride he had prayed so incessantly to win, he hoped Allah wouldn't punish him for neglecting other things. He also felt guilty being blessed before the race by a 'Christian infidel', but ' "My father's house has many mansions," ' Niall had reassured him.

The crowd, swollen by numerous fans of Mrs Wilkinson, had read of Amber's broken wrist and were fascinated to see how this handsome Pakistani would fare in her place. Rafiq had competition. Feline little Johnnie Brutus was riding Shade's Last

Quango and Killer was on Bullydozer. Bullydozer, however, who'd wasted precious energy walking his box and sweating up going down to post, had run his race before it started.

Goggles once more hid Killer's cruel, slanting, wolf-pale eyes, but the same evil smile flickered round his thin lips. Soon he was up to his old tricks. A discreet elbow in Rafiq's ribs as they jumped the first ditch nearly unseated him. At the end of the first circuit, he crept up the inner, pretending to be whacking a wilting Bullydozer, but instead the whip in his grey-gloved hand kept striking Mrs Wilkinson in her good eye, which totally disorientated her. And so it went on.

Hidden by the vast Bullydozer, Mrs Wilkinson was so small, even the television cameras couldn't pick up what was going on. But as Killer cut across them for the third time, Rafiq lost it.

'Fuck off, you bloody Paddy,' he screamed.

'Fuck off, you bloody Paki,' screamed back Killer.

As he dropped back to rest Bullydozer, Johnnie Brutus came upsides on Wilkie's left, blocking her view of the rails, bumping her, but Rafiq held her steady and still she battled on, hearing the crowd yelling, 'Wilkie, Wilkie, Wilkie.'

Even when a sixth sense told her Killer was creeping up again, she found more and more, scrabbling at the boggy turf with her little feet, beating Last Quango by a length. Bullydozer, who'd fallen away, wasn't even placed.

The syndicate went crazy. Even more so did Rafiq. 'It's a dream, it's massive,' he told Alice Plunkett as he gave Mrs Wilkinson equally massive pats, 'no money in the world can make up for it,' massive pat, 'she's tiny, but she's so tough,' massive pat, 'she's a credit to her connections. I thank them for their faith in me,' massive pat. 'Marius is great trainer, and Tommy Ruddock keeps her so well,' massive pat, 'she has one eye only but biggest heart in the world. This is best day of my life,' three massive pats, 'I am speechless.'

'Oh Rafiq, oh Wilkie.' Tommy and Chisolm hurtled up, sobbing and bleating. 'You rode her brilliant, she was so brave. That Killer ought to be shot. Both he and Johnnie were interfering with her, but she held on and you kept her straight.'

But Rafiq had been distracted by Killer riding back.

'What do you do that for?' he howled, all jockey hierarchy forgotten.

'You needed a lesson, new boy,' hissed Killer. 'Don't mess with me again, you little shit, or it'll really hurt. Fucking suicide bomber.'

Rafiq raised his fist.

'Don't hit him,' cried Tommy. 'Marius will sort it.'

This wasn't good enough for Mrs Wilkinson, who, swinging her head round, took a chunk out of Bullydozer. The much bigger horse shrank away, utterly exhausted, terrified of the beatings to come.

'Listen how they love Rafiq,' said Phoebe in delight as he and Wilkie were cheered back to the winners enclosure. 'It isn't just Amber who pulls in the crowds.'

Valent, who'd interrupted a board meeting in New York to watch the race, immediately rang Etta.

'Bluddy marvellous, Rafiq was awesome, he kept his cool and her on her feet. She looked bewildered. Well done for suggesting him, Etta.'

Marius stalked off to complain. Trilbies crowded the hat stand of that home of the establishment, the stewards' room. Gone were the days of a whisky between races. Now only coffee cups and papers littered the long, polished table.

'That was dangerous both for Rafiq and Mrs Wilkinson,' shouted Marius at the men sitting round it. 'Killer cut across her, bumped her again and again and slashed at her good eye with his whip. Then Johnnie Brutus took over. Killer should be suspended for the rest of the season and Johnnie too. Bloody hooligans.'

Alas, the Stipendiary Steward, who was a friend of Harvey-Holden, wouldn't shift. Nor was there any way he was going to suspend Killer just before the Cheltenham Festival.

'We've made our decision. Mrs Wilkinson was given the race. Nothing Killer did altered the placings. Your jockey's the green one, Mrs Wilkinson was hanging left into Killer's whip. Look at the video.'

Then came the unkindest cut of all.

'Wait till you're back with the big boys, Marius, before you start throwing your weight about.'

Back at Ravenscroft, Harvey-Holden, shivering and spitting with fury that Mrs Wilkinson had won yet again, went into Bullydozer's box with a whip and a mad, set face.

Next moment, Bullydozer had him against the feed box. Just in time, Vakil dragged his boss to safety.

'That horse is going to the sales next week,' screeched Harvey-Holden.

'Bullet through the head if you ask me,' said Vakil.

*

Valent, who was delighted by Rafiq's victory, sent him £500, which he sent straight to his family in Pakistan. Valent also sent £300 to Tommy, who wrote to thank him and suggested he bought Bullydozer.

'Jessie, who does him, says Harvey-Holden's got it in for him. Vakil hit him with a shovel yesterday and he's done a leg, but he's a good horse . . .'

Under an assumed name, Valent bought Bullydozer very cheaply at the sales. Arriving at Throstledown, the huge horse gave a sigh of relief, ate and ate, put on eight kilos in two days and stopped biting people. By contrast Jude the Obese, as WOO's guinea pig, had lost eight kilos as she and Martin pounded the Willowwood lanes.

Realizing Marius had been on the brink of sacking him before his win, Rafiq tried to be more amiable and co-operative in the yard. But it was not easy.

He was constantly aware of the government continuing to bomb and destroy the social fabric of two Muslim countries. He had recently, on the internet, watched a film of American triumphalism – joyous Tarzan howls accompanying direct hits on, among other things, an old farmer and his donkey. Another friend had just been killed by US bombs on the Afghan–Pakistan border.

Rafiq was frightened of pouring his heart out to Tommy, knowing her father was a policeman. Worst of all, Amber, whom he loved so much, was being poisonous.

When she came out of hospital, she refused to stay with her parents because she'd had a blazing row with her mother over the interview with Rogue – so Tommy and Rafiq had found room for her in their flat over the tack room, which meant Rafiq sleeping on the sofa.

Amber was obsessed with getting her career back on track. When she wasn't going to the gym or on power walks she would monopolize the only television, watching endless videos of races even when *EastEnders* was on.

Putting aside his jealousy of both Shade and Marius, Rafiq had tried with extreme gentleness to make love to her, but she had shrieked at him to go away and not touch her, only later sobbing for him to come back.

She also made constant demands on Tommy, to pull on her socks, do up her bra, unscrew bottles, wash her hair, even soap her lovely naked body in the shower.

'Do you think Tommy's a bit of a dyke?' Rafiq overheard Tresa saying to Josh.

Storming upstairs to the flat in his break, Rafiq found Amber in floods. Having chucked the *Racing Post* with a picture of Rogue on the cover into the bin, she was now, with her left hand, trying to pull it out covered in baked beans and tomato ketchup. A blazing row followed over the way Amber was treating Tommy.

A fortnight later, Tommy, who'd nipped into Larkminster during her break, returned to find Bullydozer's box empty and Mrs Wilkinson, who rather fancied him, yelling her head off.

After searching everywhere, Tommy had roused the other lads and was about to ring the police when through the blue April evening Amber came cantering towards them, popping the vast Bullydozer perfectly over the huge new Gold Cup fences. Her right hand was in plaster, her left held lightly on to Bullydozer's reins. Aware his charge was fragile, he was jumping with great care, an expression of seriousness and responsibility on his dark brown face.

Marius, who'd come back unexpectedly because Uttoxeter had been rained off, went ballistic. How dare Amber risk a valuable horse and her own life again? Secretly he was delighted he'd whipped another fantastic horse from Harvey-Holden.

101

With Bonny on tour or filming, Valent took to ringing Etta when he was in England. They spent happy evenings gossiping, discussing progress at Throstledown, grandchildren and poems they'd read, listening to music and the nightingales singing and making plans for the garden.

On one occasion they even sloped off to Larkminster and bought Valent a lovely dull-yellow jacket checked with red to wear to the races. It was so nice, they reflected individually, not to be mocked, put down and corrected.

Etta was shopping in Tesco's one morning at the end of April. She was desperately broke and dickering whether to run to another bottle of white, when the money ought to be spent on getting her shoes mended and some more deodorant.

To stink or drink, sighed Etta.

'Do you want a packer, Mrs Bancroft?' asked the checkout girl, glancing at Etta's pathetic pile of goods.

'She's already got one, I mean "wow",' said a voice, and a shoulder of lamb, a packet of mint, a bag of new potatoes, asparagus, frozen peas and a chocolate tart landed in her basket, followed by a lot of bottles. 'Let's have this for supper at my place,' said Valent, getting a card out of his wallet. 'I saw your Polo outside, nearly all Green now, Ione would be pleased.'

How lovely to be able to wash her hair and shower so the lack of deodorant didn't matter, put on her pretty lilac linen dress, and take time over her face.

She found Valent in the kitchen at Badger's Court, which, under Bonny's influence, was so like a laboratory, Etta expected to open cupboards and find poor little monkeys being experimented on. Valent, however, was playing Mahler's First Symphony, which Etta had told him she adored. There was a wonderful smell of mint, rosemary and garlic coming from the oven and a huge glass of Sancerre was thrust into her hand.

'You look smashing, Etta.'

She then brought him up to date on yard gossip. Rafiq had clocked up another win on Mrs Wilkinson, 'And there was a big piece in the *Express* about racing's new pin-up. Rafiq's terribly embarrassed but so pleased, he asked for five copies in the village shop to send home to Pakistan. Tommy's so excited for him. Amber's still a bit beady, understandably, poor child.'

Valent, who kept tabs, knew all this but he liked hearing Etta's version as he tested the lamb and the new potatoes.

She was now telling him about Amber sneaking out and illicitly riding Bullydozer over the new Gold Cup fences.

'Marius is so clever at recognizing a horse's potential. Bully's sweet, like a great puppy, and really responding to TLC.'

Valent just managed not to point out that he'd paid for all the fences and bought Bully, after Tommy's tip-off. As he turned the new potatoes, however, he couldn't resist telling Etta he'd got a lovely present that day, 'in that box over there'.

Inside was the most beautiful decanter shaped like a ship.

'Oh,' gasped Etta, 'how ravishing. What does it say on the prow? "God speed to a great boss." Who gave you that?'

'The card's tucked in the side.'

On it were hundreds of signatures, all over the inside and even on the back of the card, accompanying the words, 'With admiration from all your friends at Goldstein Phillipson'.

'Oh, how wonderful. That was the American bank you felt guilty about abandoning. What an amazing compliment.'

She listened and remembered, thought Valent.

But as Etta took the glass ship out of its box to examine it, it slipped from her hands and smashed into a hundred pieces on the floor.

'Oh God, oh God, oh God, I'm so sorry, I'm so sorry, so, so sorry,' wailed a distraught, disconsolate Etta.

'It doesn't matter, pet.' Leaving the new potatoes, Valent put his arms round her. 'It doesn't matter. It's only glass, not a heart, that's broken, please, please don't cry. Stay there on the window seat, Priceless luv, you don't want to cut your paws. Now let's find a doostpan and broosh.' Then, when Etta couldn't stop crying as she seized them from him and began sweeping frantically: 'It's all right, luv, I've got the names on the card, I was so tooched by that, that's what matters.'

Sampson would never have forgiven her, thought Etta.

Valent was so, so kind, topping up her drink, leading her out into the dusk and turning up the sound fortissimo so Mahler's second movement, a lovely galumphing dance, erupted down the valley. On cue, the sinking sun burst through a rain cloud to light up Etta's blonde curls, her smudged mascara, her still falling tears.

To stop her crying, Valent swept her into a waltz and soon had her shrieking with laughter as their feet flew over the grass.

'I'd no idea you were such a good dancer, de dum, de dum dum, de dum, de de de de dum,' sang Etta, as Priceless gambolled after them.

Next moment, Valent caught his foot round a rustic pole on the edge of the lawn and pulled Etta over on top of him in the wild garlic.

Both stopped laughing hysterically and gazed into each other's eyes.

'Oh Etta,' muttered Valent, 'you OK, not hurt?'

'Far from it, you make a lovely cushion.'

Their hearts stopped, but not Mahler. Then they both jumped.

'Will you kindly turn down that din,' roared a voice, 'or I'll call the police. There are kiddies trying to sleep here. Valent Edwards will not be pleased when he hears about this.'

It was the Major.

Valent was about to shout back, when Etta put a hand smelling of scent and wild garlic over his mouth. Then, clambering off him, she shot back into the kitchen.

'He's got his grandchildren staying,' she explained, giggling helplessly as she tried to slow her beating heart. 'I took Drummond and Poppy to tea there yesterday. Drummond pulled up all Debbie's bamboos to use in a sword fight, then he peed in the Major's rain gauge. The Major, assuming it was four inches of rain, promptly rang the Met and *The Times* – so embarrassing. I fled.'

'How's dear little Trixie?' asked Valent.

'She worries me,' sighed Etta. 'She's so miserable and ratty. I can't work out if it's normal teenage behaviour or something more serious. Oh, I'm so sorry about the decanter.'

Tomorrow she would write to Goldstein Phillipson and ask them to engrave another ship, which she would pay for, even if she had to sell the Munnings.

102

Valent flew off again, coinciding his return with Bonny having a week off from her tour of *Private Lives*, which she told Valent was proving an incredible success. Seth was so supportive, the audience so warm. The director was so appreciative of how she'd impacted on the play. The designer thought she looked so enchanting in his clothes, after the run he was going to give them to her.

She and Valent were staying in his house in St John's Wood, when one evening Bonny raised the subject of Pauline's clothes. They were still upstairs in a boxroom, which Bonny wanted to redecorate.

'Why don't you send them to a charity shop, Valent, or at least give them to Etta Bancroft or Joyce Painswick? I'm sure they'd appreciate them. They might have to be let out for Painswick, but she's so deft with her needle. You've got to move on, Valent, it's the only way you'll achieve closure.'

When he had looked mutinous, she had stripped off and begged him to make love to her on the lounge shag-pile. For the first time in their relationship, Valent had not been able to get it up. No amount of licking or sucking had worked. Bonny, saying it must be stress-related, insisted Valent consult a sex therapist.

Later, leaving a sleeping Bonny in bed, Valent had crept upstairs to the boxroom, where hung a row of dresses, crimplene and polyester, easy to iron, easy to mock. In the chest of drawers he found Pauline's handbag, black plastic – he'd never been able to cure her frugality – which the police had returned to him after the crash, which he'd never been able to bear to open.

Inside was a jumble of pens, biros, bus tickets, pressed powder, which had disintegrated, a mirror smashed by the impact, bright red lipstick, without which she felt naked, a purse in which he found a fiver, two pound coins, her credit card and a picture of himself, Ryan and the children. Above all, her perfume in a blue and silver spray, Rive Gauche – she had pronounced it 'gorsh' – was still fresh as Valent breathed it in.

The poem that had most moved him in Etta's anthology was the sonnet in which Milton described the anguish of dreaming his dead wife was alive. It ended: 'I waked, she fled, and day brought back my night.'

Last night, Valent had dreamt of Pauline. Whatever was going to become of him?

The following day he escaped to Willowwood. There he discovered the loveliest May evening, with the cow parsley foaming up to wash the weeping tresses of the willows and hawthorn blossom exploding in white grenades all over the valley. Having taken a large whisky on to the terrace, comforted slightly by the beauty of his garden and the heady smell of pale pink clematis and pastel roses swarming over wall and yew hedge, he spent an hour on his BlackBerry checking his companies around the world.

Glancing through the twilight, he noticed Etta's white and mossy green Polo had stopped outside his gates and hoped she might be coming to see him. Then he saw her leap out and put her arm round a passing Mrs Malmesbury.

At the same time Priceless jumped out and was romping up and down the middle of the road with Oxford the foxhound. They nearly got run over by a returning Debbie, who always made a ghastly din with her horn as she came round each of the five bends in the road on her way back to the village.

Picking up his binoculars, Valent realized Mrs Malmesbury was wiping her eyes, poor old duck – or goose. Then he saw Niall arrive, also putting an arm round Mrs Malmesbury and leading her home. He could hear her geese honking their welcome.

Curious to know what had happened, Valent rang Etta and suggested he wander down with a bottle for a quick drink.

Below huge indigo clouds, a scarlet sun on the horizon had turned the white hawthorn blossom pink as candy floss. Cow parsley caressed and soothed his arthritic hands as he walked down to the bungalow. He could hear the strains of Mahler's First Symphony.

'Gosh – a whole bottle of whisky,' cried Etta. 'How are you?'

'Fine.'

In fact he looked dreadfully tired. She wondered if sardines on toast would spread to two.

'What's oop with Mrs Malmesbury?' asked Valent.

'Oh, poor darling.' Etta turned down the CD player. 'A fox got her goose, Spotty, on Thursday. Mrs M nipped out to the bank at lunchtime and it was such a lovely day she didn't shut up the geese. They were sunning themselves on the grass when a fox rolled up. The ganders waddled away but poor Spotty was heavy with eggs and couldn't run. The vile fox stripped off her feathers and was sucking her blood when Mrs M got back. She rushed her to Charlie Radcliffe but it was too late.

'The two young ganders now sit on Spotty's feathers, which the fox scattered everywhere, and call for her. But what's really sad,' Etta's voice trembled, 'is poor, blind old Honky is utterly heart-broken. Spotty used to lead him everywhere, but because he can see slightly out of one eye, to comfort him, Mrs Malmesbury leaves him on the terrace, so he catches a glimpse of his own reflection in the kitchen window and thinks it's Spotty.

'Niall was so sweet to her just now, he's so much more outgoing these days. Did you know that foxes were illegal immigrants? Henry V was so enamoured of hunting at Agincourt, he brought them back here after the battle.'

Etta suddenly realized neither she nor Valent had a drink and she was chattering into a vacuum. Turning, she gasped in dismay. Like rain trickling down the side of a grey castle wall, the tears were pouring down Valent's cheeks. It was the poignancy of the old gander kept happy by his own reflection, an illusion that his wife was still alive. Next moment he collapsed on the sofa, narrowly missing Priceless.

'Oh Etta, if only I could see Pauline again – even if it was only the shadow of my own reflection in a window. I was such a workaholic, whizzing round the world, I never told her how much I luved her.'

Perching on the edge of the sofa, Etta put her arms round him.

'There, there, darling. Please don't cry. Of course you miss her, but I'm sure she knew. Please don't be sad.'

It was like holding a huge bison brought down by the hunts-man's spear. Etta just hugged, patted and handed him one sheet of kitchen roll after another. Gradually the sobs subsided, so she poured him a mahogany whisky.

'I'm sorry, I'm such a bluddy wuss.'

'You're not, you're the bravest, kindest person I know. What happened, what is it?'

Stumblingly he told her about Pauline's things and Bonny wanting him to chuck them out.

'It was her perfume that did it.'

517

'You could leave her things here, if that would help.'

'You'd have to put them on the roof,' Valent laughed shakily.

Priceless, who didn't like dramas, nudged Valent with his long nose. Next moment, Gwenny had jumped through the window on to his knee and started purring.

For a second Valent pressed a great muscular forearm to his eyes, his shoulders shaking again. Then he picked up Gwenny and plonked her on Etta's knee.

'Forgive me, Etta, I've been a wimp. I'm so sorry. Priceless needs his sofa back.'

Stumbling to his feet, he squeezed her hands, then patted Gwenny and Priceless and lumbered off into the night.

Next day he ordered Joey to install an electric fence down to the ground round Mrs Malmesbury's geese run, sent Etta lilies and altroemerias and flew off to the Far East, bitterly ashamed of himself. He had never broken down since Pauline died.

103

Towards the end of June, Alan, who was longing for the school holidays so he could see more of Tilda, took his laptop and a bottle of red into the garden and seated himself under a big lime tree which was in flower.

He could hear, like a great orchestra, the growling hum of bees glutting themselves on the sweetly scented flowers. How industrious they were, unlike him. Disinclined to work, he decided to send Dora an email, which he could use later as material for his book on Mrs Wilkinson:

Darling Dora, Please come home, we need you to cheer us up. You were so right to suggest Rafiq rode Wilkie, they were really flying – but everything seems to have gone belly up. Talk about a summer of discontent.

For a start the terrorist bomb scares have made everyone even more suspicious of poor Rafiq, who thought every policeman at the races was going to arrest him, particularly now his infamous cousin Ibrahim has been peddling propaganda on the internet.

Secondly, the stock exchange crash has screwed the hedge fund market, disastrous for my dear wife Carrie, who is putting a lot of pressure on yours truly to make some money out of writing. This makes me so depressed, I ought to interview myself for my depression book, but I've been forced to send it off to my publishers as they were threatening to tear up the contract.

In passing, I fear Carrie's soon going to sack Toby, who's on paternity leave because Bump has arrived. He's a dear little baby, but Phoebe is already expecting the whole of Willowwood to babysit for nothing.

But to return to our summer of discontent, foot and mouth

has caused hideous problems for Marius, preventing him moving his horses around. Even worse, poor little Chisolm has become such a celebrity, she's being stalked by DEFRA because she's got cloven hooves. They first suffocated some other poor goat at a nearby farm, by way of an example, then buzzed all over Marius's yard in helicopters trying to track down and kill off Chisolm. Mrs Malmesbury was convinced World War III had broken out.

In fact the bird had flown. Ione had already very sportingly allowed Chisolm to be hidden in the priest's hole at Willowwood Hall. Chisolm isn't at all grateful and keeps escaping. She's already demolished Direct Debbie's roses and eaten the piece Ione was writing for *Compost Weekly* and the minutes of Alban's quango on doctors.

Far more seriously, without her bleating friend, Mrs Wilkinson is flatly refusing to go to the races. Marius dragged her all the way to Fontwell and she wouldn't even unload. She's become a complete prima donna and a prima donna who ain't *mobile*, which means my story of her life is at a standstill.

Meanwhile everything else is horrible. All livestock movements are stopped, auctions and market places empty of animals.

What's really unnerving Willowwood is that Lester Bolton has bunged the District and Parish Councils so much, he's been allowed to install a vast moat round Primrose Mansions, not only diverting two streams into it but also topping it up with endless tankers of water. If the predicted floods occur, we're all going to be submerged. We'd better get Joey to build an ark.

As a result, all the locals blacked Lester and Cindy's arse-warming party, except H-H and Jude, Martin and Romy, and our own wank manager, the Major, who all live on high ground anyway. I went along too, reluctantly – writers have to experience everything – but it was terribly funny. The party was roaring away in Lester's underground leopardskin bar when Jude rolled up so hot and sweaty from jogging with Martin that Cindy persuaded her to strip off and go fatty-dipping in Lester's glass-bottomed swimming pool.

Suddenly the room went dark and the guests, who included lots of Lester's porn clients, choked on their cheap champagne as this vast whale, far bigger than the one in the Natural History Museum, started splashing around above us. She is *enormous*. Martin claims she's lost eight kilos, but I can't see where. Harvey-Holden was laughing his head off, he's such a shit. Evidently Lester is in line for a gong. Pity Orwell isn't alive today to write *The Road to Becoming a Peer*.

Anyway, darling, I've rabbited along for long enough, I hope you and Paris are having fun, everyone sends love. I know Trixie would adore to see you, she hasn't got a boyfriend at the moment and seems awfully low.

The syndicate's getting very fed up with no Wilkie to watch. In fact we're so starved of jaunts, we're off in July to see Family Dog run at Worcester. He's 200–1. Loads of love, Alan.

PS. Amber's wrist is recovered and she's back fighting with Rafiq over who's going to ride Mrs Wilkinson – so perhaps it's best the dear pony refuses to race.

104

July brought a heatwave – infuriating because it was the going Mrs Wilkinson loved. Etta's stream dried to a trickle, paths cracked, and Ione policed the village for illicit sprinklers, chiding those who had not created compost that would have provided moisture for their flower beds.

Valent, who'd been far too embarrassed to contact Etta after breaking down in front of her, felt compelled to ring her when a second ship decanter, duly engraved, arrived from his friends at Goldstein Phillipson.

'You shouldn't have paid for it, Etta.'

'I didn't, I didn't, they were such fans of yours they had another one made for free. They wrote me such a lovely letter.' Etta didn't add that they'd begged her to look after Valent.

'Well, that's a relief then. Come and have a drink,' said Valent.

It was another ravishing evening. Jupiter, the archetypal alpha male, blazed above Marius's yard, billowing blue-black clouds were echoed in shape by deepening green trees, the air was heavy with the scent of a thousand roses, honeysuckle, philadelphus, rank sexy elder and sweet white clover.

The nightingales had left, replaced by Beethoven's fourth piano concerto played by Marcus Campbell-Black, which flooded the valley.

'How lovely,' cried Etta. 'That was my father's favourite piece of music. I adored the Proms because for once, on Fridays, which was Beethoven night, I was allowed to stay up and listen.'

'Why were you called Etta?' asked Valent, handing her a glass of Pimm's and leading her into the garden.

'My real name's Henrietta, but my maiden name was Bullock and the girls at school kept chanting "Henry ate a bullock" so I changed it to Etta. Sampson said it sounded like a dodgy terrorist organization.'

How rarely she mentions him, thought Valent.

'What do you miss about Sampson?' he asked.

'I liked the way he used to yell at the television during wildlife programmes. When some starving meerkat had been rejected by the pack or a baby elephant had lost its mother, he'd yell, "You bloody cameraman, why don't you get out of your Land-Rover and give that poor animal some of your bottled water and egg sandwiches?" or "Why don't you warn that poor zebra a lion's bearing down on it, instead of filming it being gobbled up?"'

'How's Honky Malmesbury?' asked Valent.

'Well, Oxford's returned to Mrs M for the summer and has personally vowed to catch the fox, and Honky's fallen in love with the patio heater and won't leave it alone.'

Valent laughed. 'How are your grandchildren?'

How kind of him to ask, thought Etta, and confessed Poppy had suddenly become terrified of the dark.

'Someone told her about the ghost of Beau Regard. And I'm a bit worried about Drummond. He used to be so aggressive. But I went to watch him play football the other day, he kept kicking balls into his own goal and expecting everyone to clap, and the other boys just said, "You're so stupid, Drummond." When he was in goal, he kept looking in the wrong direction, letting goals in and getting shouted at. He was so crestfallen.'

'I'll kick a ball around with him, next time I'm down.'

'Oh, would you? Such a thrill for him.'

Etta got to her feet and wandered to the edge of the terrace. She was pleased with the roses and the delphiniums rising like dark and light blue dreaming spires. Across the valley, she could hear the roar of machinery as Marius's lads pulled up ragwort and drove round spiking up bales of hay shaped like cotton reels.

'Thank God he's got his forage in. Torrential rain's forecast for tomorrow. Oh look, there's Count Romeo with his head between Wilkie's hind legs so she can whisk the flies off him with her beautiful tail. Double pleasure. Sir Cuthbert's looking very jealous. Poor little Chisolm still in her priest's hole. She'd so love the fruit in this Pimm's. Good thing Ione thinks fitted carpets are naff. Scattered currants don't matter so much on polished floors.'

'Are you going to Worcester to watch Family Dog next week?' asked Valent.

'With any luck. Romy and Martin are taking the children away for a long weekend, so I should be free. Doggie's being given a last chance to acquit himself well after three years unplaced. Should be a laugh.'

105

Next day the rain started, and by Friday the River Severn had risen about four inches. Severe flooding was forecast. Racing had already been abandoned at Naas, Market Rasen and Brighton. Everyone expected racing to be cancelled at Worcester but it went ahead.

The centre of the course was flooded. Depressed swallows massed on telegraph poles, the Owners and Trainers was shut, and in the unearthly storm light the grass was lurid green and yellowish.

Despite dire reports of roadblocks, trains cancelled and fire brigades pumping out homes, the syndicate had pressed on. Alan had been keen to spend an afternoon with Tilda, Woody with Niall, Alban with Etta, Phoebe, already, without Bump. To the Major's disappointment, Corinna was in London, rehearsing for *Mother Courage*, which was opening in the West End.

Because of the school term, exams and general revulsion, it was the first time Trixie had joined the syndicate since *Antony and Cleopatra* in February. Afterwards Seth had bombarded her with flowers and telephone calls begging her to forget the four-in-a-bed – everyone had been plastered – and see him again. All of which Trixie had refused but she was still overwhelmed with a sick craving for Seth and had rolled up today in the hope of seeing him again, only to find he was in Bath, in *Private Lives* with Bonny.

Looking up at the unrelenting black clouds, Trixie was distracted from thoughts of Seth by worry about her grandmother.

'People have been advised to move their valuables and furniture upstairs. Granny doesn't have an upstairs.'

'She'll be fine,' said Debbie briskly. 'She can check the state of flooding on the internet.'

'Granny doesn't have the internet, and she's in a car anyway.'

'Well, as long as she keeps her mobile charged.'

'She often forgets to switch it on and she sometimes can't get a signal down at the bungalow.'

'I thought she was coming today, where's she gone?' asked Woody.

'Bloody Martin and Romy,' exploded Trixie, 'have rushed off to London to some stupid WOO launch, leaving poor Granny to drive Poppy and Drummond to Weybridge so Romy and Martin can pick them up on the way to their weekend in Kent. Bloody selfish. Granny was so looking forward to cheering on Doggie.'

Doggie was 250–1 now. There was an expression of hopeful expectancy on his broad white face as he splashed round the parade ring after the seven other runners. It had started to rain in earnest. Tommy, her elbow on Doggie's shoulder, her hand stroking his neck, had put on two rugs, one pulled up round his floppy ears.

'Worth putting on twenty quid at that price,' said Woody, the not very proud co-owner.

'Worth twenty-five after your boyfriend's blessed him,' said Joey, the other owner.

'Shurrup,' hissed Woody. 'He's such a sweet horse, I can't bear to sell him.'

His face softened as Niall waded into the paddock, put a hand on Rafiq's thigh and on Doggie's shoulder and murmured a few words.

'Can he put a call in to Allah?' asked Joey. 'Oh hell, it's worth a monkey.'

Valent landed in his red and grey helicopter just before the horses went down to post.

'Fancy him turning up here when he's so busy,' said Phoebe to Debbie. 'Toby and I thought he'd be a nice rich godfather for Bump.'

Valent was wearing his dark blue overcoat with the collar turned up and a dark blue Searston Rovers baseball cap.

'Where's your nan?' he asked Trixie, thinking how pale and tucked up the child looked. The big smile was wiped off his face when Trixie said Etta had gone to Weybridge.

'Fucking hell, in this weather? Half the roads are closed, flooding everywhere.'

'I know.'

It was raining even harder, coloured umbrellas going up like psychedelic mushrooms. The syndicate waited hopefully. Plenty of time for Valent to buy them a quick drink to warm them up before the off, but he was straight on to his mobile, checking flood lines and traffic lines, his face growing grimmer. In the distance he was sure he could see a huge black cloud over Willowwood.

'I'm so glad I didn't have a bet,' said Phoebe as Doggie, who was inspecting a flock of paddling seagulls, got badly left behind at the start. Not liking mud kicked in his face, he fell further and further behind as he ambled along, admiring stretches of water on both sides.

'He's going to be lapped by the front-runners,' muttered an anguished Woody. The crowd rocked with laughter.

'Come on, Doggie,' yelled Trixie. 'Dogs are supposed to be good at paddling.'

Doggie, however, was so far behind, he missed being caught up in a seven-horse pile-up at four out. Picking his way carefully over prostrate animals and their swearing riders, he was the only runner to complete the course, to deafening cheers. Rafiq, who hadn't bothered to pick up his whip, was grinning from ear to ear. The £5,500 for the winner meant £2,200 each for Woody and Joey, and £750 for Marius and £750 for Rafiq to send home to his beleaguered family.

Tommy couldn't stop laughing as she led Doggie into the winners enclosure and gave him a long drink of water which he didn't deserve, having hardly broken sweat. Doggie looked both delighted and astounded to get so much patting.

'He'll get hooked on success and win again,' said Trixie, who'd put on a fiver and won £1,250.

'It's because you blessed him, Rev,' grinned Joey, who'd won twelve times that amount. 'He'll probably turn up at Evensong on Sunday to fank you. Let's go and get legless.'

'And Valent can buy us lots of lovely fizz,' said Phoebe. 'So nice, now Bump's born, I can drink again.'

'Worcester Racecourse provides winners with lovely hospitality anyway,' snapped Alan.

Through the pounding rain, a jubilant Woody smiled at Niall, who next week was off to be a locum in Suffolk. Today was their last chance to be together and Woody had planned for them to steal off for a few hours to a secret woodland dell he had discovered and make love under the stars amid pale enchanter's nightshade and the papery ghosts of bluebells. It might be a bit damp – but who cared.

They laughed as they passed Alban commiserating with the

beaten favourite's owner, a rather glamorous blonde called Alex Winters. Alban was nodding so vigorously, he sent water gathered in his hat cascading down her cleavage, which involved a lot of mopping up with Alban's red silk spotted handkerchief.

Woody was just about to take his first gulp of champagne and watch Doggie's great victory in the hospitality room when Valent stalked in looking wintry.

'Put that down,' he barked at Woody. 'We're going back to Willowwood. They've had six hours of flash floods, Bolton's moat and the River Fleet have both burst their banks. Sorry to ruin your celebrations,' he told the disappointed syndicate, 'but I think you should all hurry home and enter Willowwood from the north, Alban. Any approaches from the south have been closed.'

As Woody emptied his glass into Niall's half-empty one, Niall murmured, 'Many waters cannot quench love, nor can floods drown it. Ring me when you get a moment. Good luck.'

'Sorry to drag you away from your boyfriend,' Valent told a startled Woody as they sprinted towards the helicopter. 'Don't worry about your mother, top of the village is OK at the moment.'

Why the hell hadn't he done something to stop Bolton's moat?

106

Five miles south of Willowwood, Etta drove at a snail's pace along the centre of the road. It was only twenty past six but as dark as night because the tree tunnel had been bowed down by the deluge. Ominously, there was no traffic coming in the other direction. Rain was machine-gunning the windows of the Polo, as puddles grew into ponds, streams into rivers and raindrops jumped like flying fish from the gutters.

She had to make it home. Priceless was safe with Miss Painswick, Mrs Wilkinson safe in a field on high ground at Throstledown, but she'd left Gwenny asleep on her cherry-red chair, and the rose she was grafting for Valent on a top shelf.

She patted the steering wheel, her dear Polo wouldn't let her down, but she was driving through a foot of water now.

She was terribly hot because as a suck-up gesture she had put on a wool shirt in a particularly unbecoming red which Granny Playbridge had given her several Christmases ago and which she'd never worn.

'I love it,' she had gushed on arrival, 'I've worn it loads,' whereupon a tight-lipped Granny Playbridge had removed the price tag.

Etta was still blushing, and sweating up worse than Furious, as she splashed past Marius's gates. Thank God Throstledown was high up, but as she dropped down and the water rose to meet her, she realized that the lazily idling River Fleet had turned into a raging torrent and the willows were tossing their weeping branches in an orgiastic dance of death.

Then, as the water surged over her bonnet, she gave a scream of horror. For there in the field beside the footbridge was Mrs Wilkinson. She must have tried to run home to Etta. Now, with a terrified Gwenny perched on her back, eyes rolling, neighing in desperation, she was marooned on a sliver of island which, as the raging, rising waters thrashed around it, was getting smaller and smaller.

Frantically Etta pushed at her car door, but as the water rose the pressure was so strong she couldn't open it.

'It's all right, Wilkie, I'm coming,' she screamed, as she managed to wriggle out of a back window.

Clambering over the wall, splashing down the field, she reached the river bank. If she waded through the torrent to the island she could grab hold of a now piteously mewing Gwenny and lead Wilkie to safety.

'Just stay there, darlings.'

But as she stepped into the river, she realized it was at least five foot deep and she couldn't withstand the currents. She'd better call for help. As she unearthed her mobile from her breast pocket, the force of the water swept it away.

With a despairing sob, wading downstream, she tried to swim to the island. Next minute the racing river had sucked her under. Choking on thick muddy water, she tried to regain her foothold, but the level was rising too fast. When she pushed out her arms to swim, the current again defeated her and swept her fifty yards downstream until she crashed into an overhanging willow and grabbed a branch, which cracked and gave way.

She grabbed another one, the long green leaves slipping away. Somehow she clung on and, edging upwards, caught hold of a larger branch. Digging her fingers into its mossy grooves, she gained a purchase. She couldn't drown, she'd got to save Wilkie and Gwenny. Dragging herself upwards until the raging waters were below her, she emerged through the canopy of leaves to reach the top of the tree, to be greeted by torrential rain.

You couldn't be wetter, Etta.

But looking upriver, she gave a wail of horror. Wilkie was still screaming shrilly as she paced up and down her piece of land, but Gwenny had vanished. She'd never survive in this torrent.

'Cling on, Wilkie,' sobbed Etta.

Then suddenly hope flared, as a police helicopter chugged over her head, searching for casualties.

'Help, help, help,' screamed Etta, but the thunder of the waters drowned her cries, and it chugged on.

After an eternity, by which time she had frozen solid and grown hoarse from shouting for help and reassurance to Wilkie, she heard the relentless purring rattle of another helicopter. Frantically tearing off her red shirt, she waved it round and

round, nearly losing her grip and plunging into the river, clinging on and croaking, 'Please God, help us.'

Could it be red and grey? Then, like a huge insect of mercy, the
heavenly 'copter hovered overhead. Was it moving on? No it
wasn't.

Suddenly Etta and her old greying bra and grey pacing Wilkie
were flooded with dazzlingly bright light. As the helicopter
descended, the downdraught blasted into the willow, flattening
and spreading its branches, so Etta nearly lost her balance, and
only prevented a plunge into the river by clutching more leaves
with numb fingers.

But as the canopy spread, a god descended harnessed to a steel
cable.

'I've come to tack you up,' shouted the god in a strong
Larkshire accent.

'Oh Woody,' sobbed Etta, 'oh thank goodness.'

'We're here, you're safe. Good old *Salix babylonica* saved you.'

Swinging towards her, he rested his foot on a horizontal
branch, then, slipping a harness under her arms, pulled her
towards him.

'Don't cry, this is the way we do it.'

Pressing her head against his chest, wrapping his legs tightly
round her bent-up legs, 'God, you're cold,' he said and made a
thumbs-up sign to the pilot above.

'We can't leave Wilkie, and Gwenny's in the water,' wailed Etta
as they were hauled upwards.

'Valent's ringing for an RAF helicopter which'll bring slings so
we can winch Wilkie to safety,' yelled Woody.

'Thank you, thank you for rescuing me,' gasped Etta through
desperately chattering teeth, as Valent, looking more threatening
than the black clouds massed overhead, reached out and tugged
her and Woody into the helicopter. Then, as with frozen fingers
she frantically tried to tug on her sopping wet shirt to cover herself, he roared, 'Don't put that stupid thing back on, give her my
coat, Woody,' then, completely losing his temper, 'You stupid
woman, risking your life to rescue a bluddy horse.'

'She's not a bloody horse,' shouted Etta over the roar of the
blades. 'She's the Village Horse and we've got to rescue her.'

Then, peering down out of the still open door, she gave a
scream of despair, for Mrs Wilkinson, unnerved by the helicopter
and the water swirling round her hocks, deserted by Gwenny and
her mistress, had plunged into the raging torrent. For a harrowing half-minute, she disappeared under the water, then the
strong little frame, stout legs and even stouter heart, which had

propelled her over huge fences and down the straight to snatch victory from her rivals, did not desert her.

Her white face could be seen above the frenziedly tossing white horses as she battled to safety. She was nearly defeated, disappearing beneath the water again, as she tried to find a foothold on the sodden collapsing bank. But after a heroic lurch, she found firm ground beneath a clump of bulrushes and managed to tug her feet out of the quicksand. Next moment, Tresa, who with Painswick had been manning the yard, and Priceless came racing down the hill to lead her to safety.

'"And even the ranks of Tooscany,"' Valent squeezed Etta's hand for a second, '"could scarce forbear to cheer." Sorry I chewed you out, luv, I was worried.'

As he turned the helicopter round, Woody put an arm round Etta.

'Good thing you weren't wearing a jacket, water in your pockets would have pulled you under.'

'Thank you again for rescuing me,' mumbled Etta. 'If you could just drop me off—' Looking down, she realized she couldn't see Little Hollow. It had disappeared beneath the water. 'Oh my God.'

'You're coming home,' said Valent firmly.

Mop Idol had lit a fire in a spare bedroom. Valent had buzzed off to Throstledown to reassure himself and Etta that Wilkie was all right. He returned with Priceless, who, having done nothing but eat Painswick's shortbread all afternoon and run down the hill to Wilkie, had collapsed exhausted on the bed. Valent had unaccountably disappeared again.

Etta, slowly coming to the realization how near death she had been, was distraught about Gwenny.

'I must go and look for her.'

Mop Idol, who hadn't been to the races, persuaded her not to. 'We don't want you to suffer from hypothermia, you're exhausted. Mr Edwards insisted you rest and it's more than my part-time job's worth. Cats have nine lives, Gwenny'll turn up.'

'She'll die like the first Gwendolyn,' wept Etta.

After a boiling bath, she found a beautiful pale pink silk short nightie and dressing gown laid out.

'That's Bonny's,' cried Etta in embarrassment.

'Doesn't matter. She's got too many clothes. Mr Edwards insisted you put them on and got this down you,' said Mop Idol, marching in with a bowl of game soup and a very large brandy.

'You are kind.'

532

Etta had nearly cried herself to sleep when a dripping Valent, his hair falling in wet black tendrils over his forehead, marched in and dropped an exhausted Gwenny on her pillow.

Dried off, her black fur flattened, Gwenny looked half her normal size but was purring twice as loudly.

'Oh thank you, thank you, how did you find her?' mumbled Etta. 'You must get out of those wet things.'

Was she dreaming or did Valent really take her hand, muttering, 'Oh Etta, thank God you're safe. I lost Pauline. I couldn't have borne it if I'd lost you.'

Then, dropping a kiss on her forehead, he was gone.

107

Etta was woken by Priceless squeaking to go out and Mop Idol bearing a cup of tea and full of gossip. Mr Edwards had flown to London to avoid the press, the ones who got through the flood, who were hanging around outside.

'They want to interview you. *Mail*'s got the story.' She handed the paper to Etta.

Page one concentrated on general flood devastation. On page three, under the huge headline GALLANT EDWARDS, was a picture of Valent, Etta and Mrs Wilkinson taken when he'd rolled up and turned the court case. The piece described how he had flown back from the races and saved Etta and the famous Mrs Wilkinson from drowning. He was quoted as saying how brave Etta and Woody had been and how Etta had nearly been killed leaping into the water to save Wilkie, but how in the end Wilkie, showing typical resilience and guts, had saved herself.

'They want to interview you and Gwenny,' said Mop Idol.

'Oh dear,' said Etta.

As Mop Idol sat down on the bed, Etta thought how pretty and merry she was despite working so hard and felt sad that Joey was messing around with Chrissie.

'The top of the village has no water, and neat sewage and used tampons are flowing down the high street.' Mop Idol shuddered. 'The stink's horrible. The Major's gone berserk because abandoned cars all over the place are holding up the traffic.

'Repulsive Harvey-Holden's gloating because his yard's so high up he hasn't been touched by the floods, but everyone else has. The Salix Estate has got water up to the skirting boards, and the vicar and Tilda Flood and the school have all been flooded.

Parents had to paddle across the high street to collect their kids yesterday.

'Mr Pocock was flooded. He was brilliant, he built a wooden barrier to put at the bottom of Miss Painswick's drive, stopped the water pouring in.'

Contributing to Mop Idol's good cheer was the fact that her own ground floor had been flooded out, which meant the council providing her and Joey with nice new carpets and a new kitchen.

'The Major and Debbie's garden's been flooded. Angela Rippons and Alan Titchmarshes not eaten by Chisolm were up to their necks, all the goldfish in the pond swept away. Serve the Major right for not opposing Bolton's moat,' said Mop Idol. 'Bet his rain gauge has overflowed.

'I ended up in the Fox last night, and Chris said the only funny moment was when Cindy Bolton boasted her Chelsea tractor could cope with any flood. She drove off down the high street and disappeared totally under water. Pity the Major wasn't there to rescue her.'

'I must get up,' sighed Etta.

'Mr Edwards insisted you stay here until your bungalow's recovered.'

Gwenny gave a raucous caw of agreement and snuggled up between Etta's blanketed legs.

'How did Mr Edwards find me?' Etta asked timidly.

'Trixie was worried you was driving to Weybridge. Valent tried your mobile number and when he got no answer he hijacked Woody before he got plastered like the others. Then they saw the Polo and your red shirt. So romantic, the papers want to talk to you. Brilliant to save Mrs Wilkinson, poor Chisolm will be hoppin' to miss the fun.'

Etta let Mop Idol rabbit on and her tea get cold, totally distracted trying to remember the blissful thing Valent had said to her last night. Had she dreamt it? 'Gallant Valent', he'd been so amazing rescuing her.

'Where's Bonny?' she asked.

'In Bath.'

Etta looked out of the window. The valley steamed like a victorious racehorse, everything dripped. She could see lots of people with cameras and a television van beyond the gates.

'Oh goodness.'

'You don't have to talk to them.'

'My hair's such a mess, and this red shirt.'

'Borrow something of Bonny's. A nice white shirt, she only wears things once.'

535

Having a quick shower however, Etta caught sight of an upright pink pig in the long bathroom mirror and realized it was her own plump body with its 'dinner for one' spare tyre.

Amid Bonny's battalion of make-up, needed to create that natural look, she found a magnifying mirror, in which she could see a watery sun caressing the lines on her face, her crêpey breasts and the pleated skin on the inside of her arms. As she came out of the bathroom, she noticed a huge ravishing blow-up of Bonny hanging on the wall looking down the stairwell: naked but 'tasteful, resonant and empowering'. After Bonny, how could Valent fancy an old biddy like herself? She'd been such a fool over Seth, she must stop herself falling in love with Valent. Crumpets and *Midsomer Murders* with Painswick were all she could hope for. She must stop crying.

She had put on her clothes, including the red shirt Mop Idol had washed and dried, and was just wondering what to do next – take Priceless for a swim? – when Romy swept in.

'We're back, we're back. We heard the news this morning and saw the papers. Of course it's the silly season or they wouldn't have made such a fuss, but we felt we couldn't desert you – must have been frightening. The road's cut off still so we can't check the bungalow yet, but I'm sure it will be all right when the water goes down. Anyway, for the moment you must stay with us at Harvest Home.'

'But I'm staying here,' stammered Etta.

'Mrs Bancroft's had a terrible shock,' said Mop Idol quickly. 'She's just lost her home. Mr Edwards insisted she stay.'

'One must keep a sense of proportion,' said Romy, who wanted a live-in babysitter to free up her and Martin for work during the summer holidays. 'People in the third world are much worse off. Could we be alone for a minute?' She opened the door. Reluctantly Mop Idol left them.

'Valent is a very kind man,' Romy waved a finger at Etta, 'but you can't stay here. Bonny's coming home later. With her away on tour so much, they need their special precious time together. Remember how you got the wrong idea about Seth.'

Romy in fact had met Bonny in Bristol earlier in the week to discuss the WOO launch. During a lunch of lettuce, cucumber and plain yoghurt, Bonny had begged Romy yet again to get Etta off Valent's back. 'I'm fed up with her fawning all over him.'

'It's important to know when you're not wanted, Etta,' went on Romy. 'It's so undignified to throw yourself at men at your age,' she added brutally. 'So let's get you over to Harvest Home.'

'What about Gwenny and Priceless?' whispered Etta.

'Not invited,' snapped Romy. 'Priceless is Seth's responsibility and Gwenny belongs to Pocock.'

When Valent rang Harvest Home to raise hell about the hijacking of Etta he was for once outsmarted by Martin, who thanked him profusely 'for saving Mother's life. If it hadn't been for your quick thinking, things could have been serious. Afraid you can't talk to Mother, she's actually fast asleep. I think she felt safe the moment she got to us – she doesn't want to take personal calls. The great thing is I've been down to the bungalow and the water's dropping. It'll clean up OK. Fortunately Mother kept Dad's photographs and letters on a special high shelf, and they're unharmed. She would have been heartbroken if they'd been ruined.'

Thank God he and Carrie had appropriated most of Etta's more valuable things when she left Bluebell Hill.

Poppy was the most excited that her grandmother was coming to stay, and by her adventures.

'All the same, Granny, it's a shame you didn't die, then I could have gone on television saying what a caring grandmother you were and put tulips outside the bungalow and all my friends would have cried and hugged me.'

108

From the safety of the stage at the Theatre Royal, Bath, Seth was greeted by applause even louder than the water thundering down Willowwood high street.

After a rapturously received Saturday night performance, he had returned to Willowwood on Sunday afternoon, having been summoned by an outraged Martin to retrieve his dog. Seth was relieved to discover the Old Rectory at the top of the village was unflooded, and the delphiniums in the garden had been toppled (since they laid off Pocock) by bindweed rather than downpour. Corinna was currently wowing Broadway with *Mother Courage* and Bonny had returned to Badger's Court and Valent. As the ground floor of the Fox had been flooded, Seth met his friend Alan in the skittle alley upstairs.

Outwardly Seth was in cracking form, but secretly he was irked by the fuss Bonny was making over the massive publicity afforded to Gallant Valent's rescue of Mrs Wilkinson and Etta.

There was no ice because the pub fridge had surged up from the floor, smashing the kitchen ceiling, so they had warm Bloody Marys. On the trestle tables rescued from downstairs were the framed photographs of the hunt and Marius and Harvey-Holden's horses, alongside horse brasses, drenched silks, foxes' masks and red coats.

'It was like being on the *Titanic*,' grumbled Chris, who was polishing glasses. 'Water gushed in through the walls and the floorboards.'

'Bloody bad luck,' commiserated Alan.

'This'll all make a great chapter for your book on Wilkie,' said Seth.

'Bloody needs to,' said Alan gloomily. 'I've a feeling the

publishers won't find enough bullying and sexual abuse in *Depression* for today's market.'

'Interview Bonny. She loves rabbiting on about her journey. You been flooded?' Seth asked Alan.

'Only the cellar, we found a dead rat floating there.'

'Probably Harvey-Holden.'

'*Au contraire,*' sighed Alan, 'the little weasel is very much alive and gloating because his yard's untouched, unlike poor Marius, who's had two furlongs of his new all-weather washed away.'

'Jesus – that bloke's star-crossed. How's Etta?'

'In floods in all senses of the word – poor angel. That bungalow Martin built for her nearly disappeared beneath the water.'

'Which would have benefited Willowwood aesthetically.'

'Oh, shut up,' grinned Alan. 'Even worse, bloody Romy whisked her away from Badger's Court, insisting she stay with her and Martin, but they wouldn't allow her to take Gwenny and Priceless so they've all moved in with us until—'

'That's very kind of you to take in Priceless,' Seth interrupted quickly. 'Great weight off my mind, couldn't take him on tour. Let me buy you a drink.' Seth splashed vodka from the bottle into Alan's glass, topping it up with tomato juice and Worcester sauce before filling his own. 'How's little Trixie?'

'Buttering Gwenny's paws and the house because Gwenny keeps escaping.'

'Lucky Gwenny.' Seth wondered if he dared have another go at calling Trixie to beg forgiveness for the Stratford foursome. Bonny would go ballistic if she found out.

'How's *Private Lives* going?' asked Alan.

'Fantastic – sold out in every city – possible film in the offing. Oh God, here comes the Major to bore us.'

The Major was in a high state of chunter and statistical overkill.

'Last time we had this much rain in Larkshire was in July 'sixty-eight. Folk rushed around providing portable toilets.'

'It was Bolton's moat bursting its banks wot did it,' accused Chris, handing the Major a tepid pint.

'Jude probably fell in,' said Alan.

'Willowwood should sue Bolton collectively,' said Seth.

'And the planners and the Parochial Church Council he bribed,' said Alan slyly.

The Major choked on his beer.

'Must keep a sense of proportion,' he spluttered. 'All Larkshire's been hit. Hundreds of people trapped in their cars. Thousands still without power. A hundred and eighty thousand homes without water.'

'Let them drink Scotch,' said Seth.

'Debbie is very distressed all the carp in her pond were swept away. I intend to form an action group to address the problem of flood defence.'

'I hear the banging of stable doors,' Alan shook his head.

'Whatever happens, council tax will go up,' said Chris, emptying the vodka bottle into Seth's glass.

'And how's your Tilda Flood defence, my dear?' murmured Seth to Alan.

'Non-existent, I adore her and the poor darling's school's been trashed, but shut up about it.'

'Only if you tell your sweet daughter to call me. I've got an idea for when Corinna comes back from America: we'll give an evening of Shakespeare and perhaps Noël Coward to raise money for the flood victims. Trixie loves Shakespeare. Maybe she could help. What d'you think, Norman?'

But the Major was off bellyaching about Larkminster Council who were offering free sandbags. 'But when Debbie and I rolled up this morning they were only handing out bags with no sand in them, which are utterly useless.'

'Why don't they use the obese as sandbags?' suggested Seth. 'Give them a feeling of self-worth. They could start with Jude. It'd be better than pounding the streets with Martin to raise awareness for WOO.'

'That is in deplorable taste,' exploded the Major. 'Jude is a lovely lady.'

109

Even though she'd been lucky enough to keep Priceless and Gwenny with her at Russet House, Etta was fretting about what she was going to feed them on, now the village shop had been flooded out. Priceless also needed a walk.

'I must take him,' she wailed, rearing out of bed.

'You've got to rest,' ordered Trixie, adding hopefully, 'Dad should be home in a minute. I'm defrosting a chicken for everyone's supper and I'll take Priceless out for a quick walk. I know he hates getting wet, so we'll go east across Farmer Fred's land.'

Outside, everything dripped and reeked of sewage, and Farmer Fred's fields had been replaced by huge lakes of pale brown water with clean-washed cows and very white sheep grazing on the still green high ground. Yesterday's deluge had bowed down the willows and flattened the shocking-pink willow herb growing along the footpath, which had become a rushing stream. A light breeze ruffled the yellow antlers of the wild honeysuckle.

Priceless bounded in front, picking his feet out of the water, tossing his head from side to side, to beckon her on, before charging off in search of rabbits. Despite the muggy closeness of the evening, Trixie shivered. She had been jolted by how close her grandmother and Wilkie had come to death. She must try to enjoy life more.

Suddenly Priceless gave a bark of joy and loped forward as a tall, dark and decidedly handsome man emerged from the shadowy hazel grove ahead. The smell of sewage retreated, giving way to the musky lemon scent of Terre. And Trixie's heart failed. It was Seth. She must keep her feet on the *terre*.

'Go away,' she whispered in horror, as he fell into splashing step beside her, 'I so don't want to see you.'

'Darling, please, please, please listen to me,' Seth begged, 'I only want to say how desperately sorry I am about Stratford. It was appalling. My only defence is I was so relieved the first night had gone well, I got absolutely plastered. Four in a bed was all Rogue's idea, he was so desperate to shag Bonny.' The more Seth lied, the more truthful he made it sound. 'And in vino veritas, the only thing I wanted to shag was you. I've never desired a woman,' how flatteringly his deep voice lingered over the word, 'the way I desire you. I'm afraid that night my vile animal nature overcame me.'

'Don't blame animals, they've got much nicer natures than you,' said Trixie furiously. She must not look into his face or she'd be lost. She wished her heart would stop thumping and she wished she could breathe again. But when she slipped in the mud, his hand caught her elbow and he left it there.

'Please forgive me,' his voice became hypnotically mesmerizing, 'just give me a second chance. I can't bear us not to be friends, I so adored coaching you.'

'"Come, my coach,"' said Trixie sarcastically, but as they walked on, jumping to avoid the puddles, the fingers of his left hand somehow plaited with the fingers of her right.

'"Had he come all the way for this?"' he spoke melodramatically, '"To part at last without a kiss."'

'Who said that?' asked Trixie sulkily.

'William Morris in a poem appropriately called "The Haystack in the Floods". Although he wrote it about a girl, I know I'm too old for you. I've tried to back off but I can't stop wanting you.'

As he dropped her hand and laid his, warm and caressing, on the back of her neck, she couldn't resist putting her head back to trap it. She noticed, in the setting sun, meadow browns and peacock butterflies going berserk in the nettles. Like me, she thought, giddy with relief, now he's beside me again.

'Where's Bonny?' she asked even more sulkily.

'Rushed back to minister to gallant Valent. She does love him in her way.'

'Poor sod, how can you put up with her?'

'I have to act I'm in love with her on stage. Like that silly old joke. "Did Ophelia sleep with Hamlet?" "Always on tour, but never in the West End."'

Trixie laughed. She could hear Marius's horses calling to each other. Above Throstledown, Jupiter had risen dazzling gold. The breeze ruffling the drenched trees sounded like rushing water.

The raging stream pouring across the footpath was filling up her gumboots, so Seth picked her up. Reaching the other side, wondering complacently if he was the reason she'd lost so much weight, he found her trembling mouth on a level with his, and kissed it very gently.

'Please forgive me. Can't we start seeing each other again?'

'Not if you're going to cool off. I'm not Priceless, to be dumped when you've got better things or women to do.'

'I promise.'

As Seth put her down, Priceless took off again, dispersing a party of rabbits taking refuge from flooded holes on a grassy hillock. As Trixie waded on, trying to stay in control, she caught sight of a blue plastic bag full of yellow daisies lying in the long grass.

'What's that?' asked Seth.

'Ragwort. Poisonous for horses if it's not pulled up. Gives them ulcers, kills them eventually. Just as loving you destroys me,' she said bitterly before she could stop herself.

'Darling, you mustn't say that.'

'I ought to get back.' Turning round she could see windows dimly lit by candles because most of Willowwood's houses still had no power.

'Don't go. Your dad was in the pub, but he was going straight home to look after Etta,' lied Seth. '"I do love nothing in the world so well as you: is not that strange?"' he murmured. The words always worked.

Next moment, he had taken her in his arms, warming her with the heat of his body, drawing her behind a hedge where they collapsed on a sodden bed of willow herb.

'Oh Trixie, Trixie, Trixie, my lovely water baby.' His practised hand unhooked her bra and unzipped her jeans and she was lost and a second later naked against the shocking-pink flowers. 'You are so beautiful,' Seth said truthfully.

There was no time or need for foreplay, such was their longing. But at the moment of bliss, as he drove deeply into her, she was distracted by a terrible screaming.

'What's that?'

'Hush, it's only Priceless, got some baby rabbit.'

'We must save it.' Trixie tried to leap up but Seth pushed her back.

'Not a hope, he'll rip it to shreds in an instant.' But as his lips stopped any further protest, Trixie realized that in his arms she was as helpless as that poor baby rabbit.

110

Etta was in despair. She had visited her bungalow. Everything was wrecked: the red buttonback chair, Sampson's king-sized bed, the sea-blue sofa off which Priceless had kicked everyone, the television, the ancient gramophone, all her books impossibly crinkled as though she'd dropped them in the bath, the Munnings of the mare and foal, which she'd known she could sell off if all else failed.

Suddenly 'Blot' and the tiny shady garden where she, Gwenny and Priceless had been happy and so many people, especially Valent, had dropped in, seemed immeasurably dear. So did her Polo, which she'd been forced to abandon in the road. Even if dried off it was most unlikely to pass its MOT.

Etta wished someone would butter her paws. Her mobile had vanished in the flood and no one knew she was now at Alan and Carrie's. Carrie, who'd whizzed down to assess the damage, was predictably unsympathetic.

'Don't know why you're upset, Mother, Martin and I made sure you were well insured. So you can replace everything with some nice stuff from IKEA and have a few bob left to spoil yourself.'

Etta was frantic to ring Valent, to hear his voice, to thank him, but when she finally screwed up enough courage, Bonny answered.

'He's busy,' she said icily. 'Hasn't he helped you enough, Etta? He doesn't need lascivious old "ladies",' deliberately Bonny put quotes round the word, 'invading his personal space.'

As the rain stopped and the River Fleet slowly retreated, Willowwood started the massive task of clearing up. After Bonny's cruelty, Etta was overwhelmed with gratitude when a task force of

Woody, Joey, Mop Idol, Tresa, Josh, Rafiq and Tommy descended on the bungalow like seven maids with seven mops, armed with buckets and steamers to clean the carpets and try to remove the foul-smelling mud and silt which coated everything.

She must pull herself together and think of other people. No one in Willowwood was untouched. Joey, she knew, had disastrous gambling debts, and Mop Idol wouldn't get her new kitchen because the council didn't cough up for people who owned their own houses.

Chris and Chrissie had been badly flooded and with more and more people economizing and drinking at home, the takings were right down. Even though the council had agreed to repair the Salix Estate, the stress of water swirling round her knees had driven Woody's mother finally off her head, and Woody was facing the prospect of an expensive nursing home.

The Government, trumpeting the necessity for cuts in the health service, had cancelled Alban's latest quango. Ione meanwhile had invested so much in solar panelling, wind turbines, heat pumps and court battles to install them, it would be years before she recouped in saved energy. The tiny interest on their shared capital was dwindling. Rather than jeopardize the house, an always frugal Ione's first move had been to cut both Pocock and Mop Idol down to two days a week.

More dramatically, Toby, supposedly on paternity leave, was seen on television at the Lords Test and promptly fired by Carrie. Phoebe as a result was milking it. She knew everyone in Willowwood would help Toby look after Bump while she got a job. Painswick must be due for retirement any minute and Phoebe felt sure she could handle Marius better.

Carrie, with the collapse of the hedge fund market, was in real trouble, about to lose £500 million. Alan felt the sandbag of a rich wife was suddenly emptying. Without half of Carrie's income, his dreams of running off with Tilda were in tatters.

Tilda was having an even worse time, with her classroom flooded, her library and computer wrecked. The money she'd saved to get her teeth fixed would have to go on repairing School Cottage, which Shagger had insufficiently insured for her. Shagger had also been foul to her because he felt she should have abandoned her school during the flood to shift his furniture upstairs.

Shagger admittedly was not in an enviable position. His company was facing £150 million worth of claims for flood damage. Mrs Malmesbury was one of his clients and although her geese had been saved, her house had been trashed. The flood had overturned furniture and ripped plaster and pictures off the walls. Her ancient dachshund, after sailing round and round her flooded kitchen in his basket like a little boat on a rough sea, had happily been rescued by Mr Pocock.

Gales had blown numerous slates off her roof, but when she came to claim the insurance set up by Shagger, a blonde with a laptop had rolled up and announced that the gale had been measured at 48 mph and they only paid out for gales above 48 mph.

'The only way to get anything these days is to be an unmarried mother with ten children and foreign,' grumbled Mrs Malmesbury.

Miss Painswick had not been badly flooded, thanks to Mr Pocock's help, but she was now incensed that Ione had laid him off. He'd been so loyal, never taking holidays in the growing season.

Corinna had been so delighted by her notices in New York that she agreed to herself and Seth putting on an evening of Wilde and Shakespeare in the village hall to swell the flood victims' fund, to which Valent had already anonymously given half a million.

Trouble was in store, however, because Bonny, whose tour was ending and who wanted to raise her caring profile, was determined to join Seth and Corinna and wanted the evening to take place at Badger's Court. Seth, in a weak moment, because he wanted to sleep with her, had agreed to this.

The Major, terrified of being rumbled for taking bribes from Bolton, was boring everyone with his action group on preventable flooding. Direct Debbie was heartbroken because they were now a no-carp family and because a still incarcerated Chisolm had escaped and stripped her garden of any splash of colour.

The fête was cancelled, to everyone's relief except Bonny's, who had been going to open it and Greycoats and the church, who in a normal year would receive £3,000 each from the takings.

The only person to profit spiritually from the floods was Niall. Away on his month's locum in Suffolk, he had been replaced by a lady vicar, a windbag called Susan Burrows, who was immediately nicknamed Mrs Locum.

Because it was the only warm and dry place, the church was packed to hear her first service on the Sunday after the floods. Alas, she not only forgot to thank God for saving the Village Horse and Mrs Bancroft, but her sermon was still in full flow after forty-five minutes, whereupon little Drummond Bancroft spoke for all when he loudly complained, 'This has gone on far too long.' He was firmly ticked off by his father, at which point an exasperated Ione bellowed, 'Don't reprove that sensible child. This has gone on too long. Over to you, Craig.'

So Craig Green had launched into 'O Worship the King', but as the congregation shuffled to their feet, Mrs Locum shouted from the pulpit that she hadn't finished yet.

So the congregation sat down again, whereupon Ione bellowed, 'For God's sake get up or she'll start again.'

So Craig launched back into 'O Worship the King' and Mrs Locum stormed out, refusing to hover in the porch and offer words of consolation to her flooded flock.

Having slagged off Niall for so long, Willowwood was now gagging for his return, particularly after he popped back in the middle of the month to commiserate with the villagers, many of whom were living in caravans, still with no water.

Finally, Amber was in despair. The doctors had pronounced her fit once more. Riding out on Mrs Wilkinson towards the end of July, she noticed meadow browns crowding an amethyst sweep of thistles, enduring the prickles in order to suck out the honeyed sweetness. Who would put up with her prickly cross-patch nature and love her, when she was so unlovable? Amber knew she'd been vile to Tommy and bitchy to Rafiq, of whom she was now so jealous. He had become so much less sulky and unforthcoming, even managing a win on Family Dog, that lots of owners were asking for him personally to ride their horses when the yard threw off the shackles of foot and mouth and became operative again.

Amber had also written a hundred letters to Rogue thanking him for the freesias and torn them all up.

111

It was a red-letter day for Throstledown when, on 9 August, the restrictions on animal movements were finally relaxed, which meant Marius could shift his horses and Chisolm was allowed home from her priest's hole, to the ecstasy of Mrs Wilkinson. Chisolm's little tail didn't stop waggling as she rushed round the yard greeting her human, canine and equine friends, disappearing into the bushes with Horace the Shetland before rushing back to Mrs Wilkinson.

A mad scramble ensued to get the horses match-fit for the next season. Valent's rescue of Mrs Wilkinson had attracted a huge amount of publicity for Mrs Wilkinson's trainer, and three new owners had decided to send him a total of ten horses. One, a beautiful chestnut mare called Miller's Daughter, arrived ahead of the others.

Miss Painswick had just sent out the invitations for an owners' lunch and a parade of the horses in early September, when it was discovered Miller's Daughter had a cough, a running nose and scoped dirty, indicating an illness.

Summoned, Charlie Radcliffe shook his head.

'Sorry, Marius. You'll be off for two months at least.'

Within a couple of days, every horse in the yard was coughing. The new owners had to be warned to keep their horses away, and because they wanted to run them, they took them to other trainers. Except for Miller's Daughter, who had to remain at Throstledown until she was no longer infectious. Her owner, a comely blonde called Alex Winters, wasn't nearly apologetic enough that she had grounded Marius's yard. Judging by the speed with which she'd taken her other horses to Harvey-Holden, Marius wondered if Miller's Daughter had been fed in deliberately.

548

He was on the verge of suicide. He couldn't pay his staff and had little to feed his horses, except for the forage he'd got in early. That morning he'd had a foul letter from his bank manager, who was threatening to seize the yard. Marius couldn't ask Valent for any more money. He was acutely aware that Amber and Rafiq were in despair at having no rides. At least Rogue was getting plenty from Rupert Campbell-Black.

Marius was just waiting for Painswick to go home so he could get stuck into a bottle of whisky, but she was hanging around shuffling papers. He pretended to be glued to *At the Races*, which was showing a race in Saratoga, in which Rupert's grandson Eddie Alderton, on a black horse in a white bridle, was being ponied down to the start.

'Boy's alleged to be as good a rider as Rupert,' said Marius, turning up the sound. 'Go home, for God's sake.'

Miss Painswick walked over and turned off the television.

'I'd like to say something. But first I'd like you to pour me a large glass of whisky.'

'I need the whole bottle myself, just bugger off.'

'Don't swear, it doesn't help. I know how bad things are, I do the books.'

'I'm fucked,' said Marius, getting out the whisky bottle.

'I may appear disapproving and frosty but I've enjoyed working for you, and I'd like to go on doing so.'

'I said I'm fucked, so you can't.'

Any good trainer always looks tired. Marius looked near death, black hair nearly all grey now, hollow cheeks, sunken, bloodshot eyes, teeth savaging his lower lip.

'You poor boy,' said Painswick, 'I know how hard you've tried. Things will pick up. I'm prepared to work for nothing until you get straight.'

Marius's hand trembled as he handed her a glass of neat whisky.

'That's amazingly kind.'

'I also have a few savings. You're welcome to those if you'd like them. I'd like to help out. With the floods I'm not sure how many of Mrs Wilkinson's syndicate are going to be able to pay her training fees.'

Marius slumped on to the sofa, narrowly missing Mistletoe, who jumped up and tried to lick his face, which was now in his hands.

'That is so incredibly kind, Miss P. I can't believe it when I've been so persistently bloody to you. If I could not pay you until the bloody cough's gone, and perhaps borrow a few grand?'

*

How could she have said these things, handing over her savings, wondered Painswick as she walked slowly home. Awaiting her on the doormat was a letter from her insurance company saying they couldn't pay her for any flood damage because they'd gone into receivership.

Miss Painswick was always depressed at the beginning of September. The turning trees, reddening apples and traveller's joy foaming like sherbet along the hedgerows reminded her of returning to Bagley Hall to work for her beloved Hengist Brett-Taylor.

Pocock was also depressed to have only two days' work a week. Men with spare time on their hands, however, become bossy. Pocock consequently started nagging Miss Painswick to rid Ivy Cottage of the ivy which encased it, darkening its rooms by growing over its lattice windows and even creeping inside bathrooms and landing windows.

'It'll pull out the brickwork, like chewing gum pulls out your stoppings,' he nagged yet again when he paused to pass the time of day as Miss Painswick dead-headed the roses in her front garden.

'But it's called Ivy Cottage.'

'I've lived in Willowwood since the war, place didn't always have that weight of ivy. Pretty cottage underneath.'

'I'm perfectly satisfied,' said a nettled Painswick.

'If you ever wanted to sell it, or raise a mortgage on it, it'd be much easier with the ivy off. If you don't like it bare you could always grow up a honeysuckle or a nice red rose.'

The smothering dark ivy, Pocock reflected, was rather like Miss Painswick's clothes: dark tent dresses, loosely cut coats and skirts, only occasionally brightened by a bright hat or Hengist's green and blue scarf, clothes which so concealed her body that no one had any idea what her figure was like at all.

'I could take it off for you,' he offered. 'I'm free Mondays, Wednesdays and Fridays now.'

'I'll think about it,' said Painswick.

Later she accosted Etta, weighed down from shopping in Larkminster, who since the Polo was grounded was walking back from the bus stop.

'Pocock wants to take off the ivy.'

'He's probably right about it not doing the house any good,' pondered Etta.

'It might have gone too far and he might pull the whole thing down,' said Painswick.

Next moment, Ione, on a one-woman mission to save the planet, came by on her bike, trailing jute bags of organic goods.

'Hear you're taking off the ivy,' she yelled. 'Good of you to give Pocock some work, but ivy does provide food for the bees and shelter for the birds. Ivy flowers are particularly good for late feeders in winter when there's not much food about. So think carefully about it,' and she pedalled on.

'Bossy old bag,' said Painswick with surprising ferocity. 'She didn't think carefully about cutting Harold's hours.'

They were joined by Alan, who'd been for an unlikely walk, with his shirt buttons done up wrong. He urged Miss Painswick to get the ivy off, 'Pocock's such an old pro,' and insisted on carrying Etta's shopping home.

'But what about the birds and the bees?' Etta asked him anxiously.

'I don't think Painswick knows much about them,' said Alan.

So Painswick gave Pocock the go-ahead.

After a restless night, Painswick set out for Throstledown. Marius's remaining horses were out in the fields, shaking manes and tails, kicking irritably to drive away the flies from their bellies. Heavy rain in the night had bowed down the willows, so, like George Eliot's hair, their crinkly pale green tresses divided at the top to reveal yellow partings.

Half an hour later, Pocock rolled up at Ivy Cottage, shinned up his ladder and began cutting back, tugging, pulling, clipping, sweating, swearing. By working frenziedly, he managed to get half the ivy off the first day and returned on Saturday. Collecting a cup of tea and leaving Miss Painswick to scrub the kitchen floor, he was soon up his ladder, cutting and pulling, trying to swear less.

Tugging off the ivy which was threatening to invade a rather pretty bedroom window, he nearly fell off his ladder, for there, changing to go out after a vigorous morning's housework, was a naked Miss Painswick. Pocock had to grab hold of a clump of ivy, for she had the most charming body, with full high breasts, and as she turned, a plump but firm bottom curving in at the waist. Leaning inwards, he discovered there was not a varicose vein in sight and her pubic hair was the softest mouse brown.

Scrambling down the ladder, a huge erection steepling his dungarees, Pocock frantically pretended to be draining a cold cup of tea as Etta and Priceless arrived to take Joyce shopping.

Five minutes later, hearing excited squeaks of 'Joyce, Joyce,' Painswick ran out to find Etta admiring the cottage and Pocock's work.

'Oh Joyce, the cottage looks so pretty and Harold's just unearthed the most charming little window upstairs.'

Painswick, primly dressed in her grey boxy jacket and straight skirt, stood back to look, her lips pressed ready to disapprove.

'It does look nice, very nice indeed. Thank you, Harold. You were quite right.'

'Not finished yet,' Pocock smiled, showing several missing teeth.

As he finished stripping her house, he now dreamed of undressing her as well.

Pocock wouldn't take any payment, so Painswick presented him with a lovely dark blue scarf she'd been knitting him to say thank-you and invited him round for a drink the following afternoon.

Having invested in a couple of bottles of really good red, she spent a happy afternoon making canapés: asparagus rolls, smoked salmon sandwiches, cheese straws, mushroom vol-au-vents, sweet potato wedges and little chicken kebabs, all laid out on a table spread with a pretty pale blue cloth.

On impulse, Miss Painswick removed all the photographs of Hengist Brett-Taylor and replaced them with vases of flowers from the garden. Then she settled down to read the *Lady* and *Country Life*. She loved working at Throstledown but it was nice to get away.

Harold arrived in a lightweight dog-tooth check jacket, a bright blue tie and off-white trousers. Miss Painswick thought how dashing he looked, with his ruddy face and shock of white hair, and going into the kitchen for a bottle of red, gave herself another squirt of Anaïs Anaïs.

Pocock was very touched by the banquet on the drawing-room table, and although he would have much preferred beer, he was even more touched by the seriousness of the red.

'The cottage looks wonderful, so much bigger and lighter inside,' said Miss Painswick. 'You were quite right, I should have done it years ago, thank you so much. I hope you'll help me choose some roses for growing up the sides.'

Pocock, almost too nervous to eat, nibbled at a mushroom vol-au-vent.

'Have a stuffed date,' said Miss Painswick.

Though they had never had any trouble chattering before, they found themselves embarrassingly robbed of speech and were relieved when Chisolm leapt over the back garden fence. Pausing to dead-head a few roses, she trotted bleating up the lawn, in through the French windows and greeted them both fondly, nicking a cheese straw before settling in a flowered chintz armchair.

'Do you think she's had a domestic with Wilkie?' asked Painswick. But as she rose to fill Pocock's glass, Chisolm bossily nudged her hand, spilling dark red wine all over his pale new trousers.

Painswick was distraught.

'I'm so sorry, *naughty, naughty* Chisolm, bad girl. Oh, your smart trousers, I'm so sorry.'

Salt was the answer, but she was so flustered she couldn't find the salt cellar and instead seized a dishcloth. Filling a bowl with hot soapy water, she started sponging down Pocock's trousers, furiously rubbing at his crotch.

'So, so sorry.' She paused, to wonder if salt would be better.

'No, no,' croaked Pocock, emboldened by wine, asphyxiated by Anaïs Anaïs and feeling pretty breasts pressed against his arm. 'This is much better. Oh Joyce.'

As she rubbed, Miss Painswick realized something inside his trousers was moving upwards and her pursed mouth fell open in surprise.

'You're so pretty,' muttered Pocock, putting out a rough garden-grooved hand, stroking her hair until it fell out of its prim bun. Then, cupping her head, he drew it close, glancing at her in wonder, 'Oh Joyce,' and he kissed her amazed mouth.

'Oh Harold,' sighed Painswick, 'this is a surprise,' particularly as his hand left her hair and began to unbutton her navy-blue dress so he could slide it inside her bra, where he found breasts just as thrilling as the ones he'd seen through the window.

'You're so lovely,' he gasped, as Painswick's scented softness and plumpness collapsed on top of him.

Unchecked, unnoticed, Chisolm worked her way through asparagus rolls, stuffed dates, mushroom vol-au-vents, cheese straws, sweet potato wedges and the brown bread and butter beneath the smoked salmon, and then managed *Country Life*, the *Lady* and a few pages of *Thoroughbred Owner and Breeder* for pudding.

112

Etta was delighted when a glowing Painswick confided that she and Harold were now an item. Did he propose on *Gardeners' Question Time?* she wondered. She was, however, ashamed how low she felt to think that Pocock, not she, would in future be enjoying cosy suppers of macaroni cheese and *Midsomer Murders*. Joyce had been such a staunch, comforting friend.

Far worse, after Bonny's horrible jibes about her being a 'lascivious old lady', Etta had been very off-hand with Valent and refused all his invitations. Then she grew increasingly and miserably aware of how much she had come to depend on his friendship and kindness, as snatches of music or poetry reminded her of the lovely evenings they'd spent together.

She was desperately broke. Martin was grudging about helping her repair her car and the damage caused by the floods. The blackberries she used to pick while walking Priceless were over. She'd eaten all the apples which hung over her fence from Valent's orchard. Pavarobin was most put out that she no longer mixed cake and croissants with his birdseed. She imagined the fish in Valent's pond mouthing reproachfully when she no longer passed by to tend his garden. Gwenny and Priceless had got so used to chicken and liver she felt as disconsolate as a restaurateur trashed by A. A. Gill when they flatly rejected tinned or dried food.

Conkers baked in the oven soaked in vinegar and threaded with string for Drummond's birthday were equally spurned, Drummond displaying no interest in 'boring old nuts'. Later Etta received an irate call from Romy: had she no idea how much damage conker fights caused, had she not heard of Health and Safety?

Etta longed to send the conkers to Valent, and thought wistfully what fun they could have had playing with them. Only the rose she had grafted for him, growing on her window ledge since the flood, seemed a link with the past.

Her great fear was that Mrs Wilkinson, now over the cough and match-fit, would have to be sold, because none of the syndicate could afford training fees any more.

One cold October evening, coming out of the village shop she bumped into Mop Idol and, hoping for news of Valent, asked her home for a cup of tea. Mop Idol looked so thin and pale compared with her usual lovely blonde buxom self that Etta wished she'd been able to afford to make sloe gin this year. There were only two teabags left, Etta hoped she wouldn't want a second cup, but when she asked after Joey, Mop Idol burst into tears. He had failed to keep up the mortgage payments. He was so overdrawn that the bank was threatening to repossess the house. Last week he'd put the wages on a horse which had lost and he was betting maniacally to recoup his losses.

'Isn't there still work,' Etta felt her voice go thick, 'at Badger's Court to be done?'

'Valent's away, you know how involved he gets, in the States. He's launching a night-light called Guardian Angel, made by his Chinese factory, to stop kids being frightened of the dark. Wish he could invent something to stop grown-ups being frightened,' sobbed Mop Idol.

Remembering how she'd told Valent about Poppy's terrors, Etta nearly wept too.

'Oh Etta, what am I going to do?' went on Mop Idol. 'I've got four children and I don't think I can work any harder.'

'Of course you can't.' It would be even worse if she knew about Joey and Chrissie. Thank God, Joey had not got Chrissie pregnant.

Etta felt so sorry for her, and it also brought home how in the past she'd relied on Valent for help. If she had just picked up the telephone she was sure he'd have helped Joey, but no longer.

Mop Idol then set out for the Fox, which only paid £5 an hour. 'Least it's helping in the kitchen, not in the bar, so people won't see how dreadful I look,' she said, vanishing into the night. 'Thank you, Etta, for being so kind!'

Morale was also rock bottom up at Throstledown, where the staff had had to disinfect every centimetre of yard to get rid of cough germs.

Overwhelmed with restlessness, Etta took her torch and wandered up through the rustling leaves. At least the rustle meant no rain and firmer ground for tomorrow.

At a meeting in the Fox last week, there had been a strong move, led by the Major and Shagger, to sell Mrs Wilkinson and cut their losses. Dora, however, back from New York and bursting with plans, had reminded the room that Mrs Wilkinson's website was still receiving a thousand hits a day, and the fan mail begging her and Chisolm to come back to the race track was still flooding in.

'There's a public hunger out there,' pleaded Dora. 'Racing is crying out for a really charismatic horse ridden by a really charismatic jockey.'

'Then Rafiq must ride her,' insisted Phoebe. 'A member of our ethnic minorities would be . . .'

'Far less marketable than a beautiful girl on a gutsy little mare,' snapped Dora. 'Marius is putting up Amber. They both get mare's allowances.'

Everyone recognized that this might be Willowwood and Marius's final race. The money lent him by Painswick had gone on feed bills.

As a last hope, because she was so well and rested, Marius had entered Mrs Wilkinson for a two-mile four-furlong chase at Cheltenham on Saturday. She would be running well below the handicap but what the hell. Excellent prize money of £55,000 had attracted some big hitters. They included Rogue, who was forging a strong relationship with Rupert, on Lusty and Killer on Ilkley Hall. Despite it being early in the season, both jockeys were even more fiercely competitive and travelling to every meeting to get rides where they could win.

Arriving as a vast yellow moon was rising, Etta found the Throstledown yard deserted except for Tommy, who had fallen asleep in the tack room. The others had gone to the pub to drown their sorrows and spend their lack of wages. The open half-doors of the empty boxes were like cavernous eye sockets. Etta gave an old piece of blackberry and apple pie to Chisolm. To Mrs Wilkinson she gave half a packet of Polos and a serious talking-to.

'It's your last chance, Wilkie, it'll break your heart and all ours if you have to be sold. You'd die living with Harvey-Holden,' Etta shuddered, 'and he'd sack Chisolm for starters. Jude would probably eat her for tea. Everyone needs your help. Tommy, Rafiq and Painswick will lose their jobs if you don't get your hoof out. Marius is desperate for a winner. You owe it to us, Wilkie, you've had such a long break.'

Mrs Wilkinson looked and felt wonderful, her silver mane lustrous, muscle like iron beneath her gleaming pewter coat. She pretended to be asleep. Her good eye was closed, but from the lower lid of the empty socket of her blind eye, infinitely pathetic, as if to say 'I did have life once', sprouted three long black eyelashes.

'You've been so brave and come such a long way since I found you in the woods,' whispered Etta, 'but so many people's lives have been wrecked by the floods. Please help us.'

Mrs Wilkinson pretended to be asleep but she was listening.

113

One source of help which had been withdrawn was Corinna and Seth's grand Shakespeare evening in aid of the flood victims. This had fallen through because Corinna refused to participate if Bonny was involved.

'She must be debarred from the Bard.'

Martin was so appalled that his darling Bonny should be so despised and rejected, he called on Corinna to mediate and got a bucket of water tipped over his head. All this provided a great deal of chunter-fodder in the minibus on the way to Cheltenham.

Dora, who'd fed the story to the press, pointed out that the three radio masts on Cleeve Hill looking down on the racecourse must be Seth, Corinna and Bonny playing the three witches in *Macbeth*.

'"When shall we three meet again?"/"In thunder, lightning, or in rain?"' intoned Dora, glaring at the Major. 'That's very symbolic. If the syndicate folds and this is Wilkie's last race as our horse, heaven knows when we will all meet again.'

'She's got to win,' quavered Tilda, or how would she ever see Alan?

Alas, from Mrs Wilkinson's point of view, it had rained very heavily in the night, but at least a watery sun was breaking through a gap in the charcoal-grey clouds.

When they arrived Rupert Campbell-Black's Lusty, mean, moody and magnificent, as was his master, was prowling round the parade ring, followed by Ilkley Hall looking sleek but slightly porky after his summer break. He was followed by Cosmo Rannaldini's Internetso, who'd won his last three races, and a flash French gelding called Julien Sorel, on whom Lord Catswood had rather ostentatiously spent

£250,000, as a twenty-first birthday present for his son Dare.

Mrs Wilkinson had been reluctant to get into the trailer, but the moment she and Chisolm stepped out on to the Cheltenham courtyard leading to the stables and heard the cheers of her admirers, many of whom waved 'Welcome Back Wilkie' placards, she perked up.

'You're a Saturday horse now, Wilkie,' Tommy told her fondly.

Down in the parade ring, more well-wishers fighting for space laughed and applauded as she strutted past, big grey ears flopping through the holes in a silly green straw hat Dora had brought her from Mexico as a publicity gimmick.

'There's Tommy,' cried the punters. 'There's Etta, where's Valent? There's Chisolm. There's Amber in the green silks. Isn't she pretty? There's Rafiq who rode her earlier in the year. He's hot. He's riding that big brown one today.'

Bullydozer, huge, lumbering, pouring with sweat because Vakil had shaken a fist and cursed him in the pre-parade ring, was madly in love with Mrs Wilkinson, who'd protected him and admitted him to her gang shortly after he arrived. Now he followed her everywhere and looked round in admiration as Mrs Wilkinson, who had no desire to be held up by anything, dragged Tommy across the grass, sending owners and trainers leaping for their lives, to greet her syndicate, nudging Marius in the ribs: 'I'm going to win for you today.'

'Not unless you take off that bloody hat,' grumbled Marius, as shaking hooves with Painswick, pretending to fall asleep on Etta's shoulder, showing off, Mrs Wilkinson demonstrated once again how she adored an audience.

Brandishing a microphone, Alice Plunkett sidled up to a seething Harvey-Holden. 'Nice to see your old mare back on form,' she said slyly.

'Looking like the seaside donkey she is,' snarled Harvey-Holden. 'What possessed Marius to think she's got a hope in this race? And don't think the Rev Niall giving her the last rites is going to help. She and Bullydozer don't stand a chance.'

In retaliation, as soon as Amber mounted her, Mrs Wilkinson gave three terrific bucks to show how well she was, then, thrashing her plumy tail, giving a squeal of rage, took a lunge at her old enemy, Ilkley Hall.

'Keep control of that brute,' howled Harvey-Holden. 'Neither of you have learnt any manners since you've been off the track.'

'Hear, hear!' sneered Killer, who'd been surreptitiously texting illegal tips from the weighing room.

The wolf whistles of the crowd did not appease blonde Tresa.

Being the head lad's partner had not brought her any perks. She was overworked, had not been paid for the last month and now she was leading up Bullydozer and Rafiq, who'd joined the yard long after she had.

Michelle, who was leading up Ilkley Hall, smiled at her smugly. 'Let's have a drink and catch up next week.'

'I'd keep her on a loose rein to relax her,' called out Dare Catswood from the heights of a quarter-of-a-million-pounds' worth Julien Sorel, as a hopelessly over-excited Mrs Wilkinson carted Amber down to the start.

Next moment Bullydozer, having caught another glimpse of Vakil, fled past, startling Julien Sorel, who immediately took off, scorching past Amber.

'Nice to see you so relaxed,' she shouted.

They were all out. 'Are you ready, jockeys?' called the starter. The flag fell, the tapes flew, they were racing.

As Bullydozer, a lunatic front-runner, set off, binoculars leapt to eyes, race cards were scoured, as despite competing with two ex-flat horses, Lusty and Julien, he shot fourteen lengths clear. After the first circuit he showed no sign of letting up.

'Bloody hell,' muttered Joey, 'Josh told me to back him to lose.'

Rogue, as usual, chose to hover at the back and join the leaders at the last fence, particularly as it once again gave him the bittersweet pleasure of admiring Amber's graceful haunches, lust riding Lusty.

Gradually, Julien Sorel, Ilkley Hall and Internetso reduced the gap between themselves and Bullydozer.

Tommy, knowing what was at stake, watched the race through her fingers. Marius, in the last-chance saloon, was smoking with his back to the course. Mrs Wilkinson, mid div, was bustling along easily.

'Lovely girl,' cajoled Amber.

In front of her, Internetso, Julien Sorel and Ilkley Hall were toughing it out up the hill, turning the turf black with their hoof-prints, white plumes of breath rising from their nostrils as they overtook Bullydozer, who'd run a gallant race.

'Go for eet, Amber,' yelled Rafiq as now in fourth place she passed him.

But there was no room for a little one.

'Go back to the Pony Club, snotty bitch,' yelled Killer, glancing around. 'We're not letting you through.'

Mrs Wilkinson thought different. The crowds at Cheltenham remember it to this day. Glimpsing back through her legs, realizing Rogue was about to swoop, Amber, using Ilkley Hall's plump quarters as a guideline, jinked Wilkie at a right-angle right, then right-angle left like a polo pony, then right-angle left again, three sides of a square, before putting on a phenomenal burst of speed and drawing away from the leaders.

Heartened by the crowd bellowing her name, their cheers driving her forward, Mrs Wilkinson belted up the home straight, somehow escaping her pursuers.

That same moment Bullydozer, like Count Romeo, seeing his dear mentor and protector surging ahead, responding to Rafiq's whip and pounding heels, caught the leaders on the hop, scorned Rogue's late run and passed the post hardly a length behind Mrs Wilkinson.

Marius fought back the tears but Joey had no such reserve. One had wagered £1,000 he couldn't afford on each horse, the other £500.

Pocock's hand slipped joyfully into Painswick's, Alan's into Tilda's and Woody hugged Niall. 'Thank you, dear, dear God.' Etta jumped up and down, up and down, clutching Dora, both yelling at the tops of their voices, drowned by the ecstatic roar of the crowd. Once past the post, Mrs Wilkinson slowed to a walk. Amber, delirious with joy, turned to shake hands with Rafiq.

'We did it, we did it, we beat the buggers.'

Next moment Rogue had caught up with them.

'Well done, darling, bloody good,' he told Amber, 'and as for you, you little tinker,' leaning over, he hugged Mrs Wilkinson, ruffling her mane and pulling her ears. The crowd, loving a generous loser, roared even louder.

'Thank God Rupert isn't here,' said Rogue. 'I'd be Campbell-Black and blue for getting beat.'

For a divine second, he and Amber smiled at each other, then Dare Catswood, who'd come fifth, cantered up. 'Well done, Amber,' he shouted. 'Bloody good show, Bolly's on you tonight.'

Fuck, fuck, fuck, thought Amber as Rogue's face closed up and he trotted off.

But as Wilkie, led by Dora and Tommy, entered the noisily appreciative winners enclosure, Marius noticed they were practically holding her up. For once her ears weren't pricked but flat against her hung-down head, her white face black with mud, her sides heaving, and with a lurch of guilt and gratitude he realized she'd given her all to save him and his yard.

As they posed for photographs, he put his arms round her and kissed her on her forehead. 'You're a mare in a million.' Then he kissed Amber, 'Well done.'

'You shouldn't get rid of your cast-offs so casually,' Dora taunted a hopping Harvey-Holden, who'd only managed fourth place with Ilkley Hall.

'Glad we took the informed decision to give Mrs Wilkinson another chance,' said the Major pompously.

'Oh ye of little faith,' murmured Niall.

Chisolm was less restrained. Resenting such disloyalty to Mrs Wilkinson, she lowered her head and butted a posturing Major on his posterior.

'That's why they're called buttocks, because they get butted,' said Dora to howls of laughter, as a furious Major picked himself up from the mud.

Marius was on his mobile, grinning like a lottery winner.

'It's Valent,' he said. 'He saw the race, he's over the moon, it's midnight in China.'

'Oh, let me speak to him,' gasped Etta.

'He wants to congratulate his jockey,' said Marius, handing the mobile to Rafiq, 'and to know why we're all making a fuss of Mrs Wilkinson instead of hugging Bullydozer.'

'Because Wilkie's one hell of a horse,' said Joey, kissing her.

Remembering last night's talking-to, Etta said, 'And she is a very good listener.'

114

So many lives had been ruined by the floods. As if she were truly responding to their cries for help, Mrs Wilkinson carried on winning: at Chepstow, Wetherby, Newbury, Sandown, Kempton, where on Boxing Day she pulled off an amazing victory in the King George VIth Cup to win nearly £90,000. Consequently she became so popular that wherever she raced, she put tens of thousands on the gate.

As she won, slowly the syndicate began to make money. Not huge sums because after you've taken off 10 per cent for Marius and 10 per cent for Amber, and divided the rest between ten with several people owning one share, £50,000 didn't go that far, but enough to put a smile on everyone's face.

One member who was smiling all the time was Tilda who'd at last been able to afford to have her teeth fixed. Now she could laugh and call out, 'Do your Tilda Flood face, Wilkie,' with the rest of the syndicate.

Joey had avoided the Grim Repossessor and, with his team, was repairing the all-weather gallop and, as more owners rolled up, building more boxes at Throstledown. Marius was greatly relieved to be able to repay Painswick.

Niall was blissfully happy with Woody, who by night could often be seen limping, trembling, through the frozen grass towards the vicarage. A church tribunal, tipped off by a wildly jealous Shagger, decided to overlook Niall's affair with Woody because his successful blessing of Mrs Wilkinson was such good publicity for the Church of England. The church was always packed as the congregation listened for the latest updates from Niall, who accompanied Wilkie to every race, vying with the Catholic priests who blessed the Irish horses.

Alban had a kosher quango at last: £100,000 a year to decide if sitting in front of computers all day made people obese. So far Alban had managed to avoid Martin Bancroft's attempt to forge a link with his WOO campaign.

Corinna insisted on taking a hair and make-up artist every time she watched Wilkie race, always holding up the minibus. She and Seth tried to dictate Mrs Wilkinson's campaign to fit in with their acting commitments. Marius ignored them. Bonny never came to the races, commenting bitchily how she envied Corinna having so much free time to witness Mrs Wilkinson's triumphs.

'Alas, I'm always working, but my trainer Marius Oakridge updates me on the phone and sends me videos.' (A complete lie.)

This task was undertaken by a still star-struck Phoebe, who to Painswick's irritation had achieved her ambition to work part-time in Marius's office. She was needed to cope with Mrs Wilkinson's huge fan mail, now that even letters addressed to 'Mrs Wilkinson, somewhere in England' reached Throstledown. Vats of barley sugar, Polos and carrots poured in.

'Can't we tell fans she loves champagne?' suggested Dora.

An open-top single-decker bus had been ordered, so Wilkie could ride in triumph round the village after a win.

Now his wife was the breadwinner, an unemployed Toby was making rather a success of looking after little Bump. Everyone was having bets on who would talk first.

Those around Mrs Wilkinson were also becoming stars. Amber was permanently in the gossip columns and on the cover of magazines. Tommy was interviewed for *Racing Post* and photographed from a flattering angle rushing forward to welcome a winning Wilkie. Mrs Wilkinson had such clout as a crowd-puller that Chisolm was allowed to go down to post with her. Chisolm herself had already had an *Observer* profile, and her bleat had been heard on Radio 4. Dora was ghosting a cookery book for her called *Goat Cuisine*. When Mrs Wilkinson, coached by Dora, met the Queen, she executed a wonderful bob. Chisolm blotted her copybook, wolfing a posy of primroses just presented to Her Majesty by a little girl, who didn't stop bawling until she was allowed a ride on Wilkie.

Mrs Wilkinson's photograph also appeared on a Glad to be Grey poster for Age Concern. Her willow-green browband was universally copied by the Pony Club. The press, revved up by Dora, nicknamed her the 'People's Pony'. How could anything so small contain such a huge heart?

Dora had also revamped an earlier refrain about the great jockey Aubrey Brabazon.

'Amber's up,' sang the fans, 'The money's down, the frightened bookies run / So come on punters give a cheer for Mrs Wilkinson.'

Marius's other horses, Furious, History Painting, Bullydozer, Count Romeo and Oh My Goodness, to name a few, were all doing well. It was hoped that Mrs Wilkinson's beau, Sir Cuthbert, after his long, long lay-off might race again soon.

Marius had notched up fifty wins by the end of January. He kept seeing Olivia at the races looking lovely and cherished by Shade. But when Mrs Wilkinson, despite carrying another 13 lb due to her successes, had her glorious victory in the King George, beating Playboy, Shade's Gold Cup hopeful, Olivia rang up to congratulate him.

'They talked for twenty minutes and Marius was so un-grumpy afterwards,' Phoebe delighted in telling Amber, who was still not praised enough by Marius.

But at least the sapphire and crimson flag was flying continually again at Throstledown. And when Marius complained that Killer and Ilkley Hall had once again cut up Rafiq and Bullydozer at Sandown, Killer was banned for a week and no stewards ignored Marius's objection because his wasn't a big enough yard.

The flip side was the press hanging around the whole time. Marius loathed this. Not only did it disrupt the peace of the yard, but he was far too superstitious to enjoy pronouncing on the likelihood of his horses winning races.

The syndicate, however, was reaping benefits. Because of his diplomatic skills, Alban had also got a consultancy job with World Horse Welfare, heading up a campaign to put an end to the dreadful transporting of live horses abroad. Ione had been invited to go on *Celebrity Big Brother* and as Green Queen was frequently asked on telly, usually to shout at tycoons because of their excessive carbon footprints. Willowwood's own tycoon, Valent Edwards, had been away. Following the worldwide success of Guardi, the lit-up Guardian Angel who dispelled children's fear of the dark, Valent's Chinese factory was working on other toys.

The Major was kept busy controlling the parking of all the tourists who poured into the village. All the local businesses were prospering. The Fox, renamed the Wilkinson Arms and with an inn sign of a white-faced Mrs Wilkinson with her tongue lolling out, was always packed. A betting shop called Easy Lay had opened in the high street. The village shop and post office, threatened with closure, had to stay open to cope with Wilkie's fan mail.

Painswick and Pocock, growing even closer and also padding through the frozen grass, were planning to move in together and spend their winnings and the money from the sale of Pocock's house on opening a teashop.

Miss Painswick's adored former boss, Hengist Brett-Taylor, whose photographs she had taken down in the drawing room, had meanwhile become a huge television star. A second Simon Schama, he was making a drama-documentary about the legend of Willowwood and the rise of Beau Regard the Second. He was working closely with Alan, whose publishers had suddenly become wildly excited about his inside story of Mrs Wilkinson. Both Hengist and Alan were delving into her past.

To rub acid into the wound, fans and press never failed to remind an increasingly maddened Harvey-Holden that he had let the mare who had so helped racing slip through his fingers.

Even more wickedly, Dora had taught Mrs Wilkinson to yawn for the cameras every time Harvey-Holden's name was mentioned.

115

Stardom, however, invites jealousy. Morale may rocket in a yard that brings home winners, but Josh and the other lads, who considered themselves far better riders than Rafiq, were irked by his success. It was worse now Dora had got to work, organizing features in the nationals, which led to a piece in *Hello!* that included moody, sexy photographs of Rafiq, the tigerish 'Shere' Khan of racing. This resulted in a lot of ragging, but also some snazzy clothes and a small car, thanks to Dora. She had craftily explained that, if Rafiq were given money, he'd send it straight home to Pakistan.

Furious was also becoming a cult figure, an alpha mule captivating the crowd with his wayward antics. In big races he was now allowed to miss the parade before the start because he bit and kicked both people and horses. Having refused even to be tacked up at Ascot, his finest hour had occurred in the Larkminster Cup, his prep race for the Cheltenham Gold Cup, when as the tapes went up, he turned, sending the man with a whip leaping for his life, and bolted in the other direction. Hauled round after a furlong by a screaming Rafiq, he changed his mind and belted after the high-class field. Horrified to find himself among them, he overtook the lot to beat Lusty by a length, to scenes of hysterical laughter and adulation.

Like Mrs Wilkinson, he was a character and whenever he ran, the public flocked to the track to watch the bad boy of racing. Rafiq adored him more than ever, wandering round the yard and the fields without a lead rein, Furious following him like a big dog.

'Amazed *Hello!* got a word out of him,' snarled Josh. 'All he ever talks to or about is Furious.'

Rafiq now prayed to Allah that Marius would put him up on Furious for the Gold Cup in March. He had stopped praying for Amber to return his love. Even if his career continued to soar, like Buraq the flying horse who carried the Prophet to paradise, their backgrounds were too different. Even if he came 'singing from Palestine', Amber, his lady love, would never welcome him home.

Hearing him singing his mournful songs round the yard, however, Dora had opened negotiations with a record producer. 'Rafiq's so beautiful, he's got such a lovely voice, he could easily become a pop star.

'Honestly, Rafiq,' she sighed later, 'with me around you don't need an agent.'

When Etta met Hengist Brett-Taylor she thought he was one of the most gorgeous men she'd ever encountered and totally understood Painswick's crush. He was so amused and amusing and couldn't stop laughing about his old secretary's new love.

'I cannot believe the old duck's got a drake at last, or rather a Pocock. I must tell Sally,' and he rushed off to ring his wife.

Etta also loved Hengist because he rolled up with a beautiful white greyhound called Elaine, with whom Priceless fell madly in love, and even more because Hengist insisted on having Rafiq, his gaol-mate, in his drama-documentary. Dora's boyfriend Paris was playing Sir Francis Framlingham. Rafiq, in a blond wig, plumed hat pulled down over his nose, was acting as Paris's stand-in, cantering across Larkshire on Mrs Wilkinson to recreate Sir Francis going to war on Beau Regard.

Hengist was also using Rafiq in the documentary to put forward the Muslim point of view. There was a touching moment when they were filming in the church, as a bristlingly defensive Rafiq had gazed down at the stone effigy of Sir Francis for a few moments before murmuring, 'He too went a long way for his religion.'

Rafiq had mellowed. As a Muslim he had learnt that human life was sacred, but, steeped in the ideology of the terrorist training camp, he had come to believe that his own life should be sacrificed for the cause in the holy war to wipe out non-believers. But gradually he had found himself growing to love non-believers. Not just Hengist, who had protected him in prison, or Marius, who had bought back Furious and given him a chance as a jockey most lads could only dream of, or Etta and Painswick, who'd mothered him so kindly, or Valent, who'd tipped him so generously and fought his corner. There was also his dear friend

Tommy, who worked so tirelessly on his horses, advised him so tactfully and had contributed so much to his dramatic rise to fame.

Rafiq was keeping his nose clean. He was extra careful because he was sure the police were watching him and tapping his telephone calls, hoping this would lead them to his cousin Ibrahim, who he believed was still hiding out in the lawless bad-lands on the borders of Pakistan.

To up their incomes, Josh and the other lads all passed on tips to punters. 'It's a lovely day in Willowwood' was code for a horse likely to win, while 'It's raining in Willowwood' indicated one that hadn't a chance. Rafiq had stopped even giving free tips to the friends he had made in gaol.

Tommy, meanwhile, who looked after Wilkie, Romeo, a rapidly improving Bullydozer, and Furious when Rafiq was away, was well ahead in the Throstledown points system that allocated a groom three points for a win and one for a place.

Tresa and Michelle (even though she now worked for Harvey-Holden) were wild with envy. They were a thousand times prettier than Tommy, but they didn't get the fan mail, weren't pestered for autographs or have their pictures in the *Racing Post*. Owners pinched their bottoms, but they didn't thrust fistfuls of tenners into their jeans pockets for racking up wins and turnout prizes.

To Tresa and Michelle, Tommy was the school swat, always working, always putting the stupid horses first, because she had nothing else with which to fill her life. They couldn't appreciate that the public adored Tommy because she always smiled and although no one hugged and patted her horses more enthusiastically when they won, she comforted them and their jockeys equally lovingly when they lost.

116

This festering jealousy erupted one late January evening after the Larkminster Cup, when traditionally jockeys and stable lads and lasses from neighbouring yards joined up at a Larkminster club called Electric Blue for a party.

On this occasion, the drinking was very heavy, both to celebrate Furious's victory and to blot out a hideous death. Harvey-Holden had run the lovely little mare called Gifted Child, who had never really fulfilled the promise she had shown when she was trained by Marius. He had therefore instructed his hired assassin, Vakil, who had so terrorized Bullydozer, to slip Gifted Child a bucket of water before the race.

As a result, she broke a blood vessel and her off fore, landing clumsily six out. Struggling up, she collapsed trying to jump the next fence. Her stable lass had gone home in tears. Vakil, unmoved, had pocketed £300 from Harvey-Holden, and this evening was intending to lay a stable lass or at least a prostitute. 'Why you no kiss me?' he was asking Tresa.

'Because you're not a good kisser,' she snapped back.

Vakil worked forty-eight weeks a year and sent his wages home to support his wife and four children in Pakistan, whom he boasted would one day become dentists and lawyers and keep him in his old age. Tonight he was planning to enjoy himself.

The party from the racing yards was seated at a long table looking down on a dance floor filled with writhing couples and surrounded by more packed tables. As well as Tresa and Vakil, the racing party included Josh, Michelle, little Angel and jockeys Johnnie Brutus and Dare Catswood, who'd had a second at Larkminster, and Dare's brother Jamie. Jamie was Harvey-Holden's new pupil assistant, who claimed he wanted to train horses but was really more interested in getting up at midday and shagging stable girls.

Jamie had a loud voice, wore red cords and a striped scarf – a prat in a cravat – and was accepted because Mummy had horses in training and rich Daddy was a member of the Jockey Club. Jamie was good with owners and at opening champagne bottles, and it was agreed H-H needed someone like that.

The group were all shouting with laughter. Yelling to make themselves heard over Lily Allen and the pounding of the disco, they gazed through visibility much thicker than the fog at the races earlier, in order to play a game called Snog-a-Trog. Snog-a-Trog involved each person in the party picking out a really unattractive member of the opposite sex – which was often hard through the gloom – and seeing how quickly they could snog them. Jamie, whose new job it was to time horses on H-H's gallops and who was already very drunk, was randomly timing progress with a stopwatch.

Michelle, looking sexually predatory in tight red-leather trousers and a red see-through shirt with a red bra underneath, had kicked off. She had approached a bespectacled geek in short-sleeved crimplene and with a mullet, who'd been dancing around waving his arms like an over-adrenalized tic-tac man, only to be primly told he was engaged. Josh was now across the room dancing with a girl with a turbot's face and a huge bust, which rather precluded him getting close enough to kiss her.

This caused as much mirth as the fact that Awesome Wells, who had been expected to join the party after whizzing up to Wetherby, had afterwards got into the wrong private jet, fallen asleep and ended up in Dubai.

Amber, who was also riding at Wetherby, and Rogue, who was riding at Fairyhouse, were expected later, as was Rafiq. After his great win in the Larkminster Cup, Rafiq was doing a television interview about being the latest role model for young Muslims.

Great excitement was caused by the arrival of Eddie Alderton, a very blond American flat jockey who had grown too heavy and tall to do the weights, and was trying his luck as a jump jockey at Rupert Campbell-Black's yard, Penscombe. He also turned out to be Rupert's grandson, far more beautiful and drunk than anyone else, and he was buying most of the booze.

'I wanna play Snarg-a-Trarg, I wanna play Snarg-a-Trarg,' he kept saying.

'You gotta girlfriend?' asked Tresa, licking her lips.

'Ah got five.'

'Five?' shrieked Michelle disapprovingly.

'That still leaves two days free a week, if you're up for it,' said Eddie. 'Snarg-a-Trarg.'

Lily Allen was followed by Michael Jackson, then by Lady Gaga.

'He settled beautifully, switched gears going into the last, you'd think he'd just jumped in at the start,' Johnnie Brutus was telling himself.

'I'm going to have a crack at that tarty blonde,' announced Dare Catswood, and came back very shaken. 'It's a bloke, tried to drag me into the Gents.'

'Here's Rogue,' sighed Angel, 'isn't he gorgeous?'

Rogue had had a treble at Fairyhouse today and was riding there tomorrow, but had come back for the party.

To match his eyes he was wearing a kingfisher-blue sweatshirt which said, 'I rode work for Rupert Campbell-Black and survived. Could you?'

As he walked in, girls nudged each other, tossed their hair and rucked up their dresses. Rogue glanced round, waved at Johnnie Brutus, scowled at Dare Catswood, then, clocking that Amber wasn't at the table, made his way over to Tommy. She was sitting in a dark corner, making herself as inconspicuous as possible.

'Hi,' he said, kissing her. 'Where's Amber?'

'So sorry, she's not coming.' Then, as Rogue's face fell, 'She's just texted me, she's gone to see her dad who's in hospital in London.'

'Do you know which hospital?'

'I think she said the Marsden. She didn't know you were turning up here.'

'D'you want a lift home?'

'I'm waiting for Rafiq.'

'OK, see you.' Ignoring the yells of 'Rogue, Rogue,' he was on his way to the door when Johnnie Brutus swayed after him.

'Where you going?'

'Back to Ireland.'

'You just arrived. You're working too hard, relax. I'll find you a slapper, there are a couple at our table.'

Rogue glanced at Michelle and Tresa. Having just discovered he was Rupert's grandson, they were laughing uproariously at Eddie Alderton's jokes.

'I've had them both and they were rubbish,' said Rogue bleakly, and he was gone.

'Where'd Rogue go?' protested Eddie. 'I wanted to talk to him. I want to ride Lusty in the Gold Cup but I guess Grandpa'll put up Rogue. Thinks a lot of Rogue.'

'Thinks a lot of himself,' snapped Tresa.

'Who was he talking to?' drawled Eddie.

'Tommy Ruddock, works in our yard.'

Eddie got out a pair of binoculars and stared through the gloom at Tommy.

'That's my Trarg.'

Michelle and Tresa screamed with laughter.

'Have a crack at Lotto Briggs,' advised a returning Johnnie Brutus. 'Dare peeked into the ladies' changing room at Cheltenham, said she wears grey underwear, has a forest down there and her girlfriend would geld you. But you'd win first prize, Eddie, you can't get uglier than that.'

'No, I'm going to try that Tarmy,' insisted Eddie, 'she might know something I don't know about Rogue.'

Tommy tried to make herself even smaller. She was overwhelmed with longing. If only she were beautiful, like the other girls, jumping, swaying, their blonde hair swinging like the willows of Willowwood, showing off lovely legs in jeans or the shortest of minis.

She was used to melting into the background. Sometimes, out of kindness, girls dragged her on to the dance floor. Tommy was aware that tonight she looked particularly plain. She'd been up since five, ridden out four lots, driven to the races and back and bedded the horses down before coming here. She hadn't slept last night, worrying quite unnecessarily how Furious would perform. But the rain, which had been great for him, had frizzed up her hair more than usual. The heat in the room had turned her pink face red, and she'd forgotten a powder compact to tone it down.

When she got to the races, she'd found someone had pinched Rafiq's silks and Furious's cheek pieces, so she'd had to rush round begging replacements from travelling head lads and valets. She suspected Tresa had nicked them but she mustn't get paranoid. Oh God, they were all laughing and looking in her direction.

She supposed Rafiq was turning up because he'd hoped Amber would be here. Shy about going into clubs, he had asked Tommy to wait for him this evening. She drained her pina colada, then noticed the most beautiful man in the group, white-blond and Nordic, jumping down from the platform and fighting his way across the room.

'Tarmy Ruddock,' said the softest Southern voice.

Tommy started as the Adonis put two glasses of champagne down on the table and said, 'Budge up.'

Tommy budged.

'You are a legend.'

'Me?'

'You do Furious and Mrs Wilkinson, I've read about you in the *Racing Post*. Even my grandfather wants to poach you.'

'Me?' squeaked Tommy.

Tommy couldn't believe anyone, despite squinting slightly, could be so good-looking.

'Furious was awesome for a change,' said Eddie dismissively. 'My grandpop would soon get rid of those mulish antics.'

'It's part of Furious's character, he had a deprived childhood.' As Tommy raised her glass to drink, her trumpet sleeve fell back to reveal a huge bruise.

'Jesus, your boyfriend do that?'

'No, Furious, he gets excited. I haven't got a boyfriend.'

'You have now,' said Eddie. 'Come and dance.'

'Oh look, Eddie's got her on the floor,' screamed Michelle.

'Can't dance,' said Tresa, as Tommy bounced around like a bull terrier puppy.

'Doesn't get much practice,' sneered Michelle.

Jamie Catswood was looking at his stopwatch. 'He's going super,' he told the others.

As Eddie drew Tommy against him, Tommy could feel the solid muscle beneath his blue denim shirt. As he laid his cheek against hers, he made a thumbs-up sign behind her head to the giggling table, followed by a drinking sign to tell them to fill up his and Tommy's glasses.

The Black Eyed Peas were electrifying the dancers.

'I've got a feeling tonight's going to be a good night,' whispered Eddie into a bemused Tommy's ear.

They were all convulsed with laughter when a shadow fell across the table. It was Rafiq. He was wearing, courtesy of *Hello!*, tight black jeans and a shirt the clear scarlet of runner bean flowers. His hair, newly cut and styled for the Channel 4 interview, was spiked upwards with product, showing off the flawless cheekbones and forehead usually hidden by flopping black curls. He looked arrogant and antagonistic – not quite the ideal role model for young Muslims – as he scowled across at Vakil.

'Here's the "Shere" Khan of *Hello!*,' mocked Josh.

'Rafiq, Rafiq. Great win!' called out Tresa. 'Come and join our game.'

'What game?' said Rafiq.

'It's called Snog-a-Trog,' brayed Jamie Catswood, with whom Rafiq had already had spats about the British Army's presence in Afghanistan.

'Snog-a-Trog,' shouted Michelle over the din. 'You each pick the ugliest person in the room and then have a competition to see how quickly you can snog them. Johnnie's about to get a black eye from Lotto Briggs and Michelle goofed with a geek. It's your turn next, Vakil.'

'And Eddie's chosen Tommy,' said Tresa bitchily. 'He's doing good.'

'He what?' It was like a rifle shot. Rafiq swung round. There was Tommy, laughing and bouncing around on the dance floor.

'Eddie's got a dog on his telephone already,' giggled Jamie. 'Black Lab – another dog won't make any difference.'

'Take that back,' hissed Rafiq, seizing Jamie's arm and raising his fist. 'Take it back.'

'All right, mate, calm down,' said Jamie, looking rather frightened. 'I was only pulling your leg.'

'What you mean "pull my leg"? You think I'm gay?'

'It's a figure of speech, dickhead,' said Josh. 'Means taking the piss. For God's sake, cool it, Rafiq. Get him a drink, someone.'

Eddie's hand had moved downwards. Tommy had a big butt for sure, but as she smiled up in wonder, he noticed she had very pretty white, even teeth for a Brit and a sweet pink mouth and such sweet breath it would be no hardship to kiss her.

But as he bent his head, a vice gripped the shoulder he'd dislocated last year and he howled in pain, as he was pulled off Tommy and punched in his own perfect American teeth, a blow which threw him across the room.

'Leave her alone, you bastard.'

'Rafiq,' stammered Tommy, 'whatever's the matter? Eddie only asked me to dance and bought me a drink, he was being so lovely.'

'Lovely, my arse,' snarled Rafiq, grabbing her bruised arm so she too shrieked in pain. 'We're going home.'

'He knew all about Furious.'

By this time Jamie and Josh had jumped down from the platform and closed round him, Jamie picking up Eddie and restraining him as he tried to take a pot at Rafiq.

'Cool it,' snapped Josh, 'you don't want to get stood down before Cheltenham.'

'Get out of here,' Rafiq snarled at Tommy, then as she reluctantly moved towards the door, 'go on, quickly. Wilkie's cast herself.'

The moment she'd gone, he turned on Josh and a swaying about-to-lunge Eddie.

'I'm not having her humiliated,' he spat. 'If any one of you bastards breathes a word about snogging trogs, I keel you, I keel you.' Such was his mad dog frenzy, even Eddie backed off.

'It was a game, Rafiq,' called out Tresa, who'd also jumped down from the platform.

But Rafiq had vanished into a night as dark as himself.

'My God, there was murder or rather suicide bomb in his eyes,' said Dare.

'I'd commit suicide if I had a bum as big as Tommy's,' Tresa said, giggling nervously as they climbed back up to the table.

'Well well well,' Josh shook his head, 'I thought Rafiq was hopelessly hooked on Amber.'

'Amber's well fit, I'd love to shag her,' mumbled Eddie, grabbing a napkin to stem the blood pouring from his mouth.

'Tommy'd look better if you hid her face and that frizzy hair under a burka,' said Michelle bitchily. 'Are you OK, Eddie?'

'It's your turn to choose a trog to snog, Vakil.' Jamie got out his stopwatch.

But everyone had lost their taste for the game, particularly Michelle, when the geek with the mullet and the fiancée sidled up and asked for her telephone number.

117

Tommy and Rafiq were silent on the way home. Brilliant stars glittered through the bare trees, gardens were lit with snowdrops. Rafiq was desperately analysing his feelings, his volcanic burst of rage . . . Was he merely defending his dear friend whom above all things he didn't want hurt, or could it be jealousy, a lightning strike, sudden excruciating pain to see her smiling up at the effortlessly handsome Eddie?

'Is Wilkie OK?' muttered Tommy.

'She wasn't cast, I made it up. I am sorry, Tommy. We have another early start tomorrow. I kept you waiting, I don't want you to get too tired.'

Slowly Tommy's heartbeat grew slower.

Back at Throstledown, they found Furious and Wilkie flat out and snoring. Furious looked particularly sweet, his hooves curled round his nose. Chisolm, snuggled up against Wilkie's belly, opened a long yellow eye.

Rafiq looked at Tommy. It was as if he'd seen her for the first time, through newly polished spectacles. How dare those pigs call her a trog? He walked her upstairs to her room.

Outside she stammered, 'That was such a brilliant win.'

'I learn Furious could win the Gold Cup today,' said Rafiq softly, 'but tonight I learn something much more important. I have been barking up wrong treat.'

He took her round, anxious face in his hands, flattening the fuzzy hair, seeing how long and dark were her eyelashes and how bemused with love her eyes. Unable to stop himself, he dropped a kiss on her trembling lips, which tasted faintly of champagne.

Tommy shuddered then kissed him back, keeping her mouth

shut then opening it timidly as her hands crept very slowly up his chest.

'Oh Tommy,' mumbled Rafiq and kissed her much harder. 'It is truth, I dragged you away because I was jealous.'

'Jealous,' squeaked Tommy in amazement.

'I want you to be just mine.'

Then he let her go and opened the door further.

'You need sleep,' he smoothed the purple shadows beneath her eyes, 'and we must take this very slowly because you are so precious to me. I cannot bear anything to go wrong.'

Afterwards, Rafiq couldn't sleep. He felt huge happiness and confusion. Sweet Tommy, how could he have wasted so many opportunities when they'd been alone together?

As he prostrated himself in prayer on the white fur rug Tommy had given him for Christmas, he thanked Allah first for Furious's amazing win and then for Tommy. Then he groaned. 'Oh God, when I begged for someone to love, I forget to tell you what colour and what faith.'

Reeling with ecstasy and shock, Tommy, once her door was shut, was brought down to earth by a message to ring her father whatever time she came in.

'Young Rafiq was in a fight at Electric Blue tonight,' were his first words.

'Jockeys are always having fights,' protested Tommy.

'Knocked out Rupert Campbell-Black's grandson's front tooth.'

'How d'you know this so fast?'

'We're watching him. His cousin Ibrahim is rumoured to be back in England. Find out what you can. If he says anything it's your duty to tell me.'

'I love him, Dad,' said Tommy.

In a corridor of the Marsden, Amber slumped against the wall, desperately pale beneath the fluorescent lights.

Her father, all wired up in bed, had just told her he'd got lung cancer but in his usual sweet way had belittled any horrors.

'Don't worry, darling, I'll lick it. God, I could murder a fag or a drink now.' He had started laughing and coughing, then couldn't stop.

'Does it hurt terribly?'

'A bit – just had a shot of morphine – like Oliver Twist asking for morphine.' Billy laughed again, triggering more coughing.

He reached for her hand. 'Darling – oh shit – I know it's hard but please don't tell anyone. If the BBC find out they'd probably lay me off and I've got a few bills to pay. Your mother'll want to make it public.'

Amber said she thought she ought to tell her brothers, Christy and Junior, who were both abroad.

'Not yet,' Billy pleaded. 'How's Mrs Wilkinson?'

'Good. Entered for the Gold Cup. I'll try and win it for you.'

'That's great, darling.' Billy's eyes were drooping. 'Rupert's having trouble with Eddie Alderton, who's just like Rupe when he was young. Like Bambi and Bambi's father or grandfather. Rupert's never had a son that played up before. I'm so lucky to have you.' Billy's words were slurring. He was asleep.

Amber fled into the corridor, too stunned to cry. Twenty was too young to lose a father. She hadn't spoken to her mother since the appalling interview with Rogue. She could only imagine the meal Janey would make of 'my beloved Billy's battle with cancer'. It was Janey who'd leaked the quite untrue story about Amber having a walk-out with Dare Catswood, who Milly Walton was mad about anyway. But Janey would love a rich daughter she could bum off.

I mustn't work myself up, thought Amber. She'd never felt more lonely in her life. If only she could call Rogue, but he'd be shagging some slapper in Fairyhouse or Larkminster.

'It is, isn't it?' said a voice, as a woman in a fur coat sidled up. 'We thought it was, we're such fans. How's Wilkie?'

'She's fine,' stammered Amber.

'Could we possibly have your autograph?'

She handed Amber a little red diary, and as Amber scribbled her name, said, 'Thank you so much, we're such fans of your dear father too.'

'So am I,' mumbled Amber.

Rogue, flying back to Fairyhouse, had reached Heathrow. Amber's number was engraved on his heart, as was everything she'd said about him. He wanted to call her or text her, 'Sorry about your Dad, call me,' but she'd have switched off her mobile in the hospital. He located the Marsden number, then tore it up. He'd be the last person she'd want to talk to.

Rafiq's euphoria and feeling of coming home were also sadly fleeting. Furious came out of the Larkminster Cup so well that Marius entered him for a big race at Ascot a week later, where he was a very hot favourite.

While he was riding out on the morning of the race, noticing bluebell and primrose leaves pushing through the faded leaf mould and rejoicing that spring was on the way for him and Tommy, Rafiq was startled out of his reverie by his ringing mobile.

'Furious is not going to win today,' said a voice with a thick Pakistani accent, 'or we take out your family in Peshawar.'

'You don't know my family,' hissed Rafiq, pulling History Painting into a clearing.

'Oh yes we do.' The caller reeled off names and addresses until Rafiq's blood froze. It must be some terrorist mafia.

'Just fuck off,' he stammered.

'You've been spending a lot of time with Tommy Ruddock recently. D'you want her and Furious taken out as well?' The voice grew thicker and more menacing. 'We need funds. Allah will reward you if Furious doesn't win.'

Rafiq, who was vastly brave, hung up. Determined to ignore the threat, he caught up with the others and told no one.

The terror he always felt before a race was intensified a hundredfold that afternoon when he saw Tommy leading Furious round the parade ring at Ascot. She looked so radiantly happy and newly pretty because Tresa, feeling guilty about Snog-a-Trog, had straightened her hair for her.

Eddie Alderton, who was riding in the same race, had also noticed. 'Like your hair,' he called out to Tommy. Then to wind up Rafiq: 'How about a drink later?'

But Tommy had blushed, smiled and, turning lovingly towards Rafiq, said she was sorry, she was busy.

Suddenly Rafiq couldn't bear anything to happen to her, so he deliberately pulled Furious. This he did by holding him up for too long so that two furlongs out there was still a pack of horses ahead of him. Furious had no desire to mingle with them so he dawdled and came in sixth.

'Perhaps he was tired,' Rafiq told Channel 4. 'He only run a week ago.'

This enraged Marius. 'Don't you dare accuse me of over-running my horses,' he shouted at Rafiq. Having bollocked him for careless riding, however, he gave him the benefit of the doubt.

The Ascot stewards were less lenient. They and the crowd had been looking forward to seeing Furious repeat his Larkminster Cup form. They suspended Rafiq for a week for breaching the non-trying rules.

Later Marius returned to the attack.

'If anyone thinks I encouraged you to pull Furious, I could be

580

banned from entering any horse in a race for forty-two days
(which would rule out the Gold Cup and the entire festival), and
be fined thirty-five thousand which I can't bloody afford, so don't
do it again.'

Rafiq felt bitterly ashamed but waited in terror for another
telephone call.

118

Alan for once was working flat out. From his study window, over a pile of Wilkie's cuttings and photographs, he could often see her let out for an hour or two in her New Zealand rug, trailing her devoted entourage through the frosty fields.

He had accepted the fact that his marriage was dead. He hadn't seen Carrie for days. The hedge fund market was in free fall, Carrie clinging to the wreckage. He was convinced his only happiness lay in running off with Tilda, and he needed to make a massive success of Mrs Wilkinson's story to fund it.

He knew he was neglecting Trixie and he hardly had time to see Tilda, but he found intense satisfaction in rising at dawn to write, sustained by endless cups of black coffee made on the percolator Tilda had given him for Christmas. He didn't even slip out to the Wilkinson Arms at lunchtime or in the evening. Alban and Seth missed him dreadfully, and Chris complained his takings had nose-dived.

Adding pieces to the jigsaw, Alan had been digging into Wilkie's early history, even braving Harvey-Holden.

'H-H dear boy, I must devote a chapter to Usurper's leaving her dam and spending time at your yard. It's all a bit shadowy. Who broke her? You must have had valuable input. I'm determined to portray you in a positive light.'

'Fuck off,' said Harvey-Holden, hanging up.

How had she escaped the fire? wondered Alan. Hengist remembered Rafiq being close to Jimmy Wade, one of the Ravenscroft stable lads, when he was in prison, but when Alan asked Rafiq for details Rafiq had also closed up. H-H had such a rapid turnover of staff, most of them foreign, so when they left they disappeared off home. Alan talked to H-H's ex-wife, who remembered little Usurper as being a poppet, 'But frankly my mind was on escaping from H-H, not his horses.'

Moving on to the present, they were now a few weeks away from the pinnacle of the National Hunt season – the Cheltenham Festival. After her glorious win in the King George at Kempton on Boxing Day, Mrs Wilkinson was favourite for the Gold Cup. But after every big race the bookies would shuffle the pack and a new challenger would emerge.

It had been a tremendously exciting season, with Killer and Rogue battling to be leading jockey, Shade pouring in more and more to become leading owner, and Marius, Harvey-Holden, Isa Lovell and Dermie O'Driscoll fighting to become leading trainer.

One of the greatest prizes was the Order of Merit series, which awarded a million pounds to the horse that notched up the most points for wins in the biggest races. Mrs Wilkinson, Furious, Ilkley Hall, Bafford Playboy, Internetso, Dermie O'Driscoll's Squiffey Liffey and Rupert Campbell-Black's Lusty were all in contention. But as Marius refused to overrace his horses, Wilkie and Furious were unlikely to triumph unless they won the Gold Cup or the National. Fans and press still kept reminding H-H and Shade they had let Mrs Wilkinson slip through their fingers.

The Gold Cup demanded level weights, which meant all horses had to carry 11 stone 10 lb on their backs. This, in turn, meant that Amber, who was light, had to drop into her saddle a deadening amount of lead, which didn't move and thrust like her body, to be as heavy as the other jockeys.

Mrs Wilkinson had gone up 13 lb in the handicap after the King George at Kempton and another 7 lb after a good win at Warwick. She was therefore in danger of being forced to run only in races carrying weight beyond her strength. Like running a marathon when you're giving Jude the Obese a piggyback, reflected Alan.

Syndicates, however, become spoilt, and the more Willowwood won, the more they wanted. They were now looking forward to a trip to Leopardstown where a prep race in early February, six weeks before the Gold Cup, would boost both Wilkie's large Irish fan club and sales of Alan's book, when it was published. Dora had organized interviews with everyone. A special Cheltenham Festival preview had been arranged on Sunday evening to co-incide with the meeting, where all the leading Irish trainers, owners and pundits would be holding forth and would in turn be riveted to hear Marius's views on his horses' Gold Cup chances.

Mrs Wilkinson still preferred to travel everywhere with Chisolm in the trailer. On this occasion Marius decided to fly her over to

Ireland, believing that this would be less traumatic than a long journey imprisoned in the bowels of a ferry. Mrs Wilkinson thought differently and absolutely freaked out, trembling violently, rearing, lashing out and flatly refusing to join History Painting and Bullydozer on the plane.

When the flying groom got tough on the runway and, moving in between Tommy and Wilkie, tried to drag her on blindfolded, Wilkie completely lost it and most uncharacteristically savaged him.

'Ouija Board did exactly the same thing on a trip to the Far East,' observed Alan. 'Happens to great horses.'

All the same he was pissed off. Many of the syndicate, including Etta, had been too poor to go, but those who had already booked their flights and hotel rooms were livid – particularly Alan and Tilda, who were looking forward to a five-star night alone. Unlike Pocock and Woody, Tilda was too worried about her reputation to limp trembling through the frozen grass, although, Alan teased her, she was so pretty now with her straightened teeth, not even a binocular-waving Major would recognize her.

Wilkie's defection also meant that Tommy didn't go to Dublin either, which broke her heart. She'd so hoped, away from home, she might learn why Rafiq, after being so angelically loving, had so suddenly rejected her. He had bitten her head off when not totally ignoring her, and seemed terrified of being seen near her in public.

Fuel had been chucked on the fire when Etta, finding Tommy sobbing into Wilkie's shoulder, had again most uncharacteristically shouted at Rafiq for being mean. Rafiq had shouted back at Etta to mind her own business. Everyone was on edge.

119

Amber was just as miserable as Tommy. Like Mrs Wilkinson, she should have backed out of going to Dublin. She felt dreadful abandoning her father when he was still so ill in hospital, but a distraught Dora had begged her to go. She'd set up so many interviews for Amber, which would really make her name in Ireland, and compensate a little for Wilkie and Chisolm's absence. Furthermore, the generous Irish racing authorities had offered Amber the wonderful Parnell Suite at the Shelbourne Hotel.

What had shamingly tipped the balance was the knowledge that Rogue was riding in five races at Leopardstown. Amber dreamed that on his home territory they might somehow get together, and relieve the dull ache of longing that never left her. But on arrival in Dublin first thing on Sunday morning, she learnt that Rogue too was in hospital having dislocated his shoulder in a fall at Doncaster.

'Poor sod swears he'll be OK for Cheltenham,' said a jubilant Johnnie Brutus, who'd picked up those of Rogue's rides not appropriated by Killer. 'Must be gotted. This'll lose him the championship. All he cares about these days is winning. Used to be such a fon bloke, now he never laughs any more.'

Seeing Amber's stricken face, Johnnie suggested she come out on the town with them that evening:

'Dare Catswood dropped two Viagras in Awesome's Bloody Mary on the plane out. He's had a hard-on since he arrived – convinced it's the Dublin air.'

'I can't,' sighed Amber, 'I've got to go to this preview with Marius and tell the audience about Wilkie. Mr Monosyllabic is not going to satisfy them.'

Marius was out looking at horses and the other jockeys were riding in races, so later Amber travelled out to Leopardstown with Phoebe, the Major and Debbie.

As they crossed the Liffey, blue-grey and silver, reflecting the clouds and the sun glinting through them, the taxi driver announced he used to jump off this bridge as an eight-year-old.

'Wasn't it polluted?' shuddered Debbie.

'Filthy, it was so clean you could see the mullet going through it.' As they drove past faded russet houses, Debbie shuddered even more over the litter and the graffiti.

'They've got daffies and the blossom's much further out than in England.'

'That's because the air's gentler, like the people,' said Amber, who was surprised how much she'd enjoyed her morning's interviews. All the journalists were so friendly and enthusiastic.

'Where the Pony Club's concerned, you're a bigger icon than Jordan,' the *Irish Independent* had told her.

'I must try and keep my pedestal clean,' Amber had replied.

Phoebe was now grumbling about the security at Birmingham.

'We had to strip everything off. Painswick was down to her Damart thermals and Pocock to his long johns.'

Suddenly she shrieked with laughter as they passed a signpost to a place called Stillorgan. 'That can't be Rogue's home town. He's never kept his organ still in his life.' Amber wanted to throttle her. The Irish, the soft caress of their voices, reminded her so much of Rogue before he had become angry. She hoped he wasn't in too much pain.

Arriving at the racecourse with its big grey stand, she noticed the owners' and trainers' entrance, next to the ambulance gate, a constant reminder that danger, accident and death were never far away from jump racing. Outside, with prams full of goodies, one woman was selling slabs of chocolate for a euro.

Up in the stands, Amber looked down at the most beautiful course, ringed by blue mountains and woods through which, like rosy-faced children, more russet houses peered. On the rails were ads for Deloitte, Betchronicle, Party Poker and Irish Stallions, which brings us back to Rogue, thought Amber wearily.

Typically Irish, with horses at the heart of things, the stables were in the centre of the course. The runners, legs on springs like greyhounds, could be seen dancing across the track and returning more slowly after their race.

A large crowd had turned out in anticipation of cheering on Rogue, their favourite son, and to catch a glimpse of Mrs Wilkinson. People were soon bombarding Amber with questions:

'Is she thirteen or fourteen hands?'

'Did she miss a vocation as a footballer?'

Marius's day started well when History Painting won a handicap chase for Awesome Wells, but deteriorated when Playboy pissed all over the big race, the Hennessy Cognac, for a revoltingly triumphalist Shade. At least Marius had been spared a gloating Harvey-Holden, who'd stayed at home, obsessively chasing winners, because Irish victories didn't add any points in the leading English trainers' championship. Instead he had sent Michelle and Vakil, who, because a desperately uptight Rafiq was riding Bullydozer in a novice handicap, missed no opportunity to mob up their former horse. Killer, riding a new French gelding called Voltaire Scott, had been sledging Rafiq equally viciously in the weighing room.

Here, for the first time, Rafiq had put on Valent's new colours, purple covered with dusty green stars, green sleeves and a purple and green cap, inspired by an African violet Etta had once given him.

Watching Bullydozer in the parade ring, Amber thought he didn't move or look as well as usual, perhaps because Tresa was too busy tarting herself up to get her horses gleaming like Tommy did. The big horse trembled and cringed but didn't leap away when he saw Vakil. He really didn't look right. Amber was tempted to say something to Marius, but he'd only bite her head off. Marius himself was looking funereal, wearing his dinner jacket, which he'd need for the preview tonight, over jeans because he couldn't be bothered to bring two coats. Next door a trio of pretty women, however, were drooling over him.

'That's Marius Oakridge, who trains Mrs Wilkinson. Isn't he handsome? His wife Olivia ran off with Shade Murchieson, the big fellow over there; looks a brute, I'd have stayed with Marius. He looks much gentler.'

Marius was belying this by telling a shivering Rafiq to 'Go to the front, and lynch that fucker Killer,' as he legged him up. Valent had just called Marius from China, wishing him, Rafiq and his adored Bullydozer good luck, saying he was sorry he couldn't be with them. He was up-country and couldn't get to a television.

'Safe journey,' called Amber in Urdu as Rafiq passed but beyond glancing round in terror he ignored her and rode on.

'That's JP's plane,' said one of the trio of pretty women, as a helicopter chugged over. 'He's coming to the preview tonight. He'll be flying back to Limerick to change.'

Unlike Marius, thought Amber.

Up in the Owners and Trainers to watch the race, Amber was

horrified to find herself rammed by the crowd next to Shade. Oiled up by champagne and watching Bafford Playboy's victory again in the hospitality room, he was revving up to cheer on Killer and Voltaire Scott.

As his hot-chocolate brown eyes wandered over her, Shade smiled evilly. 'How's the wrist?' he murmured.

'Fine,' snapped Amber.

'You could put it to interesting use later.'

Blushing but totally ignoring him, Amber concentrated on Bullydozer going down to post. Again, she was puzzled he wasn't pulling at all, even when Killer and Voltaire Scott thundered past, deliberately trying to unsettle him and Rafiq.

Rafiq hardly noticed. An hour ago he'd received another telephone call, ordering him to pull Bullydozer, but this time he was determined to defy it.

As they raced past the stands on the first circuit, all the runners were bunched up together, so the handicapper had got things right. But Bullydozer, who always led, was last and clearly not right. Rafiq was so terrified that Marius and the stewards would think he was pulling the horse once more, deliberately not trying, he gave him three hefty smacks and dug his heels in. Bullydozer, who normally would have leapt forward, didn't react. He was stumbling and lurching now, clearly in pain.

'All right, Bully,' called out Rafiq, determined to pull him up after the next fence, but it was too late. Bullydozer hit the top, struggled to avoid a chestnut mare fallen on the far side, turned over and crashed to the ground on his head.

Television moves on, following the leaders and the living. The fence that had caused the tragedy was hidden from the crowd. Next moment Amber saw Marius belting down the track. Rafiq, who'd been thrown free, staggered to his feet, and over to a help-lessly writhing Bully.

'Don't die, don't die,' he sobbed, collapsing on to Bully's huge shoulder.

But before the screens had closed round them both the chestnut mare and Bully had gone still.

Meanwhile an ecstatic crowd were yelling, 'Go on, go on, go on,' like Mrs Doyle in *Father Ted*, as Killer eased Voltaire Scott first past the post.

Amber was so distraught about Bullydozer it was a few seconds before she realized Shade had his hand round her waist, his fat fingers massaging her breast.

'Come and have a glass of bubbly to celebrate,' he purred.

'Celebrate what?' exploded Amber.

'A great win and another chance to teach Throstledown not to pinch other people's horses.'

'No!' Amber would have screamed at him to eff off if the 'It is, isn't it?' brigade hadn't moved in again:

'Amber Lloyd-Foxe! Do tell us about Mrs Wilkinson. We specially came to see her.'

Amber managed to be charming for a minute, then she stammered, 'I'm so sorry, a friend's horse has just been killed.'

Turning back to the course, she could see Rafiq walking back clutching his whip, saddle and Valent's purple and ivy-green quartered hat. He was now standing: tall, slim and absolutely motionless, the brilliant sun casting his long black shadow across the deserted track as he watched the rerun of the race, including the hideous fall, on the big screen. He stayed so long, tears washing the mud from his face, that an official ran up saying he was so sorry about the horse but Rafiq had better move on, as the runners would soon be coming down for the next race. When Rafiq gazed at him in bewilderment, the official took his arm and led him back to the weighing room.

Marius loved Ireland and the Irish, who put him at his ease. Trust him to have given up drink in February, quipping it was the shortest month, only to be confronted with such a tragedy.

Bullydozer had been such a sweet horse, so grateful for kindness, so full of promise and Valent's pride and joy. His body would now be on the way to the nearest hunt kennels, but there was something especially poignant about a horse dying abroad. And there was still the empty box to be faced when he got home, and Valent in China to be rung.

Not an unkind man, Marius was just ham-fisted in his dealings with people. He had found Rafiq sobbing uncontrollably in Bully's box but had been unable to comfort him. The horse had looked wrong from the off; tomorrow he'd study the video.

Marius was also very fond of Billy Lloyd-Foxe, who had often helped him in his career. Painswick had confided that Billy had terminal cancer, so Marius wanted to comfort Amber. But he had been so burnt by Olivia, he was unprepared to risk a serious relationship. Michelle had been sex with no affection, but he was finding himself increasingly attracted to Amber and knew he was foul to her in an attempt to conceal it.

Now there was this ghastly preview to be got through, when everyone would be clamouring for information about his Gold Cup chances and what tactics he was planning to use. He was far too superstitious to suggest his horses were going to win and felt

589

that admitting what tactics he intended to use would be giving the game away.

Previews were all the same: trainers, jockeys, journalists, so-called experts, talking dickheads, going on and on about which horses were likely to win over the four days of the Cheltenham Festival. Going round and round the mulberry bush when in fact in each race one horse crossed the line before the others – end of story.

120

The preview consisted of a dinner held in a big room at the Shelbourne, with the panel of pundits seated at a long table across the end and everyone else at tables round the room. Those attending were mostly men, mostly in dinner jackets, some without ties, mostly drinking champagne. Marius had put on a dress shirt but not bothered to brush off the mud that covered his dinner jacket from kneeling beside Bullydozer.

Shade, at drinks before dinner, was in his element. 'Bafford Playboy's missing Cheltenham so he'll be fresh for Aintree,' he was telling everyone. As was the Major, who looked about to pop: 'I manage Willowwood. Yes, Mrs Wilkinson, pity she missed her prep race today.' Neither man realized that the charming men hanging on their every pompous word were only interested in selling them horses.

Phoebe, who had muscled her way in with Debbie, was boasting, 'I run the Willowwood syndicate. You should see Wilkie's fan mail. Yes, she's only five hands.'

Everyone was provided with notebooks to record pearls dropped by the panel.

Then Amber sauntered in from an interview with RTE, and the room went quiet. Television make-up had lengthened her yellow eyes and emphasized her big mouth. Piled-up gold hair showed off her lovely bone structure and long, slender neck. She was wearing high-heeled brown boots and a short, flesh-coloured shift with a big butch leather belt. She'd already had several glasses of champagne. Suddenly, every man in the room wanted to know how this ravishing young jockey rated Mrs Wilkinson's chances.

During dinner, after a first course of smoked salmon,

the microphone was brought over to her and Marius's table.

'Tell us about Mrs Wilkinson.'

'Every time she stands up, she wins,' replied Amber proudly. 'Everything I ask her, she gives. She's a street fighter. At Cheltenham, there'll be enough horses breathing down her neck to gee her or rather gee-gee her up. She's absolutely gorgeous.'

'That's enough,' snapped Marius.

'There's a cloud over Mrs Wilkinson,' volunteered one of the panel. 'She's never won over three miles.'

'She won the King George – that's three miles,' protested Amber.

'Do you want to tell us about Furious?' the interviewer asked Marius, who shook his head.

'Furious is like an Alsatian,' chipped in Amber. 'One doesn't take liberties. He's like Liam Gallagher. He may not come out of his dressing room, but if he does – wow!'

The audience were captivated. A great Irish racing journalist got up and dismissed both Furious's and Mrs Wilkinson's chances.

'Furious is too edgy: never take an edgy horse to Cheltenham. Mrs Wilkinson has a wonderful jockey,' he raised his glass to Amber, who could now be seen on the big screen coaxing Wilkie over the vast Kempton fences, 'but she's too small and carrying too much weight. It's too big an ask.'

'Boo,' yelled Amber.

'Eat up your dinner,' chided the Major.

Another panellist announced that he wouldn't look beyond Ilkley Hall. Shade smirked.

'Which of your horses will win?' the interviewer asked Dermie O'Driscoll.

'Squiffey Liffey is not slow,' said Dermie carefully. 'He'll go out and run a big race. Hopefully he'll be thereabouts.'

There was also a wonderful drunk on the panel who kept interrupting and getting lost: 'That happened where we were last week, somewhere up north, the winner was called – it's slipped my memory.'

Amber, who had gone off table-hopping, was having a heavenly time.

'I've met Willie Mullins, Tom and Elaine Taaffe, and Michael Hourigan, who's going to send me a picture of Beef or Salmon, and JP, who's got such merry eyes. I've always slagged off handicappers but I met a sweet one who showed me the way to the Ladies but wouldn't follow me in in case he got arrested,' she babbled to Marius, as she collapsed giggling on the chair beside him. 'And I met Ted Walsh who's so nice but he said such a spooky thing about Wilkie, that she was like Kicking King, who was so brave and competitive he raced his heart out, literally. I'd hate that to happen to Wilkie.'

Amber had table-hopped in an attempt to avoid Shade, who with an evil, knowing smile on his big lips, seldom took his heavy-lidded eyes off her. She felt like a baby bird being eyed up by a big greedy tomcat while its mother was off searching for worms. Marius was hardly a mother bird but she stayed close to him, knowing Shade wouldn't try while he was around.

The panel was winding up. Amber was ashamed she'd written so little about the Gold Cup in her notebook. Marius had written nothing.

'Have you rung Valent?' she asked him.

'I lost my mobile at the races. It's got Valent's number; it's got everyone's number. I can't even ring Painswick.' He was ashamed what a relief it was.

'I've probably got it,' said Amber. 'I found one in my bag when I got back to the hotel. You must have dropped it when Bully, when Bully, oh Christ—' Her voice broke. 'He was such a sweet horse – so sort of humble. My father had a horse he adored like that called The Bull.'

'Let's go,' said Marius. 'They're about to start the auction, and I don't want to bid five thousand for a visit to Dermie O'Driscoll's yard. I've spent quite enough this weekend. Don't say goodbye to anyone, just go.'

Amber caught a glimpse of Shade's outraged face, the tomcat deprived of its baby bird, as Marius whisked her out of a side door.

'Come and pick up your mobile,' she said idly, 'and see my amazing suite.'

121

'Christ,' said Marius, as he followed Amber into the Parnell Suite.

There were flowers everywhere, champagne on ice, a sitting room with sofas and chairs, a desk, two minibars to mock him when he wasn't drinking, and a television set which welcomed Miss Amber Lloyd-Foxe to the Shelbourne.

On the wall, beside watercolours of rolling hay bales and distant mountains, was a picture of Parnell: dark, balding, one slanting eye bigger than the other.

'The only thing it says on his grave is "Parnell born 1846"; isn't that cool?' said Amber. 'That's fame for you. Nice name for a horse, Parnell, bound to be taken. Here's your mobile. I must ring and check up on Dad,' she added, going towards the telephone.

Marius knew he ought to ring Valent, but instead he prowled round the huge room. Amber was a star like Parnell. He was proud and grateful to her for talking up his horses this evening. She had mellowed and was so much less arrogant than she used to be.

'Dad's sleeping,' she said, putting down the telephone. Immediately it rang.

'Go to bed, Awesome,' she said, hanging up. 'He's having a sauna with Michelle and Tresa,' she told Marius.

Marius laughed when she told him about the Viagra.

'Help yourself to the minibar,' she said, 'and can you open that bottle of champagne?'

'You've had enough.'

Amber escaped to the loo and found herself cleaning her teeth, then spraying on buckets of Madame to hide the smell of toothpaste, then powdering her nose. Returning, she found herself a glass and flipped through her messages. Two news-papers and a radio station were confirming interviews for tomorrow. She mustn't be late or get too hammered.

Suddenly she wanted Marius to kiss her, but turning she saw he'd opened his briefcase and was studying Monday's schooling lists to check which lad would be schooling which horse over fences or hurdles, and flipping through the DVDs of horses he might buy. He was flying straight to Leeds tomorrow, then on to Wetherby where he'd meet Josh and Tommy, Oh My Goodness and Romeo.

'Don't you ever let up?' she said sulkily.

She had kicked off her boots, losing five inches. Wandering towards the window, she opened the curtains a fraction. Below her, bare trees tossed like a silver sea. A horse clopped past, taking someone home in a cart. On the corner of the square, a floodlit statue of a soldier cast an ebony shadow over the pale steps behind. Amber shivered, reminded of poor Rafiq, transfixed with horror by the sight of Bullydozer's fall on the big screen.

'Weren't you pleased everyone was taking Wilkie and Furious so seriously?'

She looked at Marius who looked at her, both their resolves weakening. It seemed such a waste of a splendid bed.

Marry-us, marry-us.

'Must have a pee.' Marius took his briefcase with him, which contained a toothbrush. He used it as well as Amber's toothpaste.

But then, just as she heard the lavatory flush, there was a hammering on the door. 'Bugger!' she groaned.

Assuming it was Rafiq, who she'd told to call her if he got too miserable, she opened the door a crack and was asphyxiated by horribly familiar rich, sweet aftershave as Shade forced his way in.

Amber tried patter. 'Why didn't you ring first? You know I'm allergic to droppers-in. What do you want?'

'Another ride.'

Oh Christ, they were in the passageway leading to the sitting room. She prayed Marius couldn't hear; he'd never forgive her.

Shade had taken off his tie and his dinner jacket, his white silk shirt was predictably undone to the waist. He looked so devilish she expected flames to burst from his waxed nostrils and his black eyebrows to shoot up at the corners like Mephistopheles.

'I'm tired, Shade. Very tired. I've got interviews first thing. Please go.'

'Not like you. You used to be much more friendly.' Barging into the sitting room, Shade whistled.

'Nice place, get it gratis? Who did you sleep with to get this?'

As she chucked Marius's coke tin in the bin and put the champagne bottle back in the ice, he slid his hand under her dress, fingering her bottom, exploring it intimately. 'Lovely arse.'

'Don't,' said Amber furiously.

'Don't be silly. You could be a very lucky lady and have some really exciting rides. I'd use you in all ways.'

Oh God, if Marius knew she'd shagged Shade, such was his pathological hatred, and Valent's too, they'd never forgive her. She'd be jocked off Wilkie.

'Please go,' she screamed.

'Silly girlie, this time I'll make it really worthwhile. In the sack and out,' purred Shade. 'I'll make you come until you scream.'

'What about Olivia?' gasped Amber.

'Olivia's skiing. You and I are special. A ride for a ride, remember? You loved it last time, even if you're pretending you didn't.'

He thrust his huge, ringed hand into the neck of her dress, backs of his fingers digging into her breasts, before tearing the silk, sending buttons flying, as he tore it off her. Jack the bodice ripper.

'Bloody don't,' howled Amber. 'That's my favourite dress. Mariska Kay made it specially for me.'

'Relax, I'll buy you half a dozen more. Let me loosen your girths.' Undoing her leather belt, Shade slapped her with it before dropping it on the floor.

'Beautiful breasts,' he gloated. Hot breath scorched her forehead as he greedily grabbed, squeezed and tweaked, then, sliding his hands round her back, pulled her against him.

'Let me go, you bastard,' spat Amber, but as her knee came up, it encountered his towering cock.

'Don't try that silly little game.' As Shade plunged a great slug-like tongue into her mouth, she was tempted to bite it off.

'Let me go,' she mumbled, tugging her head free. 'It's not fair to Olivia.'

'Olivia won't know a thing about it.'

'Yes she will,' said a chilling voice, 'because I'll tell her, and these horrid little things,' Marius was clicking away with Amber's oblong silver camera, 'have their uses.'

'What the fuck?' Rigid with shock and fury for a second, Shade hurled Amber across the room so she hit the table, and crashed to the floor sending the champagne flying.

'Gimme that camera.'

'Not content with stealing my wife and wasting champagne at two hundred and seventy-five euros a bottle,' drawled Marius, cool as the fallen ice bucket despite Shade giving him three stone, 'you're now trying to steal my stable jockey, you fat bastard.'

Next moment, Shade had grabbed the champagne bottle, smashed it and was brandishing the jagged edge in Marius's face.

'Fancy some surgery?' he hissed.

In reply Marius gathered up a large pale blue lamp. 'Drop that bottle or I'll brain you.'

'You wouldn't dare.'

'Oh yes I would, and call the police and have you up on a rape charge, you fucking letch.'

Marius was so unafraid that, to Amber's amazement, Shade suddenly dropped the bottle and, growling like a huge grizzly, lumbered out of the suite.

'I'll tell Olivia her ex is back fucking the stable staff and I'll bury you,' he shouted as he slammed the door behind him.

Struggling up off the carpet, Amber tiptoed over the broken glass, collapsing on the sofa, trembling uncontrollably, burning face in her hands.

'Horrible, horrible man.'

'It's all right, darling.' Marius dropped a hand on her piled-up hair, which was also collapsing.

'I'm so sorry,' sobbed Amber. 'It was all my fault. I slept with him in exchange for a ride because I was so cross with you for not putting me up on History after Stratford.'

'Was he good in bed?'

'No, vile, crude, brutal, totally lacking in finesse. "Pleased hisself," as Joey would say.' Amber gave a choked half-laugh.

Glancing up, she was amazed to find Marius smiling in delight.

'He's right.' He pulled her up into his arms, caressing her breasts with a flattened palm as if he were gentling a terrified horse. 'They are lovely and so are you. I've been an absolute shit to you, particularly over History.' Looking down at her face, he ran a bitten-nailed finger along her quivering lower lip. 'Don't cry, let's go to bed.'

'It's no good,' sobbed Amber, jumping away from him. 'I want clean sheets, not a fling to anaesthetize the pain. You're still crazy about Olivia. If we go to bed, you'll still be crazy about her in the morning. I've got too many other things to be sad about.'

'Hush,' whispered Marius, and kissed her until she stopped struggling. 'Well?'

'Oh fuck, let's have a fuck, you are so goddamed sexy and an excellent kisser, but only just this once.' Then she paused. 'Did you say "stable jockey"?'

'Yes,' said Marius, pushing her into the bedroom.

When her early call woke her, Marius had gone. Staggering replete, bow-legged into the bathroom, she found he had broken her lipstick scrawling, 'Definitely ride of the century,' on the mirror.

Rafiq had been so gutted he had retired to his bedroom and refused to go out with the other jockeys. He sat on his bed staring at the white telephone with its white pad and sharpened pencil, desperate to ring Tommy and tell her how much he loved her and why he had been so cruelly pushing her away. But he was frightened to do so in case, even here, calls were being tapped.

Hearing a thud, he jumped out of his shivering skin, then found an envelope had been shoved under his door. By the time, unfamiliar with hotel bedrooms, he'd managed to unlock and open the door, the landing outside was deserted.

His name had been typed on the envelope. His hands were shaking so much he tore the letter inside, which was wrapped round a thousand-rupee note. This in turn was wrapped round a big needle threaded with black twine. Rafiq swore as he pricked his finger, scattering drops of blood, smearing the letter which in Urdu and black capitals advised him to buy himself a shroud as he would be needing one very soon.

Jibbering a prayer to Allah under his breath, Rafiq fell to the floor. Similar love notes had been sent to victims by the warlord alleged to have murdered Mrs Bhutto. This meant the side he had once supported so passionately would turn against him unless he kept on pulling horses.

Despite all the terrorist camp had taught him about life being but a trifle, it had become very precious since he had fallen in love with Tommy. She would be devastated about Bullydozer.

Oh Bullydozer! For a moment the sense of loss wiped out all feelings of terror. Then the telephone went. What dread threats awaited him? But it was only Tresa.

'We're having a party in Awesome's jacuzzi. Why don't you join us?'

Rafiq replied that he didn't feel like partying after what had happened that afternoon.

'Oh, don't mention Bullydozer,' said Tresa, 'or you'll set me off. I'm so upset.'

122

Valent was devastated by Bullydozer's death. Could he have saved him if he'd been there on the day? A horse of David Nicholson's had recovered from a broken neck and foreleg to win the Scottish Grand National. He had been so proud of rescuing Bully from H-H and had identified with the big, shy, affectionate, bumbling horse. He had already set in motion plans to run him in a Pauline Edwards Memorial Race at Worcester on Pauline's birthday and to invite Ryan, his wife Diane and the grandchildren down for the day as a way of making amends.

With Bullydozer's death, his plans were in smithereens. Wilkie was too highly handicapped for the race and Furious would bite everyone, so Valent instead invited the family to lunch in London, with a trip to see a marvellous play called *Warhorse* afterwards. When he originally planned Pauline's race, Valent had hoped Bonny would come along and get to know Ryan and Diane, but now he was rather relieved when she told him it would be 'inappropriate' if she were present.

'It's yours and Ryan's special day, stay as long as you like, I've got lines to learn. I need to engage with *The Journey of Bonny*.' This was a dramatized documentary in which she would play herself.

Lunch and the theatre were a huge success. Valent and Ryan talked their heads off, made plans for the future, and the grandchildren were very well behaved and sweet.

Ringing the office as he was tucking into profiteroles, Valent got a message that a Trixie Macbeth had rung. She was in London. Could he spare twenty minutes to see her some time? Ringing straight back, Valent told her to come round to his house in St John's Wood in the early evening, after Ryan and the family had left for Yorkshire and before he left for China.

Trixie was shivering outside when he got home, terribly pale, her hair hidden by a black wool hat.

'Granny's hyacinths, that's nice,' she said listlessly as he showed her into the drawing room. Having sat down on one of Bonny's pure white sofas, legs in red tights sprawling like a colt's, before he could even offer her a drink she burst into tears.

'Please don't tell Mum, she won't understand,' she begged. 'I can't talk to her and Dad's so obsessed with Tilda Flood, and Romy and Martin will be so smug and judgemental. I'm pregnant. I loved him so much. I don't want Granny to be hurt, but it's Seth. He was so kind and loving at the beginning, then he backed off. It was all stop-go, stop-go. Then on the night of *Ant and Cleo*, before I realized it, I was in a bedroom. Bonny and Rogue were in there. Seth made me go to bed with them. I'm sorry, Valent, I don't mean to hurt you, it probably didn't mean anything to them. But it was gross.'

She was crying so much Valent often couldn't catch what she was saying. He just sat patting her shoulder as the story of Stratford unrolled, so angry he couldn't speak. Then he got up and poured her a brandy.

'Afterwards,' Trixie took a gulp and choked, 'I refused to see him any more, but I couldn't stop missing him. And when I bumped into him on the weekend of the floods, stupidly I forgave him and we started up again, and now I'm pregnant.'

'How long?'

'Only two months. Please don't tell Granny, she's away this weekend. She adores Seth so much. Perhaps I got pregnant to get attention. Mum and Dad just aren't interested in me.'

'You poor little luv.' Valent took her hand. 'What d'you want to do?'

'I don't know. Half of me wants an abortion, I don't want anything of Seth's. But part of me wants the baby, though teenage mums are such a cliché, more of us than in any other country, a fuck to get a flat.' The words were ugly, falling from her woebegone mouth. 'I don't want to be just another statistic. And I don't know if I could support a baby.'

'I'll help you. You're a very bright and very beautiful young woman,' said Valent. 'What you need is a job.'

Valent had been planning to fly straight back to China, where he was having problems in the toy factory over his latest brainchild. Instead he flew to Staverton airport, where a car brought him back to Willowwood. There were no stars or moon, snow was idling down, whitening the fields. There were new blondes on the block, however, hazels with their cascades of yellow catkins competing with the dark gold willows.

Valent hadn't bothered to warn Bonny he was coming. Going upstairs, he found her at her dressing table in a grey silk dressing gown, beautiful and scented. She was brushing her ash-blonde hair, like an actress in an old film, like Sir Francis Framlingham's Gwendolyn.

The bed was rumpled.

'I've been studying for so long I had to have a nap' were her first words. 'How did it go?'

'Good.' Valent sat down on a mauve chaise longue so delicate he always felt it might buckle under him, and got out his chequebook.

'How were Ryan and Diane?'

'Fine.' Valent was writing a cheque with lots of 0s. Bonny wriggled her toes in excitement in the thick blond carpet. She had seen a divine cream coat at Lindka Cierach's last week.

'I hope you've invited Ryan and Diane down here, I am so looking forward to meeting them.'

As Valent handed Bonny the cheque for £300,000 she didn't notice his hand was shaking.

'Ooooo, lovely,' she cried. 'Is this a birthday present?'

'No, it's a leaving present,' said Valent harshly. 'Get out.'

Bonny was remonstrating noisily when Valent opened the wardrobe and Seth fell out, wearing nothing but a pale pink negligee as a loincloth. He was flabbergasted when Valent shook him by the hand.

'Thanks, mate, you've done me a very good turn. Now hop it, both of you.'

'You can't end it like this,' screamed Bonny.

'Oh yes I can.' Valent's voice was as rattling thunder. 'If either of you act up, I've just been talking to Trixie. She hadn't reached sixteen when you took her to bed at Stratford, you could both go to prison.'

'She's a lying little tramp,' shrieked Bonny. 'Nothing happened at Stratford.'

'I don't think so,' said Valent. 'She knew you had a diamond in your labia, and for someone who's always making such a fuss about being abused, you don't practise what you preach. *The Journey of Bonny*'s going to look pretty damn hypocritical. Now beat it. Give me a forwarding address and I'll send all your stooff on.'

'I'll be living with Seth.'

'Good, I'll send everything round to the Old Rectory,' said Valent, noticing Seth had gone green.

' "And out of Eden took their solitary way," ' sighed Seth, as most ignominiously they set off through the snow.

'At least we can be together,' said Bonny, who had at least managed to grab a full-length mink.

'It's a bit more complicated than that,' said Seth. 'Corinna and I go back a long way and I couldn't possibly support you in the way you've been accustomed. Valent'll cool down. Come back tonight, but tomorrow Corinna's coming back from America.'

Looking out of the window, Valent could see Bonny slapping Seth's face and was suddenly overwhelmed with relief.

Going into his octagonal office, he breathed in white hyacinths and poured himself a large Scotch. His hands were shaking so much it took him four goes before he managed to text Woody to tell him to dig up the conifer hedge that had guarded both Bonny's privacy and her peccadilloes. Peccadillo, that's a nice name for a horse, he thought.

What a pity Etta was away. He longed to know why she was still refusing to see him. Conversely, he might not have been able to resist telling her about Trixie.

When Etta reached home, which still stank of flood water, the following evening, she discovered moonlight pouring in through her kitchen, drawing-room and bedroom windows. Running outside, she realized the conifers had gone – poor things, she hoped they hadn't been chucked on a rubbish heap – and had been replaced by a dark blue trellis supporting her roses, honeysuckles and clematis.

Next moment, Joyce Painswick, seeing a light on in the bungalow, rang in excitement.

'Bonny's gone, she's moved out.'

'Poor Valent, he must be devastated.'

'Evidently not. According to Woody, he gave her the push. There'll be dancing in the streets. Joey's planning a party. Even though it's winter, he wants to hire a bouncy castle.'

When Valent returned home a week later, he could see straight into Etta's bungalow and hoped she wouldn't be upset. Later he watched her coming home from putting Poppy and Drummond to bed, down the path with Priceless, clinging joyfully on to each rustic pole, trying to teach Priceless to bend in and out of them, like her Pony Club days, then Gwenny rushed forward to meet them, black furry tail aloft.

123

Excitement really kicked in the week before the festival. Television companies were flat out filming the most fancied Gold Cup horses. Channel 4 were due at Throstledown to meet Mrs Wilkinson, Chisolm, Furious and the syndicate, who were all dickering about what to wear. In church, Niall prayed for the rain to stay away, so the going would be quick enough for Mrs Wilkinson.

After twelve hours at the typewriter, keeping track of events, Alan needed some fresh air and set out round the village with a torch. Earlier he'd heard a blackbird singing, and every garden shone with daffodils. Seeing a light on in the bungalow now the mature hedge had gone, he toyed with the idea of taking a bottle down to his mother-in-law, who he hoped would go on seeing him after he'd split up from her daughter.

Reaching the top of the high street and turning right on to the village green, he flattened himself against a wall as a Mercedes with an SM1 number plate roared by and flashed its lights outside Cobblers' wrought-iron gates. A minute or two later, the Major scuttled out and opened them. Strange bedfellows. Even more interestingly, a second later, Alan flattened himself against Ione's yew hedge as Harvey-Holden, mufflered, trilby over his nose, stormed up and also turned his Land-Rover through Cobblers' gates. What could the little snake be up to?

The coup de grâce, as Alan turned for home, was his brother-in-law Martin – jogging by in a black tracksuit and a balaclava, far too busy telling a mobile telephone that he adored it to realize he was being observed. Alan longed to say, 'Boo.' Next moment, Martin had turned right through the Major's gates. What was this about?

Next day the Major emailed the syndicate, summoning them to an emergency meeting that very evening. A full house except for Seth and Corinna attended. The locals were amazed to see Martin roll up with Bonny, who looked stony-faced and blanked Etta.

'Why does that infernal dog have to occupy the entire window seat?' she said, glaring at Priceless.

Dora, who'd rushed down from London, was briefing everyone about the Channel 4 interview. 'We must get Wilkie to do as many tricks as possible, particularly yawning when Harvey-Holden's name is mentioned. Isn't it exciting,' she went on, 'Chisolm's diary in the *Daily Mirror* is pulling in ten times more readers than Rupert's column in the *Racing Post*.'

The Wilkinson bar, where the meeting was held, had been entirely papered with Mrs Wilkinson's cuttings. All one could see were backs as syndicate members read about themselves.

'We really must smarten up Etta before the Gold Cup,' Debbie was murmuring to Phoebe. 'Should one wear one's Gold Cup hat for the Channel 4 interview?'

Chris was just taking orders when the Major strode in. Rheumy eyes gleaming, bristling moustache in a state of arousal, he ordered champagne on the house. The syndicate looked alarmed, hoping they wouldn't have to pay.

Mrs Wilkinson hadn't brought in any winnings since the beginning of February. Many of the syndicate had been wiped out by Ireland. The houses of others were still wrecked by the floods. Woody, after a bad fall, was off work and having to pay for his mother in an old people's home. Phoebe, to people's amazement, was pregnant again. Shagger wanted cash; Alan wanted to run off with Tilda; Joey was worried he might have made Chrissie pregnant. The Major and Debbie had their ruby wedding coming up and, now they'd moved up a rung socially, their grandchildren's school fees to pay. Corinna and Seth were always short. Painswick and Pocock wanted capital for their teashop. Trixie, slumped in a corner, sipping Perrier and reading *Horse and Hound*, had her own money troubles. The vicar needed a new spire; Bonny wanted a new squire; Etta's Polo had failed its MOT.

As Alan got out his notebook, the Major cleared his throat:

'I bring you glad tidings of great joy. We've had a most extraordinary offer from a secret buyer for Mrs Wilkinson. I was approached yesterday. This would mean over fifty thousand for every member of the syndicate and twenty-five thousand for those with half-shares.'

Etta stopped shoving photographs of Mrs Wilkinson and

Chisolm into envelopes. 'We can't,' she gasped, 'we can't sell Wilkie.'

'I think we can,' said Bonny rudely. 'What we can't do is turn down an offer like this.'

'Certainly not,' agreed a salivating Shagger. What a shame he and Tilda only had a half-share each. 'We must accept immediately. Dermie O'Driscoll was telling me he turned down two hundred grand for a horse last year, which sold for only seven grand six months later.'

'How dreadful,' shivered Phoebe. With the rate of inflation, £100,000 would probably just cover Bump's first term's prep school fees. 'We must accept at once.'

'We can't sell Wilkie,' repeated an ashen Etta. 'Valent wouldn't allow it.'

'It's my horse, thank you,' snapped Bonny. 'Valent gifted me a share.'

'At least let's sleep on it.'

'Won't get much sleep worrying the vendor might change his mind,' said Debbie.

'Why the hurry?' asked Alan, who was frantically trying to work out the implications.

'They need to know straight away because they want to run her in the Gold Cup,' said the Major.

'What about Alan's book? It's centred round the village and Wilkie being part of it,' protested Tilda angrily. 'What about Hengist's film?'

'Add to the drama of the plot,' said Shagger, draining his glass and refilling it. 'It's only a horse. With that kind of money, we can buy a couple more and keep the syndicate going.'

Etta lost her temper. 'How dare you!' she shouted at Shagger. 'After all Wilkie's done for you and Willowwood.'

'We can't possibly sell her, it would break her heart,' said Dora. 'Who's the buyer anyway?'

'My lips are sealed,' said the Major primly. Dora imagined him being kissed by a great seal.

'It would be treacherous to sell her,' cried Trixie, roused out of her apathy. 'We can't do it.'

'You've got a rich mother,' hissed Bonny, who hadn't forgiven Trixie for shopping her to Valent. 'Lucky for some.'

'We must be told who wants to buy her,' said Etta hysterically.

'Oh, pull yourself together, Mother,' chided Martin. 'What does it matter? Think of the money you owe us on the bungalow, and you need a new car to take the kids to school,' he whispered furiously.

'What a thoroughly unpleasant man you are,' drawled Alan. 'I know exactly who's trying to buy her,' he added, glancing round the astounded room. 'Shade Murchieson has wangled a box near the winning post at Cheltenham and plans to use it to entertain five hundred of his grubby clients during the festival. All his grubby clients want is to meet Mrs Wilkinson. Shade absolutely detests Marius and Valent and so does Harvey-Holden, so does my egregious brother-in-law,' he nodded at Martin. 'So they've hatched a vile plot to snatch Wilkie from under our noses on the eve of the Gold Cup. Shade has sold so many bombs and weapons he's just paid himself a fifty million bonus and he wants to go shopping.'

There was an appalled silence, followed by an explosion from the Major. 'How dare you. You couldn't be more wrong.'

'Oh, there'll be a nice cut for you, Major, probably another villa in the Portuguese sun above a nudist beach,' said Alan, now taking flashy shorthand notes.

'That is offensive.'

'And true,' smiled Alan.

Overhead they could hear the droning rattle of an approaching helicopter.

'As Bonny so rightly points out,' said Martin, 'it's only a horse.'

'She is not,' sobbed Etta. Then, turning furiously on the Major, 'You bloody little man, we can't let her go back to Harvey-Holden, he's a sadist, he tortures his horses. Look what he did to darling Bullydozer.'

'Who would probably still be alive if H-H had him in training and that cack-handed Rafiq hadn't been put up on him,' said Shagger bitchily. 'I say sell. Let's have some more fizz, Major.'

'No, no, we can't betray Marius either.' Etta leapt forward, hammering Shagger's great chest with her fists.

'Well done, Granny,' shouted Trixie.

'Pull yourself together, Mother,' said a shaken Martin, wondering if he ought to slap Etta's face.

Next moment, all the pub windows rattled as a red and grey helicopter landed on the village green, scattering daffodils.

'It can't park there,' yelled the Major.

'Hurrah,' cried Dora, looking out of the window, 'the US Cavalry have arrived,' as sprinting up the high street came Valent. Alerted by Alan earlier, he'd been on holiday in Dubai with Ryan and the children and had just come off the beach. He was wearing a Hawaiian shirt, shorts and espadrilles. As he stormed into the room, Etta ran to him.

'Thank God, thank God, Harvey-Holden and Shade have

made a massive offer for Wilkie and everyone wants to accept it.'

Valent was so angry at first, he couldn't speak, then he roared:

'Bloody, bloody traitors, bloody turncoats. After all that little mare has done for you. Raced her heart out, put this pub back in business, saved you all, saved Willowwood, and you've just got bloody greedy. I know times are tough, but do you honestly want to go down in history as the traitors who sold the People's Pony down the river to the most evil thugs in the world? And Alan will record every word if you do.'

As he scowled round at them, most of the syndicate decided they didn't.

'If Wilkie wins, she'll be worth even more of a fortune as a brood mare. Wait until after the race and I'll top Shade's offer.' He unpinned a photograph of Wilkie and Chisolm from the wall and put it in his pocket.

'That's over fifty thousand,' hissed Phoebe.

'Examine your consciences,' Valent said sternly. 'Can you honestly let her go?'

'Where are *you* going?' squawked Bonny as he went towards the door.

'Back to Dubai.'

'Thank you, thank you,' gasped Etta, running after him into the street.

For a second they gazed at each other.

'I'm so sorry about Bullydozer,' she stammered, 'such a lovely horse. It was so incredibly kind of you to come back.'

To her utter astonishment, he touched her cheek.

'I've missed you,' he said roughly. 'You'll find a present outside your bungalow,' and he was gone.

A shell-shocked Etta went back into the pub, where reluctantly the syndicate were deciding to wait. If Valent was going to up the offer it was worth taking a gamble. But there were some very angry people and Shade and Harvey-Holden would obviously be even more determined to take Mrs Wilkinson out in the race.

Etta was too bemused to hang around. Bonny was looking daggers; Martin was clearly dying to lecture her, so she switched on her torch and walked home. Valent had come all the way back for Wilkie and said he'd missed her. She wanted to skip like the lambs already in the fields. The stream was shaking the first primroses. The palest green willow leaves were breaking out of their buds.

Clinging on to Valent's poles, she ran down the last four steps because a snow-white Polo was parked outside her house. Then she froze: the number plate was still the same, inside was still the same, all the stickers still on the windows.

A card was attached to the windscreen.

'Dear Etta,' she read in amazement, 'I'm not sure what went wrong but I'd like to rebuild our friendship, so for a start I've rebuilt your car. Love Valent.'

Inside was a new CD player. As she switched it on, out poured Mahler's First Symphony, causing Gwenny and Priceless to jump out of their skins.

'Come on,' cried Etta. 'Let's do a lap of honour,' and they all piled into the Polo and drove round and round the village.

124

The whole world seemed to have descended on Willowwood on Gold Cup morning, persuading most of the syndicate they had been right to hang on to Mrs Wilkinson. A vast crowd of camera crews, journalists, photographers and well-wishers outside Throstledown's gates had cheered her and Furious off to Cheltenham. Despite being besieged by customers, Chris and Chrissie saved the Wilkinson bar for syndicate members to line their stomachs with a massive fry-up and kedgeree made from a salmon caught by Alban.

Those attempting to pace themselves drank Buck's Fizz rather than champagne, as Dora, looking enchanting in a new short scabious-blue coat with 'I love Wilkie' and 'I love Furious' badges pinned to each lapel, handed out emerald and willow green rosettes.

'If we'd accepted Shade's offer,' Corinna looked beadily at Dora's coat, 'I too could have afforded something new from dear Amanda Wakeley.'

Neither Tilda nor Painswick had been able to afford anything new, but Alan and Pocock respectively thought how lovely they looked.

'Wilkie has received more than a thousand good luck cards,' Dora announced proudly, 'and Furious twenty-two, most of these admittedly from Trixie, his heroic new stable lass.

'If anyone didn't see the hilarious Channel 4 film,' Dora went on, 'Derek Thompson sportingly mounted Wilkie, whose legs immediately buckled like a camel and, as the camera rolled, so did Wilkie, depositing Tommo on the deck to be butted by Chisolm, after which Wilkie wandered over and sweetly nudged him better.

'The Easy Lay has already taken thirty thousand on Wilkie this morning and been subjected to an Animal Rights demo.' So as not to upset Etta, Dora didn't add that members of the demo had been shocked rigid by Drummond Bancroft's language when they tried to stop him having a bet on his way to school.

'The media coverage has been awesome,' reported Dora modestly, 'with enough cuttings to repaper the entire Wilkinson Arms. The only person to receive as much fan mail as Wilkie is Woody. "Why can't they have tree surgeons in *Holby City*?" says *Fame* magazine, but in case Niall gets jealous, we're incredibly grateful he's given up a Friday in Lent to bless Mrs Wilkinson.'

'She'll need it,' sighed Joey. 'Last mare to win the Gold Cup was Dawn Run.'

'I had the runs at dawn this morning.' Toby neighed with laughter. 'Couldn't sleep a wink.'

'When I can't sleep I count past lovers,' announced Corinna. 'I always fall asleep before I get to treble figures.'

Etta felt too sick to eat any kedgeree. It had rained heavily in the night. Walking Priceless early, she'd slipped and fallen twice in the mud. How could poor Wilkie stay upright over thirty huge fences and three and three-quarter miles?

She also banked fences when she was tired. As a dreadful omen, the rising red sun had crashed through Valent's trees, scraping its tummy on the spiky twigs. Etta hadn't seen Valent since the night he had yet again saved Wilkie and delivered her rejuvenated Polo. She had written him an ecstatic thank-you letter, but so wished her Valent Edwards had flowered in time for her to present him with his own dark red rose for his buttonhole.

Last night Valent had left a gruff message on her machine. He was aware she'd be watching the Gold Cup with the syndicate, but he hoped she'd pop into his box for a drink to meet Ryan, Diane and the grandchildren.

If only Bonny wasn't insisting on joining the syndicate when they reached Cheltenham, so she could 'engage with her public'. If Etta had been vain, she would have sworn Bonny was hanging on to her share in Wilkie and watching Valent like a warder to ensure that a 'lascivious old lady' didn't pull a fast one.

For once Etta was happy with her clothes. Painswick had turned up an old dusty-pink coat to well above the knee, Rafiq had polished her black boots and Trixie, out of her first month's pay packet, had bought her grandmother a dashing mauve velvet beret topped by a bunch of felt violets.

If only Trixie could buy her a new face as well.

Glancing round as the minibus splashed down Leckhampton

Hill, Etta noticed Corinna, glass in one hand, copy of *Hamlet* in the other, scowling in her direction.

'If we'd accepted Shade's offer,' she repeated sourly, 'dear David Shilling could have run me up a new hat.'

'Then you wouldn't have had a horse to dress up for any more,' said Painswick tartly.

As a downpour drummed enraged fingers on the bus windows, everyone groaned. Marius had refused to make a decision as to whether to run Wilkie until midday. But the pressure was great. Forty thousand extra were expected on the gate to cheer her home. Cheltenham staff had been rugger-tackling each other all week, practising crowd control.

Nor would Valent let Marius pull her. He had poured a lot of money into Marius's yard. He wanted results.

The Willowwood minibus was cheered all the way through Cheltenham, loveliest of cities, even lovelier in her party dress of pink and white blossom. Daffodils nodded in the parks like horses after a race.

The pavement swarmed with all types and ages. Seedy-looking men in shiny suits and spiky greased-up hair flogging tickets, smiling Irish turning the whole day into a party, Sloanes in little suits and boots. The Check Republic was out in force, high and low society, saints and sinners, happily mixing as they banged on the minibus window.

'There's Mr Pocock, how's your garden growing?', 'Hello, Seth, when are you going back to *Holby City*? And there's Corinna, his partner, isn't she lovely?', 'And there's Woody, isn't he good-looking, can we have your autograph?', 'And little Phoebe, how's Bump, Phoebe?', 'And look, there's Etta and Halban, hello, Halban.'

'Good God,' said Alban, going pink.

'They really know who we are,' squeaked Etta, 'thanks to Wilkie.'

'If she wins, the bookies'll be carried out on stretchers,' said Joey.

' "Amber's up, the money's down, the frightened bookies flee," ' sang the crowd as they drifted into the course.

In the hospitality boxes, waitresses were stripping down to their bras and tattoos and donning aprons, red waistcoats and trousers, to provide splendid lunches for over two thousand people. Ten thousand more were living it up in the tented village. For reasons of economy, the syndicate had not hired their own box, assuming they could watch the race from the Owners and Trainers. Now they bitterly regretted it, never having dreamt of such a scrum, as they fought to buy drinks or have a bet. It was like back-stage on *Britain's Got Talent,* as men on stilts in top hats, women in hoop dresses and ethnic jewellery, belly dancers, brass bands and gypsies brandishing white heather battled their way through the crowds.

Debbie, being used by the Major as a battering ram, was in full throttle, complaining about the dreadful smell of scampi, fish and chips, burgers, frying onions and stale fat as her huge scarlet Stetson got knocked sideways and her splash of colour was splashed with Guinness.

'How much did you pay for that heather?' she beadily asked Joey.

'A fiver.' Roaring with laughter, Joey tucked the white sprig into his woolly hat beside his gold pen. 'Gypsy wanted a tenner. I asked her where she'd picked it, she said, "Birmingham warehouse."'

Alan, who'd been typing the story of a lifetime on his laptop in the bus, invaded the press room, a hive of rattling activity, where his friends Marcus Armytage and Brough Scott descended on him for news of Wilkie. Would Marius run her?

By the window, the great John McCririck, in his check deer-stalker with brown earflaps, pored over hieroglyphics like a kindly stork.

'When I saw Rogue Rogers looking through his legs,' typed the *Scorpion,* 'I knew he had something up his sleeve.'

Having walked the course, Marius finally gave the OK at midday. It had stopped raining, but overhead, dark clouds merged with the William Hill balloon.

'The ground isn't ideal,' he tersely told a flotilla of tape recorders, 'but Mrs Wilkinson has rested since Warwick in February and she's very well in herself, and had a good blowout last week at Larkminster racecourse.'

'Course not going in that deep,' reassured Simon Claisse, the genial Clerk of the Course.

'Bend's under water,' Rafiq, who'd already walked the course twice, told an increasingly terrified Amber.

The five-star racecourse stables, with their little white clock tower topped by a galloping golden horse weathercock, accom-modated three hundred horses in Gold Cup week. Ilkley Hall had just spent half an hour in the solarium. Mirrors had been provided in Internetso's box so he wouldn't be lonely. In the past, walls had been knocked through between boxes, so an uptight horse could converse with its stable mate. Horses were offered ordinary or organic water. Nothing was too much trouble.

Many horses overnighted before Gold Cup day. Many of the Irish runners, avoiding a rough ferry crossing, had been there for several days and were as relaxed as Priceless.

To his staff's disappointment, Marius refused to let them or his horses overnight, unlike Harvey-Holden, who even booked himself into the grooms' hostel, pretending it gave him immediate access to his beloved horses but in actuality because it was cheap and gave him a chance to pull stable lasses.

As runners set off for the third race, the excitement really kicked in as Gold Cup horses were given a final polish. Michelle, polishing her own face for the parade, was debriefing Tresa on last night's party, emphasizing how badly, released from Jude's watchful eye, Harvey-Holden had behaved. This was to discourage a tendresse Michelle suspected was developing between H-H and Tresa, who she frequently caught whispering in corners.

The only person who had evidently behaved worse than Harvey-Holden was Rupert Campbell-Black's grandson, Eddie Alderton. Still celebrating winning the Bumper on Wednesday, he had got into several fights after getting off with other jockeys' girlfriends.

'Such a pity Marius won't let us overnight,' grumbled Tresa, as usual leaving Tommy to do all the work, 'but he's still convinced someone nobbled Bullydozer at Leopardstown. If we were allowed to overnight, Tommy would sleep in Wilkie's box.'

'Only thing prepared to sleep with Tommy,' sneered Michelle.

'Shut up, you beetch,' hissed a voice. It was Rafiq, come to check on the horses, his face so contorted with fury that Michelle dropped her eyeliner.

'My my, someone did get out of the wrong pigsty this morning,' observed Tresa, as Rafiq disappeared into Wilkie's box.

Chisolm was having a ball, hooves up on the stable half-door, sporting a new green suede collar, being photographed and stroked. Everyone was in hysterics because Dora had muddled the copy for Rupert's column in the *Racing Post* with Chisolm's in the *Mirror*, so Rupert's readers had been urged to 'gobble up the polyanthus round Best Mate's statue and butt Ilkley Hall and Lusty on their delicate legs if they got the chance'.

The stables seethed with the rumour of non-runners, shifting odds and jockey changes. With the rain, Wilkie's odds had drifted and Lusty and Ilkley Hall had become joint favourites.

Word had also got round that Furious had a stunning new lass. Heads kept popping over the half-door to admire her as she attempted to plait up her fractious charge, hugely embarrassed that, even with Rafiq's help, she'd been unable to clip all his coat. With her own dark hair in a long plait, her colt legs in tight black jeans, Trixie was wearing a snazzy jacket Valent had given her, striped in his dusty green and violet colours, fur-lined against the cold and long enough to conceal any bump.

At least the going would suit Furious the mudlark. Described in the *Racing Post* as 'an alpha mule who couldn't be relied on to start', Furious was 50–1.

Half an hour to the parade, Tommy the equable gave a howl of rage.

'Someone's shaved off Wilkie's whiskers, who the hell's done that? It must have happened in the last hour. I was only away twenty minutes changing for the parade. Did you touch her?' She turned on Tresa and Josh.

'I did not, I wouldn't dare touch your precious baby,' taunted Tresa.

'Someone must have done it, someone she knew well.'

'Probably Rafiq,' said Josh.

'Don't be fatuous.'

'He was down checking Furious. Feels uncomfortable in the weighing room with the real men,' said Michelle nastily.

Tresa was peering into the bin. Reaching down, she pulled out a razor with its orange lid off.

'Rafiq uses these because they're cheap. Look,' she waved it triumphantly, 'it's got black whiskers in it. You better fingerprint it. I've just touched it, so my prints are on it already. I expect Master Rafiq doesn't want Wilkie to beat Furious.'

'Oh shut up,' screamed Tommy.

'Calm down, no one's died.'

'Not yet.' Tommy had gone bright red in the face.

Taking down Furious as late as possible to saddle him up in the pre-parade ring, Trixie ran slap into Eddie Alderton dropping four Alka-Seltzers into a teacup and about to ride Rupert's second horse, Merchant of Venus.

'Oh my gard,' he yelled, utterly spooking Furious, 'you are so gorgeous. Will you come out with me tonight? Oh my gard.'

Then he caught sight of Rafiq. 'Oh deah, you've got that Rottweiler as a minder. And there's Tarmy, hi Tarmy.' He gave her a kiss which made Rafiq even crosser. 'Better take a rain check,' and he ran off laughing.

'Who is he?' gasped Trixie. 'He's hot.'

'Rupert Campbell-Black's grandson,' sighed Tommy.

'By the way Eddie's putting himself about, Rupert'll be a

great-grandfather soon,' giggled Dora, 'which wouldn't be good for his image.'

Tommy felt a tug at the heartstrings. Rafiq was still avoiding her. Had he, like Eddie and everyone else, fallen for Trixie?

125

To add to the excitement, Rupert Campbell-Black, a rarity on the National Hunt scene these days, had four runners. Rogue had already won races on two of them for him and was hoping for a treble on the mighty Lusty in the Gold Cup.

After dumping all Shade's horses in St James's Square because Shade had made a pass at his wife Taggie, Rupert had decided he was fed up with owners, who were even more rich, spoilt and difficult than himself, and had given up training other people's horses.

Instead he was concentrating on breeding then running his own horses on the flat and, less frequently, over fences. Lusty was the son of Rupert's most successful stallion, Love Rat, who'd won the 2000 Guineas, the Derby and the Arc. It would be a splendid advertisement for the yard and Love Rat's prowess if Lusty, at the venerable age of ten, won the Gold Cup today.

Rupert had met Valent in Dubai and they'd got on so well that today they were sharing a box near the winning post. It was turning out to be the ritziest and noisiest of the festival, particularly as someone had smuggled in a CD player which was belching out loud music.

Another connection was that Rupert's beautiful daughter Bianca was the girlfriend of Feral Jackson, Ryan Edwards's dazzling new striker, who had been a contributory factor in Ryan's team going to the top of the second league this season.

Valent and Rupert's box was therefore packed with hunky footballers and WAGs tossing more long blonde hair. They were thoroughly over-excited to meet Rupert and naughty Eddie, and all were putting fortunes on Lusty and Rupert's second horse, Merchant of Venus, in the Gold Cup.

Shade, glowering from a nearby box, was particularly insulted that Rupert, who always made him feel socially inferior, was captivated by a yob like Valent. Both had recent Dubai suntans, while Shade's was getting a bit yellow.

Meanwhile, Rupert's god-daughter Amber was coming apart at the seams. Last night, Marius had watched videos of former Gold Cups and of the morrow's main runners with her and Rafiq to work out strategy, but her brain had retained nothing. All she longed for was a pair of arms round her but Rafiq was indifferent to her now, and after that glorious night at Leopardstown Marius had cooled as though it had never happened. Shade must immediately have told Olivia, who maybe had had a go at Marius.

Unable, like Rafiq, to cope with the badinage and dropped towels in the weighing room, she now had taken trembling refuge in the women's dressing room. Her father was still in hospital. Never had she needed his comfort and guidance more. She had lost five pounds in the last fortnight, so had to carry even more lead in her saddle, which wouldn't help Wilkie. Her wrist was agony from signing autographs. Someone had stolen her new lucky pants.

The expectations of the crowd and particularly the syndicate had got to her. If she wasn't placed they'd forfeit their bets, any prize money, any hope in the Order of Merit and the half-million Shade and H-H had offered them to buy Wilkie. She must save her from that fate.

She'd got in such a panic, she'd nearly called Rogue at 4am. Today she hadn't seen him. When he wasn't winning races, he was touring the boxes giving them tips at £300 a visit.

Cabals were now gathering in the paddock. Broad backs turned to broad backs as Marius blanked Shade and Harvey-Holden, and Rupert blanked Isa Lovell, who had once worked for him.

Out came the jockeys, pulling on their gloves, ashen faces in contrast to their brilliant silks. Amber, as the only girl, was comforted by the great cheer from the crowd as she joined Marius and the Willowwood syndicate.

'Wilkie's spot-on today,' Marius told her, 'but Harvey-Holden's in an ugly mood. Tuck yourself in at the back, keep clear of the pack, stick to the inner all the way round. The bend's under water so take it easy. Good luck,' for a second he dropped his guard and his face softened, 'be careful.'

'Daddy, Daddy,' little India Oakridge, in a blue coat with a velvet collar, seized Marius's hand, 'come and talk to Mummy and Shade.'

'Not now, darling,' said Marius, striding over to Rafiq, who, surrounded by Valent and his pack of footballers, was about to mount Furious.

'Furious is stepping up in trip, meaning a longer race,' Marius explained, 'so I'm asking Rafiq to hold him up as long as possible or he'll wear himself out.'

Harvey-Holden and Shade were now in a huddle with their three jockeys. Dora, who'd been practising lip-reading as a valuable journalistic tool, noticed Harvey-Holden's thin lips kept widening over his teeth in a G then pursing them out in a W.

'I know he's telling them to Get Wilkie,' she hissed to Etta, then leapt behind Debbie to avoid Rupert, who was not pleased to have had Chisolm's diary switched with his.

At least Mrs Wilkinson was adoring every moment, aware of the vast crowd admiring her as she came knuckering up to the syndicate.

'Safe journey,' they chorused as Marius legged Amber up.

'Just come back safely,' cried Etta. Turning away to hide her tears, she caught sight of Valent, the turned-up collar of his navy blue overcoat caressing his suntanned cheek. Lucky coat, thought Etta, he was so gorgeous. As though drawn by the intensity of her longing, Valent swung round and caught sight of her looking so adorable in her purple beret.

'Good luck,' they mouthed at each other, then Valent made a drinking gesture. 'See you in the winners hospitality room, I hope. If not please come oop and drown your sorrows in our box.'

Etta was brought back to earth by Dora tugging her sleeve.

'Guess what, someone's just put three hundred and fifty thousand on Wilkie.'

'Bookies must be praying and laying,' said Joey.

'You better get praying to counteract them, Vicar,' said Debbie briskly.

Niall put his hands on either side of Wilkie's face and, as she nudged him lovingly in the belly, he kissed her white forehead and told her in a choked voice:

'May God bless you, little Village Horse, and bring you and Amber home safely.'

'And first,' said Joey.

To their horror, they were then joined by Bonny. She erupted into the parade ring ravishingly understated in a little fawn check suit with a nipped-in waist, a skirt five inches above the knee and

618

a little green trilby the same green as her owner's badge. She'd show the Sloanes how it was done.

'This is the first of the Bonny Richards Collection,' she told the hovering press, who immediately trained their lenses on her rather than Mrs Wilkinson.

As the syndicate fought their way out, they met Corinna in a dark crimson picture hat, radiant from hair and make-up and signing lots of autographs, coming the other way. Then she caught sight of Bonny and promptly dragged an only-too-willing Phoebe off to the racecourse shops to buy an even more opulent hat than Bonny's 'stupid trilby' to lead in Mrs Wilkinson: 'We've got masses of time, they've still got the parade to get through. Let us through, let us through.'

Past legends watched over the paddock. Arkle from under his pale weeping willow, Golden Miller from the roof of the tote bar, Best Mate in his sea of polyanthus, the great mare Dawn Run on the chute down to the course, wished the runners God speed as they came out.

Up in the Owners and Trainers, so happy to have talked to Valent, Etta rejoiced in the wonderful panorama in its bowl of hills. Everywhere she could hear Irish accents, soft as the amethyst blur of spring on the Cleeve Hill woods. Just visible through the mist and drizzle were the three radio masts with their pointed hats.

Every woman's hat seemed lavishly trimmed with feathers.

'Bald ostrich day,' murmured Alan into his tape recorder. Below he could see the enormity of the crowd, seething and bubbling like Ione Travis-Lock's wormery.

'Wilkie's put about fifty thousand on the gate,' said the Major proudly. 'I should think they'll close on a hundred thousand.'

'Word must have got round that Bonny Richards was putting in an appearance,' Bonny told Seth and Alan. 'Extraordinary to think that about a hundred times that number watched *The Blossoming* on Sky last week.'

Helicopters, including Shade's, Rupert's and Valent's, could be seen gathered on the far side of the course like a flock of pterodactyls. Bonny needed another rich man.

To the left, the syndicate could see into the box which Shade had paid over the odds for and which he'd covered in photographs of himself and the famous to wow his customers. These were coming out on to the balcony, creatures of the night, thugs in black coats and hats with waxy faces, their women in black too, pashminas thrown over bare bulky shoulders.

'Black to match the body bags,' said Alan. 'Horrible-looking bunch.'

' "Now thrive the armourers," ' murmured Seth.

Glamour was provided in Shade's box by Olivia in a soft grey cashmere suit. 'How can she put up with that hood?' shuddered Alan.

Now joining them were Romy and Martin and Jude the Obese, who took up most of the balcony.

'They could fly her instead of the William Hill balloon,' said Seth.

'Whale-iam Hill,' quipped Alan.

'I thought Martin was jogging with her every night so she could be a role model for WOO.'

'That's rather fallen by the weighing scales,' said Alan, as Bonny smirked and gave Martin a discreet wave.

Glancing further to the right, Bonny's lips tightened as she noticed Valent, Rupert, Ryan Edwards and his family plus footballing friends having a ball. And omigod, they'd been joined by Cindy Bolton, shrieking, jangling and half naked.

Now Cindy was smiling up at Valent.

'It distresses me to see Valent today,' Bonny told Seth and Alan earnestly. 'If only he'd received some counselling over Pauline, I'm sure he could have achieved closure.'

'I'd rather achieve winners enclosure,' said Seth, handing his hipflask to Alan, who was making notes as the colours of the Gold Cup runners were superimposed on the course.

To kick off, great Gold Cup winners of the past, including Rupert Campbell-Black's Penscombe Pride and the late Roberto Rannaldini's Prince of Darkness, sauntered down the course, relaxed as ex-prime ministers, no doubt agreeing that in their day the fences had been much higher and darker.

Huntsmen in red coats then led out the great horses of the present, gloriously gleaming Gold Cup runners, with two lads to each horse. A cheer went up from Shade's box as Ilkley Hall passed. He was led by Vakil, sinister as an undertaker in his dark suit and tie, and by Michelle, who with her pale face and rippling red forest-fire hair was H-H's only stable lass whom Shade's magenta and orange colours suited. Her sexy sidelong smiles distracted the punters from a lacklustre Ilkley Hall, who'd been relentlessly overrun in pursuit of the Order of Merit.

Bonny's lips tightened again as the occupants of Rupert and Valent's box fell over the balcony, joining in the massive cheer for their pin-up boy Rogue as he passed by on the vast liver chestnut

Lusty. Lusty's plaits seemed tiny on his huge arched neck as Rogue unravelled the two nearest to hold on to.

The women in the crowd cheered louder as they admired Rogue's jutting lower lip, his blond streaked curls and his hefty shoulders broadened by the horizontal blue and green stripes of Rupert's colours. Cool outwardly as the minus-140-degree chamber he'd been plunged into to cure his dislocated shoulder, which was now hurting like hell after two wins, Rogue had convinced the doctors he was fit to ride and smiled up at his admirers to prove it.

'Going to take a lot of beating,' brayed Alban. 'Oh, here comes Wilkie, hurrah, hurrah.'

But his words were drowned by a vast collective bellow, as led by a beaming Dora and Tommy, ears pricked, head up, striding out with pointed toe, totally unfazed by the masses, lapping up the adulation, came Mrs Wilkinson.

'If she could wave her hoof like the Queen, she would,' giggled Dora, as ecstatic admirers brandished 'I love Wilkie' posters, opened their jackets to show Wilkie T-shirts and yelled, 'Hello, Tommy. Hello, Dora.' Chisolm, having hastily hoovered up the polyanthus round Best Mate's statue, gobbled up any posies offered by fans.

The crowd, as Mrs Wilkinson passed, also clocked her green browband. Noting the black patch over her blind eye, they were moved by how small she was and how slight her ashen young jockey, and cheered even louder.

'Isn't it lovely the crowd love her so much?' laughed Tommy, wiping her eyes. 'You'll soon have a statue and a bar here named after you, Wilkie.'

But though she smiled, Tommy still fretted about the shaven whiskers. Like a cat, Wilkie used them to check a gap was wide enough for her to push through. CCTV in the stables would have captured the theft. Pray God it wasn't Rafiq.

Furious, after a whisk round the parade ring, had been allowed to miss the parade and go straight down to the start, which proved counterproductive as he ran slap into a large crowd gathered to catch a glimpse of Mrs Wilkinson. Despite his half-clipped coat, he was shivering, sweating up and looked a shaggy and unplaited mess.

He had tugged off Trixie's bandanna that morning and eaten it, her arms beneath her purple and green jacket were covered in bruises, but he had started knuckering whenever she arrived in the morning, and she could see why an equally shivering, sweating Rafiq loved him so much.

'What's that?' demanded Rafiq as they splashed round to keep warm while they waited for the other runners.

'The Pakistani flag for you to wear round your shoulders when you win.'

'Don't count your hens,' growled Rafiq.

He had been thankful to miss the parade as the Mafia had threatened him with another hideous call last night. But his resolve had hardened. He had bottled out as a suicide bomber, thank God, and he was not going to pull Furious today. Last night Valent had texted him, countering Marius's instructions: 'Don't hold him up. Give him his head. Let him enjoy himself.' Rafiq was touched that both Hengist Brett-Taylor and sarcastic Sergeant Gibson, who'd run the prison stables, were in the crowd but he couldn't stop shaking.

'Get off and let me give you a hug to calm you down,' begged Trixie.

'Any hug from you would make me anything but calm. You are so pretty, you rocket my blood pressure,' said Rafiq, but at least he smiled.

126

Cheltenham was also on edge. A hundred million pounds had been bet on the race. Too many horses had died in jump racing recently. Animal Rights were threatening reprisals. On the big screen the horses were circling, dwarfing Mrs Wilkinson.

'I can't see her,' wailed Etta.

'Napoleon liked small horses,' said Alban.

Killer O'Kagan was keeping up his barracking.

'That horse has shrunk even more,' he sneered at Amber.

'Shut up,' snapped Rogue, putting a hand on Amber's trembling shoulders. 'Good luck, angel . . .'

'Our Father, which art in heaven,' said Awesome through chattering teeth. The Irish jockeys crossed themselves. The starter had mounted his rostrum, shouting, 'Settle down, settle down,' in a high Dalek voice at the jockeys, all desperate to get in front through the gate and not waste any more time.

Etta wished she could have watched with Valent. She needed his big, warm, reassuring hand holding hers so badly.

'Where the hell's my wife?' grumbled Toby.

'Shopping,' said Shagger. 'They'll never get back through the crowd now.'

'At least we won't have to give Phoebe a running commentary,' muttered Seth.

The tapes flew and like a tidal wave dragging down the shingle of the world there followed the Cheltenham roar, enough to unsettle any horse, particularly Furious, who shot to the front.

'Bloody, bloody fool,' groaned Marius.

Harvey-Holden had put in Voltaire Scott, another really fast pacemaker from the flat, to exhaust Mrs Wilkinson but he was no match for Furious, who'd taken off like a superjet.

'I hate it when they're so far ahead at the start,' moaned Dora, who'd joined Tommy in the stable lads' stand where the chute joins the course.

Amber had never known anything so terrifying, the great stiff fences of unrelentingly massed birch twigs racing up to meet her, crashing against Wilkie's belly, the thunder of hooves, the huge horses blotting out the light on all sides, the crash of landing, the jockeys howling at each other, turning the dull grey sky blue with their language.

She was lying tenth, keeping quiet except that Harvey-Holden's third horse, Last Quango, was sitting on her tail, like a driver in a narrow lane pushing her into error. Then Cosmo Rannaldini's Wriggoletto cut in front of her trying to seize the inner, kicking a lump of mud into Wilkie's eye.

Drawn into a barging match, Wilkie couldn't see and panicked. Ahead on the rails Voltaire Scott was being deliberately held up by Johnnie Brutus. Amber was forced to pull out to overtake them but as she passed, Johnnie swung right, knocking Wilkie off course. Instantly Last Quango slid up and took Wilkie's place, on the inside rail, further blocking her vision. As she lost her bearings, Wilkie was unable, without her whiskers, to feel her way through the solid line of horses in front of her.

'Wilkie, Wilkie, Wilkie,' roared the crowd.

'Let me through,' screamed Amber, 'give me some daylight.'

Then she saw Killer's teeth flashing beneath his black goggles, like a highwayman chancing on a coachload of bullion. Thrusting Ilkley Hall up on the left between her and Last Quango, he edged her even further away from the rails. Wilkie was also having trouble tugging her feet out of the mud but somehow she scrambled over the big fence four out on the first circuit.

Ahead loomed three out, flanked by trees and daffodils, known as the Field of Hope, but there was no hope for Wilkie. To avoid Killer, she jumped wildly to the right, skidding across the wet grass on landing. As Amber struggled to stay put, Wilkie tipped over, crashing to the ground, throwing Amber into a pounding seven-strong pack of horses.

The crowd's massive bellow of encouragement, briefly drowned by whoops of joy from Shade's box, turned to screams of horror and anguish as both horse and rider lay motionless, Amber's face whiter beneath the mud than Mrs Wilkinson's.

The convoy of doctors, vets and paramedics accompanying the runners screamed to a halt.

As silence fell over Cheltenham, a hundred thousand hearts broke. Despite the tracking cameras following the other runners up the hill on to the second circuit, all eyes were turned down the course to the People's Pony and her brave jockey, as the screens hid them from sight.

Valent's binoculars swung round to the Owners and Trainers. As Etta's hands flew to her face, he saw Seth put an arm round her.

'Doesn't necessarily mean a fatal accident,' quavered Debbie.

'Where are the loose horses?' sobbed Etta, peering through the mist in the hope of seeing Wilkie appear over a fence.

'Here's one,' said Niall hopefully, but it was only a returning Merchant of Venus who'd dumped Eddie Alderton, fortunately, out in the country, because Eddie's language was worse than Drummond's.

'My book,' groaned Alan. As he put down his pen Tilda slid a hand over his in sympathy.

The Major was looking almost smug. If they'd listened to him . . .

'What a fucking tragedy we didn't sell her last week,' Shagger echoed his thought.

'Shut up, you revolting man,' screamed Tilda.

'I hope she's properly insured,' said Bonny.

'Shagger should know,' hissed Woody, then, taking Niall's hand: 'Pray for us.'

'Our Father,' began Niall in a choked voice.

Marius, who always watched races on the members' lawn, had vaulted over the rails, run across the track and jumped into an official's dark green 4×4 Mitsubishi, ordering it to drive him down to three out. Legendarily concerned only with the welfare of his horses, he leapt out, pushing open the screens, totally ignoring a panting, supine Mrs Wilkinson and, to the horror of the ambulance men, gathered Amber up into his arms, his face frantic with worry.

'Amber, darling, oh my baby, please be all right.'

'She's been kicked in the back and the head, for God's sake,' hissed a paramedic.

With infinite effort, Amber opened her eyes. 'I'm so sorry I let you down,' she mumbled. 'Is Wilkie OK? I couldn't hold her together. The bastards blocked us in, she couldn't see. She's so little. I'm so sorry I screwed up.'

'You didn't. You rode a blinder.'

'Hardly the operative word. Wilkie's only half-blind.'

Realizing she could still joke, Marius's grip tightened.

'Oh Amber,' his voice cracked as, looking into her mud-freckled face, feeling her body protector rough beneath her green silks, unable to resist a temptation that had taunted him since Leopardstown, he kissed her passionately and at great length, only pausing to groan, 'Thank God you're OK.'

Mrs Wilkinson, meanwhile, was most put out. She had been given oxygen, had the ignominy of a hunky horse ambulance man sitting on her head to keep her down. She had had needles poked into the coronet bands of her pretty feet, her tail rotated to see if she was suffering from a spine injury, and her legs tugged back to see if they were broken.

Mrs Wilkinson was a serious horse. Seeing her trainer and her jockey locked in each other's arms, she nudged them. When they ignored her, not amused by such dalliance, she struggled groggily to her feet.

A deathly silence hung over Cheltenham. The public address system was playing up, it was hard for the stricken crowd to understand what was going on. A second horse ambulance was hurtling towards the screens from one end of the course, Chisolm and a sobbing, frantic Tommy from the other. The syndicate (even Shagger at the thought of the money he might have made) was in floods.

Then next moment, to the crowd's incredulous delight, a dirty white face, also speckled with mud, pushed the screens apart. Mrs Wilkinson looked round for her competitors and rubbed her hooves together. Was it really her? A great bellow of joy split the air as, stirrups and reins flapping, she set out at a cracking pace. The bellow grew even louder and the entire crowd rose to cheer her home as she jumped the last two fences down the straight into the arms of a distraught, tearful Tommy, with Chisolm bleating joyfully round her. The cheers escalated in hysterical relief as Tommy led her back, hugging, kissing her and pulling her ears. Despite losing so much money, the crowds were so relieved and delighted she was safe.

Mrs Wilkinson, on the other hand, was extremely hurt and annoyed not to be allowed in the winners enclosure.

127

Meanwhile, in another part of the forest, a race had been going on. As the runners reached the second circuit, Furious, the horse hater, the unpredictable, the 50–1 underdog, started to look like the over-dog, jumping majestically, unsettling the competition by the gallop he continued to take, never touching a twig, meeting each fence so exactly, landing, galloping, flustering both Ilkley Hall, who was exhausted anyway, and Last Quango, who was hitting every fence.

The crowd couldn't believe their eyes as Furious's white star came bobbing towards them like a satellite at night. Lusty must make a move soon, or Wriggoletto, or Internetso, but they were like Minis trailing a Ferrari.

Rafiq couldn't believe it either.

'Good boy, good boy. "Singing from Palestine, hither we come!"' Talking nonsense, Rafiq crooned to him as Furious's ginger ears flickered back to listen. His eyes were red-rimmed, his nostrils filled with foam, but he kept going faster. As they reached three out, with yellow chevrons and a man with a flag directing them round it, Rafiq noticed the screens and ambulance men but his pace didn't slacken. 'Come on, Furious.'

Slowly, slowly Lusty was gaining on him but at three out Lusty's jockey took a closer look, glimpsing a slumped iron-grey body and crumpled green silks, lost concentration momentarily, but somehow forced himself to carry on.

As Furious stormed up the hill, Rafiq glanced back through his legs. Lusty was still six lengths behind, with Squiffey Liffey, Internetso and Ilkley Hall, who was having the shit thrashed out of him by Killer, even further away. Even if the Mafia got him and Furious, they would die gloriously. Flying over the last two fences like Buraq himself, showing Lusty a muddy pair of heels, Furious stormed first past the post.

Joey's shout of joy that he'd just won £12,000 was only exceeded by Rupert's howl of rage when, ten seconds later, Rogue crossed the line, but, able to bear it no longer, tugged Lusty round and hurtled through oncoming runners back to Amber. Reaching three out, he leapt off his frantically blowing horse, hurling his reins to a groundsman.

'Can you undo his girths?' he yelled. 'I'll weigh in later.'

But as he ran in panic towards the screens – please God, let her be all right – his heart stopped pounding abruptly and most painfully as he caught sight of Amber in Marius's arms. Changing tack, he escaped into the trees. The Field of Hope had failed him too.

Up in the stands, Valent's box had erupted. Drunken footballers and WAGs screamed their heads off as Valent's dusty green and purple winning colours were superimposed over the grass at the end of the course and other jockeys rode all over them before swinging round to shake Rafiq's hand and congratulate him. Even Killer O'Kagan put his arm round Rafiq's neck, pretending to kiss him before hissing in his ear:

'We'll get you for this, you little shit.'

But Rafiq was too dazed to care. He could hardly stammer out a sentence when Derek Thompson rushed up waving a microphone, except to say that Furious was worth a million horses, and Valent was wonderful owner, and Marius wonderful trainer.

Fortunately Rafiq couldn't hear the commentators banging on and on about how he and Furious had met in prison and what a triumph it was, Rafiq putting his criminal past behind him.

Next moment Trixie had panted up, sobbing with joy and flinging the green and white Pakistani flag round Rafiq's shoulders before throwing her arms round Furious, who was so amazed by the cheering crowds he forgot to bite her. Nor was he even fazed by the deafening roar that greeted Wilkie when she emerged from the screens.

Nearly as loud a cheer went up as Marius emerged with his arm round Amber. As the Mitsubishi dropped them both off at the medical room, Edward Gillespie, Cheltenham's charismatic managing director, tapped Marius on the shoulder. 'You're wanted in the winners enclosure,' he said with a smile. 'Your other jockey's talking to connections.'

Slowly it dawned on a dazed Marius that he might have won the Gold Cup.

The loudspeaker had announced a stewards' inquiry; punters

had been advised to hang on to their betting slips. Killer and Johnnie Brutus were in the stewards' room, about to be banned for extremely careless riding and interfering with Mrs Wilkinson. Killer was employing all his thespian skills to persuade the Stipendiary Steward that Mrs Wilkinson, with an inexperienced rider on her back, had been wandering all over the place. Difficult not to cut her up.

'Listen,' Killer kept saying, 'listen.'

'I've done quite enough of that already,' snapped the Stipe, who was not looking forward to the blazing row he would have next, when he suspended Rogue for infringement. The grounds-man had not only undone Lusty's girths but also removed his saddle, which made it no longer possible for Rogue to weigh in or Lusty to come second.

To complicate matters, Furious's victory, as a rank outsider running way above his handicap, was so unexpected that as a formality he'd have to be dope tested in the sampling unit after the presentation.

With two Cotswold Huntsmen flanking him, Pakistani flag around his shoulders and the broadest grin splitting his face, touching his hat shyly to acknowledge rather muted cheers, an utterly dazed Rafiq had been led into the winners enclosure by a joyful, still tearful Trixie and an ecstatic Valent punching the air.

Furious, still enchanted by all the applause, neither kicked nor bit anyone. Marius the reticent also found himself being hugged by everyone, so he hugged everyone back and, as they all posed for photographs, informed the seething media that Wilkie and Amber were both all right.

'Tommo told me to enjoy the moment,' sighed Trixie, hugging Valent. 'Oh, thank you for giving me this chance.'

Finally, after what seemed an eternity but was only twenty minutes, the loudspeaker crackled.

'Here is the result of the Cheltenham Gold Cup: first Furious; second Squiffey Liffey; third Internetso; fourth Ilkley Hall.'

A jubilant Valent, taking Ryan, Diane and the grandchildren with him, went up and accepted the Gold Cup from the Princess Royal, whom he admired because she worked as hard as he did. The Gold Cup turned out to be a gleaming golden bowl with bites out of the rim as though Furious had enjoyed a good supper out of it.

A shell-shocked Marius went up next for a smaller Gold Cup and a louder cheer for a great trainer who'd come back after too long in the wilderness. A large police presence moved in, security guards fingering their guns, as Rafiq, the first Muslim to win the

Gold Cup, received a little gold replica and told the Princess, 'Furious is so honest.' Finally they were joined by Trixie, in her purple and green striped jacket with her black plait unravelling, who accepted a silver photograph frame to a chorus of wolf whistles.

But as Marius stepped down from the platform, Rogue, who hated stipes because they treated jockeys like other ranks, and who had come out of the stewards' room with the possibility of being banned until long after the Grand National, clinched the matter by ducking under the rails and hitting Marius across the winners enclosure.

'Keep your hands off Amber, you fokker,' he howled.

'How dare you hit my daddy,' screamed little India Oakridge, rushing up and kicking Rogue on the shins.

Rogue was about to be arrested by the posse of policemen watching Rafiq when he was grabbed by Rupert Campbell-Black roaring, 'Come here, you little bastard,' and dragging him off to perdition.

'Nothing much wrong with Rogue's shoulder,' observed Awesome. 'That cold treatment works wonders.'

Meanwhile Phoebe, who'd spent a fortune on a rocking horse for Bump, and Corinna, wearing a vast turquoise Cavalier hat trimmed with a plume of Prussian blue feathers, had fought their way back from the shops. Having earlier heard the roars of 'Wilkie, Wilkie, Wilkie,' they had assumed Mrs Wilkinson had won and were outraged not to be allowed into the winners enclosure.

Bonny was equally incensed. She too was denied access and couldn't pose beside Valent to show off the debut outfit in the Bonny Richards Collection.

'Where's bloody Seth? I need a vast drink,' snarled Corinna.

Bloody Seth, however, lust reignited, had accosted Trixie and Furious on their way to the sampling unit.

'Darling, well done, how terrific you look, are you going to put my picture in that smart silver frame?'

Trixie gasped and recoiled in horror. Furious, who'd behaved well for too long, was just flattening his ears when a mud-caked Eddie Alderton swooped and seized Trixie's arm.

'You're too late, Grandpa,' he told Seth. 'She's putting my picture in that photo frame. And once she's settled Furious she's coming back to my grandpa's box to celebrate, then she's coming to the Lesters' with me tomorrow.'

'Am I?' asked Trixie excitedly. Seth was looking absolutely livid.

*

Cheltenham racecourse was ringing with the sound of high words. Even Killer turned pale as Shade and Harvey-Holden bawled out him and Johnnie Brutus, who were awaiting news of the length of their bans. 'How could you be so fucking stupid to get caught out? You've probably lost us the Order of Merit.'

'If you're not back for the National you're fired.'

'The hoss was exhossted,' protested Killer.

'Don't make bloody excuses.'

Rupert was even more drastic. 'You lost me the bloody Gold Cup, you cunt-struck bastard,' he was yelling at Rogue. 'You'd have won it if you'd kept up the momentum. You're fired. You'll never ride for me again and I'm going to sue you into the next county for the loss of prize money.'

Olivia Oakridge pretended to be incensed by Killer and Johnnie Brutus's poor showing but her fury was directed more towards her husband.

'God, Marius has got hard. Not giving a damn about poor Mrs Wilkinson, only interested in snogging Miss Lloyd-Foxe in the middle of a Gold Cup. Lost the plot completely. No wonder Rogue hit him.'

Chisolm, who'd been intending to snack on the oxblood and mushroom-pink orchids round the Queen Mother's bronze in the winners enclosure, was even crosser.

A tear-stained Tommy, who'd been ricocheting between hell and heaven, having bandaged and settled Wilkie, was belting back to listen to the press conference when she ran slap into Rafiq, returning to check on Furious. Next moment they had fallen into each other's arms.

'Well done, well done, I'm so proud of you and Furious, he ran brilliant,' cried Tommy, quite giddy with relief.

'Oh Tommy.' Rafiq gave a sob as he buried his muddy face in her neck. 'Wasn't he wonderful, I miss you so much, please be patient. One day I explain why I'm so cold, for now, please keep away from me,' but as he reluctantly pushed her from him, from the shadows he saw Vakil leering at them both.

631

128

Valent's box was a riot with the CD player blaring out, 'We Are The Champions', and the binoculars of half the men in the crowd trained on the balcony where Cindy Bolton and assorted WAGs screamed and tossed their manes in the breeze.

Etta wished she had a stable pass so she could go and console Wilkie and Tommy and congratulate Trixie, Rafiq and Furious. But even more, she longed to go up to Valent's box and congratulate him, but he was probably still drinking champagne with Lord Vestey and Edward Gillespie in the Royal Box. If he'd really wanted to see her he could have called her on her mobile.

In an overcrowded marquee beyond the weighing room, Valent in fact was controlling the press conference. Having dispatched Rafiq before any awkward questions were asked about his past and Marius before anyone asked him about snogging Amber, Valent, who didn't want to talk about Bonny, was winding things up.

He needed a drink. His euphoria at winning the Gold Cup had been tempered by Etta not even bothering to ring him. Perhaps she was too gutted about Wilkie.

'Thanks, guys,' he said, getting to his feet to a flickering firefly orgy of flashbulbs.

'What's the state of play between you and Bonny Richards?' asked the *Scorpion*.

'I can tell you,' cried a joyful voice and in swept Bonny, looking utterly radiant in her little fawn suit. 'Valent and I are definitely together. He's backing me in my fashion dream.' She did a twirl for the cameras. 'This is the first in the Bonny Richards Collection.'

Then, floating up to Valent, she seized both his hands,

swinging round to the furiously snapping cameras and scribbling journalists: 'I want to congratulate him on a great victory. I've realized I've made a terrible mistake. The age gap's utterly unimportant, it's you I love, Valent, the journey of Bonny must end here.'

Next moment, she had reached up, put her arms round his neck and pressed her smiling lips against his.

Valent's face was inscrutable. Then, putting an arm through hers, he frogmarched her towards the exit. 'Now is not the time or the place,' he said grimly, 'I've got a win to celebrate and guests up in the box.'

'Valent, Valent, Bonny, Bonny, Bonny,' screamed the photographers.

Outside, Valent had to put his arms round her to protect her from the scrum.

Seeing his stony face, Bonny whispered, 'I just miss you so much. We need to talk. Can't we go back to London?'

'I'll give you a lift. We've got to look in at the box first.'

Battling their way through the crowd, Valent didn't notice a hovering, stricken Etta.

Still incandescent with rage at having lost the Gold Cup, Rupert dropped into the box in search of Valent and found his letcherous old father Eddie in situ and surrounded by WAGs, including a drunken Cindy Bolton. 'I got a Casanova for *Little Miss Muff Diver*, Eddie,' she was screaming, 'and another for *Juicy Snatch*.'

'I got a Casanova for *Scottish Girls Wee in Glasgow*,' countered a Celtic Rover WAG in a micro-kilt, 'and for *Splash Gordon*.'

'Oooh, there's Rupert,' squawked a third.

'Rupert, Rupert,' they all cried, tottering towards him on their six-inch heels.

Christ, thought Rupert, deciding it was better to laugh than cry. Next moment a thunderous-looking Valent entered the box.

'I'm pushing off,' Rupert called out to him.

'Not just yet,' said a laughing voice. 'We haven't met yet, but I'm enchanted to meet you, Rupert – I'm Bonny Richards.'

Marius told Tommy, Trixie and the rest of the lads that they'd all go out to dinner on Monday and celebrate Furious's victory, but for the moment he was going to take Amber back to Throstledown and put her to bed. They both felt shell-shocked. Rogue had hit him very hard and the medical officer said Amber would be very sore tomorrow. They both needed some peace.

*

Marius's syndicate meanwhile were most unhappy. They had no box to ply them with free drink. Euphoria that Wilkie was safe had given way, as they came down from champagne, to rage. They'd each lost a fortune. A share of the Gold Cup takings would have brought some of them as much as £20,000, not to mention money from winning bets. Joey with his white heather was the only one who'd backed Furious big time. Would Valent honour his offer to buy Wilkie now she had lost? After the King George, everyone had taken their picture and clamoured to interview them. Now no one seemed interested. How fleeting was fame.

'I'd never have paid such a fortune for that rocking horse if someone had told me Wilkie hadn't won,' wailed Phoebe.

'Rocking horse'd have more chance,' snarled Shagger.

As they were leaving, Etta saw Bonny and Valent hurrying towards Valent's red and grey helicopter and tried not to cry. It had been ridiculous to assume they wouldn't get back together again.

On their way out, kicking tins, crunching plastic glasses underfoot, avoiding drunks, the syndicate passed the entrance to the stables, where a crowd was hanging over the rails. Reluctant to bid farewell to the festival for another year, they were watching horses being loaded up for the journey home.

A great cheer went up as Furious sauntered out in his black rug which said 'Totesport Gold Cup Winner' in big gold letters. His ears were pricked, his eyes confident. 'I am the king,' he seemed to say as he looked round at the crowd before bounding on big bandaged legs up the ramp of Marius's lorry. Here, Trixie tied him up with his head near the driver so his long upper lip could nuzzle Rafiq's ears.

Then Tommy led out Mrs Wilkinson. For once her white face wasn't covered by lipstick. She looked bewildered, utterly deflated, her head and tail hanging down.

'I am the one who gets the praise, the clapping, the patting, the hats and race cards thrown in the air,' she seemed to say. 'Am I written off completely?'

For once she loaded instantly, so as not to cause any trouble, but Etta could see her one eye, huge and sweet, anxiously gazing out of the window.

'She should have been allowed into the winners enclosure,' wailed Etta, longing to run to her. 'She looks so sad.'

'She didn't bloody win,' snapped Corinna.

As they walked back through the drizzle to the minibus, which had been parked in Wellington Square to avoid traffic jams, the crowd going the same way were muted, as is usual when a favourite is beaten. With rain in their dry throats, the birds were singing so sweetly that spring was on the way.

Searching in her bag for a handkerchief, Etta realized she had left her mobile switched off.

'I knew Bonny and Valent would get back together again,' crowed Phoebe.

'Don't worry,' Painswick tucked an arm through Etta's, 'Wilkie'll live to fight another day.'

As Valent clambered into the passenger seat of Rupert's dark blue helicopter a quarter of an hour later, Rupert demanded, 'What have you done with that pretty girl? She seemed rather keen on you.'

'She's going back to London in my chopper.'

'Isn't she expecting you to go with her?'

'Yes, but I'm not, I've got things to sort out here.'

As Rupert's helicopter took off into the lilac evening, Valent caught sight of an utterly outraged Bonny beckoning from the window of his red and grey helicopter.

'Funny old day,' said Valent.

Rupert was still brooding: 'A man would have been able to fend off that kind of bullying from Killer and Johnnie. Amber's too slight, and what the hell was she doing necking with Marius in the middle of a Gold Cup? World's gone mad.'

Perhaps Amber needed a father figure now Billy was on the way out; Rupert was overwhelmed with sadness.

Valent felt ashamed. He'd just won one of the greatest races in the world, and had no right to be depressed because Etta hadn't bothered to ring him and had deliberately switched off her mobile. Business, however, prevailed.

'I've got to come clean, Rupert,' he said in embarrassment. 'What am I going to do about six hundred thousand cooddly Wilkinsons and four hundred thousand cooddly Chisolms arriving from Kowloon?'

'You what?' Over the engine Rupert wondered if he'd heard right.

'If they'd been delivered as promised before the Gold Cup,' said Valent, 'I'd have sold the lot, but the ship got held oop by pirates. Probably expected liquor or cocaine but didn't have much use for a cooddly pony, even one who shakes hands and sticks her tongue out. The cooddly Chisolm's almost cuter, got a primrose in her mouth.'

'And her bloody diary got confused with my column. Remind

635

me to murder Dora when I see her,' said Rupert, who was trying not to laugh. 'Are you talking about stuffed toys?'

'A million of them,' said Valent gloomily. 'That's why I offered to buy Mrs Wilkinson, to stop any infringement of copyright.'

'How much for?'

'Six hundred thousand.'

'Jesus.' Rupert thought for a minute then he said, 'Your only hope is to enter Mrs Wilkinson for the National. The public still adore her.'

Etta would like that, thought Valent, her favourite book was *National Velvet*.

'I'll train her for you,' said Rupert. 'We've got three weeks.'

'I'd have to check with Marius.'

But Rupert was leaping ahead: 'And once you've bought her you can dump that ghastly syndicate. Harry Herbert copes brilliantly with syndicates at Highclere, but I'm not being pestered by your job.'

129

Over at Throstledown, the crimson and royal-blue flag was flying again. Furious had won the Gold Cup and as the first Muslim to ride the winner Rafiq received massive publicity. He had also notched up a tenth win and could qualify to ride in the National, but his delight was tempered. Every newspaper led on his amazing turnaround, his jailbird past.

'"Marius rescued us both,"' wrote the *Scorpion*, beneath a lovely photograph of Rafiq hugging Furious. '"Furious and I found each other in prison."'

Before, only a sprinkling of people were aware he'd been inside and was a possible terrorist threat. Now the whole world knew.

He'd switched off his mobile but he knew the Mafia would soon return with their death threats, ordering him to pull Furious and other horses. After all this publicity, the sophisticated techniques of MI5 would also soon find out he was speaking to the enemy and pack him off to a detention camp in Eastern Europe, never to return. What would they do to darling Tommy? Vakil, whom he distrusted, had caught them kissing – so Rafiq went back to ignoring Tommy, hurting her dreadfully.

Nor were Marius and Amber very happy with the press as they woke up, on the morning after the Gold Cup, in Marius's double bed where the sheets had hardly been changed since Olivia walked out. If only they could have confirmed their commitment and reached insensibility having sex all night! Alas, Marius suspected Rogue had fractured his jaw, Amber had been kicked everywhere, and even after a lethal cocktail of champagne, whisky and Nurofen, any lovemaking had resulted in 'Ouch, ouch, ouch.'

Neither was into masochism so they fell into a fitful sleep, to be woken by Painswick bringing them cups of tea with averted eyes and pursed lips. Once again she had found her office a tip, with papers all over the floor, empty bottles, glasses everywhere and a disgusting smell of burnt tinned tomato soup.

As Florence Nightingale, Marius was clearly a washout.

'People have been leaving messages all night asking after Wilkie and congratulating you on winning the Gold Cup,' said Painswick tartly. 'Her Majesty, the Prime Minister and the Archbishop of Canterbury all sent texts. Flowers, consignments of Polos and carrots keep arriving. And the press are at the gate.'

'I'll shoot the buggers,' snapped Marius, reaching for a cigarette. 'Bring me a large whisky – please. How's Wilkie?'

'Terribly depressed. She walked out sound but she won't eat up. Furious seems fine. The press want to know what time Furious and Rafiq are going to make a victory parade through Willowwood and when's the party. And they all want to talk about you and Amber and Rogue.'

'I'm not talking to anyone, I've got a black eye.' Amber peered at herself in the dusty mirror.

'Neither of us has anything to say to the press,' snarled Marius. 'Amber's moved in. End of story. Has anyone done the declarations?'

'Not yet, and you're not going to like this.' Painswick dropped the *Scorpion* on the honeysuckle-patterned counterpane.

'Omigod,' groaned Amber, a few seconds later. 'Bloody, bloody Mum's done it again. THE LIVING NIGHTMARE WHEN I THOUGHT MY AMBER HAD DIED. Oh my God.'

Janey Lloyd-Foxe must have written and filed her copy as fast as any of the journalists in the press room at Cheltenham. There were big pictures of Marius, Amber, Rogue and Mrs Wilkinson.

' "Two of the most charismatic men in racing fighting over my baby," ' read out Amber in increasing horror. ' "When she was a teenager, my Amber had pin-up photographs of sexy champion jockey Rogue Rogers. But she also used to refer to handsome Marius as MFH, which stood for My Future Husband, and now it looks as though her dreams have come true. Our photographer caught Amber locked in Marius's arms. Heart-throb Rogue could not contain his jealousy and swung his mount round and later hit tasty Marius across the winners enclosure. Rogue has lost the race and his job as Rupert Campbell-Black's jockey. What a price to pay for love. But there was a happy ending for handsome Pakistani Rafiq Khan, my daughter's former boyfriend, who put his dark prison past behind him and stole the show." '

'The bitch, the bitch. Oh God, I'm sorry.' Amber clutched her head and shrieked with pain.

'It's all right, darling.' Marius seized the *Scorpion* and thrust it at Painswick. 'Of all the bloody tactless things to produce. Get out,' he thundered at a reporter who'd climbed up the flagpole and was peering in.

'They're all the way down the drive,' sniffed Painswick.

'You get out as well, get out,' roared Marius, rearing out naked from under the duvet, so Painswick scuttled. Then, turning to Amber, he saw she was in tears.

'Doesn't matter, we're what matters. You stay there, I'll go down and sort things out.'

Admiring the flat broad shoulders, the taut high bottom and the long muscular legs, Amber thought what a pity that Marius ever had to get dressed at all.

Painswick found Dora talking to Mistletoe in the kitchen.

'Lemme go upstairs and see them.'

'No, you can't.'

'All my contacts want a statement. Someone's got to deny that crap written by Janey Lloyd-Foxe. Poor Amber, what a cross to bear, even worse than my mother. Have they both got black eyes? People who look alike are supposed to be attracted to one another.' Dora sighed. 'Wilkie's not speaking to anyone, I better go and interview Chisolm.'

Furious got his parade through Willowwood, wearing his black Cheltenham Gold Cup Winner rug, and managed not to kick or bite anyone. Perhaps Trixie's euphoria, resulting from a pocketful of greenbacks from Valent and the prospect of Eddie taking her out on the toot that evening, had rubbed off. Wilkie stayed at home, still depressed.

'Mrs Wilkinson doesn't want to steal Furious's thunder,' Dora told the press.

Afterwards, having ascertained from Charlie Radcliffe that Wilkie had suffered no ill effects from her fall, Valent called an emergency meeting of the syndicate at the Wilkinson Arms, which Shagger quipped should now be called the Furiosa.

Here, to everyone's delight, Valent honoured his pledge. He offered to buy Mrs Wilkinson for £600,000 and, even better, allowed the syndicate to retain a 1 or a 0.5 per cent share each, 'so we can keep her in the family, so to speak'.

To this, a majority vote agreed joyfully.

'And we can still enjoy being part of Wilkie without the uncertainty and expense of the bills,' said Tilda. 'Thank you so
much, Valent.'

Expecting a party, the syndicate were somewhat deflated when
Valent immediately pushed off to discuss the new arrangements
with Marius.

'That's about sixty thousand each,' worked out Alan, who still
hadn't got to the end of his book.

'Isn't he kind?' sighed Etta, whose eyes Valent hadn't met once.

'Pocket money to him,' mocked Shagger.

130

Journalists were still hanging around outside Throstledown as Valent arrived. Telling them to bugger off, he checked on Wilkie, who was indeed so low she refused a bit of barley sugar.

In the office, Valent found Amber wearing a blue and white striped shirt of Marius's. Having enquired after her bruises and given her some grapes, Valent also told her to 'shove off, luv'. His meeting was only with Marius.

Amber retreated upstairs and went on the rampage.

Like Miss Havisham's house, nothing seemed to have changed since Olivia left. In the wardrobe, Amber found lots of pastels and blacks. Skirts had got shorter since Olivia had left Marius, she'd need to have everything turned up if she wanted to wear them again. Hatboxes were piled under the dressing table, boots under the chaise longue. On the walls were photographs of Olivia with terriers, with India, with horses, jumping them, leading them up, posing with winners. Even her jewels were still in their case.

Had Shade, the control freak, wanted to excise the Marius years and ensure everything Olivia owned had been given her by him?

On the dressing table were bottles of scent, many of which had lost their individual smell through age. One sweet and peppery scent called Silver Rain she remembered smelling on Olivia before the first point-to-point and had occasionally caught wafts of in the paddock. Perhaps Silver Rain had been an affair present from Shade. Olivia had left a bottle of cleansing cream upside down in a loo roll, draining out the last drop. She and Marius must have been terribly short of money. There was arnica for bruises – Amber rubbed some underneath her eye – and even a bra still in the dirty clothes basket, although that could have been Michelle's.

Loathing herself, Amber found a couple of whisky bottles inside Marius's bedside cupboard. Inside Olivia's she found a Dick Francis and Jenny Pitman's autobiography face down. In a Bible, she found a handsome photograph of Shade and a letter: 'My darling, Everything awaits you.' Another picture fell out. Goodness, it was Alan Macbeth, so like Niles in *Frasier*. Her hand shaking, Amber felt under the cupboard's lining paper. The pain was ridiculous as she pulled out a photograph and a letter from Rogue, who never wrote letters. 'Darling Olivia, Sorry I came too soon. Better fuck next time. Yours always, Rogue.' Amber had heard rumours. God, would she never get over him? She slumped on the bed, face in her hands.

How strange that Marius was so incurious, he'd never bothered to open Pandora's box. All over the house were pictures and sculptures of horses galloping, yet time seemed to have stopped at the starting gates, waiting for Olivia to come back.

Down in the office, Valent thought how pale and exhausted Marius looked. *At the Races,* turned up sforzando, was showing a race in Kentucky with lots of little Eddie Aldertons in long white trousers and ankle boots riding large horses which were being ponied down to the start by large men on little ponies.

He knew Marius was anxious to get out to evening stables, so, having accepted a can of beer, he immediately broke the news that he'd bought Mrs Wilkinson.

'Shouldn't chuck your money away like that.'

'Got enough for the rest of my life.'

'Not if you start buying racehorses,' said Marius, examining the schooling list for tomorrow.

'Will you turn the foocking television down and concentrate, Marius? I'll have to put you in a flooffy noseband.'

'Stupid time to buy her anyway,' went on Marius, 'I'm going to turn her away for the summer. She's had a long hard season.'

'Rubbish,' said Valent, 'she's been very lightly raced, only did one round of the Gold Cup. I want her to go in for the National.'

'Too late, it's all been handicapped. And she's much too small.'

'You entered her and Furious ages ago.'

'Painswick did. I never had any intention of running her, unless she'd missed the Gold Cup or hadn't won the King George. They announce the National weights in the middle of Feb, after the King George in fact, which means she'd be top weight. You can't expect her to carry 11 st 10 lb, 10 lb more than Playboy. I've lost too many horses in that race.'

'Why are you running Sir Cuthbert then?' asked Valent sulkily.

'Because we've finally got him right, he's twice as big as Wilkie and he stays for ever. Wilkie's too gutsy, her heart's too big. I'm not running her. If you're determined to take her to Aintree, enter her in the Mares Only on Friday.'

Marius topped up his whisky without water, turned up the television and picked up the *Racing Post*.

Valent flipped. 'Turn that foocking TV down.'

Despite his great generosity, Valent was first and foremost a major player who always aimed for the top. Ryan was back in his life, excited at the prospect, and there were 500,000 cuddly Wilkinsons to shift out of the starting stalls.

The Gold Cup was the mecca of the National Hunt world, but the National was something else. Every housewife in England had a pound on it, 600 million people watched it on television. It was an Everest with vast romantic and historical associations. Valent also remembered Etta saying she still read *National Velvet* once a year.

'Wilkie'll make a fortune as a brood mare if she even runs well in the National.'

'Rubbish.' Marius looked up from the *Racing Post*. 'Great race mares don't necessarily make good brood mares.'

'Aintree would love to have her,' said Valent proudly. 'It'd be great box office to take her there. Aintree's flat, it would suit her better. You know, Marius, the Gold Cup's for horses with a great cruising speed and a turn of foot which Wilkie doesn't have. National's for out-and-out stayers. Anyway, small horses tend to jump more carefully and concentrate.'

Marius looked at him beadily.

'You've been talking to Rupert.'

Valent drained his beer and got up.

'I'm sorry, Marius, Wilkie's going in for the National.'

'She is bloody not. It's less than three weeks away. Don't tell me how to train horses, Valent, go back to inventing robots and importing toys.'

Valent glanced at a photograph of Olivia taking part in the Ashcombe point-to-point – she and Bafford Playboy stretched over an open ditch.

'National's only an oopmarket point-to-point,' he said.

Hearing shouting and Valent's car storming off down the drive, Amber shoved back drawers and ran downstairs.

'Everything OK?'

Marius, pouring himself another large whisky, couldn't speak for rage. Mistletoe cowered under the desk.

Amber crouched down to stroke her. 'Whatever's happened?'

'Valent's taking Furious and Mrs Wilkinson to Rupert.'

'He what!' Amber was aghast. 'They'll loathe it, he's far too rough on horses. Like going to Borstal.'

'He's entering them both in the Grand National,' said Marius bleakly.

'He can't,' whispered Amber. 'Rupert doesn't approve of women jockeys. He can't put up that spoilt brat Eddie Alderton, he wouldn't get her over the first fence. Nor will Furious ever run for Eddie or Rogue.'

'Rogue's banned until after the National.'

'Wilkie's uptight enough as it is. If he takes her away from Tommy and all her friends, it'll destroy her. And what the hell will it do to Rafiq? How dare Valent do that, after all you've done for Furious and Wilkie.' She put her arms round him. 'Come to bed. I'll make it better.'

But later, when she put her lips round his cock, nothing happened.

'Flag's the only thing going up round here,' said Marius bitterly.

Rogue came out of the cottage in Penscombe, from which Rupert had evicted him, to find the paparazzi out in force. Why had he turned his horse round, why had he hit Marius? Was he gutted because Amber had shacked up with Marius?

Rogue shrugged, 'I guess on the day I was beaten by a better horse,' and jumping into his Ferrari, he drove straight at the paps, sending them leaping for their lives.

He had screwed up the best job in racing and probably his best chance of winning the National. His shoulder was giving him hell, but nothing like the pain of being banned for a month. To avoid the press, he decided to go on holiday and flew out to Portugal. Having sat on the beach for ten minutes, surrounded by vast women with massive tattooed thighs, he decided to fly home again.

He felt utterly miserable. For two years he'd been fighting the fact that he was crazy about Amber. He'd give up all the girls in the world for her. Nothing had equalled the agony when he'd seen her motionless body at the Field of Hope.

He must be lunatically smitten for it to take his mind off winning the Gold Cup, but even that agony was nothing to the red-hot-poker rage when he saw her in Marius's arms. It was entirely his fault, he'd taken the piss out of her so often, and now he'd lost her and screwed his career.

As he walked into the Arrivals lounge at Heathrow, his mobile rang. It was Diana Keen from Sunset and Vine, the ace production company with the massive task of covering the Grand National for the BBC:

'Hi Rogue, Billy Lloyd-Foxe is ill and won't make it, Bluey Charteris has got pneumonia. How'd you like to come and help us with the commentary on the Grand National?'

131

Rupert Campbell-Black had moved almost entirely away from National Hunt to the flat, winning the big races with the progeny of his stallions to advertise their potency. As each stallion was capable of covering 150-odd mares a year, at a massive stud fee, the riches were unimaginable.

The great Irish trainer at Coolmore, the sheikhs in Dubai and Rupert all respected and liked each other and bought each other's foals. Although he was a martinet, Rupert's jockeys and stable staff would jump through fire for him. Now he was fifty-six, not too many miles from sixty, his record-breaking three-thousandth win was expected before the end of the season. But Rupert was not happy.

For a start, he was faced with the problem of the two Eddies. His father Eddie had been such a hit on *Buffers*, the television show in which retired military men argued about wars, that the public had even started shoving Rupert out of the way to get Eddie's autograph. Eddie, however, was slipping into senility, resolutely exposing himself in the orangery, addicted to pornography, sliding DVDs entitled *Eight Hours of Big Tits and Dicks* into a machine and his hands up girls' skirts.

Even Painswick, who'd helped Eddie out with his fan mail when things had been slack at Throstledown, wasn't out of bounds and Pocock was threatening to call Eddie out. Rupert, woken by moaning the morning after the Gold Cup, thought it was Banquo the Labrador desperate to go out, but discovered it was one of Cindy Bolton's Casanovas which a naked Eddie was watching in the study.

More stressful, however, was Eddie the second: Edward Alderton, Rupert's twenty-year-old grandson by Perdita and Luke

Alderton, both international polo players, so Eddie could ride before he crawled.

Arrogant, spoilt, opinionated, Eddie had already achieved considerable success as a flat jockey in America, but having grown too tall and heavy he'd decided to try his luck over fences and had come to spend a year with Grandpa Penscombe and Taggie.

Like Rupert nearly forty years ago, this gilded brat thought he knew everything and was very rough on horses. The rows between him and Rupert were pyrotechnic. Poor Taggie, Rupert's wife, was desperately attempting to keep the peace.

Racing was different in America. Even apprentice jockeys only ride out from six thirty to ten thirty in the morning, while stable lads, mostly Mexican, look after the horses. Painkillers banned in England are allowed in the States to enable horses to run. Jockeys are ponied down to the start. Eddie refused to admit how terrified he'd been when, in his first race in England, he had to find the start by himself and his horse had carted him. Eddie had also taken some time to overcome his terror of Rupert's kamikaze downhill gallop. Now he scorched down, taking every liberty.

Young Eddie had also palled up with old Eddie. They watched porn together with howls of laughter and encouraged each other in all sorts of silly behaviour which drove Rupert crackers.

Also contributing to Rupert's unhappiness was the fact that his beautiful chestnut avenue, a towering candlelit vigil in spring, shedding conkers like a bed of fire in autumn, which he had planted when he first started showjumping back in the sixties, was dying of some incurable fungus, its bark cracking. It might soon have to be felled.

Finally Rupert was devastated because his greatest friend, Billy Lloyd-Foxe, was dying of cancer. Rupert, despite his Olympian caprice, had troops of friends but none equalled Billy for tolerance and sweetness and a sense of humour. He and Rupert were joined at the hip, read each other's minds and finished each other's sentences.

On the surface Billy was too kind, easy-going and generous, but he had won Olympic medals for showjumping and had become an adored BBC commentator. Somehow, too, Billy had managed to stay married to his rackety, promiscuous journalist wife, Janey. But to cope with the strain, Billy had always drunk and smoked to excess, which had now taken its toll. Billy made light of the pain but his stocky figure had dwindled away, the thick curly grey hair was sparse, and only the huge smile dominating the emaciated face was the same.

Although Billy remained in hospital, he was still hoping and fighting to be well enough to fly up and swell the team of BBC presenters covering the Grand National.

The National was the only big race that had evaded Rupert and he had caught Valent up in his desire to crack it. He therefore made colossal headlines by announcing that from now on he would be training Furious and Mrs Wilkinson at Penscombe and they would both be joining Lusty in the National in three weeks' time. Despite his love-hate relationship with young Eddie, he would have adored his grandson to ride his three-thousandth winner on one of the three horses.

Most of the Willowwood syndicate were absolutely thrilled by the move to Rupert. Not only had they cleaned up financially with their share of the £600,000 Valent had paid for Mrs Wilkinson, but there was also the 1 per cent share they'd retained in her, and Valent had promised to fly them all up to Aintree where he'd taken a box.

'Marius who?' mocked Shagger.

'Rupert's two top stallions, Peppy Koala and Love Rat, charge stud fees of a hundred thousand,' announced Alan.

'I'd pay that to sleep with Rupert,' said Corinna.

'If we all put in fifty thousand we could have a gang bang,' chortled Phoebe, then, although she'd never visited Mrs Wilkinson at Badger's Court or Throstledown, she added, 'I hope we'll have lots of access to Wilkie so she won't get lonely.'

'I'm looking forward to seeing Rupert's wonderful yard,' said Tilda.

So was Alan, for his book, but he was not sure how accommodating Rupert would be.

' "At the base of these aristocratic races," ' quoted Seth, ' "the predator is not to be mistaken, the splendorous Blond Beastie avidly rampant for plunder and victory." Never underestimate Rupert.'

Etta had missed the meeting held on the Monday after the Gold Cup, at which the Major told the syndicate of the move to Rupert's. Romy and Martin had buzzed off to London for an evening fundraiser, leaving Etta with the children. She therefore heard the news later in the evening from an outraged Painswick and was so distraught she immediately rang Valent:

'How dare you desert Marius after all the love and work he's put into Wilkie, and what about poor Tommy! They know what she's capable of – not bloody Rupert Campbell-Black.'

'I thought he was your pin-oop and you'd be pleased to have him training Wilkie for the National.'

'The National?' screamed Etta. 'How could you!'

'You were always saying your favourite book was *National Velvet* and as a little girl you dreamed of winning the National.'

'The Pie in *National Velvet* was huge, Mrs Wilkinson's had all the stuffing knocked out of her by the Gold Cup and she's only fourteen two.'

'So was Battleship.'

'Everyone quotes bloody Battleship. Anyway *National Velvet* was fiction.'

'I don't oonderstand you, Etta,' snapped Valent and hung up. Priceless sighed.

The rest of the syndicate tried to talk Etta round.

'You're being too harsh on Valent, Granny,' protested Trixie, remembering the greenbacks after the Gold Cup. 'He loves Mrs Wilkinson and he's saved her so many times, look at the time he came all the way back from Dubai to talk the syndicate round. And think how exciting it will be to see Rupert's yard.'

Rupert's yard was indeed glorious, with its lovely honey-gold house lying back against its pillow of beeches, now showing a green blur of spring. The old showjumping yard had been enlarged to house his racehorses, but he had colonized the entire valley to build the stud where his stallions strutted their stuffing and the boxes for his brood mares and their foals. Electronic security gates and CCTV cameras monitored operations in field and stable.

'It's a good thing they didn't operate in the old days,' said Dora, 'when Rupert was pulling every girl groom in sight.'

There were multi-screens in his office to watch his horses wherever they were running as well as a gym, spas and a salt-water pool, plus equipment and flat and uphill gallops to replicate every fence, hurdle, surface or course in the world.

None of this, however, impressed Mrs Wilkinson, who was above all a home bird who never slept in strange stables. She was desperately homesick and frightened at Rupert's. No one played Beethoven to her. No one laughed when she stuck out her tongue, no one gave her a Polo if she tried to shake hooves. Refusing to eat, walking her box, driving everyone crackers yelling for Chisolm, she desperately missed Tommy, Etta, Rafiq and all her horse friends at Throstledown.

Nor, to their rage, was Rupert going to give that 'ghastly syndicate' access or allow any journalists or fans into his yard, so Mrs Wilkinson missed their adulation as well.

The acquisition of Mrs Wilkinson was a two-edged sword. Red postal vans were soon buckling under her fan mail, as tons of

Polos, carrots, barley sugars and get-well cards arrived at Rupert's gate. Chisolm sent her a bleatings card. These had been redirected by Painswick, who remembered Rupert as one of the most subversive and difficult parents at Bagley Hall.

'It's your problem now,' she sourly told Rupert's very diplomatic PA.

132

Dora, however, was a great friend of the Campbell-Blacks.

'It's absolutely dreadful for Marius, Tommy and Rafiq,' she told Etta apologetically, 'but I can't diss Rupert because I'm writing his column for him.'

Always on the hunt for a story, Dora rolled up at Penscombe to see her friend Bianca, Rupert and Taggie's daughter.

Mrs Wilkinson, temporarily roused out of her black depression, was touchingly pleased to see Dora, practically clambering out over the half-door of her box.

'How is she?' Dora asked Lysander, Rupert's assistant, who was a genius at bringing on horses. Infinitely patient, refusing to push them, believing that it didn't matter if they came fifth or sixth as long as they looked forward to their next race, Lysander praised and encouraged them to the skies. So far he wasn't having much success with Mrs Wilkinson.

'She's absolutely miserable,' he sighed. 'Rupert's put her in a ring bit and a cross noseband to teach her to jump straight. He's taking her drag hunting tomorrow so she gets used to jumping big fences at speed.'

'She's refusing Polos, she must be dying,' said a worried Dora.

'She's also come into season.'

'Ah, will Rupert still run her?'

'Only one in ten mares runs better in season or when they're cycling,' said Lysander, 'so the odds aren't great.'

'We better enter her for the Tour de France then,' giggled Bianca.

Mrs Wilkinson sank back into gloom, whinnying piteously then retreating to the back of the box, head drooping, tail down, so Dora asked if she and Bianca could take her for a walk. Lysander, who was quite used to dealing with temperamental stallions but who had turned deathly pale at the prospect of sorting out an impossibly fractious Furious, said that was OK.

The yard for once was very quiet. All the lads were on their breaks. Rupert was at the World Cup in Dubai. Lysander had clattered off to the indoor school. Bianca, who was madly in love with Feral Jackson, Ryan Edwards's brilliant new striker, wanted to know if Dora thought seventeen was too young to get married.

'You're a WAG anyway,' said Dora, who wasn't listening.

They were passing Billionaire's Row, a yard of boxes housing Rupert's top stallions, who weren't let out into the fields but lunged or walked in hand for a couple of hours a day.

'They've got to be kept fit if they're covering four mares a day,' explained Bianca.

Beside each stallion's door was a brass plaque listing the races they'd won.

'That's Peppy Koala.' Bianca pointed to a wild-eyed chestnut, who was chewing at his half-door. 'He's worth forty million. He never gets ridden, poor thing, he'd take off. Eddie jumped on Love Rat the other day, nearly ended up in Scotland. That's the practice mare,' went on Bianca, pointing to a dozing dapple grey. 'She stands still and the stallions practise on her.'

'Cheap date,' said Dora, 'no champagne or flowers.'

'Mares travel from all over the country for our stallions,' said Bianca proudly, 'like women used to run after Daddy before he married Mummy.'

'Still do,' said Dora, thinking of Corinna and Phoebe.

'Love Rat had three hundred and twenty applications this year, but he only accepted a hundred.'

'Sounds like the waiting list at Bagley.'

'Here's the covering yard.' Bianca showed Mrs Wilkinson and Dora a huge barn with shredded black tyres over the floor and rubber padding round the walls so the horses didn't hurt themselves.

'See that little ramp, it's for smaller stallions to stand on.'

'Like jockeys,' said Dora.

'Some stallions are very slow and take at least ten minutes.' Bianca rolled her huge brown eyes. 'Others only take ten seconds.'

'Just like jockeys, according to Amber,' said Dora, who, not having had any lunch, was eating Mrs Wilkinson's Polos.

'You need five people for each covering,' continued Bianca. 'One man to hold the mare with a twitch, one to hold the stallion, one to hold the tail out of the way, one to see if the stallion has ejaculated and one to guide the penis in.'

'Poor mares, just like a levee after a royal wedding,' said Dora indignantly.

'Whatever. Talking of weddings,' said Bianca, 'should I marry Feral?'

'Bit young, he's lovely but only twenty.'

It was a beautiful evening, robins and blackbirds singing their heads off, tree shadows striping the frost-bleached fields. A little foal in a paddock below, his beige coat darkened by rain, was attempting to shag his mother.

'That's one of Love Rat's,' said Bianca, 'starting early.'

'God, I love foals,' sighed Dora. 'Where is Love Rat?'

'Here,' said Bianca, turning right.

Unlike Rupert's other stallions who were confined to barracks, Penscombe Love Rat, father of Lusty, had a low boredom threshold and was allowed to roam free for part of the day in an electrically fenced field.

With his huge hindquarters, barrel chest and noble head he was a splendid sight, particularly as, like a teenager, he tossed his long blond mane, through which the setting sun was streaming. From the branch of a huge sycamore, already putting out acid-green buds, hung rubber tyres, even a rubber horse to keep him amused.

Love Rat's stud fee was £100,000 but the mares frequently presented to him did not flutter his pulses. He was a free spirit who disliked formalized cover.

'Are you sure your father's in Dubai?' asked Dora, as Love Rat wandered up to them.

'Quite,' said Bianca, but she turned paler than Lysander when Dora suggested a bit of nooky, known in the trade as 'stolen service'.

'Daddy'd kill you.'

'He won't know,' said Dora airily.

'One of the screens in Daddy's office looks straight into this field,' protested Bianca.

'Go and switch it off,' said Dora. 'It's the ideal time, March or earlier. The gestation period is eleven months so she'd foal in February.'

'What about the National?' quavered Bianca.

'They can run up to five months,' said Dora, scribbling excitedly in her notebook.

Dora and Bianca put covering boots like great fluffy Uggs on both Mrs Wilkinson and Love Rat so they didn't hurt each other, then fed Mrs Wilkinson into Love Rat's field.

Instantly she became very skittish, whinnying, bucking and flashing her fanny at Love Rat. They then had a heavenly time consummating the marriage.

'At least nine minutes,' said Dora proudly. 'Much better than jockeys. And they didn't need five humans to guide anything.'

Afterwards Love Rat nuzzled Mrs Wilkinson and licked her very fondly.

'He doesn't do that normally,' said Bianca.

'Just rolls over and goes to sleep,' grinned Dora, and rewarded Love Rat with the rest of Mrs Wilkinson's Polos.

As a result Mrs Wilkinson cheered up no end and ate a large tea when she returned to her box.

'Eating for two already,' said Dora happily. 'Love matches are best.'

'Then I should marry Feral,' declared Bianca, 'and Daddy won't bully me to get a job.'

'What are you two laughing about?' asked an ashen Lysander, limping back after being bucked off and attacked by Furious.

Dora couldn't resist telling him. Lysander nearly fainted:

'Christ, Dora! Rupert'll fire me, and send you a bill for a hundred thousand.'

'You'll have to sell a lot of stories for that,' said Bianca. 'Better not put it in the *Racing Post*. The marriage has been arranged between Love Rat Campbell-Black, and Mrs Usurper Wilkinson.'

'Don't call her Usurper,' shuddered Dora. 'That's what hideous Harvey-Holden called her.'

Mrs Wilkinson sank back into gloom. Young Eddie, who'd been ordered on to Furious by an absent Rupert, didn't want to get savaged so instead he put the horse on the horse walker for the first time. Instantly Furious went berserk, and nearly wrecked himself and the horse walker, kicking the sides out.

Over at Throstledown, Marius, despite Amber moving in, was absolutely devastated by the departure of his two star horses. He'd picked himself up from the floor once too often. Chisolm was on hunger strike and bleated incessantly for her friend. Mrs Wilkinson's box was left empty. All the horses, particularly Sir Cuthbert and Count Romeo, peered in hopefully. The lads, in despair, even missed being bitten by Furious.

Rafiq had cried and cried when Furious was taken away. Even though trainers were offering him rides, the media were avid to interview him and agents desperate to handle him, he could hardly force himself up in the morning, he was missing Furious so much.

Tommy soldiered on but bled inside, missing Wilkie, desperately sorry for Marius, spurned by Rafiq. Trixie was devastated. Her difficult but endearing charge had been whipped away. None of Marius's other horses had the same appeal. Eddie promised he would put in a word when Rupert came back from Dubai.

The papers, however, which had led on Glorious Furious's spectacular victory on Saturday and spent endless column inches working out why Mrs Wilkinson fell at three out, were by Tuesday slagging off Valent and Rupert for taking the horses away from Marius. Both men were getting hate mail.

Marius, however, was a gentleman. He had already given Rupert details of the fads and feeding habits of Furious and Wilkie, although he forgot to mention the tricks she did for a Polo. When he heard from Dora that both horses were going into a decline, he offered to lend Tommy, Rafiq and Chisolm to Rupert until after the National. The move wasn't entirely altruistic. He was fed up with Rafiq's tantrums, and he wanted his horses, particularly Sir Cuthbert who was entered for the National, to get some sleep.

It was a measure of Tommy and Rafiq, and particularly their love for Wilkie and Furious, that they were prepared to go and work for the hated enemy. But despite young Eddie's pleas, there was no way Rupert was going to allow a schoolgirl like Trixie loose in his yard.

133

Rupert tolerated Tommy and Chisolm moving in, but he didn't want the moody, darkly resentful Rafiq, who looked at him with such loathing, muttering what sounded like curses under his breath. Rupert's sweet wife Taggie had made matters worse by insisting 'poor Tommy and Rafiq' stay in the house. 'It's only for a few days, and they must be so devastated losing both Mrs Wilkinson and Furious.'

On the first morning, a silent, sullen Rafiq sat in Rupert's Land-Rover watching Mrs Wilkinson and Furious being taken over National-size fences in a tiny forty-by-twenty-metre school to teach them to jump more carefully. Neither of them performed well with Eddie Alderton. Rafiq expressed disapproval of Mrs Wilkinson being restricted by a cross noseband and a ring bit.

'A great jockey called Terry Biddlecombe,' Rupert felt he was being extremely decent to explain, 'travelled five miles in a four and a half Grand National because his horse wandered. Mrs Wilkinson hangs left; she's got to learn to run straight.'

Mrs Wilkinson looked listless, then terrified as they moved on to Rupert's uphill gallop, and Eddie, his feet practically touching the ground on either side, got out his bat to make her go faster.

A horrified Rafiq dropped his guard:

'You are crazy. If you knock her about she stop trying, and Furious, I know he seem vicious but he is insecure and if he's threatened he get more angry. Both horses need treating gentle.'

'Both horses need experienced riders on their backs,' snapped Rupert.

'That's why he win Gold Cup with me,' spat Rafiq. 'And you should put Amber back on Mrs Wilkinson. They are twin soul.'

'Amber is beautifully balanced and controlled going over

fences. But she lacks the power to hold up and to force a finish.'

Why, wondered Rupert, was he bothering to justify himself to this arrogant little shit?

Reaching the top of the gallops, they were greeted by a wonderful view of fields and donkey-brown woodland in a geometric pattern of stone walls stretching to the horizon. Spring seemed to have gone into retreat as a bitter east wind flattened the grass and Rupert's long lake had gone grey, mirroring the lowering skies above.

Leaping out of the Land-Rover to escape Rupert's antagonism, Rafiq gasped at the cold, then gasped in horror as Eddie Alderton suddenly swung Mrs Wilkinson off the gallops, straight down the rollercoaster ride. Now Eddie whooped and yelled, and it was Mrs Wilkinson's turn to be terrified so witless she closed her eye until she reached the bottom. If it had not been for the pain caused by the ring bit, she would have scraped Eddie off by running under the branches of the nearby beech. Next moment Tommy came panting up.

'How dare you!' she shouted at Eddie. 'How could you be so cruel! You'll set her back years. Don't you know what a terrible past she had, her eye gouged out, look at the scars on her body. Someone was obscenely cruel to her, and now you're being obscenely cruel all over again. There, there, my pet,' Tommy caught Mrs Wilkinson's reins. 'That bloody bridle's made her mouth bleed, you bastard.'

'Oh, put a sock in it.' Eddie pretended to play a violin.

Rafiq's mood was not improved later in the day when Eddie brought Tommy a bunch of daffodils picked from Rupert's garden, apologized for upsetting her, and took her off to see the stud and the stallions in her break.

'They're so beautiful,' sighed Tommy as Peppy Koala was led past. 'Jump horses like Lusty and Sir Cuthbert go on for ages, awful to think flat horses end their glorious careers so early.'

'I don't know,' drawled Eddie, 'I'd much rather fuck all day than be thrashed within an inch of my life for not running round a racetrack fast enough.'

Rafiq, who was hovering, could see a blush creeping up Tommy's cheek.

'Is it easier racing in England?' she asked.

Eddie grinned. 'Sure, the horses are slower.'

Meanwhile, every time Dora drove in and out the press accosted her.

'Which story are you doing? Marius and Amber, Bonny back

with Valent, Wilkie and Furious going to Rupert, or Rogue Rogers wrecking his career for love?'

'All four,' replied Dora happily.

Chisolm was having a lovely time, her column in the *Mirror* getting more and more unbridled:

'Here I am at Penscombe. Never a dull moment. Excellent primroses and violets. Love Rat, Rupert's top stallion, whinnies to Mrs Wilkinson every time she passes. Furious kicked Rupert's black Labrador Banquo yesterday. Rupert very cross. Why can't he talk to the rest of us in the loving, "Come to Daddy" way he talks to his dogs?'

'Watch it,' snapped Rupert.

Great reservoirs of rage kept bubbling up over Rogue losing him the Gold Cup and forcing him to sack him. If only he could get him back. Agents were never off the telephone offering him lousy replacements for his three National horses.

Valent and Hengist Brett-Taylor, who was still making his film about Beau Regard, Mrs Wilkinson and the Willowwood legend, kept trying to persuade Rupert to put Rafiq up on Furious. Rupert, however, had been poring over the videos of Rafiq's races, noting the ones when his horses should have won, and concluded Rafiq was bent. That horse Bullydozer had certainly been nobbled at Leopardstown.

The police had already warned him to watch out.

'Rafiq's OK,' insisted Hengist. 'He learnt his lesson inside.'

'Bollocks,' said Rupert. 'Bang up heavy-duty villains together, they just learn more skills to continue their villainy.'

Nor was Amber finding it easy at Throstledown. None of the stable staff liked the new hierarchy. Would Miss Toffeenose end up as the boss's wife?

Her allies, Tommy and Rafiq, had gone to Penscombe. Painswick, who'd been devastated by the departure of Wilkie and Furious, didn't approve of Amber in Marius's bed. Wandering down to the yard one morning, Amber found Tresa reading *OK!* and gossiping to Josh.

'Amber's always got to the top on her back,' she was saying.

'Rubbish,' shouted Amber, making them both jump, 'I got to the top on Wilkie's back,' and stormed off upstairs.

Amber found it such a bleak house. Marius, however kind he was to her, was above all a trainer, one-track and focused, who worked a seventeen-hour day, rising at five and not going to bed until after the ten o'clock news. No time really for love. Mistletoe the lurcher, who now shadowed Amber, was her only friend.

Poor Amber was in such a muddle. She was finding the relationship with Marius too frenzied. He was too needing of comfort and he still talked in his sleep about Olivia, whose presence was stamped all over the house.

Then she read, in Katie Nicholl's column in the *Mail on Sunday*, that Olivia had been seen this week having a discreet drink with Rogue, and Amber felt the same searing red-hot-poker jab of jealousy. Rogue's colours were superimposed on her heart rather than the racecourse.

She must get back on a horse. She longed to ride Sir Cuthbert in the National but Lady Crowe had a soft spot for goofy Awesome and insisted he was given the ride on her old horse. Amber had been gutted to be jocked off Wilkie. She couldn't bear the thought of Eddie Alderton beating her and yanking her around.

Finally, she was sick with worry about her father, who'd told the BBC he couldn't cover the three days at Aintree but hoped to fly up to interview Amber if she got a ride in the National. He didn't realize he simply hadn't the strength.

Feeling horribly disloyal to Marius, knowing the press would have a field day, Amber rang her godmother Taggie to discover when Rupert had ten minutes free and drove over to Penscombe. She had spent a lot of time there as a child, but always been aware that Rupert was the rich man in his castle, the Lloyd-Foxes the comparatively poor men at his gate. Rupert's daughter Tabitha had won Olympic Gold for eventing and another daughter, Eddie's mother Perdita, was an international polo player. Suddenly Amber had a desperate urge to be up with them.

Taggie hugged her, loving as ever, but she looked harassed. 'I'm afraid Rupert's very uptight.'

Amber found Rupert in his office, which had two doors so he could escape from people he didn't want to see; probably her as well, when she begged him to let her ride Mrs Wilkinson.

'Dad's only got a few weeks to live. He'll never see another Grand National.'

'You don't have the experience,' said Rupert flatly, horrified how thin and pale she looked. 'It's too tough for a slight girl on a very small horse. Aintree has made heroic efforts to make the entire course, and particularly the fences, more forgiving, but there are still thirty of them. Thirty fences, four and a half miles, loose horses careering everywhere, like no other race. Statistically half the field don't come home. No mare's won for years. No woman rider's ever won. No grey's won since Nicolaus Silver. The odds are against you. Like girls playing rugger against Martin

659

Johnson.' Rupert took a deep breath. 'I don't want to risk you or Mrs Wilkinson's lives, angel.'

'Mrs Wilkinson will be much safer if I'm riding her. Her whiskers have grown, we'll slide through the gaps. Please, Rupert, for Dad's sake.'

Bitterly regretting there would now be no chance of Eddie riding his grandfather's three-thousandth winner on the People's Pony, Rupert agreed to let Amber ride her instead.

'But you're going to have to build up some muscle. Tomorrow you're taking Wilkie drag hunting, four runs over really fast, high black fences to give her some practice.'

Feeling sick with guilt, Amber drove back to Throstledown. Marius was so proud, would he regard her riding Wilkie as the final betrayal and chuck her out? Mistletoe ran out to welcome her, but Painswick had fortunately gone shopping. Amber was about to break the news to Marius when a car drew up and a lot of terriers and India Oakridge fell out.

'Daddy, Daddy,' screamed India, rushing into the office, 'look what Mummy's just bought me.'

They were the first cuddly Wilkinsons and Chisolms.

'They're absolutely awesome. Wilkie neighs, sticks her tongue out and shakes hands and Chisolm bleats and butts people. Look, she's got a flower in her mouth. Aren't they lovely?'

'That is neat,' said Amber, picking up Wilkie, 'and just like her. Where did you get it?'

'Cavendish House, they're galloping out of the shops,' said India's mother, walking in wearing dark glasses.

'Look at Chisolm,' cried India. Having wound up the goat, she put her on the table, where she promptly butted Marius's whisky on to the floor.

'Well done, Chisolm,' said Olivia coolly. 'Daddy shouldn't be drinking whisky in the middle of the afternoon anyway.' Then, turning to Amber, 'And you can get out. This is where I belong.'

If it hadn't been for the split-second lighthouse beam of hope and happiness on Marius's face, Amber might have put up a fight.

'OK, I'll pack my things.'

'Amber, wait,' called out Marius, but he didn't follow her upstairs.

There wasn't much to pack, she'd lived in Marius's shirts since she'd been there.

Back in the kitchen she found India had escaped to see the

horses, and Marius and Olivia gazing at each other as though they were playing statues.

'I'm off,' said Amber. 'I just want to say one thing, Olivia. Marius loves you. He and I only got together because we both desperately needed someone, but we aren't making each other happy. He's a brilliant trainer, and you were a brilliant team together, but he's done really well in the last year without you, so don't mess him around any more.' For a second she crouched down to stroke Mistletoe. 'And please look after this sweet dog because she's got a lousy home here.'

'How dare you,' exploded Olivia, but Amber had turned to Marius. 'Thank you for having me to stay. Sorry I won't have time to write a thank-you letter, but I'll be too busy revving up to ride Wilkie in the National.' Then, gratified at the outrage on the faces of both Marius and Olivia, she sauntered out. 'See you at Aintree.'

Her mobile rang as she hurtled down the drive. It was Taggie.

'I've left Marius,' gasped Amber.

'Hurrah,' said Taggie, 'come and stay at Penscombe.'

Next morning Amber took Wilkie drag hunting and Rupert was just pondering whether he dared risk putting up Eddie on Lusty in the National, when Lusty broke a blood vessel on the gallops, spraying blood all over Eddie. Later the horse scoped dirty, proof of a virus, which probably explained why Furious had beaten Lusty in the Gold Cup. This freed up Eddie to ride Furious in the National, giving Rupert a legitimate excuse to jock off Rafiq.

Eddie, who detested the way his grandfather insisted he work in the yard, feeding and skipping out horses, had been winding up Rafiq all morning. For a third time, he flicked droppings over the partition into Furious's box, narrowly missing Rafiq.

Then Rupert came out and broke the news that Lusty was a non-runner and Eddie would be riding Furious.

'I'm not riding that goddam awful pig,' protested Eddie, throwing down his shovel with a clatter.

Emerging from Furious's box, a distraught Rafiq launched into a stream of Urdu expletives.

'Don't speak of Furious like that,' he yelled. 'I'm riding him in the National.' If he said it loud enough someone might believe it.

'Afraid not,' said Rupert, 'you don't have the experience.'

'You're just a bloody racist,' snarled Rafiq.

'I am not,' replied Rupert in outrage. 'I have two black children, my son is going out with a Muslim girl whose Pakistani parents I get on with extremely well. Don't you dare call me a racist.'

'Prove it,' said Rafiq haughtily, 'let me ride Furious.'

On cue Furious put his head out of the box, laying it on Rafiq's shoulder.

'Loosen up, Rafiq,' drawled Eddie, 'National's for the big boys.'

At which Rafiq jumped on Eddie and tried to throttle him and four other lads had to be called in to pull him off.

Tommy's father had rung Rupert that morning, warning him yet again to watch Rafiq, so Rupert sacked him, banning him from the house and the yard.

The moment he cooled down, Rafiq was devastated to be leaving both Tommy and Furious, and realized he had nowhere to go. He couldn't return to Throstledown and the sneers of Tresa and Josh. Rupert offered him £500, which he threw back at him. He still had his Gold Cup winnings. Clutching the little gold replica of the cup he had won, he fled, howling vengeance, down the drive.

An utterly distraught Tommy, who had been riding out and missed the drama, pleaded with Rupert to change his mind. 'Rafiq's been on edge because he loves Furious so much. Even if he doesn't ride him, let him stay on to do him, you'll have a million times better horse.'

'He's a security risk,' Rupert told her coldly, 'and your father feels the same. He rang me today.'

It didn't help that the son of Rupert's great friend Drew Benedict had been killed by a roadside bomb in Afghanistan the day before.

134

The Grand National approached. All the media were featuring cuddly Wilkinsons and Chisolms, expressing the hope that the speed they were careering out of the shops – resembling the cavalry charge up to the first fence – was a good omen for Mrs Wilkinson on Saturday.

Adding a bestselling toy to his other triumphs, however, had not made Valent happy. Rafiq being jocked off was the last straw. Etta was still refusing to speak to him.

Valent also felt guilty about the syndicate, who were observing a faint media neglect of late. There were no badly parked journalists' cars or television vans for the Major to chunter over. Would Niall be allowed to bless Wilkie? Would anyone visit Painswick and Pocock's teashop? Mop Idol was desperately trying to prevent Joey putting his £50,000 on Wilkie. Woody was busy trying to find a cure for Rupert's chestnut avenue, their grey trunks cracked and slashed as though Rafiq had taken a sword to each one. The ladies, Phoebe, Corinna, Debbie, Bonny, even Tilda, were outraged to have been denied access to Rupert and his yard. Trixie was desolate not to have been summoned to cherish Furious. Alan was frantic for an ending to his book.

To cheer them up and to tempt Etta out of her mega sulk, Valent invited the syndicate to a pre-National get-together on the Thursday before the race. He'd have liked to hold it at Badger's Court, but to swell Chris and Chrissie's depleted takings he chose the Wilkinson Arms.

Etta was terribly torn. Her tears had watered the Valent Edwards rose, which was about to bloom. She so longed to see him, yet so passionately disapproved of the action he had taken.

All in an April evening, hummed Etta, going out into the soft twilight. Now the conifer hedge had gone, she was able to see a little gold crescent moon. As galaxies of primroses and daffodils twinkled all over Valent's garden, Orion and his dog star, Arcturus, Capella and the Great Bear glittered overhead. Was it global warming that made them so bright?

The willows were at their fluffiest, little green leaves, tiny yellow catkins at roguish right angles to their gold stems. Earlier she'd noticed the ground cracking, which meant good going for Wilkie. It was such a magic evening, she couldn't bear to stay away. She was comforted by the way Valent's face lit up as she entered the pub.

'Oh Etta, so pleased you've come.' He shoved a glass of champagne into her hand.

'Wilkie's really well,' he told her by way of mitigation, 'and cheered up. She's so happy to have Amber on her back. Tommy's fussing over her, and Tommy, Chisolm and Furious have driven up today with a nice Irish lad of Rupert's called Michael Meagan. They're staying tonight and tomorrow in some quiet yard owned by friends of Rupert about fifteen miles from Liverpool, so she won't be subjected to all the madness and boostle till Saturday morning.'

The rest of the syndicate waved but were too busy playing with cuddly Wilkinsons and Chisolms, who were bleating so loudly it sounded like market day in Larkminster.

As Valent wandered off to welcome Alban and Ione, Phoebe joined Etta. 'How are you, stranger? Aren't they adorable?' she cried, winding up a Chisolm. 'I'm going to pinch a pair for Bump, who's walking now.' Then, at Etta's expression of disapproval, 'Valent can spare one, he's making a fortune, the only reason he insisted Wilkie run in the National was to boost sales.'

'I'm sure that's not true,' protested Etta, taking such a slug of champagne it spilled over her face. Debbie then came up to ask if Etta had heard from Rafiq. 'I was shocked Rupert jocked him off, but I suppose it stands to reason, Rupert wants the mount for his precious grandson,' she sniffed.

'Eddie's a very good rider,' said Trixie sharply.

'Bit mean to sack Rafiq as well,' said Phoebe.

'He what?' asked Etta incredulously.

'Sacked him,' said Shagger, joining the group. 'According to Painswick, Rafiq never even bothered to collect his stuff from Throstledown. He's utterly deranged evidently, I hope he doesn't start blowing people up.'

Seeing the outrage on Etta's face, alarmed she might bolt, Valent was checking everyone had full glasses.

'When's little Bonny travelling up?' asked Shagger fondly and to wind up Etta.

'On Saturday,' said Phoebe happily. 'She's coming straight to Aintree.'

Valent banged the table, welcomed everyone and said he was looking forward to seeing them all at the Grand National, and hoping to fly up as many of them as possible the following evening to stay at the Radisson Hotel.

'Can we each have a couple of owners' badges?' asked Shagger.

'Not sure there'll be room in the parade ring, it might be a bit of a croosh, but we can certainly watch from the Owners and Trainers.' Valent cleared his throat, blushing slightly.

'I'd also like to say none of us would be here today if it weren't for Etta Bancroft, who found and rescued Wilkie in the first place and saved her life,' he raised his glass to a furiously scowling Etta, 'and I'd like to make a presentation.

'My factory in Kowloon needed guidance on how to recreate a realistic cooddly Mrs Wilkinson. Knowing her aversion to aeroplanes and long journeys, it wasn't possible to fly Wilkie to China, so I commissioned this portrait of her by Dora's brother Jonathan Belvedon . . .'

'Must have cost him,' muttered Shagger.

'It did,' beamed Dora.

'. . . for them to work from,' went on Valent, 'and I'd now like to give the portrait to Etta as a token of all our esteem.'

The picture was propped against the wall. Dora turned it round and proudly carried it to the table:

'Isn't it great, Etta?'

'That's beautiful,' cried Tilda.

'Wilkie to a T, dear little soul,' sighed Painswick.

'Jonathan painted her left side, so you see her good eye and her sweet expression,' said Trixie.

'What a lovely thought,' said Debbie. 'That must cheer you up, Etta. You'll have Wilkie on your wall for ever now.'

Everyone was smiling at her.

'I don't want it,' gasped Etta. 'It's appallingly bad luck for a horse to have its portrait painted before it retires. This'll bring disaster on Wilkie on Saturday.'

'Don't be ridiculous,' exploded Valent.

'Don't be so ungrateful and ungracious,' accused Phoebe.

'It's bad luck and I'm not coming to the National either,' shouted Etta.

*

The little gold moon and the glittering stars had retreated behind a black cloud by the time she got back to the bungalow. Neither Priceless nor Gwenny could comfort her.

'I don't know what's the matter with me,' she sobbed.

She knew she was being horrible and everyone was fed up with her. But Rafiq and Marius had been betrayed and Valent had only bought Wilkie to help sell his bloody stuffed Wilkinsons and Chisolms. She must stick to her principles, no longer the cowardly lion, and refuse to go.

But she wept even louder as she remembered Amber would be wearing Valent's colours, which he'd chosen from the African violets she'd given him. Worst of all, if she were truthful, even if Wilkie won the National, it would hurt too much to see Bonny and Valent rejoicing there together.

135

Rupert always got uptight before a big race. Matters weren't helped on the eve of the National when he sat Amber and Eddie down to watch tapes of the other runners, and Eddie, whose nerves took the form of ragging, got bored and inserted one of Old Eddie's porn videos, crying, 'Look how good she's riding him.' Rupert had gone into orbit and nearly jocked Eddie off.

Amber was as uptight as Rupert. The knowledge that Rogue would be part of the BBC team made her even more nervous, he was sure to take the piss. She was also demented with worry about Billy, who had struggled out of bed and travelled up to Aintree in the hope of watching her ride, but had collapsed and been taken to hospital. Rupert had persuaded Amber to get some sleep and fly up with him, Taggie and Eddie tomorrow.

Trying to keep down a cup of coffee the following morning, Amber was slightly cheered when Taggie dragged her to the kitchen window:

'Look, round the bird table, look, three magpies for a girl. That must mean you and Mrs Wilkinson will be the first girls ever to win the National.'

'Goat's given you a good plug,' drawled Eddie, who was reading Chisolm's column in the *Mirror*. ' "Winning the National is going to be a breeze," she writes, "after Wilkie's day drag hunting. When she and Amber came to a vast oxer, the horses of the master, the joint master and two whippers-in all refused. But my friend Wilkie cantered up, stood back on her hocks and cleared it easily. Look to your laurels, Bafford Playboy." That goat is getting above herself.'

It was a good thing Chisolm had departed for Cheshire. She'd already shredded Taggie's fur hat, eaten Eddie's passport and regurgitated Amber's new, new lucky pants.

Despite the quietness of the Cheshire countryside, Tommy couldn't sleep, fretting about Wilkie and those vast fences and even more about Rafiq. He had rung once since he left Penscombe and she'd been stupid enough to express her fury at the rough way Eddie was treating Furious in an attempt to break his spirit.

She had, however, enjoyed spending time with Rupert's stable lad, Michael Meagan, even if he did believe 'a dirty hoss was a happy hoss' and left her to do both Wilkie and Furious. He also had a terrific crush on Tresa, who'd no doubt be poncing about at Aintree as she led up Sir Cuthbert.

Grand National day dawned at last very cold and grey. Michael Meagan drove Rupert's dark blue lorry, Carl Davis's music from *Champions* blaring, towards Aintree. As they passed houses with boarded-up windows, decorated with surrealistic paintings of Liverpool and Everton shields, and drove down streets full of pitbulls and schoolgirls socking each other at bus stops, Tommy thought how different was Liverpool to the pastel Regency houses and lovely parks of Cheltenham.

Over in the BBC tent, Rogue, at his first production meeting, was staggered by the enormity and professionalism of an operation covering three days of Aintree, culminating in today's broadcasting of the greatest race in the world to 600 million viewers.

More than two hundred people, including presenters, many of whom were ex-jockeys, talking heads and crew members, had been employed by the production company Sunset and Vine. Having breakfasted royally at long tables covered with blue gingham cloths, they were flipping through pink running sheets and easing bacon out of their teeth, as the day ahead was scrupulously mapped out.

'There were a few hairs out of place yesterday,' said Dermot, the young, good-looking programme producer, whose own hair was gelled upwards like a hedgehog rolled in olive oil, 'but it will be fine today.'

Everyone had been very welcoming, but Rogue was aware how cast down they all were by the absence of Billy Lloyd-Foxe. Despite the cock-ups and the outspokenness – 'That jockey couldn't get a jump in a brothel' – Billy had been so engaging, good-hearted and adored by the public.

Rogue had been asked a lot about Wilkie and whether Rupert would transform her. He had also been subjected to a lot of ribbing about turning Lusty round and thumping Marius. Discussing the run-up to the race, Dermot the producer, over the noise of the racecourse generator, was briefing the presenters: 'You'll each have a camera in the parade ring, so grab any jockey coming towards you.'

'Bags I grab Amber Lloyd-Foxe,' said Robert Cooper.

'Not if you don't want to get laid out by Rogue,' quipped Richard Pitman.

'Don't rise,' murmured Jim McGrath, the genial commentator, who was busy trying to memorize all the colours.

Rogue didn't rise. One day he would be forced to give up racing. He didn't want to screw up a potentially lucrative career in television before it had even started.

The production team had secretly decided that, bearing in mind Rogue's volatile disposition, he'd better not be let loose in the parade ring with a roving mike in case he got into a fight with Rupert or Marius. So apart from the odd assignment round the racecourse, he would be positioned in the 'studio', a raised desk near the parade ring, where his input on the day's events would be invaluable 'and we can kill his mike if he suddenly goes over the top'.

'We must come to him a lot,' said Deirdre, a production assistant, 'he's so gorgeous-looking. Really interesting if he could interview Rupert or Amber.'

Down the table, a group of Sloanes in looped pashminas, hair in little knots on the crowns of their heads, were also gazing at Rogue in wonder. Known as 'spotters', recruited from their local hunts, they would later be stationed by each National fence, armed with radios to feed through to the BBC and the Aintree PR service the news of any fallers.

'Haven't you ridden a race on Mrs Wilkinson, Rogue?' they asked eagerly.

'We never started,' grinned Rogue. 'I was silly enough to give her a smack at the start and she dragged me off under the rails. She's tough.'

'Would you like to come to our party tonight?'

In the dark blue control room next door, a wall of monitors showed the director everything, policemen turning to watch the Liverpool ladies arriving in their finery, wonderful sepia film of charismatic past winners coming out of peeling stables, the paddock, the bookies, the stewards, jockeys in the weighing room reading about themselves in the *Racing Post*, snatching sleep on benches, Johnnie Brutus admiring himself in the mirror, Awesome Wells struggling with the crossword.

'Pretty tame this year,' giggled Deirdre, 'without Rogue dropping his trousers and flashing his tackle all the time.'

'Basically,' Dermot, glancing down at the running sheet, told the marquee, 'this is where we move into position for the big race, so grab any winning trainers and ask them for their take on the National and on Rupert's three-thousandth win.'

It was not worth even Clare Balding approaching Rupert, Dermot added regretfully. He'd only tell her to eff off.

'He wouldn't even let us film Mrs Wilkinson at Penscombe,' grumbled Deirdre.

'We'll be showing film of Tipperary Tim winning eighty years ago,' went on Dermot. 'Any anecdotes about Tipperary Tim, Rogue?'

But Rogue wasn't listening because on the monitor he could see Amber being interviewed, lovely pink lips parted over lovely white teeth, soon to be covered by a gum shield. Dear God, don't let a hair of her head be hurt. I've broken every bone in my body, he thought despairingly, why can't I recover from a broken heart?

'Now we move on to Richard Dunwoody and Rogue discussing iconic moments in the Grand National,' Dermot was saying, giving Rogue a stab of regret. He'd have liked to create one of those moments himself. He must get his career back on track.

'To sum up then,' said Dermot, 'we start with the titles, horses crossing the course. We go back to the runners and riders, followed by film of old winners and heroes, all contributing to the sense that we're about to witness something special.

'After this meeting, Rogue, we've got a job we know you'll enjoy, interviewing some Liverpool lovelies.'

Clare Balding smiled at Rogue:

'Did you know there are more sunbeds per capita in Liverpool than anywhere else in the world?'

The syndicate had reached Aintree on Friday, and Debbie had gone straight to heaven when she was awarded a Citroën car as a prize for the Best Dressed Mature Lady.

Where would the Major find room to park it?

Everyone was frightfully excited to be staying at the pukka Radisson Hotel. Alan, however, made a note for his book that outside the vast Littlewood's building opposite, the sculpture of its founder, Sir John Moores, a big, smooth-featured, handsome man whose eyes looked straight through you, bore a spooky resemblance to Shade Murchieson.

'Do you think this is too see-through?' asked Tilda as they set out for the racecourse next morning.

'No, it's Liverpool,' said Alan.

136

Having dropped in on Billy at the Royal Liverpool Hospital, Amber found him conscious but drowsy from a morphine injection to kill the pain.

'She's the People's Pony, darling, just bring her and yourself back safely. God, I wish I was calling you home.'

It had started to snow as Amber took a taxi back to the course. The driver pointed out the Catholic cathedral known as Paddy's Wigwam and the Church of England cathedral topped by vertical spikes, as though coaxed up by the product Billy had always refused to use on his hair. As they drove past red houses, purple dustbins, shivering flowering currant, an off-licence called Quencher and the Co-operative Ireland Funeral Parlour, the driver told Amber that as a child he used to watch the Grand National from the roof of the pub belonging to his father, who had drunk and gambled away all the family money.

As Amber leapt out, he asked for her autograph and wished her and Mrs Wilkinson good luck. 'And good luck to your dad, a lovely man.'

A somewhat optimistic sign by the entrance to the course said: 'John Smith thanks you for drinking responsibly.'

'Amber!' Despite the bitter cold, a swarm of half-naked orange-skinned girls in huge hats and party dresses came tottering towards her on six-inch heels, cuddly Wilkinsons in one hand, glasses of champagne in the other.

'Can we have your autograph? We've all backed Wilkie. Girl Power.' They punched the air, sprinkling champagne. 'Is Chisolm here too?'

Amber was warmed by their friendliness but overwhelmed by the hugeness of Aintree. The stands were like vast chests with their drawers pulled out and already overflowing with people. The John Smith Stand, layered with hospitality boxes, soared like a glass mountain. Cheltenham was the country; Aintree the town. The Check Republic was less in evidence here, Alban wouldn't know everyone, but there was a terrific atmosphere of jollity and camaraderie, like a huge party where everyone spoke to everyone.

At the prospect of 600 million people watching him fall at the first fence, even Eddie's chatter was stilled, as he walked the course with Amber and Rupert.

'Get a good gallop across the Melling Road until you come to the first,' Rupert told them at the first fence, 'then stand well back on your hocks.'

They came to Becher's. A terrifying five foot high with a seven-foot drop, it was composed of piled-up branches of spruce, on which the snow was settling, which were already scattering pine needles. Amber broke off a sprig to take back to her father. Rupert advised them to jump near the middle where the drop was least.

'Go wide at the canal turn,' he continued, as they reached another bogey fence. 'It's a right angle, if you cut the corner you can easily get interfered with by the people going wide. But don't go too wide, particularly in the second circuit, or you'll lose too much ground, then straighten up and go hell for leather for Valentine's.'

Seeing television cameras everywhere, Amber kept looking for Rogue.

'Don't forget two fences are missed out on the second circuit. Crucially – are you listening, Amber?' snapped Rupert – 'don't pick up your whip until you get to the elbow,' the slight bend into the home straight. 'Unless you've got a fifth gear you're fucked. It's the longest run-in in the world.'

Noticing how white she'd gone, Rupert bore Amber and Eddie off to look at Red Rum's grave, on the left of the winning post. It was scattered with bunches of red tulips and daffodils and the Polos he loved so much.

'He won three times and second twice,' exclaimed Eddie. 'That is cool!' and he helped himself to a Polo.

'Eddie,' cried Amber, shocked, 'fans gave Rummy those. What does it say on his grave?' She crouched down to read.

> 'Respect this place, this hallowed ground
> A legend here his rest has found

673

His feet would fly, our spirits soar
He earned our love for ever more.

'God, how sweet,' she sobbed into Rupert's coat, 'I just wish Dad was calling me home.'

For a second, they clung to each other.

'Come on, let's go and have a drink.'

Getting across Aintree with Rupert was rather like taking Muhammad Ali to a boxing match. The crowd mobbed him all the way, asking after Wilkie and Furious and how Taggie was.

Rupert took them to the Old Weighing Room, which had now become a bar and a shrine to heroism.

'It used to be the old unsaddling enclosure as well,' said Rupert as he handed them both tomato juice. 'You're supposed to see ghost horses at night.'

On the walls of the bar were photographs of former winners, their silks, saddles and whips.

'Oh look, there's Red Rum's maroon and yellow colours, and there's Foinavon,' Amber told Eddie, 'a rank outsider, one of a handful that finished in 1967. And there's the huge saddle of gallant Crisp, ridden by dear Richard Pitman. He gave Red Rum twenty-three pounds and led all the way round, only giving in to Rummy in the run-in. So Wilkie could beat Bafford Playboy.'

So much history, she thought, I want to be up there too. Then, overwhelmed by the enormity of the task, she fled to the Ladies, throwing up only tomato juice and then bile.

But on the wall on the way out she noticed a 1930 plan of the Grand National course. Along the bottom of the green picture frame had been listed the names of all the thirteen winning mares including Charity, Miss Mowbray, Jealousy, Sheila's Cottage and Nickel Coin, ten of them in the nineteenth century, only three in the twentieth, the last way back in 1951, and none in the twenty-first.

'We're going to change that, Wilkie,' said Amber grimly.

No lady rider had ever won the Grand National. History said top weight never won either. Bugger history, thought Amber.

If only she had a ride in an earlier race to distract her. It had started to snow again. Coming out of the bar, they went slap into Rogue interviewing wildly excited Liverpool ladies.

As it was the north, many of the horses running were still in their winter coats. The ladies were not. They were showing acres of cellulite, tattoos everywhere, visible panty lines, mobiles instead of earrings, and an inch gap at the heel of their stilettos in case their feet swelled up. Hailstones were now bouncing off their gooseflesh.

'Who have you backed?' Rogue was asking them.

'Mrs Wilkinson,' came the reply, 'she's the People's Pony. It's girl power, innit.'

'You all look stunning,' Rogue told them, 'but aren't you frozen and aren't those shoes killing you?'

'To be in fashion you've got to suffer pain,' said the blondest and prettiest, who was eating scampi out of a cardboard box. 'I bought my outfit back in August.'

'Paintree,' laughed Rogue. 'Jump jockeys are the same. No gain without pain.'

'Why aren't you riding in the National, Rogue?' they asked him. 'You're the best jockey.'

'It's rather a long story.'

'Will you come to our party tonight?'

Rogue was very dolled up in a lovely pale grey suit, a sky-blue shirt and pink silk tie covered in blue elephants. He was also wearing television make-up. His curls were brushed flat, he looked gorgeous, thought Amber, and as usual surrounded by girls.

Catching sight of her, he yelled out, 'Amber.'

'Not today, thank you,' snapped Rupert, frogmarching her back into the crowd.

Alban knew fewer people than he did at Cheltenham, the Major was fretting about who to lean on to get planning permission for a second garage for Debbie's new car, but they were utterly compensated by so many ravishing half-naked girls everywhere.

The men who drove the horse ambulance had parked near the crossing by the Melling Road, so they could have a laugh as the stilettos of more ladies pouring into the ground got stuck in the thick sand. They needed a laugh. Later they might have the grim task of fatally injecting some beautiful horse that had fallen.

At least Chisolm was enjoying herself. While Wilkie was in the farrier's box, she'd hoovered up the azaleas blooming outside. Now, jumping on to Wilkie's back, she was wolfing pansies growing in the hanging baskets above the saddling-up boxes. Debbie agreed they were the best hanging baskets she'd ever seen.

137

A terrific tension and feeling of menace was building up. Animal Rights, revving up for Horse Awareness Week, were out for blood. Would they sabotage the race?

The combination of Mrs Wilkinson, Rupert and the possibility of his three-thousandth win had whipped the crowd into a frenzy. The bookies had already taken a massive £200 million.

Bafford Playboy, the course specialist, was favourite, particularly as he was being ridden by Killer, who was wearing the gold armband of the jockey with the meeting's most wins. But with punters worried the fences and the extra weight would be too much for her, Wilkie's odds had drifted to 20–1.

Many of the vast crowd, fifteen deep round the parade ring and waving 'Where there's a Wilkie, there's a way' posters and cuddly Wilkinsons and Chisolms, were unhappy and booed Rupert and Valent, shouting at them to give Wilkie back to Marius. They also booed Eddie for replacing Rafiq on Furious.

Their animosity had been exacerbated by Dora's leak to the press that Etta, whom the crowd loved because she'd rescued Wilkie in the first place, had stayed away because she so disapproved of the move to Rupert and felt Wilkie was far too small for the National.

Unlike a heartbroken Etta, however, Rafiq couldn't bear to stay away. Disguised as a treader, in woolly hat, gumboots and dark glasses, he had stolen away from the course where he was pretending to replace divots, and joined the crowd round the parade ring.

There was his darling Tommy, proudly leading up Mrs Wilkinson, whose lack of inches nothing emphasized more than

Rupert's dark blue rug with the emerald-green binding almost trailing on the grass.

'Painswick should have turned it up,' giggled Dora, who was hanging on to Chisolm. She'd escaped earlier and been found running round the lorry park.

For the first time, Mrs Wilkinson, like Furious, would be running in Valent's violet and dusty green colours. In defiance, on her quarters, now hidden by the rug, Tommy had imposed a weeping willow.

After the Gold Cup win, Furious was 12–1 and evoking vast interest. He looked both glorious and potentially victorious, but he'd sweated up and as he dragged along Michael Meagan and another of Rupert's lads, his rolling eyes, eternally searching for Rafiq, showed how unhappy he was.

Rafiq longed to call out, knowing he could calm him in a trice. It was cold comfort that when the arrogant American bastard Eddie came swaggering out, female screams at his beauty were drowned by boos and cries of 'Bring back Rafiq.'

Amber was panicking again. Even in the paddock she had borrowed Rupert's mobile and having illicitly rung the hospital had failed to get beyond the switchboard.

'I don't want to look at your swine flu website,' she was yelling, 'I want to talk to my father, Billy Lloyd-Foxe. I know he's there. I'm about to ride in the Grand National, yes I bloody am, I want to say goodbye to my father in case I don't come back.'

'That's enough.' Rupert took the mobile from her.

At least this altercation distracted her from the embarrassment of seeing Marius and Olivia. Olivia, wearing dark glasses and a rather dowdy olive-green suit, which Amber recognized from her wardrobe at Throstledown, clung on to Marius's arm. She looked tired but so relieved to be back with him, which couldn't have improved Shade's temper. Ringed by the orange and magenta backs of the four jockeys riding his horses, Shade and Harvey-Holden had their heads together, plotting devilries and death to Mrs Wilkinson.

Incarcerated at Rupert's, Mrs Wilkinson hadn't for ages seen any of her horse friends, except Furious who she loathed. Suddenly, ambling half asleep towards her, his long grey face lengthened by a lack of noseband, came her sugar daddy, Sir Cuthbert. Mrs Wilkinson went crazy, rushed over, nuzzling and nudging, knuckering and exchanging whiskery kisses.

Towed up by Chisolm, Dora turned to Bianca.

'I wonder if she's telling Cuthbert Love Rat's got her up the duff,' she whispered.

'Shut *up*,' hissed Bianca, going pale. 'Daddy'll kill us.'

Mrs Wilkinson had also seen Niall and Valent, and bustled over to welcome them like a party hostess, then started looking around hopefully for Etta.

Realizing how tiny she was, how huge the other horses and how challenging the fences out on the course, Valent suddenly felt ashamed of himself. Why the hell was he endangering this darling horse? No wonder Etta hated him.

'Hello, Valent, got butterflies?' said a hearty voice. It was Martin Bancroft, who with Romy had flown up last night with Harvey-Holden. Both of them were avid to meet Rupert.

'Where's the syndicate?' asked Romy.

'Oop in my box. Only room for Niall and Dora in the parade ring,' said Valent.

'Mother up there too?' demanded Martin.

'Couldn't make it,' Valent said grimly, 'doesn't approve of the Grand National.'

'What!' exploded Martin. 'Thought she was definitely coming. If we'd known we'd never have bothered to fork out a fortune for a sitter.'

'I'll phone her and tell her to hotfoot over to Harvest Home and relieve Sarah,' said Romy, edging out of the mob and switching on her mobile. She was back a minute later, crimson in the face. 'Your mother told me to bugger off, she was watching the National.'

Valent grinned broadly, and seeing him looking more approachable, Clare Balding sidled up:

'Mrs Wilkinson's looking well.'

Forty horses were now circling the parade ring. The uptight ones, principally Furious, were causing logjams as they jigjogged into the backs of those who were calmly walking.

Bafford Playboy and Ilkley Hall both looked magnificent and very large. Vakil, leering in an even sharper black suit, looked very sinister.

'Michelle must be sleeping with Harvey-Holden,' whispered Dora to Bianca, 'for him to allow her to lead up Ilkley Hall in stilettos. I'm sure it was her or Tresa who let Chisolm out this morning, Michael Meagan's so besotted with Tresa he wouldn't have noticed.'

Niall was praying his heart out to compete with the Catholic priests and their rosaries, who were busy blessing Dermie O'Driscoll's Squiffey Liffey and the other great Irish horses.

'Squiffey is even plainer than Not for Crowe,' said Dora. 'I wonder if they're related.'

'Squiffey's very full of himself,' Dermie was telling Clare Balding. 'Hopefully he'll be thereabouts, but the race is going to be a triller.'

The paps were everywhere, hoping for a fight. Would Shade punch Marius for getting Olivia back, would Marius punch Rupert for taking away his best horses?

Marius was giving last-minute instructions to Awesome Wells: 'Don't fiddle with Cuthbert, just sit still and let him make his own way. Give him plenty of daylight, start picking them off in the second circuit.'

'I will,' said Awesome, who was the colour of the tiny leaves thrusting out of the sticky buds overhead.

'I'd give instructions to Cuthbert, he knows his way around,' murmured Lady Crowe, Marius's most loyal owner.

Sir Cuthbert was so old that the grey dapples on his coat had turned white. It had taken years of sweat and vet's bills to get him right. Despite her gruff exterior, Lady Crowe adored her ancient horse as once she'd loved Marius's father.

'Good luck, old chap, come back safe,' she said, scratching Cuthbert's neck with a claw-like liver-spotted hand. 'And good luck to you,' she called out to Awesome, as Tresa led them off to join the parade.

'That horse'll need a Zimmer to get round,' yelled Harvey-Holden.

Awesome for once was paying enough attention to turn round and give him a V-sign.

Winning trainers were being grabbed by BBC presenters and asked for their take on the race. Rogue, in the studio, had been asked for his most iconic National moment.

'Now, today,' he'd replied in a choked voice. 'Mrs Wilkinson is the smallest horse carrying the most weight, a brave and beautiful girl on her back,' and 600 million viewers cheered in agreement.

The crowds bubbling over with excitement, the clattering of police horses' hooves and the fanfare from red-uniformed trumpeters with radio mikes on the end of their instruments shredded the horses' nerves as they set out in the parade led by Mrs Wilkinson carrying the top weight.

The BBC had each horse's details ready in order, but everything was screwed up by Furious, who was used to having Rafiq on his back and going straight down to the start. Catching Michael Meagan off guard as he gazed at Tresa, Furious took off, taking half the runners with him.

'What would be going through your mind at this moment, Rogue?' asked Richard Pitman.

'Irritation at the hold-up, wanting to get going,' said Rogue.

It was eerie and very cold at the start. The huge crowd had gone so quiet you could hear the distant cries of the bookies as punters scurried to put on last bets. Treaders edged in final divots. Spotters checked their walkie-talkies.

Dora had gained the scoop of a lifetime, riding along in a car with the BBC camera crew filming the race. As they waited, she watched the jockeys taking their horses to look at the first fence.

Mrs Wilkinson couldn't see over it, Sir Cuthbert, who resented missing lunch, was trying to eat it and spitting out bits of spruce. Other horses were having their manes raked or their ears pulled, anything to calm them.

For a second Tommy clung to Mrs Wilkinson.

'Just come home safely, darling, and you too, Amber.'

'I want to say thank you for all you've done for me, Tom,' muttered Amber, about to cover her frantically chattering teeth with her gum shield. 'If I don't come back, I want you to have all my jewellery.'

Tommy thought her heart would burst.

138

As forty horses circled together, the sun came out to see them off. All the Irish jockeys were crossing themselves.

'Our father,' Awesome intoned.

'Defend oh Lord, this thy child and her horse,' murmured Amber. She thought about Rogue and then about Billy, then she thought of nothing but the race as they hustled in a cavalry charge over the Melling Road for three hundred yards to the first fence rising as huge as a green block of flats. A great cheer went up as Mrs Wilkinson stood back on her hocks and flew over.

'That bar used to be a railway siding, where people watched the race from the train,' said a BBC cameraman as they hurtled Dora along beside the track.

'Wilkie's jumping really well,' crowed Dora. 'Can we go a bit faster?'

'We mustn't go too fast or the horses start racing us, which infuriates the jockeys.'

As Rupert had told her to hunt round the first circuit, Amber was actually taking it very easily. Rupert had had a good effect on Wilkie, she was running much straighter. Furious, even further behind, was loathing having horses all round him, and exhausting himself battling against the brutal strength of Eddie, who'd been instructed to hold him up.

Shade's pacemaker Voltaire Scott was as usual going much too fast. Out of the forty runners, six horses, trying to keep up, fell at the first fence, eight at the second, seven at the third. Soon loose horses were galloping all round Amber.

At each fence the leaders ripped away a forest of fir tree and put up a cloud of dust it was difficult to see through. Amber was trying to get a clear run, but every time she landed, she had to avoid fallen horses and jockeys on the ground.

Now it was Becher's, vaster than Etta's conifer hedge and with its seven-foot drop. As Rupert had instructed, she steered Wilkie towards the middle and even though she felt they were falling off the edge of the world, they landed safely.

When would Harvey-Holden start employing his team tactics? Gradually on her left she was aware of a dark shadow growing closer, Johnnie Brutus and Ilkley Hall edging up on the rails, then Bafford Playboy sliding up on her right, and she realized in terror they were trying to box her in and once again block Wilkie's good eye.

Somehow they scrambled over Foinavon and were scorching towards the Canal Turn, where the course jinked ninety degrees and where, because of Animal Rights trouble in the past, no crowds were allowed.

Through a haze of fear, Amber tried to remember what Rupert had told her.

'Go wide round the bend, take it at an angle, then swing left in the air, straighten out and go hell for leather for Valentine's.'

Shoved out by Johnnie Brutus on the inner, unable to go wide because of Killer threatening her on her right, Mrs Wilkinson forgot Rupert's lessons and jumped wildly to the left to reach the safety of the rails, cutting across Furious who was just behind her.

Losing concentration, distracted by the swearing and the shouts of the jockeys and by loose horses on all sides, Furious took off too early, hit the top of the fence and seeing a horse writhing just below him, lunged to the right. Next minute he had fallen heavily, taking Eddie with him.

Eddie sat with his head bowed, his right hand thrashing the cut-up ground with his whip, he'd done something awful to his left shoulder. He'd let Grandpa down, no three-thousandth win.

'Fucking, fucking horse, fucking stupid animal,' he screamed, until the rest of the field had moved on and the sun had gone in in embarrassment.

The crowd and Rafiq watching on the big screen had yelled in relief as, ever gallant, Furious scrambled to his feet and broke into a canter. The cameras moved on, but those nearby gasped in horror as they realized his hind leg was swinging loose as if to drop off and he was running on three legs. When an official managed to catch his reins, Furious bit him.

Ilkley Hall, who'd been the horse writhing on the ground and who'd been raced three times in three weeks, chasing the Order of Merit for Harvey-Holden, had not got up.

The screens went round both horses. Rupert's assistant Lysander, having grabbed an official car, was at the scene as quickly as possible, by which time a course vet had decreed that Furious must be put down and moved to the side of the course before the runners came round again. Furious, who'd been initially sedated by an injection, was for once standing docile.

Next moment a screaming, hysterical treader in a woolly hat and dark glasses had shoved aside the screens and, sobbing wildly, flung his arms around Furious.

'Don't shoot him. We can save him, Martin Pipe saved Our Vic, please don't kill him, please don't.'

'Rafiq,' gasped Lysander as he and a security man and two spotters managed to tug him away. Rafiq immediately struggled free, clutching Furious, smoothing back the blond mane, at which Furious whickered lovingly to see him.

'Look, he know me, he's OK. He's all right.' Rafiq looked beseechingly up at Lysander. 'We can mend him.' His sobs increased. 'I'm going to give you a wonderful home.' He dropped a kiss on Furious's white star.

'Please be quiet, you're upsetting the horse,' snapped the course vet. 'We've got to get it out of the way.'

This time it took two security men, two spotters and Lysander to drag Rafiq off and restrain him as a horse ambulance man held Furious while the course vet put a gun to his white star and pulled the trigger.

There was blood everywhere as, with maddened strength, Rafiq fell back on to Furious's body.

'You kill my horse, he shouldn't have died,' he howled at the course vet.

A shadow fell across them. It was Valent, who put a hand on Rafiq's shoulder.

'Nothing they could do?' he asked Lysander, who was also in tears as he shook his head.

Ilkley Hall, meanwhile, who was whimpering in the most pathetic way, had struggled to sit up like a dog. Putting his ear to the horse's back, the vet heard a crunch.

'Back's broken. We've got to get them to the side of the course.'

Eddie Alderton, spitting out mud and grass, had staggered to his feet. Johnnie Brutus lay still. Glaring wildly round, utterly deranged, Rafiq watched Harvey-Holden, with a strange, almost excited look in his reptilian eyes, approaching to see his horse dispatched. This time there was no whickering of recognition from Ilkley Hall. As the trigger was pulled he writhed, kicked violently and went still.

As the horse ambulance men winched the two horses to the side of the course, Rafiq turned like a viper on Harvey-Holden.

'At least you get the insurance like you did after that fire you started. I know everything about you, you evil bastard.'

As he whipped out a knife, everyone jumped back, except Valent, who stepped forward: 'Give that to me, lad.'

But Rafiq only wanted to cut off a lock of Furious's mane.

'They've killed my horse,' he yelled at Valent, then dropped a last kiss on Furious's shoulder, covering himself in blood.

'I'm awful sorry, Rafiq,' muttered Eddie, who, supported by an ambulance man, had joined the group.

For a moment, Rafiq fingered his knife.

'I'd have kept him out of trouble,' he hissed. 'He hate any horses round him, but it was Wilkie's fault, she hung left. She brought him down.'

'They're coming. Get off the course,' yelled a security man as the runners on the second circuit came thundering towards them. By the time they had gone and new fallers were waiting to be picked off the floor, Rafiq had vanished.

139

News had flashed round the course that both Furious and Ilkley
Hall had fallen and the screens had gone round but few knew the
outcome or could hear the commentary because of the roar of
the crowd.

Only fifteen horses were left. Ilkley Hall's stable mate was
faring well. On the big screen, Playboy could be seen beginning
to work his fatal magic on the race, eating up the miles, sweeping
past the field as though they were standing still. Killer on his back
was hunting him round – a day out with the Beaufort.

Sir Cuthbert was up with the leaders, in with a chance. To the
joy of the crowd, Mrs Wilkinson, tongue flapping, was in eighth
place, leading the second group.

Amber was dying of pride, as she crouched over the neat grey
plaits, watching the grey ears twitching, listening to every word of
encouragement. Now Wilkie was grinding her teeth in her deter-
mination to catch the leaders.

'You can do it, Wilkie, you can do it.'

One furlong to go, two horses crashed at two out. Only Squiffey
Liffey, Sir Cuthbert and Playboy were ahead. Then Julien Sorel,
who'd unshipped Dare Catswood at the open ditch on the second
circuit, lumbered past like a maddened buffalo determined to
influence the race, and did so by spurring on Mrs Wilkinson.

'Come on, Wilkie,' roared the ecstatic crowd, as she overtook
him.

Killer, bounding up to the last fence, a four-foot-six cliff of
green, was so convinced he was going to win, he lost concentration and let Playboy take off too early so he banked the
fence, scattering spruce, losing ground.

Reaching the elbow, he moved his whip into his right hand to guide Playboy to the left and into the home straight. Deafened by another roar, he glanced between his legs, arched like the John Smith horseshoe, and was flabbergasted to see his nemesis, a white face in a green browband, bearing down on him.

Never had a roof of blue sky been so raised at Aintree. Watching the huge bay and the little grey battling it out was like seeing a father racing his child. The difference was that Killer, mad with rage, was thrashing the life out of Bafford Playboy.

'Such a fight to the death,' yelled Jim McGrath from his commentary box. 'This is the battle of the sexes. First time a mare's won for nearly sixty years, first time a woman's ever won it, making history in the battle of the sexes.'

Mrs Wilkinson was so exhausted, humping her great burden of weight, she could scarcely put one foot in front of another. She'd given her all. Would the post never come?

In the BBC control room, they could see the Liverpool ladies screaming in ecstasy, the stewards leaving their polished table and running cheering to the window. Even the policemen in their yellow flak jackets turned round to smile and cheer as Wilkie pulled ahead.

'Mrs Wilkinson is about to join the great legends of the winter game,' shouted Jim McGrath. 'She's coming up on the inside rail, she's scraping the paint, this is un-be-liev-able.'

This is the longest time I've ever been on a horse. Keep asking, keep asking, Amber told herself.

Foam was flying from Wilkie's mouth, the veins on her grey coat stood out like pipelines, but she pricked her ears and, still with a little left in the tank, she thrust her head forward.

But Killer, riding with balls of steel, bringing his whip down again and again, was coming from the right again. He was ahead.

'Get your bat out,' Amber could imagine both Rupert and her father yelling. She could hear the crackle and slap of whips behind her. How many horses were going to overtake her? Glancing round she could see Squiffey Liffey and Sir Cuthbert bearing down.

Kicking and kicking with her heels, thrusting her body forward and forward, she caught sight of the post and Red Rum's grave on the left, 'Earning our love for ever more.'

'Rummy's calling you, Wilkie.'

As if by magic, Playboy's cavernous nostrils were receding, now level with Wilkie's ears, now with her sweat-darkened withers.

With a supreme effort as though her heart would 'burst the

buckles of her armour', Mrs Wilkinson hurled herself past the post.

All heart, all heart, all heart.

Aintree erupted.

'This is focking unbelievable, focking unbelievable,' yelled Rogue to the delight and horror of the BBC's 600 million viewers. 'The smallest horse, a little mare with one eye carrying a young girl and 20 lb more than Bafford Playboy. We knew she had gots, like David, she's dispatched not one but forty Goliaths. What a marvellous ride, well done, Amber darling.'

'That's enough, Rogue,' said a not unamused director into Rogue's earpiece.

All over the course there was pandemonium – hats, scarves, cuddly Wilkinsons and Chisolms being thrown into the air. Even people who hadn't backed Mrs Wilkinson were yelling their heads off.

A second later, to Amber's amazement, Killer was shaking her hand and kissing her cheek.

'Well done, baby, great ride.'

Next moment Awesome, ecstatic at coming third on Sir Cuthbert, had cantered up, hugging Wilkie and pulling her ears:

'Brave little girl.'

He was followed by the handful of jockeys who'd managed to finish, hugging, kissing Amber, banging on her helmet. She'd joined the band of brothers at last.

The yelling and cheering increased deafeningly as Tommy, crying her eyes out, and Valent, who'd just made it back, came running towards her, and turned to shouts of laughter as Chisolm, to avoid the scrum, leapt up and hitched a lift behind Amber.

'Bluddy marvellous, well done, both of you,' Valent had to yell to make himself heard over the crowd, and two fingers to Etta, perhaps she'd forgive him now. Tommy flung a Union Jack round Amber's shoulders and her arms round Wilkie. A fanfare of trumpeters and two police horses accompanied them back to the winners enclosure.

Raising her own two fingers to the Pony Club, Amber undid her cheek strap and hurled her hat into the crowd, then shyly touched her head to acknowledge the tumultuous applause. Her heart swelled to see an overjoyed Rupert, the handsomest man in England again, with a smile plastered across his face.

'Well done, angel. Christ, that was marvellous. How could I ever have doubted you? Well done, Wilkie,' and the little giant killer disappeared under a frenzy of patting from her supporters.

Burly Valent and Ryan then escorted Amber through the rugger scrum to the podium in the winners enclosure, so she could weigh in and be drenched in champagne by the other jockeys clapping her from the weighing-room steps, then back to Mrs Wilkinson for photographs and more patting.

Meanwhile, high up in Valent's box, the syndicate had erupted with joy the second Mrs Wilkinson passed the post. The cavalry charge to the Melling Road was nothing to Corinna and Bonny, who hurtled down the stairs to get in the photograph.

'Who came second?' asked Alban.

'Who the fuck cares?' crowed the Major.

'Penny in the swear box, Daddy,' chided Debbie.

'I can afford it,' laughed the Major, 'I've just won two grand.'

Even Shagger, who'd worked out they'd each get £8,000 prize money, was looking quite cheerful.

'Our horse came third,' cried an overjoyed Painswick, fox-trotting round the room with Pocock. 'Good old Sir Cuthbert, Marius will be so delighted.'

'Your prayers did it, Niall,' said Trixie, who was so excited she spilled her drink all over the man in the box below, who promptly asked her out to dinner.

Alan, with his laptop on his knee, ecstatically writing the perfect ending, could hardly bear to stop to take a call from Etta in Willowwood.

'Wasn't she wonderful, wasn't she wonderful? Please tell Valent, I was so stupid to make a fuss over that portrait, one must never listen to old wives' tales. Please give Valent all my love and congratulations.'

'Fine, fine,' said Alan, typing with one hand, 'I'll ring you later, darling. We've got to belt down to the winners enclosure. No, I'm not sure what happened to Furious. Wish you were here.'

By the time he'd finished his paragraph and accepted a kiss and a glass of champagne from Tilda, Alan had forgotten all about Etta.

Marius was so enchanted with Sir Cuthbert coming third for Lady Crowe, and Mrs Wilkinson winning, that he and Olivia hugged Rupert, Taggie and Valent. Mrs Wilkinson, her little sides heaving, was so exhausted, she nearly fell over as she tried to shake hooves with her beloved ex-trainer. Instead she rested her weary head on Marius's shoulder.

Tommy was in heaven.

'I look after Wilkie, I do everything for her, I love her to bits,' she was jabbering to Clare Balding. Alas, her euphoria was

688

fleeting as an ashen Lysander pushed his way through the crowd.

'Brilliantly done, Wilkie and Amber.' He gave Wilkie a huge pat and kissed Amber. 'Sorry to spoil things,' he turned to Rupert, 'but Furious had to be put down, broke a leg at the Canal Turn. Ilkley Hall broke his back at the same fence.'

'Oh God,' Tommy's tears of joy turned to horror, 'poor Furious, poor Rafiq.'

'Rafiq was there,' explained Lysander, who seemed still in shock. 'He was sobbing his heart out, begging the vets to save Furious. We had to drag the poor bugger off.'

'What about Eddie?' asked Taggie quickly.

'Might have put his shoulder out,' answered Valent, 'but he was able to walk to the ambulance.'

'How d'you know?' asked Rupert.

'I got there joost after they'd shot Furious, but I doubt if we could have done anything, it was a hideous break. Rafiq was absolutely demented, crazed with grief, he ran off down the course.'

'Why didn't you tell me?' snapped Rupert.

'I didn't want to spoil Wilkie's moment.'

And he managed to lead her in, keeping his unhappiness to himself. That was so brave, thought Taggie, giving Valent a hug.

As his overcoat fell open, she noticed his shirt covered in blood. 'I know how fond you were of him.'

'How the hell did it happen?' demanded Rupert.

'Evidently Wilkie jumped across Furious, cut him up. We'll see on the rerun.'

All this was going on while a frenzy of press and well-wishers were desperate to congratulate and interview them.

'Don't say anything to Amber,' said Rupert sharply. 'She's trying to get through to the hospital.'

'Dad's asleep,' said Amber, switching off her mobile.

As they all posed for photographs, with Chisolm still bleating on Wilkie's back, Rupert turned to Valent.

'Sorry about Furious, as Hen Knight said after Best Mate died, "If you have livestock, you have to have deadstock." It's a risk sport. You can go to the races with a full lorry and come home with an empty one. I know it's hard.' He turned to Taggie, who was comforting a sobbing Tommy. 'Can you try and track down Eddie? He's probably been taken to the Fazakerley. We've got the presentation in a second and then Amber, Valent and I've got to face a press conference.'

'Well done,' murmured back Taggie, 'your first Grand National and your three-thousandth win,' and she kissed his rigid cheek.

'I'd forgotten about that.'

689

Walking back from the bookies down a side alley and carrying a bulging suitcase, Rupert bumped into a man in a black woolly hat. Then, seeing murder in his eyes, he recognized Rafiq and said, 'I'm sorry we couldn't save him.'

'You killed him,' said Rafiq hysterically. 'Wilkie took him out, cutting across him. But it was the fault of your precious grandson holding him up, allowing him no daylight. Now he never see daylight again.' He gave a strangled sob.

'I'm sorry, we'll try and bury him at Penscombe.'

'I bury you first,' hissed Rafiq, spitting in Rupert's face before he disappeared into the crowd, upsetting Rupert more than he cared to say.

140

On the television screen, after a rerun of the race the BBC showed Mrs Wilkinson's name being painted in gold letters on the Grand National winners' list.

'Not since Aldaniti,' observed Rogue to Richard Dunwoody, 'has an entire country been behind a horse.'

Clare Balding had made the presentation and Amber was now in the media centre facing the post-race press conference with Rupert and Valent, their early euphoria diluted by the death of Furious. Amber, her sweat- and champagne-drenched hair unloosed, sat looking vulnerable, still wrapped in her Union Jack and clutching her big silver winner's plate like a shield to ward off trouble.

Clancy Wiggins, the racing correspondent of the *Scorpion*, kept putting the boot in. 'Would Mrs Wilkinson have won if she'd stayed with Marius? How did Amber feel when Mrs Wilkinson was taken away? Was Marius upset when you opted to ride for Rupert?'

'Marius behaved impeccably,' said Amber crossly. 'He lent his best lads, Tommy and Rafiq, to Rupert.'

'But Marius still threw you out the next day.'

'He didn't.'

'Well, his wife kicked you out.'

'Shut oop,' snapped Valent, 'this has nothing to do with the National.'

'The course rode beautifully,' insisted Amber.

'Furious died in the race,' persisted Clancy. 'Why didn't you let Rafiq Khan ride Furious rather than your grandson, who couldn't stay on his horse either in the National or the Gold Cup?'

'We're not talking about Furious,' Amber said irritably. 'His death was a complete accident.'

'He was brought down by Mrs Wilkinson,' said Clancy, 'cutting across him, hanging left.'

'Was he?' gasped Amber, turning to Valent in horror.

'Am I going to have to come over and throttle you?' bellowed Valent.

'Amber has achieved the impossible,' began Rupert, then, pausing to answer his mobile: 'Yes, OK, we'll come at once.' He beckoned to an Aintree official, and after a few words rose to his feet.

'Sorry, guys,' he told the protesting room, 'we've got to go. Valent will answer any questions, thank you, everyone.'

Such was his chilling blue glare and his air of suppressed menace, no one tried to stop him.

'Your father's taken a turn for the worse,' he told Amber outside. 'He's conscious but he's sinking. He can't see any more but he heard the race on the wireless. We've got to move fast.'

Aintree provided Rupert and Amber with a VIP car. As police horses had escorted her back from the winning post, now a policeman on a motorbike led them out of the course, weaving his way through the happy home-going crowd.

They passed the horsebox car park where horses were being led out with huge bandages on their legs, hay nets were being loaded into lorries for the journey home, and the lads were calling out: 'Thank you for having us, see you next year.'

I won't see Dad, thought Amber in terror.

The car had to weave its way through a swaying, limping forest of Liverpool ladies carrying their stilettos and queuing up to buy flip-flops, which were selling almost as fast as cuddly Wilkinsons.

Drunks slept peacefully in the gutter.

There was the sign by the exit: 'John Smith thanks you for drinking responsibly'.

Dad never did, thought an anguished Amber.

The nurses clapped her as she entered the ward.

'Your dad couldn't see the TV but Nurse Jenkins held the radio to his ear. He heard everything, he was so pleased and proud,' they told Amber.

'He's just been given another injection to relax his muscles, stop him tensing up against the pain and control the rattle in his throat,' said Nurse Jenkins. Amber looked at her round kind face in bewilderment.

'Is he dying?'

'He's near it. Go in and tell him you love him. Try not to cry, it's the last thing he'll want to hear when he's leaving this world.' Nurse Jenkins put her arm round Amber's shoulders. 'You couldn't be braver than you were this afternoon.'

Down the passage Amber could see her mother Janey blubbing into her mobile.

'Amber and Rupert have just arrived, my sons Christy and Junior are on their way home.'

Amber ran into the room and shut the door.

'Daddy, it's me, I love you.' She took his hand.

Billy was lying on his side, the flesh on his face fallen away. She had to lean close to hear him.

'Oh darling,' he gasped, 'I don't need to go to heaven any more. I've been there today, most wonderful moment when you headed Playboy, and Rupe's three-thousandth win. What a brave little mare.'

Next moment Rupert stalked in with a briefcase and scattered thousands of notes over Billy.

'Two hundred grand,' he said.

'Should have done it both ways,' muttered Billy. 'Thank you, Rupe. It's your inheritance, darling. You rode so well and Wilkie, what a sweetheart.'

Billy's voice was hardly audible as Rupert sat down on his other side, putting a hand on his shoulder.

'Do you remember how The Bull hated water, Rupe? I hope I see The Bull again.' Billy's hand in Amber's went slack.

Out of the window against a rose-pink sky, Amber could see the black silhouette of Paddy's Wigwam and the Church of England cathedral with its spikes coaxed upwards.

After a minute Rupert, his normally deadpan face contorted by anguish, managed to say, 'I'm afraid he's gone.'

And Amber felt free to burst into agonizing sobs.

'I did it for Dad, I did it for Dad, I wanted Dad to call me home.'

Rupert was still patting her shuddering, champagne-soaked shoulders, unable to comfort her, wishing Taggie was here, when a figure appeared in the doorway and a soft Irish voice said, 'God called your father home.'

'Fuck off,' snarled Rupert, desperately wiping his eyes on a sheet.

Amber looked up in bewilderment to see Rogue, still with the mike in the lapel of his beautiful grey presenter's suit, still in his television make-up. But no eyeliner or shadow was responsible for the concern and tenderness in his eyes.

'What are you doing here?' she sobbed.

'Come to take care of you,' said Rogue, as she stumbled into his arms. 'I know when I'm wanted.'

Word had galloped round and the press prowling outside the Royal Liverpool surged forward as Rogue and Amber came out twenty minutes later. Amber was white and trembling, but warmed by Rogue's right arm round her shoulders. Before anyone could ask questions, Rogue raised his left hand.

'I want to say something. Amber and I are together now,' he ran a finger down her ashen cheek, 'for always. This afternoon, Amber achieved a miracle winning the Grand National,' loud cheers, 'but she has also just lost her father, Billy Lloyd-Foxe, an absolute hero just like herself.'

Even the most hardened members of the press groaned in dismay and sympathy.

'So I beg you to respect her need to mourn the loss of a truly sweet man and leave us alone.'

For once Rogue's handsome face was drained of laughter. His shoulders were twice the width of Amber's. They were the same height, but at that moment he seemed ten feet tall.

Tape recorders were switched off, cameras put down. As a car slid forward, Clancy Wiggins leapt forward to open the door for them.

'Godspeed,' he shouted, banging the roof of the car, as they set out for Rupert's helicopter.

141

FOREVER AMBER! NATIONAL TREASURE! LADIES FIRST! Mrs Wilkinson and her jockey dominated the headlines. The country reeled with happiness. Journalists writing emotionally and beautifully ran out of superlatives. National Hunt racing was thrilled to be so positively in the spotlight. Billy's death only served to add a poignant and heroic dimension to Amber's huge achievement. Rogue, another favourite son, riding to the rescue provided a comforting and happy ending.

Chisolm and Mrs Wilkinson, with her red and black John Smith's Grand National winner's rug still flapping round her fetlocks, because any turning up would have lopped off the word 'winner', went on a triumphant tour of the Cotswolds in her open-top bus adoring the adulation.

Rupert, fed up with the volume of Mrs Wilkinson's fan mail, was contemplating returning her to Throstledown. To distract himself from Billy's death, he was in an insufferably triumphalist mood, winding up both Shade and Harvey-Holden, who was being accused of overracing his horses at Sandown, Ayr and Perth in a desperate attempt to clinch the leading trainer's title.

Nor was Rupert's press entirely flattering. Charges of nepotism and racism hovered. Why had he jocked off and sacked rising star Rafiq and put up his clearly inexperienced grandson? What a tragic waste of glorious Furious.

Throstledown felt the same and found it hard to rejoice whole-heartedly in Wilkie's and Cuthbert's victory now Furious had gone and Rafiq vanished. Tommy kept her mobile on twenty-four hours a day, praying he'd make contact.

Etta, desperately disappointed that Valent had never rung her back, had to admit that Mrs Wilkinson's portrait had brought the reverse of bad luck. Valent, however, had not offered it to her again, instead presenting it to Chris and Chrissie to hang in the Wilkinson Arms. And serve Etta right, thought many of the syndicate, for not supporting Wilkie at Aintree, where they delighted in telling her they'd had such a brilliant time.

'Corinna, Bonny and Phoebe were saying you ought to be more media-friendly, Etta,' Romy had even more delight in passing on.

The snow which had fallen on Grand National Day had melted except for the occasional frozen fragment on verges or beneath the trees across the valley. With these Etta identified – somehow she couldn't unthaw. She was also devastated about Furious and petrified that Rafiq, on the loose with nowhere to go, might do something terrible to avenge him. And that was Valent and Rupert's fault too.

Distraction from such sadness and recrimination was provided the following Saturday by the Equine Hero of the Year awards, known as the Horsecars, which were being televised at Rutminster racecourse after the day's racing.

Mrs Wilkinson had been nominated, as had Rupert for his three-thousandth win, Amber for her heroic victory, and Billy posthumously for his contribution to equine sports. Votes were pouring in but Mrs Wilkinson was hot favourite. Despite tickets being like gold dust, Valent, who felt they deserved a treat after all their hard work, had managed to secure enough for both Rupert's and Marius's lads.

The syndicate were extremely miffed at not being invited.

'All Etta's fault for rejecting that picture and blacking the National,' grumbled Phoebe.

A despairing Etta felt totally to blame.

There was still no word from Rafiq. But as Rupert was interviewed by his old friend John McCririck before the 3.15 on Saturday afternoon, suddenly behind them, amid the waving, winking punters on their mobiles to alert friends they were on telly, Rafiq's pale, cold, murderous face appeared briefly.

142

The races were over; a rising moon was casting the dim grey shadow of Rutminster Cathedral across the course. The horses had gone home, except Mrs Wilkinson and Chisolm, who, parading that afternoon and giving a display of their footballing skills, had upped the gate by tens of thousands. The People's Pony was now housed in one of the course boxes, tended by Rupert's laziest stable lad, Michael Meagan.

Tommy had been extremely reluctant to relinquish this responsibility, but Valent insisted that she attend the awards ceremony and have some fun, particularly as she'd been nominated for Groom of the Year. Valent had thrust a mega wodge of greenbacks into her jeans after the National, ordering her to buy a new dress. Taking herself glumly off to Monsoon, she was amazed to find herself size twelve and voluptuously curved for the first time in her life. She had stopped eating since Rafiq vanished and could now squeeze herself into a dress of dark blue lace, which enhanced her big cornflower-blue eyes, her splendid cleavage and her smooth no-longer-bulging shoulders. Embarrassed but delighted by the compliments – even Rupert had told her she looked gorgeous – wishing Rafiq could see her, she was now getting tanked up and singing, 'Here's to you, Mrs Wilkinson', in the bar with the rest of the lads.

It had been noticed that special red rush matting had been laid up to the podium, which could mean that Wilkie . . . expectations were sky-high.

Gossip also centred around how the hell Tresa, on a lad's salary, could afford a slinky black dress, cross-laced back and front and saved from indecency by strategically placed ostrich feathers, and secondly, whether the nasty cuts on Johnnie

Brutus's pretty face, which had needed stitches, had been caused by a fall into barbed wire or by an enraged Harvey-Holden slashing him with a bridle after the demise of Ilkley Hall in the Grand National.

Michael Meagan, meanwhile, was fed up with being left down at an otherwise deserted stables with Mrs Wilkinson and Chisolm. His crush on Tresa had increased since the National. He wanted to be beside her in the bar, fending off competition. He was disconsolately reading the evening's programme, salivating over the details of the three-course dinner. Frankie Dettori had been nominated. Tresa was nuts about him. He had just seen Zara Phillips, Alice Plunkett, Claire King and Katie Price rolling up.

Michael's sense of injustice intensified. God, he needed a drink. Suddenly Mrs Wilkinson gave a whicker of welcome, Chisolm an excited bleat. Looking up, Michael crossed himself as Rafiq padded up on panther feet.

'How'd you get in here?' asked Michael.

'Hung on to my stable pass when Rupert sacked me.'

'Everyone's looking for you. You've been nominated for Conditional Jomp Jockey.'

Rafiq didn't seem interested. He appeared about to lose it as he patted Mrs Wilkinson, who nudged him lovingly in the belly. Chisolm bounced the football to get attention.

'Sorry about Furious,' said Michael, noticing how Mrs Wilkinson tossed her head and winced as Rafiq's fingers clenched her neck. 'Eddie didn't get anyting out of the horse, who was in a terrible state without you, ran his race before it started, completely different animal to the Gold Cop horse. I'd never have run him but Rupert was distracted. Billy Lloyd-Foxe died that afternoon.'

'That was after the race,' said Rafiq bleakly.

'Rupert's terribly cot op.'

'Good.'

'Great party going on up there,' said Michael, wistfully. 'They'll be going into dinner soon.'

'Why don't you nip up there for half an hour?' suggested Rafiq idly. 'I'll look after Wilkie.' He smoothed her silken mane, which smelled agonizingly of Tommy's shampoo. 'She's not Furious but I got very fond of Wilkie. I'm leaving England soon and I'd like the chance to say goodbye. What's that button on the side of the stable door?'

'Some security device, I guess,' said Michael, getting out a comb, dipping it in Mrs Wilkinson's water bucket and slicking back his hair. 'Are you sure?'

'Sure. Go on, hurry,' urged Rafiq. 'How's Tommy?'

'Heartbroken, can't stop crying over Furious. She's coming out later to relieve me and if Wilkie wins she'll lead her up.'

'Give her my best, love, no, my very best love, now hurry.'

Rafiq shook hands formally, but in the lights from the conference centre Michael could see how much weight he had lost, how wildly his hollow eyes burned and how his emaciated face was green-tinged and glistening with sweat. Cock ruling his head, Michael ignored these signs.

'Are you giving an award or getting one?' celebrities were asking each other as Michael slid into the hall.

Green candles on every table flickered on pink tulips and roses and on ice buckets full of pink champagne, as diners tucked into smoked salmon and prawn timbales. Beautiful girls with gleaming brown bodies and waterfalls of shining hair were everywhere. Flat jockeys seemed to attract them. Stroppy little buggers, always getting into fights like Jack Russells, thought Michael dismissively, but they certainly pulled the girls.

Tomorrow was Good Friday, one of the few days like Christmas Day when there was no racing, so they could all get plastered, away from the tyrannical treadmill of win, win, win or, for those less fortunate, the awareness of not getting rides.

The jump jockeys were a different breed, bigger, more muscled, comrades united in war. Conscious of their superior courage, they were watching clips on a big screen of the year's worst spills and thrills, fascinated by the falls of others. The audience, who were not jump jockeys, put their hands over their faces with horror. There were Furious and Ilkley Hall tipping up in the National, there was Wilkie falling in the Gold Cup.

On a side table on the right of the platform, the Horsecars, silver models of jockeys crouched over galloping horses, awaited their recipients. Amber, tipped as leading lady jockey, was too sad still about her father to show up and collect her award, which Rupert would probably accept on her behalf.

Penscombe, to Harvey-Holden's fury, was expected to do very well. Valent, to everyone's surprise and disappointment, had made his excuses and flown to Milan to watch Ryan's team on the first match of a mini-tour. Cuddly Wilkinsons had sold out and the Kowloon factory was working on a virtual reality game in which you imagined yourself on Mrs Wilkinson winning the National. Valent was also fed up with the syndicate, none of whom, except Alban, Alan and Painswick, had bothered to write and thank him for ferrying them up to the National, all assuming it was the privilege of the rich to pick up the bill.

143

Richard Phillips, the handsome trainer and the funniest man in racing, was warming up the audience with a joke about one trainer ringing up another trainer, only to be told the tragic news that the second trainer's wife had just died.

'Are you going to Towcester?' asked the first trainer.

'No, we're going to bury her,' said the second trainer.

Howls of laughter greeted this, distracting the audience from the serious business: who was going to win awards?

With so many Irish mates to hail, it took Michael ages to battle his way to the Throstledown and Penscombe table and find Tresa being chatted up by Rupert's lads. Fortunately Tommy, who would have reproved him for deserting Mrs Wilkinson, had gone off to thank Valent and show him her lovely new dress. Disappointed to find he was in Milan, she got sidetracked talking to Marius and Olivia.

As she had left her second course of roast lamb and dauphinoise potatoes untouched, Michael took her place, scooping them up and helping himself to a large glass of red.

'You'll never guess who I saw,' he whispered to Josh. 'Rafiq.'

'Christ, where?'

'Rolled up at the stables. Offered to keep an eye on Wilkie.'

'Is that wise? Million-pound horse now.'

'She'll be OK, I'll go back in a minute.' Michael helped himself to another drink and forked up another mouthful of dauphinoise.

Like napalm, the news flickered round the table, until it reached Tresa, stunning in her black cross-laced dress, as always on her mobile but smoky eyes undressing Michael as she did every man.

'Oh look, there's Zara Phillips,' said Josh. 'She's well fit, I wouldn't mind . . .'

'Nor would I,' said Michael. 'Oh, here comes Tommy, she looks lush too, I should have made a move at the National. I better go. I'll call you later.' He buried his lips in Tresa's soft white shoulder.

Smirking Tresa switched off her mobile. The moment Michael had disappeared into the melee, over the raucous applause for Katie Price mounting the platform to hand out the Jump Ride of the Year award, she shouted across to Tommy, 'Guess who's looking after Wilkie?'

'Michael is.'

'He is not, he's just left this table. It's your friend Rafiq.'

Tommy knocked over her glass of red, dousing two candles with a hiss, as she leapt to her feet:

'You're winding me up.'

'Go and look.'

Charging through the diners and then the crowd round the roulette tables, past equine stars looking down with unseeing eyes in the Hall of Fame, out through the double doors, breathing in the cool night air after the heat, Tommy ran towards the stables and was just crying, 'Rafiq, Rafiq,' when a colossal explosion rocked the entire racecourse. Tommy felt a searing pain in her left shoulder as shock waves blew her off her feet.

Complete pandemonium followed. As dinner-jacketed and bare-shouldered diners stormed the doors and fought their way out of the hall, a smothering tornado of black smoke could be seen rising from the stables.

'Wilkie! Rafiq!' screamed Tommy, her lovely lace dress shredded, her shoulder spurting blood. She staggered to her feet and, wiping more blood out of her eyes, stumbled in the direction of the stables.

'Please move away from the hall into the centre of the car park,' said a voice over the tannoy. As the building emptied of guests, waiters and waitresses, one was still clutching the plates she'd been clearing from the table.

Searching desperately through the gloom, Tommy could see little flickers of flame rising from the blackness as straw and wood caught fire. There was a dreadful stench of burning. As if some giant chimney sweep had been at work, everything was coated in soot.

A jangle of fire engines was soon joined by a howl of police cars and ambulances. Tommy was staggering onwards when Rupert caught up with her.

'Christ, Tommy, are you OK? Where did it get you?'

'Wilkie, Rafiq,' mumbled Tommy.

'Come back from there.' Rupert had just put his dinner jacket round her shoulders when he caught sight of another swaying figure. Beneath the blood and soot, only the thick Irish accent was recognizable.

'Michael, oh Michael,' sobbed Tommy, 'did you get Wilkie out? Where's Rafiq?'

'Rafiq was here,' explained Michael in a dazed voice. 'He asked for a few moments alone with Mrs Wilkinson to say goodbye. Said he was leaving England for ever.'

'He was leaving the world for ever,' howled Rupert, 'fucking suicide bomber! You stupid fucker, leaving him alone with her.'

Through the black smoke, they could see the stables had been bulldozed to rubble, with a great crater gaping in the centre.

'Don't go any nearer, Mr Campbell-Black,' ordered a policeman. 'You must all come into the centre of the course. The ambulance has arrived. Can you walk that far or do you need a stretcher?' he asked Tommy and Michael.

'Has Michael been killed? Has Michael been killed?' Tresa shot past Tommy, then, recognizing Michael, threw herself into his arms. 'Thank God you're safe.'

Next moment, Chisolm raced towards them with a singed and blackened face, bleating frantically.

'Oh poor darling,' cried Tommy.

'There, there, poor little duck,' Rupert grabbed Chisolm's collar, 'poor little girl.' He stroked her head.

'If Chisolm's escaped, perhaps Rafiq and Wilkie have too,' gasped Tommy, and fainted.

As the crowd shambled towards the middle of the course, police and bomb disposal experts were already checking the car parks for further bombs.

No one was allowed to leave, which caused several shouting matches.

'My stable lads have got to get back to the yard to look after the horses,' yelled Rupert.

'I'm on GMTV tomorrow,' screamed Harvey-Holden.

Several of the jockeys had seen fit to take bottles from the tables and were having parties. But as the news got round that Mrs Wilkinson had been blown to kingdom come, laughter turned to tears and the racecourse went quiet.

144

Later, when questioned by the police, a patched-up Michael in his bloodstained shirt remembered Rafiq asking about a button on the side of the stable door, which the Clerk of the Course vouchsafed would not normally have been there. It was deduced that the bomb had been triggered off by a mobile that anyone could have rung from the hall or beyond. But this was a bomb with a difference. The killer had used Obliterat, a sophisticated substance which literally obliterates everything within forty yards and renders even DNA analysis inoperative.

Guests, sponsors, caterers and racecourse staff were compelled to sleep in makeshift accommodation in schools, village halls and in the great concert hall of the Rutminster Symphony Orchestra. They were only released the next day. A heavily sedated Tommy was rushed to Rutminster Hospital, where surgeons removed several splinters of wood from her left shoulder. She had been lucky they didn't puncture an artery, she was told, even luckier they had missed her heart.

Tommy, wiped out by the loss of Rafiq and Wilkie, didn't believe they had.

The nation – nay the world – joined her in mourning. After Furious and Ilkley Hall's deaths in the National, Animal Rights were suspected. So was Islamic terrorism, particularly when police, after a tip-off, raided the bleak room in Larkminster where Rafiq had taken refuge after he'd been sacked by Rupert. Piled up in a corner, they found film footage of 9/11 and the beheading of hostages, tapes of ranting sermons from radical preachers, militant literature, a picture of Bin Laden and flyers claiming that 'Allah loves those who fight for him.' Not entirely incriminating evidence, but traces of Obliterat were also discovered along with photographs of Furious, Amber and Rafiq's family in Pakistan.

Why the hell, reasoned the police, hadn't he covered his tracks, unless he intended never coming back?

Michael, in spite of being rushed to hospital, was in the dog-house. If he hadn't abandoned Mrs Wilkinson . . . Tresa, however, was in her element. What a good thing she'd had her hair high-lighted yesterday. Still wearing her lovely black dress from last night, slightly bloodstained from hugging Michael, she visited him in hospital before a long session in a side room with hand-some Chief Inspector Gablecross.

'Amber broke Rafiq's heart, Chief Inspector. Rafiq and I were friends, he talked to me a lot. I'm a good listener, he was lonely. He utterly adored Furious. He only wanted to make money as a jockey so he could one day buy Furious. Mrs Wilkinson and Amber brought Furious down in the National. Rafiq was devoted to Marius and felt Valent had betrayed him by taking his horses to Rupert, particularly after the Gold Cup victory. Then Rupert jocked Rafiq off and fired him. Rafiq detested Eddie Alderton – American bombs had wiped out so many of his family. Eddie screwed up on Furious.' Tresa opened wide her smoky grey eyes, made more appealing by the shadows beneath them. 'May I call you Timothy, Chief Inspector? This bomb was pure revenge, the only way of destroying them all.'

This seemed to be the general consensus.

More upset than anyone was Valent, who had deeply loved Mrs Wilkinson. Told of her death during a victory dinner in Milan by Rupert's ringing from the racecourse, the hard man of football amazed everyone by breaking down and having to flee the restaurant. He was crying as much for Etta as himself. He had been deeply upset she never rang to congratulate him after the National, and had later assumed it was because Furious had been killed. Now, with Wilkie and Rafiq gone, she'd never forgive him.

But he must be brave. After a quadruple Scotch, he called her. 'Etta, luv, I'm so sorry.'

'It's all your fault, if you hadn't entered her for the National she'd never have been nominated for that award. Please leave me alone.' Etta knew she was being unfair, but she was crying so much she had to hang up.

Priceless sighed and rubbed his nose along her thigh.

'You still have me.'

Etta was one of the few people who publicly defended Rafiq.

'Rafiq adored Mrs Wilkinson,' she told the press. 'He stayed up all night with her once when she had colic. He was overjoyed when he won a race on her when Amber broke her wrist. And he was far too fond of Tommy to destroy the horse she loved. It doesn't add up.'

'Rafiq would never hurt an animal,' protested a numb, tearful Tommy from her hospital bed. 'Marius could hardly get him to use a whip. He always worried if Mistletoe's water bowl wasn't filled up. He loved animals.'

Tommy's detective sergeant father tried to convince her otherwise. 'Rafiq wimped out as a suicide bomber last time. He wanted to prove to Cousin Ibrahim that he was one of the boys.'

'He didn't,' wailed Tommy, and as she left the hospital she defiantly told the massed journalists and television cameras, 'Rafiq didn't want twenty-seven virgins in heaven. The only reason he'd want to go to heaven would be to see Furious again.'

But Etta and Tommy appeared to be Rafiq's sole champions, particularly when Ibrahim was alleged to have rung in claiming Al-Qaeda's responsibility. What remained uncertain was whether Rafiq had perished with Mrs Wilkinson or had escaped and was still alive.

The syndicate took it very hard.

'St Peter needn't open the Pearly Gates,' observed a choked Joey. 'Mrs Wilkinson'll jump clean over them.'

'At least she'll know Furious up there, and Best Mate, Dessie, Arkle, Rummy and Sefton will form a guard of honour,' said Woody stoutly.

'She united us like a band of brothers,' wept Painswick.

Poor Alan's book was screwed because of the mass coverage. The bandwagon creaked as Corinna, Bonny and even Cindy leapt on it to convince the media of their deep sense of personal loss and sent out photographs of themselves hugging Mrs Wilkinson. Willowwood was a sea of flowers.

'Now thrive the florists,' sighed Seth. 'Amsterdam will be stripped of tulips.'

Chisolm was much too upset to write her diary in the *Mirror*.

'You must be able to cobble something together, Dora,' pleaded the features editor. 'Readers have the right to know.'

'Chisolm's probably the only one who knows the truth,' confessed Dora, whose stolen service had also gone by the board.

'Did you know that Mrs Wilkinson was going to be a mother?' she sobbed to Trixie.

'You let her run that huge race when she was in foal?' exploded

Trixie. 'How could you, Dora? If you hadn't, she wouldn't have brought down Furious or been nominated for that award.'

'I know, I'm so sorry,' bawled Dora.

And if Willowwood was weeping, so was the nation. Like Shergar, Mrs Wilkinson was a martyr to terrorism. The government stepped up security. At racecourses all round the country, the jockeys wore black armbands and a two-minute silence was observed.

Mrs Wilkinson's box was left empty, both at Penscombe, where Love Rat's great stallion's bell rang out for her, and at Throstledown, where even though she'd departed a month before, Sir Cuthbert, Count Romeo, History Painting and Doggie still peered in hopefully every time they passed. Her bridle with its green browband hung empty from the manger. The People's Pony was no more.

145

There were no bodies so no funeral but a memorial service was planned, first in St James's, Willowwood, then, because of the demand, it was moved to Larkminster Cathedral.

Niall was revving up to help the bishop take the service. Major Cunliffe was organizing parking and a video of Mrs Wilkinson's finest hours – so many of them. Ione would do the flowers with Direct Debbie, draping the cathedral with willow branches and never a splash of colour. Chris and Chrissie and Mop Idol were organizing food for the syndicate and friends afterwards. Seth and Corinna were doing readings but all the syndicate wanted to say a word, except Etta. She looked at Mrs Wilkinson's betting slips and then at the coloured pieces of string, like a child's ball, which had attached her owner's badges to her handbag. She knew she was being wet but she also knew that she was incapable of paying tribute to Mrs Wilkinson without breaking down. Day and night she longed for her deep-throated whicker.

Mrs Wilkinson's portrait had brought the worst luck in the world, but at least if Etta hadn't hurled it back at Valent she would have had a reminder of how sweet Wilkie had been and how Valent had tried so hard to please her. He and Alban had completely disappeared. And his last memory would be of Etta screaming at him to leave her alone.

She was comforted by Poppy and Drummond.

'Are you sixty, Granny?' asked Poppy.

'No, nearly seventy, alas.'

'So you'll go to heaven like Mrs Wilkinson soon.' Then, when Etta looked really sad, 'Don't worry, Granny, you'll die soon anyway.'

'If you can't sleep, Granny,' Drummond put an arm round her, 'you wake me and we'll talk.'

'I think they'd better have counselling,' said Romy.

Amber was also crippled with guilt that her photograph had been found in Rafiq's room. 'I didn't realize he still cared. Rafiq would never have blown up Mrs Wilkinson if I hadn't jilted him and, far, far worse, brought down Furious. He had a double motive.'

As he tried to comfort her, Rogue reflected it was a pity they couldn't hold Billy's memorial service on the same day. Amber's mother, Janey, was making such a meal of it.

Shagger wondered if they'd get insurance.

'Does this count as an Act of God?'

'Whose god?' said Alan bleakly. 'We'd only get 1 per cent anyway.'

On the morning of the memorial service, which coincided with a heatwave, Seth had the temerity to roll up at Etta's and ask her to hear his reading. Now he'd shaved off his beard and moustache to play a rather old Brick in *Cat on a Hot Tin Roof*, she realized what a weak, self-indulgent face he had compared with Valent's. She was tempted to tell him to go away, but let him in because she was so desperate for news of Valent. Priceless greeted his old master with much flashing of teeth, but showed no desire to get off the sofa.

Seth had no news to report, except what hell Bonny was to rehearse with. 'She's insisting on reading a passage from *The Journey of Bonny* this evening.'

Through the open window Etta could hear Pocock practising 'Here's To You, Mrs Wilkinson' on the church bells.

'Bonny won't be pleased,' Seth went on. 'It doesn't look as though Valent's going to make the service. I guess he's lost interest in Willowwood. Badger's Court's on the market for six mil. Can you just bear to hear this, darling?' He handed over a poetry book.

' "Brightness falls from the air," ' read Etta. ' "Queens have died young and fair,/Dust hath closed Helen's eye." '

The words made her cry and she certainly couldn't face the memorial service now. No one would want a sobbing, emotional grandmother.

As soon as Seth had gone, disappointed she hadn't offered him a drink, Etta threw Priceless into the back of the Polo and drove south-west towards her old house. She had forgotten how ravishing Dorset was, particularly in early May, with wild cherry blossom and cow parsley decking out the countryside, like the young bride she had been when she and Sampson moved to Bluebell Hill.

She went first to Sampson's grave in the churchyard and was just leaving a bunch of white roses when she noticed a small posy of crimson-flecked geraniums. Attached to them was a little note: 'Darling Sampy, never a day goes by, all love Blanche.'

In a trice, Etta remembered her own anguish when she had found the same geraniums, which she herself had specially propagated, growing in a pale blue tub on Blanche's terrace, obviously given her by Sampson. It must have been a special bond between them and, twenty-five years later, here they were on his grave. He and Blanche must have really loved each other.

Now Etta loved Valent so helplessly, she could understand and forgive them and not feel jealous any more.

'I'm sorry,' she whispered as she placed the white roses in their vase of water on the grave beside the geraniums. 'I'm so sorry for not loving you enough.'

Then, as if sleep-walking, she found herself driving to Bluebell Hill. Bluebells were appropriately staining sapphire the wood-land floor behind the soft russet house, and the peonies and irises were in their pink and purple glory. On the lawn was a tank, a football and a push-along dog, which had belonged to Trixie. The swing still hung from the chestnut tree.

Ariella, who lived there now, was thrilled to see her, asked her in for a cup of tea and some rather stale Swiss roll, then showed her over the house, which was nice, messy and lived-in. A large ginger cat snoozed on an unmade bed.

One of the children was out playing with a friend, the other, now a chubby eighteen-month-old, who hadn't been born when they bought the house, had just tipped a whole packet of Rice Krispies all over the floor. Ariella proceeded to shove them back into the packet.

'Ruthie cleaned the floor this morning. She always speaks so fondly of you, Mrs Bancroft. There are so many things I wanted to ask you. Did all your streams dry up in the summer and do you take those lovely agapanthus into the greenhouse in winter?'

'May I wander round the garden?' asked Etta.

An outraged Priceless, nose rammed against an open inch of car window, glared as the ginger cat wandered after her, rolling lasciviously in the catmint. There were an awful lot of weeds; slugs had eaten most of the young delphiniums. Etta found a plastic JCB in one flower bed, a rocking pig in another and the see-saw that went round and round and up and down, which Sampson had made. At least someone had weeded round Bartlett's grave.

709

Etta sat on a stone bench gazing into space. After a while Ariella came and sat with her:

'So pleased you came. Heard you were heartbroken to leave here. I don't blame you. It's such a happy house, despite the awful things that happened to you.'

'It needs children and laughter. There wasn't much laughter in my husband's last years.'

Seeing Etta was crying, Ariella took her hand.

'So terrible to lose a husband and a lovely house.'

And the rest, thought Etta wearily.

But as they walked back to the house, Ariella said:

'We had another visitor recently, Valent Edwards.'

'*The* Valent Edwards?' squeaked Etta, going scarlet.

'He just knocked on the door, apologized, said he was driving through and loved the house. I showed him all over. He said we could name our price. I said we didn't want to sell. Cally had just got into a lovely local school and we were so happy here. He gave me his card in case we changed our minds. I suddenly realized it was *the* Valent Edwards. He looked tired and older than his photographs, but he's still very dynamic and attractive for an older man. He said he wanted to buy it for a very special lady. I expect it was one of those glamorous A-list celebs he runs around with.'

'How long ago was that?' said Etta faintly.

'Last week, no, the week before. Said he had a horse running in the National. I said I was sorry I didn't know anything about horses. Johnnie said it was crazy of me not to take him up. I told him how sad it was you couldn't bear to come back. Everything reminded you of Mr Bancroft.'

It's not true, Etta wanted to scream.

She drove home in turmoil, twice losing the way. Valent probably hadn't been buying it for her and if he had, he'd have changed his mind now, thinking she still loved Sampson and remembering how vile she'd been to him. She drove slower and slower.

She must remember people in tsunamis and earthquakes and forest fires, with whole families wiped out. She must pull herself together. She still had Trixie, Poppy, Drummond, Priceless, who was now resting his head on her shoulder, and Gwenny to live for.

The sun was an hour off setting as she drove into a totally deserted Willowwood. She noticed Valent's gates padlocked as she passed. Would he ever come back? Would he make the memorial service, which would be starting in a few minutes?

710

It was still terribly hot. Etta had a shower and pulled on her old jeans and a faded blue denim shirt from the sixties she couldn't bear to throw away. Then, overwhelmed with restlessness, she took Priceless and Gwenny for a walk in the woods.

Down by the pond, on the edge of Marius's land, she found his horses turned out. There was Count Romeo, History Painting, Not for Crowe, Sir Cuthbert, still a little stiff from the National, Doggie and Oh My Goodness. Suddenly, they all formed up and started hurtling round the pond, weaving in and out of the willows, snorting, kicking up their heels, stopping then galloping on again. Who could say horses didn't enjoy racing?

146

Over in Larkminster Cathedral, Tommy, who'd agreed to say a few words about Mrs Wilkinson, wondered how she'd get through it without losing it. She'd lost so much more weight, nothing fitted. Etta had lent her the black dress with a frilled collar which she'd once worn to Ione's party. The only colour in Tommy's newly hollowed face were eyes red with weeping.

Revving up for the memorial service, she'd hardly had time to think, but afterwards, how could she go on without Rafiq, Furious and Mrs Wilkinson, the three things she cared most about in life? How could she survive never feeling Mrs Wilkinson's whiskery nose in her hand, or nudging her in the back, or hearing a low whicker of love, or being cheered up by her silly faces or by her particular way of carrying her lovely head to the right so she could see ahead out of her left eye?

Tommy still refused to believe Rafiq was behind it, but there had been a third sighting this morning near Bagley Hall, so she wrestled with hope and dread. If he were innocent, why hadn't he got in touch?

The funeral bell had finished tolling. The same trumpeters who'd played at Aintree were up in the gallery, poised to launch into the Dead March from *Saul*. The cathedral was draped most beautifully with weeping willow branches intertwined with cow parsley. The place was absolutely packed, swarming with press and television cameras inside and out, as the procession came slowly up the aisle.

Huntsmen in red coats were followed by jockeys wearing black armbands (Rogue and Amber hand in hand) and stable lads and lasses from both Throstledown and Penscombe, who had dressed all in black. There was no coffin, Mrs Wilkinson's Grand National winner's rug and her head collar had been blown up with her.

The children from Greycoats occupied the front rows on the left. Tilda had been coaching them all week in a farewell song, 'Goodbye dearest Wilkie, whose coat was so silky', at the end of which they would wave goodbye.

The syndicate, all fighting back the tears, occupied the front pews on the right. Behind them were Marius and Olivia, a stony-faced Rupert and Taggie, Bianca and Feral and an ashen Eddie Alderton, who had learnt a few lessons in the last week.

In the front row of the next block of pews sat Harvey-Holden with Jude the Obese, who took up most of the pew, which left little room for their caring new best friends: Martin and Romy Bancroft. Harvey-Holden had offered a massive reward.

'I and the entire racing world,' he had told *The Times* in an interview that morning, 'will not rest until we have tracked down Mrs Wilkinson's killer. I once owned this remarkable mare. She was stolen from me by gypsies and when I tracked her down at Etta Bancroft's, I realized they had bonded and it would be heartless to part them, so I made the supreme sacrifice.

'Now I and my wife Judy are offering not only two hundred and fifty thousand pounds as a reward to anyone who leads us to the truth, but also two hundred thousand pounds to the Sampson Bancroft Memorial Fund, as an expression of our deep sympathy for Etta Bancroft.'

No wonder Martin and Romy looked like cats who'd got majority shares in Dairy Crest.

Deliberately timing their entrance just before that of the clergy came a very handsome couple, Shade Murchieson and Bonny, radiant in black velvet and new diamonds. Sauntering up the aisle like models on the catwalk, they didn't seem to mind having to sit very close to each other as they squeezed into Harvey-Holden's pew.

'What a revolting pain,' exploded Dora, but she was too sad to ring the press.

Bringing up the rear of the procession were the bishop and Niall, his blond pallor set off by his black robes. Woody felt so proud he wanted to reach out and touch Niall's hand as he passed. They had both been torn apart by the death of Mrs Wilkinson.

Pocock put a reassuring arm round Miss Painswick's shoulders. There was an empty seat between Trixie and Alan, who whispered across to her, 'I don't think Granny's going to make it.'

'I'm going to sit with Eddie then,' said Trixie, nipping back to the seat beside him.

Debbie Cunliffe was sobbing openly.

'Pull yourself together, woman,' hissed the Major, wiping his eyes.

Ione's face was expressionless. Travis-Locks didn't weep in public but she was comforted when Alban's hand crept into hers.

Corinna and Seth were checking their make-up and mouthing the pieces they had to read.

Then came the heartbreakingly lovely sound of a lone piper playing 'Amazing Grace' as the lone figure of Tommy came slowly up the aisle, holding Mrs Wilkinson's bridle with its willow-green browband, with Chisolm trotting listlessly beside her.

'They've both lost so much weight,' muttered Trixie.

'Tommy's really pretty now,' murmured Eddie, wincing as he remembered Snog-a-Trog.

After 'Now thank we all our God,' which raised the vaulted roof, Niall walked down the chancel steps.

'We have a video of Mrs Wilkinson in her finest and most precious moments and several readings from people who loved her,' he told the congregation, in a commendably steady voice, 'but first let us have two minutes' silence to remember our little pet.'

A minute and a half passed – like an eternity. Then suddenly over the muffled sobs, there was a clip clop, clip clop, clip clop on the flagstones outside, followed by a shrill whinny. Chisolm, roused out of her torpor, bleated back in bewilderment and hope. Then a hauntingly beautiful man's voice could be heard singing:

> 'Gaily the troubadour touched his guitar,
> When he was hast'ning home from the war.
> Singing from Palestine hither I come;
> Lady love, lady love, welcome me home.'

'Rafiq,' gasped Tommy.

People were looking at each other incredulously, tears drying and then falling on their faces. 'Could it be?'

Then cautiously a white face came round the great studded oak door, angled to the right so she could see with her left eye, and Mrs Wilkinson entered the cathedral with Rafiq on her back. His face was as hostile and haughty as a young kestrel. He was wearing only black jeans and a torn grey shirt, pale rider, pale horse. Into the cathedral they came and up the aisle.

There was a stunned silence, broken only as people rose to their feet, screaming and yelling with joy, climbing on to pews and chairs, throwing their hats into the air, leaning out of choir stall and gallery, blowing joyous blasts on trumpets and hunting horns and giving Mrs Wilkinson the greatest standing ovation of her career.

As this was nothing that Mrs Wilkinson wasn't used to, she carried on, ears pricked, looking from side to side, graciously acknowledging the pandemonium, whickering at friends and the children who broke into the aisle to pat her again and again.

Next moment, Chisolm had shoved through their legs, dancing and bleating and joyfully rubbing noses with her dear, dear friend.

Only Harvey-Holden, his face far whiter than Mrs Wilkinson's, was hysterically writhing with rage.

'Arrest that man,' he screamed.

'No,' roared Valent's voice over the loudspeaker, 'arrest *that* man.'

Mrs Wilkinson quivered with terror, her dark rolling eye showing so much white that it seemed for a second she would bolt out of the cathedral. Harvey-Holden's eyes were also darting from side to side, desperate to escape. But as the great cathedral door slammed shut, police poured in from all sides, two of the largest flanking Harvey-Holden.

'Silence, please be quiet,' shouted Valent, who'd followed Rafiq into the church and bounded up the steps of the pulpit. 'Let Rafiq speak.'

Tommy leapt forward, seizing a trembling Mrs Wilkinson's reins. Smiling down at her, Rafiq patted Mrs Wilkinson and turned coolly to Harvey-Holden. The cathedral was so well miked up, his every word could be heard.

'I know, Mr Harvey-Holden, that it was you who set fire to your own yard. You burn your own horses to death to hide that they were dying of starvation and so you claim insurance.'

'This is nonsense,' thundered Jude the Obese.

'Denny Forrester learn this when he was your head lad,' went on Rafiq, 'so you murder him and fake his suicide, and pretend he started the fire.'

'Utterly preposterous,' jabbered Harvey-Holden, foam flying from his lips.

'You were jealous of Mrs Wilkinson when Shade sent her you for training, because your then wife loved her.' Rafiq was continuously stroking Mrs Wilkinson's quivering shoulder. 'To get her into the starting stalls, you used electrodes on her legs. You denied her food for months to break her spirit and finally drove your Land-Rover into her, catching her legs in the bumper and the radiator. The only reason she miss the fire was you left her out in a freezing field that wouldn't keep a budgerigar,' Rafiq's voice was even more filled with hatred and contempt, 'so you had to get her away quickly, but she refuse to load. For two hours you beat her unconscious with a shovel, so she lost an eye. Then you dragged her into the lorry, digging out her microchip and dumping her in Willowwood on the coldest night of the year, where Etta found her.'

Dora and Alan were scribbling frantically on their service sheets.

'This is fabrication,' shouted Jude with less conviction.

'I'm sure it's nonsense, dear.' Romy put a caring hand on Jude's vast arm.

The rest of the congregation, many in tears, were hanging on Rafiq's every word with increasing dismay. Even Chisolm, recovering her appetite but not finding any of Debbie's bright flowers to eat, was listening intently.

'Jimmy Wade,' continued Rafiq relentlessly, 'was in prison at the same time as me, banged up for giving tips for reward, because you pay him so little. He tell me every terrible thing you did, and that he was going to expose you, but you had him murdered the moment he was released. I was terrified you murder me too, so I keep very quiet, but I was so upset about Furious, I blow gaff at National and told you I knew you started fire.

'You panic that I'm on to you. You're so frantic to get rid of me and Mrs Wilkinson that you plan to blow her up at Sport Personality Award and frame me, by planting all that Al-Qaeda propaganda and bomb equipment in my room, helped by your evil bugger friend, Vakil. Lucky my cousin Ibrahim tip me off.'

Harvey-Holden was just clenching his fists and muttering rubbish now.

'He's barking,' hissed Dora.

'Lucky too,' went on Rafiq, turning mockingly to the assembled policemen, 'I learn in the past a little about making bombs, so I recognize device fixed to stable door. One of Mr Murchieson's latest inventions. It only need mobile phone to set it off from fifty yards. I had so little time. Fortunately,' Rafiq turned and smiled at Michael Meagan, who was blushing among the stable lads, 'Michael want to see Tresa, so I am able to ride Mrs Wilkinson out of empty racecourse. I am very good rider,' he nodded haughtily at Rupert, 'Mr Campbell-Black should have never jocked me off National, and Mrs Wilkinson turn out excellent cross-country horse. We escaped to friend who hide and protect us and Mr Harvey-Holden blow up empty stable.'

Shade, meanwhile, had jumped to his feet. 'I've never heard so much rubbish in my life,' he roared. 'I want my lawyer.'

'This is all nonsense,' screamed Harvey-Holden, 'all lies. Rafiq blew up Usurper because he's a dirty little terrorist and he loathed her because she took out that brute Furious.'

Maddened, he leapt forward, trying to claw Rafiq to the ground, but Mrs Wilkinson was too quick for him. Shuddering with recognition, squealing with rage, she lunged at him, catching his shoulder in her teeth, shaking him like a rat.

'Get off, you bitch,' he howled, raising his hand to punch her in the eye.

Next moment the police had swooped and grabbed him as well as Shade and Vakil, who were both racing towards the door.

Rafiq, who was thoroughly enjoying being centre stage, then informed the congregation that he had forgiven Mrs Wilkinson for taking out Furious.

'I love her,' he added, pulling her ears, 'and I love Tommy and I would never do anything to break her or Etta's hearts.'

Leaping off Mrs Wilkinson, he took a sobbing, deliriously happy Tommy in his arms and everyone burst into delighted applause. It then turned to tumultuous boos, as Harvey-Holden was led away.

'This is a wonderful turn of events,' said the Bishop.

'It's a miracle,' said Niall, seizing the mike. 'Our little pet has risen like Lazarus from the dead.' Then, muttering to the Bishop: 'How on earth do we disperse this lot?'

'Perhaps we could see just the video, which is after all a celebration,' suggested the Bishop, 'and the children can sing their song and wave hello rather than goodbye.'

'Then end with a few prayers?' asked Niall.

'And those invited can repair to Willowwood,' murmured the Bishop, who hadn't had any lunch, 'where I hear there are some excellent refreshments.'

'What about my reading?' demanded Corinna furiously.

What about my £200,000 cheque? thought a shaken Martin. Which would be more advantageous, to comfort Jude or Bonny?

Rafiq was still ecstatically kissing Tommy, so Amber grabbed hold of Mrs Wilkinson.

'Where's Etta?' demanded Valent, his ruddy face for once paler than Rafiq's. Ignoring Bonny's cries of 'Valent, Valent,' he ran down the steps of the pulpit.

'Etta couldn't handle the service,' Amber told him. 'Oh Wilkie,

717

I'm so pleased to see you again.' Then, turning to Rogue: 'Look, darling, isn't she gorgeous?'

'I'm not leaving any of you in charge of a national treasure,' snapped Valent. 'I'm taking my horse home.'

147

The sun was setting, firing the trees, turning Marius's horses a glowing pink. Etta started to cry again at their carefree happiness. Covered in mud, their shaggy manes held rakishly off their foreheads by burrs, they once more weaved in and out of the willows, as she had once so deliriously weaved in and out of Valent's rustic poles.

So many willows still weeping for Beau Regard and Gwendolyn, who poor Sir Francis had lost, as she herself had lost Mrs Wilkinson and Valent. How had Sir Francis carried on living? wondered Etta. As if in sympathy, a dark whale of cloud had drifted in front of the sun. The horses had stopped to drink from the pond, then, as if deciding on a last race, they re-formed and, snorting with excitement, set off again.

Calling for Priceless, who'd as usual pushed off rabbiting, Etta set out wearily for home. Then she froze, cried out in terror and crossed herself before clutching an overhanging willow branch for support, because the pack had been joined in the twilight by a ghost horse with a pure white face. Was it Beau Regard back from the dead? Could it be the ghost of Mrs Wilkinson?

Etta's heart was hammering louder than the hooves on the parched ground as the other horses raced on, then they too double-took in amazement, slithering to a halt, whinnying, squealing with joy and bewilderment, circling the newcomer, whickering, nuzzling, nudging and nipping her for staying away. An overjoyed Count Romeo laid his dark head on her shoulder. Sir Cuthbert kept butting her, making sure she was real.

Then, ecstatically, they all took off again, round the pond, swishing through the willow curtains, but the little ghost horse led the pack. At her hurtling approach, Etta caught her breath and clutched the willow branch again, because the ghost horse had an iron-grey body, a white face with one big, wise, dark eye and a pink tongue lolling out.

Etta longed to call out, but no sound came. It must be a double, some cruel trick of similarity.

'Wilkie,' she croaked.

The ghost horse stopped in her tracks, then squealing in irritation as Count Romeo and Not for Crowe collided into the back of her, she peered through the pale green waterfall of leaves, searching everywhere. From whence had come that beloved voice?

'Wilkie' – it was a strangled whisper – but Mrs Wilkinson heard and, thrusting aside the branches, charged over to Etta, nearly sending her flying, whickering again and again, nudging her joyfully, nosing in her pockets for Polos, holding out one foot and then another, until Etta, who could only raise half a Bonio, tugged at a clump of grass for a reward.

She really was Mrs Wilkinson. There was the microchip scar and the scar above the closed right eye – battle scars now she was home from the wars. Flinging her arms round Wilkie's neck, she breathed in her lovely, distinctive, newly cut hay smell.

'Where have you been, darling, where have you come from?'

Then as her stroking fingers crept over Mrs Wilkinson's face to check that she really was no ghost, they encountered a letter tied with a brown shoelace to her head collar. With frantically trembling hands, Etta ripped it off. Child- and OAP-proof, she thought as she wrestled with the knot and finally smoothed out the paper.

'Darling Etta,' she read incredulously, 'I've never stopped loving you. Dearest lady love, please welcome me home. Yours ever, Valent.'

The sun had set, but rosier blushes swept Etta's face, as her eyes darted round.

'Valent,' she cried.

And spitting out his chewing gum, letting go of an extremely restless Chisolm, the man himself emerged from behind an ancient oak.

'Where did you find her?' whispered Etta, as rocked by the pounding of her heart she clung on to Mrs Wilkinson.

'Rafiq had her the whole time.'

'I don't understand.'

'He had a tip-off from Ibrahim that she was going to be blown up, so he talked his way into the course, smuggled her out, then discovered he was the major suspect and was too terrified to come out of hiding.'

'My God, oh the poor boy.' Etta was too confused and shaken to meet Valent's eye. 'How did you flush him out?'

Valent clocked the letter which was shaking like a captured seagull in her hand, but he answered quite matter-of-factly.

'Alban's been bluddy marvellous. Put messages on the internet and Arabic and Pakistani stations begging Rafiq to come back, that we troosted him. Ironically, what did it was Tommy on the news saying Rafiq didn't mind about twenty-seven virgins in heaven, only about seeing Furious again.'

Etta laughed shakily. She was passionately relieved Rafiq was innocent, but all she wanted to do was reread Valent's letter.

'Who planted all that stuff in his room?'

'Harvey-Holden, he's a psychopath. Hated Mrs Wilkinson obsessively. Each win, he loathed her more and more. Wicked thing was the bastard had been using Vakil to pretend to be the Mafia. They've been blackmailing Rafiq for months, saying they'd take out Tommy or his family in Pakistan unless he pulled Furious, among others, so Shade's horses could win. Shade's all tied up in it. Knows all about sophisticated explosives and he wanted to bury Marius.

'And Tresa was in on it too.' Valent's voice hardened. 'Rafiq reckons she and Vakil nobbled Bullydozer and she shaved off Wilkie's whiskers before the Gold Cup.'

'How terrible,' said a dazed Etta, 'poor Rafiq. How did you flush him out?' she asked a second time.

Realizing she wasn't taking anything in, Valent said he'd explain later. Then, as Mrs Wilkinson and Chisolm wandered off to talk to their horse friends, he added roughly, 'Where the hell have you been?'

'I went down to Dorset. It's Sampson's birthday, though I forgot actually and dropped in on our old house. Such a lovely girl living there now. She said that . . .'

Valent scuffed the ground with a laceless brown shoe.

'I went there.'

'She said you had.'

'Smashing place. I recognized some of the flowers and the colour combinations. Must have hurt you leaving it.'

'Not that,' Etta almost shouted. 'What hurt was losing Mrs Wilkinson, Furious and Rafiq, but most of all you. I'm so pleased you've got her back.'

'You've got her back, she's yours,' blurted out Valent. 'She need never race again if you don't want her to. Not for a bit anyway, she's in foal.' Then, at Etta's look of amazement: 'Dora organized a stolen service with Love Rat. Rupert was livid and was going to bill Dora, now Mrs Wilkinson's alive he's tickled pink. Bugger off, Chisolm luv, we're busy, and you too, Gwenny.'

Valent was once more slumped against the ancient oak, Etta against a willow, because their legs wouldn't hold them up any more.

'Rupert thinks—' Valent began.

'I don't give a damn what Rupert thinks,' cried Etta, 'I've been so unhappy. I didn't believe it was possible to love anyone like I love you. It's made me realize I never loved Sampson.'

Valent said nothing, but he went very still.

'I went to apologize to him for not loving him,' stumbled on Etta, 'and to say goodbye.'

'I thought you adored him and then that it was Seth, then Sampson again. I was so jealous,' confessed Valent, then added bitterly, 'and Romy said you could never love a yob.'

'The bitch, that's vile,' stormed Etta. 'You're not remotely yobbish. I've loved you for so long, it began the first night when you were so sweet about Wilkie staying at Badger's Court. Seth was a stupid crush. He's got such a weak face.'

Somehow they'd both left their supporting trees and almost sleepwalked towards one another. Etta put a hand up to Valent's cheek, stroking it:

'You've got the strongest, kindest face in the world. I was always so happy when I was with you. The world lit up.'

Valent took her hands, kissing them slowly, lingeringly:

'Same for me. The times we spent together were the happiest of my life, discovering poems, listening to the nightingales and the Proms, planning the garden. I felt so cherished and peaceful, no more compulsion to work my arse off, free to be completely myself . . .'

'Oh, so did I.'

Etta looked up into Valent's face properly for the first time, noticing how unusually pale and drawn it was, the circles beneath his eyes as black as his dark eyebrows.

'I don't believe it was just Alban that got Rafiq and Mrs Wilkinson back,' she protested in wonder. 'It was you working flat out night and day that did it.'

And as she found herself in Valent's arms, face against the yellow-check tweed jacket they'd bought for him to wear at the races, she realized how much weight he'd lost.

'I didn't know how to get you back,' muttered Valent, 'but I knew I wouldn't have a moment's happiness until I did. I bought Wilkie in such a cack-handed way to stop Harvey-Holden and Shade getting her.'

'That and the beautiful portrait I was so vile about, please can I have it back?' begged Etta. 'And all the other sweet things, mending the Polo and Sky in Switzerland and the rustic poles.'

'Hush,' said Valent and he kissed her, very tentatively then passionately, until they both had to collapse on a conveniently mossy bank.

'That was so earth-shatteringly lovely,' sighed Etta and then, cast down, 'but oh Valent, I'm not glam enough for you. I was so jealous of Bonny. She's so beautiful – and young.'

'And daft as a brush. Don't be so bluddy stupid.' Valent tried to kiss her again, but Etta stopped him, really perturbed.

'I'll probably horrify you with nothing on, all saggy and varicose.'

Valent laughed softly.

'I saw you in the bath on the night of the flood. I barged into the bathroom with Gwenny and shot out before you realized. I didn't want to embarrass you but you looked bluddy gorgeous.'

'But not like Bonny,' wailed Etta.

'She's for a weekend, you're for always. I want a playmate, not a plaything.' Valent stroked her hair.

'And I'm heavily into yob-satisfaction,' giggled Etta, trapping his hands under hers. 'You are so bluddy gorgeous too.'

Valent smirked.

'Where do you want to live?' he asked. 'I thought you'd like Bluebell Hill back.'

'No I would not.' Etta decided it was time to be assertive. 'I love Willowwood, we've got so many friends here. Little Hollow's a bit small but I'd love to stay at Badger's Court with you.' And she kissed him, putting her hands on either side of his face, unbelievably touched to feel the tears spilling out of his eyes.

'Ouch,' she squawked as a jealous Priceless, back from rabbiting, nudged her in the ribs.

'Ouch,' yelled Valent, as Gwenny shimmied down the oak tree and landed, claws out, on his shoulder. Next moment Mrs Wilkinson and Chisolm had wandered up to join the party.

'With this menagerie, we're going to need Badger's Court,' said Valent happily, 'particularly if we've got to find room for Mrs Wilkinson's foal,' and probably Trixie and her baby too, he thought, but he'd tell Etta about that tomorrow.

The stars were coming out, the moon rising to witness their joy, when suddenly, sweetly, over the bowed willows floated the pealing of church bells.

'Oh how heavenly,' sighed Etta, 'Pocock must be back from the memorial service.'

'They'll be ringing for us in a week or two,' Valent tucked his arm through Etta's, 'and Niall can marry us.'

'Oh yes please.' Etta gave another sigh of happiness.

As Pocock started ringing 'Here's To You, Mrs Wilkinson', Valent said, 'We'd better get her back to face the world's press. She'd hate to miss them.'

'My mother always said VE were the most beautiful initials in the world, because they stood for Victory in Europe,' said Etta, kissing his cheek, 'but my most beautiful initials are VE because they stand for Valent Edwards.'

And I'm going to be Mrs Valent Edwards, she thought in ecstasy.

As they wandered back through the wood, followed by Priceless with Chisolm and Gwenny both hitching a lift on Mrs Wilkinson's back, Etta said it was like the end of *The Incredible Journey*.

'Do you think Romeo and Sir Cuthbert will call Love Rat out when they learn Mrs Wilkinson's in foal?'

'No, Auntie Chisolm will put paid to that.'

148

On the village green, amid scenes of riotous celebration, a hastily assembled disco had taken over from the church bells. Ione was twisting with the Bishop, Old Mrs Malmesbury was teaching an absolutely plastered Joey the Charleston, the Major foxtrotted with Tilda, Shagger bopped with Debbie.

Niall, his black vestments flying, jived with Woody, each congratulating the other on saving the Willowwood Chestnut as they gazed up at its multiple moonlit candles. Woody was particularly excited that he and Valent were getting close to a cure for chestnut fungus and might save the great chestnut avenue of Rupert, who, for the past hour, had been nose to nose discussing horses with Marius. Trainers didn't change, their wives, Taggie and Olivia, were fondly agreeing.

Alan the incredible journalist was dictating an even more exciting ending into a tape recorder. Dora was on her mobile to the *Daily Mail*: 'Mrs Wilkinson is to become a mother, Mr Dacre,' she was shouting over Robbie Williams. 'I can confirm Penscombe Love Rat is the father, rather an exciting mating.'

Martin, also on his mobile, was desperately calling his bank to find out if Harvey-Holden's cheque had gone through.

Alban, ringed by admiring journalists, was explaining how his numerous languages had enabled him to track down Rafiq and Mrs Wilkinson. He was delighted to have another quango: £300,000 a year for one day a month to find out if immigrants mostly come from abroad.

Toby was dancing round with Bump in his arms, making the gorgeous blond little boy scream so much with laughter that the photographers competed to take their picture. Then Phoebe, determined to get in on the act, snatched Bump away and started dancing with him, whereupon Bump bawled his head off and, to loud cheers, uttered his very first words: 'Want to go back to Daddy.'

Painswick and Pocock sat hand in hand outside the pub, planning their teashop. Seth and Corinna were enjoying posing for photographers and plugging work in progress. Seth was keeping one eye on Romy, who was getting bored with comforting Jude, and the other eye wistfully on Trixie, who was sitting on the edge of the duck pond, cooling her swollen feet and talking to Eddie Alderton.

'You mustn't feel guilty about Furious,' she was saying. 'He was glorious but mad, one day he'd have done something dreadful.'

'And you mustn't worry about the baby,' said Eddie. 'My mom was illegitimate and she's done good. Let's have dinner tomorrow.'

Whenever the disco stopped, the Greycoats children sang their song about Mrs Wilkinson, but were somewhat distracted to notice their favourite teacher snogging Mr Macbeth.

A big screen was showing the Major's film of Mrs Wilkinson's finest moments.

'Pity it didn't include her stolen service with Love Rat,' giggled Dora.

Hanging around for Seth, Martin or Valent, Bonny noticed a beautiful youth with white-blond hair jumping out of a badly parked car and cried, 'Who is that *most* appealing young man?'

'My boyfriend,' snapped Dora, briskly dictating Chisolm's diary to the *Daily Mirror*, 'and he's taken.'

Chris and Chrissie, having made sure there was enough food and drink on the trestle tables, joined the party, deliriously happy that at last Chrissie was pregnant.

'I do hope the baby doesn't come out in a woolly hat, waving a betting slip,' murmured Woody to Niall.

Oxford, Priceless, Cadbury, Araminta, Mistletoe and half a dozen of Olivia's terriers, aware that the minds of their owners were on other things, had just emerged from the pub kitchen licking their lips.

On a bench beneath a cherry tree dropping white petals on to them like confetti, Amber and Rogue were locked in each other's arms. As they broke off, Amber caressed Rogue's face with a hand on the third finger of which glowed a beautiful sapphire.

'I am so sorry,' she whispered. 'I was so vile in the past, I love you so much and I take back everything I said about jockeys being rubbish in bed. And I adore the idea of Dad and Furious bonding in heaven. Dad was always great with difficult horses.'

'If you're definitely going to hire Rafiq Khan as your stable jockey next season,' Rupert was saying to Marius as they helped themselves to another mahogany whisky, 'I'd better have Rogue back to make sure of beating you.' Over Marius's shoulder, Rupert raised his glass to his goddaughter.

The press were frantic to talk to Rafiq, but he had escaped to Penscombe with Tommy. They were both shell-shocked, clinging together in case the other vanished.

'I was so terrified you were dead,' said Tommy.

'I was so terrified they'd kill you if I made contact,' said Rafiq.

Overhead the moon hung like a little gilded banana.

'Imagine Wilkie peeling it,' said Tommy. 'Thank you ever so much for saving her.'

As they breathed in a smell of wild garlic tempered by a faint sweet scent of bluebells, they could hear the idle stamping and neighing of Rupert's horses. But Tommy led Rafiq on, past the tennis court to the animals' graveyard. Her torch flickered over the names: Badger, Gertrude the mongrel, Rockstar, and came to rest on a beautiful headstone which Joey had only finished engraving that morning.

'In Loving Memory of Rafiq's friend Furious, winner of the Gold Cup. Allah finally called him home,' Rafiq read incredulously, and fell down on the wet grass to pray.

The tears were still pouring down his cheeks as he rose to his feet, so Tommy wiped them away and told him, 'There was rather a row because EU regulations don't allow you to bury horses at home any more, but Rupert said, "Bugger Europe," and brought him back. Joey carved the stone.'

'Let's return to the party,' said Rafiq, taking her hand. 'I would like to thank Rupert and Joey.'

Back at the village green, everyone was saying, 'Where's Mrs Wilkinson?' particularly the press, who wanted to make sure she was really alive. None of them had got any sense out of Rafiq and Tommy or Rogue and Amber, so they were enchanted to witness hysterical scenes of rejoicing when Mrs Wilkinson and Chisolm finally arrived in their open-top bus, driven by Joey with Etta in the passenger seat, giggling on Valent's knee.

Seeing so many friends, Mrs Wilkinson had to leap out and bustle round, greeting everyone. She had been far too busy to eat except for a few snatches of grass earlier in the day, so she was delighted to be offered a big bowl of bread and butter pudding from the pub. Chisolm's long yellow eyes soon lit on the hundreds of floral tributes propped against the church railings in memory of Mrs Wilkinson and she began tearing off the cellophane.

Valent was in no mood for a press conference:

'I'll talk to you guys tomorrow.'

For a photo opportunity, however, he did agree to stand in the village green goal posts and fend off shots from Mrs Wilkinson, Chisolm and the local children. He was just congratulating himself that he hadn't lost his Cup Final touch when Chisolm, to roars of applause, headed one into the top left-hand corner.

'That's enuff.' Valent chucked the football to Drummond and turned to a watching Etta. The sight of her laughing face so filled with love made his heart turn over. Next moment, Phoebe had sidled up to her.

'Could you possibly hold Bump for a min, Etta, so I can have a dance?'

'Sorry, Phoebe, actually she can't.' Martin had strode up and grabbed his mother's arm. 'Can you take Poppy and Drummond home, Mother, and put them to bed? You're hardly dressed for a party anyway. Romy and I can't miss an opportunity with so many press and big hitters about.'

'No she can't,' roared the biggest hitter of them all, so that even Martin backed off. 'From now on,' announced Valent proudly, 'your mother will be much too busy putting her new husband to bed.' Then, at Martin's look of outrage: 'Etta has done me the huge honour of agreeing to be my wife.' Seizing her hand, he beamed down at Etta. 'And we want to be together, so we're going home.'

With the cheers ringing in their ears, Valent and Etta, followed by Chisolm, Priceless and Mrs Wilkinson, who was not letting her mistress out of sight for a second, set out for Badger's Court, through the willow wood, where they were joined by Gwenny.

'And into Eden took their solitary way,' said Valent triumphantly.

'Oh Valent,' sighed Etta in rapture, 'if Mrs Wilkinson has a colt, do you think Ione might possibly plant a willow for him?'

Acknowledgements

No horse staggering past the post in the Grand National can have been more relieved than I when I finished *Jump!* Yet I was overwhelmed with sadness that I would no longer have the excuse to devote myself solely to the heroic, thrilling, yet hugely friendly world of jump racing.

Early in my research, I was lucky to meet one of its funniest, most charming characters: trainer Richard Phillips. Over a splendid lunch at the famous Pheasant Inn near Lambourn, Richard explained that, in racing, one must regard the owners as the parents and the horses as their children at very expensive private schools, at which the trainers are the headmasters, under huge pressure to deliver the goods.

Consequently few people work harder than trainers and their wives. I was therefore hugely touched that so many made time to both talk to and entertain me. They include Martin, Carol and David Pipe, at whose glorious yard I shook hooves with National winners Comply or Die and Minnehoma.

At Paul Nicholls's yard, I had the excitement of watching Denman and Kauto Star skipping over huge fences in a tiny school like gymkhana ponies. I even stood beside the sublime Venetia Williams when her horse Mon Mome won the National.

I am also eternally grateful for the help and inspiration given me by Nicky Henderson, Nigel Twiston-Davies, Bob and Nell Buckler, Charlie and Susannah Mann, Sally Mullins, Tom and Sophie George, Kim and Claire Bailey, Tom and Elaine Taaffe, Carl Llewellyn, Philip Hobbs and Alan King.

Writing a novel is not unlike wading through a raging river. On blissful occasions you stumble on a stepping stone that helps you on your way. One such stepping stone was meeting the insouciant

Henry Ponsonby, who invited me to join one of his super racing syndicates. This involved taking a share in a lovely dark bay called Monty's Salvo, trained by Nicky Henderson.

Soon I was watching Monty thunder up the gallops, studying the meticulous expertise with which Nicky brings on his horses and setting out on joyful jaunts to the races with other syndicate members. At Worcester we felt ecstasy when Monty only lost by a whisker in a photo finish, followed by the agony of him breaking down irrevocably on the same course a week or so later. One of the saddest days of my life, however, became a poignant chapter in *Jump!* and convinced me to base my story round a syndicate. I would therefore like to thank Henry and his girlfriend Kish Armstrong and the rest of the syndicate, including particularly Bernard and Glenys Cartmel, for all the wonderful fun we had.

Addicted to syndicates, I was delighted to be asked shortly afterwards to join Thoroughbred Ladies, a local group of delightful, larky women, whose syndicate is run by Sophie George from a glorious yard overlooking the Slad valley. Since then we have had the intense excitement of seeing our horse Island Flyer, with Paddy Brennan up, win three times on the trot. I would like to thank Sophie for her wonderful hospitality and the other ladies for their friendship.

Others who inspired me were Eddie Kearney, who belongs to a riotous local syndicate, and James and Nicky Stafford, who run the highly successful Thurloe Thoroughbreds. At one of their splendid evenings where newly acquired horses are named, I met Compton Hellyer, who stylishly, on two pages of my diary, set out the basic finances of running a syndicate, which proved absolutely invaluable. I also spent a miraculous day at Highclere, mecca of syndicates, run by Harry Herbert, where I watched a wonderful parade of stallions and their offspring, and enjoyed a fabulous lunch.

Without owners there would be no racing. As a very new owner I was knocked out to be allowed into the Owners and Trainers bars and stands and to meet and form close friendships with other owners. These include dear Jim Lewis, owner of Best Mate, and his lovely new wife Jennifer Harrison. The wonderful Liz and Peter Prowting entertained me endlessly at Cheltenham, as did the very generous Nigel and Penny Bunter.

David and Caroline Sebire, Roger and Carol Scan, Jim Jarvis, the ebullient greyhound lover Harry Findlay, Laurence and Elaine Nash, Piers Pottinger, Jenny Allen, Baroness Arlington and many others were all willing to share hilarious and heroic anecdotes about their horses.

It would be impossible to over-estimate my admiration for jump jockeys, that band of brothers, putting their lives on the line with every race, yet always able to banter and joke in the face of danger. For all their inspiration and help, I would like to thank: A. P. McCoy, Tom Scudamore, Choc Thornton, Paddy Brennan, Andrew Tinkler, Sam Thomas, Rhys Flint, Felix De Giles, Barry Geraghty, Timmy Murphy (for a brave and touching book), Hannah Grizel and Alex Charles-Jones.

Before I began *Jump!* I was privileged to count among my friends three times champion jockey Richard Dunwoody and ace amateur jockey Brigadier Andrew Parker Bowles who heroically finished the Grand National with a broken back. Retired from racing, these amazing men have worked tirelessly to raise money for charity, particularly when related to injured jockeys or the welfare of race horses. I salute them both and thank them for all their help.

There are many heroes in National Hunt racing, not least the stable lads and lasses who labour unceasingly and devotedly looking after their charges. I would particularly like to thank the gorgeous Lorraine Hunt, Leroy Jones, Rachel Field and Michael Kissane and the excellent head lads Corky Brown, Clifford Baker and Gordy Clarkson for all their wisdom.

Among the unsung heroes are the redoubtable trainers' PAs, whose job resembles that of Horatius holding the bridge. Not only do they manage incredibly busy offices and keep everything running smoothly, but they also ensure that owners, jockeys and their often extremely demanding bosses are happy and at bay. I am hugely indebted to Rowie Rhys-Jones, Jo Saunders, who gallantly read the manuscript, Georgina Philipson-Stow, Clare Jones and Lauren Thompson.

I was very lucky that my son Felix is mad about racing and gallantly accompanied me to many horsey events. We had a heavenly time at different racecourses, particularly at our local course, Cheltenham, truly the jewel in the National Hunt crown. I cannot begin to thank Edward Gillespie, its managing director, and Simon Claisse, Clerk of the Course, for their intense kindness, inspiration and willingness to answer my questions while constantly providing dazzling spectacle and loving care for both horses and their connections.

My thanks also go to the chairman of Cheltenham racecourse, Lord Vestey; Andy Clifton, head of communications; Tim Partridge, manager of buildings and facilities, and Liz Cole, who so charmingly holds sway over the ladies' loo.

I am devoted to Worcester and its splendid welcome provided

by Jenny Cheshire and Sue Page, and Henry Pratt who runs the lorry park. I must also thank Marilyn Peachey and Tricia Cavell for splendid Ladies' Day lunches at Worcester in aid of the wonderful St Richard's Hospice. Two other favourite courses are Ludlow, where I must thank Clerk of the Course Bob Davies for his help, and Stratford, where Steven Lambert, Clerk of the Course, also helped me and where chairman Captain Nick Lee conducted a splendid auction.

I have a hugely soft spot for Newbury, not just for its stylish beauty but for the most delicious glass of champagne I and other Thoroughbred Ladies enjoyed in the royal box, after our horse Island Flyer won his race. My thanks to joint managing director Stephen Higgins, Jeni Sieff and Natasha Berkeley.

More thanks to Louise Mitchell and Phil White for a Kentucky Challenge evening at Kempton Park, the perfect night out, and to the beautiful Becky Green for a gloriously funny summer evening at Fontwell where Richard Dunwoody, Honeysuckle Weeks and I judged an eco-beauty competition.

I loved my visit to Wincanton, but sadly failed to get to Wetherby to research an important chapter in the book. Invaluable help, however, was received from Jonjo Sanderson about the course and from Josephine Shilton about the famous White Rose restaurant.

I owe a bumper debt of gratitude to Sarah Driscoll, peerless press officer at Aintree, for providing so much information and to Andrew Tulloch, Clerk of the Course, for all his advice.

I was guided to another massive stepping stone by Richard Pitman, one of the most delightful and helpful men in racing, when he introduced me to Diana Keen of Sunset and Vine, the ace production company employed by the BBC to broadcast the Grand National to more than 600,000,000 viewers. Dear Diana allowed me to sit in on a vast production meeting on the morning of the National, marvel over multi-monitors in the control room and hurtle round the course before and during the race in a BBC car with rigger driver John Anderson and cameraman David Taylor. This unique privilege enabled me to witness the making of a beautiful film about a heroic race.

Fiona Macdonald, one of the team of Spotters who report on fallers at every fence, and Harriet Loxley from the Royal Liverpool Hospital also provided invaluable information.

Jump racing is one of the most dangerous sports in the world. Where else, as A. P. McCoy pointed out, would you be permanently followed by a convoy of vets, doctors and ambulances? Horses and jockeys win, suffer injury and die. I would, however, like to stress the valiant efforts made by the people who run race-courses to make both track and fences more forgiving.

On the same subject, I would particularly like to salute Sebastian Garner, a wonderful horse ambulance man, who at both Aintree and Cheltenham allowed me to witness the kindness and quiet competence with which he eased the pain of injured horses and dispatched the fatally injured into the next world.

Any horse's death is tragic, but I wish animal rights activists would direct their fire more towards the ghastly long distances that horses have to travel to slaughterhouses abroad, or against vicious, deliberate cruelty.

In *Jump!* my horse heroine, Mrs Wilkinson, is discovered appallingly mutilated in a wood in the snow. Researching this, I spent a harrowing yet uplifting day with Ted Barnes, the awesome field officer of World Horse Welfare, who showed me how horrifically neglected, even tortured horses, reduced to mere skeletons, are rescued and lovingly restored to healthy, happy and confident working lives.

Another stepping stone was meeting Helen Yeadon, who with her husband Michael runs the most wonderful sanctuary for retired and rescued racehorses at Greatwood in Wiltshire. Here these great animals are rested and nursed back to health and often new careers. In this Garden of Eden they bond not only with impossibly naughty Shetland ponies, goats and dogs and a rooster called Rodney, but most touchingly with autistic children who regularly visit the sanctuary. Helen herself gave me invaluable advice on restoring Mrs Wilkinson to health and happiness.

I'd also like to thank Janet Perrins, Greatwood's fundraiser, Emma Cook of World Horse Welfare, and the Blue Cross and the Brooke Hospital for their help in horse rescue work.

My horse heroine, Mrs Wilkinson, loses an eye before she is saved so it was crucial to meet two gallant one-eyed mares, who won many races as well as the public's adoration, to see how they coped with the argy-bargy of the racetrack.

The first mare was Material World, or Daisy, a terrific character as tough as she is adorable. Owned and trained by Suzy Smith and Sergio Graham-Jones down in Brighton, she is now happily in foal to Shirocco. The second mare is Barshiba, trained by the great David Elsworth, who recently won a major race at Haydock with Hayley Turner up.

One of my heroes does a stint in gaol where he finds huge satisfaction in looking after one of the rescued racehorses being restored to health in the prison stables. I am therefore grateful again to Andrew Parker Bowles, founder and former chairman of Retraining of Racehorses (ROR), and to Di Arbuthnot, its director of operations, who pioneered a similar scheme at Hollesley Bay Prison in Suffolk.

Leaving prison, my hero works in a yard and dreams of becoming a jockey. Like many stable staff, he realizes this dream by taking a course at the excellent Northern Racing College in Doncaster. Again, I must thank the racing school's training co-ordinator, Michelle Beardsley, for her help.

It was also a great thrill to watch Leroy Jones, a stable lad at Tom George's, come fourth out of a large field when he made his debut in the Berkeley Hunt point-to-point at Woodford last year. I would like to thank John Berkeley, president of the hunt, hunt secretary Tom Whittaker and Louis Purvis, head of the hunt supporters, for a marvellous afternoon.

One of my favourite characters in *Jump!* is Chisolm, a goat, who becomes Mrs Wilkinson's inseparable companion after being rescued from a dreadful fate. I would like to thank Southern Animal Rights Coalition, and especially Niccy Tapping, for their help on this subject. Marilyn Sheppard, a goat addict, told me some wonderful stories about these idiosyncratic creatures. I am hugely indebted to Hazel Johns for sharing her wonderful knowledge of geese and ganders and for her take on the mysteries of nature.

I must thank Tom and Sophie George for inviting me to a Lawn Meet at their house, where I was able to witness in glorious surroundings how hunting operates after the ban.

Another stepping stone in the book was meeting Tom and Sophie's then head lad, Sally (Minnie) Hall, who is encyclopaedic in her knowledge of horses and racing, and spent hours discussing my story with me. To see her working with horses was also an inspiration and although we miss her in Gloucestershire I am glad she is now a trainer herself in Bedfordshire and one of her young horses, Clerk's Choice, has already notched up three wins.

The winter game, as jump racing is romantically known, produces, like Minnie, the most marvellous women: strong, combining beauty with kindness like Shakespeare's Sylvia, capable of rising in the dark to ride out, partying until first light, yet retaining a work ethic to die for. Glamorous Amazons – I call them Glamazons.

Two Glamazons – Liz Ampairee, marketing guru, and Jacques Malone, who runs her own PR company in Dublin – truly looked after me while I wrote *Jump!*, endlessly answering questions, coming up with ideas, taking me to the races, introducing me to owners, trainers and jockeys, and entering wonderfully into the spirit of the book.

Jacques, in particular, took me and Liz on a magic trip to Dublin, which included a day at Leopardstown races, for which I must thank Jane Davies, a glorious dinner in the evening given by J. P. and Noreen McManus and a fascinating and illuminating Cheltenham Preview at the Shelbourne Hotel hosted by Betchronicle the following night. All this provided terrific copy for the book. I cannot begin to express my thanks enough to Liz and Jacques.

Another Glamazon is Carey Buckler, daughter of trainer Bob Buckler, who came for a couple of days' work experience and ended up regaling me with marvellous tales about everyone in racing. Another was Charlotte Kinchin, who after waitressing at the Pheasant Inn, riding out and driving round trainers, was a mine of glorious gossip.

Hospitality in jump racing is Olympian. Nothing lifts the spirits on a bitterly cold winter's day like a Bull Shot or a glass of champagne in a warm box. I am, therefore, eternally grateful to my dear former editor Veronica Wadley and her husband Tom Bower, John Boyle of Boyle Sports, the team from Betchronicle, Harriet Collins at Johnno Spencer Consultancy, John Woodhatch of Equine Effects, and Emma Jesson the weather queen.

Libelling humans is to be avoided in books, and even worse is to libel a horse. So I tried very hard, particularly with badly behaved horses, not to give them names that had been used before. Huge thanks therefore to Rachel Andrews and Emma Day at Weatherbys and Jo Saunders for checking these names for me and I hope none has slipped through the net.

There is quite a lot of sex in *Jump!* – some of it equine. I am therefore most grateful to John Sharp of Weatherbys' stud department for his advice and to Ali Rea for arranging a miraculous visit to the Darley Stud in Newmarket. Here Richard Knight took me on an exhilarating tour of the breeding yards and the stables, where I was thrilled to meet the mighty New Approach.

I would also like to thank Ed Sackville, an ace bloodstock agent, Jane Mead and Corrin Wood who told me about rearing thoroughbred foals. My neighbour, Penny Smith, a Highland pony breeder, whose mares and foals and visiting stallions across the valley are a constant joy, waxed lyrical on the equine delights of 'stolen service'.

Most of the people who helped me in the writing of the book are experts in their field, but as *Jump!* is fiction I'm afraid I only followed their advice when it suited my plot. My woman jockey, for example, breaks the rules by remounting in a point-to-point around 2005 and, as I believe in miracles, criminally maltreated horses recover and win big races.

And talking of miracles it would be difficult to overstate my admiration for the racing press, who file such immaculate, exciting and poetic copy at such lightning speed. Icons include Brough Scott, Marcus Armytage, Alan Lee, Julian Muscat, Charlie Brooks, Jonathan Powell, Colin Mackenzie, Marcus Townend, Alastair Down, Andrew Longmore, Robin Oakley, the great revered John Oaksey and Ivor Herbert, and the late lamented Clement Freud.

The *Racing Post* is another miracle, as readable as it is all-embracing. I am so grateful to its editor, Bruce Millington, and associate editor, another greyhound lover, Howard Wright. *Horse and Hound* frequently inspired me and one of the bonuses of being an owner has been the monthly arrival of *Thoroughbred Owner and Breeder*, which is as sparky and as beautiful to look at as the horses it features.

Normally I write in a gazebo at the bottom of the garden, but I abandoned this for the top of the house so I could watch racing coverage on Channel 4, the BBC and the glorious *At The Races* while I worked. I must thank all three for the beauty, information and entertainment of their programmes and would express particular gratitude to the great John and Booby McCririck, Richard Pitman, Robert Cooper (who loves Material World), Jim McGrath, Mike Cattermole who took me up to the commentary box at Cheltenham, Clare Balding, Johnnie Francome, Matt Chapman, Sean Boyce, Alice Plunkett, Luke Harvey, Nick Luck and the irrepressible Derek Thompson.

Jump! is largely based in a Cotswold village called Willowwood, which in a way resembles our lovely village of Bisley, which has a beautiful church, a great school and a golden stone high street. No one in the story, however, is based on any living person and any similarities are purely coincidental, unless the person is so famous, like John McCririck, that he appears as himself.

Many other people helped me with *Jump!* Our own delightful vicar, Simon Richards, and curate, Stephen Jarvis, were eloquent on church matters. Tree surgeon Tim Bendle and Simon Toomer, who runs the glorious Westonbirt Arboretum, advised me on trees. Phil Bradley, who drove me all over the country, initiated me into the skills and hazards of goalkeeping. Rupert Proctor advised me on betting. Inspector Mark Ravenscroft of Operational Services and Chris Miller were brilliant on explosives, and my super lawyer, Graham Ogilvie, wised me up on the law. Adam and Nat Phillips inspired me on houses and cockpit-shaped offices as did Judy Zatonski on greyhounds. Bill Holland with his usual sweet nature answered the most obscure musical queries. Wonderful Stephen Simson at Hatchards as usual tracked down endless books. Susanna Franklyn was witty and illuminating on the theatre. Bob and Derelie Cherry enlightened me on rose grafting as did Mariska Kay on lovely clothes and Anne Spackman of Kenneth Green Associates on lovely scent.

I would also like to thank my wonderful bank, Hoares, and especially Bella Hopewell and John Gallop for looking after me.

On the veterinary front, I had great advice from my own vet, John Hunter and his staff at Bowbridge Veterinary Group, from Shirley Bevan and, particularly on hairline fractures, from Emma Ridgeway at the Willesley Equine Clinic.

Pat Pearson and my own doctor, Tim Crouch, advised on medical matters, and my super dentist Terry Mason on straightening buck teeth.

Of the younger generation, Poppy and Charlie Stirland, Harry Luard and Kit Cooper educated me on teenage slang, and Luke and Freddie Mander on excellent speeches.

Willowwood is threatened by widespread flooding in *Jump!* A huge thanks therefore to our local neighbourhood warden, Ashley Nicholson, for providing graphic descriptions of wrestling with the Gloucestershire floods and the helicopter rescues these entailed. Our own local papers, particularly the *Stroud News*, the *Citizen* and the *Gloucester Echo*, also covered these events most dramatically.

Meanwhile, Martin Meade and pilots Robin Gibson and Garry Hodge advised me on helicopters; photographers Gavin James and Les Hurley kept me supplied with wonderful pictures of racing and horses.

There was huge excitement recently when our Bisley Compost Scheme won an MBE for all their hard work. One of the scheme's pioneers, Liz Howlett, and Anna Shepard, Green writer on *The Times* and author of the wonderful *How Green Are My Wellies*, gave me marvellous advice on ecology. I have to confess to a slightly irreverent portrayal of Mrs Travis-Lock, my eco-warrior in *Jump!*, but as a character she is staunchness personified.

Over the past few years, a ravishing Queen Anne house across the road has been gutted and lovingly restored by a team from Ward & Co. of the Ryeford Industrial Estate, headed by their general manager Gary Perrins. During this period, they regaled me with hilarious stories of work in progress. Despite the roads closed and traffic hold-ups, we missed them hugely when they went.

I must also thank Shaun Moore, an expert on graffiti on white vans.

My friends, as always, provided magical input; they include Maria Prendagast, my sister-in-law Angela Sallitt, Rudolph Agnew, Peregrine Hodson, Susan Kyle, Antony Winlaw, Suzie Dowty, Laura Cooper, Mandy Pitman, Rupert and Ollie Miles, David Cull, Miriam Francome, Deborah Waters, Janetta Lee, Lucy Lane-Fox, Jemima Khan, Arthur Wade and Pete Curtis.

I have listed the names of so many people but to my shame I took down the telephone numbers of many others, but never found time to follow them up. For this I apologize, and even more so to anyone whose help I sought and haven't included.

Now to the book itself. I am utterly blessed in my publishers, Transworld, who truly know how to cherish and inspire. I cannot thank Larry Finlay, my darling editor Linda Evans and her hawk-eyed PA Joanne Williamson enough for all their kindness. Claire Ward and Henry Steadman produced a most stylish jacket, and I am honoured that Neil Gower, who won Jacket of the Year for *Lord of the Flies*, has drawn such a beautiful and witty map.

Deborah Adams tackled the copy-editing, while Katrina Whone and Vivien Garrett ably managed the progress of the book through its copy-editing and proof-reading stages. For the typesetters, Betty Leggett amended the text with inimitable speed and accuracy.

One of the reasons I love finishing a book is because I can work again with the divine Nicky Henderson, my freelance publicist, and the fantastic publicity team at Transworld, headed up by the lovely Patsy Irwin.

I am also blessed with the most wonderful agent, the wise and warm-hearted Vivienne Schuster. She and Linda Evans must have felt like midwives delivering elephant quads as I laboured to finish *Jump!* but their sweetness and encouragement never faltered. I am also delighted Viv has taken on a bright and beautiful assistant, Felicity Blunt, who gave me excellent advice on developing characters.

Once again, the true heroines are my friends, my PA Anna Gibbs-Kennet, Annette Xuereb-Brennan, Mandy Williams and my former PAs Pippa Birch, Pam Dhenin and Pam's daughter Zoe. They dropped everything to produce a huge and beautiful manuscript in record time, typing long into the night, wrestling with my increasingly indecipherable writing, then carrying out a million corrections, pointing out errors and making suggestions. I cannot thank them enough, or Sue Kilmister for also helping me with a later draft.

I would like to add an extra thanks to dear Anna Gibbs-Kennet, who not only masterminded the production of the manuscript but kept my office running smoothly at the same time and dealt with a million loose ends.

I must also praise the kindness and resourcefulness of Steve Perry, my husband's carer, who spends a lot of time looking after me. He was brilliant, sorting out various computers when they started playing up and checking facts. When Steve is away, Hazel Johns steps in and cheers us all up with her sweetness and expertise.

Nor would I survive for a second without my wonderful house-keeper Ann Mills, who has somehow put up with our family for twenty-five years. Ann and her great friend Moira Hatherall skip out our house as cheerfully and heroically as any stable lads, always leave it beautiful and provide so much comfort and love.

My own family has, as always, been beyond reproach. My brave husband Leo, a great publisher, who gives me wonderful advice; Felix and his wife Edwina and their daughter Scarlett; my daughter Emily, her husband Adam, their three sons, Jago, Lysander and Acer; Feral the cat, and our collective dogs: Feather the grey-hound, Bobby the Labrador and William the mongrel, have once again provided their essential mixture of love, fantastic copy and good cheer.

I am also deeply grateful to Monica, my ancient manual type-writer, who, when computers crashed, never put a key wrong.

Finally, I would like to thank thoroughbred horses everywhere for racing their hearts out and for the joy and excitement this brings the public, and plead that their lovely, sensitive and trusting natures should never be abused.

Jilly Cooper is a journalist, writer and media superstar. The author of many number one bestselling novels, she lives in Gloucestershire with her husband Leo, her rescue greyhound Feather and her black cat Feral.

She was appointed OBE in 2004 for services to literature, and in 2009 was awarded an honorary Doctorate of Letters by the University of Gloucestershire for her contribution to literature and services to the County.